F   Ross-Macdonald, BRANCH
ROS   Malcolm.

        An innocent woman

$18.95

DATE			

BRANCH

An Innocent Woman

Also by Malcolm Macdonald:

A Notorious Woman
His Father's Son
Honour and Obey
The Silver Highways
On a Far Wild Shore
Tessa D'Arblay
For They Shall Inherit
Goldeneye
Abigail
Sons of Fortune
The Rich Are with You Always
The World from Rough Stones

An Innocent

WOMAN

Malcolm Macdonald

St. Martin's Press
New York

for Douglas Hill

Library of Congress Cataloging-in-Publication Data

Ross-Macdonald, Malcolm.
    An innocent woman / Malcolm Macdonald.
        p.   cm.
    ISBN 0-312-05448-3
    I. Title.
PR6068.0827I45   1991
823'.914—dc20   90-15545
                                                            CIP

First published in Great Britain by Judy Piatkus Limited under the writer's pen name Malcolm Ross

First U.S. Edition: January 1991
10 9 8 7 6 5 4 3 2 1

PART ONE

MARKET JEW ST ~ PENZANCE

Ménage à deux

1 THE TRAIN DREW INTO the terminus at a few seconds past 6.35 that Friday evening, the 1st of June. "More than seven minutes late," Mr Hervey commented severely, making a jotting in his notebook. "I shall write to the company about it. Six minutes at Worcester, eleven at Bristol, four at Plymouth, and now seven at Penzance. Always late, you see. Never ahead of the timetable. It's too bad."

"And why on earth we had to wait half an hour at Truro ..." Jane began.

"Ah, but that is clearly shown in the table, my child," her father pointed out. Within the family circle – which was now reduced to himself and Jane – he considered he held the monopoly in complaints, or, at least, in those that were justifiable. "In fact," he pointed out, "it is a *forty*-minute wait at Truro."

"Yet for no apparent reason," she said, as if anticipating his objection.

But Mr Hervey had no objection to *that* delay, for, as he said, it was clearly shown in the company's timetables. Annoyed that she should even hint at putting such words into his mouth, he said, "Now I wish you to go to the head of the platform, where you will see an archway to your left. Go through it, turn right, and wait for me just outside. I don't want you getting smuts all over your dress. And I don't want you beneath my feet while I see to our luggage."

Jane obeyed. She did not even think of discussing the matter. True, she was dressed in black from head to foot, being still in mourning for her mother, who had died last November. And true, that same black dress had endured a steady rain of smuts over these past two days of travel from Leeds to Manchester, to Worcester, Bristol ... and all those other places in her father's catalogue of late arrivals. But, dearly as she loved him, it was so pleasant to escape beyond the range of his all-organizing voice, if only by a few dozen yards, that she did not demur. At the head of the platform, before making for the arch, she turned and glanced at him. His tall, almost cadaverous figure, though bent now with age, was easy to discern; yet even had he been of ordinary stature his gestures would have distinguished him – wagging his finger, counting boxes and trunks and bags, ticking off lists in his ever-handy notebook. She shook her head in fond exasperation and made for the arch.

A warm, westering sun was gilding the granite walls of the station. Jane put up her parasol. Beyond was a yard where drays and hansoms might load and unload. Through the railings along its farther side she could see the whole of Penzance harbour, bobbing with boats as far as the seaward breakwater, a couple of furlongs away – or chains or cables or however nautical people expressed it. There were trawlers and lobstermen, colliers and steamers, sailing boats and Trinity House tenders. No other sight could have marked better the difference between the life she had left behind her and the new one she was about to begin. Yesterday morning she had bidden farewell to the industrial landscapes between Leeds and Manchester;

3

now here was an industrial scene of a different kind – maritime, yet just as busy, just as casual, just as dirty.

She sniffed at the strong and surprisingly cool breeze from the harbour. What should have been the unalloyed, salt-laden air off several thousand miles of ocean was freshly tainted with the aroma of decaying fish, tar, train oil, and, as in every other town in the land by now, the ammoniac, sulphureous reek of the gas works. She wrinkled her nose and prayed for her father to be done with his fussing as soon as possible. Why had he brought them to this odious end of the world, where they had neither family nor friends?

She became aware that a woman, respectably dressed and about her own age, was standing a few paces off, staring at her with an expression of some doubt. Unfortunately, that was the moment when Jane wrinkled her nose, and, though she was staring through the woman rather than at her, it must have seemed insulting.

Jane smiled. "I'm so sorry. Do forgive me. I was miles away." She moved an inch or so nearer the arch, making symbolic room for the other in case it were her wish to stand beside her and enjoy the warmth of the stone, too.

It apparently was her wish for she settled herself, or, rather, her bustle, a few inches clear of the wall and turned to face the sun; like Jane, she shielded her skin from its harmful rays with her parasol. "Do you have lodgings?" the newcomer asked quietly, giving Jane only the briefest of glances.

"Oh, yes, thank you. My father has bought a house in the district, in fact. Montpelier, in Breage. D'you know it?" She pronounced the name of the village as if it were French: *bree-ahje*.

Her companion frowned and then, with a smile of enlightenment, exclaimed, "Oh, *breeg*. Or, as the Cornish call it, *brayg*. How pleasant for you."

"Silly me! Of course I know it's pronounced *breeg*. That's my French upbringing coming out. Perhaps I should introduce myself? I am Miss Hervey. Jane Hervey. Is it a pleasant place?"

"More salubrious than this." She dipped her head with distaste toward the messy sprawl before them. "I am Miss Esther Wilkinson."

"D'you live in Penzance? Are you waiting for someone off the train, perhaps?"

"In a way." She laughed awkwardly. "Don't you recognize me?"

Jane thought it an extraordinary question. "I'm afraid not, Miss Wilkinson," she replied. "I have never visited this part of the world before. Indeed, I have only ever lived in Paris and the North Country."

"Ah, Paris," Miss Wilkinson murmured. Then, with a sigh, as if turning from dreams to mundane things, "And what shall you do in Breage?"

"Manage my father's household, I suppose – until someone else asks me to manage his. The usual thing, you know."

"Yes. The usual thing. I see you are in mourning. Is it a recent ..."

"My mother died last November."

"I'm so sorry to hear it. You must still miss her, especially at such a time as this. Both my parents are dead, but I could not afford to ..."

She broke off. A man – and a gentleman by the cut of him – paused before Jane and stared at her in rather an insolent manner.

4

"I think you're looking for me," Miss Wilkinson said. She led him a little way off; they exchanged a few words; Miss Wilkinson returned and resumed her former place. "A small matter of business," she said lightly. "Well, I wish you luck in your search, Miss Hervey."

"Search?"

"For a household to manage."

The ambiguity of the explanation, and the irony in the tone, made Jane pause. Had she implied to this young woman that she was looking for a post as housekeeper? If so, how could she correct the impression? She was still floundering for a response when her father suddenly appeared, red in the face. "Be off with you, you baggage!" he shouted at Miss Wilkinson.

"Father!" Jane cried.

Miss Wilkinson stared him out coolly. Jane, who had turned to apologize, was mesmerized by that look in the woman's eye – calm, unabashed, yielding nothing to any man. Oh, to be able to be like that when a total stranger turned on you in such a bullying fashion!

"Come, child!" Her father grasped her by the wrist and jerked her back into the station concourse.

"Goodbye!" she called over her shoulder.

"Goodbye!" Miss Wilkinson laughed.

"I had no idea," her father said – several times. "Until that porter told me, I had no idea. If only Manette hadn't given in her notice – this sort of thing would never have happened." He turned and stared at Jane. "You weren't ... you didn't ... she didn't ...?"

"We passed the time of day," Jane said defensively. "That's all. Her name is Miss Esther Wilkinson."

"A fig for her name, miss! You didn't speak to her? You didn't permit her to address you?"

"She was a very pleasant, respectable young lady."

He closed his eyes and shook his head. "She didn't ... *tell* you anything?"

"Lots of things. Father, why are you behaving in this ..."

"What did she tell you?" He grabbed up her wrist again. "Speak, girl! I must call in the police."

"She told me that *bree-ahje* is pronounced *breeg*. She said the Cornish ..."

"You told her where we live?" He was aghast.

"What is wrong, Father?" Jane grew agitated. She had obviously done something dreadfully wrong, yet for the life of her she could not think what.

He stared at her, first in one eye, then in the other, as if they might tell different stories. "You have no idea what she ... I mean, who she is, that woman?"

Jane thought it most curious that Miss Wilkinson should have asked the identical question, though in different words. "All I know is that her name is Esther Wilkinson and she lives in Penzance, or somewhere locally, anyway, and she's waiting for a person off a train – someone who's going to transact some business with her. And she obviously has no idea what he looks like because ..."

"Business?" Her father picked up the word and stared at her intently.

5

Jane shook her head. "I'm sorry. She gave no hint of what that business might be." He smiled then, a smile of relief which he sought to make genial. "Come!" Now his tone was gentler. "It is a storm in a teacup. Our carriage is up in the main street. We shall be home in an hour."

As they set off along the coastal road her thoughts returned to the strange encounter at the station. Obviously Miss Wilkinson was somehow involved in their lives. Her father had recognized her at once, and she had expected Jane to know her, too. In some way she must be connected with those shadowy years when, although her mother and father had been secretly married, they had been compelled to live apart. Indeed, they had lived in different countries and her mother had always claimed that her husband was dead. From her father's behaviour, she guessed the woman's connection with them was tainted with scandal.

Would Manette have recognized her? Her father had implied as much. Manette had been Jane's French maid but she had given in her notice the moment she had heard they were off to such a barbarous place as *Cornouaille,* which she had regarded as even worse than Brittany. There was freedom for you! The servant said, "No thanks, I'm off." The mistress had no choice but to go. Yet how could Manette have known Miss Wilkinson? She'd only been engaged by the family two years ago.

Was Miss W perhaps a love-child of her father's brother, her late uncle James? She had no very precise idea what a "love-child" might be, but she knew it tainted people's lives. She had never met Uncle James, nor been told anything of him other than that he had existed; but whenever his name was mentioned there was a certain *je-ne-sais-quoi* in the air. She could hardly be a love-child of Jane's father's! He was so proper; he'd never let any sort of taint into his life.

Were love-children related to the normal kind? Good heavens! If so, she had just stood there, outside the station, chatting with her ... cousin? Half-cousin? Step-cousin? But how exciting! As far as she knew, she had no living relatives of her own age. And to find one as pleasant-looking and well-spoken as Miss Wilkinson – or Esther, as Jane would certainly call her if she were a cousin ...

"The sooner you're safely married, the better," her father muttered, more to himself than her.

Silently Jane hoped she might have some say in the matter but, knowing her father, it would at best be the power to say no. "I wish ..." she mused.

"Yes, yes, what?"

"I wish that I might be allowed to direct the servants at Montpelier. And to arrange our unpacking, and our rooms ..."

"But you will only make a mess of it," her father pointed out.

She sighed, not being able to deny it. The problem was that she could never fuss and fidget with half the devotion *he* put into it. If she had her own household, she knew she'd manage it all perfectly well, but as long as he was there, hovering around, topping up, as it were, her inadequacies as a fusspot, she would, indeed, make a mess of it. "How shall I ever learn?" she asked.

He smiled sympathetically and gave her arm an affectionate pat. "Have no fear," he told her. "I certainly shall not try to teach you. We should only fall out and become enemies for life."

6

"Father!" She leaned her head against his shoulder. "As if we could!"
He sighed lugubriously. "Not that I shall live for ever. Next year I reach the biblical three-score-and-ten, you know."

She knew. He had reminded her of it often enough since her mother's death. Sixty-nine years old! It was unimaginable to her. "Born 1791." How often did one see that sort of date on tombstones already white with lichen. By grisly coincidence, the three nearest her mother's grave at Adel, north of Leeds, were all dated 1791. She would never forget the look on his face as the realization dawned, when he turned from her newly filled grave and saw it. "God works in mysterious ways, indeed," he had said as he wiped away a tear.

"Born 1841." What would it be like to see her own year of birth on a tombstone? There must already be thousands, of course, yet she'd never seen one. It wouldn't make her dwell morbidly on her own mortality, she decided. Rather, she'd think of that poor young person lying there with so many dreams and desires unfulfilled.

"Well," her father went on, "I'm not going to risk the loss of your amity. I value your little bird brain and your cheery smile and your warm heart too much for that, my child. No, I have an idea."

"What?" she asked in an intrigued tone, snuggling against him like a child about to be told a story – which was something she had never had the chance to do when she truly was a child, for he had not entered her life until she was about twelve. It often struck her that much of their intercourse was like that – making up for those missing years of father-child association. Half-pretending it was there to be revived.

"Well," he said, just as if his next words would be, "once upon a time ..." He leaned forward and let the window down slightly. "I think we may risk a little sea air now we're clear of the town," he explained. "Now tell me – what's going to happen once we start settling in, eh? People will leave cards. People will call. And the first among them will surely be a lady of eminent respectability, a leader in local society – Helston society, I suppose. A lady with time on her hands ... perhaps her own daughters have fledged and flown ..."

"Then she will be fat and fully fifty," Jane complained. She could see this dowager already, with her fine, downy moustache ... not a fastidious washer ... and a little pug dog under her arm.

"She might be younger and childless." He offered it more as a bribe than as a genuine probability. "Anyway, were she Methuselah's wife, no matter. As long as she pulls all the strings in the neighbourhood. And when she hears the size of your dowry ... well, I never met a woman yet who didn't adore being generous with other people's money. And if she can't arrange for a trooping of at least three dozen eligible young men for you, then this isn't England."

The implication, Jane reflected glumly, was that it would be an ungrateful girl, indeed, who couldn't say yes to one of three dozen. But she could just imagine them already – clodhopping sons of squires and tin-mine owners, curates with a crozier in their knapsacks, poor officers hoping for better regiments, junior solicitors or doctors with an eye on a larger partnership. The world was full of young men for whom a nice, fat dowry would turn dream into fulfilment. Sometimes she thought life would be so much easier if she weren't an heiress, if money weren't so all-important.

7

Funnily enough it hadn't been important for most of her childhood – when she had been too young to appreciate the fact. Her mother must have spent it like water. She remembered their beautiful villa in the Faubourg-St.-Honoré, and all her mother's friends there, during their years of unaccountable exile from England and separation from her father. They were the sort of men she'd really like Mrs Stringpuller to parade before her by the dozen. What a choice – the dashing cavalry officers in those breathtaking uniforms ... the Chevalier this and the Baron that with their impeccable charm ... the fashionable artists ... the pale-skinned poets ... She still could not understand what had made her mother give up all that dazzling society to come back and resume her marriage with this elderly gentleman now at her side. Oh, a decent, kindly man, to be sure; easy to live with if you did what he said. But he wasn't in the same class as those dazzling Parisian friends. They probably wouldn't even have spoken to him – a mere tea merchant!

She stared out through the window for quite a while before she realized she was looking at St Michael's Mount. "Oh, how disappointing!" she cried. "In Turner's engraving it looks so ... magical."

Her father, who was ticking off things in his notebook again, looked up briefly and said, "Oh, yes." But, she realized, there was no one you could write to and complain about it. Turner was dead, and anyway, artists had "licence," which was the freedom to lie and generally behave worse than ordinary people.

The carriage rattled on over an indifferent highway; St Michael's Mount, viewed from an ever-changing angle, grew on one; probably from close-to it looked as imposing as Turner had made it appear from an enchanted distance.

They paid the toll at Marazion. The two horses made heavy going of the hill but once they were up on the Helston turnpike their pace was brisk and they bowled along in the evening sunshine. Jane felt herself awakening to the charm of the countryside. The intensity of the colour was astonishing, especially now, with an almost horizontal sun drawing it out like some inner fire. The entire world was suddenly ablaze with the most saturated hues of green and brown – all made a hundred times more resonant by the deep violet of the twilight half of the sky. Even the granite of which the more substantial houses were built seemed compounded of scintillations of pure colour, which the eye, unable to discriminate among so many, decided to call mere grey.

As they went down into the long, shallow valley above Praa they were overtaken by a featherweight gig driven by a woman of about forty – quite obviously a local eccentric. Her jet-black hair was cropped almost as short as a man's and was covered by nothing more substantial than a sort of Tyrolean hat with a large feather stuck in its band. She stood on the driving platform like a Roman charioteer and cracked her whip fiercely over the head of her horse, which must have had Derby winner's blood in his veins. Jane half rose and, holding on to her own more elaborate headgear, risked the top half of her head outside the window to watch the progress of this amazing Diana.

The charioteer raised a battered bugle to her lips and blew a nearly musical blast upon it. The dust of the turnpike had almost obscured the legend on the tail of the gig but Jane could just make out: ROSEWARNE'S ALES. That, she reflected sadly, was

8

the sort of thing you could do if you weren't an heiress. The image of the eccentric lady, a figure gilded by the sun, driving like a fury, eyes all aglow with the pleasure of it, lingered long after her dust had drifted away inland.

They paid no further toll at Ashton, being by then in their own parish. The charioteer-bugler had driven straight through as well, so she must also be fairly local. Then a few more twists and turns brought them within sight of Breage and to the gates of Montpelier House, on the seaward side of the road.

"Do our grounds go all the way down to the sea?" she asked.

"In a way. They are cut across by a public byway. But we own the cliffs beyond and a couple of little coves at their feet – as far as the high-tide line, anyway."

It gave her visions of tripping down for an early-morning dip, but she did not like the sound of the byway. Perhaps if it were a hardly used byway it would be all right.

The gatekeeper, a bald old arthritic, came hobbling out of his lodge, wiping the supper from his lips. "Welcome Mr Hervey, sir," he cried in a strange sing-song as he opened the first gate. And then, as he skipped painfully to catch the second, which swung open of its own accord: "And you, too, Miss Hervey, ma'am. Welcome to your new home."

"Pengilly," her father murmured wearily, as if the three syllables said all that needed to be said about *that* man.

"He's rather sweet," Jane replied.

As they drove past she stared at him and nodded a gracious thank-you; only then did she realize he was quite blind. She leaned out and called back to him, "Thank you, Mr Pengilly."

"No need for the mister," her father chided.

"That's my French upbringing," she told him – thinking at once how odd it was to have given that explanation twice within the hour.

After a pause he said, "My dear, I wish you to say as little as possible to local people about your upbringing in Paris."

"Is it a secret?" she asked excitedly.

"No, no, if we make a secret of it, that will only whet their curiosity. Just volunteer nothing. Answer courteously if asked, but in the briefest fashion that is consonant with good manners." After a pause he added, "And it might be best to say nothing about that strange childhood illness of yours – the one that damaged your memory. It would do nothing to help you get a husband."

The drive curved gently, first right, then left, for about a quarter of a mile through rhododendrons and azaleas, some still in the last of their bloom. Then the view opened over a half-furlong of well-clipped lawn and rose beds, from which reared the pleasing granite façade of Montpelier House. It was what they called "a house of the middle size." A great landed family would class it "a shooting box"; a retired tea merchant would affect to call it "my place," but he would think of it, secretly, as a mansion – which is what, in simple truth, it was.

On the ground floor it had a morning room, a drawing room, a dining room, a ballroom, a library, and a business room – though the estate whose business had once been transacted there had long since been sold off to Squire Pellew of Skewjack Hall. There was also a splendid antechamber and hall, with a grand staircase like a Y curved back on itself. The first floor had a dozen or so bedrooms, boudoirs, and dressing rooms; and there were as many rooms again for the female servants on the top floor, which was arranged around the square of the entrance hall and its domed light. The menservants slept in cubicles and dormitories in an annexe that linked the house to the stables – except for the butler and one footman, through whose bedrooms one had to pass to reach the silver safe.

Jane knew all this from her father's descriptions and from the plans he had brought back with him to Leeds. What she had not been prepared for was the sight of all the servants lined up on each side of the pillared portico – thirteen indoor servants to her left, twelve outdoor to her right.

The butler, Hinks, introduced the three footmen and her father's valet; then the housekeeper, Mrs Tresidder, introduced the two upstairs maids, Mrs Gill, the cook, her assistant, and the three scullery maids. The head gardener, Silcock, introduced his four assistants and two boys, then Veryan, the head groom, who had driven them out from Penzance, introduced his second and the three stable lads.

"We'll dress for dinner and dine in about an hour," her father told them as they dispersed to their stations.

"I thought you might welcome a bath after such a fatiguing journey, Miss Hervey," said Mrs Tresidder as she ushered her into her new domain – or, rather, as he had already made clear, her father's new domain; the arrangements for dinner ought really to have come from Jane.

One of the upstairs maids, Margaret Banks, was to act as her lady's maid until she found a replacement for Manette. She was a rather stolid, watchful woman in her mid-twenties, not addicted to smiling, yet pleasant enough and she seemed quite as efficient as Jane might have wished.

The footmen carried the pails of hot water from the kitchen to the stair head, from where Banks and another maid carried them into the bedroom and filled the bath. In fact, there were two baths, one in her father's bedroom as well, so the footmen worked double tides. Two baths was a luxury that not even their house in the Faubourg-St.-Honoré had boasted.

"The range must be covered in pans for all this hot water," she commented, seeing the depth to which they had filled the bath. She stepped in and gasped with pleasure at the heat of it.

"Oh no, miss," the maid told her, "they've put in a new boiler as draws its heat directly off the fire in the range. You can have all the hot water you do want, and any time you do want, day and night."

Wonders would never cease! She wriggled as the maid tipped in the last of the pails. The heat swirled around her like living tendrils.

"Mr Matthews do make them," she went on. "He belonged to be steam engineer up Wheal Vor afore it closed."

"Was that a tin mine? I've been reading about them, but I didn't notice any on our way here."

"No, you wouldn't, not from the turnpike. A lot do go round Goldsithney, see, to avoid the toll. You'd of seen them all if you'd a' done that. Over to Carleen. 'E's only two mile away up the valley. The other side Trigonning Hill."

"Is that the big hill opposite our front gate? I'll tell you one thing I did see – a most extraordinary sight. A woman driving along like a demon, blowing a bugle for all she was worth."

The maid laughed. "That's Mrs Moore. She's some famous in these parts. She and Dr Moore do live up Lanfear House. That's on the Penzance side of Trigonning, like. She do own Liston Court in Helston, too."

"Ah, no doubt I shall be meeting her."

"I shouldn't hardly think so, miss."

"Why? Is there some scandal? Could you just scrub that bit I can't reach – just at the bottom of my shoulder blades?"

After a pause the reply came, "She don't go about much, as the saying is."

"Well, she was certainly going about this evening! Oh, that's lovely. I feel so much more refreshed now. If ... what's the other maid's name, Kemp? – if Kemp has finished unpacking the larger trunk, you may lay out my pale-blue evening gown. We've dropped full mourning *en famille*, but I'll wear the purple sash. Oh, and bring me some clean underwear."

Dressed for dinner she felt like a new woman. She went out onto the gallery at the head of the stairs just as her father emerged from his dressing room. He paused and shook his head vigorously, as if to clear it of something. "For a moment you looked so like your mother." He smiled and stepped out to join her.

She took his arm and they started down the stairs. "I'm sorry."

"No, no. I'm proud of you."

"I can't *not* wear her clothes. She had so many, it would be a wicked waste – and I've grown to fit them exactly."

"As I've just been made uncomfortably aware! But you are right. You must use her things as often as possible. Make them your own. Her memory does not need that trivial sort of protection."

"No, indeed."

They continued in an easy, reminiscing sort of silence to the foot of the stair. There, just before they went into the dining room, he said, "I hope you'll feel safe here, my dear."

"Safe?" she echoed, a little surprised at the word.

"Yes. We had to be so careful in Leeds, your mother and I, notwithstanding my elevated position in the community. With a marriage as unconventional as ours had been – until your mother came back to England, anyway ... well, we had to be so careful. But here" – he drew a deep breath through his nostrils – "don't you already smell a certain freedom?"

She sniffed the air as he had done, and laughed. "If it has the same sort of aroma as veal casserole, yes, I do."

In the moments before sleep claimed her that night she thought back over the strange things that had begun to happen from the moment they had arrived in Cornwall. First the enigmatic Miss Wilkinson, who was somehow mixed up in Hervey family affairs; then the amazing Mrs Moore, to whom, despite Banks's refusal to confirm it, she felt sure there attached some scandal; and finally that strange word of her father's: *safe.* Why safe? she wondered.

11

Had they been under some kind of threat in Leeds? She had never been aware of it. They enjoyed the usual circle of friends that the family of a prosperous wholesale tea merchant might expect to enjoy, all of whom had seemed as affable and charming as such people ought to be. Why would her father talk of being *safe* from them?

And as for her companions at Miss Moreton's Ladies' Academy ... she thought of Sally and Eglantine and Gervaise and Barbara ... and almost burst into tears at the realization they might never meet again. To talk of feeling safe, because all those dear, dear people were several hundred miles away, was absurd.

So her thoughts returned in those moments before sleep to that puzzling question: Safe – from *what?*

2 JANE RETURNED THE calling cards to their boxes, hers on one side, her father's on the other. "Things are different in the country," she sighed, echoing his words. In Paris, and even in Leeds, newcomers and established families called or left cards indiscriminately; but in the country it was the strict and invariable rule for the newcomers to wait until called upon and then to return a call with a call or a card with a card. "And we do want to do these things properly," she added – a further echo of her father's sentiments.

But all that week no one called. Her father could not understand it. "They must assume we need time to settle our domestic arrangements," Jane suggested. To herself she thought, *Little do they know you!* For, naturally, he had left reams of lists with Hinks and Mrs Tresidder so that, by the evening of their arrival, the domestic machine was already running at full tilt. It continued to do so all week – except that between the hours of three and five in the afternoon, when Jane took particular care to be at home in the social as well as the literal sense, no one paid a "morning" call and no cards were handed in. It was unnerving to go to church on Sunday and not be able to talk to anyone or even nod to them – except, of course, the vicar. And even there Jane made a small blunder.

She said, in the way one does say such things, that she hoped there'd be some means by which she might assist in the work of the parish. It was as good as asking for an introduction to a member of the Ladies' Committee, who were, of course, all about them in the departing congregation; but he, poor man, being in no position to effect such an introduction, was reduced to saying, vaguely but effusively, that he, too, hoped she might "in the fullness of time assist in their parish labours." It was a kindly way of telling her she must first be assured of her acceptance into local society; a delicate slap on the knuckles, in fact.

So Jane filled in the days as best she could. She sorted her gloves by material and then by colour, dreaming of the day when she could go back into colours again. She picked and arranged the flowers. She discussed the menu with Mrs Tresidder. She inventoried the silver with Hinks. And, when she was not waiting "at home," she went for walks, with Banks as her chaperone.

Her father saw how she fretted. "Profit from this enforced lesson, my dear," he advised. "We are not being ostracized, of course. No question of that! And yet it is *as if* we were. So now, as you rattle around this unvisited mansion, seeking some timely distraction, learn what a perilous thing it would be to lose society's good graces for ever! And just see what a pathetic, lonely, useless thing is a woman without a place in it! That is why I say, so often, a woman's reputation can have no price. It *must* be kept unspotted."

He was – as always – right. The very thought of a spotted reputation made her shudder. He, to be sure, had his books and memoirs, *My Interesting Life in Wholesale Tea*, to occupy him. The ways of the world were so easy for men. And yet one could not complain of that. Society's rules had been fashioned by women, not men, and none were more jealous to maintain them than those favoured ladies who were "In."

"Banks," Jane asked her maid after several idle days had passed, "who would you say is the local queen bee? Whose hand are we waiting to knock at our door?"

The woman had to think. "If you was married, Miss Jane, I s'pose 'twould be you. I mean, Montpelier's the biggest *house* hereabouts."

"Yes, well I can hardly start the social whirl in train by leaving cards on myself."

"Well next in line, now, if you're talking about Helston, would be Mrs Samuel Troy. Now Mrs Ramona Troy's dead at last. Only Mrs Sam is ailing, too, and they do say as she may never recover after that little baby boy in the spring. So then it ought to be Mrs Anthony Moore of Liston Court."

"The lady with the bugle?"

"Yes, except half the ladies hereabouts won't even give she so much as a nod. Then, if you're just meaning Breage parish – which is Breage-with-Germoe, like – then it ought to be Mrs Pellew, Squire Pellew's wife of Skewjack Hall, or Mrs Leonard down Pengersick. But they're both in Mrs Moore's circle, see – so a lot of ladies in the parish are a bit cool with them, too."

Jane busily committed every name and alliance to memory, for these were the hand- and toe-holds she would need if she was not to fall into the abyss during her perilous explorations of local society. "So who does that leave?" she asked.

Banks considered the matter. "I calculate that'd be Mrs Lanyon of Parc-an-Ython, which is half-way between Breage and Sithney parishes. But then Breage and Sithney do go together, like."

"What does her husband do?" She meant, of course, what was the basis of her claim to be among the leading local ladies.

"He do own a lot of land, like, and he's mineral lord, too, over most of Sithney."

"I see – and what sort of lady is she? Is she old?" If her father's plans came to pass, it would be this Mrs Lanyon, or someone very much like her, under whose wing she would be sheltering until a suitable marriage could be arranged.

"No, I wouldn't say she's yet thirty."

That sounded promising. "And children?"

"She haven't had none yet. They do say as she can't never have none, neither."

"Oh, the poor woman. But in herself, now – is she placid and equable? Or has she a temper? What do her servants have to say about her?"

Banks cleared her throat. "I'm not sure as 'tis my place, miss."

"Perhaps not as upper maid, Banks, but I'll tell you a secret. The chief office of a *lady's* maid is to bring her mistress all the useful information she can lay ear to." After a pause Banks asked carefully, "Does that mean I'm to be your lady's maid then, Miss Jane?"

"That is not my decision, Banks. But you will never hold the place *without* practising its duties."

There was a further pause before the maid replied, "She's a very strict and upright woman by all accounts, miss. And that's all I could rightly say."

Childless, strict, and upright. The early promise was already receding.

The following Saturday morning, after more than a week of idleness, Jane set forth with Banks for the summit of Trigonning Hill, which, according to the guidebook, offered views of the whole of western Cornwall. The day was fine and warm, so she wore her lightest black dress. The two young women toiled up the slope between stout Cornish hedges, which are, in fact, thick walls of dry stone "mortared" with soil, in which anything grows that can set down roots. There was a mass of early summer blooms, drowning in the murmur of bees. When they reached the upper limit of the cultivated slopes Jane was disappointed to see how far away the hilltop still was; from the road at its foot the area of heather and ling, which now stretched above them, had seemed so small.

There were two figures silhouetted against the clouds: a woman and a child. Jane asked Banks who they might be. The maid replied, "The little giglet is Miss Moore – Hannah Moore, that is. And the other is her nanny, Mrs Temple – Hilary Cardew as was. Her husband, John Temple, is coachman to Dr Moore." She looked shrewdly at Jane. "You want to know all about they, too, do 'ee?"

Jane chuckled. "Why? Is there much to tell?"

"Enough to burn your ears."

Jane frowned. "Well ... not if it's anything indelicate."

Banks said nothing.

"Do begin then," Jane coaxed. "Or we shall be upon them."

They paused for a brief rest. "Hilary Cardew," Banks began, "and her li'l sister and two brothers was left orphans after a big parish fight between Breage and Goldsithney, 'bout ten years backalong."

"Good heavens! D'you mean their mother was killed in a brawl?"

"Her and a couple of dozen beside. The Big Randy, they do call 'n. There hasn't been nothing quite hardly so big since."

"I should just hope not!"

"Well ... they do go in for fighting a lot – miners and farming folk. Anyway, Mrs Cardew was killed in that one. Her husband got crushed to death down Wheal Vor before that. So Dr Moore, he helped stitch a lot of sore heads together that day she died, and he took the four of them in, like."

"Took them in where?" They resumed their climb.

Banks turned and pointed it out. "Lanfear. That's his place down there."

Jane saw a substantial but modest two-storey house of granite.

"'Course, he'd just bought it then so he never had no servants at all, 'cept a cook and one maid-of-all-work."

14

"He must be a man of great charity. They could hardly have earned their keep at their ages."

"They done well enough since, miss. The younger girl is now schoolteacher over to Stithians and the two boys do work in Mrs Moore's brewery in Penzance."

"Ah, *that* explains the device on her gig. So she inherited a brewery, did she?"

"No, she built it, miss. She started out brewing the ale herself, down there in the stables at Lanfear, and selling it door to door – and now she's got the biggest brewery in the West of England, so they do say."

Jane could just imagine the sort of woman who'd do such things – coarse, manly, red-faced, and as plump as her own barrels. The raven-haired, blue-eyed Diana she had spied on the evening of her arrival did not fit at all. "And you say the child is their daughter?" she prompted.

"Her daughter," Banks replied carefully. "She was still plain Miss Johanna Rosewarne when little Hannah come along."

"Ah." Jane blushed. No wonder the woman's rise in the world had divided local society. She was one of those Free Thinkers, no doubt. But what could one say of people like Mrs Pellew, the *squire's* wife, befriending such an abandoned creature?

"They do say as she crawled three miles out of Helston, and through the worst storm in living memory, to be sure the babby was born at a certain place – the *crows-an-wrea,* the croft of the witches." Banks pointed it out, for they had just reached the shoulder of Trigonning, half a mile from the actual summit, which was now to their north. The croft itself was too far off to discern, but Tregathennan, the hill at whose foot it lay, was landmark enough.

However, Jane's eye was now more taken by the landscape immediately below them, a waste of mines and spoil heaps among which tiny stone-girt fields jostled for elbow room. Obviously the miners and farmers were at constant war, not just on occasions like the one Banks had mentioned. The maid, seeing her interest, began to point out the mines, which were distinguishable by their engine houses, square towers of stone with pitched slate roofs, each of which was attended by a tall, round chimney, stone at the base, brick above: "Wheal Fortune, Scott's, Grankum, Wheal Metal, Pallas Consols, Wheal Vor ... 'course, Wheal Vor's been shut down this dozen years or more, but they do say as there's more tin left down there unmined than ever come out."

"And how much did come out?"

"Over two million pounds' worth, as I heard tell."

"Goodness gracious! One can't imagine all that wealth. Oh, I should so love to see down a tin mine."

"Well, that's one thing you'll never do, Miss Jane – go down a bal. They do never let a woman below. 'Tis the greatest misfortune, they do say."

"Oh do they, indeed! And in Yorkshire the women haul the coal from the face – and children, too."

"And there's no misfortunes to follow?"

"A great deal, I fear."

"They let a woman down Wheal Unity a few years backalong, and next day all the stopes was fell in."

15

Jane smiled. "And even then it never crossed their minds we might come cheaper than blasting powder?"

Banks laughed, never having thought of it that way.

"Can we see Parc-an-Ython from here?" Jane asked.

Banks pointed out a substantial stone-built house about a mile away on the far side of the valley between Breage and the neighbouring village of Sithney.

Though Jane still thought of Cornwall as the end of the world, she had always felt a certain affinity for the county, chiefly because her mother had kept a small map of it in her pocket book. Perhaps she had had some thought of ending her days in the county? The possibility had reconciled her to her father's decision to settle here in his retirement.

The resumed their walk to the summit. Here on the shoulder of the hill the slope was much gentler than on the climb itself and they soon drew near the child and her nanny. "Good morning, Miss Banks," the woman said. She dropped Jane a curtsy.

"Good morning, Mrs Temple," the maid replied. And then, to the child, "Morning, my lover. How are you digging in that pit, then?"

Young Hannah was using a broken furze branch from last Midsummer's bonfire to grub up the sand in a shallow pit beside the path. "My Uncle Terence once found a George the Third penny here," she explained. "He says the ancient physicians dug this when they came here looking for tin and didn't know any better."

"That's very like a physician," Jane could not help commenting, though she had not intended any intercourse with the girl.

Hannah rose and nodded gravely. "How d'you do. I am Miss Moore. You, I believe, are Miss Hervey. We hope you will find the district to your liking."

"How kind," Jane said awkwardly.

"My father's a physician, too," Hannah added, "but not an ancient one."

"Yes, so I hear. In fact, he's very modern, isn't he. He's done some splendid work among the miners, I'm told." It annoyed her to hear herself gabbling on, especially when she'd intended nothing more than a polite nod and, at most, a comment on the weather. But the girl was so engaging.

"Yes," Hannah agreed, with an edge of doubt to her voice. "Of course, they can't organize, not to save their lives. My mother has to do all that."

"Now then, miss," her nanny said. "People don't want to hear all that old cooze." She gave the others an apologetic smile.

Hannah was unabashed. "That's where I live." She pointed out Lanfear House.

"What splendid views of the bay you must have from there," Jane said.

"My father sent me a telescope from America. I can count the sails on all the ships, even on the horizon." She grinned. "And I can see Montpelier, too."

"And what can you count there? The kerchiefs on the washing line, I suppose?"

Hannah giggled and Jane made a mental note to be sure the curtains were carefully drawn in future. "Well," she concluded, "I promised myself I'd go to the very top of this hill, and one should always keep promises, you know, especially those one makes to oneself."

When they were out of earshot she asked Banks what the child had meant by saying her father had sent a telescope from America.

The maid chuckled. "She do mean her real father – Hal Penrose. I don't suppose she do catch on yet to the difference, like, between the father of the child and the father of the family."

She made the girl's ignorance sound so charmingly infantile that Jane did not like to confess that she was in the same quandary herself. How could one say, "so-and-so is that child's father," if there was no marriage? By what process did fatherhood get pinned on a man who was not the woman's husband? .

At various times people had told her that babies were "found in the garden, like eggs at Easter," or, "the doctor brings them in his big black bag." But she knew by now that those were little fibs designed to protect children's innocence. But from what? She had worked out for herself that babies grew in women's bellies. She'd seen enough of them *enceinte*, as people said, or "in an interesting condition," to observe that their sudden return to normal size coincided with a new and lusty young voice from the regions of the nursery. For years, too, she had known there was something shameful attached to the business, so that one no longer asked the innocent questions of childhood. And yet now that she was nineteen, everyone seemed to assume she had somehow acquired the answers to all those unasked questions, anyway. It was most vexing.

"How did they *know* he was the father?" she asked, and held her breath for the answer. You never knew what might slip out between the lines.

"Oh, he made no secret of it, Miss Jane," the maid replied. "He give she the babby before he went to America, see."

"To look after?"

Banks laughed. "No, he never even knew he done it. Hopeful Harry, just like every man. She was named from the pulpit and all. The very day that young girl there was born, the vicar preached her mother from the pulpit."

Jane closed her eyes and shivered. Most of Banks's reply was gibberish to her, but the degradation of being named from the pulpit was well within her understanding. "I suppose she had to leave Cornwall for a while," she commented.

"Not she!"

"She sounds utterly brazen to me. It's a wonder she had such a charming little girl. Is she an only child?"

"No, miss. She got two brothers and a sister – in wedlock, of course. And that Mrs Temple, she got three of her own, too, much of an age. And they do all grow up together in the same nursery."

"Oh!" Jane was at a loss for words; she just shook her head at such depravity. She would most decidedly *not* be at home to this Mrs Moore person if she called.

They reached the summit of the hill, from which she had expected to gain a splendid view over the countryside to the north. Instead, the land dipped slightly and then rose to a second, lower eminence, which Banks told her was Godolphin Hill. "We must go up there one day," Jane said. "I love these aerial views. It's like looking down on toy farms and toy villages."

Breage was a perfect example – the twisting roads, the wind-bent trees, the little whitewashed houses ... the idealized picture of Everyman's village. But from here you could also see something that was much less obvious from down there, when you were actually in the place: the cankerous sprawl of miners' hovels, lurking behind hedges and down nameless little lanes. "Goodness," she exclaimed. "Look at all those little shacks and things. It's more than twice the size of the village. And all the way up the valley, too – in every little copse and spinney. They're like ants."

"Emmets," Banks said.

Jane turned and faced west, looking across a dozen miles of a much gentler landscape, with hardly a mine chimney in sight. And beyond that again, half swallowed in the summer haze, rose the pale, blue-gray humps of the Land's End peninsula. "It is so different from our Yorkshire Dales," she said. "Yet I think I could grow to love it just as well."

At last they turned to go. "We must hurry home," she said. "We have *such* a busy afternoon ahead of us!"

Her father met her at the door. "Who were you talking to?" he asked. "You were seen talking ..."

"To a little ten-year-old girl playing in a sandpit. And her nursemaid." Jane stroked his arm soothingly. "Nothing to be alarmed about."

A faint smile flickered across his face. "Well, I do worry. I don't want you to ..."

"Miss Wilkinson wasn't there," she added by way of a joke.

It baffled him. "Miss Wilkinson? And who may she be?"

"Oh ..." She sought for the easiest explanation. "Just some local batty old creature. Never mind."

How could he have forgotten her already, especially after making such a song and dance at the very sight of her last week? Was it an early sign of senility? Or did he perhaps know her by some other name?

*　　　*　　　*

Jane's ironic comment – that she had such a busy afternoon – was prophetic. She had barely settled in her drawing room before Hinks opened the door and announced, "Mrs Jesse Lanyon."

Swallowing her heart, which was threatening to leap out of her throat, she rose to greet her inquisitor-guest (to name her roles in the order of their importance). "Mrs Lanyon, how very kind of you to call. I am Miss Hervey, Jane Hervey. Where will you sit?" She resumed her own chair and left her visitor to choose.

Mrs Lanyon selected the next closest. She was a plain woman at first impression, a light brunette, slightly above average height; but she had a fine, healthy skin, neat features, and kindly, hazel eyes, which, Jane felt, had summed her up in the first four paces from the door. "I do hope I am not too early?" she murmured, then, seeing Jane glance at the clock, added, "No, I mean too soon after your arrival in Cornwall. I can just imagine how much there is to do on moving into a house this size."

Jane smiled as if imparting a secret. "My father is the world's greatest organizer, Mrs Lanyon. You would have found me At Home for a week, so you are, indeed, very welcome. Hinks, tell my father Mrs Lanyon is here."

"Oh, pray do not disturb him on my account."

"He would never forgive me." Jane smiled.

Mrs Lanyon smiled back. "You are kind to say so. Then you must be an organizer, too, Miss Hervey?"

"I fear not. I merely swirl along in his wake like an autumn leaf behind a carriage." The faintest of frowns crossed Mrs Lanyon's face. In her view, clever turns of phrase – indeed, anything that hinted at a superior mind – were not to be indulged in by young girls who had not yet caught their man.

Jane saw it and felt constrained to add, "As he puts it."

"Ah." Mrs Lanyon was content again. "You have been lucky with the weather, Miss Hervey."

"Yes, indeed. I'm told a week without even a shower is something of a rarity in Cornwall. Let us hope it persists, for the farmers' sakes. I was up on Trigonning Hill this morning and I noticed the green just beginning to fade from the corn."

"Ah? You are interested in agricultural matters?"

"As an observer, merely. I cannot help noticing how much further the season is advanced down here than it was in Yorkshire."

"Really? Yorkshire would be your native county, then?"

"No." Jane laughed. "I am a Parisienne by birth."

"Paris?" It was the first genuine – or, at least, lively – interest the woman had shown so far.

"Yes. I lived there until I was fourteen – five very long years ago, it now seems." There was another question answered without being asked. Now for a few more – the difficult ones. "My father, as you may know, was in the tea business and travelled extensively. My mother, who was born in Wales, found the English climate not at all to her liking and, being able to indulge whatever choice she might make ..."

"Fortunate woman."

"Indeed, in some ways. Sadly, she was orphaned and without close relations at the age of four – but was left very well endowed."

"And so she chose Paris, when she could? Nothing can compensate the loss of a parent, as I see you know."

"Indeed." Jane's eyes fell, though less in sorrow than in shame that she had felt far more grief at the death of her old nanny. Her mother, by contrast, had always seemed remote and angelic. Jane glanced out of the window. Two children, supposed to be turning hay, were enjoying a romp. The smell of the hay, drifting in through the partly opened sash, reminded her of the Bois de Boulogne.

Mrs Lanyon, too, was thinking of that city, which she had visited a million times in her imagination. "Yet to live in Paris," she said, "must have been a partial recompense at least. Do you miss it, my dear?"

"I did when we first moved to Leeds. Yes, I suppose I still do at times. I hope I don't sound ungrateful, for I'm sure my father's house was ... was ... all one ought to wish for." She gave a wan smile. "One day perhaps I shall go back."

Mrs Lanyon smiled, too. "And – don't think me intrusive, pray, but are *you* also well enough endowed to ..."

Her father entered at that moment. Jane presented him. "How kind of you to call," he told her. "Jane and I have been so looking forward to meeting *you*, Mrs Lanyon, for I'm told there is no more discriminating arbiter of local society."

"Oh ... well ..." The woman produced a menagerie of self-deprecatory noises. "And I propose to make use of you straight away!" he went on with a twinkle in his eye. "Tell me now – put our minds at rest – in the circles we have just left, one would never have offered a caller refreshments before four o'clock. Yet I'm reliably informed that in some West Country circles it is considered discourteous not to offer refreshments whenever a caller may arrive. What are we to do, dear lady? We shall be bound by your decision."

She dipped her head in happy acceptance of the compliment. "You have obviously moved in very correct circles, Mr Hervey – as, indeed, I would expect, now that I meet you and your charming daughter. Some of the" – she smiled tolerantly – "how shall one express it? Some of the less ..."

"Discerning?" he offered.

"Just so! Some of the less discerning ladies – even, I am distressed to confess it, in my own circle of friends ... dear, good, kindly souls that they are – they will press their tea and cake or sandwiches and ale upon one no matter what hour one calls. One does one's best, you know, with a discreet cough, a lifted eyebrow, but it's like water off a duck's back ..." She smiled conspiratorially at Jane and added, "... as Lanyon always says."

Jane gave Hinks an almost imperceptible nod, a signal that he was to go and tell Banks and one of the footmen that they were not to prepare tea before four o'clock. He did not grasp the point. Mrs Lanyon, who noted the exchange – or lack of it – waited to see how well Jane controlled her annoyance. The result pleased her; it was just sufficient to let a servant know he had erred, without intruding on the company. Young Jane Hervey began to impress her. Obviously, to have lived in Paris had given her enormous social advantages – poise, ease of manner, an instinctive feeling for the *niceties* of a situation.

Hinks announced a Mrs Menadue. Jane noticed a slight darkening of Mrs Lanyon's countenance; it was swiftly masked by a smile that was both brave and faintly weary.

Mrs Menadue was of average height, well fleshed but by no means stout; she had enough energy for half a dozen. She advanced across the room with the broadest of smiles. "My dear Miss Hervey, welcome to Cornwall! Why, you must feel you've come to the end of the earth. I know I did when Menadue first brought me down here." She nodded in passing at Mrs Lanyon but the outpouring did not stop. "Well, let's have a good look at you. Oh, is this your father? Mr Hervey, you're welcome, too. Let's hope you'll bring some changes now. You've certainly brought some fine weather down with you."

"Yes," Jane began, "I was just saying ..."

"Changes?" her father echoed, shaking the woman's hand.

Mrs Lanyon – as etiquette demanded – yielded her chair to the newcomer; but she hesitated long enough to make it quite clear that etiquette alone had moved her.

"Oh yes," Mrs Menadue bustled on as she occupied the vacated chair. "This house ought to be the hub of the district. I've always felt that. Indeed, I said as much the moment I clapped eyes on it when Menadue first brought me down in the world – as I like to put it." She giggled. "Yet for some strange reason it never has. Never quite got the right people." She glanced about her. "I'm too early for tea, I see. Well, as I was saying, let's have a look at you. Come on, up you get!"

She herself rose and held out both her arms as if she and Jane might dance a quadrille together.

A bewildered Jane complied, giving Mrs Lanyon an uncertain glance out of the corner of her eye. Mrs Lanyon raised her gaze to the ceiling and sighed heavily. "I think I really must be going," she murmured.

"Oh, must you, dear Mrs Lanyon?" Jane asked unhappily. There was so much more she wished to learn from this woman who was acknowledged as the doyenne of local society.

"Let me see you to your carriage, dear lady," Hervey offered.

Mrs Lanyon raised a surprised eyebrow; the length of their acquaintance hardly warranted such courtesy. It smacked of something foreign and overdone.

"Well," Mrs Menadue was saying as she turned an embarrassed Jane this way and that, "here's a sight will turn many a head at the next ball, eh, Mrs Lanyon? What is the next ball, by the way?"

"But I am still in mourning, Mrs Menadue." Jane spoke in as sharp a tone as her unhappy situation allowed.

Mrs Lanyon, pleased at this revival of the girl's spirit, decided she could safely part company. Jane shook her hand warmly, was so glad she called, and asked when she might be At Home.

"On Tuesday, my dear." She beamed. "Come early."

"And work up a thirst," Mrs Menadue muttered.

"I beg your pardon, Mrs er ...?" Mrs Lanyon said.

"I said, 'And you still won't be first,' Mrs ah ... Your At Homes are so popular." She gave a tiny sniff and added, "I'm told."

As soon as Mrs Lanyon had gone, the other woman collapsed with a sigh of relief and said, "Poor you! I'd have called earlier except that I've been shopping in Plymouth most of the week. I knew *she'd* be first." She gave a contemptuous backward shake of her head, which half dislodged her bonnet. "But she's not the pattern for the neighbourhood – as I'm sure you'll be relieved to hear. Was it she told you not to serve tea until four?"

Jane smiled icily. "I believe it is not done in the best circles, Mrs Menadue."

The other stared at her with large, amused eyes. Jane suddenly felt as if she were fourteen again.

"I see," Mrs Menadue murmured sadly as she took out her card case. "Well – that would appear to be that! I'll leave my husband's card. And I'll turn the corner down. But consider it a mere formality. I shan't be offended if you don't repay this call."

She rose and they touched fingers briefly. "Indeed," she added as she bounced toward the door, "it takes a great deal to offend me. I hope you'll remember that when you're just a *little* bit older."

At the door she paused and, holding up her husband's dog-eared card, said, "In Paris – as you'll of course know – they turn the entire edge down. Doesn't that worry you?"

"Why should it?" Jane asked.

21

"Well, they can't *both* be right, can they." She grinned and, jerking her head in the direction Mr Hervey and Mrs Lanyon had taken, said, "You know what that's all about, I hope?"

"I beg your pardon?" Jane was cool again.

"You'll observe, no doubt, that we haven't heard a carriage depart yet? Could it be that your father and your undeparted guest are settling your entire future between them? Has someone misinformed him that she is the one to arrange it all?"

"I'm sure that is his business," Jane retorted.

"Then you *are* a fool," Mrs Menadue replied, as affable as you'd wish.

3 WHEN MR HERVEY saw Mrs Lanyon to her carriage she felt an uneasiness within him, which made her uneasy, too. "Your daughter is a charming young girl," she said warily.

"Yes." Though he spoke the word firmly enough he followed it with a little sigh. "It is proving rather hard for me. Until her mother passed over I was not aware how much ..." He left the sentence hanging while the valet-du-jour opened the door.

"Oh, your gardens are an absolute picture!" she enthused as they went out. When the door had closed behind them she went on, "I can imagine your difficulties, Mr Hervey. I remember how it was between my own mother and me at that age. So much passed between us that needed no words. There is such an amazing sympathy between mother and child." Her eyes rose sadly to the crest of Trigonning. "But it seems I shall not ..." She paused and began again. "Our union has not so far been blessed with children − as you may know."

"I'm sorry. I had not heard." He lied to spare her the embarrassment of knowing he had discussed her so intimately with others. "But you are young yet, surely."

She thought fleetingly of all the times she and Jesse had tried − then she hastily suppressed the memory. "It seems not to be," she said.

"Then you are called to your womanly duty in some other way," he assured her. "As I have been called to pilot young Jane through these turbulent seas of love and courtship into the safe anchorage of a good match. A daunting prospect, indeed."

They arrived at her carriage. He was reaching for the door handle when she said, "Would you think it dreadful of me if I asked to stroll about your garden, Mr Hervey? It is so long since I ..."

"But nothing could give me greater pleasure, Mrs Lanyon, especially if you will permit me to be your guide."

"Oh, I don't wish to deprive your other callers of your company."

He nodded at her footman. "Be so good as to ask my valet to bring out my hat and gloves." With a smile he offered her his arm and added, "If you don't object to my going bareheaded for a step or two?"

The valet caught up with them at the farther edge of the main lawn, where they had paused to admire a splendidly geometrical display of cineraria, salvia, and petunia. "Not a leaf out of place," he said. "Or not so as to show."

22

"You have a treasure in Silcock. He learned his craft at Trengwainton, you know – the Bolithos' seat near Penzance. He'll rival their gardens yet if you give him scope here."

The moment Mr Hervey was properly dressed he became easier in his manner; and now that they were among the literal bushes there was no more beating about the metaphorical ones, either.

"She is a good girl," he said. "Obedient, tractable, and willing ..."

"And handsome, too," Mrs Lanyon put in. "Oh, she has many advantages."

"Indeed, indeed, ma'am, as you rightly say. But the enormous gulf between our ages troubles me, I must confess. It is so hard to ..."

"Come! Is it so enormous?" Mrs Lanyon asked, moving to an arm's length and peering archly at him.

"I am in my seventieth year," he told her.

But his solemnity was belied by a twinkle in his eye. A temporal echo of a younger Wilfrid Hervey smiled gravely down at her and she saw that he must have been quite a ladykiller, in his day – which, come to think of it, was when ladykillers were first invented. Indeed, he was not without his charms now, "in his seventieth year"; so correct in his thoughts, so courteous in manner, so firm in his opinions. Such men had always excited her admiration. "Now there you surprise me," she assured him. "I would not have guessed a day over ..."

"Come, come." He smiled and patted her hand in the crook of his arm. "Whatever you might have guessed, dear lady, it would still represent an enormous gulf." He became crisp and businesslike again. "The reason I prefaced my remarks with a certain immodest praise of my daughter's character is that I was going on to say that she is, nonetheless, a young girl. And even the most virtuous of that species, brought up on the strictest principles, must nonetheless have in her blood some taint of the original Eve. Our Creator Himself has ordained it so, even as He has charged us to be on our guard against her wiles. The wiles of Eve, I mean, of course."

Mrs Lanyon cleared her throat delicately. "I trust you speak from general principles, Mr Hervey?"

"Indeed, dear lady. Scriptural principles."

"Quite. I mean, you have detected nothing in *particular* to cause you any unease?"

Mrs Menadue's carriage could be heard departing. "Well, your daughter gave *her* short shrift," Mrs Lanyon added approvingly. She, too, now became easier in her mind. "I had my doubts about leaving them alone, I confess. But etiquette is so particular upon the point of yielding to a new caller that I really had no choice. But top marks to Miss Jane! She is obviously to be trusted to make her own judgements, to some degree at least." She glanced up at him. "Or do I now trespass upon your own thoughts, sir?"

"No trespasser was ever so welcome, ma'am. The worry of it poisons my dreams. The innocence and purity of a young girl is such a treasure. Its possession is so delightful to her; its example so enriching to society at large. Yet there is always that worm in the bud: the Old Eve. She is so apt to cloak herself in the raiment of purity even as the serpentine temptations are coiling themselves within, ready to sink their fangs in that daintiest of flesh."

Mrs Lanyon nodded sagely. "Your decision to move to Cornwall," she said. "That was not in connection with ... I mean, these considerations played no part in it?" "No, no," he said firmly, "thanks be to God. Naturally, an anxious father, so unversed in the ways and thoughts of young girls, would always be aware of the temptations and opportunities afforded by a large city, especially one like Leeds, which, I must admit, is disorderly to a degree."

"Do you say so?" she asked emphatically.

"Oh, Mrs Lanyon, you can have no idea! To answer your question, I chose Cornwall because you have preserved here the old-fashioned modes of regulating society and of restricting access to it. I do not wish to seem to slander my good Yorkshire neighbours. We knew many of the utmost propriety ..."

"I'm sure."

"... and yet the uphill task we all faced there since the general rise in prosperity has brought affluence to quite unsuitable people – I can hardly convey it to you. Men and women whose greatest intimacy would once have been a respectable tipping of the hat or the dropping of a curtsy, now clap one on the shoulders and ask how it goes!"

"Mercy!" Mrs Lanyon was dutiful in her surprise. "Mind you," she added, "something of the sort has happened here, too. Every revival of the tin trade sees another dozen gigs on the roads. And when people buy a gig they seem to think they have also purchased the automatic right to bow at one across the street and smile at one in church ..."

"Church!" he barked. "Now there you have it, dear lady. The Church is much to blame in this. I assure you it was quite possible in Leeds for young people, socially quite unsuited yet smitten with those feelings that thumb a nose at society and its demands ... it was quite possible for them, one Sunday, to nod at each other across the pews in church; next week they'd bow; next, exchange a remark on the weather ... and very soon after, within a few months, they'd be conversing on terms of ease!"

Mrs Lanyon tutted her disapproval. "In church, you say?"

"Indeed, dear lady, in church! And never mind that one lot of parents were cutting the other lot dead, while *they*, of course, were egging on their youngster to widen this breach in the wall. Now an impressionable young girl, even one most correctly brought up, cannot but help relax her standards where such grossly improper behaviour becomes commonplace."

"She's well to be out of that," Mrs Lanyon agreed. "I had no idea such depravity could flourish in what ought to be the most respectable of *milieux*."

They went under a pergola and emerged into a small courtyard-garden of stone troughs and alpine plants.

"But in our particular case," he concluded, "my anxieties are compounded by the fact that Jane has been left a considerable heiress by the tragic death of her mother."

"Ah," she said. "This sun is more powerful than one supposed. Do you think we may sit awhile."

"But of course. How thoughtless of me."

They sat on a stone seat in the shade of a little arbour and she was able to ease the strings of her bonnet. "Your wife seems to have been a lady of independent means,

24

then, Mr Hervey?" she prompted. "Jane was telling me she chose to live in Paris after she herself was orphaned."

There was a short silence before he said, "Instinct is such an uncertain guide, and yet there are times in one's life when one simply has no alternative. I have an instinctive feeling, Mrs Lanyon, that this brief acquaintance between us – which I look upon as one between our two families – will mature into something stronger."

"Well, I earnestly hope so, Mr Hervey. You may take it that my husband is associated with everything I say and do. We are of one mind, he and I."

"I am reassured to hear it, ma'am – though I would never have thought it to be otherwise. I feel I must make a certain confession to you, slender as our acquaintance may be, for fear that you might otherwise think we entered society down here upon false premises. You may suppose, from my conversation today and from my unremitting efforts to preserve my daughter from harm, that I am now and always have been a most conventional member of society. Alas, that is only half true. The half that is true is that I am now. But it would be a deceit to claim I was always so. Perhaps that is why I am so particular with Jane – who thinks me a dreadful old fusser. But I know what blood runs in her veins, you see."

"Mr Hervey," Mrs Lanyon interrupted. "Pray do not feel you have to tell me these things. After all, which one of us can cast the first stone?"

"But I have a particular reason, dear lady. Two particular reasons. First, I am assured that your voice carries great weight in these parts. So if you know the entire truth you will feel sufficient moral assurance to quash those nasty gossips who learn bits of it and let their disgraceful imaginations fill out the rest ..."

"... without revealing what I know, of course."

He smiled at her and she felt suddenly warm and privileged. "You understand me so perfectly," he said. "My second reason is that I have a favour to ask of you – which would be a monstrous imposition if you did not know everything."

"Rely upon me, sir," she assured him, "and if it be within my power ..."

"Say nothing as to that until you have heard me out," he warned. "In any case, I could not possibly expect an answer today. You must give it your most solemn consideration, you and Mr Lanyon both." He drew a deep breath and began his tale.

"I have told you I was not always the most fervent supporter of society's conventions. As a young man I was rebellious and headstrong. I kicked against the pricks at every chance I got. But the pinnacle of my revolt came when, against not merely the advice but the express command of my parents, I fell most desperately in love with and eventually married Jane's mother, Angwin."

"That's a Cornish name," Mrs Lanyon interrupted.

"Ah, indeed? Well it is Welsh, too, for that is where she came from. We married in secret and it was our intention to run away together and begin a new life. We hadn't two farthings to rub together, but what we lacked in coin we made up for in dreams and youthful vigour."

"But I thought Jane said ..."

He held up a finger. "I'm coming to that. The day before our departure, which was some three or four months after our clandestine wedding, my father was crippled by a stroke. At first I feared it was on my account – that he had heard of my deceit and was stricken with an apoplexy. But no – thank God he never learned the truth. The events were quite unconnected."

"He died without knowing?"

"He died a few months later, of a second stroke. The first had not affected his mind, which was as sharp as ever, and it had even left him some power of speech. He called me to his bedside and confessed to me that our family business was – not to put too fine a point on it – on the rocks. He begged me to say nothing that might distress my mother and sisters but to work all the hours God sent in an endeavour to restore our fortunes."

"This was the tea business," she said.

"Wholesale. Yes. What I did not know – and what Angwin did not tell me for some time – was that little Jane was already on the way by then. With the benefit of hindsight I can say that we grew a rod for our own backs, Angwin and I. Chiefly I, of course, for, like Jane, she was always guided by me. I ought to have grasped the nettle and confessed all to my mother. She was a stronger person than I then gave her credit for being. At the time I feared that the shock of my treachery, coming so soon after the shock of my father's illness, would finish her. So I continued to live a lie. And once one has put one's hand to that particular plough, one must turn the furrow to the end of the field, for when the treachery is continuous, time can never diminish it."

"Poor man," Mrs Lanyon murmured.

"Ah, well, it is all so long ago now. The one to pity was poor Angwin, who had to do what many another poor young woman in her condition had done – and does still – and without the benefit of a wedding ring. She at least had that, though she could not show it. But the height of my folly was revealed when a distant relative of hers died and left her a considerable fortune – amounting to some twenty thousand pounds, in fact. Had I not been so adamant in what I thought were kindly white lies, we could have revealed our marriage *and* the parlous state of the family business *and* the means of rescuing it the very next day. They would surely have been reconciled to Angwin then! But, in my pride, I could not admit I had been such a consummately good liar. In my pride, I wished to rescue the business by my own efforts not by my wife's charity. I thought it would take seven years. In fact, it took twelve. Of course I made frequent visits to Paris 'on business.' Angwin found life there so congenial I had not the heart to insist on her return to England after Jane was born. But the hardest part for me was to watch her growing up from a distance. We thought it wiser to pretend at first that her father was dead – it being easier for a young child to accept than a father who is there one minute and gone the next. Later, I was introduced as her uncle – though she says she has no memory of it."

He threw up his hands in resignation. "Again, with hindsight, I cannot claim that these were the right decisions to have taken. All I can say is that, at the time, there were cogent reasons in their favour. Be that as it may, when Jane was about twelve my mother passed on. The business was by then in good order once more. Do not think me boastful but it was ten times greater than ever it had been, even at its peak, in my father's day. So I confessed the truth at last to my sisters. They had always liked Angwin and were delighted to hear she was now one of the family ..."

26

"Are they still alive?" Mrs Lanyon asked.

He shook his head. "If they were, I doubt we should be having this conversation. No, both were carried off in a cholera outbreak about three years ago – the last of my near relations. They were ladies of impeccable standards. I would have entrusted Jane's coming out to them in the smallest detail, so I feel their loss as keenly now as when they died, though for different reasons."

"And that is the favour you wish to ask of me?" Mrs Lanyon said.

"Let me put all my cards on the table, dear lady. When I first came down here in search of a property in which to retire, this problem was already vexing me. I inquired among the gentlemen I met – not in particular terms, you understand, but as to which ladies were taken as the arbiters and setters of standards in local society, and the one name that recurred, again and again, was yours. So, though I may seem to be making this proposal on the slimmest of acquaintances, it is not truly so. However, I do not expect a hasty answer."

She rose. "Shall we return?" she suggested. "I feel we have exposed poor Jane to the rigours of entertainment too long." She took his arm and they began to stroll back toward the house. "You call it a proposal ..." she prompted.

"Yes. I need a guide, philosopher, and friend to advise me in seeing my daughter well matched and settled."

"And a hostess," Mrs Lanyon pointed out. "Jane could hardly preside over a ball whose purpose was to introduce her to likely suitors!"

"Exactly. I hope I need not add that any out-of-pocket expenses you may incur, should you decide to honour us in this way, would gladly be reimbursed."

"Oh, but there's no need for that ..." she began to protest.

"I would insist upon it. And if one or two of your favourite charities might need a donation, I should be generous. It is as well to have these things understood from the start. I should also perhaps say that none of these payments would come from Jane's own inheritance. I regard them as a father's responsibility."

Mrs Lanyon was silent for a while. At last she spoke. "It would be so easy for me to say, 'Oh yes, I know so-and-so and thingummy-bob and what-d'you-call-im' – eligible bachelors all. Indeed, I could probably name you a dozen without even thinking. But it would be tragic to saddle a dear girl like Jane with someone who, though a perfectly decent man in himself, is utterly unsuited to her." Her voice rose a little as she added, "Parents who merely choose a partner for their daughter on the grounds of his social eligibility and his decency of character do not understand what monstrous and bitter disappointments they may be ..." She gulped and checked herself. "Still ..." She gave an embarrassed little laugh. "... that hardly applies here. All I'm saying is that in our commendable efforts to see that our young are well settled we often overlook their equal need to be well matched. And, as I was about to say, I do not know Jane at all. It may seem an absurd suggestion but I make it in all seriousness. I should like to invite Jane to stay with us at Parc-an-Ython – for at least a month. Perhaps, while she is still in mourning, and before the giddy social whirl can begin, this would be an appropriate time?"

He paused and took her hand between his. "Dear lady!" He sniffed rather saltily. "Your goodness overwhelms me."

"No, Mr Hervey," she replied. "Your predicament has stirred something within me – more than you can guess at. You said earlier that I am called to my womanly duty in some other way than in the rearing of my own family. I'm sure you did not mean *this* particular service, yet the moment I guessed where your conversation was tending I felt my response rising within me – yes – very like a calling."

He blinked back his tears and nodded at her, no longer trusting his voice at all.

In a different tone she added, "I should, of course, need to know the size of Jane's inheritance – if only to strike from the list those whose own fortune is their chief recommendation."

He cleared his throat, and, relieved to be back on home ground, replied, "Thanks to careful husbandry, it has augmented to almost thirty thousand pounds. And, of course, my own estate, which ... well, let us say it is of a somewhat larger order ... will also descend to her. Quite soon, perhaps."

She smiled at him. "At last, sir, you have spoken words I find impossible to believe. I think you will be with us for many years yet. I certainly hope so."

He chuckled at her flattery. "I did not yet tell you your greatest qualification for this task, Mrs Lanyon. Forgive me for saying so, but from the long perspective of seventy years, you and Jane seem much of an age to me. Of course, I know it is not so. I remember when I was nineteen what decrepit old creatures men who were not yet thirty seemed! Nonetheless, you will be closer to her in both age and sympathy than anyone else of whom I might conceivably ask this favour. So to find that you are also by far the most qualified is to me a miracle."

Now it was she who nodded and blinked and did not trust her voice.

As they reached the gravel of the drive he added, speaking almost as much to the air itself as directly to her, "Jane is the apple of my eye. I love her almost too well for her own good. Since her mother passed on, all my hopes and emotions have become focussed in her. You, I think, will restore that necessary distance which our judgements will require."

She, too, spoke as if to the air about them. "How odd it is. When you speak like that I cannot believe some forty years separates our ages."

4 THE TWO CARRIAGES stopped as they drew level. Mrs Menadue lowered her window all the way and leaned out. "Is it you, Mrs Pellew?" she asked.

The other window dropped, too. "Why yes, Mrs Menadue. Have you been away?"

"Plymouth. Shopping. Just paid a call on the new people at Montpelier."

"Ah, we're on our way there now. I have my two young nieces staying with me. D'you remember Angelica and Jemima Pellew of Swanpool?"

Mrs Menadue's head bobbed this way and that as she peered into the gloom of the carriage interior. "Oh yes. We've met. Hello you two. Remember me? The beach at Praa. You brought me a pair of live crabs. You've grown."

Angelica laughed. "You were very understanding that day, Mrs Menadue. How nice to meet you again."

The woman nodded and returned to the aunt. "Take my advice, turn about. You're wasting your time. She's an insufferable little prig."

"Dear me. D'you say so? How old is she?"

"Been stuck at fourteen for the last five years, I'd say. Mrs Jesse Lanyon was there. The little creature hung on her every word. Wouldn't serve a sip of tea, though I dropped a hint as big as the Logan Rock."

"Ah!" Mrs Pellew consulted her carriage clock. "Well ..." she said vaguely.

"Go on, go on," Mrs Menadue urged. "Don't take my word for it. See for yourself. And stop by for some cribbage this evening, if you mind to."

"I take it Madame Lanyon will have left?" Mrs Pellew asked.

"She was still there a few moments ago. Measuring the gardens with the father – a dry old shank of eighty if he's a day. They're settling the future of that poor pinioned dove between them, mark me. They'll have her married off to one of her cronies before you can turn round. I warned her but it was like talking to porcelain doll. On with you, then – see if you fare any better."

The coaches drew apart. Two stone carriers and a farmer in his cart, all of whom had waited in respectful patience, hastened into the gap.

"She hasn't changed," Jemima commented.

"Nor ever will," her aunt replied. "She's the salt of the earth, though. There are two women to whom I would turn in an extremity. One is Mrs Moore, and the other is that one. I think, my dears, we shall simply leave cards on the new owners of Montpelier House, and go on at once to ..."

"But, Aunt!" The nieces protested that they had been *so* looking forward to meeting Miss Hervey, the heiress.

"Very well," she relented. "But we shan't stay long. Ten minutes at the most."

When they drew up before the porticoed entrance, her footman descended to inquire whether Miss Hervey were at home. The question caused no small consternation in the drawing room. "I think you are *not* at home," advised Mrs Lanyon, who was now taking her leave for the second time, having returned briefly to make arrangements for Jane's stay at Parc-an-Ython.

"I shall be guided by you, of course, dear Mrs Lanyon." Jane turned Mrs Pellew's card over and over in her fingers. "But would it not be more correct to accept the call and then fail to return it?"

Mrs Lanyon gnawed unhappily at her lip. That was, indeed, the correct course and there was no point in denying it.

Her discomfort turned to alarm when, on her arrival at the carriage sweep, she saw Mrs Pellew descending in the company of her two nieces, girls with a fairly incandescent reputation in local society – especially in that part of it where she herself was proud to move.

"Mrs Lanyon!" trilled the squire's wife, as warmly as if she truly meant it. "How good it is to see you – and looking so well again."

"Mrs Pellew," she replied, with a cold little nod; but she could not help echoing that puzzling word: "Again?" She knew it was a mistake the moment she spoke.

"Yes." Mrs Pellew smiled sympathetically. "That little unpleasantness – quite over and done with, I trust?"

"I'm afraid I don't understand?" Mrs Lanyon countered. "You must be confusing me with some other person."

"Ah, very probably," the other agreed – but in that soothing tone which implies: *You obviously haven't been told about it, so I'm extricating myself as best I may.*

"My carriage!" Mrs Lanyon snapped at the valet-du-jour – quite unnecessarily since the vehicle itself was already approaching.

"Aren't we petty?" Mrs Pellew murmured as she watched the woman depart. "I blame you girls. You're a thoroughly bad influence on me." She braced herself for what she was now sure would be a stiff encounter.

"Miss Hervey!" she cried as she sailed across the drawing room. "Welcome to Cornwall! I had hoped to be the first to say it, but I see that dear Mrs Lanyon has preceded me. Such a stalwart!"

Jane acknowledged her greeting, presented her father, said all the right things. Her welcome to Angelica and Jemima was also impeccable. Mrs Pellew, searching diligently for any sign of the girl's true feelings, found none; it impressed her greatly. Jane was surrounded by an aura of calm. Her eyes rapidly scanned her three visitors, from the topmost feathers in their hats to the fringes that swept the floor. The older woman knew she had noted every detail, yet there was no impertinence in it.

They conversed on all the safe topics for the statutory ten minutes; meanwhile their silent evaluations of one another continued, unhindered by any need to think what to say. The topics themselves were utterly unimportant. Neither party had time for actual thought; each was far too busy studying the other's gestures, tone of voice, deportment – all those vague but vital traits summed up in that supremely vague but vital word: *mien.* After they had parted, each had to confess herself quite taken with the other's mien.

"One hardly believes Mrs Menadue met the same girl," Angelica commented as they settled themselves back in their carriage. To her sister she added, "I see you've forgotten your pocketbook. Are you going to remember it now, or in a minute?"

Jemima smiled sweetly back as she descended again. "Now, I think."

"Larkin will retrieve it," her aunt called; but the girl was already at the door.

"She's going to suggest a bathing party tomorrow morning," Angelica explained. "Just the three of us. Get her alone and start unravelling her. We don't believe anyone can really be so adamantine as that!"

Meanwhile Jane was saying: "She is quite different from what Mrs Lanyon led us to expect."

"Nonetheless, I would trust her judgement." There was a warning edge to her father's words.

"Without question," Jane replied at once. "Yet one cannot simply suspend one's own faculties in that regard."

"Perish the thought, my dear. But one must allow them to be guided by those with more experience of life in general and of local society in particular."

"Talking of *particular* local society" – Jane smiled archly – "I thought you were quite taken with the two nieces. I know they were bowled over by you."

30

"Oh?" The news startled him. "Do you think so? Surely not." He moved to the window, squinted at the sun, pinched the bridge of his nose.

"Dearest father, you are so practical and down-to-earth. Do you really not notice these little *tourbillons du coeur?*"

"Speak English," he commanded gruffly to hide his delight.

"Eddies of the heart? Dust-devils of the heart? It's not the same at all."

Jemima herself entered at that moment, giving a mere token tap on the door. Jane marked her down for it; a lady should never knock before entering a drawing room. "I'm so sorry," the girl said. "I appear to have mislaid my pocketbook."

"This?" Mr Hervey stooped and retrieved the small, silken bundle; he caressed it absently as he carried it to her.

"Oh, Mr Hervey, what superb eyesight you must have," she gushed. "I'm sure I should never have found it."

Jane knew than that the girl must have eavesdropped on at least part of their conversation. Neither of the two nieces had, in fact, paid anything more than the usual scant attention two young girls might pay to an elderly gentleman; she had merely said that to divert him. But now here was Miss J, taking the words for her cue.

Then, to her amazement, her father did likewise – making a gallant offering of his arm to escort her quite needlessly back outside. In taking it the girl managed to convey, by a subtle tilt of her head, a momentary lifting of her brows, an unvoiced whistle, that its firmness and bulk astonished her. "Are you fond of dancing, Mr Hervey?" she asked amiably – a question that would have seemed wayward indeed to someone who had not just had his muscles and joints so nimbly assessed.

"I have cut a caper or two in my time," he allowed.

"Then I hope we shall see you at many of our balls when you are out of mourning again." Before he could reply she glanced back over her shoulder and said, "Oh by the way, Miss Hervey, there is a dear little secluded cove where your land meets the bay. Angelica and I have swum there from our childhood." She turned to the father. "I trust we may continue to do so, sir?"

"But of course," he cried, overflowing with benevolence.

"How generous you are. In fact, we were thinking of taking a dip tomorrow morning. Would you care to join us, Miss Hervey?"

Jane, who wanted nothing more, began to demur. There was so much still to be done. She wasn't sure ...

"She'd love to!" her father assured the young woman. "And I'll put a man there to make sure you aren't spied on or disturbed."

"Oh, Mr Hervey!" She blinked at him several times and added with artless enthusiasm, "We were saying to one another in the carriage just now – how good it is to have two such fine neighbours."

When she had gone Mr Hervey appeared rather thoughtful.

"Provincial ways have a certain undeniable charm," Jane suggested.

"I believe you are right," he replied. "That is, one ought to make up one's own mind about people. It is a kind of duty, in fact."

*   *   *

31

The breeze off Mount's Bay was sultry and close. Where it struck the shoreline it almost immediately formed clouds – a curious phenomenon whereby the entire silhouette of West Cornwall was, so to speak, painted across the sky in a template of fleecy vapour. The sun, peeping beneath this blanket, gilded the shoreline so that the three young women passed from a grey overcast into brilliant sunshine on their half-mile walk between Montpelier and the clifftop. Margaret Banks and the sisters' maid, Millie Tredwell, followed at a respectful distance with their towels and caps. At their side was Tom Collett, one of the footmen.

"Listen!" Jemima stopped suddenly.

"I can't hear anything," Jane said after a while.

"That's the unusual thing," Jemima told her. "Normally we'd have to raise our voices from here on, over the roar of the waves. That shows how calm it's been."

"Smugglers' weather," Angelica commented.

Jane asked why it was called that.

"The little Breton boats bring cognac over and leave it in lobster pots on the seabed. There are so many lobster fishermen – who can tell which of them is hauling up what?" She gestured at the bay, where, indeed, they could see men in half a dozen small boats rowing from marker to marker and hauling up their pots. The waters were as flat as glass.

"I've only ever seen it like that twice before in my life," Jemima murmured. "It's like ..." But she couldn't think what it might be like. "It's not like Cornwall, anyway."

"What do we smuggle to France in return?" Jane asked.

"Nothing," Jemima answered stoutly. "The French know how to live. They don't tax all the good things in life." She turned to Jane. "Of course, you've lived there, Miss Hervey, haven't you."

"Until I was nearly fourteen. Then my family moved back to Leeds."

"You must have been heartbroken," Angelica commented. "I know I should have been. Oh Paris!" She sighed.

"You have been there, Miss Pellew?" Jane asked over her shoulder.

"No!" they chorused emphatically, looked at each other, and laughed.

"Perhaps," Jane said, "to avoid confusion, we might drop the handles? I was really asking Angelica – may I call you that? The way you sighed when you said the name."

"My uncle has a whole shelf of Baedekers. I love to read them before I snuff out my candle – always in the hope of dreaming about ... oh, Vienna ... Constantinople ... Rome ... and, of course, Paris. The one for Paris is all in French, which is especially thrilling."

"*Vous aimez mieux que nous parlons Français?*" Jane asked.

From then on they spoke mainly in French. Jane, a native speaker, was pleased to discover that the two sisters were also pretty fluent.

"I expect you lived in one of the finest houses there?" Angelica prompted.

"And had the most superb chef?" her sister added.

"And your parents were always going to the opera and the grandest balls?"

"And I'll bet you had the most divine lingerie, even at fourteen?"

"Stop!" Jane laughed and put her hands to her ears. "Do you want to be disillusioned? Life in Paris was very like life anywhere else. For a little girl, anyway."

"But it can't have been! There must have been *something* special."

They came to the edge of the cliff, where they stood awhile and peered down at the mirror-calm sea. "Quicksilver," Jane murmured. Then, more practically, "It's a long way down."

"It means we can't *really* be spied on," Angelica replied. "Your father needn't have bothered sending Tom Collett."

"Though it was very kind of him," Jemima added. "Our way down is over there."

She led now, off to their right, where the coastguard path skirted a marshy hollow from where, in normal times, there was a slimy, slithery scramble to the rocks. Today, however, it was dry, and the waterweed was brown and dying on the stone.

"There must have been *something* special about Paris," Jemima insisted as they walked gingerly across the dried-out marsh.

"My mother did entertain a great deal," Jane admitted. "I was kept in the nursery, of course. The French are even more insistent than the English on that point. But I could see all the grand carriages – the phætons and open landaus – drawing up. And the people getting out. And the officers in their uniforms, and the diplomats in court dress. And the aristocrats! They're not supposed to have an aristocracy any more, but they do, of course."

"And their wives," Anglica said. "I'll bet their gowns were sumptuous. They have such a flair, those French ..."

"No," Jane replied. "Now that *is* a difference between France and us. From what I remember, French men seem to go out to soirées and things without their wives. My mother had a sort of salon, I suppose you'd call it."

"Where artists and writers could meet and set all the world to rights."

"No, that was Madame de Meyron and the Comtesse ... I forget. But they were the two big artistic salons. Every hostess had her own preferences. My mother's was for ... well, military and diplomatic people, as I say."

"And aristocrats."

"That's what most of them were, of course."

Jemima hesitated at the very edge of the cliff, which was here only a dozen feet above the rocks. "I can't imagine it," she said, staring over the sea toward France. "Think of our lives and think of theirs! Our greatest excitement on most days is to be served an extra slice of caraway cake. And to think, while we are saying ooh! and ah! – all that ... that *glister* is going on!"

"All *what?*" Jane asked.

"It's something I can't imagine. But it must be ... oh, to live in that world every day! You are so lucky to have been part of it. And how you can *bear* to ..."

"But I told you – I wasn't. I couldn't even name one of them. I wasn't supposed to do so much as look out of the window. I got punished for doing that."

"But didn't you creep into the grown-ups' part of the house and spy on them through the banisters?" Angelica asked. "We always did."

Jane shook her head. "All the doors were kept locked," she explained. "My mother was most particular as to that. The moment callers came, the nursery doors were locked and I was to stay away from the windows."

"How extraordinary!"

By careful manoeuvring of their skirts they arrived at the rocks without a tumble. "Really, we are silly," Jemima commented. "What's the difference between taking our things off here and a hundred yards farther along!"

Nonetheless, they made their ungainly but fully clad way over the rocks, sweeping their hems up and back to be sure their feet were going where they ought among the little clefts and barnacles. At last they arrived in the sandy cove at the foot of the cliffs. "They seem even taller from down here," Jane said, shielding her eyes to stare up at them; they masked the strange cloud formation, leaving the vault of the sky a veiled, milky blue.

Tom Collett gave an exaggerated salutation and withdrew ostentatiously out of sight. "We're safe from prying eyes now," Jane said.

The sisters laughed as if she had spoken in jest. They undressed in a most novel way – loosening their crinolines and then crouching down inside them, as if they were tents, while they struggled out of the rest of their clothing. Jane followed suit, laughing at the absurdity of it, but unwilling to fall out of step. And "struggle" was the word in that confinement, with much giggling and many a cry of *botheration!*

Margaret Banks and Millie Tredwell stood a little way off, watching the three apparently empty dresses shivering like giant jellyfish. They shook their heads and murmured, "Well, did you ever!"

At last the girls were done. "Ready?" cried one of the crinolines. "Ready!" answered the other two.

And, "Tararaa-dee!" cried Angelica as, like Venus from her shell, they ducked out from beneath their respective hems.

That is to say, the two sisters were like Venus from her shell; Jane was still in her chemise. "Oh!" she said; and "Ah!" they replied.

"I didn't realize," Jane began. The scene was suddenly unreal, as if it had been transferred from life to an art gallery; she had never before seen grown women – or mature girls, anyway – in a state of nature, except in art galleries – in those pictures she had been advised she might look at but not linger over.

"Do you always wear a chemise?" Angelica asked.

"Every day. Don't you?"

"It's not just for swimming?"

She shook her head. "I've got my dry one for going home in. One of you could borrow it if you like."

They laughed and thanked her but said they'd stick to their own arrangements. "Aren't you coming in?" Jemima asked the two maids in English as they passed on their way to the water's edge. Millie handed them their caps and stared askance at the water, giving a theatrical shiver. "Come on, slowcoach!" they turned and called back to Jane.

Watching them, still undecided, she was reminded even more strongly of those classical paintings she had never been encouraged to linger over. The two women had figures that would have made any painter scrabble for his brushes. Suddenly her chemise felt absurd; she saw herself as if in a painting, and dressed like that, and somehow it was far more ... what was the word? Wrong? Blush-making? "Ah well," she exclaimed and eased the buttons from their holes. Banks came forward and picked up the chemise as she stepped out of it, handing Jane her cap at the same time. She skipped after the other two as she tied it up and tucked her hair inside; her bosoms were larger than theirs, which made running more awkward. Behind her the tide-soaked sand marked her trail in shimmering puddles.

"D'you know," she cried as she drew near, "the last time I bathed *au naturel* was when I was eight. One blistering hot afternoon in August in the Bois de Boulogne. I'd forgotten what a lovely, free sensation it is."

"Goodness! D'you wear a chemise when you bath yourself?" Angelica asked.

"Of course not. But that's just stepping off the hearthrug into the bath and out again. It's not like this." She pranced and skipped like a faun, turning and spinning at each leap. "I wonder if I can still do a cartwheel?" She tried – and three-quarters succeeded, collapsing in a heap of laughter and wet sand. "Now I'll have to go in. Goodness, it's cold!"

Angelica and Jemima exchanged satisfied glances. If their sole ambition had been to induce their prim and correct young hostess of yesterday to unbend, they were achieving it handsomely.

Jane struggled to her feet and lurched at the other two with hands mired by the clammy, wet sand. "Go on, you try," she urged.

They scattered from her, screaming with laughter, galloping into the water and sending up great sheets of silver like starbursts around them. Still pursuing them in that same madcap dash, Jane suddenly became aware that the water was the coldest she had ever encountered. In fact, merely to call it "cold" could in no way describe the shock of its chilling grip. It encircled her calves, her knees, her thighs ... like that medieval torture called the "Iron Maiden" – a close-fitting skin of metal embellished on its inside with nails – only this was like a million fine needles instead of just a few spikes.

She stopped just as the water reached her midriff and stood there wondering where she would even find enough breath for a gasp – and whether she would get back to her lovely warm clothes before she died and turned to a single block of ice.

"She who hesitates is lost," shouted the other two, who had launched themselves up to their necks as soon as the depth permitted and were now sidestroking vigorously to keep their circulation going.

"You didn't warn me it'd be so co-o-o-old!" Jane complained, hugging herself with futile tenderness.

"But it's always like this. Come on – after a minute or two it'll seem boiling. Promise." They turned around and began swimming back to where she stood.

Tiptoeing forward, inch by inch, and knowing she was only prolonging the agony, Jane edged deeper into the icy water. At last the decision was made for her, when Jemima and Angelica arrived and started splashing her with all their might. Then, in a fury of white water, shrieking with pain and pleasure mingled, the three girls launched themselves full length and struck out in an overarm-underarm sidestroke as if only France would stop them. "See?" Jemima gasped when they were level with the headland and hoping for second wind. "Doesn't it ... feel warm?"

Jane trod water long enough to take stock. "Boiling," she agreed. "Actually, it's very invigorating. Oh, I haven't felt so free of ... so free, since ... I can't remember."

"We used to swim every single day when we were younger. Starting before Easter and going on almost to bonfire night. If you think *this* is cold ...!"

"Not ..." Jane faltered. She had been going to say, "Not Sundays?"

"Not what?"

"It doesn't matter. Not here, I was going to say, but, of course, you must know dozens of places."

"We'll show you lots and lots if you like."

How odd it seemed, three talking heads amid the quicksilver ripples; and in that cold layer of unmoved air immediately above the surface their breathing showed as steam, just as in winter. "I'd love it," she agreed, wondering if Mrs Lanyon would permit it.

Then part of her reacted against that thought. Mrs Lanyon was not going to be her gaoller. It was not a question of permit or forbid, surely?

Surely not?

Perhaps it would be as well to make that clear from the start.

"It's sand at the bottom here, you know," Angelica cut in. "I'm going down." She clasped her nostrils and plummeted.

"Her hair'll get all wet," Jane commented.

"And all dry later," Jemima added. "Can you swim underwater?"

"I don't think I ever tried." Tentatively she pinched her nose.

"You don't need to do that," Jemima told her. "If you breathe out just a tiny bit all the time, you can swim with both hands and it's much nicer. Like this." She puckered her lips into a rosebud, almost blocking her nostrils.

"You look like a baboon or something," Jane told her.

But the other had already slid from sight. Moments later two babboon-like hands groped for her ankles, grasped them, and jerked her below; fortunately she was already trying out the technique – and even more fortunately, it worked. She kicked her way back to the surface, drew a lungful of air, and did a sort of surface pike dive that carried her down ten feet or more – where she opened her eyes on an out-of-focus fairyland of pale light, shimmering sand, and mysterious, ultramarine distances. She rolled onto her back. Jemima was just above her, gliding through the water, just a foot or two beneath the surface, with her eyes clenched tight, a thin trail of bubbles peeling backward from her nose.

Jane wafted herself down until she was squatting on the sand, but the moment her feeet touched she uncoiled herself and darted, arrow-straight and with hands upraised, toward Jemima. She caught her by the waist and, such was her impetus, she lifted her almost clear of the surface when they emerged.

When they had finished laughing and had recovered their breath, Jemima said, "Can you keep your eyes open underwater?"

"So it seems. Where's your sister?"

"She'll be over among the rocks ..."

At that moment Angelica broke the surface about twenty yards away, her pent-up breath exploding like a seal's. "You should swim underwater like me," she called out scornfully. "You're missing the best of it." And she drew another breath and vanished once more.

The other two looked at each other, devilry in their eyes. "Shall we?" Jane asked. "Indeed we shall. Didn't she ask for it?"

They swam over to where she had disappeared, whereupon she emerged again, only five or six yards away now. "Come on," she cajoled.

They followed her down. For a moment Jane was completely disoriented. All the usual clues to distance were missing – perspective, loss of detail, changes in texture and colour; the entire submarine world was one kaleidoscopic blur of movement. Then she saw it was the seaweed, anchored to the rock and drifting gently this way and that with the minute stirring of stray currents. If the seas had been stronger, the motion would have been uniform and she could have taken her bearings from it; but on a day like this it was so random that she felt herself lost in a seething restlessness of green and brown.

There was a nudge at her side, though she was so cold she hardly felt it. She turned to see Jemima gesturing toward a forest of long-fronded weed ahead – Jemima with both eyes open. Jane pointed to her own eyes and then at Jemima, who smiled and nodded back, but went on pointing at that clump of weed. In its depths Jane now and then glimpsed a pale shimmering that could only be Angelica.

Jemima pointed to herself and made an elaborate encircling gesture. Jane nodded her agreement and watched the other go arcing over one of the taller rocks to ambush her sister from the other side. She herself now edged toward the weeds.

When she drew closer she saw they were anchored in a deeper pool; some were those very dark green, leathery ribbons that grow on their own "handles" and which small boys love to pretend are carter's whips; others were much lighter and even broader ribbons, crinkled and crimped. But what held her fascination most of all were the extraordinary antics of Angelica, who had let go her nose and was swimming like a minnow, this way and that among the fronds of the weeds. She had her hands stretched out before her and had discovered some trick of letting a wriggle pass all the way down her body, from the tips of her fingers to the ends of her toes. And as she moved onward, slowly but steadily, the fronds wrapped themselves around her in dozens of soft tendrils.

Jane was so fascinated she momentarily forgot that they had intended to ambush her. But the very instant she remembered and launched herself at the unsuspecting girl, Angelica grew short of breath and kicked herself up to the surface once more. Jane and Jemima met among the fronds, pulled a face at each other, and themselves went up for air.

"What on earth were you doing down there?" Jane asked when they had all got their breath back.

"Haven't you ever done that? You should try it. I call it my Ophelia game."

Jane, who, for a split-second, heard "oh-feelier game," thought it quite a good name; even in her brief skim through the fronds she had discovered they did not feel as clammy and repulsive as they looked. But when she realized what Angelica had actually said, she was puzzled.

"I think to myself," the other explained, "I'll stay down here until I die. Like Ophelia, you know, among the weeds. And all those fronds and tendrils suddenly become like a hundred enticing fingers, caressing me with their friendship and begging me to stay. I go on and on thinking like that until I just have to come up and breathe again." She laughed at her own simplicity. "But it's great fun, too. It really does feel like a kind of dying. You get a heavy, choking sort of feeling in your chest and your heart thunders like a galloping horse. Just try it."

Jane glanced at Jemima, who gave a why-not sort of shrug. They all drew a fresh lungful and sank back into the enchanted forest, which was broad enough for each to claim her own portion to try out the Ophelia game. And it was just as Angelica had described it, Jane discovered. The fronds of weed lost their slimy, clammy quality and turned into countless fingers, cool but friendly. If on dry land one could be suspended on a curtain of air while being wafted through a forest of ostrich plumes and peacocks' tails, the sensation could be no more thrilling than this.

Angelica was right, too, about that seductive, flirting-with-death languor which seized one during the Ophelia game. The underwater swimmer's obsessive thought, "I can't stay down here too long ... must get back to the air ..." was, for however brief a moment, suspended. And during its absence Jane felt almost as if she had turned into a mermaid and could now remain below the waves forever. What utter bliss it was to drift in this forest of gentleness, with all these amiable hands supporting her, caressing her, reassuring her she was safe here ...

Safe at last. Her father's singular phrase kept coming back to her.

How strange it was to be so repeatedly comforted by notions of *safety* when, in fact, her peace of mind did not feel threatened in any way.

The fondling weeds brought her to the sandy floor of the pool. Eel-like she turned over, then over, and over again, wrapping herself in their tendrils. She giggled a bubble and watched it buffeting its fussy way to the surface, spawning silver children in its wake. After several more spins she was half-clad in weed. She'd once seen a dancer at a circus in Vincennes spin herself into a swaddling of bandages just like this; it gave her an idea.

She crouched on the seabed and sprang toward the sky. The weeds yielded their tenuous purchase on sand and rock and clung to her still. Only when she broke out into the air did she realize how desperate had her need for it become; the cold water and the strange delights of the Ophelia game had intoxicated her beyond a sense of danger. The other two girls were already at the surface, gulping for air as well. "You don't realize ..." Angelica said, gasping between each word.

"I'm wrapping myself in seaweed." Jane spoke in the same disjointed fashion.

"Why?" Jemima asked.

"Because it's fun." And she slipped beneath the surface again to complete her submarine *couture.*

"See that fellow in the nearest lobster boat," Jemima said quietly. "He just threw a lobster back in disgust. A big one, too."

They laughed and vanished after Jane to try the new sport. Soon the surface was mottled with fragments of green and brown, floating in that strange, sticky spume which comes from lacerated seaweed.

"I'd swear I'm almost presentable again," Jane said when they next returned to the surface. "Let's go out and show ourselves to each other. I want to see what we look like, all in our weeds."

Hobbled as they were it took some time to wriggle and scoop their way into waters shallow enough for standing.

Angelica said, "It reminds me of that time I had to wear two pairs of corsets because both had split in different places."

"We could pretend we were mermaids," Jemima suggested breathlessly. "Swim along under the cliffs until we saw some mussel pickers or something and give them a fright. We could get into the papers."

"With the little weed you're wearing," Jane told her with mock severity, "there would be easier ways of doing that!"

They were less than knee-deep by now, and laughing so much they failed to notice that the "disgusted lobsterman" was rowing ashore for all he was worth.

Angelica saw him first and gave a little cry of horror. In the same moment he called out, "Sorry about this ladies, but it's going to get worse. You'll have half a dozen customs men coming through in five minutes."

"How dare you?" Jane shouted at him. "Look away."

He did not take his eyes from hers. "Did you notice any at the top of the cliff on your way down?" he asked coolly.

"Let us turn our backs to him," she told the others.

They complied but it annoyed Jane to see the way they kept looking over their shoulders and giggling – not loud enough for him to hear, but still giggling. "Has he gone?" she murmured.

"No, he's just standing there, staring at us – and with *the* most insouciant grin."

"Hera, Athena, and Aphrodite," he called. "I'll leave you a bottle – my apology."

They were so surprised to hear educated sentiments – and in such cultivated tones, too – from such a rough-looking fellow that they all half-turned to him, not quite believing their ears.

He was a powerfully built, dark-haired young man in his mid-twenties, dressed to the last stitch like a common fisherman; but there was an arrogant glint in his eyes that declared him a free man who touched his forelock to none.

Those eyes now dwelled in Jane's and she felt an almost overpowering pressure from them, bearing her back, pinning her to the air as a wrestler pins an opponent and asks for submission. When she did not yield, he smiled. "I leave it for the fairest among you, of course," he added as he turned to go.

The effrontery of his glance was as nothing compared to the conceit of his voice. Jane had never taken so instant and so powerful a dislike to anyone in her life. "How dare he," she repeated quietly to the other two as they watched him lift his clanking lobster pots and hasten away up the shelving beach.

"There's precious little we can do about it," Jemima replied.

The words stung Jane to action. "Isn't there!" She stooped, picked up a small, smooth pebble, and hurled it after him.

The sisters gasped as – more by fluke than by practice, as Jane would have readily admitted – the missile sped with unerring accuracy toward the middle of his back. She had a sudden, dreadful vision of fracturing his spinal column and leaving him a hopeless cripple for life; her innards fell away inside her and she bit white flesh into her lips.

Fortunately he turned just as it arrived, so that it took him on his arm, a little above the elbow. Even so it was excruciating and, though he managed not to drop his precious burden, he bellowed at her, "What did you do that for?"

Jane, knowing she ought to apologize but feeling she'd sooner die, started striding toward him, clutching the weeds about her and just hoping she was decently covered. "You're no gentleman," she cried.

"Well, you didn't need to half kill me to tell me *that.* I've never claimed to be one. Nor sought to be one. Nor felt the remotest desire to be one."

She had the first intimations that this exchange was descending into farce; she brushed them angrily aside, ignoring the smile that was beginning to reestablish itself on his lips.

"Furthermore," he went on, "if the mark of a gentleman is that he deny himself this vision of sheer beauty" – he gestured with his elbow, ambiguously, at all three of them or merely at her – "then I hope a may never sink into that unhappy status." He darted a look somewhere just above her head and cried, "Damnation!" Then, with a final glance at her, as if he would say more – much more – he began to run in long, easy strides over the rocks toward the footholds that led to the cliff path.

"We saw no coastguards," she shouted after him before she could stop herself. She heard him laugh but he did not turn around.

5 MRS PELLEW HAD grown so accustomed to her nieces' birdlike chatter that it took her a moment or two to register what they had said. She raised a monitory finger. "A stone?" she asked. "A real stone?" The finger wafted vaguely over the litter of plates, signalling the servants to clear away the last of their luncheon.

"A pebble," Angelica said. "But quite a large one."

"And she hurled it at him?"

"Yes," Jemima confirmed. "And if he hadn't turned at the last minute ..."

"She was absolutely mortified after," her sister cut in.

"One at a time," her aunt commanded sharply. "If he hadn't turned ...?"

"She said she had visions of ..."

"It would have struck him in the spine."

"And he would have been paralyzed for life."

"My goodness – that prim and proper young miss! Mark me, there are hidden fires there." She smiled contentedly. "I wonder if dear Mrs Lanyon quite realizes what she's taking on? And who was the man, did you say?"

"Nobody knows," Angelica said.

"A smuggler, obviously. Did she take the brandy he left?"

"Yes," Jemima replied. "In the end. But she wouldn't carry it indoors. She gave it to Tom Collett to guard for her. She said she'd have to pick the right moment to explain it to her father."

"She wouldn't touch it at first," Angelica added. "But then we told her how smuggling is an ancient tradition of the gentry down here."

Their aunt cackled happily. "Yes, that's the way to recruit her!"

"Funny," Jemima went on. "Talking about her father, I could swear I saw him over on the Trewarvas cliffs, while we were swimming. Not by our mine but in the scrub at Trequean. There's no one else of that height hereabouts, is there? Not in a frock coat and top hat, anyway."

"Your uncle was there this morning," Mrs Pellew said. "It's odd he didn't mentioned meeting him. Still, never mind all that – I'm far more interested in the young fellow who provoked Miss Hervey to such an extremity. Did none of the servants recognize him?"

Angelica said, "Margaret Banks muttered something about how he might be one of the Jagos of Greenbank, but she wasn't sure. She's never met any of them."

Mrs Pellew nodded sagely. "But she'd be the one to know. Her mother is a cousin by marriage to the Penalunas of Coverack, and Edward Penaluna is the biggest smuggler between there and Porthleven. They'd certainly resent anyone from the Falmouth side of the Lizard elbowing his way in over here." She peered more sharply at her nieces. "But surely you know more about the Jagos than we do – living so near?"

Angelica gave an awkward shrug, meaning there was no easy way of summing up so complex a family as the Jagos. "They're the sort of ne'er-do-wells who ne'er do too badly, either."

The last of the footmen withdrew, carrying the silver crumb tray with him. Mrs Pellew leaned back in her chair and smiled. "I remember the father, Kinghorn Jago, very well. He had a powerful tenor voice. A fine figure of a man. Not tall, mind you, but somehow always ... impressive."

"He still is," Jemima cut in. "We often see him in Falmouth."

"He has a finger in every pie," Angelica added.

Their aunt raised an eyebrow. "So you know him well enough by sight. And did you see no resemblance between him and our mystery smuggler?"

The two sisters glanced at each other and shook their heads. "No," Angelica said. "This fellow was tall and dark."

"Sort of Spanish-looking," Jemima confirmed.

"Then the enigma remains," said the aunt.

*   *   *

It was a fairly quiet dinner at Montpelier that evening, though the silence was more thoughtful than strained. Jane, still shaken by the surprising violence of her response to the impertinent smuggler, had daydreamed the afternoon away with a dozen alternative scenes in which she maintained her dignity and yet saw the fellow off, hanging his head in shame. The trouble was, she could not imagine *that* strutting cockerel feeling shame over anything.

Even worse, if she dropped her guard the merest fraction, he was apt to take over her daydream and engage her in all sorts of impudent conversation. Even now, here at her own dinner table, she could not help imagining him beside her, pretending to be so attentive, holding her with his great, dark eyes – and all the while smiling that

41

supercilious smile which said he knew everything about her ... all her silly thoughts and childishness ... and generally just toying with her. It made her so angry she almost wished the stone had broken his back and left him helpless.

Then, of course, her finer half was mortified that she could even think such things. What was happening to her? A month ago she'd been a perfectly calm and contented young lady, supervising her father's household in Leeds, and not a care in the world. Sorrow, yes, and a certain nostalgia for her life in Paris, which seemed to have vanished for ever. But that was all related to the past. True, it was probably sinful, in the very strictest sense, to hark back like that – as if you were saying to God that you were happier with the previous hand He'd dealt you; yet, as the curate himself had assured her, if such hankerings were merely passing thoughts and fancies, they were part of the general human condition of sinfulness and nothing especially wicked; they only became that when they turned into obsessions and took over so much of your life that you were unable to face all God's present challenges.

A little *frisson* of fear twisted inside her. Was she now in danger of that snare – making ... whatever his name was, the smuggler ... making him into an obsession that would leave her unable to face life's other challenges? And they were many. She seemed to have moved from that calm, serene world of a month ago to one that was full of disturbing nuances, subtle threats that never revealed themselves but that were all the more insidious for their clandestine silence.

She shook her head to snap herself out of it. "Did you enjoy your walk, Father?"

"Walk?" he echoed, looking at her a little askance.

"Oh, perhaps it wasn't you after all. Jemima said she thought she saw you over on Trewarvas Head while we were swimming."

"Ah yes." He smiled and tapped his forehead, as if it had slipped his mind. He chewed his lip and stared at the table. "She must have a good pair of eyes."

"She said it was the sunlight glinting off your glasses, but I said that's absurd – you only wear glasses for reading."

"Indeed, I was reading – in a way." He smiled. "I met your two friends' uncle, Squire Pellew. He owns the mine at Trewarvas, you know, and he got the mine captain to bring out the map. D'you realize it goes far out under the sea? All the while you were disporting yourselves so prettily, there were hordes of little muscley men hacking away at the rock tens of fathoms beneath you."

She closed her eyes and shivered. "Oh, I should die rather than go down there. And for such a pittance. Banks was telling me that few of them earn more than ten shillings a week."

"It's what they're accustomed to, my dear. She shouldn't tell you such things. I shall speak to her about it."

"It was I who asked her, I'm afraid."

He frowned. "That's not like you."

She nodded. "In Leeds we hardly ever saw any poor people, not the really poor, unless they actually came begging at our door. But here you cannot walk a mile in any direction without being made aware of them, quite forcefully sometimes. I know I don't really understand the ins and outs of it but it does seem wrong – not that such inequalities exist but that they are so very great."

He smiled and petted her arm. "And all credit to you for that, my child. But all the more reason to leave the financial cares of this world to the wiser heads of us men. You women would have us all in one great democracy – and believe me, the wretched creatures who so tug at your heartstrings now would be the last ones to thank you for it." He leaned back and placed his fingertips together. "Suppose our men of science discovered some elixir for making the whole of mankind three inches taller; and suppose a benevolent government, following your tender-hearted, female principles, decreed that everyone was to take a teaspoon a day, so that after a month or two the whole world was, indeed, three inches taller – where would the advantage then lie?" He smiled happily at the beautiful simplicity of his logic. "Mankind, you see, does not wish to be three inches taller, though – and here's a pretty paradox – each individual within it may want it for himself!"

"All the same," Jane said as the glow of satisfaction died, "I feel I must undertake *some* charitable work. I cannot daily walk past such poverty 'on the other side'."

He nodded fervently. "That is an altogether different affair, my child. To carry gifts of nutritious scraps and uplifting sentiments to the deserving poor is another matter. But we must guard against the arrogance of desiring to visit upon mankind in general the charity that rightly belongs to individuals."

How firm and wise he was, she thought; for a moment all her doubts were dispelled. But then he spoiled it. "I did not wish to ask," he went on, "but since you raise the matter yourself ... I could not help but notice, even though I was a mile or two away at Trewarvas ... did I see a lobsterman pull ashore on our beach?"

She nodded unhappily, blushed, fiddled with the edge of the tablecloth. "I was mortified," she replied.

"Confounded impudence! What was his name? Did the servants know him? I'll have him up before the bench for trespass."

She shook her head and, still avoiding his eye, said, "No one had ever seen him before." Why did she not add that Banks thought he was a Jago of Greenbank? She reached for a pear and began to peel it for him – the season's first.

"Those customs men obviously knew him." He chuckled. "I followed every detail of the chase through the squire's ... I mean, we saw it all."

"At least we were respectably clothed again by the time they came through. It was like Headrow on market day. We certainly shan't bathe there again!"

"Oh, I think you may," he said swiftly. "What happened today was pure misfortune. It'll probably never happen again. And next time bring your two friends to luncheon with us. You must cultivate your acquaintance among those of your own age, you know."

Jane smiled fondly. "Dear Father! You always think of me. But it will all stop next week when I go to stay at Parc-an-Ython – remember?"

He nodded. "I hadn't forgotten." A slight frown creased his brow. "I have had maturer thoughts on that. I believe that, on the whole, looking at the matter all round, it might be even better if you were to spend four days a week with dear Mrs Lanyon and return here each Friday to Monday. You are, after all, mistress of this house and you should not lose your grip upon it." He brightened. "And you could nurture your friendship with ... whatever their names are ..."

43

"Angelica and Jemima." She set the pear before him, peeled and quartered. "Just so. You could see them on Fridays and Saturdays."

Jane gladly accepted the suggestion though in her heart she felt some misgiving. She liked the two sisters immensely and enjoyed their bright company; and yet there was something about them that merely added to that general malaise she felt about ... about what? About herself? About having moved to Cornwall? About ...? She could think of nothing else that might disquiet her. It was all as vague as her father's strange insistence that here they were *safe*.

Later the image of the insolent smuggler kept her from that sleep which usually came so easily. The way to dispel it, she thought, was to give free rein to her fancy – let it burn itself out, so to speak. She then allowed herself to imagine the disaster that had so nearly happened. She saw the stone strike his spine, heard the hollow thwack of it, saw the man fall unconscious – paralyzed for life. She wallowed in her mortification to such a degree that she burst into genuine tears; but then, in an unguarded moment, she found herself at his bedside, feeding him broth, helping him shave ... tending him night and day. And there was such poignant sweetness in it she had to force herself to stop.

And even when she imagined the stone breaking his neck, it required but the smallest leap to set her at his graveside, weeping inconsolably at what she had done. And then visiting it every year on their anniversary ... no, no! Not *their* anniversary. *The* anniversary.

She fell at last into fitful slumber, but he rose from his grave and pursued her into her dreams – true dreams that the mind could not censor. He came at her downhill on a velocipede, holding an oar toward her like a battering ram and grinning that cocksure grin. And she, though in no way shackled or fettered, was somehow rooted to the spot and could not, dared not, flee. Before the oar actually struck her, the whole scene changed into something equally footling. Finally, after a whole series of scrappy incidents, full of people she'd never met and never wished to meet, she found herself alone in his lobster boat in the middle of a vast ocean as still as the sea had been that morning. At the back of her mind she knew she wanted to return to the forest of drifting seaweed; in her dream she knew she could stay down there forever without drowning. But, although she could say the name "seaweed," she had lost the power to imagine it. Below the surface of her dream sea there lay ... absolutely nothing.

When she awoke the following morning she was filled with a profound unease, almost a fear; it was all to do with that nothingness.

*   *   *

At around the time Jane was peeling her father's pear, Mrs Pellew was politely refusing a second helping of strawberries at Lanfear House, where she was dining *en famille* with the Moores. Also of the party was Hamill Oliver of Leander Cottage. At least, people still referred to him in that manner although it was now some months since he had moved into Pallas House, his mother's childhood home. Now forty-odd, he had, some ten years earlier been hopelessly in love with Johanna Rosewarne, now

Mrs Moore; but he was well over that. It had been no more than a late infatuation, for his first, last, and only love was Cornwall and all things Cornish.

Mrs Pellew had not been at all surprised to find him there; the Moores kept open house where friends were always welcome, and Oliver himself was the biggest dropper-in in the county. She was surprised, however, to find him squiring his cousin, Morwenna Troy, who was rumoured to be informally engaged to one of the Vyvyan boys. She was most decidedly not the sort of young lady who dropped-in on anyone. On the other hand, Mrs Pellew reflected, her late grandmother, the redoubtable Mrs Ramona Troy had – against all the odds – been one of Mrs Moore's most steadfast champions in the period when her behaviour had divided the entire locality, causing a rift that persisted to this day. Morwenna had adored the old woman and would have accepted her judgements against all her own instincts to the contrary.

Toward the end of the meal, Mrs Moore turned to Mrs Pellew and said, "I hear your nieces were almost overwhelmed with smugglers and excise men down at Megaliggar today. Do tell us all about it."

With remarkably little embroidery, the squire's wife repeated what the two girls had told her. "The greatest mystery," she concluded, "is the identity of the young man himself. I'm almost certain he is a Jago. No one else would be so foolhardy as to come smuggling over here in Penaluna's bailiwick. And Margaret Banks was quite certain one of the Jagos is so engaged."

"She should know," Mrs Moore said, screwing up her face as people do when trying to remember some little fact that has momentarily escaped them. "I seem to recall something about the Jagos ... about twenty years ago, when I first came to live here at Lanfear ... conversations that were nipped in the bud as the grown-ups became aware of my presence." She eyed Mrs Pellew speculatively. "You wouldn't have been old enough, either, my dear."

The woman licked her lips and smiled. Through her family connections, she did, in fact, know most of the story, and fairly incandescent it was, too. But she was hoping Hamill Oliver, who had the hide of a rhino, would spare her the embarrassment of repeating it. Mrs Moore twigged her dilemma and turned to him. "Do you know what happened?"

"Oh, it was the usual thing," he said offhandedly.

"Good!" She rubbed her hands in delight.

Oliver and Mrs Pellew laughed; Morwenna stared at the tablecloth.

"Miss Troy," Dr Moore interjected. "You were asking earlier about those antirrhinums – shall we go into the garden and select the ones you want?"

Morwenna half-rose in her seat.

"She'd learn more if she stayed," her cousin said, but his tone implied that he knew she'd go. To the other two he said, "It all happened twenty or more years ago. I don't suppose either of you dear young ladies remembers the name of Angie Vyvyan? For years it was only spoken in whispers."

Morwenna sat down again at once; Dr Moore yielded to her decision and tried, by certain gymnastics with his eyebrows, to warn Oliver to tone his story down as far as possible. Mrs Pellew suppressed a smile; it was the name Vyvyan, of course, that had changed the girl's mind – so there was probably something in the rumours, after all.

45

"Angie was the apple of her father's eye," Hamill began.

"Aren't the Vyvyans somehow kinsmen of the Jagos?" Mrs Pellew asked.

"I'm coming to that. Angie was of that branch of the Vyvyans who live out near Mawnan Smith – who are obviously related to the Vyvyans at Wendron, but not too closely. Originally they must all come from Penvivian, up near Davidstowe, but the name has been widely distributed in Cornwall since at least the thirteenth century. Neither the place nor the family is mentioned in Domesday, but nonetheless ..."

"Yes, Hamill, dear!" Mrs Moore chided. "It's Miss Angie we're interested in."

"Ah yes. Sad. Very sad." He turned suddenly to Mrs Pellew. "Come to think of it, the mother of your two charming nieces, Agnes Pellew – now she'd be the one to tell you all this. She was a Vyvyan and, indeed, a sister to Angie. An elder sister."

Mrs Pellew smiled knowingly. "They never, never, never talk of her. What I wish to know is *why?*"

"Well, I can tell you. She was to be married to some cousin of the Bolithos, someone from up in England. She went into Falmouth one day to order her bridal dress and had the misfortune to set eyes on Kinghorn Jago, who would then have been ... what? Twenty-odd. Within a week they had eloped!"

The two women leaned forward eagerly, their eyes sparkling. Even now the name of Kinghorn Jago was one to conjure with among the dove-côteries of West Cornwall. Morwenna, too, hung upon her cousin's lips.

"But Angie's father, old Redvers Vyvyan – he's still alive, by the way – somewhere up in Somerset, I believe – must be in his eighties now. Anyway, he and the thwarted bridegroom – can't recall *his* name – set off in hot pursuit and caught up with them in Bristol. There was a fight, of course, and the constable had to arrest *someone*. And when it's a choice between a justice of the peace, the son of a lord-lieutenant, and a man whose only commendation is a fine tenor voice and a way with young ladies' hearts ... well, it's an easy one to make."

He sipped his brandy with relish before he continued. "They dragged poor Angie back to Cornwall but they soon realized it was too late. She and Kinghorn had" – he glanced briefly at Morwenna – "jumped the starter's flag, as they say. So – the wedding of the year was called off." He smiled around at them as if that were the end of his tale.

"And?" the two women almost shrieked in chorus.

"And what?"

"Hamill, stop it!" Mrs Moore snapped. "You know jolly well *what*. What became of Miss Vyvyan – and why do you call her 'poor' Angie? I thought you were all in favour of people doing whatever they want."

"Oh, I don't know." He shrugged. "They sent her abroad, of course. Vienna or somewhere like that."

"But presumably she returned? They usually do."

He shook his head. "Not here. She was never seen again."

"Did she die?"

"Perhaps she did."

"Well!" The women exchanged glances of vexation. "I call that a most unsatisfactory story." Mrs Pellew summed up their feelings. "It tells us nothing."

Dr Moore interrupted with a laugh. "It tells us that Kinghorn Jago was then as he is now – an unrepentant ladies' man. It tells us that the ladies have only themselves to blame – for all the encouragement they have lavished upon him down the years."

"Do we detect a note of jealousy in this unbridled tirade?" his wife asked.

"In extra helpings!" Dr Moore confessed happily. "It also tells us that, when the last double line is drawn, it is the woman who foots the bill. It is therefore a highly moral tale and Hamill – for once – is to be commended."

For a moment his wife's eyes dwelled in his. "The woman is often happy to do so," she told him quietly.

"Ah!" He turned again to Hamill Oliver. "Now there, old fellow, I agree with the distaff side of this table. It is the single most important thing you have not told us. Was poor Angela Vyvyan happy, in the teeth of it all?"

"Not Angela," Hamill replied. "Angwin. The Vyvyans were always keen on real Cornish names for their children."

Dr Moore waved the correction aside.

Hamill licked his lips and glanced uncomfortably at his cousin. "To tell the truth, she did write to me once," he confessed. "About a year after she went away."

"So," Mrs Pellew cut in, "she didn't die in ..." She left the word unspoken.

"Vienna." Dr Moore supplied another.

"Lord alone knows why she chose *me*," Hamill went on. "I don't suppose we'd spoken together above half a dozen times. But she said I was the one truly disinterested friend she had."

"And did she say she was happy?" Mrs Moore asked. She seemed to take the young woman's fate quite personally.

"Not in as many words. But there was no hint of despair in it – or even remorse. She missed Cornwall dreadfully, and all her old friends. They were always a sociable lot, the Vyvyans of Mawnan Smith. But she'd made a new circle. She wasn't outcast and alone."

"Did you reply?" Morwenna asked.

"She gave no address. It was sent from Paris, but that was to muddy her tracks, I'm sure. Her cousin, Luxon Vyvyan, was a secretary at our Paris embassy and I'm sure they wouldn't have embarrassed him by sending her there."

"Did she marry in the end?" Mrs Moore inquired. "Did she say anything about a husband in the offing?"

He paused long enough to let them know that the word "husband," though close, was not *quite* what Miss Vyvyan had found. Then he said, "No."

"Why did she bother to write at all, I wonder?" Morwenna asked.

"She wanted me to tell people, I suppose. She couldn't openly crow that they'd cast her out and it had proved no punishment at all. I mean, she'd landed well and truly on her feet."

The two older women exchanged fleeting glances of amusement, each understanding that it was quite a different part of her anatomy on which the outcast young woman seemed to have landed.

"And did you tell people?" Morwenna insisted.

"I have now."

The conversation turned to other matters. Mrs Pellew seemed somewhat withdrawn; a little smile played about her lips as if she contemplated something highly pleasing to her. Eventually Dr Moore asked her what entertained her so.

She complied eagerly, having been dying for someone to notice her amusement and ask. "I was just thinking – wouldn't it be the most exquisite irony if history were about to repeat itself?"

"In what way?" Mrs Moore prompted.

"Our young heiress, the new mistress of Montpelier House, is to move shortly to Parc-an-Ython, it seems, there to live under the tutelage of dear Mrs Lanyon, who will bring her out and – no doubt – arrange a suitable match."

"And?"

"And I will lay a thousand guineas that her idea of a suitable match is someone like Thornton Coad or Richard Vyvyan." She avoided Morwenna's eye as she spoke the name. "But from what my young nieces tell me today, the sacrificial dove in question is already powerfully taken with Daniel Jago ..."

"If, indeed, it is he," Hamill murmured.

"Don't spoil it," Mrs Moore chided; then, to Mrs Pellew: "I begin to see what you mean, dear. Suppose she were to flee from the altar into the arms of young Jago – another young Jago! – and a chip off the old block – pursuit – a fight in Bristol ... and, er, profitable exile abroad?"

Mrs Pellew's tinkling laughter spread a sheen of silver over the happy picture.

"There's only one difference," Dr Moore pointed out.

They turned to him, already half annoyed that he was about to tarnish it for them.

"Miss Angwin Vyvyan wasn't an heiress." He avoided his wife's eye as he added, "Money does make such a difference."

6   ON THE LAST Monday in June the dog cart was brought around to the front door of Montpelier House. Two trunks containing Jane's last-minute things were put aboard and she and Banks set off in great excitement for Parc-an-Ython. Her main luggage had gone before her the previous Saturday. The drive was all of three miles, first down, then up the deepest valley in the district; but the two houses were just out of sight of each other. Had they been mutually visible, she thought, the adventure would have seemed a great deal more tame, somehow.

Banks, whose immense local knowledge more than compensated for her lack of refinement, was now confirmed as her lady's maid; she, too, was quite excited at the prospect of their weekly move, even over so short a distance. There would be new servants to talk to, new information to share with them – and, naturally, to pass on upward. With servants, as with their masters and mistresses, their worth often depended less on *what* they knew than on *whom*.

Part of Jane's excitement lay in the unspoken purpose behind these weekly peregrinations, to and fro – the fact that she was a wealthy young heiress upon whose choice of husband the fate of landed or commercial dynasties might depend. It made her feel more important than at any time in her life – which, admittedly, was not difficult, since she had never before felt of the slightest importance at all.

She experienced little guilt at this self-indulgence; her importance did not really attach to her*self*, not to what she was, but rather to what she quite accidentally possessed. The queen, she supposed, could justly be proud of being the queen without letting that pride taint her own private soul. Nevertheless, in practical terms the difference was hard to discern. *She* was the centre of attention; *she* was the subject of society talk and the object of its members' ambitions – or of a goodly few among them, anyway.

As she dressed for dinner that night, she broached the subject with Banks – or rather it was the maid who accidentally opened the way by disagreeing with Jane's choice of dress. The moment the maid held up the one she would have chosen, Jane saw she was right and, slightly to her own surprise, yielded the point without argument. Banks, to repair matters, said with a kind of angry intensity, "You're going to be the best-turned-out young lady in the whole of Cornwall, if I've got anything to do with it."

Jane was instantly mollified. "Where have you acquired your taste?" she asked, genuinely curious.

"Dunno, I'm sure, miss. I've always been interested in clothes and fashions and colours and things. I do read every ladies' journal I clap eyes to. And days off and that I belong to go in Penzance and look in all the shops and see the fine ladies."

"Really?" Jane rubbed her hands in glee. "But then there's no need to wait for a day off. There's nothing I should love better, myself. Let's go in this Friday."

"Or sometimes I belong to go down Falmouth," Banks added with studied carelessness.

There was a pause before Jane said, "Penzance, I think." A moment later she added, "I saw a very prettily turned-out young lady there the very evening we arrived. Just outside the station."

Banks merely laughed and held up two silk mantillas for Jane to make her choice – deliberately indicating no preference of her own.

"Which d'you think?" Jane asked.

Smiling contentedly, Banks laid one down and draped the other around her mistress's shoulders.

"That's my favourite, too," Jane said. "D'you think I should let my hair grow longer? I was looking at Miss Angelica's when we were swimming today, the way it lay on the water all about her. I felt quite envious."

The maid lighted the little spirit stove and prepared to give her mistress's curls some last-minute attention. While the tongs were heating she spread a plain muslin cape over her shoulders. "You could have it cut so short as Mrs Moore's and you'd still command more attention than Miss Angelica and Miss Jemima and half a dozen others beside, all rolled into one."

Jane had a fleeting mental glimpse of Mrs Moore as she had seen her that first day, standing up in her gig with her face all aglow, driving like Diana out of the setting sun. "I wonder," she said speculatively.

"No!" Banks laughed. "My dear soul! I only said that to make you see you needn't worry overmuch *what* you do look like — so mebbe 'tis just so well Mother Nature made you nice and eyeable, anyway."

"Don't be absurd!" Jane blushed and then grew solemn. "Still, if what you say is true — about it not mattering, I mean — then it's rather sad, isn't it? I'd like to meet someone who has no idea who I am, nor my prospects or anything like that ... someone who'd like me just for being me."

"I think I know who you mean."

"Why d'you speak in that tone? I don't mean anybody in particular. This conversation will stop if it's going to turn stupid."

Banks tested the temperature of the tongs, holding them within a whisker of her wrist; satisfied, she began a series of deft crimpings that took care of every last stray wisp on Jane's head. "And what if he liked you not for being you but just for being eyeable, then?" she asked. "A doxy maid as we do say."

"But that would still be me, wouldn't it? Assuming I am 'eyeable,' just for the sake of the argument. It would be a shallow affection, I grant, but it would not have been kindled by something completely outside my and my control, like my inheritance." She looked up and caught Banks smiling in the looking glass, the sort of smile people make when children say something charming. "That's enough!" she snapped. "I'm sure my hair will frizz and fall off with the heat."

"A face is an inheritance," Banks said, calmly finishing the last two curls. "And men can squander prettiness so well as any legacy."

"I don't know what you mean, I'm sure."

The maid slipped off the muslin cape with a curiously operatic movement, as if performing an unveiling ceremony. "There!" she said, holding it up as a backcloth.

Jane stared at her reflection and was amazed at the difference those last little touches had made. She had never worn this combination of dress and mantilla before; it was almost a new person, or, rather, a person subtly different from any she had seen before, who stared back at her.

"I mean they can use it and pass on," Banks said.

It still made no sense to Jane. How could anyone *use* an object of beauty? How could you use a beautiful painting, for instance — except to grace and ornament a room? She was dimly aware, however, that this conversation was bordering on that unspoken grown-up conspiracy whose protocols she was supposed to share though they had, in fact, mysteriously passed her by. "Yes," she replied, "that is true, of course. One forgets it so easily."

Banks appeared to think that a strange sentiment, indeed; but there was no time for more. The dinner gong rang out and Jane was determined not to be late on her first evening with the Lanyons.

Her hostess met her at the foot of the stair. "Oh, my dear," she exclaimed, spreading wide her arms in welcome, "you are as pretty as a picture!"

They pecked the air beside each other's cheeks. "Poor Lanyon broke a shoelace," she added, "but he won't be long. Meanwhile, try to remember this: Dull Men Eat Very Brown Bread."

Jane repeated the strange sentence and asked what it meant.

50

"It is the order of precedence of the English Peerage: Duke, Marquess, Earl, Viscount, Baron, Baronet. My mother taught me that and I have never forgotten it. I shall try to pass such useful little fragments on to you from time to time.

"Dull Men Eat Very Brown Bread," Jane said happily.

The dining room, like everything else to do with the house, was solid and comfortable rather than grand. The paintings, though numerous, did not crowd each other upon the walls; the porcelain that gleamed in the two large cabinets "had room to breathe," as her mother would have said. Jane looked about her with approval, but Dorothy Lanyon must have misinterpreted her glance. "At Pallas House," she said, "they have just relegated all Sir William Troy's old furniture to the servants' attics, you know. But I think that is a terrible jolt to a house, don't you. I admit that Chippendale and Sheraton are not the most elegant of styles, but they are perfectly serviceable still." She ran her gloved fingers over the back of the chair that was to be Jane's. "There is something almost sinful about discarding them before they have reached their natural span."

Jesse Lanyon joined them at the moment. His wife presented him to Jane. She curtsied and thanked him for the honour he and Mrs Lanyon were doing her; he paid her all the expected compliments, which, once he saw her, he had no difficulty in making sincere. Then, rubbing his hands in anticipation of a good dinner, held her chair while she took her seat. The hoops of her crinoline lifted her dress clear of her lap so that she had the strange sensation of sitting there with nothing on below her waist but her underwear.

The butler helped his wife to her place; he himself managed to sit down quite unaided. He spoke warmly of her father, of how pleased the whole district was to see new life at Montpelier ... pity, in a way, that the lands had gone from it ... but then, on the other hand, estates were something of a mixed blessing – not to say an out and out burden ...

Objectively, Jane thought, examining him as he spoke this monologue, he could not be considered an attractive man. He was well up in his forties, with a head more than half bald and a pate as shiny as a pippin. He had a high-domed forehead that suggested intellectual rather than manly interests. His eyebrows were finely drawn but his eyes were close together, crowding the almost knife-thin bridge of a nose that was both aquiline and pointed. His lips were thin, too, but not cruelly so, and at least his jaw was nicely cleft and firm. He was clean-shaven and his skin was like a pale parchment, tautly stretched over the bone of his cheeks and brow.

And yet, unprepossessing as each individual feature might be, Jane could not help warming to the man. It was his eyes, she decided at last. They were a pale greeny-gray and genial – but their kindly light owed nothing to sentimentality, rather to a suggestion of wisdom that seemed to lurk in the depths of them. Once he stopped mouthing these expected platitudes, she thought, a different and altogether profounder man would be revealed.

She was pleased to make this discovery. Her conversation with Banks had left her most dissatisfied. They had spoken of the most paltry things as if they had been deeply philosophical; now she felt she wanted some real conversation, about things that were truly important. Her chance came while they were still on the soup.

"I expect that Yorkshire and the life you led there must already seem long ago and far away?" he asked her.

"Indeed." She nodded. "I was thinking of it only this morning – of the train journey down here, in fact. It is a strange thing about trains is it not? Their purpose is both to join and to separate. I mean, that train has joined me to you and all my other new friends here in Cornwall, and yet it has separated me from all my old ones."

In the corner of her eye she saw Mrs Lanyon begin the same patronizing smile as Banks had smiled earlier. It annoyed her – though she had to admit that her thoughts on trains, which had seemed quite philosophical in her own mind, sounded a great deal less so when expressed in her clumsy words.

But Mr Lanyon was onto them at once. "How very true," he said. "But it does not end there. Think of first, second, and third class, all in the same train – united in one sense, divided in another. What interesting thoughts you raise, Miss Hervey."

Delighted, she risked a further *pensée*. "It made me wonder *why*, you see. When you really consider the matter, everything that happens involves a separation-from that is also a joining-up."

"Goodness!" Mrs Lanyon exclaimed, looking from one to the other and wondering how to get the conversation onto the lines she preferred.

Her husband chuckled. "We are separating this soup from its plate and joining it up with ourselves! It raises the whole question of purpose – as you so rightly say. We eat to nourish ourselves – our bodies. We nourish our bodies to give our minds scope. We give our minds scope in order to improve ... whatever we may. Selfishly – our own conditions and prospects. More nobly, perhaps – our circle of friends, our community, our civilization. And we seek to improve these things ... why? Now that *is* a mystery."

"Is it?" Jane asked – thinking if only Banks could hear her now, what a very different opinion she would form. "Isn't it self-evident?"

"Not to me." His smile was so genial that she saw at once it was by no means self-evident that mankind in general should want to improve anything.

"When we are gone," he continued, "it cannot possibly matter to us whether our successors inhabit a world that is better, or worse ..."

"My dear!" his wife interrupted.

"Mmmm?" He gave her that same gracious smile, showing not the faintest annoyance. Jane could not help thinking how her own father would hate to be stopped in full flight like that.

"Miss Hervey is not dressed in mourning, I know, but that is only because we are *en famille*. It is a little unfeeling to talk of passing on."

"Oh, please!" Jane protested. "I grieve for my dear *Maman*, of course, but in a very philosophical sense. We were never close. Don't think me unfeeling, but she was not the sort of person to encourage ... closeness." There was a silence. Jane added, "And yet ..." not really knowing what sort of qualification she might mean – merely wishing to soften any unintended harshness in her sentiments.

"Yes?" Mr Lanyon prompted.

She sighed. "I don't know. I've never said this to anyone – well, there's never been anyone to say it to. But I often felt that she wished for a warmer intimacy between us.

You know that certain look people get when there's something they'd really like to do, only they think it's their duty not to do it – whatever it may be? Well, she often got that sort of look in her eye when there was a danger of some tenderness arising between us."

"Why d'you say 'danger'?" Lanyon asked at once.

"I don't know." Her use of the word now puzzled her, too. "I suppose I mean that is how *she* would have seen it."

Mrs Lanyon interjected, "You have to remember – hers was a most difficult situation."

"Was it?" Jane asked, turning to her for more.

"So I believe," she replied awkwardly. She was furious with Lanyon for starting this hare when there were so many important matters to discuss. "Of course, I only know what your father has told me."

"And I only know what I saw." Jane chuckled. "We probably have two quite different pictures in our minds, you know."

"And what did you see?" Lanyon asked.

"My dear!" his wife expostulated.

Genial as ever he accepted his wife's rebuke and, turning to their young guest, said, "Well then, tell us about the friends you have made since the Great Western Railway joined you to us."

But Jane was back in her sunlit nursery in sunlit Paris; there must have been gray days, stormy days, but her memory had discarded them. "I remember music and laughter – her laughter – drifting up through the green baize door to our part of the villa. I remember seeing her in an endless succession of silks and cottons and furs and hats, strolling in the garden with this officer or that one, stepping into her carriage on the arm of her favourite ambassador ..."

Husband and wife exchanged wary glances. Jane, her lips parted in a smile, her eyes closed upon her memories, went on: "... returning with a whole retinue of dukes and marquesses, none of whom" – she smiled at Dorothy – "ever ate brown bread, I'm sure. I remember my nanny telling me she was 'the toast of Paris.' La Vivie, they called her. Of course, I never met any of these people. I'm sure that, in her salon, there were as many cross-currents of spite and ill-feeling as in any other small circle, but I never heard a voice raised in anger or even derision." She smiled apologetically at her hostess. "I can remember nothing I would call a 'difficult situation,' I'm afraid – though I'm sure my father is right."

Mrs Lanyon conjured some warmth from somewhere and put it all into her smile. "I meant only that she was married to a husband whom painful circumstances prevented her from acknowledging. That would be distressing to any woman."

Jane nodded thoughtfully. She had never thought of her mother as one who suffered hardship with a noble spirit but she supposed it must have been so. "I'm sure she was greatly consoled by her friends," she added.

Lanyon avoided his wife's eye. "I say, this soup will go cold," he warned.

When the course was finally cleared, he drew breath to speak. His wife caught his eye and gave an imperceptible shake of her head – which turned to an approving nod when he said, "You were going to tell us of your new friends here in Cornwall."

And Jane babbled on just as eagerly about them as she had about her mother's laughter-filled days of self-sacrifice and resignation in Paris.

Later that night, in those precious moments before sleep, she reflected on her good fortune at being befriended by two such splendid people as these. It proved that a concern for propriety did not necessarily go hand in hand with dullness and gloom – as Angelica and Jemima were forever hinting. Mr Lanyon especially showed it. What a razor-sharp mind he had! She could say the most ordinary things and he'd pick them up and show her what deep thoughts lay just beneath their surface – thoughts she'd almost had herself but had just failed to grasp. Perhaps, if she had enough conversations with him, some of that intelligence might rub off on her. It would be better, she decided, to choose moments when she'd otherwise be in Mrs Lanyon's way. She was the dearest, kindest soul but she seemed most intolerant of her husband's flights of philosophy. No doubt she appreciated his many other qualities, of which Jane as yet knew nothing.

At that same moment, the man himself was lying at his wife's side, saying, "A charming girl, my dear."

She nodded, not quite as enthusiastically as he might have expected – considering the eagerness she had shown before Jane's arrival.

"A good-looker, too."

"Mm-hmm."

"Not that she needs to be, mind – with her inheritance."

"No." She turned to him and pulled his nightcap fully on again.

"It's a warm night," he complained. "D'you really think I need it?"

"You know how easily you take cold."

After a silence he went on. "Has it all come from wholesale tea?"

She sighed. "From the way he spoke, the mother had independent means of her own – I mean, not from any allowance he might have made her. No, in fact, it certainly didn't come from wholesale tea. I remember now. His firm was in dire trouble when her inheritance came to her. He said it would have put the firm back on its feet but he was too proud to let his mother and sisters know."

"Sounds pretty rum to me, what?"

"People are apt to do stupid things, dear. He didn't want to admit he'd been living a lie. Also, I suppose he wanted to effect the rescue by his own efforts. Pride in a different sense."

"You suppose?" he echoed. "Or did Hervey tell you as much?"

"Oh, he told me. I must say, it sounded very reasonable then. I never felt a moment's ..." She let the word hang.

"Until these tales of Gay Paree!" he commented.

She nodded – and resettled his nightcap yet again.

"What if there's something in them?"

She swallowed hard before she replied. "I'd have to drop her, of course."

"Completely? Don't you think that's rather harsh?"

"There can be no half measures in something so ... so ... I mean, it's the very bedrock of society. Besides, it always comes out, something like that."

"The truth, you mean?"

54

"No. The seed. The pedigree." She smoothed out several wrinkles in their sheets. "Pedigree is all. However ..." She rallied and became more cheerful. "I simply cannot believe it of them. He is so charming and so respectable. And you've seen the girl – as pure and innocent as the day. We're worrying our heads over nothing."

"Suspend judgement, eh?" He slipped his hand onto her thigh and gave her a friendly squeeze.

Without a word she rolled up the hem of her nightdress, lay back, and loosely parted her limbs for his nightly assault upon her childlessness. It was always without a word now. In earlier days he had talked to her, explained how it would quicken her, how there was no other way, how it was her duty. But in time his little homilies had come to seem like an accusation, branding her as barren. Then being the decent, kindly man that he was, he said no more.

Being a man he thought silence was no sort of accusation.

7 DURING JULY AND AUGUST, although there was no formal season, there was a seemingly endless round of teas and At Homes, of croquet and tennis parties, all of them well attended by the eligible bachelors on Dorothy Lanyon's list – the sons of landowners and mineral lords, plus a good sprinkling of rising professional men. There was no one from the business classes. From Truro came the somewhat lethargic Spry twins of Tregolls and a more sprightly young Devonshire of Newham; from Carclew, a juvenile Lemon, "rather sweet," as Jane wittily said; Carwythenack House near Trevennen sent a moody young Hill, while Bosahan, nearby, supplied a fine specimen of a Grylls. Acton Castle, at Roost, paraded Captain Praed; but the military man who most captured her fancy was Richard Vyvyan from Trelowarren. As a mere naval ensign he would be unable to marry, but if there were a serious possibility of his winning Jane's hand, the family would think it worthwhile to buy his captaincy, whereupon he could marry away to the utmost limit of the law.

These and two dozen more young eligibles ("young" being an elastic term that could stretch with a bachelor into his forties) vied with each other to hand her tea and cut her cake, to partner her on the lawns, to fetch her cushions, to turn her page at the piano, to join their tenor, baritone, or bass to her mezzo-soprano, to enthuse over her sketches ... and all those other activities by which Society has determined that young people shall not become so well acquainted before marriage that they shrink from the very idea of it altogether.

"You are so lucky, my dear," her hostess told her, "to have such a choice. You've no idea of the scheming and contrivance I and my sister had to endure merely to meet one eligible young man. There is a law of nature that girls must marry as soon as they can, while men must avoid it for as long as possible. And the only power that can suspend this law is the power of a goodly inheritance."

Jane did her best to feel lucky.

She also began to go about the district – discreetly, only to the smaller, informal occasions, and always in half-mourning. But it hardly widened her circle. At Home with Captain Pread she would meet the Spry twins, a Devonshire, a Lemon ... At Trelowarren there would be a Lemon, a Devonshire, a brace of Sprys, and all the rest of that increasingly familiar company. Sometimes there would be a new face – a Moyle or a Michell from Bosvigo or Comprigny, a Millet Thomas from Killiow, say – but they were new in the sense of "more" rather than of "different." Her list might be expanding; her choice did not.

When it came to drawing up the invitations for the next occasion, Dorothy Lanyon noticed with satisfaction how frequently her young protégée would ask, "And is Mr Vyvyan not to come?"

She would have felt less satisfied had she known that Jane was secretly taking an interest in the Lanyon's solicitor, Vosper Scawen of Helston, who made occasional calls upon the house by way of business. As the weeks of that summer wore on, they became more frequent – and he almost always found occasion to pass the time of day with her. But in the very nature of things, Dorothy could have no inkling of what was going on. The idea, the very *idea*, that Jane might be interested in someone of that class did not even cross her mind.

Vosper Scawen, a handsome man in his twenty-eighth year, had a commanding presence and an easy, affable manner. To Jane he seemed the embodiment of all that was calm, collected, and rational; but what made her warm to him most especially was that he did not treat her in the way that other men did. Most of her would-be suitors seemed to regard her as a delightful child; they wore that special smile which people keep for youthful enthusiasms and opinions. Their attitude said, "Let us do nothing to spoil this charming vivacity." But Vosper Scawen – perhaps because he knew his suit would be hopeless – treated her like ... well, almost like a colleague. She would even have said "like a brother," except there was that certain twinkle in his eye, that restrained electricity between them, too.

Actually, to be fair to him, young Richard Vyvyan was also very easy with her – though, come to think of it, he *was* more like a brother.

Banks was an invaluable antidote to Mrs Lanyon's enthusiasms. Jane would send her up to her room with orders to mend this or sort through that – tasks she knew to be already completed – thus giving the woman time to sit behind the lace curtains, invisible to the world while she quizzed it at her leisure through Jane's high-powered binoculars. They were almost too high-powered, for, despite the milky haze of the out-of-focus curtains, she was once able to count the individual bristles in Captain Praed's ears.

Later, when Jane was taking her bath and dressing for dinner, there would be a delicious post-mortem in which suitors fell like autumn leaves.

"And what of Gervase Pender of Budock Vean?" Jane might ask.

"Was he the one with the bit of hair at the back that wouldn't lay down?" Banks would say, which made Jane laugh and confess she had not remarked it at the time but, yes, that was, indeed, the man.

"Then he's a fidget. He'd drive you mad in a week. Took his kerchief from this pocket, put it in that, took it out again, mopped his brow, stuck it up his sleeve, took it out again ... never still. Jingles his knees. Rattles the coin in his pockets. He'd make you want to scream."

A man's entire character and prospects could be written off in half a dozen words: "Picks his nose and chews it" – or: "Studies himself dearly in the glass."

Sometimes her inexhaustible local knowledge rather than her direct observations supplied the coup de grace. This man's family had a terrible fight against the demon drink; that one was a notorious womanizer and known to keep company with drabs.

"You couldn't say any such thing of the young Nicholls boy from Antron," Jane commented. "He's taking Holy Orders and they say he'll surely be a bishop one day. He got a double first in Greats, whatever that means."

"You'd admire to be an archbishop's wife, would you?" the maid asked.

"If I'm to be a clergyman's wife at all, yes. I mean there's no sense in going in for something if you don't intend to go in for it as hard as you can, is there."

Banks seemed dubious.

"Also, there is something very inspiring about a man who is so *naturally* virtuous as Argus Nicholl, don't you find?"

"Mebbe." Banks shook her head. "It doesn't sound much like the Church of England to me, though. I mean to say, Church of England is a one-day-a-week faith – six days hunting and fishing and Sundays in the pulpit. I don't believe they reckon much to such a great old show of virtue as Mr Nicholl do put up."

"So you don't think he has the makings of an archbishop?"

"I wouldn't go so far as that, Miss Jane. All I say is he'll have a harder road than most if that's where he do want go."

Jane sighed, reluctant to discount the young man entirely. Such conspicuous virtue was rare; and he made it seem so light a burden, so effortlessly borne, that she had hoped a closer association might work the identical magic for her. "Oh to be good," she murmured, "without ever having to *try!*"

But Banks, as usual, had the last word: "Good enough is good enough for most folks." And Argus Nicholl, no matter how virtuous, was put lower down the list.

*   *   *

In all this talk of marriage Jane never once thought back to the impudent young smuggler – at least not in that context. Yet hardly a day went by when the memory of him did not at some moment cross her mind. Usually it was at the dying end of the evening, when her prayers were over and done with, and sleep was drawing on. She liked to dedicate those moments to a brief survey of what she had done, or left undone, that day, renewing her determination to profit from her errors and so make the morrow a little better. In the very last minutes, though, when she honestly could not trawl her memory for one more lapse, a picture of the fellow would come stealing in at the edges of her awareness; and before she knew what was happening, he had taken over the stage.

At first she had fought it, giving herself many a restless, sleepless hour. Then she had discovered the trick. She only fought to banish his image because she thought of it as a product of her own mind – or, rather, of that heedless tendency to vice that is

57

part of all human existence and which no son or daughter of Adam can escape. Latterly, however, she began to feel quite certain that he was deeply ashamed of the way he behaved that day and now wanted nothing more than to sue for her pardon and draw strength from her to be a better, finer person in every way.

That, at least, was what he told her, night after night, as he crept into her mind. In those circumstances, of course, it would be unchristian to turn him away. She wondered if the chance to put her charity into practice would ever occur. Angelica and Jemima had invited her to Swanpool, which wasn't a million miles from the Jago clan at Greenbank (if he was a Jago); but they had then themselves been invited to a cousin's in Scotland and would not be back until autumn – "Betrothed, like you, let us hope," as they said at their departure.

One morning, the first to carry a hint of autumn on the air, Jane and Dorothy set off to look out new dress materials at Nicholls's in Helston. They had just negotiated the turning to Sithney Common Hill when Dorothy exclaimed, "Oh dear!" and nodded toward a gig about a furlong away and approaching them, slightly erratically. Its driver was a young lady, respectably dressed as far as one could tell at such a distance, and alone. "I think I know who that is," she added.

"The horse seems agitated," Jane commented.

"Transmitted down the reins, I believe. This, unless I'm mistaken, is Mrs Wender of Skyburriowe."

Jane stared at the woman in the gig, and then stared again to be certain. "Her daughter, don't you mean?" she asked.

"No – the lady herself. She married very young. It must have been just before you came. Early June, I think – and what are we now? Mid-September." She heaved a sigh. "I've been half-expecting this."

"She must have been very young." Jane could now see the girl quite clearly; she looked as if she'd hardly left the nursery.

"She was all of fifteen," Dorothy replied, almost defensively. "I was very surprised at her mother, I must say."

There was no time to pursue the matter further; young Mrs Wender was now too close. Her smile was brave rather than warm. "Mrs Lanyon! Do I call at an inconvenient hour? I was so hoping to find you in."

"Mrs Wender, what a pleasant surprise. We are, in fact, on our way to Helston, but not on business of any great import. Nothing's amiss, I trust?"

"No. Oh no. Certainly not. It's just been such ages since I saw you."

Looking at her, and hearing her speak, Jane found herself wondering if the girl was even fifteen.

"Yes, hasn't it. And Dr Wender, he's well, too, I trust?"

She gave a light laugh – more of a forced giggle, in fact. "He says he's as well as any doctor has a right to expect."

"Splendid," Dorothy said and made a slight movement of the reins, as if preparing to prepare to move on.

The child (for Jane still could not think of her as a married woman) looked hopelessly about her. "Would it be ..." she stammered. "I mean what morning would ... I'd so enjoy a chat ..."

Jane's heart went out to the girl. "Dear Mrs Lanyon," she said. "Our visit to Helston is really of no consequence – and the poor horse looks quite lathered." She meant it as an excuse, so as not to say that the poor child looked quite lathered, too; but the poor child herself took it in a different spirit. "He's quite hard to control, Miss Hervey," she snapped. "It is Miss Hervey, I take it?"

"Yes," Dorothy stepped in. "Permit me."

The introductions over, Jane smiled and said, "Perhaps a brief rest at Parc-an-Ython will settle him. Has he had many outings lately?"

The girl, too agitated to maintain any mood for long, smiled back gratefully; her eyes seemed unnaturally bright and both women had the feeling she might be close to tears.

"You go on, my dear," Dorothy told her. "I'll turn by that gate and follow you." When the girl was out of earshot Jane said, "I hope you don't mind? She seemed so agitated."

"No, dear." The other sighed. "I'd have come to it myself, I'm sure. If I seem a little reluctant, it's that I foresaw all this – and told the mother so before the betrothal was announced. It's too late now for anything but balm and bandages."

"Does her mother live far away?"

Dorothy gave a single, mirthless laugh. "A mile up the road, in Sithney."

"Why doesn't she go to her?"

"Because she'd come away with a flea in her ear. The poor woman has three other daughters to settle. The last thing she wants is for them to gain a reputation for weeping and whining and running home to mother. So now it falls to me to put some backbone into her! Still, I suppose Lanyon and I have as much interest in seeing them well married off as the woman herself."

"Are they kinsfolk of yours?"

Dorothy laughed at the very idea. "If you'll stop asking questions, I'll tell you the whole sad story. Or as much as we've time for. That girl's father, Owen Delamere, was our agent for the farms we own in North Cornwall. They live in a tied cottage of ours in Sithney, as I said. He died over a year ago now. Tragic. Got kicked in the head by a horse in the backyard of an inn in Launceston. He was a charming man – and good at his work, too. Lanyon couldn't speak too highly of him. He was the second son of the Earl of Mere and everyone was quite certain he'd inherit one day. The older brother had been married for years with no issue and the wife well past the age by then. But one should never count one's chickens in the egg, you see. The old wife died, the brother married again – a slip of a girl no older than little Bessie – and lo and behold, within the year, a bonny, bouncing young heir! So poor May Delamere, the mother, has seen her prospects fall from the dizzy heights of thirty thousand a year to a pension of ninety-five from us. And her only hope of bettering herself now is to marry again – which no man in his right mind will offer until those other three girls are settled." She smiled wanly. "So, as I said, Lanyon and I have as much interest as the mother in making young Bessie see sense. She must on no account upset the applecart. Indeed, she ought to be helping her mother find husbands for her sisters."

"She's the youngest, I take it," Jane said.

59

"No, she's the third. Fanny's fourteen. Rosa and Susie are ... what? I suppose eighteen and seventeen. She could help her mother find husbands for them – and the best way of all would be to advertise her own happiness and sense of marital duty as widely as possible. And I shall tell her so. They are good girls. Good breeding, you see." She smiled and patted Jane's arm. "It's so important. It always comes out – no matter what."

"It would still leave ... Fanny, did you say? The youngest. She could hardly marry, at her age."

"Why not? A girl may marry at twelve, my dear, if needs be."

"But I thought you said you were surprised at the mother marrying off Bessie at the tender age of fifteen?"

The older woman frowned in bewilderment. "But I didn't mean her age. I agree, it might have been better to wait a year or two – especially as Dr Wender has already buried three wives. On the other hand, Bessie's not as frail as she looks, you know. And beggars must be no choosers, either."

Jane gave a perplexed little laugh. "Forgive my returning to the point, Mrs Lanyon, but what was it surprised you in the mother's action, then?"

Dorothy sucked in her breath in that ambiguous Cornish manner which can mean so many things (and therefore, as often as not, means nothing at all). "I'll tell you later," she said. "There's no time now." They turned in at the gate.

"Oh, I do wish I could help in some way," Jane cried.

"A sentiment that does you great credit, my dear." They halted and began to dismount. "But I suspect this is going to be a married woman's problem, which only another married woman can resolve."

Jane understood very well that she was being tactfully excluded from whatever interview might now take place; she said she would welcome the opportunity to finish one small corner of her embroidery.

But before she even took up her needle she saw Lawyer Scawen coming up the drive. Realizing that Dorothy Lanyon could hardly entertain him, what with Mrs Wender in her present state, she went down again to do the sociable thing.

Vosper Scawen was all apologies in case he was detaining her from something important. She eased his none-too-troubled conscience on that score. He said that he was delighted to have the chance of talking to her again. For one appalled moment she thought he might be about to propose – something for which she was in no way prepared – but all he said was, "As a matter of fact, I was only calling to find what day might suit you and Mrs Lanyon for me, your father, and a Commissioner for Oaths to attend upon you." He smiled encouragingly, as if suggesting an ordeal. "There is a small document that needs your signature."

While he spoke, and her fears subsided, she tried to study him objectively, wondering what sort of a husband he might make. Dorothy Lanyon had told her she must not expect to marry for love – or not entirely or even chiefly for love. So much money and property were at stake that to pile it all upon the frail craft of love would be to risk sinking it entirely. Numerous examples of such a tragedy had been paraded before her and she was willing to accept not only that the head must rule the heart in her case but that the head which did the ruling might not even be her own.

He'd be a very acceptable husband, she decided. He was certainly good looking. You'd be happy enough to go on meeting that face over the breakfast table. And he was cheerful, conscientious, and very hard-working; everyone spoke most highly of him. He was certain to be a circuit judge one day, they said; perhaps he'd even rise higher, to the high court itself. Baron and Lady Scawen? It sounded very nice. Just fancy – little Jane Hervey ending up a baroness! Perhaps Dear Mrs Lanyon was being just a teeny bit short-sighted in sticking so rigidly to the social calendar of the moment? Who knew what the future might bring?

At that moment he reached the end of his explanation.

"Does it need such a ceremony?" she asked. "Why can't I just call in at your office and you can get the man for the oaths and ..."

"But I wouldn't dream of troubling you to call on me, Miss Hervey." The very idea seemed to shock him.

"But I'm going in to Helston, anyway. If we hadn't met Mrs Wender, you'd have passed us on our way in to Nicholls's. I expect we'll go when Mrs Wender leaves. And we'll have luncheon at The Angel, as usual. Then I could call on you, at half past two, say. I'd like to see where you work, anyway."

He conceded with a smile.

He should smile more often, she thought. It was the best thing about him, so warm and genial. On the other hand, a young lawyer who went about looking warm and genial would probably never reach the eminence of a barony. Which was the better? Warmth and geniality, she decided – and then smiled at herself, for she could just hear her father saying that showed how young and inexperienced she was.

"I hope Mrs Wender has not brought bad news," he commented.

"Mrs Lanyon has told me of her mother's and sister's situation," Jane replied, thinking the lawyer would certainly know the full story.

"A painful case," he said vaguely.

Jane took the plunge. "Just before we turned in at the gate, Mrs Lanyon said that everyone was surprised at Mrs Delamere's handling of the marriage. I thought she meant because Mrs Wender was so young, but apparently that wasn't it." She raised her eyebrows and challenged him to fill the silence.

He became aware that she was making this some kind of test of him – or, rather, of his attitude toward her. He smiled again, while he rapidly scanned the truthful answer for anything that an unmarried girl ought not to hear.

"I know what surprised a great number of people," he replied at last, "including me. Perhaps that's what Mrs Lanyon means? You see, there was no settlement on Bessie in the marriage contract."

"I suppose she didn't have much choice," Jane said thoughtfully.

He made a precarious balance between his two hands. "Nor did he. To put it baldly, the number of wives a doctor can afford to lose must surely have some limit this side of four!" He studied her response closely.

Against her will she giggled, covering her mouth like a naughty girl and staring at him with wide, slightly alarmed eyes that stole his heart away. Actually he could not have said anything more likely to endear him to her, for by treating her as one of his own set, which was no doubt as worldly wise as you might wish, he was paying her the highest compliment. Her spirit swelled to be thought worthy of such trust. "One shouldn't laugh," she said, "but you're quite right, Mr Scawen. I take it there was no suggestion of – you know – with the deaths of the first three wives?"

He shook his head. "No, not even his sworn enemy could say anything like that – apart from which they were all treated by other doctors, of course. His first wife died in a hunting accident. The second after – well, of what they call post-puerperal fever. And the third had a cancer. Even so, no matter how innocent their deaths undoubtedly were, they hardly left him strong in trumps when it comes to courting his fourth. The mother could have screwed him to some sort of a settlement if she'd been better advised. Now, without such protection, young Bessie is at the mercy of his will, you see."

"Both during his life and after his death," Jane murmured.

He glanced at her sharply, as if he had not expected so astute a comment from her, or not so swiftly. "Fortunately for *you*," he said, "your father is one of the cleverest and most far-sighted men I know."

"What is this signature you require?" she asked.

"Oh ..." A little trill of his fingers dismissed it. "Just the transfer of some property. Your father has arranged it all."

"Property he owned in Leeds?" she asked, wondering how her signature might be required.

Again that smile. "You needn't concern yourself with the details, Miss Hervey. They are most fearfully dull and complicated."

She sighed. "I suppose we must be grateful to you men, that you can manage to understand such things and are willing to endure the tedium of it all."

"We cannot manage without the inspiration that ladies provide, though. That easily outweighs the rest."

A short while later Dorothy Lanyon came hurrying into the morning room, bristling with apologies and positively glowing with the satisfaction of a job well done. Behind her came a much happier Bessie Wender.

Jane was by now intensely curious to discover what had troubled the girl so and what Mrs Lanyon might have said to bring about such a radical transformation. Before she could stop herself she said, "Oh, Mrs Lanyon, I'm sure you and Mr Scawen have a thousand matters to settle. And I have just arranged to call at his office after luncheon, so ..."

"Call at his office?" Mrs Lanyon was scandalized.

Jane smiled. "The matter is pressing, I understand. And we can kill two birds with one stone – this commissioner-for-oaths business, as well, you know?" Seeing Mrs Lanyon beginning to waver, she added, "And I do want to choose the right material – and you know how dreadfully I prevaricate when the choice is so rich. So, wouldn't it be best if I accompany Mrs Wender to Helston, leaving you and Mr Scawen to complete your business? And you can catch me up at the milliner's."

Dorothy turned and stared uncertainly at Mrs Wender. "You have quite recovered yourself?" she asked.

The girl nodded eagerly. "Quite."

"Oh, very well." She yielded with good grace.

Jane took temporary leave of Vosper Scawen. "Excuse me for just two shakes," she said to Mrs Wender, and hurried upstairs.

Behind her Mrs Lanyon was saying, "I'll see you to your gig, my dear." The offer did not immediately strike Jane as slightly odd ... a little out of character. At the top of the stairs she found two gardeners carrying out the soil bucket she had hoped to use. She turned and went to the downstairs closet.

But for that circumstance she would never have overheard Mrs Lanyon talking to Mrs Wender.

8 DOROTHY LANYON CANNOT have realized that the closet window was open – still less that Jane was inside and able to overhear every word; indeed, she had led Bessie Wender out of doors to prevent any such accident.

She took the girl's arm and walked her gently down the side path to the stable yard, where one of the grooms had brought her horse to cool him off slowly and get him resettled. The thin, silvery sunshine turned their brief promenade into a pleasure. "Now do remember, my dear," she was saying as she drew within earshot of Jane, "Miss Hervey may be four years older than you, and she may speak as if she knows the ways of the world; but she is, in fact, as delightfully innocent and free of that burden as when she came into it. I know you will do nothing to destroy her childlike charm."

"Of course not, Mrs Lanyon." The voice was so young and clear Jane had to remind herself that the girl was a married woman.

"I'm sure you still recall – perhaps with a certain wistful nostalgia? – your own happy innocence."

"Indeed."

"So let her enjoy *her* innocence while she may. Time enough to learn of our burdens."

Bessie said nothing.

"And since you know you ought to love your husband, for he has been very good to take you off your mother's hands, it is surely a small thing to endure for the sake of his happiness?"

Still Bessie was silent. Was she nodding, or just staring with those childlike eyes?

"You can think of other things. That's what I do. I'm sure it's what all respectable women do."

"Yes, Mrs Lanyon," the girl said at last.

Jane went out to join them in a most curious state of mind. She seemed almost to be swimming; the hall, the front door, the garden ... all these familiar landmarks had suddenly taken on the dreamy, drifting unreality of the seaweed pools in the "Ophelia Game." Some small part of her, deep inside, resented Dorothy Lanyon's warning and hated being cast as the innocent child; the rest of her closed around that anger, shielding it and its intentions from the censorship of her conscious mind. The result was this curious, drifting vacuum of purpose. Her feet carried her where she neither willed nor did not will them to go.

And when, a minute or so later, she and Mrs Wender were out on the road to Helston once more, she became, as it were, a spectator to her own curiosity – watching, listening, digesting ... doing everything but take part. Her tongue formed words that her thoughts had not prepared.

"Dear Mrs Lanyon is so wise," she heard her voice say. "What a great pity she has no children of her own."

"Yes." The girl shifted uneasily on her seat.

"But then she would have less time to help the likes of you and me."

"That's true."

"Often, when I have felt myself close to ..." She broke off. "Don't think me proud or presumptuous, my dear, but – since you seemed to know my name before we were introduced – I suppose you know something of my situation?"

The girl laughed drily. "I know you are in the happy position of being able to choose among a dozen eligible suitors, Miss Hervey."

It was Jane's turn to laugh. "Who was it said, 'my neighbour's fields are ever the greener'? I'll tell you truly, I do not relish being at the centre of so much attention."

"Do you say so?" Her bluntness surprised young Bessie out of her reserve.

"I do, indeed. I can never forget that if my inheritance were to vanish, so would they all. It is not *me* that captivates them."

"Well, I would not mind that so long as I had the choice. You must think of that."

Jane said nothing.

"Choice," Bessie repeated.

There was another silence before Jane said quietly – and as much to her own surprise as to Bessie's, "What if none of them were my own true choice? What if there were another who lives far outside that approved circle?"

Bessie, though still inhibited by Mrs Lanyon's warning, could not help smiling, leaning a little forward, encouraging Jane with an amused eye. "And is there?"

"No, no!" Jane retreated at once. "I'm only saying there might be. There could be. Then *that* man would be my true choice, but I should not be permitted to make it, you see? So, while that very possibility exists – even if there is no such person – which there isn't – just the possibility, you understand – even so, it still means my choice is not entirely free. And therefore it is not entirely mine, either."

Bessie reined the horse back to an even slower walk, but she made no reply. Looking at her, Jane found her expression quite unreadable. "Do say you agree?" she prompted.

"I had such a man," she said in a remote, faraway voice. "If I'd been the last of my sisters to marry, I'd have been left do it. If only Wender had picked on Rosa or Susie!"

"And why didn't he?" Jane asked rashly. Then she was all confusion. "Oh, do forgive me. What an impertinent question. Please, let us talk of other ..."

But Bessie herself now seemed under that same coercion as had seized Jane earlier. "Because he'd already had a bride of twenty, and a bride of eighteen, and a bride of seventeen. He considered them too old to bend to his ways."

After a pause Jane plucked up the courage to ask, "And did you know that when you married him?"

As she heard her own astonishing question reverberate in her mind, she suddenly realized that a door had just closed behind them. Society, society's ways, decorum, manners, the constraints of common etiquette ... all these fetters had been shed; they strewed the ground beyond that closed door. Here, on this side of it, in some strange limbo where the very idea of rules was alien, she and her unhappy young companion were held by a compulsion to talk that no power could stay.

"I knew nothing then," Bessie said.

Jane recognized the compulsion, not because she was familiar with it – quite the opposite. Indeed, she had never encountered it in her life before now. But she had certainly read of it in those odd little books her mother used to leave about the house. *The Sagacity of Innocence* she remembered particularly well for its stirring, almost feverish language and the utter vagueness of its content. In one sultry emotional passage after another it had warned of the dangers of heated emotions, of the "invincible compulsions that overwhelm young bosoms and limbs when their owners are rash enough to encourage the intimacies of thought, feeling, and gesture that are to their affections what fecund hothouse soil is to the orchid and the passion flower." How odd, she thought that such a vague but powerful admonition should at last make sense here in a Cornish lane, in a lurching gig driven by an inexpert hand, on a morning more chill than tropical!

"Perhaps it's as well to know nothing," Jane said with all the pat complacency that usually lards the sentiment.

Bessie's unseeing eyes were fixed on the road ahead. "I don't see how anyone could have told me. Mrs Lanyon says that the woman has the sweeter nature and must bend herself to forgive the man."

"But is it possible?" Jane asked. She, too, was gazing at the road ahead, and straining every nerve for the girl's reply.

"She says it can only get better. She says every wife goes through this during the first year and it should be easier for me, being so young and adaptable. What if I was thirty, and set in my ways? she says. And you can't say no to any of it, can you. So I suppose she must be right."

"It's hard to think of being thirty when you're not even twenty yet."

Bessie looked at her in bewilderment. "What *do* you know?" she asked.

"Not as much as you, obviously."

"Mrs Lanyon says you're innocent as a babe." She laughed harshly. "But she said the same about me before I married. At least I knew what men and women *do.*" After a pause she added, "Or are supposed to do."

Jane framed the question a thousand ways in her mind; all of them risked the sort of laughter that would shrivel her up. In the end she dared venture no more than: "What do they really do?"

They had reached a steep part of the hill. Helston was spread before them like a map, beginning down in the valley and straggling up its farther side. Automatically Jane reached for the brake.

"Yes," Bessie told her. "Thanks. Pull hard."

"What do they really do?" Jane repeated, emboldened by the grinding of the brake block, which half-drowned their conversation and robbed it of portentousness. Bessie continued staring at the road ahead. The words came in cryptic eruptions; in the intervening silences, her jaws ground, her breathing was short and staccato. "Bind you hand and foot." The hedgerow passed in unreal clarity. "*Hoard* you like a miser with his gold." Words of everyday meaning suddenly had no meaning whatever. "Practise abominations upon you."

"Hurt you, you mean?" Jane held her breath.

"Only in the beginning. After a time or two it gets like any other ..." She shook her head as if clearing it of an unpleasant dream. "Still, I know what to do now."

"What?"

"What Mrs Lanyon told me. Close my eyes. Close my mind. Just try to think of my dear mother and my poor sisters, who are so lonely without the comfort of a ..." And at that she burst into tears.

In putting her hands to her face she jerked the reins and checked the horse harshly in his mouth. He gave out a whinnying scream and started crabwise across the road, on a course that, had Jane not snatched the reins from her and brought him back in hand, would have caused them to lock wheels with a heavy stone cart going up the hill, which would, in all likelihood, have smashed both vehicles. The beast was calm in a moment, allowing Jane to throw an arm around the unhappy girl's shoulders and hug her warmly. "Oh, Bessie, dear Bessie," she said. "You sound so lonely and wretched. May I be your friend? I can't bear to see you miserable like this."

The floodgates opened. The little thing buried her face in both hands and began to howl. Jane looked about them and, seeing a narrow lane leading off to their right, pulled over and backed the gig into it, going just far enough to tether the horse to a gatepost, hard against the road.

"Come on," she said, taking up a rug she found in the body of the vehicle. "We'll stroll in that field out of people's sight until you're yourself again."

Bessie shook her head. Her face was still buried in her hands but her sobs had abated to mere sniffles.

"I have a little chocolate in my bag," Jane added.

One eye peered out between a vee of two fingers.

Jane smiled and fished it out, popping it back at once, as if half the treat lay in being tantalized like that.

Arm in arm they strolled over the stubble, aimlessly, this way and that, slowly zigzagging up the slope to where the ground levelled off a little and they might spread the rug and rest. Every time Bessie started to speak she lapsed within half a dozen words into incoherence. "Calm yourself," Jane urged. "We have all the time in the world."

When they reached the level, or less sloping, ground she spread the rug and they sat gratefully, for the climb had been stiffer than it had seemed from the gate. "Lucky we're neither of us in big hoops today," Jane commented as she smoothed out her skirts.

Bessie sighed and leaned back on rigid arms, staring out over the sunlit valley and town below them. "I never saw it from up here before," she said.

Looking at her, at her arms and the double-jointed bend in her elbows, Jane realized she still had the body, the stance, the manner of a child. The disjunction between that and her status as a married woman – the female to whom all the mysteries of life were at last revealed – was unnerving. She turned away and stared at the town, too. "Think of all the lives being led in all those little ... *hutches,*" she murmured. "I often wonder about them, don't you? When you're driving past other people's houses, or looking into their back gardens from the train. I remember on the journey down here from Yorkshire, one particular garden just after Exeter. Nothing at all grand. But they were holding a party of some kind. People playing croquet ... and archery targets. And the girls pretending they couldn't hold the mallets or the bows properly so the men had to put their arms round them and show them – and then scoring a bull or roqueting their opponent for six into the shrubbery. And maids carrying out jellies and plates of sandwiches. And footmen with seltzer and ginger pop. And I just wanted to stop the train and run across the fields and join in. I always feel that – other people's lives are so much more interesting. They're secure. They live in the same house for always and always. I don't think I'll ever have that feeling about me."

Bessie cleared her throat in a particular way.

"Sorry!" Jane laughed and offered her the chocolate, which was wrapped in kitchen paper.

"I shan't eat it if you won't," Bessie said, helping herself to a piece but not putting it into her mouth.

Jane took it from her, nibbled a corner, and handed it back. "I'm not really hungry," she said. "So that'll have to satisfy you – a token sharing. If boys can be blood brothers, I don't see why girls can't be chocolate sisters."

Bessie chuckled as she popped the sweet between her lips. "You're a funny one," she said. "I've heard people talk about you. They say you're all prim and proper and always doing the right thing and never saying a word out of place. But you're not a bit like that."

"You mean I talk scribble."

"No!"

There was pain in her denial, though Jane had only meant to make a joke of it. At once she became serious. "Perhaps it's because I'm afraid of talking like this – seriously – and behaving like this. I don't know what to do or say to you, Bessie. Can I call you Bessie? Mrs Wender doesn't seem very appropriate now."

"I don't know what to do, either," Bessie said.

"I knew from the way your horse was behaving – long before Mrs Lanyon recognized you and told me who you were – I knew then what sort of a state you were in."

"I can hardly remember it myself. Getting up this morning. Coming out here ... everything. It's all ... everything's just ..." She shook her head and fell silent.

"And you emerged from your interview with Mrs Lanyon all brave smiles and head up – but I could see nothing had changed. Except that you were more alone than ever."

"How could you tell that?"

"I just knew it." She nibbled the corner off another piece of chocolate and passed it over, saying, "Well, now you're not alone. I don't want to pry into all your secrets. That's not why I'm saying this. I probably wouldn't understand it, anyway. I'm just *here*, that's all. Just so that you know you're not alone."

Bessie blinked back more tears but this time there was no risk of a flood. She laughed to clear the sudden lump in her throat. "I can't mingle with high-quarter folk like you, Miss Hervey ..."

"Try Jane."

"Jane, then." The girl dipped her head in submission. "It makes no different. By any name, I can't mingle with you."

Jane chewed her lip in thoughtful silence, until it actually hurt. "Who makes these rules?" she asked vehemently. "What *are* they meant to protect?"

"The doctor wouldn't allow it anyway. I shall be chastised for coming out like this, on my own. I'm to have no acquaintance except those of whom he'll approve in due course – when I'm more tractable, he says, and more broken to his will."

Jane closed her eyes and tried to imagine she had not heard these words. "I am not a rebel," she said at last.

"I'm prepared for it," Bessie assured her. "I'll do what I must for the sake of my mother and sisters."

"At least – I never thought of myself as a rebel before. I always thought rebels were girls like Angelica and Jemima. They pretend to conform but inwardly they're looking for every chance to be naughty. That's what I thought rebellion was – just being naughty." She turned to Bessie with a smile. "But it isn't, is it?" She passed her the last piece of chocolate, again after taking a token nibble. "In fact, merely being naughty is like paying a kind of tribute to the rules. Rebellion goes much deeper." She stood up and dusted herself off. "Come on! I want to get into Helston now."

"What for?" Bessie accepted her offer of a helping hand to rise.

Jane, no heavyweight herself, found her light as a feather. "I want to try my hand at it," she said grimly. "One tiny little act of rebellion. And we'll see where we go from there."

They said their goodbyes at the Grylls Memorial at the bottom of Coinagehall Street. Jane hugged her tight and told her to have courage. "I don't know what to do yet, but I'll do something."

She saw Mrs Lanyon coming up the hill and waited for her to draw level. "You look very pleased with yourself," the older woman said as she climbed into the gig.

"I hope not," Jane said. "Pleased with life, perhaps."

"The older you grow the closer those two pleasures become. What, er, what did you and Mrs Wender talk about?"

Jane made an expansive gesture. "Girlish prattle. She's very young still in so many ways. We spoke of the harvest, the prospect from the top of the hill ... the joy of peering into other people's gardens. Oh, and we shared some chocolate ..."

"And – forgive me for interrupting – but before we leave Mrs Wender, she seemed quite herself again?"

"Completely. I don't know what you said to her but its effect was like magic." Mrs Lanyon seemed satisfied.

They passed a pleasant hour at Nicholls's, choosing dress materials for when Jane came out of mourning, and another pleasant hour in the private dining room at The Angel. Then, it being fifteen minutes past the appointed hour, they strolled up Wendron Street to the offices of Scawen and Conway, Solicitors at Law.

Everything gleamed; not a paper was out of place; the air was drowsy with lavender-scented beeswax. Jane's keen nostrils also detected the odour of dust – not venerable dust lying thick on every surface, such as you might meet in an antiquarian shop, but that same dust when it has been freshly disturbed. The clerks must have spent the rest of the morning, after Scawen's return from Parc-an-Ython, chasing it about and flapping it out of the windows. Now the place was the very model of a good solicitor's office.

Scawen himself met them at the door and conducted them through to his inner sanctum. There Jane found her father already waiting. Though they had parted only two days earlier, they greeted each other tenderly before he waved his hand in a flourish toward the table. It was a sturdy piece of the kind known as a "partners' table," broad enough for two to share facing each other, each with his own set of drawers. The top was finished in leather, dyed in red and green and ornately gilded. And there, in Scawen's half, lay a sheaf of documents, beautifully engrossed and bound in red tape – and sealed, she noted, with her father's own device. Beside it lay a freshly cut quill and a crystal-glass inkwell with its silver lid already open. "All in readiness, as you see," Scawen told her. "Mr Visick will administer an affidavit when you've signed."

A man she had not previously noticed stepped out of the gloom beyond her father and bowed. Jane nodded back. She drew a deep breath and lifted a corner of the deed and riffled its pages. "I think," she said, drawing a further deep breath on top of the one that was already filling her lungs to near-bursting, "I think I should like to read it first."

9 IF JANE HAD SUDDENLY revealed herself as an anarchist, bomb in hand, sputtering fuze and all, she could not have produced a greater sensation. "It's just ... you see ... oh dear. It's just that I have no idea what this deed *is* that you all wish me to sign."

For some reason the men turned to Mrs Lanyon, as if they thought she might be able to explain this astonishing outburst. The woman gave an awkward laugh. "My dear – I think we may safely leave all such questions to the gentlemen, don't you? They understand these things."

Jane remained silent, staring round the circle, trying to read the unreadable eyes.

"Surely you agree, child," the older woman said sharply.

She turned to her father. "Dearest Papa – I've so often heard you say one should sign nothing unless one fully understands what one may be signing away."

Her tone, she realized, was not at all what she intended. She had quite made up her mind to be firm, respectful, and ladylike, without a trace of truculence or shrillness. In fact, to her own bewilderment, the voice that spoke her words was wheedling, gay, almost coquettish. It threw her off her stride for a moment, until she realized it was exactly the way her mother would have spoken. It sent a shiver up her spine to think that in some strange way her mother, like some ancestral puppetmaster, might be playing old games in her.

Her father saw the likeness, too – she could read the shock in his eyes. He just stood there, staring at her, mouth agape, trying to remember how angry he had been only moments earlier.

Mrs Lanyon replied for him. "I'm sure that is an excellent precept for a man, dear child. But when your solicitor – on the instructions of your own dear father – has swept the path before you, it would be presumptuous in the extreme to question their good faith and judgement."

Jane turned to Vosper Scawen. She wished merely to ask him if there were any good reason for her *not* to read the document, but quite different words came out of her mouth. "Humour me," she said in her most flirtatious voice. "You know I'm going to sign in the end, so what's another day? I simply have a desire to know *what* I'm signing." She turned to Dorothy Lanyon. "May he come and explain it to me this evening at Parc-an-Ython? After supper, perhaps? And we could play a hand or two of whist as well."

Poor Mrs Lanyon hardly knew what to make of this. For a solicitor to make a social call was unthinkable – well, almost. But she saw the mute plea in Mr Hervey's eyes. To secure Jane's signature upon this document was more important to him than anything else in the world at the moment. She did not understand the ins and outs of it herself – something to do with their residual property in Paris, in which the girl had an interest – but she knew that he considered it vital to all their plans for her. "Well ..." she faltered, turning to canvass Scawen .

The lawyer glanced at her father, who gave a curt nod. "Well," Vosper said, "I'm only sorry Mr Visick has been troubled."

"Please!" Visick beamed at Jane. "No lawyer should ever feel himself discommoded by a client who wishes to be cautious."

"My sentiments exactly," Vosper rejoined, though he looked daggers at the man.

"Well then!" Jane's smile was genuine enough for she had never imagined she would carry the day so easily. She picked up the deed. "I'll make what I can of it," she told Vosper. "At least I'll have read it by the time you arrive. About eight, shall we say?" She glanced respectfully at Dorothy Lanyon, who nodded curtly back at her in tight-lipped agreement.

She took tender leave of her father, who remained gruff and withdrawn. She straightened his lapel quite needlessly, saying, "Now the days are growing cooler make sure that Ogilvy puts out some warmer clothing for you. That red flannel cummerbund I gave you." She stood on tiptoe to kiss his cheek, which threw him into a fresh confusion. It was the first time in her life that she had fussed over him like that. Normally, although he liked nothing better than to fuss over others, he hated being the object of such attention. Only her mother had been able to do it.

70

This new-found power, which must have been lurking within her all unsuspected, was exciting. But why had it suddenly shown itself, today of all days? Why, in the middle of her conversation with poor Bessie, had she suddenly decided on this one trivial act of rebellion – which was, in any case, no more than a token. She would sign the thing tonight, or tomorrow if Visick had to be there, so what did it prove?

Dorothy Lanyon's thoughts, though starting from different premises, converged with Jane's. "I don't know what you think you've gained by all that," she said frostily as they walked back to the Angel yard, where their gig would be waiting.

Jane tried to give it a reasonable gloss. "Mr Scawen said it concerns the transfer of some property. Now, if that requires my signature, it must mean I own it – or have some interest in it. But I didn't know I owned any property or had any interest in anything like that. So of course I'm curious and want to know more. Wouldn't you?"

The woman shook her head crossly. "If word of this gets out!" She tutted with vexation. "Well, of course it'll get out. Visick was grinning his head off. He'll tell that sister-in-law of his, Mrs Moore. She'll pass it on to Mrs Pellew. And then it'll be all over Penwith. And let me tell you, my girl, it'll do your reputation no good. Heiress or not, no man wants a wayward and disobedient wife. If you had reservations about signing this document, you should have made them in private and beforehand."

Jane thought back to the way Visick had behaved. It had reminded her of something but for the moment she couldn't think what. Then it came to her: His attitude had been that of a tradesman hoping for new custom. All that benign tolerance, those sugared words – that was how a draper might speak to a rival's customer. Then it struck her that was how Vosper Scawen had taken it, too, with his: "My sentiments exactly!" But his look of fury gave the words the lie. He had thought Visick was fishing for her custom at some indefinite time in the future.

It was another exciting glimpse of power to her. The same power? she wondered – and decided, on the whole, that it was not. She had won over Scawen and her father by a combination of gesture and tone of voice – by coquetry, though she would not have used the word of herself. But Visick had been swayed by something else ... his knowledge of what was in that deed, perhaps. In his eyes she was a woman of property; that was the power to which he had responded.

"You have some fences to mend, miss," Dorothy Lanyon said sharply.

Jane began to wonder what sort of behaviour would work best on her hostess – and then immediately felt ashamed of the thought. It was all rushing to her head – these vague glimpses of ephemeral power. Chastened, she tried to think of something suitably contrite and soothing to say, but the words no longer came easily. Something had happened to her today – to do with Bessie's strange half-revelations, of course, though the precise connection was still obscure to her. But there was no doubting one thing: The Jane Hervey who had woken up this morning, determined to be sober, honest, industrious, obedient, helpful, cheerful, grateful, admiring ... and all the other things that come so naturally and easily to the well-brought-up young girl – that Jane was no longer so instantly accessible to the rather more thoughtful girl who now walked down Coinagehall Street.

Her silence unnerved Dorothy Lanyon, who could so readily have coped with anything else. "What has happened to you, child?" she asked.

71

Her very tone betrayed her uncertainty; it was neither peremptory nor cajoling; instead, it handed some small, experimental initiative to her protégée.

Jane realized that the question with which she had shamed herself – what would "work" on her hostess – had, nonetheless been answered: silence was best.

*   *   *

Vosper Scawen, seemingly indifferent to the high honour he had been accorded, was shown directly into the drawing room, where Jane was reading the deed yet again.

"Oh, you have it the right way up," he said in apparent admiration, and then laughed to show he was joking.

It annoyed her nonetheless. "Wait here one moment," she said and, before he could recover from his surprise, strode from the room. There was once a Jane who would have added that she had forgotten her handkerchief or some such rigmarole. "Send Banks down to me, will you," she told the footman. She returned to the drawing room to find Scawen deep in thought. He looked up and smiled as he heard the door close behind her. "Shall we sit at the card table?" he asked. "We can have the deed between us then." When they were seated he added, "And what have you gleaned?" in a tone that expected the answer, "Precious little."

"I can hardly believe it," she replied, "but it seems I own our old villa in the Faubourg-St.-Honoré. I thought it was sold years ago – the lease, I mean – when we returned to England. I never realized my mother owned it. I always thought we were just tenants there." She tapped the deed. "Or is this, in fact, just to dispose of the tail end of a lease? What does *fee simple* mean?"

"Is that the only obscurity?" He shook his head and smiled again. "We lawyers must work a little harder on our language. It is obviously becoming much too intelligible to the layman – and woman. But you've grasped it well enough, Miss Hervey. You own the villa outright. Lock, stock, and barrel. In fee simple, as we say, or *propriété libre,* as they prefer."

"But I don't understand how. I thought all my mother's property belonged to my father. I mean, I didn't realize a married woman *could* own her own property. Doesn't everything pass automatically to her husband?"

He nodded. "Unless there are specific exclusions in the marriage settlement. In fact, your mother' will left everything to your father – which should have been sufficient. But an English will cannot dispose of property in France. So when your father's executors tried to appoint French agents to sell the villa in Paris, they discovered he had no title to it. In fact the title is yours."

"Automatically?"

Banks slipped into the room at that moment, seated herself by the window, and took up some sewing.

Vosper stared at Jane as if he expected her to tell the maid she needn't stay. "Automatically?" Jane repeated.

He gazed at her a while in silence and then said, "No. It transpired that your mother signed a deed – under French law, of course – dated sometime in February, 1843 – conveying the villa to you."

Jane was stunned. "But how extraordinary! There must surely be some mistake? I was only two at that time. Why did she not leave it to my father?"

He shrugged noncommittally. "Who knows what advice they were given? I'm sure your parents would have acted only on the very best advice."

"And why did *she* own it anyway? Everything she inherited from her Welsh connections became his. I remember her telling me that."

Another shrug. "Again, I can only surmise it was done on the best available advice. It's not hard to think of reasons why an Englishwoman, forced to live alone for most of the time in France, should be given the security of her own freehold. Especially when you remember the political situation in the 'forties. And, indeed, at the present moment, public order in Paris is hardly any better. I know that is why your father is most anxious to sell the villa. The next riot might leave it a worthless heap of ashes."

Jane smiled. "Ah, Mrs Scawen, you don't know the people of Paris, the so-called 'mob.' They would never do such a thing. During the trouble in 'forty-seven our villa was a hospital for the wounded of both sides. I was only a child at the time, but I remember it as if it were yesterday. It was one of the few occasions when I was allowed into the grown-ups' part of the house." She closed her eyes and leaned back in her chair. "It is utterly magnificent, you know. Montpelier House is a mere charcoal-burner's shack in comparison. All those sumptuous rooms, filled with the wounded and dying. But when it was over, they carried my mother shoulder-high through the streets, and the gendarmes just smiled and looked the other way."

Vosper thought he had never seen her looking more beautiful than at that moment, her eyes closed, her lips parted in a smile of happy reminiscence.

She came out of her reverie suddenly and startled him; it was a rare moment, when she could peer into his eyes, which were usually so carefully veiled, and see the man. His longing for her could not have been plainer. "You may set your mind at rest," she assured him. "The rioters of Paris would burn down every last house before they touched ours." She paused and corrected herself: "Mine."

He nodded. The customary veils fell and he became the proficient lawyer once more. But that glimpse of his longing, unguarded and without reserve, lingered in her memory, exciting her with hints of a new power within her.

"You understand the position at least," he said as he folded up the deed. "Are there any particular clauses you'd like me to clarify?"

"No, it's fairly straightforward. What is that list of names?"

"It's the descent of the title to the land and buildings. French deeds are like English ones in that respect."

"So the previous owner was Baron de Puisne."

He opened the document and checked. "Yes, until January, 1843."

Jane chuckled. "Poor Mamma – she only owned it a month! And just think – all those times I was punished for peeping into the grown-ups' part and warned never, never to go there – I was actually being ordered out of my own house! I do wish I'd known." When their laughter at her fancy died she added, "I wonder what she paid for it? I know it's vulgar to ask, but is it recorded anywhere?"

He smiled as if to prepare her for something almost incredible. "It seems the Baron gave it her for nothing! Of course, that must have been some device to keep the transaction beyond the reach of the tax farmer, but it was dressed up as an out-and-out gift. I didn't dream of asking your father – and naturally it's not recorded in the deeds themselves – but I imagine there was a quid-pro-quo somewhere, an equivalent property, perhaps even in England. The Baron wouldn't be the first Froggie to find a second home here in time of revolution."

Jane began to feel bored with the topic. The main thing was, she owned the dear old villa.

"Are you going to sign now?" he asked casually.

After thought she said, "I'll talk it over with my father. I'm sure we don't actually need the money. And if all he's worried about is losing it in the riots ..."

Scawen was shaking his head. "He'll be most unhappy to hear this," he warned.

Inspiration came to her rescue. "The riots and the unsettled state of the French government will surely have depressed prices?"

He had to admit that was so. He even threw in, quite gratuitously, that the present tenant, a Colonel Esterhazy, whose wife was a German princess and who entertained lavishly, had twenty years of his lease still to run – and that alone was enough to depress the price.

"There you are then." She buried the topic with a waft of her hands. "Since we're not desperate to sell, we ought to consider holding on for better times – which would mean better prices. I'll talk to him about it."

The Lanyons came in at that moment to begin the promised round or two of whist. Banks slipped silently away, giving Jane a meaningful look as she closed the door behind her.

All through the game, which gave her many excuses to observe Vosper's face, for he was her partner, she tried – as with all the men who came her way – to picture him as her husband. Here they were, Mrs and Mrs Vosper Scawen, playing a quiet game of cards with their old friends, Mr and Mrs Jesse Lanyon. The calm, self-contained lawyer was hard to imagine in that context; but she remembered that other, less disciplined young man she had briefly glimpsed when his guard was down. Alas, he, in turn, was overlaid by other, vaguer images, planted in her mind by poor young Bessie's rambling confessions, which had revealed nothing even while they hinted at so much.

To her surprise she found she could quite easily imagine this quiet, orderly young man – how had the girl put it? – *hoarding* her like a miser with his gold. Her mind shied away from those other dreadful images, hovering in the wings of that not altogether distasteful scene.

Later the same evening, when Banks was combing out her hair and putting it in papers for the night, she asked what was the general opinion of Dr Wender.

"They do say he's some good doctor," the maid replied guardedly.

"Yes, but I often wonder what that actually means. Does he keep teetotal old ladies happy with elixirs full of ardent spirits?"

Banks chuckled. "I don't suppose he's got much time for that sort. Some lawdy-daw lady went to his surgery once saying she was distracted with the discomfort in her mouth. And she peels off one glove" – the maid mimed it with precious, finicky gestures – "and she sticks one long finger between her teeth and says, 'Theeah!' And old Doctor Wender, he peers in and sees a little old pimple no bigger'n a pinhead. So he pulls on one glove, just the way she did it, puts his hand to her bustle, and pushes her out the door. 'Theeah!' he says! And that's the only word he spoke." When they had finished laughing at this really rather disgraceful behaviour, Banks added, "But he took little Tommy Weeks's appendix out on the kitchen table and sat up all night with the boy — saved his life, no doubt of it. And he wouldn't take a penny for it, neither, because old Bert Weeks had just been made idle by Penrose Estates. So if you got something really wrong, he's some burr old doctor. But a lady with the vapours — she must look elsewhere."

"It seems he hasn't much time for females," Jane commented.

"That Bessie's his fourth wife."

Jane just stared at her in the glass.

"No," the maid admitted. "I don't suppose he has."

"Why does he keep marrying, I wonder?"

Banks returned the brush to its drawer and went to turn down the coverlet on the bed. "A man can need a wife and still have no time for her. You want a drink of milk, do you — with a spoon of honey? Cook says she wants it used up because Mr Lanyon, he says if we get junket just once more this week, he'll tip it down her neck."

Jane laughed at the imaginary scene and said she'd quite like a glass of warm milk with a spoon of honey. When the maid returned with the brew, she bade her sit awhile at the bedside. Then she told her about the extraordinary discoveries she had made since refusing to sign the deed that afternoon. "The thing is," she concluded, "if I own that villa in Paris, I don't think I want to sell it. I loved that place, and if we don't really need the money, why can't I keep it?"

The maid shrugged awkwardly. "'Course, you do know your father better'n what I do, Miss Hervey, but he do seem to me like the sort of man as, if he's got his mind set, he won't welcome contradictions and refusals."

"That's putting it mildly! We've enjoyed an uneasy sort of calm these last few months, but there have been quite different times." She did not elaborate.

"He wants to see you nicely wed."

A dozen thoughts were packed into those few words, none of which needed spelling out to Jane, who replied, "Mind you, I've done nothing to provoke him, either. We've both had our reasons for wanting domestic calm. But I think it might be about to end."

Banks dry-soaped her hands abstractedly. "You think 'tis worth it, do 'ee?"

"A villa in Paris? Worth it? Don't you think any suitor who's interested in me now would be doubly interested if he knew I owned such a beautiful house in the most beautiful city in the world? I can't understand why there's this eagerness to sell."

"Well, 'tis all over my head," Banks said happily.

"And mine. Everything seems to go over my head."

Banks went on looking at her hands in her lap.

"First, Bessie Wender," Jane continued. "I couldn't make head or tail of what she was saying ..." She paused, hoping that the woman would prompt her to repeat some of it, but all she got was a worried, sympathetic smile. Jane went on anyway. "She said she felt trapped in her marriage — bound hand and foot, were her actual words.

And trapped by her husband's jealousy, too. D'you know, he'll chastise her for this, just for driving out to call on Mrs Lanyon? I couldn't believe it. He's supposed to be her husband. He took a vow to love her and cherish her. But she says he just hoards her, like a miser with his gold. She's to have no friends until she's broken to his will. Then he'll choose them for her. What can she do?"

Banks just shook her head. "Reflect that it's still better than a decline into poverty as a useless old maid – which is all that waits her mother and sisters."

"But she was only fifteen, Banks! Surely there'd have been other chances? She's a bit skinny, I know, but she's quite good looking, with nice, homely features. Someone better would have come along."

Banks shook her head. "You ask her sister Rosa. She's eighteen and as good looking as any – but never a caller. She must be desperate now. She'd soon tell 'ee who was the lucky one, her or Bessie."

After a thoughtful moment Jane said, "Then I truly do not understand it. Nothing is as we are taught it should be. Love, marriage, companionship – all those things at the very core of our lives, they're not ... not quite as I have been taught." She wanted to put it more strongly but felt that what she had said was already daring enough.

"Yes, well, if that's all, Miss Hervey?" the maid replied.

When she had gone, Jane added the thought, *And who is there to teach me? Not Banks, obviously. She thinks it's more than her job is worth.*

She lay in the dark, relishing the gathering warmth between the sheets, and turned the problem over in her mind. Suddenly, out of the night, came the surprising thought that Vosper Scawen might carry her some of the way toward enlightenment. The speed of his response that afternoon to what he perceived as Visick's interference revealed that she had some value to him as a client, quite independently of her father. And look at the way he had stayed quite neutral in what could have been an unpleasant contretemps; if her father was the only one with any sway in all this mysterious business, she had no doubt but that Vosper Scawen would have stood shoulder-to-shoulder with him at once.

It seemed odd to be thinking about her likely future husband in this way; but, in view of what she was learning about the true state of matrimony, perhaps it was best to go into it clear-eyed and with few illusions. Anyway, Vosper's behaviour hinted that she might hold a certain sway, too.

Also, come to think of it, wasn't that odd, the way he threw in the tidbit about Colonel Esterhazy? It was one more piece of ammunition for her to use in any skirmish with her father. But why should Vosper do that, all unasked? She began to admire him more than ever, seeing him as a deeper and more mysterious young man than she had yet given him credit for being. He'd never openly come out and say, "Look, my dear, if that is your intention, then this is the way you should go about it and here are the arguments you should use." But he would leave them casually in her path for her to pick up if she had the wit to recognize them for what they were – these nuggets of vital information. What strength that must take – strength of will and of character.

In a way, he was paying her a far higher compliment than anyone else in her life had ever paid. He might speak like the rest of them – making patronizing little jokes like congratulating her for at least getting the deed the right way up – but his real joke (on them, not on her) was to treat her as if she were the most sharp-witted woman around, able to see through his casually dropped clues and take in their real substance. Now, of course, she regretted her annoyance at him for that joke. She must be careful in future to see such things as part of a never-to-be-mentioned conspiracy between them.

She settled herself to sleep, thinking happily of this new-found strength in him. What *would* it be like being married to him? Suppose he were here now, beside her in this bed ...?

She tried to picture it but her mind was an absolute blank.

She let one hand foray in search of him; instead it found the iron frame of her bed. Memories of Bessie's words returned to her: "bound hand and foot." Had she meant it literally? Jane wondered. She imagined her wrist was lashed to the frame – so vividly that when she tugged, her arm would not move. Intrigued, she slipped her other arm out until it touched the opposite frame. Then one ankle. Then the other.

It was a most curious sensation to be lying face-down, spread-eagled like that. She had not exerted herself and yet her heart was beating like mad and her breast felt congested and short of air. Then she became aware that her mind had veered off its image of Vosper Scawen and had fastened on ... no, she was not going to name him. "I only saw you once," she shouted at him in her mind. "It's utterly absurd for you to keep bobbing up like this. Go away!"

She struggled with her fetters but, so powerful was her imagination, she was as good as pinioned there until her fancy decreed release. A moment of panic almost made her scream aloud; and then he touched her. Gently his hand rested on her back – actually in the small of her back. And then he began to *hoard* her like a miser with his gold. What that actually entailed she could not say; she no longer felt the touch of him. Rather her body seemed to go drifting off in a sea of fleeting sensations, like muted electric shocks or the dying moments of pins and needles. There were stars in her veins and the taste of honey revived in her throat.

When it passed and she was free to move her limbs again, she found she was perspiring; and yet the calm that now possessed her was like the certainty of salvation. In some remote corner of her mind she was able to acknowledge that great storms now lay ahead, but for the moment she was inviolate. No harm could come near her. Almost at once she fell into a profound and dreamless slumber.

10 THEY GAVE JANE no warning. The following week, on the first Tuesday in October, she was summoned directly after breakfast to the morning room. Her heart sank the moment she entered, for there was her father, looking as stern as ever she'd seen him, and Dorothy Lanyon, with her lips compressed to a thin red line, ready for battle, and Mr Lanyon, pale and ill at ease, and Vosper Scawen, as unreadable as ever.

Of course I shall yield, she told herself; she almost said it aloud. *I shall offer a little token resistance, for my own self-respect, and then I'll capitulate.* She smiled at them all. Only Vosper smiled back, and guardedly at that.

"No Mr Visick this time?" she asked.

"Certainly not," Mrs Lanyon snapped.

It struck Jane then that they were expecting her *not* to sign the deed. She was amazed. Couldn't they detect how feeble was her resolution? Couldn't they hear the flutter in her voice, see how painful it was to maintain this smile, feel her terror just pouring out of her? Obviously not. They fully expected her to dig in her heels. They had come prepared for it. So what would they now think of her if she meekly caved in and did as they wished?

Suddenly it was no longer a battle over signing or not signing this wretched deed. Behind it an even more important principle was at stake; what happened here this morning would set the pattern for her foreseeable future. If she meekly submitted to her father's wishes, merely because they were his wishes and without any explanation whatever from him, then meek submission would be her lot for ever.

"Tell me one thing, Father," she said amiably. "Do we actually *need* ..."

He was at her like a slipped greyhound. "I'll tell you one thing, my girl: I require you to sign this deed. That is all I shall tell you and that is all any dutiful daughter should wish to know."

"My dear," Dorothy said, hoping to soften the words by her tone if not by her sentiments. "Your father is quite right."

Jane felt her resolve grow. "Is the duty of a daughter no more than the duty of a hired servant, then? To hear is to obey?" She turned to her father again. "Is that all the intercourse you wish with me, sir – authority on your side, flunkeyism on mine?"

Vosper, standing a little behind the others, risked a wink of approval.

"In this matter, yes," barked her father. "It is too important for anything else."

"Too important even to engage my understanding? Can you not even explain why we must sell when the price is sure to be ..."

"*Must* sell?" he sneered. "There's no must about it. It has no bearing whether we sell or not. The only *must* is that you must obey me, your father."

Dorothy, knowing Jane well enough by now to realize that this was a disastrous argument, stepped in quickly with, "What your father means, my dear ..."

But he would have none of it. "What I mean, ma'am, is what I say. And I'll thank you to keep out of this."

"Oh!" She gave a little shriek, like a toy steam engine, and turned to her husband.

"Come now, Hervey," he said gruffly. "This is our house and we have arranged this meeting for your convenience."

The old man closed his eyes a moment and nodded. "I'm sorry," he murmured. "I am beside myself this morning. Please accept my humblest apologies, dear Mrs Lanyon. How could I be so discourteous?" He turned to Jane. "It is all your doing, miss. I ask you one last time – will you sign?"

"Yes ..." Jane said. There was a collective sigh of relief, into which she added, "... the moment I understand why it was once considered important enough to draw up this deed. I accept your assurance that it no longer matters a fig."

There was a long silence in which nobody breathed; she dared not look at Vosper.

"Go to my carriage," her father commanded. "You will see no one, communicate with no one, entertain no one, until you have submitted to me."

She bowed stiffly. "I'll tell Banks to pack."

"I shall do that. You will give no more orders to anyone. The servants will be instructed to ignore any command you may attempt to issue."

She turned and swept from the room with all the dignity she could muster.

Ashen-faced, her father turned to the others. "My dear friends! What must you think? I have never seen her like this – not since she was fourteen. Ah, there we have it! It is her French upbringing, of course. They absolutely spoil their children."

"Please, Mr Hervey!" his hostess exclaimed. "I fear it is I who have failed. For these past days I have done nothing but point out to her the consequences of her disobedience, but obviously to no avail. What more might I have said?"

The old gentleman shrugged. "I cannot think why she has chosen to dig her heels in on *this* particular point." He turned to Vosper Scawen. "Can you, perhaps, enlighten us, young man?"

"Perhaps I can," the lawyer said carefully. "May I first ask, sir, if you really intend to be as severe with her as you have just indicated?"

"Every bit!" He bridled. "Why, what is that to you?"

"Simply that I do not believe the punishments that were so effective when she was only fourteen will …"

"I repeat," the old man said more sharply, "what is it to you?"

"She is of marriageable age and she feels she is being treated like a child."

"But she is a child – my child. She always will be my child. I did not ask you to meddle in all this, Scawen. I simply wish to know why she has decided to dig her heels in now? What does she suspect?"

The question surprised Vosper; though his profession had brought him into contact with every variety of human failing, he had never imagined there might be cause to *suspect* this particular transaction. "She is inordinately attached to that villa," he offered. "It seems she was very happy there."

"Well, of course she was! Didn't I just say it – utterly spoiled."

"If it were explained to her why it is now necessary to sell the place …" He let the conclusion hang.

"Explain?" Dorothy Lanyon sputtered. "Is it not enough that her father wishes it?"

But the old man held up a finger. "Go on," he said. "The girl is no longer present. Let us at least consider the point."

This potential sacrifice of principles that only moments earlier had seemed so dear to the old man gave Vosper more food for thought. It was obviously important to Hervey to be rid of this villa – almost regardless of the cost. He dangled the bait: "I think she might very well sign – and quite happily, too – if the whole business were explained to her … if she were made to feel a party to the decision."

Hervey licked his lips thoughtfully. "And, pray, would you undertake such a commission, sir?"

The other made a noncommittal gesture. "To be quite candid, Mr Hervey, I myself am a little uncertain as to the reasons. The villa is tenanted on a long lease and Paris is seething with unrest. Either fact on its own would depress the price. Together ..."

"Pshaw!" the old man exploded. "What does she know of such things?"

"That is not my point, sir. My point is that *I* know of them. They make me wonder why it is so urgent for you to sell, when the price you realize will be trifling. If you could explain it to me, I could then perhaps explain it to her in terms she would understand. And then, as I say, I'm sure she'll agree."

Hervey stared at them like a man in a trap. Vosper could see him considering a dozen explanations. But in the end the only reason he offered was, "It is the past − the useless lumber of the past. I tell you, I would *give* it away to be rid of it."

Vosper just stared at him. Hervey shifted uncomfortably. "Well? Can't you dress that up in some pretty way to please her? What sort of an advocate are you?"

"Mr Hervey," the lawyer said quietly, "the reasons you have just given for selling are the very ones that Miss Hervey advances for holding on."

The old man communed with himself for another long moment. Vosper longed to know what was going on in that cunning old mind, for he was now certain that the old man had not even begun to tell the truth about the entire transaction. In the end all Hervey said was, "Then it's a plain battle of wills." He smiled savagely. "She won't last twenty-four hours! I know her of old, believe me − twenty-four hours!" And he turned on his heel and left.

Lanyon, playing the host still, followed him out.

"Poor Jane," his wife murmured; Vosper detected no depth of sympathy there.

"I wouldn't be too sure," he said. "It may be the crowning of her."

"Hah!" The woman looked at him askance. "It's a crowning of thorns then − the death of all her prospects. Would *you* want a wife with so rebellious a spirit?"

He merely smiled at her.

"Would you?" she challenged triumphantly, thinking even a skilled lawyer could not tell so bold a lie.

"The man who marries Miss Hervey," he said calmly, "will presumably love her, too? In which case, he will find that there are no circumstances in which he would *not* want her as his wife."

He studied her response closely, knowing well what a risk he had taken, even in saying so little as that. If Mrs Lanyon were not so utterly set in her ideas of a *suitable* match for Jane, she would have read quite easily between his lines. Her reply was entirely in character: "If you are so cool and detatched, Mr Scawen, will you still be able to act for Mr Hervey?"

He scratched the back of his neck and grinned; so a lawyer could not possibly entertain feelings other than those of his clients! "My dilemma, Mrs Lanyon, is somewhat parallel with Miss Jane's: Is a lawyer a mere flunkey, to do precisely as he is bid, or must he think independently − in his client's best interests?"

She took it as a genuine question. "He must think for himself, of course," she rejoined stoutly, seeing no conflict with her earlier question.

He gathered up the papers and stuffed them in his case. "What's sauce for the gander ..." he murmured.

*   *   *

Jane sat beside the coachman, shivering with rage. The more indignities her father sought to heap upon her, the greater grew her determination not to submit.

"What are you doing up there?" he barked as soon as he saw her.

She stared directly ahead and spoke to thin air. "I did not suppose I still enjoyed the status of an inside passenger."

"Come down at once! You are being absurd."

"I am taking my own medicine," she said.

"And what may you mean by that?"

"If no one is to obey me, then I shall obey no one."

"Veryan!" he snapped at the coachman.

"Please, miss?" the man begged her under his breath. "'Tis very ockard for I."

Jane descended but, instead of going inside, she set off down the drive.

"And where d'you think you're going?" her father called after her.

She did not respond.

He mounted the carriage and told Veryan to catch her up. The front drive was short so she was out on the road by the time he drew level. He let down the window and said, "I asked you a question, miss. Where are you going?"

"To Montpelier House." She darted behind the coach and chose the old lane to Breage, far steeper than the new toll road.

Veryan hesitated. "After her, man!" shouted his master.

"Us'd have to turn back at Trelissick gate, sir. This one mare'd never pull we up Breage hill."

Beside himself with fury Wilfrid Hervey watched his daughter disappear down the lane; the swish of her long dress through the autumn leaves was like laughter.

There was precious little laughter in her, though, by the time she reached Trelissick gate. This gesture would have been better made had she not been wearing thin cotton slippers. Her pride would not let her go back and change into her leather boots; she had no choice but to soldier on. Halfway down the hill, however, the last shreds of cotton wore out and she was as good as barefoot beneath her dress, vulnerable to every thorned twig, every bit of loose gravel.

"You'm in some fine old dalver, my lover."

The voice came from behind the hedge to her right. She knew of the cottage, of course, having passed this way many times by now; she had considered it as a possible source of aid and comfort and had looked in vain for smoke from its two chimneys, but she had been unaware of the old man out in the garden.

"Good morning." She came to a grateful halt. "Is your wife at home may I ask?"

"Not these thirteen year," he answered cheerfully. "I don't suppose you'd volunteer, now?"

She laughed at his insolence. "I'm Miss Hervey, by the way."

"I do know very well who you are, Miss Hervey," he responded mildly. "I'll bet you can't say the same of me?"

Jane thought furiously. Dorothy Lanyon had, in fact, told her this man's name. She remembered now that his wife was dead. There was a story about it. The old woman had been ailing for months and whenever people asked after her he always said, "Better, thanks," or "Bit worse today, thanks." And one day Dorothy had asked him and he'd replied, "Dead, thanks," in exactly the same tone. But what was his name? What did Dorothy used to ask? "How is Mrs .... Mrs ..." what was it? Ridden? Redden? Riddick! "How is Mrs Riddick, today?" That was it.

"You're Mr Riddick," she told him. "Billy Riddick of Roseladden Cottage."

"Well, I'll go to Copperhouses!" he exclaimed. "I never thought you'd know that. Cast a shoe, have 'ee?"

She nodded ruefully. "You wouldn't have an old pair of boots I might borrow?"

"I might." He scratched in the stubble of his chin.

"I'd be so grateful."

"Is that a fact? They do let in water, mind."

She laughed. "There's not much fear of that today, Mr Riddick. Might they be too big for me?"

"Well, maid, since I can't see your feet, I can't give 'ee no answer as to that." She hobbled toward his gate. "At least let me try them."

"They do need a bit patching," he warned.

Inspiration came to her. "I'll get them patched and returned to you. Is that a bargain, Mr Riddick?"

He nodded sagely. "That do sound fair 'change to me, Miss Hervey."

He stuffed them with the newspaper that had wrapped his winter onion sets; he said it would keep the carrot fly off her toes, and for a moment she thought him serious. When he helped her lace them up, which the hoops of her dress made difficult for her, he told her she had the prettiest pair of ankles he'd seen in thirteen long years. No one had ever spoken to her like that. Very daring, she gave his nose a playful tweak and told him she still wasn't applying for the post.

He laughed and pretended she had hurt him. On her way out through his gate he slipped his hand around her waist and gave a gentle squeeze. "Ah yes!" he sighed, letting her go at once. "Ah yes!" – as if he had almost forgotten.

As she walked away she knew his eyes were upon her, delighting in her figure. How absurd, she thought, to feel flattered by that attention. Yet it made her feel young and free.

Yes, she realized with surprise: free! Despite the terrible times in store, she felt as if her heart was pumping bubbles of joy. At the bend in the road, where he would pass out of sight, she turned round and wagged an admonishing finger at him. He laughed and waved her away. "You'll do, maid," he called after her.

She had no idea what he meant – nor, she suspected, did he. But it capped that miserable morning and filled her with fresh courage for what lay ahead.

Despite the padding, those stiff old boots rubbed the skin off both her heels by the time she reached Montpelier gates. There, remembering what her father had said about the servants, she called out, "Pengilly?"

He came from the lodge at once. "Yes, Miss Jane? Are you on foot?"

"Has my father's carriage returned yet?"

"Yes, miss."

"And did he tell you anything?"

"He told me the leaves needed sweeping, miss."

"Nothing else?"

82

"No, miss."

"Very well." She got him to help her off with the boots and gave instructions about mending them and returning them to Billy Riddick of Roseladden Cottage. "But they're to send the bill to me. D'you understand?"

He promised to do all she had asked.

Jane, her feet now bleeding slightly, hobbled off down the drive.

Her father was so appalled at the condition she was in that he almost relented. But he checked himself and banished her to her room, where Mrs Tresidder was sent to tend her.

"Here's a sorry turn, miss," the housekeeper commented.

"I'd give anything for it to be otherwise."

The woman looked at her hopefully.

"Almost anything," Jane added. "Where are my books?"

"The master says you may have the *Holy Bible*, the *Book of Common Prayer, The New Whole Duty of Man,* and *The Sagacity and Morality of Plants.* Everything else we had to clear away. And we had to take your linen sheets out and the woollen blankets and put cotton and shoddy in from the servants' cupboard. I'm sorry, Miss Jane. I tried to reason, but ..."

"Oh, you shouldn't have done that. You needn't worry. I've been brought up to this sort of thing – ever since my father reappeared ... well, anyway – I'm used to it." She smiled. "Well trained, as they say."

"You aren't going to submit, then?"

"Never."

That evening her father brought her a single candle, as if the gesture were the most enormous concession. "Won't you soften and yield, my dear?" he asked.

"Won't you at least explain it to me?" she replied. "That's all you need do to end this whole stupidity."

The following day her feet started throbbing like mad.

"What does the villa mean to you, anyway?" he asked when he brought up her bread-and-water luncheon.

"It's no longer about the villa. It's about treating me like a little child."

That afternoon she began to feel feverish. By nightfall she was delirious; her feet were hot and swollen and her skin burned scarlet. Her father sent Tom Collett for Dr Trelawney – and he also remembered to tell Mrs Tresidder to restore the proper linen to the bed before he came.

But Tom Collett learned that Dr Trelawney had gone off to Devon on urgent family business; Dr Moore was standing *locum tenens* for him. He came immediately, took one look at Jane's feet and legs, and told them to turn all the bread in the house into poultices – and then to go down to the baker's in Breage and get half a dozen loaves more for the same purpose.

He lanced the suppuration and applied the poultices as hot as he dared. "Has she been eating well?" he asked.

Mrs Tresidder glanced at her master.

"Everything that's put in front of her," he said.

"That's good. She must have all the nourishment she can manage."

He stayed for over an hour and changed the poultices twice, watching for any sign that her fever might be abating; but she did not even regain consciousness and when he left, her fever was as high as ever.

"I'll send down a nurse," he told her father on his way out, "and I'll come back myself at around half-past-two. I think that will be about the height of this crisis."

"Crisis?" the old man asked.

"If any of those wounds turns gangrenous, I doubt we'd be able to arrest it."

"And then?"

The doctor sized the father up, wondering how blunt he dared be. "Then it will become a very serious serious matter indeed."

11 DOCTOR MOORE ARRIVED home only minutes after his wife, Johanna, whom he found discussing a cast shoe with their groom. "I bought that pub in Perranwell today," she told him, taking his arm to go indoors. He narrowed his eyes and whistled. "This means war with Falmouth Ales."

"I know," she sighed. "I just couldn't dither any longer. And if they want a fight, we're ready. Have you been out on a call? I thought it was your free evening."

They went in by the kitchen door. "This was an emergency. I just hope ..." He crossed his fingers and pulled a glum face.

"Who is it?" she asked.

He waited until they were out of earshot of the cook and maid. "Miss Hervey of Montpelier House. A most peculiar business if you ask me, my dear." He poured two small measures of ginger cordial and gave one to her. "Here's to poultices."

"She has an infection?"

He nodded. "In both feet. They said she chafed the skin with a pair of new boots. But she'd rubbed great areas raw on both heels. She didn't do that in just a few minutes. I wonder if she's lost the power of sensation in her extremities? That would be very serious – I mean even more serious." He gave a guarded smile. "I shall have to see her again tonight, I'm afraid."

"You haven't forgotten that Tony and Alison are dining with us tonight?"

"No, I mean in the small hours."

"Oh, poor dear. Well, we shan't stay up too long, then."

Later, at dinner, Johanna Moore returned to the subject of Montpelier House. "D'you know what Hilary told me while I was dressing this evening? She heard it from Millie Tredwell, who got it from Margaret Banks. Apparently there was an argument between Miss Hervey and her father and she got out of the carriage and tried to walk home – in little cotton slippers, mark you! And she borrowed a pair of boots from Billy Riddick down Roseladden." She turned to her husband. "Which explains matters. Hilary said old Pengilly, the blind gatekeeper, took a pair of boots to Harry Snell for patching, and they had marks of blood inside them. I must say, I never thought she had such spirit. I wonder what the quarrel was about?"

Alison Visick cleared her throat delicately and looked at her husband, who responded with an embarrassed shrug. She persisted. "She's no client of yours, my dear. You just happened to be in the office to administer an oath when it happened."

"Oh, Terence – now you've got to tell us," Johanna urged.

"Mrs Moore!" her husband cried with mock severity. "If it's a professional secret, it's sacrosanct."

"But Alison says it isn't. Come on, *cher cousin* – or do I get it from Alison while you and this walking encyclopedia of professional ethics swill the port?"

He yielded with a weak little laugh. "You're going to be frightfully disappointed, I'm afraid. It's nothing at all incandescent – just some property the old man wants to sell and for some reason he needs the girl's signature."

"And she won't give it," Alison added.

Terence held up a pedantic finger. "She didn't actually refuse. She just said she wanted to read the deed first and for someone to explain it to her."

"Good for her!" Johanna cried. "She goes up and up in my estimation. What did the father say to that?"

"He was black as thunder, of course, but he agreed. Scawen was to go out to Parc-an-Ython that evening and explain it to her over a game of whist. This was on Monday. What was all that about blood in some boots?"

Johanna looked toward Tony, who sighed uneasily. "All this is bordering on the unethical, you know. She may not be a client of Terence's but she is a patient of mine. For the moment."

Johanna turned to the others. "As I said, it seems she quarrelled with her father – at Parc-an-Ython and most likely over this deed she wouldn't sign – and tried to walk home on her own – borrowed these ill-fitting boots – took an infection from them, and is now being poulticed for it."

They all turned to Tony. "The infection itself looks manageable," he said guardedly. "But she was in a coma when I left."

"Is that bad?" his wife asked.

"According to the great Sahl it's the chief indication for a radical amputation."

Alison put her hand to her breast and gasped. "You mean she could lose her foot?" she asked.

"Or feet?" Johanna put in.

"Legs," he said gravely.

*   *   *

"Dr Armstrong!" Jane said the moment Tony entered the room. It was two o'clock on a fine, frosty night.

His relief was enormous. "I'm afraid Dr Armstrong's away, Miss Hervey. I'm Dr Moore, *locum tenens* for him."

"Oh, do forgive me. I've never met Dr Armstrong, you see."

He chuckled. "Well, I'm delighted to find you sufficiently recovered to make such an understandable error, Miss Hervey. You had us all worried for a while. Let's have a look at these feet, eh?"

He nodded to the nurse, who peeled back the covers and said, "The swelling started to go down about an hour ago, doctor."

She held the lamp while he peered and prodded at the inflammation. "Well, here's an improvement," he said at last. "I know *why* you haven't seen Dr Armstrong, young lady – you must have a first-class constitution."

"It hurts a bit," she told him.

"I don't wish to sound callous, but that, too, is good news."

He gave her laudanum to dull the pain and promised to call again after breakfast.

When he returned home he tried to get back into bed without disturbing Johanna; but she was already awake and waiting for him. "Well?" she asked.

"I still haven't forgiven you," he warned.

"I know. But how is she?"

He told her the good news and they settled to sleep. A moment later he chuckled. "I met the old man on my way out – beside himself with worry, of course – and over the moon when I told him the good news. But then he followed me down to the door and asked me if she was to be kept on a good, nourishing diet for much longer."

"What an extraordinary question!"

"I thought so too. I told him of course she was. And then he asked for *how* long. So I said until she was completely mended but there'd be no actual harm in feeding her properly until she reached old age."

Johanna laughed. He went on: "That was my response, too. But he looked sour as vinegar at me. Of course, it didn't strike me until I was almost back here. He's been punishing her on bread and water. I'll bet that's it. And the moment he knew the crisis was over – that's the first thing he thought of – when could he start starving her again! How's that for an uncompromising father?"

Johanna shivered. "Poor girl!"

"You say she has spirit. I think she's going to need it."

A few minutes later Johanna murmured, "We never asked Terence where exactly this property is."

But he was by then fast asleep.

*   *   *

By the following week the swelling had completely gone and the wounds on Jane's heels were no more than delicately scarred patches of tenderness. Dr Armstrong, who had by now returned from Devon, assumed control of the case. On the Tuesday, one week after Jane's ill-advised gesture, she was well enough for the nurse to leave; the following day Armstrong himself said, "Well, young lady, these scabs look as if they'll take care of themselves now. You can be up and about again tomorrow. Bathe them in the sea, if you will, but otherwise keep them dry. And try not to scratch them if they itch. Send for me at once if there's any trouble. I'll call again in a week."

Her father came to her as soon as the doctor had gone. "My dear girl!" He embraced her warmly. "Thank heavens it's over! Oh, we were so worried."

"And I'm only sorry for all the worry I caused you. My wretched temper! If only I'd had the grace to ask you calmly and courteously, I'm sure you'd have explained the

86

whole business to me in a matter of seconds and I'd have sat down and signed it at once. Why didn't we do that? Instead I had to go at it like a bull at a gate and *demand* an explanation – and of course you'd be bound to take umbrage. Can we wipe the slate clean and begin again, please?"

"I'd like nothing better, my child. I'll bring up the document and pen and ink and you can sign immediately and we'll never say another word."

"Oh." Jane was crestfallen. "What I meant was, can we start where I ask you calmly and courteously and then you explain it all in a few simple words? Of course I'll sign. You know I'll sign. I never had any other intention."

He turned on his heels and left her – too angry even to speak. She was back on bread and water that same evening.

From that day on her father insisted on being present whenever a servant went into the room. Each mealtime she was brought two trays, one furnished with succulent food whose steam carried the most mouthwatering aroma to her nostrils; on the other was nothing but bread and water. "Will you now sign?" he would ask. After a few such encounters Jane would merely tap the tray of bread and water and motion to the maid to put it down.

There were, however, occasions when, for decency's sake, she and Banks had to go behind a screen. Though conversation was still not possible the maid was able to pass her notes, which Jane read and returned at once. Most of it was the simple gossip of the neighbourhood but one day, the day before Dr Armstrong was due, the note read: "Your father has dismissed Pengilly without a character over the business of the boots."

Jane drew breath to cry out her protest but the maid put a finger to her lips and pleaded desperately with her eyes.

All that night Jane fretted and fumed at the unfairness of her father's action. Poor old Pengilly had simply obeyed an order. She was mortified that it should have led to this. Who else would take him on, blind and old as he was? He'd have to go straight to the workhouse. It would kill him. When she remembered his cheery face and his happiness to oblige her, it reduced her to tears. For herself she could hold out for ever. The more her father insisted on treating her like a child the more determined she became to prove she was not. But this was a different matter. She'd have to sign now, explanation or no explanation – but only if Pengilly got his old job back.

The following morning, just as she was about to surrender to his "which tray" question, he said, "Dr Armstrong will be here in half an hour. There's no need for your perversity and shame to receive wider currency than it already has, so while he's here we shall behave as if everything were normal."

She saw one last chance. While Armstrong was poking and prodding at her ankles she said, "Oh, by the way, Father dear, it almost slipped my mind. I gave the boots that caused these wounds to Pengilly to get them repaired. May I take the money for it out of the housekeeping?"

He responded with gruff, noncommittal noises.

"And I must find out from Pengilly which cobbler he took them to."

More throat-clearing.

Armstrong said, "Yes, where is the old fellow? I didn't see him on my way in."

Mr Hervey muttered something about a touch of something. "I'll have a look at him on my way out," the doctor promised. "Absolutely no need for that," the old man told him. The doctor insisted it would be no trouble at all. "I forbid it!" Hervey shouted.

Armstrong noticed the pallor of his cheek, the tic in one eye, the trembling of his hands. "I say, Mr Hervey, are you quite sure you're all right?" "I never felt better," he snapped.

The doctor looked at Jane in bewilderment. She tilted her head on one side and gave a brave little smile, much as to say that the household was rather used to this erratic sort of behaviour. Hervey saw it and almost had an apoplexy. His head swam, his knees buckled. "Father!" Jane ran to him and just caught him in time to guide him back a pace, into a convenient chair. "Are you all right?"

Her consternation was now genuine; she had meant to provoke him to anger but not to anything so serious as this. She loosened his cravat and took out his front collar stud. But he, still supposing she was provoking him, only became angrier still.

"See here, Mr Hervey, this won't do at all, you know." Dr Armstrong took charge. "Go on like this and there's no knowing where it'll end." He grasped him firmly by the wrist, put a finger to his pulse, and took out a large, impressive Hunter.

This authoritative gesture at least prevented the old man from stoking up his anger still further. Breathless and coughing slightly he stared malevolently at the pair of them. Jane's only thought now was to undo the harm she thought she had caused. "I'm afraid this is all my doing, Dr Armstrong," she confessed. "My stupid prevarication has driven him to this. Father – listen to me now. Send for Mr Scawen and I will sign that deed. No more shilly-shallying, no more beating about the bush. As soon as he arrives, I will sign."

He stared at her suspiciously.

The doctor said, "I never felt an overheated pulse cool off so fast."

She rose, took down the Bible, and, holding it aloft, added, "I give you my word." While replacing it she pulled the bell cord. A minute or two later Banks appeared. "Father?" Jane said.

He gave an unhappy nod. "Send to Helston for Mr Scawen," he told her.

"And Pengilly?" Jane added. "Please?"

He looked daggers at her, at the doctor, at Banks, and then gave an angry nod of assent. She ran to him and knelt at his side, throwing her arms about him and kissing his cheeks and neck; but he pushed her away gruffly.

Dr Armstrong said, "I have several more patients to attend, but if you take this to my house, my assistant will make it up for you." He dashed off a prescription and handed it to Jane. She thanked him and said she would see him to the door.

Her father rose and followed them, though the doctor told him he ought to go and rest. He would have none of it, however. The lack of trust implied by this gesture left Jane feeling humiliated; but the die was now cast.

When Vosper Scawen arrived he was shown directly into the morning room; moments later Jane and her father joined him. "She's given in at last," he crowed. "Didn't I promise she would?"

Jane took up the quill and signed the document. "There," she said evenly.

Her father, still giggling like a schoolboy, sent the papers skittering across the polished table to the lawyer. "Now you witness it, you witness it," he said.

He was in such high spirits he poured two double and one half measure of brandy and passed them around. "And now," he told Jane, "I shall give you my reason. I wish to sell that house in order to protect you from the harm its ownership might still be able to cause you."

"Father, truly there is no need for ..."

"No. I've said I'll tell you, and so I shall. I know how happy you were there, my dear. To you it was a house full of gaiety and music and laughter, but, believe me, there were shadows there, too – things of which a child can know nothing, things which even now you could not guess at. I see those shadows growing longer each year, reaching out to darken your life, even here, so many hundred miles away. All the joy that house ever had in its gift it has already given. From the moment you and your dear mother left Paris, it has had nothing but darkness to offer you. I know these things – and it is well they go with me, unspoken, to my grave. Which, in the nature of things, cannot now be long."

She touched his arm gently. "That was all you ever needed to say, Father dear."

But he shook his head. "More than that I needed to know you'd still obey me."

The clock struck nine. Vosper tossed off his brandy and began to gather up the papers. "I'll see you to the door," Jane said, glancing at her father for permission. He nodded happily.

Out in the hall, Vosper said, "It makes a difference to know that, I suppose."

"Not a bit," she said fondly. "He just loves to fuss over me. He's done it all his life. That house holds no such threats for me. It's just that he likes to fuss."

"Why did you sign, then?"

"Because he was keeping me confined to my room on bread and water."

He stopped dead. "You mean you signed because it was the only way out of that situation."

"Yes. What does it matter now?"

"Of course it matters. You signed *in vis et metus* – in force and fear. The deed is not valid."

"Ah well," she said dismissively, "I suppose it's all water under the bridge now." She took a step further toward the door.

"By no manner of means," he said, holding his ground. "Even if it's of no concern to you, it is to me – now that you've told me. I'm not only your lawyer, I'm also ..."

"My *father's* lawyer," she corrected him.

He stared at her for a long moment and then said, "Yes, that's true. I was going to add I was also the witness to your signature. On both counts I cannot ignore what you have just told me." He half turned back toward the morning room.

"Where are you going?" she asked him.

"To apprise your father of this new turn of events."

She went at once to his side and took his arm. "I'd be obliged if you'd postpone it until tomorrow, Mr Scawen. There's something you don't know." She applied the gentlest pressure on his elbow, in the direction of the front door.

"What might that be?" he asked, moving only with reluctance.

"Earlier this evening Dr Armstrong called – really to see me – but he ended up far more worried about my father, who suffered some kind of ... well, I'm afraid he is in a highly nervous state. The doctor's given us something to help calm him but I don't want him further upset."

"Which is also why you signed?"

She nodded. "Is that also 'fish and meat,' or whatever you called it?"

He chuckled. "It is the usual human mixture of motives, Miss Hervey. Pure love, pure hate, pure altruism, pure selfishness – they don't really exist."

"Goodness! Where does that leave purity itself, I wonder?"

"In the obituaries, I suppose," he replied.

They were at the front door. "I might as well walk round to the stables myself as stand here waiting," he observed.

"I'll go with you." She held on to his arm, enjoying his nearness and solidity.

"I'm glad you've come through this ordeal so unscathed," he remarked.

"You knew of it?"

"Oh yes. Actually, I never doubted you would. You pretend to all the expected feminine weaknesses, Miss Hervey, but actually you're as strong as ..." Unfortunately, the only images that occurred to him were far too unladylike; he floundered.

She rescued him. "Well, I'm not as tough as Billy Riddick's bootleather. We know that much, anyway."

He chuckled. "You weren't. But now ... who knows?"

"I'm certainly not going to try to find out." In a different tone she went on, "D'you really think I'm strong?"

"Oh yes," he said again. She found his use of "oh" like that very endearing.

"Why are you talking to me like this?" she asked. "So frankly, I mean – and all of a sudden, too. We've had plenty of snatched moments alone and you've either been aloof or ... what can one call it? Conventional. Conventionally playful."

"And now?"

"You're talking to me like ... well, like an equal."

After a short pause he cleared his throat and said, "Does it not strike you that you are behaving in exactly the same way towards me, Miss Hervey?"

She shook her head impatiently. "I don't know why I started this hare at all. It's just something that flitted through my head. What I really wanted to ask you was ..."

"At least six months," he interrupted, giving her a knowing smile.

"What?" she asked in surprise.

"I expect it will be at least six months before the villa is finally sold."

"But that's astonishing," she gasped. "How did you know I was going to ask that?"

One of the stable lads brought out the lawyer's horse and started backing him between the shafts of his gig.

"Luck," he said casually, and then added, "not *pure* luck, of course."

Laughing, she stood back to wave him farewell.

His last words that evening, spoken solemnly over the shoulder as he passed, were, "By the way, if you ever need a lawyer ..."

PART TWO

Ménage à trois

12 JANE HAD NOT FORGOTTEN her promise to Banks that they would go window shopping at the first opportunity. One week toward the end of October she reminded her father that she would soon be out of mourning entirely and the bonnets that had been so chic in Leeds last year would get her laughed at now, even in so remote a corner of the country as this.

"Chic?" he grumbled. "What is chic? Do not last year's bonnets still keep out the rain and the hayseeds? Are they threadbare? Do the mice in your brain complain of the cold?"

She knew he was delighted to be able to rail at her in this manner once more. "It's just a little promenade around Helston," she said soothingly.

"Oh, very well." He yielded at last. "I suppose if I'm to get you off my hands as effectually as possible, I shall have to made the best advertisement of you that I can. And if that means chic-chic-chic instead of cheap-cheap-cheap, so be it."

They had a light luncheon at noon and set off shortly afterward in the brougham because her father had said he'd need the phæton himself. They had intended going to Helston, as she had said, but at the main gate she changed her mind and told the groom to go to Penzance, instead. It was a pleasure to see old Pengilly back in the lodge, grinning like a little elf as he skipped to his duty. To Jane the outing felt like a parole from prison.

"The master's a different man now you've given in," Banks commented.

Jane answered with a rueful smile. "I still don't think I was entirely wrong to want to know." After a pause she added, "I wonder what makes him say that villa has ghosts. Or shadows, as he puts it. D'you think something happened there, toward the end – something that would go straight over the head of a child?"

"If the master says so, then it must be."

Jane stared out of the window. "I suppose you know the names of all the people in all these houses," she murmured.

The maid followed her gaze. "It isn't no more than a dozen, Miss Jane."

"But you know them all."

Banks admitted it, still not thinking it any great achievement.

"I've just realized," Jane went on. "I've never lived anywhere where I could say the same. I never knew any of our neighbours in Paris – well, only one, and only because they had a son the same age as me. And in Leeds I knew three people in one street, two in another, four in another – all scattered. I've never lived in a village where I'd know everybody. Don't you think that's sad? Tell me who lives in all these houses. Tell me everything you know about them."

The maid complied eagerly. The largest house in view was Lanfear, so the bulk of her story was about the Moores.

"To think she was once a prisoner in that house," she said. "As good as, anyroad. She was a orphan from the time she was about twelve and her aunt and uncle, the Visicks, took her in."

"From Visick to physic," Jane commented. Then the name rang a bell. "There was a Mr Visick, another lawyer, at Scawen and Conway's that day."

"He's her cousin. Some folks do say he's the father of Hannah, her firstborn. They say he got Hal Penrose to take the blame because he'd fathered so many hereabouts it didn't hardly matter one more. And she was very sweet on him for a while."

"How did he manage it?" Jane asked, hoping once again that some casual remark would reveal the whole secret.

"Some men are like that. Nineveh Bull, they called him."

"How biblical!"

"Nineveh's a big house over to Hayle, by the village of Joppa."

"Goodness, did one of the Lost Tribes settle there? Have you ever met him?"

"Once. One evening in Helston Harvest Fair."

Jane saw by the gleam in her eye that the memory was still alive. "What was he like?" she asked.

"Big and strong, very handsome – proper 'ansum, as we do say – yet a gentleman. He was with her that evening, Mrs Moore – or Miss Rosewarne as she was then. He won the prize down the wrestling booth, and my Aunt Ena – Ma Rogers, everyone called her – she was famous for her mint humbugs and other niceys. And she had a stannin, as they call it, in Coinagehall Street where she sold niceys and fairings on market days and fairs. I belonged to help her sometimes. And he come walking up there from the wrestling, with two black eyes and a broken rib, and Johanna Rosewarne on one arm and some pretty lady on the other. And my aunt gave him a packet of humbugs, which I never saw her do before nor since. And he looked at me ... 'course, I wasn't but ten or eleven then, but I shall never forget it." She sighed happily. "That's the first time a man ever stirred me up like that. And that's the sort of man he was."

"I know that feeling," Jane confessed. "What does it mean, I wonder?"

Banks laughed. "It means if he offers you a mint humbug or any of Ma Rogers's fairings, you say thank you so fast as you can."

"Why?"

"That's a local custom. If a girl do take a nicey off her man – her shiner, as we do call him – and if she never says thank you for it, that's as good as letting on she'll go a strolling with him down Castle Wary and tarry in the bushes a while."

"And ...?"

The maid looked at her askance. "He do count the blades of grass and she do count the stars." She grinned knowingly.

Jane responded with what she hoped was a knowing grin and tried another tack. "Is that why you think he's the little girl's father – rather than Mr Visick?"

The maid shook her head. "It's because of how she waited for him, see? All while he was out in America, she waited. She could have married Dr Moore any time, because he was ready and willing. He'd have given her child a name and she'd have had a good home and everything. But not Johanna Rosewarne! No, she stayed spinster and she waited for the Nineveh Bull. And when he come back from America, after he found gold, she was on the quayside to meet him."

Jane chuckled. "Well, if he'd found gold, who could blame her!"

"That's what everyone said. But then – this'll just show you how contrary she can be – she refused him, too. He'd come back all that way to marry her, and she said no thanks! Two weeks later he married her cousin Selina, Terence Visick's sister, and took her back to America. So there, now!"

Jane closed her eyes and shook her head, struggling on the borders of incomprehension. "Don't other people lead such amazing lives, Banks. Why is ours so dull?"

The maid gave an ironic laugh. "I wouldn't say your life was all that dull lately, Miss Jane."

"No, but it's not the same."

"How?"

"Well ..." Jane floundered for a moment. She knew the cases were different but could not say why. "I mean, they were able to make decisions. Mrs Moore – or Miss Rosewarne, as she was – could decide to marry or not to marry. Think how tempting it must have been. Disgrace and loneliness on the one hand. A husband and protection and a position in society on the other. Yet she chose the first. Chose it! And all for love!"

Banks gave a little smile. "I don't think love came into it all that much, if you ask me. She worked for a time as housekeeper at the Golden Ram, over Goldsithney – when old Charley Vose was landlord. He brewed the best ale in the whole of West Cornwall, but he was too lazy ever to sell it, see – except in his own bar. She started that. She belonged to go out with a little trap and a few barrels, selling it door to door. She'd blow her little bugle and folk would come out with their jugs."

Jane chuckled delightedly. "She still does – blow the bugle, I mean. I heard her that first evening we arrived."

"Well, she's more or less obliged to, now. She's what we do call a character. She's stuck with it. But that's how she started. Selling ale door to door. And when poor old Charley Vose got transported, she took over the brewing as well. And now JR ALES, or Jars, as they do say – Jars do brew for all the pubs in West Penwith. And export, too. And they do say that when Nineveh Bull came back and saw what she'd done, he told her to sell it and marry him. That was her choice, see? Her love or her business."

"Her freedom," Jane murmured.

"Same thing," Banks said.

"So I'm right," Jane added more briskly – slightly surprised to be able to make the claim. "When she chose not to marry Doctor Moore, she pretended it was for the sake of love, but really she kept her freedom. And then, when her love came back, she turned him down. She still chose her freedom. That's the difference between us." After a pause she added, "I'm beginning to think I was wrong to give in like that. I didn't put up much fight, did I."

Banks stared out through the window a long moment. They were past the Pentreath turn now, almost at the Falmouth Packet inn. "I only know about half the people here," she said. Then, as if the thoughts were connected, she added, "She chose a man's way, Mrs Moore. She had a good business and she used it to get what she wanted. But women have other ways of fighting, if they mind to."

"Like what?" Jane sighed. "I can't see I could have done anything else. My father was in such a state I thought he might have a seizure – and at his age ..." She left the conclusion unspoken.

Banks sniffed. "He recovered pretty quick, too."

Jane ignored the implications of that comment. "Well, perhaps I could have had fainting fits of my own, and gone into a decline ... and so forth. I know there are women who get their way by such means. But I shouldn't have known what to do with it. If my father had yielded instead of me, if he'd said, 'All right, daughter, have it your own way,' what would I have done? I needed advice more than anything. I needed to sit down calmly with a lawyer and talk the whole thing over. What if I do this? What if I do that? That's the only sensible way to decide these matters. Instead, rather than risk my father's health, I just gave in and signed." After a pause she added, "I feel ..." She was going to say "inadequate," but the words that came out were, "as if I've let myself down."

Banks said no more on the topic. For the rest of the journey they spoke of more general things – amusing tales about this or that character in the villages they passed, the prospect of rain that evening, the new fashions in bonnets for the coming winter. When they arrived in Penzance the groom told them the horse was unused to the bustle of a town so he'd wait for them in one of the quieter side streets.

"Outside an inn, I suppose," Jane commented. "I warn you, if there's a taint of hops or spirits on your breath when we return, I'll drive home and you can send for your things."

He looked daggers at her but said he understood – and she wouldn't smell liquor on his breath, nohow.

Jane added, "Nor onion nor horseradish nor peppermint, either."

"You can put your foot down when you mind to, then," Banks said admiringly as they walked away. She wondered how a girl could be so worldly-wise and assured in some directions and so innocent and trusting in others.

They walked up and down Market Jew Street, looking not only in the bonnet shops but in all the milliners and haberdasheries, imagining the dresses and cloaks and gowns and mantillas and things that could be made up out of the patterns and fabrics on display – and which would go with which, and what ribbons or broderie or lace would best trim them, and would the sleeves be ruched or gusseted or what. At last Jane decided they were both dying for a cup of tea. Banks told her there was a very select tea room on the Esplanade.

Jane chuckled. "I did tell my father we were going on a promenade. I suppose esplanade is close enough not to be a complete fib." She became serious again, "But how can we sit at the same table? I don't wish to sit alone and you out in the kitchen or somewhere."

"Say I'm your companion."

Jane eyed her critically. "You don't look it," she complained. "I tell you what. We will buy a bonnet after all – the one I liked in that little shop up by the Town Hall. And you can borrow it for today."

They hastened back up the street and entered the shop, which was, in fact, a long, narrow little half-shop; the twin half next door sold small notions in leather. There was only one other customer, a statuesque lady browsing in the gloom at the back. The proprietor was a stout, taciturn woman, also in mourning. She said the newest London fashions would be in next week. Jane tried on several other bonnets before choosing the one she had her eye on in the first place. She approved of it, tried it on Banks, approved of it even more, and then handed the woman her father's card with her own name written beneath his. "I like your stock," she said. "I think we shall open an account here."

The woman peered at the card; the fading light made it difficult to read. "Miss Hervey? Montpelier House?"

Jane confirmed it.

"My terms are monthly," the woman explained. "My stock is not large and nor is my capital ..."

The other customer squeezed past at the moment, muttering, "I'll call back later, Mrs Brown."

"Right-oh my lover."

She brushed into Jane, who turned to exchange smiling apologies and not-at-alls. But the woman clutched her bonnet to her in such a way as to hide her face. Jane saw enough, however, to cry out, "Why, Miss Wilkinson!"

The woman hurried on out without once looking at Jane. The bell on the door jangled behind her like mocking laughter.

"How extraordinary," Jane commented, then, turning to Mrs Brown, asked, "That was Miss Wilkinson, wasn't it?"

The shopkeeper gave an uncertain little laugh. "Why, I've no idea, Miss Hervey. I'm not sure I've even seen the lady before."

"But you ... ah well, perhaps I was mistaken. I only met her once, after all. Anyway, I'll take this bonnet for now and will you send me a postcard when the new fashions are in?"

The moment they were out in the street Jane started searching for the woman she had taken for Miss Wilkinson. Banks, knowing her purpose, plucked at her arm and said, "Oh come on, Miss Jane, I'm all of a dalver to put up this bonnet."

"There!" Jane cried, pointing down the street. "I knew it was her. And doesn't that just prove it? Look who she's with."

"Where? I can't see her." Banks turned away impatiently.

"Just below the bookshop."

The maid saw them and froze. "That's never her," she protested.

"With my father. Of course it is. Look – they're just turning in down that little side alley. That's why he needed the phæton – and why he was so secretive." She noticed a look of consternation on Banks's face. "What's the matter?" she asked. "Is something wrong?"

The maid took a grip on herself. "I'm sorry, Miss Jane, but I'm almost sure that's not the same woman as was in Mrs Brown's just now. And I'm *quite* sure that was never Mr Hervey with her." She smiled encouragingly. "It's a hallucination through being so thirsty, I expect."

Jane fell in beside her and they went up past the Town Hall before turning down Church Street toward the Esplanade. Just round the corner they came upon her father's phæton. An urchin was holding the horse. Veryan, the coachman, was nowhere to be seen. "Banks," Jane said slowly, "that was Miss Wilkinson and it was my father. And what is more, you did recognize both of them. So tell me – what do you know about that woman?"

Banks stared at her in surprise. "What do *you* know about her, Miss Jane?"

"Only that she is ... I don't know – it sounds absurd – but she is in some way mixed up in our family's affairs."

"And how might you know that?"

Jane explained what had happened on the day of her arrival at Penzance station. "And now there they are, together again. Doesn't that prove it?"

Banks looked about them, seeking a rescue that was never going to arrive. "Perhaps he felt he was a bit sharp with her, see – shouting at her, and all. Perhaps he's just come in to say he's sorry."

Jane was hardly listening. "That's why she left the shop in such a hurry, too. She was browsing away quite happily until Mrs Brown read out my name. Then she couldn't leave fast enough – hiding her face and everything."

"Why that's easily explained," Banks assured her.

"I'd like to hear you try."

"Well – he probably arranged this meeting to apologize, see, like I said. But then she got so taken up with all they bonnets, she forgot. And then when she heard your name, it reminded her!" She gave out a sigh of relief. "Yes! That's why she was in a hurry, see."

Jane had already lost interest in such nonsense. "And there's another curious thing. Mrs Brown's behaviour. She knew it was Miss Wilkinson. She had guilt written all over her face when she denied it. But why *should* she deny it? She never saw me before in her life. Until I handed her my card, she didn't even know of our existence. And yet she knows immediately that she must deny any knowledge of Miss Wilkinson. Why? It's the same with you – denying it was her, denying you knew her, denying it was my father ... You're all hiding something about that woman."

"Here," the maid laughed, "can I turn companion now, Miss Jane? Can I try on the bonnet?"

Jane helped her settle it properly, tucking her curls in and straightening her collar. She wished the top of the woman's head could be removed as easily, so that she could reach inside and scoop out this preciously guarded secret concerning Miss Wilkinson.

Banks set off at a smart pace, leading her down to the Esplanade. But Jane would not give up. "Miss W must have said something to her."

"You'll see all the Trinity House buoys in a minute," the maid promised. "When you spy them out to sea they don't look no bigger than fishing floats, yet here they're twice so big as a man."

"To Mrs Brown, I mean. She must have said something like, 'By the way, if ever people by the name of Hervey come in here asking after me, pretend you don't know me.' That's the only explanation for Mrs Brown's behaviour."

"And I suppose it also explains why Miss W was smiling so warm and friendly at your father just now!"

"But you said you didn't see them."

"And nor I did. You told me. I'm going by what you told me."

"I didn't say anything about her smiling. But it so happens she was – therefore you must have seen them." She waited for the maid to respond. When nothing seemed . forthcoming she said. "So are you going to explain it or not?"

Banks, who now looked more like a companion than a maid, took her arm. At first Jane was affronted at this unsought intimacy; then she realized it was actually more in the nature of a plea for support. "Ask me anything but that, Miss Jane – I beg you. I'll tell you anything else you want, but not that. I wouldn't even know how to begin explaining all that."

"Hah! So there is something to be explained."

"Yes, but nothing like what you think, miss. I'm as certain as I'm standing here that Miss Wilkinson never heard the name Hervey before that evening you arrived. She didn't know you. She didn't know your father – nor anything about you. I'd stake my life on that."

"But my father knew her."

"He knew her type."

"What do you mean?"

"She's not the type of woman you'd want to know anything about, miss. And that's my first and last word on the subject."

She made to take her arm away but Jane, now wanting that intimacy for her own purposes, put her hand over the maid's and trapped it there. "Will you really tell me *any*thing else?" she asked playfully. "You promised."

Banks sighed. "Go on."

"While we were on our way here this afternoon you spoke about the Nineveh Bull and Mr Visick arranging between them as to which was to be the father of Mrs Moore's little girl – Hannah. That's the child we met up on Trigonning Hill?"

"The very same." Banks's heart felt like lead.

"I wish you'd explain to me how men can arrange the business of fatherhood among themselves like that."

Banks nodded glumly.

"In fact," Jane added, "I'd like you to explain the whole business of fatherhood."

"You don't know anything at all about it?" the other asked hopefully.

"Well," Jane gave an easy little laugh, "of course I know something. I mean, I know that ... I know ... that is" – she stared up the Esplanade – "no, I don't know much at all. Everyone thinks I do. I can see it when they make certain guarded references – the way they look at me. And I always give a knowing nod – because nobody likes to be thought a fool. But all I know is that there's something shameful that people won't talk about, and they think I know it, and I don't." She chuckled, regaining something of her normal ebullience. "And I'm a bit tired of it – that's all. So now, are you going to keep your promise?"

Banks nodded toward the house on the next corner. "That's where we're going. And I couldn't sit in a public tearoom and tell you something like that. So either we forego our tea and I'll tell you on the way home – which is just about the time it's going to take, anyroad. Or you curb your impatience until we come out again."

To a daughter of Paris the "tearoom" hardly deserved the name. It was nothing more than a private house whose drawing room had been given over to half a dozen tables and chairs. Still, they were the only customers at the moment, so the enforced intimacy of five empty tables hardly mattered. Jane said it was charming and chose the table nearest the window, where they had an excellent view of the bay from Mousehole to beyond St Michael's Mount.

Since the day was turning chill and raw, they chose toast and beef dripping in addition to the strawberry jam tartlets with clotted cream. Despite their being the only customers, Banks would not relax her embargo on the Great Unravelling. Jane returned to the other topic that had been nagging her ever since their talk about freedom, during the coach drive. "D'you think I'm spoiled?" she asked.

The woman replied at once: "Now that's one thing no one would ever say about you, Miss Jane – nor ever has in my hearing. Why ask that all of a sudden?"

"Angelica and Jemima Pellew – something they said. They told me their biggest surprise was to find I'm not spoiled. I mean, those were their actual words. They said they didn't know how a girl in such an enviable position as me could avoid being spoiled. I could hardly believe my ears. I never thought of my position as enviable." She peered hard at the maid and said, "Would you change places with me?"

Banks drew breath to reply, but Jane held up a warning finger. "Before you answer, my girl, I should tell you I have a genie in a bottle, here in my pocketbook. And if you say yes, I'll let him out and you can have your wish come true."

She was so convincing for a moment that Banks stared at her in some trepidation. Jane smiled and said, "What I mean is treat the question seriously – as if I really could make it happen."

After a long moment's though Banks looked up at her and said, in a soft, rather sad tone, "No."

Jane, quite serious herself by now, nodded. "And you're right. I never thought about it until I was made a prisoner last week. I woke up one night when my ankles were itching like mad and I couldn't get back to sleep. So I went over to sit at the window and look out over the gardens by the moonlight. And suddenly everything became clear to me, my life, my situation ... everything. I thought to myself, 'This is your true condition, my girl – locked up here like this. All the freedoms you apparently enjoy, the apparent mistress of this grand house, with your own maid'" – she waved a hand at Banks – "'and all the other servants – that's just an illusion you're permitted to enjoy as long as you behave.' It was quite a shock, suddenly to see it all so clearly. At last I realized what 'behave' means. It means obeying my father's commands. And when I'm married, it will mean obeying my husband's commands. I shall never be anything but a prisoner out on my own parole."

Banks gave a dour smile. "We're all prisoners like that, Miss Jane, one way or another. It's all a matter of making the best of it."

Jane sighed, thinking she was about to be served a potted sermon out of *My Treasure* or some such rag. But instead the maid said, "There's little tricks and things you could use – to turn the key in the lock, see."

"Such as?"

"Every women learns them in time. Some do have them natural, like."

"Throw a fit of hysterics, you mean?"

"If nothing else works. But there's better ways. Men do use them, too, mind. See how your father got you to unbend so fast?"

"But he really was ... I don't know. Not a fit. But he was afflicted with something."

"Yes – and then he saw how it frighted you. He'd have to be some burr old fellow not to play up to that, wouldn't he. So he puffs and groans and rolls his eyes, till you're all in a dalver. But when you says as you'll give in – just see him then! Skipping round like the goat before Camborne Silver Band."

"You mean it was all pretence?"

"Yes and no. I mean he played a woman's game with you – and you could have beat him at that if you'd set your mind to it. He's just so fond of you as what you are of him, so 'tis all a question of who'd give way first."

The waitress came with their tea and dripping toast.

"I'll pour," Jane said. "You can cut my toast into fingers. Actually, I'm not sure we should be talking like this. What would you have done – in my position?"

Banks needed no second asking; she'd plainly thought it all out. "I'd have tooken to my bed and sickened. I'd have got my lady's maid to tell the most fearsome and bedoling tales of my decline. I'd have got her to suggest that Lawyer Scawen was Mr Hervey's only hope of preserving my life."

"But why?"

"Because he's a lawyer. You said yourself, you needed a lawyer to tell you what's what. He's the only one your father would have let see you."

"But he's employed by my father. He'd never be so dishonourable as to ..."

"Honour's like sealing wax, my father always says. It's one thing cold and another hot. Anyroad, Mr Scawen's so nicketty-nock over you, he'd do anything you ask."

"What do you mean?" Jane was both excited and frightened at this revelation.

"You do know." Banks nodded confidently. "When he's with you, his heart goes so hurrisome he can't say if he's standing on his head or what."

"D'you think so?" Jane looked dreamily out of the windows at the gathering dusk. "We must go soon," she murmured mechanically, still thinking of Vosper.

"Your dripping's going cold."

Jane took her first bite and relished its salty succulence. "Oh!" she cried when her mouth was empty again, "one forgets in between how good it is. Actually, Vosper Scawen is the only man I know who doesn't treat me like a child."

Banks agreed. "I never liked the man myself," she confessed, "but since I've seen him with you – well, either he's changed or he's not the man they say he is."

"And what do they say of him?"

Banks hesitated.

"Go on, you can tell me. I'll make up my own mind, anyway."

"I've heard tell as he's cold – so cold as a quilkin in a cundard, as the saying goes. And calculating. And very close with his opinions and sympathies. And very concerned for one person above all the rest – Vosper Scawen."

"He's not like that at all," Jane replied scornfully.

101

"Not with you. I have to give him that. He do worship you."

"Come, come, now Banks!" Jane blushed and stuffed another dripping finger into her mouth.

"It's true. I believe he's as mismazed by it as anyone – and frighted."

"Why?" Jane was surprised into speaking with her mouth full.

"Because he do know you could provoke him to folly." She smiled, as if to suggest she realized she was being over-dramatic. "Perhaps 'tis a blessing you don't know how that power works."

Something in her manner roused a memory in Jane. "When they first expected me to sign that deed – in the office in Helston that day – I don't know why I decided not to. It was something to do with poor little Bessie Wender. She seemed so hopelessly trapped in her situation and I wanted to feel I had at least some tiny bit of control over mine. (I mean to write to her, by the way. Remind me when we get home.) Anyway, I'd made up my mind to go in there and be terribly calm but absolutely firm about it. But instead I found myself wheedling and ... I don't know, almost teasing them. And I couldn't think why I was behaving like that – it reminded me of someone else, not me, but I couldn't think who. And then I remembered – it was the way my mother would have behaved." She grinned. "I say, Banks, you *are* a companion, you know. What a pity you can't be." As soon as the words were out she added, "And yet – why not? If I were to put my foot down and insist ..."

"No, Miss Jane." Banks laughed. "There's many more important battles than that to fight."

After their tea they walked back through the town in the gathering dusk. Jane wanted to go by the harbour front and see all the boats riding at anchor, but Banks would not hear of it; that was no place for respectable people at this time of day.

As soon as they were in the brougham and on their way home Jane said, "Now! Your promise."

Banks sighed. "I won't break it, miss. I've given my word and I'll keep it. But not today ..." She spoke on over Jane's protests. "I'll tell you why. If word ever got out that I'd told you what you wish to know, I'd be turned off without a character. And if they could put me up before the beak, they'd do that, too. But there's one person could tell you – and none would say a word against her. So all I'll do is to beg you be mindful of the situation you've put me into and ask her instead. And if she won't tell you, *then* I will. But please don't hold me to it now."

"Who must I ask then?"

"Can't you guess?"

13 DOROTHY LANYON WAS Honorary Secretary of both the Ladies Committee and the Social Subcommittee of the Helston Philosophical Society. The Chairwoman was Mrs Troy, but she was still ailing after the birth – in her forty-second year – of her son Bill, and could play no part in this season's festivities. Her

duties therefore fell to Dorothy – alas, without the authority that would have made their discharge easy.

"I honestly don't know what way to turn next," she complained to Jane one day. "If I proceed and hire these rosettes and bunting, they'll say I have exceeded my powers. And if I wait for their say-so after the next meeting, Mr Blatchford will tell me the Volunteer Rifles or the Ebenezer Social Club have taken them for that day, or the day before, and there won't be time to clean them and hang them up." She heaved a dramatic sigh. "What am I to do?" The question was rhetorical; she did not for one moment suppose that Jane might actually have an answer.

"I thought the meeting was tonight," Jane said.

"That's the Ladies Committee, not the Social Subommittee. I am Honorary Secretary of the *entire* female side of the society, my dear."

"Well then," Jane went on, "who knows *Mrs* Blatchford best?"

Dorothy turned to her with a weary smile, as if she were about to say, "I know it's very kind of you to try to help, my pet, but ..." Then she grew thoughtful, saying, "Indeed, that's a very good question." She put her fingers to her temples, like skewers, and murmured, "I've been thinking in predestinate grooves – committees, minutes, authority ..." And now the smile was anything but weary. "Bless you, dear. It so happens that Mrs B is a cousin of May Delamere's. I'll have a word with her."

"Oh, do let me," Jane said. "Now that *is* something I could do. And it would give you time to write up your minutes for this evening."

"Oh that would be so kind. Do you know where they live? Well, Banks does. You could walk if you like. It's less than a mile. Otherwise take the gig."

They decided to walk. "You know Mrs Delamere is Bessie Wender's mother?" Banks asked as they set off.

It had rained heavily overnight but the dense clouds had passed, leaving shoals of fleecy cumulus and a fair bit of blue sky. A strong northwesterly breeze swept blotches of sun across the hills and fields, changing the aspect every few moments.

"Yes," Jane replied. "That's partly why I suggested doing this. I long to see what sort of woman could marry her fifteen-year-old daughter off into such misery."

"One who was all past and nothing to come," the maid commented. "And three more to be rid of."

"Rosa, Susie, and Fanny," Jane murmured.

"You got some memory."

"For faces and names." She smiled acidly at Banks. "I'm often right about them."

The maid acquired an unwilling smile and a sudden interest in the puddles.

The grace-and-favour cottage allowed by the Lanyons to the widow and her daughters lay just around the corner beyond the church. From the front it seemed to be no more than a two-up, two-down miner's cottage; but climbing roses and winter jasmine, just coming into flower, gave it a more genteel air. They obviously had one maid-of-all-work, for she was kneeling in the doorway scrubbing the front steps. Rosa and Susie, to judge by their ages, were "streaming" the windows with pails of water, one inside and one out; every now and then they paused to tell each other which flecks were on whose side of the glass. They all turned to stare at Jane when it became clear that she was not simply passing by.

She introduced herself when she still had one hand at the gatelatch, adding that she was on a small errand from Mrs Lanyon. The effect was electric. The girl doing the outside jumped down off her stool, snatched off her pinny, wiped her hands in it, flung it at the maid, plucked down her sleeves, buttoned them up and advanced smiling upon Jane with her hand outstretched – all in five paces across the pocket handkerchief of a front lawn. "How d'you do, Miss Hervey. We've heard so much about you. It's a pleasure to meet you at last. I hope it's not too late to say welcome to Cornwall?" She had short, curly blonde hair, deep-set eyes of pale blue, a slightly retroussé nose, and cupid's-bow lips. "I'm Rosa Delamere."

Jane was impressed by her aplomb but demurred at the little curtsy she offered. "Oh please," she exclaimed, "none of that. I am plain Miss Hervey – as you are, well, not-so-plain Miss Delamere. I hope this is not an inconvenient moment for you. It is a very small errand and I could quite easily discharge it out here."

"May I not offer you a cup of tea?"

"I'd adore one – but I'd hate to take you away from such absorbing work."

"Oh yes!" The girl laughed and held out a hand that ushered Jane firmly toward the front door.

Banks said, "If you please, Miss Jane, my sister's husband's cousin do live just back there foreanenst the church gate ..."

Jane waved her away without turning round. "Look out for me on my way back."

The Delamere's maid had already moved her pail out of the way; she now stood aside to let them pass. They stepped carefully over her work. "Is that Margaret Banks?" Rosa asked.

"Yes." Not for the first time Jane envied the Cornish their ability to thread the spider's web of marriage ties and kinship; it was part of that sense of belonging which she felt would never be hers to enjoy.

"My mother will be sorry to have missed you," the girl went on. "In fact, she's only just over the road in the church, looking out some cassocks that need attention. Bridget will fetch her if you wish."

Jane said it was a minor matter and she'd look into the church on her way back.

The house proved to have three downstairs rooms, a parlour to the left, an everything-else room to the right, and a kitchen built lean-to at the back. The hall that ran down to it was divided by the steepest stairs Jane had ever seen. She noticed Susie, or at least the back of her, busy over a tray in the kitchen.

"Won't be long," Rosa said as she showed her into the parlour.

"Nothing elaborate, please," Jane replied.

The ornaments in the two china cabinets were well spaced out, no doubt to hide the gaps where once-treasured knick-knacks and heirlooms had been sold off to keep up more important appearances.

Susie followed them in with the tray. She introduced herself, without a curtsy, the moment she had set it down. She was quite different from her sister, with long, dark, straight hair gathered into a bun, a nose of a kind more common in France than in England – straight, fine, and slightly pointed – a square jaw and a rather prim mouth; but her eyes were of a hauntingly pale green flecked with hazel. "Fanny made these cakes," she said.

"Yes, where is she – with your mother?"

"No, she's not feeling too grand today, Miss Hervey. She's staying in bed." Susie lifted her eyes to the ceiling.

"Oh, I'm sorry to hear it. Nothing serious, I trust?"

Rosa said casually, "It's that time of the month – and only her second visitation."

"Rosie!" Her sister blushed furiously and fussed with the napkins as she handed Jane hers.

"I'm sure it's no mystery to anybody present," Rosa answered wearily.

"What lovely embroidery," Jane said, examining the monogram and the coloured bordering of her napkin.

"Rosa did that," Susie told her.

"Susie embroidered the firescreen," Rosa countered. "Let's see what else. Mr Treloar plastered the ceiling – but he's already married, so I don't know why he bothered to do it so well. Bridget laid the fire – not much competition there ..."

"What's the matter with you?" Susie asked angrily. "I'm sure Miss Hervey doesn't wish to hear such things."

Rosa smiled disarmingly at Jane, who now began to realize that the curtsy had been ironical. "What do you wish to hear Miss Hervey? Shall we recount the giddy brilliance of life at Jasmine Cottage? Perhaps you do not know it, but you are sitting at this very moment in the social hub of Sithney village."

"Pay no attention to her Miss Hervey," Susie said angrily. "I expect you're in the throes of preparation for the first grand ball of the autumn? Or will you not be out of mourning by then?"

"No, I shall be back in colours this Sunday. In fact, my errand for Mrs Lanyon is in connection with that ball. But also" – she turned to Rosa – "I must plead guilty to your accusation of curiosity."

"I was only joking." Rosa was alarmed at the thought of being taken seriously.

"Many a true word ..." Jane reminded her. "I met your younger sister, Bessie, a few weeks ago – and took a great liking to her, indeed."

"You mean he's allowing her out and about already?" Rosa was half surprised, half envious – as if, until now, she had felt Bessie's virtual imprisonment to be a just punishment for her good fortune in finding a husband before any of them.

"Not at all," Jane replied evenly.

"Oh, I see." Rosa relaxed again.

"Poor little Bess," Susie said in a rather perfunctory tone – then, seeing Jane's lifted eyebrow, she added, "In this house, Miss Hervey, sisterly sympathy droppeth not as the gentle dew from heaven. You have sisters of your own, perhaps?"

"I am not so fortunate, Miss Susie." Jane tried one of the cakes. "She has a light touch, your sister Fanny."

"We have not been taught to cook, you understand," Susie explained. "Just one or two dishes so that, if our hubands ever fell ill, we should be able to nourish them back to health with some little delicacy from our own hands."

"So if you happen to have one or two cast-off suitors who can't get enough egg custard ..." her sister added with a heavy wink, tapping her own breast.

"Rosa!" Susie exploded angrily. "That's quite enough. You go much too far."

105

Jane, who had been bottling up her laughter ever since Rosa's last outburst, gave up the struggle; she had to set her teacup down hastily to avoid spilling it. Susie was so relieved that she joined in, even though she hadn't thought her sister's remarks the least bit amusing. And at that moment Mrs Delamere returned from the church, weighted down with half a dozen heavy cassocks.

She dropped them guiltily when she saw Jane, who, without that gesture, would never have dreamed that the woman intended to patch them herself. "Miss Hervey," she said. "It is Miss Hervey, isn't it? I've seen you about with dear Mrs Lanyon." Her eyes ran nervously over the tray, the cups, the colour of the tea. She was a slender, energetic woman, still the right side of forty at a guess, with wavy auburn hair, a white, lightly freckled complexion, a little rosebud mouth, and pale green eyes. "They haven't served you those wretched cakes of Fanny's, have they?" she added.

"I was just saying how delicious they are. I only wish my cakes would come out as light as hers."

They all looked at her in astonishment; in their fantasies an "heiress" wouldn't be able to find the kitchen, much less the baking powder.

"It was really you I called to see, Mrs Delamere," Jane went on. "Mrs Lanyon's in a quandary and was hoping you might have a word with Mrs Blatchford ..." And she explained the dilemma.

Mrs Delamere said that nothing would be easier, and then added, almost in the same breath, that it must be marvellous to be assured of a ticket to the ball ... and if there were any going begging when the lists were exhausted ... even one ...

At which point Rosa broke in to say they had nothing to wear, anyway, so such dreams were futile.

"What are you talking about? You have that beautiful saffron-coloured gown."

Rosa bit her lip and looked uncertainly at Jane. "Will the Grand Old Duke of Wellington be there?" she asked.

"Pay no attention to this nonsense," her mother and sister spoke almost in unison.

"Why d'you ask?" Jane laughed, for everyone knew the First Duke had been dead for almost ten years now.

"He might recognize it, you see. My great-great-great-great-grandmother wore it for the Waterloo Ball."

"Tsk-oh!" He mother stamped a foot in vexation.

Jane laughed again, challenging Susie to resist; but with her mother there, the younger sister was made of sterner stuff. On impulse Jane said, "I'm sure I have plenty of dresses to spare, if that's the only obstacle." One pace brought her to Rosa's side, where she stood shoulder-to-shoulder and measured herself. She looked at Susie. "And I'm sure I have some I can no longer quite get into."

"Oh ... oh, Miss Hervey!" For one awful moment Jane thought the mother was going to fall to her knees. In that absurdly overdone gratitude, bordering as it did on farce, she gained a starker insight into the woman's despair over her spinster-daughters than all the tales about her, and all the exercise of her own imagination, had yet achieved. She began to feel almost saintly in her generosity. Then she caught Rosa's eye, which was looking at her as at a madwoman.

"What now?" Jane asked.

"Don't you realize what you're doing, Miss Hervey? Why, in *your* gowns we shall sweep all the young men off their feet and there won't be any to go around for the rest of you. I should reconsider if I were you."

Jane smiled at the mother. "The dresses are all at home, so I'll call by in the carriage tomorrow morning at ... what shall we say – half-past-nine? And we can all stay for luncheon at Montpelier House, because it won't just be the gowns. There'll be shawls and mantillas and capes and fans ..."

"Glass slippers, gilded coaches ..." Rosa cut in.

Trailing an effusion of thanks Jane went in search of her maid. "Oh, I do wish Mrs Lanyon had introduced us before," she said. "I asked her if there were any girls my age and she never mentioned them."

"She wouldn't call them suitable at all," Banks warned.

"I hope you're wrong." And Jane went on to describe what had happened.

Banks said Mrs Lanyon wasn't going to like that one bit.

"But why ever not?"

"Well – treating them like they're in society. Did you see that Rosa's hands? Even mine are smoother than that."

"But their father was the Honourable Owen Delamere. He'd have succeeded to the earldom if his older brother hadn't remarried – and those girls would have been Lady Rosa, Lady Susan, and so on. How can anyone say they're not in society?"

"Because it's touch and go whether they'll end up in service, that's why. Don't take my word for it. Mrs Lanyon'll tell you soon enough, I'm sure."

Banks was right. Dorothy Lanyon was not at all pleased with what Jane had regarded as a good morning's work.

"But they're charming," Jane protested, "and completely respectable."

"Well, of course they're respectable," Dorothy replied. "No one is questioning that. But so is the vicar. So is the doctor. One hardly expects to meet *them* in society, though, does one."

Jane had to admit the truth of that, but she did not entirely give up. "Doctor and Mrs Moore will be there," she pointed out.

"But not because he's a doctor, dear – or they'd all want to come. He's there as one of the largest manufacturers and employers in the area – and a great benefactor, with all his clinics and the hospital in Redruth."

"Oh, I didn't realize. What is he a manufacturer of?"

"He's a brewer, dear. Wholesale, of course – I thought you knew that."

"But isn't that ... I mean, I was told it was his wife ...?"

"Yes, yes," she snapped, as if Jane were being pedantic in the extreme. "I can tell you've been talking to that pert young Rosa Delamere. That's just the sort of provocation she delights in."

Jane staged a little tactical withdrawal. "I'm so sorry to have distressed you, dear Mrs Lanyon. It's the last thing in the world I'd willingly do."

"So I hope that's the last we'll hear of that. But make your mind up on one thing – they are not coming to my Ball."

That evening, while her hostess was battling with her committee in Helston, Jane wandered into Mr Lanyon's library in search of a new book. She had started to reread *Pride and Prejudice* but had found its themes too close to present reality for her comfort. She found Mr Lanyon sitting there at his leather-topped desk, poring over a technical description of some new battleship.

Of course – it was Tuesday, his day for Engineering. Wednesday was Natural Philosophy, Thursday – Zoology, Friday – Philosophy … and so on. With Biblical Study on Sundays, every day of the week had its benison of fact and speculation to enlarge his mind. ("Though he's still size seven-and-a-half in hats," his wife liked to comment.) Jane envied him that steady round of purely disinterested study. When she was older and her family had grown up and gone, she'd set out her week in just such a fashion, and make the rest of the world conform.

He looked up from his journal and smiled. "Lost?" he asked.

"I'm sorry, Mr Lanyon, I didn't wish to disturb you."

He closed his journal with a flourish. Each subject had its own blue calfskin binder with the Lanyon badge blocked upon it in gold. "A battleship made entirely in iron," he said. "Would you sail in such a thing, even at double pay? But it looks as if they really intend to build her." He slipped the binder back in its proper place – Monday, Tuesday, Wednesday … read the spines.

"Why don't you put the subjects on the back instead?" Jane asked.

"Because I change the order each year," he explained. "Last year, Engineering was on Thursdays, d'you see?" He spoke as if he thought the concept might actually lie just beyond her powers of comprehension.

She still wondered why he didn't put the subjects on the folders and simply shuffle their order each year, but all she said was, "Ah, I see. So much learning! It's a wonder the mind has room for it all."

"Oh, Jane!" He smiled at her earnestness. "We stand but at the threshold today. But what excitements we can sense already, eh? Evolution, now – there's an idea for you. A soaring, noble, grand idea! It has changed my entire perception, I can tell you. I used to walk about our lanes here, marvelling at the wisdom and order of our Creator – that everything should have its place – and in such variety and abundance. But no longer."

"No?" Jane forced her eyebrows to rise.

"No! For every blade of grass that grows, a dozen have withered, and a thousand seeds have failed even to germinate."

"And some fell upon stony ground?" She hoped to shorten his lecture by leaping to its conclusion.

He laughed. "No, nothing so simple. That was an elementary parable for a primitive people. But Our Lord is still putting parables in our path if we have but the eyes to see them. And he does it through the minds of great men like Mr Darwin, who has shown us not that 'some fell upon stony ground' *once* – a sort of unfortunate accident that befell a handful of seed. What Darwin has shown us is that some are *always* falling on stony ground – that *that* is part of the Grand Design. There will always be more contenders than victors, always more applicants than places, always more seeds than soil to nurture them. Life and death struggle, you see? That's how things get better and better, because only the strong survive. Or the intelligent." He tapped his forehead and beamed at her.

"I'm sure we must still strive to end all discord and bring about peace and happiness on earth," Jane said.

He chucked her under the chin. "Bless you, child. These considerations happily do not apply to you. Those whose struggles have led to your fortune have placed you in a charmèd circle where the base laws of nature are abrogated."

"I see," she told him.

"And what did you come in here to seek?" he went on. "Another pretty little tale?" He turned the spine of her book toward him. "Ah yes, very droll."

"Only when written about," Jane agreed, "and got up into a tale. But when one sees the wretchedness of it in the flesh, it is harder to smile." She realized with a shock that she and Mr Lanyon were the same height; his position as master of the household had always somehow made him seem taller, but here they were, eye to eye with each other.

He took her elbow gently between his thumb and forefinger and guided her toward the fire, releasing her with a tiny flourish that more or less wafted her into one of the easy chairs. She expected him to take the other, but he preferred to stand with his back to the blaze and look down at her. "One must be philosophical about these things," he said.

It was so easy, she thought, for people who were well married and settled to take that attitude. "I've been thinking about them all day," she told him, "those poor Delamere girls. D'you know, they actually envy Bessie!"

He dipped his head and raised his eyebrows. "Is that so wrong? She has a comfortable establishment with an assured future, a husband of some means and excellent learning. His contributions to our Philosophical Society meetings have been splendid. If she studied his interests, they might enjoy a many a of stimulating conversation. Instead she came whimpering to us. That's no way to go forward."

"She's only fifteen, though. Don't you think ..."

"She was old enough to accept his proposal – and young enough, I would have thought, to adapt to his wishes." He smiled reassuringly. "But she'll come round in time. I'm sure of it. She was always such a cheerful, willing little thing – the pick of that bunch, in my opinion. If I were you, Miss Hervey, I'd save my pity for women who don't marry until they're in their twenties, when they're more fixed in their own ways and are much less adaptable to the requirements of a husband. They're the ones who have a hard time of it. Which also shows the importance of marrying young." His smile positively twinkled. "And how fortunate *you* are in that respect."

Jane nodded glumly. "I remember once, in our garden in Paris, when the apples ripened and there was a particularly succulent-looking cluster on one branch, and I was jumping up and jumping up and just couldn't quite reach them. And then the gardener came along, and he couldn't lift me up because his hands were all soiled, but he turned his wheelbarrow over and put a pail upside down upon it, and let me climb up. He didn't actually assist me, I mean by grasping my arm or anything, but he was there to catch me if I fell. And then I found I could stand there and pluck them with ease. And it's like that with Rosa and Susie Delamere, I think. They're leaping for something that's just out of their reach, but if they could get a start from a little bit higher, there'd be no difficulty at all."

"Well, it would be interesting to see if you're right."

"Yes, it would have been."

He noticed her slight change of tense and quizzed her with his eyebrows. She explained what had happened that morning and added, "I do hope I haven't upset Mrs Lanyon. I truly thought she'd be pleased. And you, too, indeed."

"Really?"

"Yes. I thought – suppose they do capture the hearts of one or two young men at the ball, it would be such a relief, wouldn't it? Not only to Mrs Delamere but also to you and Mrs Lanyon, surely? People think you're absolute bricks to go on supporting them with a pension, of course. But it can't be a satisfactory permanent answer. Or can it? I know so little about such matters."

He tugged thoughtfully at his lower lip. "There is that to be considered, of course. Er ... you say Mrs Lanyon was annoyed at what you'd done?"

"At what I suggested. I haven't actually done anything, fortunately. I think she was mostly annoyed that I hadn't consulted her – and quite rightly so. It was the grossest impertinence on my part and I blame myself entirely. Perhaps if I'd discussed it with her and explained it all carefully ... well, she might even have made the suggestion herself?" Seeing him teetering on the brink she added, "Banks, my maid, says I was quite in the wrong."

He bridled at once. "Oh does she, indeed! Well, we don't let our servants dictate to us in matters like this." He became genial again, almost confidential. "Leave it with me, my dear. You are probably right that Mrs Lanyon's refusal has more to do with her annoyance at the manner of the affair than at its matter. I shall talk it over with her and perhaps cooler counsels will prevail."

"I should not like Mrs Lanyon to suppose that, having lost with her, I came to you," Jane told him anxiously.

"But that would not be true. It was I, not you, who raised the subject, after all." He stared at her uncertainly. "I did raise it first, didn't I?"

Jane lifted *Pride and Prejudice* toward him.

"Yes," he cried. "That was it – when I saw your book."

She rose and restored it to its place in the shelves. "I think I shall not read tonight after all," she said. "I have such a busy day tomorrow."

14 JESSE LANYON LAY BACK comfortably in his marital bed, stretched all four limbs to their utmost, and gasped at the goodness which seemed to flood his veins. "It is surely the moment when we are nearest to the Divine," he murmured.

Dorothy rolled down the hem of her nightdress and did Dr Foley's exercises for conserving the precious, life-giving seed.

"Indeed," Jesse continued, "if the act of *pro*creation is considered as assisting the Creator in a new act of creation, then its divinity is our right."

Dorothy said nothing. Often, when he trapped her into speaking on this distasteful topic, it excited him into another assault. And for that he also had Dr Foley's encouragement. "The more the merrier!" Revolting little man. No pedigree at all. "Our reward." He offered it like a correction.

Dorothy yawned discreetly.

"We make such difficulties for ourselves by our silence," he went on. "I don't know what the answer is, but I cannot believe this shamefaced silence is right."

She straightened the blankets back over her.

"Is it never to be discussed at all?" he asked. "Not even in the abstract?"

Dorothy cleared her throat as if she were about to say something ... and then stifled a further yawn.

But his next comment found the mark: "I see it happening all over again with young Jane. And what is little Bessie Wender's problem, if not that?"

"Jane?" she asked warily.

"Yes." Now he'd engaged her at last he swiftly moved away from the particular. "But it is a manifestation of a more general failure. A failure to inform our young people, to enlighten them. What *would* we say of parents who reared their children to be lion-tamers (as all parents rear their children to be married) but who never showed them a lion (as we never show them a true picture of marriage) and who never once told them that lions are ferocious by instinct and have teeth and claws to match (as we never speak of the ferocity of our procreative desires and the claws by which they hold us)? I'm sure we'd call them monsters of carelessness and neglect."

She smoothed the blankets yet again.

"Don't you think so?" he asked.

Her sigh was one of bewilderment. "I honestly don't know what to say, Jesse. I mean, what precisely are you proposing one should tell young girls? A girl like Jane, for instance?"

Faced with it so directly he could not answer.

She pushed home her advantage. "I see no halfway house between total knowledge and total ignorance."

"The sort of total ignorance that nearly destroyed our union? And one whose legacy even now renders you incapable of reasonable discussion on the subject? Not even with our own doctor!"

"I'm not going to argue that all over again. Dr Foley was highly recommended."

"Yes, but his chief advantage was that he was three hundred miles away in London. And even then we took false names. It's so shabby. Can we not do better?"

"Tell me what else," she insisted, seeing that as his greatest weakness.

"I don't know. But we'll never devise anything better as long as we maintain this utter silence on the topic."

She closed her eyes, plunging herself into a warmer dark. She thought she'd rather sit through another committee meeting like tonight's than continue this distasteful conversation.

"It used not to be so," he went on. "Girls of our parents' generation were somehow more informed. They told each other ... things."

"And got up to all sorts of ... you know what, when no one was looking."

111

"I think they *were* looking, you see. And I think they were wiser than we. For if anything happened – if the girl broke her ankle, as they say – a marriage could be swiftly arranged."

"What a way to start!"

"At least they didn't start in catastrophic ignorance."

She exploded in scorn. "Why, it would be a heartbreaker's charter. Every Lothario in the country would go about sowing his wild oats and leaving a string of respectable females belly-up." A harsh note crept into her voice. "I know what's behind all this! If *we'd* been able to ... do before marriage what we've done ever since, we'd have discovered that I'm barren and then you needn't have married me at all! That's what you're really thinking of."

He drew in breath as if she had physically struck him. "How dare you!" he said in a low voice, full of menace.

A little thrill of fear, and of something more than fear, ran through her. "I'm sorry," she stammered. But she was angry, too – with herself for having blurted out words so mean, and with him for having provoked her to it.

"That was unpardonable," he growled. His dark shape rose at her side.

"I said I'm sorry." She hit him as she spoke, meaning the punch to be more playful then hard. But it caught him awkwardly and hurt him.

"What's got into you, woman?" He grabbed her wrist and pinned it to the bed.

"No." she pleaded. "No, you're not to." Yet there was an unaccustomed disturbance growing within; it panicked her into hitting him again, intentionally hard now, with her one free fist. Something within her exulted at it, knowing that even her feeble worst would not hurt him – and knowing, too, that he would soon grasp that fist, pin her to the mattress, and force her to submit.

What followed left her shattered, disoriented, profoundly uneasy.

In the morning the maid brought them their tea, half-drew the curtains, and told them it was going to rain later – oh, and the postman had gone by without stopping.

"Nobody loves us," he commented, reaching for the *West Briton.* But he let it lie in his lap. "You remember what we were talking about last night?"

"My committee?"

"Our excessive caution in all matters female."

"Oh, Jesse, not that again!"

"Not in the way you think, my dear. Something much more practical. I refer to two young ladies whose future should be of especial concern to us – I mean the two older Delamere girls. And little Fanny, in time, too. These modern customs – always trying to make society more exclusive than it already is, always seeking new ways of keeping people out – perfectly respectable people like those Delamere girls – it's all very well, you know, but it's going to cost us a fortune. And I mean *us,* you and me, not society in general." After a moment's thought he added, "And its cost to society is not negligible, either."

"I don't see that," she said guardedly.

"I should have thought it most obvious, my dear. Those girls have been brought up to gentility. Their only possible occupations, apart from marriage, are as companions or nursery governesses. They hardly have the education to make proper governesses.

So if, with one hand, we deny them every chance of meeting a potential husband, we can hardly complain if the other hand must dip deep into our purse to maintain them in that unhappy state.

Dorothy was astounded. "I presume you'll cease to support them after they come of age, my dear. No one could possibly say ..."

"I care not a fig for what the world may say, my angel. I speak to my own conscience in this as in all important questions. If their father were alive, then the very fact that he was the *Honourable* Owen Delamere would have given them *entrée* everywhere. But he died in our service. I am in conscience bound to support them as he would have done."

"And you would continue it until they were married?"

He nodded gravely.

She was silent a long while.

"My dear?" he prompted.

"I think I see an answer," she said slowly. "The only difficulty is that they have nothing to wear. I wonder ..."

He gave a baffled laugh. "If I had the slightest idea what was on your mind, perhaps I might help?"

"Never fret." She patted his arm effusively. "Jane is a good soul. A dear, kind soul. I'm sure she'll be able to lend them something. It will have to be delicately managed, though. Listen, if you'll just vanish on some errand immediately after breakfast, I think I know how to persuade her."

*   *   *

Jane called at Jasmine Cottage promptly at half-past-nine, exactly as she had promised; Banks was not with her. She found both girls in a high old state of excitement, and each coping with it after her own fashion. Rosa parodied it, fanning her face and fluttering her hand at her breast; Susie pretended to be as cool as a moss house.

"How many dresses have you got altogether?" Rosa asked the moment they were Montpelier-bound.

Jane was in a quandary. To reply, "I don't know," was not only untrue it would also sound blasé. But to reply with the truth, "One-hundred and seventeen," would sound boastful in the extreme and would, moreover, put her in a different universe from the other two – the very opposite of what she desired.

"Strictly speaking," she said, "I had only two or three dresses before my mother died. I simply inherited all of hers, since they require very little taking-in to fit me. I haven't worn any of them, of course – except in private at home, to try them on. And because it pleases my father to see me in them."

"Yes but how many?" Rosa insisted.

"Some of them are centuries old." Jane went on back-reining desperately. "And you have to remember that in Paris you're *dead* if you turn up in the same dress twice in the season. So what might seem foolish extravagance here is quite the accepted thing over there."

113

"Are they all Parisian dresses?" Susie was shaken out of her assumed calm.
"Yes. There was very little need to extend her wardrobe in Leeds!"
"I'll bet it's over fifty!" Rosa enthused. "How many days in a season in Paris?"
"None." Jane laughed at their bewilderment. "It runs to about a hundred and twenty nights."
Their jaws fell. "A hundred and twenty dresses?" they asked incredulously. She nodded. "If you include my three."
"Goodness, your father must have had oodles of oof!" Rosa cried.
Susie raised her eyes to the heavens at this vulgarity and apologized to Jane with a shrug of her shoulders.
But Jane wanted to scotch that notion. "I think he was too busy rescuing his family business – which he did entirely by his own skill, you know. But he certainly couldn't have afforded all those dresses. In fact, my mother inherited some money from her family in Wales." She blushed to hear herself talking in this dreadful, mercenary way; yet she did so wish to cultivate their friendship. She wanted them to understand she had not been born into the purple – nor reared in it very much, either.
Rosa grinned. "Don't worry. We, too, were taught never to speak of money."
"And some of us remember the lesson," her sister said sharply.
"You'll find it terribly easy to remember as long as the money's still sort of *there*, you know."
"Have you heard from Bessie?" Jane asked.
The sisters exchanged glances. Rosa shrugged.
"I feel so sorry for her," Jane went on. "And so helpless, too."
After a brief pause, Susie responded. "We've a saying in Cornwall – 'You've made your bed, now you must lie in it.'"
Rosa smiled wanly. "Rather apt."
"Could she have refused Dr Wender's proposal?"
Again that awkward exchange of glances. Rosa said, "I suppose not. Her life wouldn't have been worth living if she had – at home, I mean."
"We didn't know how it was going to turn out for her," Susie added defensively.
"And now," Jane concluded, "there's nothing to be done." She nodded at Rosa. "As you say – very apt."
"I don't think it can be *so* bad," Susie put in. "Of course Dr Wender's keeping her on a tight rein for the present. It's only natural when you remember how inexperienced she is. But as she grows older I'm sure he'll allow her more scope. And when she comes of age she'll be fully mistress in her own household." She smiled reassuringly. "Anyway, *any* sort of a husband is better than mouldering away at home. Spinster!" She shivered at the very word.
There was a ruminative silence before Rosa spoke next. "Does dear Mrs Lanyon know about this?" she asked. "I mean, does she approve of our getting invitations to the most exclusive ball of the season? Where is it to be held, by the way?"
"I think she said someone called Leggat ...?"
"Liggat! Is he lending Liston Hall for the occasion? How swell!" Rosa clapped hands. "That means they can hardly refuse Dr and Mrs Moore. She owns the house. My, shan't we just see the fur fly!"

114

"Oh, but they'd be invited anyway. Mrs Lanyon told me. It's because he's such a large employer, with the brewery and so on. I said I thought Mrs Moore was the one with the brewery, but she told me I was just being pedantic. I gather she doesn't like Mrs Moore much."

"When did this conversation occur?" Rosa's eyes narrowed. "Yesterday?"

"Yes, why?"

She smiled knowingly. "So you were talking about who was in and who was out as far as invitations go, eh? I'll bet she didn't want to ask us. Did you talk her into it? I don't want to thank her *too* effusively if she was against us to start with."

"Knowing you," Susie sneered, "that's just what you would do. In fact, you'd *only* thank her effusively if you were quite certain we were under no obligation whatsoever to her."

Rosa grinned at Jane as if she had just been congratulated. "There's not much love lost between either of us, Mrs L and me. But you didn't answer my question. Did she want to exclude us?"

Jane nodded, trying not to smile.

"And you talked her out of it? Bless you!"

"It wasn't quite so straightforward as that. I had a little talk about it with Mr Lanyon, after dinner, when Mrs L was in Helston. I hope I wasn't disloyal."

"And?"

Jane shrugged. "I really don't know what he said to her, but by breakfast time this morning she'd changed her mind completely."

Rosa leaned forward, seized her hands, and shook them heartily. "Oh, I *adore* people who can do things like that! I always go at opposition bull-at-a-gate, and I know it's the worst possible thing. What is the secret, Miss Hervey? And did Mr Lanyon realize what you were doing? I often think men do realize but they don't mind. Women mind it a lot more."

Jane's spirit swelled under this barrage of praise. Yes, she thought, she had managed the Lanyons pretty well. Then Susie pricked the balloon. "Don't listen to her, Miss Hervey. It's not true. She's a past-mistress at it. She's doing it to you now."

Rosa pouted and plucked her hands away.

Jane said, "I think we might drop the formalities, don't you? Let's be Jane, Rosa, and Susie from now on? Tell me, what are your favourite colours?"

"More to the point," Rosa said, "what were your mother's favourite colours?"

"Oh, she had everything. She used to say the opera was crimson, the Bois always green or brown, the Luxembourg all ochre and blue ... and so on. She had to have all possible colours for every place and occasion."

"Scarlet, then," Rosa said decisively.

"You can't," her sister protested.

"You needn't stand next to me. I know what *you're* going to choose – clerical gray and mustard trimmed in a positively shrieking olive green, I shouldn't wonder."

They arrived at Montpelier House only to find that her father had gone on business to Penzance; he was not expected back before evening. "But I thought Friday was his usual day there," Jane said.

Mrs Tresidder shrugged awkwardly. "It's Wednesday this week, Miss Hervey."

115

"Oh well, I'm sure it'll be all right. After all, they are my dresses now." And she led the way upstairs.

The two Delamere girls could hardly believe their eyes. They had never before seen such a treasury of gowns and costumes and suits and skirts – not to mention the capes and mantillas, the shawls and muffs, the gloves and shoes and pocketbooks ...

"She had *five* riding habits," Susie exclaimed.

"And half a dozen different styles for mourning," Rosa added.

"Ah yes," Jane said. "I remember Clothilde coming into the seamstresses' room with them one day. That one's in case the emperor died. That's for members of the government and so on. That's for a military funeral. I can't remember the others but they were all like that. One is for country funerals, I know."

This explanation only made the array seem even more wonderful – to think that mourning could be so finely graded by rank and geography.

"And the letters of condolence," Rosa asked, "did they have black borders of differing thickness, on the same principle?"

"Probably," Jane replied guardedly, unable to tell whether the question was serious or not.

Of course they found it impossible to open all the trunks and choose from the entire selection. But some twenty evening gowns were already hanging in cupboards and Susie made her choice from those – a gray dress, as her sister had predicted, but shot through with the new colour "mauve," which had been such a sensation at its first appearance last season. Made entirely of silk it had three tiers of flat puffs in dark mauve at the hem; and the bodice and flare of the skirt were formed from draw pleats. Drooping epaulettes in the same darker mauve emphasized the steeply sloping shoulderline.

"This fashion was made for you," Jane said admiringly. "Look, if you gather your hair in two tresses like this, one each side, and plait them in a fine, intricate pattern – and perhaps work a bit of mauve lace in, too ... just imagine it!"

Shyly the girl inspected herself in the glass, letting her mind's eye do as Jane had suggested with her hair. The transformation was so breathtaking she could not speak. She turned, shiny eyed, to Jane, who, fearing an embarrassing outburst of gratitude, let her hair fall and turned eagerly to her sister. "Now for the really difficult one," she said grimly.

"Thank you!" Rosa exclaimed. "Just for that I intend to be exceedingly difficult."

But only four trunks later she found exactly what she wanted – a long, sweeping gown in two shades of crimson taffeta with broad lozenges of black lace that fell in panels from the waist to within twelve inches of the hem. The zigzag edge thus formed was matched by a zigzag band of the same black lace whose bottommost points touched the hemline. The same lace was used for the epaulettes and, as ribbon, down the sleeves.

The moment she put it on she seemed to gain inches; she became statuesque, almost regal. She seemed to be aware of it, too, even without seeing herself in the glass. "Doesn't it make a difference?" she murmured, letting her hands run out over the flare of the skirt. "I hardly dare look at myself."

"But what shall we do about that hair?" Jane asked. "Why did you cut it so short?"

"I was in one of my rare rebellious moods," Rosa explained. "I looked like an accident at the wigworks."

"Before or after?" Jane slipped a long but very lightweight mantilla, also in black lace, over her head. She tried several variations before settling for a fold just below the hair line. "Don't look yet," she said and dashed to a box of trimmings, returning with a pair of silk flowers, both scarlet – a rose and a camellia. She checked their hue against the dress before she pinned them into the mantilla. "Now!" She turned the girl to face the glass.

The difference between the two sisters could not be made plainer than by their reactions to a transformation that was, in both cases, enormous. Rosa's eyes gleamed at what she saw. Her smile was almost savage in its exultation. "I warned you, Jane," she intoned, not taking her eyes off herself for one moment. "In this dress Richard Vyvyan is mine."

Jane, who had the measure of her humour by now, said calmly, "Perhaps so – but you'll never induce him to wear it."

Susie's eyes went wide in shock; so did Rosa's, until she could maintain the pose no more and broke down in helpless laughter.

"Why did you pick out his name?" Jane asked evenly, as the laughter waned.

"Oh, well" – Rosa's gaze could not meet hers – "all the world knows you and he are intended for each other."

"Do they, indeed? Then I'd be greatly obliged to you for paying him particular attention at the ball, and doing your very best to captivate him, for the world's choice is not mine."

"Who have you decided on then?" they asked avidly. Rosa added, "It's no use my picking on someone you don't want in the first place. I'm not going to waste my powder like that."

"I haven't even begun to make up my mind," she admitted.

Later, when they were back in their everyday clothes and taking luncheon, Jane made a further admission: "You were talking about choosing among my ... *suitors.*" She spoke the word with ironic overtones. "The fact is, I don't even know how to go about the business of choosing."

They were incredulous. "What can possibly be the difficulty?" Susie asked.

Jane was glad she had dismissed the footmen. They could perfectly well serve themselves – and talk in much greater freedom. "Well, my father and Mrs Lanyon speak very properly about it. I mean, I'm sure their advice is of the very best. I mustn't be misled by superficial things – like, I mustn't choose a man simply because he's handsome ..."

"You mean they are allowing you to choose?" Rosa asked. She seemed a little surprised to hear it.

"Yes and no," Jane admitted. "I may choose whom I like and then they'll approve or disapprove. If they disapprove, I must choose again, so it's not entirely free. And they want me to think of things like will he be a good provider? Has he a fine reputation? If he's on the poor side – they don't rule that out, you see – do people speak of him as up and coming?"

"That's Richard Vyvyan, all right," Rosa commented.

"And I've no doubt it's all very sensible and wise. I mean, if you're going to have to settle down under the same roof with someone for the rest of your life ..."

"And share the same bed," Rosa put in.

Susie stared at her in outraged shock; she didn't even dare look at Jane.

"Oh come on, sister dear," Rosa said wearily. "We are all out of the nursery here." She turned to Jane for confirmation.

Jane, seeing that something was expected of her, said, "I've often wondered about that. Is it absolutely necessary, do you think?"

Susie stopped being shocked. Now both sisters stared at her suspiciously, wondering if this weren't some elaborate attempt to out-joke anything Rosa might have tried. Jane hastened to explain. "I've never shared my bedroom with anyone, you see. I've always had it to myself and I don't think I'd like to change now, not after so many years. On the other hand, I suppose men expect it of one. If any man proposed to me, I think I'd have to tell him that."

"I agree," Rosa said heartily. "And if anyone proposes at the ball – or any time when I'm around – do let me know. I'd love to study his expression."

"Rosa!" he sister said sharply. "That's enough." She turned to Jane. "I think you ought to discuss this with Mrs Lanyon, you know. I'm sure she'll have an answer to your dilemma."

A log fell out of the fire at that moment. Rosa, who seemed about to choke on her food, dashed to the wall and tugged at the bell pull.

"That one doesn't work," Jane told her. "Anyway, surely we can lift it back ourselves." She picked up the tongs and deftly returned the log to the heart of the fire. As she replaced the implement she noticed a scrap of paper sticking out beneath the draught regulator. With delicate tweaks she extracted it – revealing three-quarters of a scribbled note. The ink was sepia and the page scorched but she was able to decipher:

Dearest W:-
It'll have to be tomorrow, Wednesday, not Friday this week. Usual time.
Ever yours, E.W.
P.S. I have the articles you so desired!

The handwriting was the neatest she had ever seen. She folded it small and slipped it under her bodice.

"Something interesting?" Rosa asked lightly as she returned with gusto to their interrupted meal.

"Puzzling," she replied.

"A scandal?" she rubbed her hands delightedly.

Jane laughed. "Certainly not. That's one thing you may be absolutely certain of."

118

15 THE HELSTON PHILOSOPHICAL SOCIETY had been in existence for almost half a century and, like many institutions of such semi-venerable age, had long ago deviated from its original purpose. It still maintained a library and reading room in Wendron Street – not far, in fact, from the offices of Scawen and Conway; and it still held regular meetings between September and April, when matters of great moment were debated. Topics for the current season included evolution (which was, of course, top of every list in every philosophical and debating society in the land in that year), child labour, disestablishment of the church, phrenology, and rational-dress reform. But these were now subsidiary to its main purpose, which was social – first to provide a focus for the secular life of the town, and secondly to regulate it in the best interests of those who were *in*.

As the society's philosophical importance had yielded to its gathering social power, so the ladies' committees had become more vital than those of the gentlemen – and competition for places grew increasingly fierce; hence Dorothy Lanyon's open and behind-the-scenes skirmishes with her fellow members.

The first grand occasion of the season was the Winter Ball, held on the last Friday of the month, which in that year fell on the 23rd. It had enjoyed no fixed venue since the old Coinage Hall had been pulled down. Recently it had found a home in the Assembly Rooms, the Mission Hall, and the covered market – none of them quite grand enough for the grand people concerned. This year's ball, however, would be entirely satisfactory on that score, for, as Jane and Rosa had surmised between them, it was to be held at Liston Court, the largest and most elegant private house in town. Though built around the same time as that other stately home of the district, Pallas House, and in the same classical style, it was urban Georgian rather than rural. Originally owned by the Brookes family, it had been bequeathed by the last surviving widow of that line, Lady Nina Brookes, to Mrs Moore, who had been her companion. The Moores, having no taste for the grand life, had let it to a Mr John Liggat, a retired partner of Liggat & Mowbray, publishers, printers, and booksellers of Paternoster, London.

John Liggat, having endured for years the ill-rewarded and thankless life of a publisher, barely managing to keep body and soul together, had finally given up the struggle, choosing instead to retire to this quiet and unpretentious backwater in the Duchy of Cornwall. That had been five or six years ago. Since then, such are the utter vagaries of fate and fortune, he had blossomed into an affluence and leisure rare among the practising members of his trade.

To most people he was an enigma. He ought to have been considered a public scandal, ostracized and ignored. He was a bottle-a-day man whom no one had ever seen drunk, though none could be sure they'd ever seen him sober, either. One of his chief reasons for retiring to Cornwall was the plentiful supply of contraband spirits of the highest quality; duty-paid brandy that would have cost him over five shillings a bottle in London could here be got for one and fourpence. He was also a bachelor, rash enough to employ as companion-housekeeper a pretty widow nearly forty years his junior, a Mrs Fenella Morgan, whose husband had died under Gough at Aliwal. She was, he claimed, his niece; many felt sure she was even closer to him than that – and fairly regularly, too.

But the pair of them attended church assiduously; she was a tireless worker – and he a generous contributor – in several good causes in the parish; and if there was, perhaps, a certain irregularity in their association, they never flaunted it to the smallest degree. On their public occasions and in their private hospitality they never betrayed the smallest sign that their personal arrangements might be anything other than they seemed. He was, moreover, an engaging man, steeped in the guarded effusiveness, the raffish respectability, the canny munificence of his former profession. Gentlemen sought his acquaintance because he was almost one of them; and those bits of his character that were "not quite the ticket" offered, as it were, a safe porthole through which to glimpse a world that was altogether more dangerous and exciting.

Ladies liked him for quite a different reason. He understood so well their need for "inside stories" of the famous, for the latest buzz, for the whispered confidence – in short, for what an uncharitable observer might call "gossip." He maintained a voluminous correspondence with every quidnunc in London and so was always in a position to oblige the appetite. When the *Cornhill Magazine* was founded that year, with Thackeray as editor, the ladies of Helston knew it before the ladies of Mayfair; and they felt quite certain that the ladies of Mayfair never knew how deeply its publishers were indebted to dear Mr Liggat for his sound advice and gently corrective hand. And if ever they wanted advance sight of some about-to-be-published book – *The Woman in White* and *The Mill on the Floss* were recent examples – it was, "Why, of course, dear lady – I just happen to have one by me. And, talking of this 'George Eliot,' did you know ...?"

How fortunate they were, they assured each other, to have such a latter-day Mæcenas among them, to grace their tables and share with them his inexhaustible fund of intelligence. The general satisfaction in the town, then, could not have been higher when it became known that Liston Court, the court of this prince, was to be the locus of this year's start-of-season ball.

Dorothy Lanyon almost suffered a collapse over the final arrangements for the decoration of the ballroom; indeed, she would have done so had it not been for the indefatigable Mrs Morgan, who seemed to have the knack of always appearing at the height of an impasse, of sorting it out with the smallest possible fuss, and of effacing herself immediately after. Thanks almost entirely to her, Dorothy was able to leave at four o'clock, in perfect time to have a bath and lie down for two hours and unfray her nerves.

The band arrived at six. The string section, being culled from church players in all the neighbouring parishes, was more used to playing Handel, whereas the rest would have been happier with military marches and revivalist hymns, being a motley "pick-up" from the Helston Brass Band, the Camborne Silver Band, and the Penryn Temperance Players. But half an hour under the firm yet jovial baton of John Blight, the local music teacher, found them playing as spirited a gavotte and enjoying as lively a Sir Roger as the most energetic dancers could have wished for.

The catering for the occasion had been farmed out, as always, to the Angel Hotel, and all day long there had been a steady stream of trunked, crated, and packaged wonders down the hill to Liston Court, ranging from hayboxes of fricasseed chicken

120

to a brand-new portable seltzer machine. By seven the whole western side of the dining room comprised one long, groaning buffet of tempting delicacies – and even then the best of it was still in the ovens and saucepans, both up at The Angel and down in the kitchens at Liston Court.

Long before the first guests arrived, the excitement and gaiety of the occasion had already infected the house. Maidservants returning empty-handed from the dining room and ballroom would hear the strains of music and join hands for a twirl or two of an impromptu waltz; footmen would bow and scrape before them in ironic gentility; and the butler and housekeeper would merely look at each other and smile.

At half past seven the rubicund Mr Liggat, his nose and cheeks shining like blood oranges, descended into the fast-dwindling bedlam; his niece was on his arm, as demure and wholesome and unruffled as ever. While she made her last-minute checks with the butler, he stood ready to receive the Social Committee, who would, in turn, receive the guests.

Meanwhile, at Parc-an-Ython, Jane, Rosa, and Susie were helping to tighten each others' laces in an attempt to pinch themselves in two. There were all the usual complaints at being unable to breathe, at having to live through such torture, and at the certainty of expiring before midnight – together with all the usual hopes that the music would be gay, the refreshments delicious, and the gentlemen worthy of so many pains.

For two hours they and the maids deputed to them for the evening worked ceaselessly at their preparations, curling and combing their hair, snipping and singeing it, patting it, pressing it ... trying it this way, trying it that, and then going back to the beginning and trying all over again. They struggled into their dresses, disliked what they saw, tried one trimming, then a second, and settled for a third – and still were unsure. They raided Jane's jewelry box with shrieks of joy – until they realized how devastatingly it increased the permutations of colour and sheen, of grace note and accent, now available to them. Were these earrings too long? Was this brooch or locket too gaudy? Could those hairgrips be too large? Would anyone see this adorable little diamond pin at all? Agony by agony they readied themselves for the year's most joyous ordeal.

As a leading light of the committee, Dorothy Lanyon had to be there promptly at half-past seven, even though no one else would turn up until eight. So, as it would reflect very poorly on the girls to be there so early, it was decided that her husband should remain behind and escort them in at a more fashionable time. His kindness almost ruined the evening.

At half past seven he tapped nervously at their door and was almost bowled over by a chorus of invitations. The sight that met his eyes was such a vision of youth and beauty that for a moment he could only stand there with his jaw open, staring at them in disbelief. Three jolly little cygnets had transformed themselves into the most regal swans. In a way Jane, the stateliest of all, was the least of his surprises. Though the sight of her was still enough to take his breath away, it was nonetheless the sort of change he might have expected. The transformation of the Delamere girls was altogether more astonishing. Susie had always seemed to him a slightly gawky, spindly young thing; Rosa, though pretty enough in her way, was an unmistakable hoyden, even when viewed from a distance of half a mile. Yet here they were, two elegant and graceful young ladies, simply radiating poise and charm. His hope of an early release from his obligations began to soar.

"Flowers," Jane said.

"Yes," he murmured.

"No – these." She came to him and touched the posies in his hand.

"Oh yes." He recovered some of his startled wits. "Yes, I brought these to grace you. But now I see it is you who will grace them."

"Fairy roses," Susie commented.

"They must have cost the earth!"

This cheery vulgarity brought him smartly back to earth. "Thank you, Rosa," he chuckled. "You do make a virtue of consistency, don't you."

They effused gratitude, sniffed the posies, and held them at arm's length.

"Now you collect yourselves together," he concluded. "All your little last-minute things. I'm about to have the coach brought round, so we'll foregather in the hall in precisely five minutes."

"Pink!" Rosa exploded the moment he'd left them. "They don't go with anything we've got."

"They're all right with your red," her sister grumbled. "They're even passable with Jane's blue. But with mine!" She held her posy to her mauve dress and pinched her nostrils – an unusually blunt sort of comment from her.

"You think it's all right with this blue?" Jane asked. "All *fright* would be nearer the mark." She nodded at Rosa's bunch. "It's not nearly so bad with your red."

"Not nearly so bad." She repeated the words as if testing them. "Yes, well, I suppose you could say that being sick after one bowl of rice pudding is 'not nearly so bad' as being sick after a dozen. What are we going to do?"

Susie plucked at her posy. "They're jolly well made," she grumbled.

"And they've cut off all the thorns, so we can't use that as an excuse either."

"Our only hope," Rosa said lugubriously, "is that some other girls there have fathers or friends who are equally colour-blind, and they'll agree to a swap."

"Come along!" Their host's voice boomed up the stairwell and they trooped out to the slaughter wearing the bravest of smiles.

Their dresses were so voluminous that poor Lanyon was quite crushed into a corner of the carriage. "Are you wearing perfume?" he asked, slightly shocked.

"No! Of course not! The very idea!" they assured him, crossing fingers in the dark.

"It must be your lovely posies," Rosa added.

"Ah, indeed, indeed. I'm so glad I thought of them. Oh, what an evening it's going to be!"

The girls kept up an excited chatter all the way in: What gentlemen would be there … what they looked like … what their people did or owned … what were their prospects in life. And in those rare moments when one or other of them was not actually speaking she was biting her lips and surreptitiously pinching her cheeks to redden them. As they turned into Cross Street there was a sudden panic that they might be the first to arrive; but Mr Lanyon opened the trap and inquired of Veryan, who assured them that at least two other parties were ahead of them.

The magnificent carriage sweep at Liston Court had been lighted for the occasion with a dozen lamp-oil braziers, whose soft radiance bathed the façade and wings in a flickering warmth; near the portico two naphtha flares burned with a colder, steadier brilliance. The ballroom windows were bright and the strains of the first gavotte were already to be heard. A small crowd had gathered in the street, pressing their faces to those parts of the railings not obscured by laurel and escallonia, informing and misinforming each other avidly as to each new arrival.

"It's terribly bright," Rosa said dubiously.

"Over a thousand candles," Jane told her. "That's what Mrs Lanyon said. There'll be two servants who do nothing but tend candles all night."

"And spill hot wax all over us."

They descended as nonchalantly as they dared and, like three stately galleons on a fair breeze, sailed indoors.

Even though Dorothy Lanyon had seen the dresses and had discussed down to the last stitch exactly what the girls would wear with them, her response to the actual sight of her three young beauties as they advanced toward her through the radiance of the portico was no less astonished than that of her husband, some half an hour earlier; indeed, she quite failed to notice him, ushering them forward like the fussy paterfamilias he would never be. But she recovered enough to whisper, "The posy is wrong, my dear," to Jane as they embraced. "What on earth made you choose it?"

"Not wishing to hurt a Certain Person's feelings," Jane murmured, with a tight little shake of her head toward her host.

"Oh dear! Just leave them upstairs. I'll make it all right."

Angela Lang was waiting to pounce on them the moment they passed through the official welcoming line. "It's terribly bright," she whispered loudly as she led them upstairs to take off their cloaks and attend to some last-minute cheek pinching and lip biting.

"Does that matter?" Jane asked.

"Of course it does. It makes your eyes look small and piggy. I've put a few drops of belladonna in mine. D'you want some? Look."

She stopped and turned so abruptly that they almost bowled her over; but her eyes were, indeed, beautifully large and dark and mysteriously shining. The moment they saw it the three girls knew they had to have the treatment, too. It was the first thing they did when they were safely in the principal bedroom – which was designated the ladies' cloakroom for the evening. Only when the last two drops were placed on Susie's quivering eyes did Angela add, "It puts everything out of focus and leaves you blind as a bat, but at least you won't look like some sharp-eyed little shrew."

"Do my eyes look large and liquid and mystical?" Susie asked anxiously.

Rosa, parodying blindness, assured her they were as limpid as a moorland pool in the moonlight – but the eyes she stared into so deeply were Jane's.

"Who's here all ready?" Jane asked Angela.

"My brothers, Hubert and Denis, of course. We're early because my father had to go on and certify a lunatic. And the Lemons are here – Hartley and Millicent and ... what's the other sister?"

"Olive?" Susie suggested.

123

"No – she married 'Piggy' Tiddy," Rosa said. "So would I if my name had been Olive Lemon. It must be Barbara."

"Barbara!" Angela agreed. "And I noticed the Gryllses came in just after you – Teresa, Ben, and Norman, so we're going to be a jolly crowd. Norman's an utter dream in the cotillion ..."

And on and on it went, their nervous, excited chatter, bridging the gap between the ordeal of their arrival, now behind them, and that of filling their programmes, soon to begin.

When they were ready, just before they returned to the company, Angela put a finger to her lips and said, "What d'you make of this?"

Greatly daring, she opened the larger of the two wardrobes in the room – which proved to be filled with lady's clothing. "In *his* bedroom!" she whispered loudly and turned to stare at the bed itself. "Imagine!"

"He's the little fat man who was standing a little bit back from the stairs when we came in," Susie told Jane.

Rosa was still staring at the bed. "And she's so young and handsome." She shivered theatrically. "Imagine!" She looked at Jane.

"Yes," Jane said, not to be left out of it, "just imagine!"

Then, laughing as if they hadn't a care in the world, smiling as if they did this every day, they descended the grand staircase like four proud queens. Indeed, they were so impressive that Morwenna Troy and the two Blight girls, Constance and Martha, felt impelled to wait at the foot of the stairs until they had passed. "I'm going to wake up soon," Rosa murmured, "and find this is all just reality."

Giggling, they attached themselves to Mrs Lang, their chaperone until Dorothy became free again, and were escorted into the ball.

Standing a little way back in the shadows, watching every flounce of their descent, Liggat murmured, "Women, God bless 'em! It almost makes you wish you were eighteen again, don't it, eh, Lanyon?"

"I'd still make the same choice," he replied.

"Me, too. Me, too." He laughed. "But the dreams that assisted it would be grander, don't you know."

Jesse, feeling his earlier comment had been too prim, said, "The two in the middle are the orphans of my late agent. The one behind is Jane Hervey ..."

"Ah – the heiress. Yes, of course, your wife's bringing her out. I remember now." He looked at him slyly. "So you drove in with that little bevy!"

Jesse smirked. "I'd not admit it to anyone else, hark'ee, Liggat, but I don't mind telling you – it made me think how dashed unfair Old Mother Nature can be. Three young beauties like that – any one of whom would set the senses on fire – and not the faintest thought or notion of the pleasures of Venus in their heads!"

"Don't you believe it!" the other chuckled.

"Oh but I do. It is surely true – and I know all our leading authorities in the field agree. The vast majority of decent women are as far above such thoughts and feelings as we wretched men are sunk in 'em. Their pleasures are entirely to be found in the nursery and the domestic round, as ours are in them. Dashed unfair, though, what? They have no idea of the torments they cause us."

124

Liggat watched the next bevy of beauties descend. "The vast majority of decent women, eh?" he murmured. "Then I must have met every single member of the minority, that's all I can surmise. But see here – no bragging contests, eh? I'd sooner boast of the very fine brandy in the smoking room – if you feel able to slip away?"

Jesse was just turning to accept the offer when his eye was caught by a tall, handsome, well-built man taking off his cape with a flourish and handing it to a footman; most impressive of all, he didn't even look to see if the fellow was there. "Who's that?" he asked. "Striking young fellow."

Liggat chuckled. "My tame smuggler – since you ask. He's on my list of guests. I hope your wife's committee won't disapprove too strongly. He's not exactly *comme il faut* – but interesting enough for all that. If you like, I'll fetch him to join us."

"You'll have a job tearing him from the ladies, by all appearances."

"Oh, he knows how to treat *them*, never fear."

And the old boy went forward to intercept his guest at the end of the welcoming line. He brought him directly back, saying, "Lanyon – allow me to present Daniel Jago of Greenbank. This is Jesse Lanyon of Parc-an-Ython."

"I'm honoured to meet you, sir," Jago said. "I've heard a great deal about you."

Lanyon smiled. "Your name seems somewhat familiar, too, young man."

They shook hands warmly and went off to the smoking room for the promised brandy. "D'ye know the best thing about the modern woman?" Liggat asked. Without waiting for reply, he told them: "She's greatly in surplus, don't you know – thanks to all this emigration. And she knows it! Oh my, don't she just! And don't it just concentrate her mind wonderfully?"

16 BEFORE THE THIRD DANCE Jane's programme was already three-quarters full; discreetly she kept several vacancies around the half-way mark and toward the end, since not all possible partners had arrived yet – Vosper Scawen and Richard Vyvyan, to name but two.

Her fourth dance, a two-step, was with Argus Nicholl of Antron – the one whom everybody except Margaret Banks thought might one day be a bishop. "How long ago it seems," he commented.

"Summer," she replied. "Indeed."

"You look especially charming tonight, Miss Hervey – if I may be so bold."

She would have liked to reply with some comment on his appearance but she was experiencing considerable difficulty in focussing on anything nearer than about six feet – an effect of the belladonna, she assumed. "Thank you, Mr Nicholl. It is pleasant to be out of mourning at last."

"It must be," he said. He cleared his throat. "Yes." He missed a step, apologized, and went on, "Indeed, that was the only reason I forebore to say what it has been in my mind to say for some time."

"Really?" Jane prayed he couldn't possibly mean what she hoped he didn't mean.

"Truly. I have pondered long and deep upon the matter – it is, after all, of some gravity. I wondered whether I should write, or seek an interview with your father, perhaps." He gave an embarrassed laugh. "I even set out to meet you, as it were, by accident in the lanes near Parc-an-Ython, but I fled in ignominy the moment I even heard you approaching." He giggled to show he was exaggerating.

"Dear me, Mr Nicholl. It distresses me to be the cause of so much perturbation." Would this dance never end?

"Oh, I promise you, Miss Hervey, that is the merest soupçon of the torments I ... well, well. At all events, I resolved that if the chance arose tonight, I should grasp it or account myself the most abject coward for ever."

"Mr Nicholl, I think I should ..."

"No no, hear me out, please, or I shall never rest. I am, as you know, soon to take holy orders, and I think I may say without breaching the requirements of modesty that I managed moderately well at Oxford ..."

"A double first in Greats, I heard."

It seemed to please him enormously that she knew of it; he glanced at her slyly, as if he could guess why she took the trouble to find out. "A fluke, of course," he admitted. "I couldn't have picked better questions if I'd set the papers myself. However, what you may not know is that the Bishop of Truro has been kind enough to take a direct interest in my entry into the church – and will doubtless do the same for my advancement through its many subtle gradations and ranks. Colonel Bolitho told my father that he had heard the bishop say he wouldn't be surprised if I were to be found one day wearing the gaiters of his office."

She had never known a two-step go on so long. "How extremely encouraging, Mr Nicholl. However, I do feel obliged to ..."

"I have nearly done, Miss Hervey. Pray do forgive me, but if I stumble now, I shall never rise again. I mention all this merely to assure you that, even without the assistance of any fortune, my prospects within the church are of the rosiest hue. I am not, of course, poor, but I lack that degree of wealth which might allow me to make the very occasional – and, I assure you, most carefully considered – charitable gesture. The sort of gesture, don't you know, that speaks louder than a thousand pious words. The sort of gesture that does not go unnoticed. So you may imagine my delight, Miss Hervey, when – having found you to be the modest and agreeable young person you are – I also ..."

"Why, what had you expected?" she asked. "Of me, that is."

For a moment he was nonplussed. "Well, coming from Paris, you might, I supposed, be rather *smart*, you know. But not a bit. Quite the reverse."

"Thank you!" she said.

Her gratitude delighted him. "Yes," he enthused, "you don't put on airs about your cleverness, you see. You're not one of these modern young misses who loves to prove at every turn how sharp a wit she has. In short, Miss Hervey, I ... I ... I speak of my delight at finding you so modest and agreeable – yes, those are the very words – modest and agreeable, I also found you to be an heiress."

He did not appear to notice this slightly awkward change in tenses. Jane realized that what he had done was to pick up the syntax of his earlier sentence at precisely

126

the point where she had interrupted him. Over his shoulder she caught Rosa's eye; the girl winked at her and pretended to turn a clockwork handle sticking out of her partner's back. It was so apt to her own partner that Jane had a hard time of it suppressing her giggles.

" ... in short," he concluded a sentence whose beginning she had missed, "may I have the temerity to offer you my hand in marriage – and the audacity to hope you will honour me with an affirmative?"

"No, Mr Nicholl," she said at once, surprising them both at her decisiveness.

"I beg your pardon?" He was so astounded that he stopped dancing.

Her momentum carried her onward, still with her right hand in his left, so that they peeled apart for a bar or two. "No," she repeated, doing a reverse turn back toward him. Her momentum started them off again.

He was bewildered enough to follow. "But I don't understand. Surely you can see that what I'm offering ...?" He glanced around the room. "I mean ... well, young Vyvyan's never going to amount to much ... but if you want a husband who's away at sea three years on end and who'll be lucky to achieve a command by fifty ..."

"I do assure you, Mr Nicholl, it is none of those things. Indeed, if you were the only ..." She broke off. That would be a little cruel, she thought.

He smiled knowingly. "Aha! You cannot say it. But have no fear, Miss Hervey. I understand. I do understand. I understand you very well."

"Indeed? I have no idea what you may understand, but I am happy for you, nonetheless. It is always highly agreeable to learn that one understands *some*thing."

The dance ended at last – but he did not. As he led her back to Mrs Lang, he said, "I understand very well that young ladies think it *de rigeeur* to refuse a proposal of this sort when it is first made. But ..."

"I'm afraid I should mislead you grievously if I allowed you to believe I am playing any such silly game, Mr Nicholl. You could make it half a dozen times more and still I should ..."

"Yes, I know that is the way nowadays. And why not? It puts us men on our toes and stokes up the fires, what? Yes, why not? Since it is the Christian duty of a wife to defer to her husband when he *is* her husband, why shouldn't she assert her brief independence while she may? What decent, amiable fellow could carp at that?"

So saying, and vastly gratified with his achievement, he left her to what he was now sure were the also-rans.

"How was *your* automaton?" Rosa asked.

"He proposed to me."

"Yes, but I mean *apart* from that?"

"He *what?*" Susie asked, all excited.

Jane turned and looked at her. "Actually, Susie, he'd probably do very well for you. And I don't imagine you'd object to being a bishop's wife for twenty years before he won his gaiters, would you? Shall we ..." She broke off.

"What?" Rosa followed her gaze to the door and saw the handsome, well-built stranger. "Ah yes," she exclaimed. "Now that's more like it. Who is it?"

"I don't know. I *think* his name's Daniel Jago."

"Have you met before?"

She nodded tersely. "And wish I had not. Lord have mercy, he's seen me! If he asks me for a dance, I shall most certainly refuse." Her heart began to hammer in her throat for he was striding toward her in the most determined fashion. "What shall I say?"

"Tell him your programme's full, of course." Rosa spoke wearily, as if she were explaining that the way to walk is to place one foot before the other.

"My programme. Oh yes, my programme." She raised it for inspection but, such was the effect of the belladonna, could make out nothing. She held it at arm's length to see if that might help. And at that moment he arrived.

"How very obliging you are, Miss Hervey," he said, taking it from her and writing his name at once in the next available space.

She opened her mouth but no words emerged. The tightness of her lacing was suddenly a torture, for she seemed unable to draw even half the air her lungs now craved. A waltz began at that moment. He checked her card. "And how very timely, too," he said, offering her his arm.

Rosa accompanied her a few paces toward the floor. "If that's your notion of a refusal," she muttered in Jane's ear, "don't for heaven's sake permit him to ask you for anything else!"

Jago was an effortless dancer. After half a dozen paces Jane knew she could relax and surrender the lead to him – but it only threw into sharper relief her utter lack of relaxation in all other ways. *Please don't let him mention that day* ... she prayed.

"I once saw a mermaid the very image of you," he said.

To her amazement she heard herself – or some cultivated instinct for light conversation – replying, "You must see a lot of such creatures in your line of work, Mr Jago."

His laughter was more than a little surprised. "That'll teach me," he said, more to himself than her; but he followed her unintended lead: "None of them may boast the beauty of that particular siren."

"Oh really?" she asked in Vosper Scawen's tones. Where was he, by the way? "So she sang to you as well."

"In my mind's ear."

"What refrain, I wonder?"

She could hear the smile in his voice, even if she could only infer it from the blur that was his face. "A most damnable refrain."

"Mr Jago!"

"Oh indeed. Don't you sometimes get a tune on your mind and it won't go away ... until in the end you want to throttle that mental musician – if only you could get your hands on her? Well, this mermaid sang just such a song to me."

"The minx!" Jane was now relishing their banter. "What were her words, pray?"

"Ah, it was one of those wordless tunes – the sort that are so powerful. Words are invoiced by the lips – and though hers were comely enough for any mortal creature, this song arose from all of her being, body and soul. That is why it will not let me go."

The sheer pleasure of dancing with so fluent a partner overcame the last of her reserve. "You almost make me wish I owned such a fertile imagination as you," she remarked. "But why are you telling me all this?"

"Forgive me," he begged, without a trace of contrition. "I should have explained at once. It was, in fact, on *your* land that I encountered this vision of pure loveliness. So when I heard you were to grace this occasion tonight, I sold my soul for a ticket."

"Goodness! I hope ..."

"And now that I see how marvellously you resemble that divine apparition, I feel sure you have some sway over her, too."

"And if I do?"

He chuckled. "I observe you do not deny it."

"I do not deny that I am sufficiently intrigued to suspend my disbelief in all you have been saying – which otherwise I would take for the most trivial persiflage." She felt his muscles harden, and was thrilled by it. Plainly he had not expected such mettle from her – and nor, if she were honest, had she. "You wish me to call her to heel?" she suggested.

The tension remained in him as he said, "On the contrary, Miss Hervey. I wish you to tell her that her song has driven me to distraction. That I think of her night and day. That I have never known such strength of ... such passion."

Jane's heart had gone from the easy trot it needed to sustain her dancing to a full gallop that barely kept pace with the wild race of her emotions. "Oh," was all she could say.

"Will you tell her?" he asked. "What d'you think she will reply?"

"I can hardly answer for another," she faltered.

"I believe you can," he insisted. "I think there is some powerful sympathy between you two. Answer me then as if it were you I had asked."

She made a superhuman effort to gather herself. "I think if some ... woman from the element of earth came to a mermaid with such strange tidings ..."

"A woman from the element of earth," he murmured, relishing the description. "... she would reply that such passions were strange to her. She would ask me their name – and their purpose, too, indeed."

"And you would tell her. The woman from the element of earth would tell her – for surely she knows the name of those passions without being told."

"I, too, would wish to know their purpose."

"How can you know what they know not? Purpose is as alien to them as is common sense, self-interest, peace of mind ... all of mankind's pursuits. Even happiness itself." She felt him relax again. "But try her," he urged. "At least tell her what I have said. Perhaps she is wiser to our earthbound ways than you suppose."

"And how may I get her answer to you?" The words were out before she could bite off her tongue; it had become such a delightfully abstract game that she had lost touch with the reality lurking behind its charm. Fortunately the waltz was ending.

"Ah now that's the easy part," he said suavely, winding them into one final spin. "There is a ball at the Greenbank Hotel next Thursday. Perhaps the enchantress will seek an invitation – once she learns of the occasion? Failing that, I dine at that same hotel every Friday. It is a most convenient place for passing along messages of all kinds." He led her back to her chaperone.

"Oh dear!" Rosa sighed, looking directly at him. "This next dance is quite empty for me."

"Then grant me the honour?" he asked over his shoulder as he bowed to Jane.

"Rosa!" Susie and Jane exclaimed in angry concord.

But she was already away in his arms, and the other two girls were soon claimed by their promised partners.

"Who are you?" Rosa asked. "You're much too interesting to belong in this company. No. On second thoughts, don't tell me. It'd spoil it. But aren't you afraid of being found out?"

He leaned a little away from her, trying to size her up. At last he grinned. "I think we're all afraid of that, Miss Rosa. You see – I already know your name, and I can assure you it doesn't spoil it in the least."

Their eyes dwelled in each other's and twinkled with merriment.

"Why did you do that?" he asked. "Invite me so blatantly to this dance?"

She moved her head about awkwardly. "Oh ... I don't know. I just felt it was so unfair for Jane to have all the luck. Actually, I'm doing the pair of you a great favour, you know."

"Are you? I'd like to know how."

"You're a lovely dancer. How many hearts have you broken, eh? Just roughly."

He laughed. "I can't keep up with you."

"Oh, I promise you I haven't broken any." She grinned evilly and added, "Yet."

"I don't mean that. How are you helping Miss Hervey and me?"

"Because she's such a ... I mean she doesn't know ... I'm making her jealous – that's how. Look at her! She can't keep her eyes off us. No, you fool! I don't mean *actually* look at her. Can't you look at a person without looking? You know that at least five men will have come to this ball with the express intention of proposing to her? They've just been waiting for her to emerge from mourning. So you're going to need a friend at court – like me."

He was silent a while.

"Oh!" she exclaimed in exasperation. "He's going to *think* about it!"

"And now," he said in an altogether brisker tone, "he's going to tell you what he's been thinking. He's been wondering why you are going to these lengths. Bluntly, Miss Rosa, what's in it for you?"

"If I give you a good reason, will you believe me?" She grinned. "Or does it also have to be true?"

He laughed again. "Give me any reason you like, and let me be the judge of it."

"All right, then – er ... it's Friday. Will that do?"

"That's no reason at all."

"All right. I'm just trying to find out what sort of judge you are."

"Well, I'm something of a judge of females – I'll tell you that. And you're among the ... strangest I ever met."

She gave a tiny, gurgling laugh. "That's not quite the word you wanted, is it."

He stared at her uncertainly and then said, "Come on, give me your reason."

"I'm not so strange, really," she said, becoming all at once serious. She disengaged her hand for a moment and tapped her forehead. "Not when you look at it from inside here. It's just that I haven't much time. My reason is that I've grown fond of Jane Hervey and I want her to be happy. No, no – don't interrupt now. As I say, I haven't much time. But Jane is such an amazing mixture of shrewdness and innocence – truly babyish innocence, which you'd have to see to believe – that I'm afraid she'll stumble into the most ghastly error and be too honourable to get herself back out again."

She spoke so solemnly he almost believed her – except that "fondness" hardly seemed sufficient motive for so much earnestness. "Error with me, you mean?" he asked. "You wish to save her from me?"

She just stared at him with a mild contempt.

This waltz, too, drew to an end. "Well" – he recovered swiftly enough as he returned her to Mrs Lang – "if ever you should need to communicate with me, by messenger or" – he kissed her hand – "in person, I dine every Friday at the Greenbank Hotel in Falmouth." He gave a final bow, plus a smaller one to include Jane, and left them.

Jane could not help overhearing his closing words. "Why did he tell you that, too?" she asked.

Rosa stared about, seeking the Recording Angel. "See what I mean?" she asked him. Then, to Jane, "He's yours if you want him. Just crook a finger."

Jane stared at her, shocked at first, then angry at being patronized in that way. "The very idea!" she sneered.

"Ah! So you don't want him?"

"Not if he were the last man on earth! I can tell you that now."

Rosa nodded placatingly. "Of course you can, darling. And why not throw in that the moon's made of stilton? And while you're about it, try convincing me that it's Friday today. Why not?"

The anger turned to a puzzled frown. "But it *is* Friday," she protested.

Rosa's eyes bubbled with secret amusement as she replied, in the most earnest of tones, "You see - be warned! That's the trouble with telling lies – it's almost impossible not to slip up and tell the truth eventually."

Jane laughed despite herself. *"You're* impossible," she said.

Rosa agreed sadly. "Even that requires practice."

The ball wound on through more two-steps, a schottische or two, a Sir Roger, quadrilles, polkas, and more waltzes – and still there was no sign of Vosper Scawen. Jane eventually asked Dorothy Lanyon if she had any news of him, but she, too, could not understand it. Daniel Jago danced with everyone – especially, Jane noticed, with the shyest wallflowers and with unprepossessing girls in their twenties whose hopes of any other kind of partner were fast dwindling.

"I'm absolutely furious with that wretched man Liggat for inviting such a scoundrel," Dorothy remarked. "But I suppose it's the price we must pay for using this magnificent house." After a pause she added, "Talking of which, I'm surprised we've seen nothing of the egregious Mrs Moore yet. I'd have thought she'd positively enjoy turning up here to gloat over us all."

Jane wondered why it would be gloating but was not sufficiently curious to ask.

In fact, Mrs Moore did not turn up until half-past eleven, when the ball was nearly over. If she gloated at all she compressed it into the five paces between the door and Dorothy Lanyon's party, for whom she made a beeline.

"Good evening, Mrs Lanyon," she said coolly enough, though something plainly agitated her.

"Good evening, Mrs Moore. We were wondering where ..."

"I'm afraid I have some ... that is, I've come on rather an urgent matter. May I have a word with you?"

They were gone about five minutes, during which the girls got in one more dance. When they returned, Dorothy was pale and shaken. Jesse was with her, also looking most grave. "I'm afraid we must all go home now," he said.

He avoided both Rosa's and Susie's eyes – which Rosa at least was swift to notice, for it certainly had not been his habit earlier in the evening. "What's the matter?" she asked. "It's to do with us, isn't it."

He nodded. "I'm afraid it concerns you very much. I'll tell you in the carriage on our way home."

They made no move. "It's mother!" Susie exclaimed in the same moment as her sister cried, "It's Fanny!"

He shook his head. "It's neither, I'm afraid. Do come on now. I'll tell you everything I know as we ..."

"It's Bessie!" Jane almost shouted. And without further ado she ran out into the hall – where, a moment later, Dorothy caught up with her.

"What are you doing, child?" she asked.

"I'm looking for Mrs Moore."

"Come home, my dear. I promise you – there's nothing we can do. It's a terrible, terrible thing, but there's nothing we can do."

Jane caught sight of Mrs Moore at that moment. She had collected her cape and was going back outdoors. The distraught young girl ran to her, almost bowling her over, such was the sail-like momentum of her wide ball gown. "Where are you going?" she asked the woman urgently.

Mrs Moore looked at her anguished face, saw that she had been told all, and said, "Back to the gaol, of course."

Jane thought furiously and flung out a wild guess: "To see Bessie Wender?"

"Of course. Er ... Miss Hervey is it not?"

Dorothy caught up with her at that moment. "Now come along, my dear," she said, in a curious mixture of wheedling and threat.

Jane's heart was now beating so fast she thought it would surely leap right out of her. "I'm going up to the gaol," she said.

"Out of the question!" The threatening tone took over completely.

Jane went on as if she had said nothing. "Whatever you do, don't say a word of this to Rosa and Susie until you're back at Parc-an-Ython. Tell them anything else you like but not this – whatever it is. But if it concerns Bessie ..."

Mrs Moore turned pale at these words. "You mean ... you didn't know?"

"Of course not!" Dorothy exploded. "Trust you to come meddling in ..."

"Be quiet!" Jane cried – so loudly that the entire company obeyed – and turned to look at her. She coloured furiously but stared them out. "Here are Rosa and Susie now," she said in a near-whisper, speaking close to Dorothy's ear. "So understand this. If I have to walk – if I have to *crawl* – I shall go up to the gaol tonight to see poor Bessie. If you have the slightest hope for my continued friendship, you will find some way to make that possible."

She had meant it as a vague and general threat, but the calculating gleam that suddenly entered Mrs Lanyon's eye revealed it as one of some potency. She saw that the Delamere girls had gone up to get their cloaks so she followed her words up quickly with, "I never was more serious about anything in my life."

"But you cannot befriend Bessie Wender now!" Dorothy was in anguish.

"I can't think why not. It sounds as if she never needed friends more."

Dorothy leaned close and whispered – in tones that declared it as the ultimate shame – "Because she has tried to take her own life!" She drew back a little and added, "There! Now d'you understand?"

17 JESSE LANYON CAUGHT up with Jane as she was climbing into Mrs Moore's carriage. "And where do you suppose you may be off to, miss?" he barked.

"I implore you, Mr Lanyon," she replied. "I must go to poor Bessie Wender."

"But that is out of the question," he said at once. "I do not know the particulars of this case but they are certain to be highly unsavoury and not at all suitable for the ears of a respectable lady."

Jane hesitated; it was, indeed, a compelling argument. She glanced at Mrs Moore but saw no immediate support from that quarter. "The particulars of the case?" she echoed. "But to me it is not a *case* at all, Mr Lanyon. Bessie Wender is my friend. You cannot know what powerful sympathies there are between us, or you would not seek to prevent me."

His eyes appealed over her shoulder to Mrs Moore, who responded, "I'm afraid there is a great deal in what Mr Lanyon is saying, Miss Hervey." But then, looking at Jesse, she added, "On the other hand, innocence may be a greater shield here than all our worldly caution."

"I cannot rest until I have seen her," Jane interjected. "That is all I know."

He sighed. "This disobedience, child, is highly distressing. I would not have expected it of you, I must say."

Jane swallowed heavily. "I'm sorry you think me disobedient, sir, but ...."

"No buts, miss. I now command you – or, rather, forbid you. I forbid you to have anything whatever to do with this affair. I say this with absolute confidence, for I know your father would not deviate a hairsbreadth from my injunction. Come."

He turned to go, fully confident that Jane would follow. Instead she drew a deep breath, took her courage in both hands, mounted fully into the carriage and said, "I shall go to see Mrs Wender." She was shivering with anger at him – and with fright at what she was doing.

Lanyon turned back in a fury, but Mrs Moore intervened. "If I may make a suggestion?" It halted him long enough for her to add to Jane, "If Mr Lanyon forbids it, you must understand that I cannot possibly convey you in my carriage."

"Then I'll walk." She half-rose in her seat.

But the older woman stayed her. "That would make a fine how-d'ye-do in Helston, wouldn't it! And it certainly wouldn't help calm people's feelings against Bessie Wender – which is what should be uppermost in all our minds at this moment, don't you think?"

"*Against* her?" Jane asked, stunned at the word.

"She doesn't understand, you see," Lanyon said. "You don't understand, child."

"But I think I might be able to explain it to her, Mr Lanyon," Mrs Moore cut in. "If she may accompany me – I give my word she shall not go into the gaol – I believe I can make her understand."

"Well ..." Lanyon sniffed dubiously and stared at Jane, whose face was far more adamantine than her spirit. "On those conditions ... I suppose ..." He bowed stiffly to Mrs Moore, and left them. After three paces, however, he turned and wagged a finger at Jane. "We shall have more words on this, Miss Hervey."

The moment he was gone Jane's true feelings came out of hiding. She closed her eyes, shivered, and said, "Oh dear."

Mrs Moore rapped with her knuckles against the roof. "Yes," she said as the carriage rumbled off, "I imagine that fairly well puts the cat among the pigeons."

Jane smiled wanly. "Tomorrow's battle," she commented. "Tell me what you know about poor Bessie. And why is she in gaol of all places?"

"May I first ask how you come to know her, Miss Hervey? Dr Wender hasn't exactly permitted her to go about."

Briefly Jane explained the circumstances of their meeting and how, even in so short a time, such sympathy had developed between them.

"And what had you intended doing to help her?" Mrs Moore then asked.

Jane gave an awkward shrug. "I hardly know. I couldn't have done anything very much until I was out of mourning, but I thought I might invite her to tea ... or we might accompany each other on visits to Falmouth."

"You obviously don't know Dr Wender," Mrs Moore said ominously.

"Is he such an ogre, then?"

"He is one of those people, my dear, whom men find ... how can I put it? Absorbing? Fascinating? Jolly good company, anyway. But women – or at least the women I know – feel there is a certain ... something you can't quite put a finger on. I shouldn't really be saying such things. I've only met the man half a dozen times, but from the beginning I had that feeling about him. He looks at you as if you're a sort of adversary, before you've even opened your mouth."

Jane made no immediate reply.

"You don't have to go through with it, you know," Mrs Moore told her. "If you're beginning to suspect these are deeper waters than you bargained for."

"You didn't tell me why she's in gaol."

"Because attempted suicide is a crime. Didn't you know?"

"I know it's a sin. But I can't believe Bessie would do such a thing. She's such a dear little ... she must have been driven to it. She must have been driven to the end of her tether by him." She brightened. "Could we call on Vosper Scawen? He'd advise us, I'm sure."

Watching the girl floundering between the constraints of ignorance and the demands of delicacy, Mrs Moore was impressed at this sudden flash of practicality. The choice of lawyer was also interesting. "Why him?" she asked.

Jane smiled. "He's the one I could most easily persuade."

"Against his better judgement, you mean? Good for you, Miss Hervey. Despite knowing so little about it, you nonetheless have an intuition of what may be involved. But let me put your mind at rest. Mr Scawen is already engaged in this business – and at my instigation, too."

"Yours?" Jane was surprised.

The woman nodded. "I'm an interfering old busybody."

"Oh, but I didn't mean to imply ..."

"Let me explain." The carriage began to labour up the hill to the Town Hall. She glanced out of the window and said, "Oh, we should have gone by the back lane. Anyway, I just happened to be in Helston police station, seeing about some alehouse licences, when they brought poor Bessie in ..."

"How had she tried to ...?" Jane did not like to finish the question.

Mrs Moore sized her up carefully before replying. "She tried to sever the arteries in her wrists."

For a moment the whole world swam before Jane's eyes, but she knew the woman had answered so bluntly as a kind of test, so she checked herself and asked, tight-lipped, "Is she still in any kind of danger?"

Mrs Moore shook her head. "Dr Wender is also the police surgeon, so they could hardly ask him to deal with her. In fact, it was he who brought her in to the station and gave her in charge."

"His own wife?" Jane was aghast. The horses needed whipping up the steepest part of Wendron Street. She felt her thigh muscles straining in sympathy with them.

Mrs Moore smiled. "And he, in his turn, could hardly have expected to find me there on other business – and, as it happened, my husband, too. You know he is also a doctor, I suppose? Naturally, the sergeant asked him to examine and treat the girl. Wender didn't like that one bit, I may tell you."

"Excuse me, Mrs Moore, but when did all this happen?"

"Oh, several hours ago. So then, when my husband told me what he had discovered, I asked him to go out to get a solicitor – Mr Scawen, in fact."

"*That's* why he didn't come to the ball."

"I'm sure the fact that you noticed his absence will be compensation enough to him, Miss Hervey."

"And what has he advised?"

"I don't know – not yet. He and my husband took Dr Wender aside. All I can say is that it appeared to be a most animated conversation. I slipped away to tell the Delamere girls, or, rather, whoever happened to be chaperoning them tonight. It would be awful if they heard of it from some good-natured friend."

The carriage reached the gentler part of the slope; Jane relaxed in sympathy with the horses, though she could hear their stertorous breathing above the rumble of the tyres. "That was indeed kind of you, Mrs Moore," she said. "Actually, they are not influential enough to have friends of that calibre."

The woman laughed, which emboldened Jane to continue: "Would it be impertinent to ask whether you have any particular reason for helping Bessie?"

"As I told you, I'm an incurable busybody."

Instead of making the expected protestations Jane sat awhile in silence. Then she said, "It makes me realize how little I know."

"About what?"

"About anything. And how shall I ever learn when people keep brushing my questions aside?"

Now it was the other's turn for silence. "I'm sorry," she murmured at last. "I didn't mean to brush you aside." She gazed out of the window and added, "Oh dear – and we're almost there."

Jane followed her gaze and cried out "Bessie! Isn't that her? I'm sure it's her. Oh, I wish I hadn't used that belladonna!" She opened the door and sprang from the carriage – inasmuch as anyone can spring in a broad crinoline ball gown.

The girl was walking between Vosper Scawen and Dr Moore. "Bessie!" she cried again and, dashing up the path to the police station, threw her arms about the poor creature and hugged her half to death. "Thank God you're all right – thank God they reached you in time!"

All vitality seemed to have deserted the frail little girl. She allowed herself to be hugged and kissed; she just stood there and let it happen.

"Bessie?" Jane said. "You remember me, surely? Jane Hervey? We met at Parc-an-Ython that day."

"Of course I remember you." Her voice was little more than a whisper. She let go of the men, put her bandaged arms about Jane, and hugged her as fiercely as her exhaustion permitted.

Feeling her body through her thin dress Jane was reminded of a starved little thrush she had once picked up in the depths of the snows in their garden in Leeds. The bird had died of fright in her hands.

"She should get into the carriage out of this chill," Dr Moore said. He and his wife helped Bessie, as docile and biddable as could be, down the path. Jane held out both her hands and said, "Vosper! How good you are to help her."

"Vosper?" he echoed. "Well, well! I'm sorry to have missed the ball."

"You missed nothing," she assured him. "Are they letting Bessie go?"

He nodded. "All charges dropped – though in fact Sergeant Clements hadn't committed a word to paper, wise man that he is." He still held both her hands in his. The touch of him was warm and comforting.

"I don't understand what's been going on," she said. "Not any of it."

He nodded. "Just as well."

"You're not angry I came here?"

He shrugged. "I'm astonished that Mrs Moore brought you – and that Lanyon permitted it. However" – he gave her hands a final squeeze before letting them go – "you'll be a great comfort to Mrs Wender, I know. I think they wish to depart." He took a pace to her side and started walking back up the path with her.

She slipped her arm through his. "I'm glad you helped her," she said. "Even before Mrs Moore told me she sent her husband for you, I suggested it."

He paused, though they were still a few paces from the gate. "Jane?" He hesitated and then asked, "May I?"

"Yes, Vosper."

"Don't press poor Bessie with questions, eh? Not that you would, of course, but don't let anyone else, either. There are things she would do best to forget entirely. Also, those sisters of hers aren't the most considerate of girls. The poor thing's very confused still. Just comfort her all you can."

"Of course I will. You didn't need to ask it."

"I know. I know." He started walking again and, in a brisker tone, added, "I imagine the Moores will take her under their wing for a while."

Jane had other ideas but she said nothing.

"There is still much to be decided but it can wait until she is quite recovered."

They had reached the carriage steps. She gave his arm a final squeeze. "Goodnight, Vosper."

"Goodnight, Jane." It seemed to her that he was a great deal more worried than his tone and the substance of their conversation had revealed.

They set off as soon as she was in the carriage; Bessie almost fell into her arms. Jane smoothed the girl's hair and rearranged her bonnet and told her to try to sleep.

"Of course, you've already met my husband," said Mrs Moore.

"How are your heels, Miss Hervey?" he asked – rather jovially, Jane thought, considering the circumstances.

"Completely better, thank you, Dr Moore. Indeed, I've danced all evening without once thinking about them."

"There a thing I meant to ask you – are you by any chance descended from the great William Harvey, who discovered the circulation of the blood?"

"I think not," Jane replied. "I have never heard of such a connection." She thought it unfeeling of him to attempt small talk at a time like this. Then it occurred to her that doctors were perhaps more used to such shocking incidents than other people.

"It would be a most illustrious connection, if you were," he commented.

Or perhaps it was his way of telling her gently not to make too much of what had happened – for Bessie's sake. She gave the girl a little hug and whispered, "Don't worry any more, chérie. It's over. Whatever it was, it's over."

To her amazement the girl began sucking her thumb like a baby. The Moores, too, watched in fascination.

They travelled in silence for a while, lit only by the fitful glow of the single carriage lamp – which hardly mattered to Jane since the whole world was still a blur to her. "Dr Moore," she asked, "how long does it take for the effect of belladonna on the eyes to wear off?"

He chuckled. "It depends on how much you used. Anything from one to three days. But why did you bother, Miss Hervey? You of all people."

Jane thought of explaining that everyone else had used it, but, as that did not show her in a very flattering light, decided not to. "I never saw it before," she said. "I just thought I'd try the effect."

They reached the first gaslamps, at the top of Wendron Street hill; a square as bright as bright moonlight passed backward through the carriage. Then another. By the light of the third Jane noticed that Dr Moore's gloved hand was pointing at Bessie. She glanced down and saw that the girl's thumb had fallen from her mouth and that she was now fast asleep.

"You have a way with her, Miss Hervey," he murmured.

"Are you taking her back to her mother and sisters?" she asked equally quietly.

She heard Dr Moore draw breath to reply but it was his wife who said, "Is that what you would advise?"

"Not at all."

"You sound very definite upon the point."

"I'm afraid her sisters have little patience with what they see as mere tantrums. They believe it damages their prospects of securing a husband, you see."

"Hah!"

Jane saw Dr Moore's hand move across to cover his wife's and soothe her.

"They're probably right, aren't they?" Jane commented.

"Only if they wish to marry into wealth and idleness – which, of course, is all their mother can even think of."

"My dear," her husband murmured.

"It's the truth. I blame her for ..." She gestured toward Bessie but the word she uttered was "... everything. There's a dozen shopkeepers and tradespeople who would have snapped up all four daughters – and the mother, too. Not to mention farmers, mine captains, engineers ... good people, all. But she's an arrant tuft-hunter. That's the root of all their troubles."

"Well, my dear, it's your opinion, but I daresay it isn't Miss Hervey's – nor a good many others' beside."

"What is Miss Hervey's opinion, I wonder?" There was a smile in his challenge.

"Is this young one not too badly hurt, Dr Moore?" she asked, nodding toward Bessie, now snoring gently. "It would seem heartless to talk in this vein if ..."

"Her wrists, you mean," he replied. "Candidly, I have my doubts as to how serious a project it was. I doubt if she lost very much blood. I'd say it was more a cry of despair than an actual attempt at *felo de se*, as Sergeant Clements insists on calling it. No, it's not her wrists that are damaged ..."

A square of light flashed across them just in time to catch Mrs Moore in the act of elbowing her husband sharply in the ribs.

"I was about to say," he added heavily, "that her spirit will take longer to heal, her *anima*, her inner self."

"Yes," his wife said contritely. "Of course."

They had reached the bottom of the hill on which Helston stands. "Are we dropping you off at Parc-an-Ython, Miss Hervey?" he asked. "Or Montpelier?"

"Are you taking Bessie to Lanfear?" she asked in reply.

"For a while."

"I could not sleep tonight, anyway. May I come and sit beside her bed? Please?"

"She won't need that kind of nursing," he assured her.

"But if she wakes up in the night – alone, in the dark, in a strange house? Someone should be with her. I'll sleep with her, if you're worried about me. I certainly couldn't sleep at home if I thought she was alone."

138

Their unhappy silence told her she had a point.

"You would need your father's consent to such an arrangement," Mrs Moore said at length. "Or Mrs Lanyon's."

"Not Mrs Lanyon. Would you mind very much calling at Montpelier on our way?"

They went by Parc-an-Ython as well, and found the place still lighted. Jesse Lanyon came out at the sound of their arrival and she told him she was going home. He said he thought that a capital idea – and that she would not be welcome back under his roof unless she were preceded by a letter of apology.

When the carriage drew away Jane had the strongest feeling that Mrs Moore's eyes were fixed upon her, observing how well or ill she responded to this challenge.

Despite her brave words Jane fell asleep going up the long hill into Breage – and did not awaken until the scrinch of the tyres changed from macadam to gravel, signifying that they were pulling onto the drive at Montpelier.

It was a quarter past twelve and her father came down in his nightcap and gown, though he did not seem to have been asleep. He always claimed that the older he got, the less sleep he found he needed. He assured her he had been reading. He made her step away and pirouette while he admired her – and he even danced a pace or two with her himself.

However, when she told him what she wished to do, all his geniality evaporated. It was absolutely out of the question, he said. What could she be thinking of? A woman who'd deserted her husband and tried to kill herself – Jane's reputation would be worthless if she assisted and comforted such a wanton creature? And what could Mrs Lanyon have been thinking of to allow her to mix in such company?

Jane went out and bade a tearful farewell to Bessie, who had passed beyond tears. She promised to come and see her as soon as she could.

Back indoors she swept past her father with a cold, "Goodnight, sir," and stumped up to her room.

The following morning Banks brought her a breakfast of bread and water. "The ups and downs of life!" she said cheerily.

He told her that he expected a written apology for her behaviour of the night now past – together with a promise to have nothing further to do with Bessie Wender or the Moores.

After luncheon he sent up to say that he was going in to Penzance, and had she any communication for him yet?

She said, "No."

And she went on sitting at her window, indulging one impossible daydream after another – mostly involving Mr Lanyon and her father approaching her on their knees, craving her pardon. It struck her that in the space of a few hours she had passed from a position of extreme privilege, or apparent privilege – the belle of the ball, sought by all, the focus of admiration, attention, and jealousy – to one of utter subjection, just as she had done two months earlier.

She decided to run away at the first opportunity. Well, she could make the opportunity herself at any moment – just write the wretched letter, pretend she was going to be the girl of *their* expectations from now on, choose her moment, and give them the slip.

She'd ask Mrs Moore for a place at one of her inns; the woman herself had done that sort of work once, so it couldn't be too bad. On the other hand she doubted that even the independent-spirited, snook-cocking Mrs Moore would fly in the face of local society to quite such a degree as that.

Dreams of other positions flitted through her mind – governess, nanny, housekeeper ... all of which were shattered on the rock of her Character – not her actual character but the written reference to it from her previous employer, which, naturally, she would be unable to provide.

It even occurred to her to wonder what Miss Wilkinson did. Whatever it was it kept her in fine style; and she had a cheerful, roguish look about her that bespoke independence – she certainly had no chaperone to hamper her. Perhaps she'd go and see her and ask if it were something she might attempt as well.

Around three o'clock her hunger brought a new realism to her thoughts. It would be far less dramatic, but far more sensible, to pretend to fall in with her father's – and the Lanyons' – expectations. It would buy her time to work with Vosper Scawen to achieve true independence of them all. That villa in Paris must be hers still.

Yes, she decided, that was the most promising line of attack.

She was half-way through her letter of apology when Banks came to tell her that her father had died of a seizure that afternoon in Penzance.

18 FOR THE SECOND TIME in little over a year Jane watched the interment of a coffin containing the last remains of the person she loved best in all the world. When it sank from daylight into that ultimate darkness she felt the weight of her grief as if it impelled her from behind, thrusting her forward, downward into that same black maw.

"You killed him." A voice, not her own, spoke with surprising clarity in her mind's ear. "His heart was broken by your wilful disobedience."

Tears at last broke through the dazed paralysis of her sorrow. Dorothy Lanyon, at her side, misunderstood and smiled; she tightened her light grip around Jane's waist, pulled her head down onto her shoulder, and murmured, "Let it come, my precious. Don't stint it now."

The formal accusation from Jane's conscience, which merely confirmed the feeling she had had in her bones from the moment she was told of her father's death, was too shocking for her to repeat aloud. To do so would be like seeking to share her guilt with others, to diminish its burden, to place their bland reassurances between herself and the cut of its lash. She knew she must endure her punishment alone and for as long as that stern inner voice dictated.

In an odd sort of way, her readiness to undergo the ordeal was measured by the corresponding desire to hide its wounds from the eyes of the world. The more punishment she was able to accept in stoic silence and secrecy, the more fitting and meet that nemesis would be.

She knew well enough what they were thinking. Wilfrid Hervey had reached his allotted biblical span of three score and ten – years that had brought him all he had aimed for and the due rewards of his success; he had left his affairs in good order; his daughter was enviably set up for life; and he had not had to suffer a long and painful decline. In fact, he had died in a barber's chair, in the middle of a shave – chatting and laughing one minute, out like a light the next. That was the way to go. One really didn't know whether to mourn the man or envy him.

Yes, that was what they were all thinking. She could see it in the ease with which they wore their public sympathy. It coloured all their condolences as they parted with her in the graveyard: "He enjoyed a good, long life, my dear. Try to remember that. And you were the crowning of it." These and other comforts she accepted with a wan smile of gratitude, and never once gave hint of the tormenting whips that flayed her soul without mercy. "Sensible girl," they told each other as they went in search of their carriages. "She'll pull through all right."

Mrs Moore was there, too. She offered her own condolences and those of her husband, who was on duty that day. "Poor Bessie also wishes you to know how very sorry she is," she added.

"I'm glad she didn't tax herself by coming out. I hope she's improving now?"

"She is. In body, at least. The other business will take a long time."

"Of course. Do come on to Montpelier now, Mrs Moore – unless you feel you have to get back to Bessie?"

Mrs Moore caught Dorothy's eye and said, "I rather think I'd better get back."

"Tell her I'll come and see her as soon as ever I can."

"You'll be welcome at any time, Miss Hervey." Mrs Moore smiled sadly, as if she, too, regretted that the easy intimacy they had all discovered on the night of the ball had now vanished.

The funeral tea at Montpelier was a much smaller affair – mostly the Lanyons and their circle. Vosper Scawen, who had been at the graveside, was, however, absent. Jane, who would have welcomed the support of his society, took his absence as a fitting though obscure comment on her unworthiness. He had already told her the important news – about the Lanyons' being made her guardians until she was either twenty-five or married; why should he linger?

Mrs Delamere and her daughters were there, and Jane at last met young Fanny, a thin, frail, nervous child with large front teeth. But Jane saw none of these disadvantages; instead she envied the child her innocence, her clear conscience, her untarnished soul. She tried speaking to her but poor Fanny was terrified out of her wits in such, to her, august company. She mumbled her replies, sucked her lips inward over her teeth in a desperate attempt to hide them, and kept her eyes fixed on the floor.

"Come," Jane said at last. "Let us slip away for a moment. I have something I wish to give you. Something especially for you."

And she led her upstairs, all the way up to the storerooms in the attic, where there were two large trunks that had not yet been unpacked. She opened the nearer of them and found the very thing she was seeking, lying at the top. *There, she thought, surely that is an omen.*

The centrepiece of this little mystery was a doll – not a child's doll but an antique fashion doll that had been used in the French court to show the grand ladies what their counterparts were wearing in Vienna, Rome, Madrid, and so on. She had an exquisite little face of white porcelain with rosebud cheeks and pale blue eyes – "Like a Watteau," people often said when they saw her.

"The Duc de St.-Omer gave it to my mother," Jane explained. "She had the most wonderful friends in Paris. They were always giving her things. And now I want to give it to you."

The transformation in Fanny's face was a joy to see. At the very most she had expected to be allowed to play with the doll; but to be given it to keep for ever was beyond her dreams. "I couldn't," she said at once.

"You would hurt me very much if you refused," Jane assured her.

After that what could she say? Except to promise to treasure it for always and always, and to thank her a million times over. Jane stared into those radiant eyes and knew she had done at least one good thing since her father's death; it felt like the first step forward in her rehabilitation. "Bring everything down to my bedroom." She cut across the embarrassing flow of undeserved gratitude. "You can play with them there until it's time to go."

At the top of the attic steps they met Dorothy Lanyon, who said, "Ah, there you are!" in such an effusive tone that Jane found herself wondering if she hadn't been standing there all along, listening.

Almost immediately she regretted the suspicion. It was precisely the sort of wilful, independent thought that had led her into the rebellion that had killed her father. One step forward, two steps back. She felt the whips descend again.

"And what have we here?" Dorothy asked, reaching out a hand toward the bundle Fanny was carrying.

The young girl turned the doll face out but clutched it tightly to her bosom. The woman's eyes gleamed, just as Fanny's had done. "Oh, but how beautiful! How utterly exquisite! And Miss Hervey has allowed you to play with it, eh? Aren't you a lucky girl."

"I've given it to her," Jane explained proudly.

Dorothy's eyes flickered from on to the other. "I see," she said at last. "Well, come downstairs, dear. We shouldn't absent ourselves from such a gathering too long, should we."

They left young Fanny in Jane's bedroom, or boudoir, as Dorothy called it; Fanny, no doubt, called it Seventh Heaven. As they reached the foot of the main staircase Dorothy said, "You go back to the others, dear. I just want a little word with Fanny."

Jane felt a great deal better as she returned to the gathering. At least she had done one good thing. She might later slide back a dozen times, and a dozen times a dozen, but nothing could gainsay that one good action; now if she could add to it another, and then another – one a day, perhaps – while at the same time punishing herself for every little act of rebellion and self-will, why, she'd soon turn the tide in favour of the goodness within her. And if she made her life one long process of self-denial and charity, she might, if she lived out *her* own biblical allotment, finally expiate the crushing sin of patricide.

142

When the last of the mourners had gone Dorothy said, "Are you sure you wouldn't prefer me to stay, dear? Mr Lanyon can easily take the Delameres home, you know." Jane shook her head and thanked her and told her how wonderful she had been.

"And you know you're welcome to stay at Parc-an-Ython, if you wish. As long as you like."

Once more Jane shook her head. "It is just the sort of generosity I would have expected of you, dear Mrs Lanyon, but I must pick up the threads again as soon as possible. That is what my father did after my mother's death. I thought it unfeeling at the time but I soon saw how very wise he was. And now I shall do the same again. It is what he would have wished. I want to do everything now just as he would have wished it. I feel …" She almost tumbled into confession but rescued herself with: "I feel he was such a *good* man. Almost saintly, you know. And now I must strive in every possible way to deserve having been granted such a man as my father."

Dorothy was too moved to reply, except to embrace her for a long moment. Then she was sufficiently mistress of herself to add the assurance that, despite those little *contretemps* that arise from time to time in any normal family, Jane had brought his declining years the profoundest joy. "Often and often he told me so," she added.

Just as they were leaving, young Fanny thrust an envelope into Jane's hand and ran to the carriage. Jane did not read the note until she was alone. In an unformed, childish hand, it ran:

Dear Miss Hervey,

Mrs Lanyon has explained to me how people in the depths of their grief do and say things they later regret and it is now clear to me as it was at once clear to her that your outstanding generosity in wishing me to have that beautiful doll and all those lovely clothes was such an action. Now I understand that, I cannot possibly accept your gift but believe me I shall always treasure the memory of your kindness.

It was very wicked of me to take advantage of your weakness at this time of grief and I feel utterly wretched and miserable at my wickedness. I only hope you can one day find it in your heart to forgive me and that we can be friends for the rest of our life.

Yours in sincere mortification,

Frances Delamere.

The letter fell from Jane's fingers as she raced upstairs to her bedroom. The doll was neatly laid out on her counterpane and all the dresses folded beside it. She snatched it up and, clutching it to her, flung herself down, buried her face in her pillow, and wept herself to a standstill.

Why did everything she touched turn to dust and ashes? Why did she seem destined to turn the sweetest things in life to bitterness and despair – from the grand joys of parenthood to the small pleasure of a friendly gesture? What an utterly wicked and degraded soul must be hers.

Outside, upon the stairs, Margaret Banks picked up the letter, read it, shook her head, and, filled with profound misgiving, went to see what her mistress might want for supper that night.

"Nothing," Jane said. "How can you even ask it?"

"You've got to keep your strength up, miss," the other answered evenly. "There's a lot to do in the days ahead. You've got letters to write to your father's cousins and all your old friends in Leeds. There's the reading of the will tomorrow – you want to keep your wits about you for that."

"Banks!" Jane exploded. "How can you! For shame, how can you!"

Banks smiled with satisfaction at this show of spirit. "I'm only telling the truth," she observed.

They compromised on an egg custard, which she took at nine that evening, and then pretended to settle to sleep. But the moment she was alone she got out of bed, stripped herself naked, and knelt in the middle of her carpet for a vigil of prayer and mortification until dawn.

It was a cold, frosty night at the turn of November. Within minutes the chill seemed to have eaten its way in to her very bones and she began to shiver violently. Every particle of her clamoured to be back between her sheets; she cast many a longing glance at her bed, with its thick feather mattress and heavy eiderdown quilt. But by sheer force of will she resisted every urge. The only movement she made was to roll away the carpet so that she could kneel upon the bare wooden floor.

After a while the gooseflesh left her – and in the most extraordinary manner, too. It was as if a giant hand had passed over her, literally wiping them off her skin, which was left cold and hard and almost entirely without feeling. And from that limbo of her sensory being her mind seemed to extract the strangest feelings. She found she could say to herself, "I am hot," and at once there was a sensation of scalding all over her. And when the pain from her knees almost made her cry out in torment, she could tell herself it was not in her but in a different Jane, a girl whose life ran closely parallel with hers and yet was ultimately apart. And then indeed she could *see* that other Jane, a blurred replica that partially overlapped her, as images do when you make yourself cross-eyed.

In a while the two images were quite separate. She was in one of them, the spiritual Jane who could exist outside pain and cold and punishment, looking across at earthly Jane, imprisoned in the hurt of her self-immolation, imprisoned in her sinfulness, imprisoned in silver rime, in the frosty square of the moonlight. And at last she understood the Mercy of God and how inexpressibly deep it was, how utterly different from the mercy of men, which is little more than the clemency of pity. For here God was showing her that though there was, indeed, one Jane who was cloistered in pride and self-will, there was another, as yet unsullied, who could rise above that mire of sin – to forgive which would be no mercy at all.

Her spirit burst into a silent hymn of love and joy – that her first unworthy prayers for understanding should be so richly answered. She continued to float there, outside and above her suffering self, watching the silver finger turn her to stone.

*   *   *

In the far wing of Montpelier, in Mrs Tresidder's room, the housekeeper and Banks sat darning stockings and mulling over these sad events. The maid explained what had happened in the business of Fanny Delamere and the doll, insofar as she was able to surmise it from the letter. "I don't think that was right," she said. "The girl would have tired of the doll in a month or two and then Mrs Lanyon could have put

144

it to her, all quiet and reasonable. But now she's gone and broke her heart – and Miss Jane's, too. 'Ti'nt right nor fair, I say."

"Is it a valuable doll?" Mrs Tresidder asked, holding her darn up to the light. "I don't know what they do to the wool these days. Look at that."

"It'll never show," Banks encouraged her. "I only got a glimpse of it, up in her room just now. But it's worth twenty guineas, I'd say, if it was worth a penny. Poor lamb, crying her eyes out. So there's two made miserable for what was meant in kindness, and that's not right."

"What'd make her give away such a thing?" Mrs Tresidder asked. "That's what I'd like to know. 'Tisn't as if she and the Delameres are all that close."

"Well ... she did lend the two oldest they ball gowns. Perhaps she thought she ought to do something for the youngest, too. Or ..." She hesitated.

"What?"

Banks shrugged. "Dunno. It's just a feeling I got – from little remarks she's dropped this last day or two. I think she feels she's the one who killed the old feller."

"Don't be absurd!" Mrs Tresidder exclaimed in one breath – then, in the next: "How?"

"Just like I said, from one or two remarks she let drop. She's starting to talk like the old man was some kind of saint." She gave a dry little laugh. "And when you think how he really *did* die ..."

The housekeeper glanced nervously toward the door. "That's enough of that talk, my girl," she said. "Anyway, you don't know it for certain. You weren't there."

"I was in Penzance. He was still warm when I got to him. Died being shaved? And the stubble on his face as even as arrishes! No mark of a razor. And where's that red flannel cummerbund he always wore in winter, eh? That was never found."

The other shook her head in bewilderment. "I just don't know what to think."

"I'll tell you then, for nothing. *She* forgot to put it back on him when she dressed him, that's what. She was in such a panic to get him dressed again and safely over the street in the barber's chair, she forgot. And that's top and tail to it."

"We don't even know the woman exists," Mrs Tresidder pointed out scornfully.

"I do. I've seen her. I've stood closer to her than what I am to you now – in Mrs Brown's bonnet shop in Market Jew Street. And you should have seen her start up the moment Miss Jane handed her card over and Mrs Brown read out the name and address!" She licked her lips and glanced anxiously at the other before she continued. "And then, not five minutes later, didn't we see the master and that same woman arm in arm, turning down that little passage that comes out by the gasworks?" She sniffed. "If you go that far, which I'm sure they didn't."

The housekeeper looked up sharply. "You never said that before."

Banks shrugged. "I didn't hardly like to. Didn't seem no point ..."

"And Miss Jane saw it, too?"

"Before me."

"Well then, how can she think he was some kind of saint?" Mrs Tresidder asked triumphantly, determined to prove Banks wrong on at least one count.

"Because she haven't got no notion about it at all." And she went on to explain what Jane had said about that first accidental meeting with Miss Esther Wilkinson outside Penzance station on the evening of their arrival, and all the false conclusions she had drawn from it. "There's not a thought in her head about all that sort of thing," she concluded. "She asked me once how anyone could say such-and-such a man was the father of a woman's child. If the man and the woman weren't married, how could he be the father – that's what she asked. I didn't know where to look."

Mrs Tresidder chuckled. "She was pulling your leg surely."

"She was not. She's so ignorant as a babby on all that sort of caper."

"Well!" The housekeeper was lost for comment.

Picking her words carefully, Banks went on, "I say it'd be a crying shame if Miss Jane was to think her father was some kind of plaster saint and it was her stubbornness that fretted him to death – when the truth is he bursted his heart in the arms of that woman."

"Banks!" Mrs Tresidder exploded.

"I'm not saying he was a plaster devil, neither. Just mortal clay like any on us. She shouldn't go fretting her heart out, thinking she was to blame for his death."

"His memory is sacred to her. I can't think of a worse sin than to desecrate it with such tales of filth."

"Even if they're true?"

"'Specially if they're true. And I hope you're contemplating no such treason against his memory – because that's what it would be."

The maid drew breath to reply but Mrs Tresidder held up a monitory finger. "Because if you did," she went on, "you'd be out of this house and no Character within the hour. And that's telling *you* for nothing."

At eleven o'clock Banks parked her darning needle and gave a loud yawn. "I think I'll just go and look in on the mistress," she said.

Two minutes later she was back, breathless and wide-eyed. "Come quick, come quick!" she cried. "The poor mite is lying out cold and stark on the floor."

Mrs Tresidder came as fast as her legs could carry her. "Is she ... she's not ...?"

"She's breathing easy," Banks replied. "Lord knows what she was doing. She's rolled the carpet up and all." They dashed into Jane's room. "I tried to get her into bed," she explained needlessly.

Jane was still in a heap beside the bed, stirring, giving out voiceless moans. The two women got her back between the covers. "Poor mite!" the housekeeper exclaimed. "She's chilled through to the marrow. What was she thinking of?"

"I fear to wonder," Banks said slowly.

Their eyes met; Mrs Tresidder lowered hers first. "I'll get a warming pan," the maid volunteered.

"No, you stay here." The older woman assumed charge. "Take off that dress and get in beside her. Warm the bed for her. I'll send Gillian Kemp up with the pan and I'll bring up some beef tea. Come us on, skip lively!"

Banks did as she was bid. Her mistress was so cold that even though her skin was soft and her joints pliant, she felt like something inanimate – a statue brought nine-tenths to life but still lacking that quickening spark of warmth. However, she was at least breathing deeply and evenly; the moment her head had been laid upon that pillow she had ceased her stirring and those little whimpers had fallen to silence.

A sleep-sodden Kemp came with the warming pan. Banks told her to leave it on the floor and go back to her bed, which the girl did willingly enough. As soon as she had gone Banks rolled Jane into the part of the bed she had warmed and then set about reheating the side her mistress had chilled. When Mrs Tresidder came with the beef tea she agreed it would be a shame to awaken the girl; they got her back into her nightdress and drank the tea themselves.

The moment she was back in bed, Banks, too, fell sound asleep. She had never before passed the night on so soft a mattress, with sheets so fine, and an eiderdown so weighty and warm. Against all her habit she slept right through until gone seven the following morning, when the first fingers of dawn came stealing in at the windows, between curtains she had forgotten to draw in all the excitement last night.

"I'm sorry," Jane whispered the moment she saw the maid's eyes flicker open. "Did I give you a fright? I must have done."

Banks struggled to hold onto the last remnants of a pleasant dream – and failed. "What were you thinking of?" she asked, rubbing the bricks from her eyes.

Jane rolled on her back and stared at the ceiling. "I don't remember."

"Well, I'd best turn out." She drew up her legs beneath her, luxuriating in the soft touch of the sheets for the last time.

"No, stay!" Jane reached over and grasped her arm, clasping it to her like a doll. "Oh, I was having such a pleasant dream."

"Me, too." Banks gave her arm a token tug, though she was far from reluctant to linger in that ocean of warmth and softness.

"I'll tell you mine if you tell me yours."

"I've forgotten it already, miss. I just remember it was very nice. I'd better get them to bring my bed down here, if you don't mind. I don't think you should be alone for a day or two."

"Oh!" Jane closed her eyes tight and held her breath.

"What now?"

"My father," she replied tonelessly. "I'd forgotten."

Her tightly clenched eyelids relaxed and two salty slugs of tears wandered down across her temples and fell into her hair.

Feeling awkward, Banks took a corner of the sheet and dabbed at their followers. "That's it, my lamb," she murmured. "You weep all you want."

After a while Jane said, "He's better off without me."

"Yes, yes," Banks said soothingly.

"He is."

"That's what we do call gawpus talk, that is. Look at your hair, all pitched! If I was you I'd turn off your lady's maid for leaving you go about with hair like that. Let me fetch a comb to it now."

She sprang from the bed and returned with the implement. She made her mistress sit up; she pampered her with pillows and the eiderdown; she deftly combed out every last tangle. And all the while she talked. But no matter whether it was soothing and gentle or light and inconsequential, nothing could shake Jane from that glumness which had descended on her the moment she remembered what had happened.

147

It persisted right through the day. Even the appearance of Dorothy Lanyon and Vosper Scawen did nothing to lighten it.

He read the preamble to the will, watching her closely between times. Whenever she saw his eye upon her she nodded sagely. "And now the actual bequests," he said in the same legal voice. "All my white mice and elephants I leave to my dear old servant, Rumpelstiltskin." He looked at Jane, who continued to nod in that same knowing way as before. He turned to Dorothy. "Perhaps some other day?"

She patted the girl's arm. "What is it, dear? What has happened?"

Jane gave that shake of the head which people give to dramatize the fact that they had been a thousand miles away. This would not do. The whole point of her self-inflicted punishment was that no one should suspect it was happening; as far as the world was concerned, she was making the normal, steady, utterly expected recovery from her grief. "I'm sorry." She forced up a smile that made Vosper's heart turn over. "I had a disturbed night last night." She turned to Vosper. "Just tell me, my dear. I don't think I could take in a lot of detail. Don't tell me figures or anything like that. Just ... you know."

He looked at Dorothy, who nodded. "As you wish," he said.

Jane gave a sympathetic little laugh. "Oh, would it have been very dramatic? Have I cheated you out of one of the great scenes of your legal career?" She reached forward as she spoke and squeezed his arm.

"You'll see." He grinned and patted her hand good-naturedly.

Jane silently assured herself that she wasn't going to marry him. She wouldn't inflict herself upon any man. So – paradoxically – there was no harm that she could see in accepting these much lesser crumbs of comfort.

He continued: "There are a few small bequests, the largest of which is some eight hundred pounds to your former housekeeper in Leeds ..."

"Mrs Daniels."

He hunted among his papers. "The very same. There are about a dozen like that, going down to fifty pounds for your old gardener ..."

"Robson."

"Yes. I've drawn up a list, in fact." He passed it across the table to her.

She ran her eyes down it. "Oh, I'm glad he remembered them all. They'll be so pleased. But then he would. He was such a very good man."

Though the comment was not at all out of place, it nonetheless struck the other two as slightly odd. They exchanged glances before he continued. "The rest is all left in trust to you for life with remainder to your surviving children. You are a ward of Mr and Mrs Lanyon until you are twenty-five or until you marry – as I've already told you. And that's really it. You ask me to spare you the figures, so all I'll say is that you've been left in extremely comfortably circumstances. Oh, and in the event of your marriage there are a number of complicated provisions of the usual kind, to provide a generous dowry to your husband but to prevent the rest of your fortune from falling under his control."

Her eyebrows shot up in surprise.

"Oh, that's quite common," he assured her. He smiled at Dorothy and added, "Thank heavens! Or what should poor country lawyers live on, eh?"

Jane remembered to smile, too. She would, of course, give away every penny she could get into her control; the idea of profiting from her father's death was absolutely unthinkable.

"That villa in Paris," Dorothy said suddenly.

"Yes?" They both stared at her in surprise.

"Is it sold yet?"

He shook his head. "Absolutely nothing has been done about that." He turned to Jane. "I must confess, I was rather surprised that your father didn't pursue it – having been so keen at that first ... well, that meeting which came to nothing in my office, if you remember."

Jane closed her eyes and remembered.

"I asked him several times after that," Vosper went on, "you know – should I not ask Mr Visick to attend again, to administer the oath for the affidavits the French courts required. And he'd say, 'Yes, yes ...' But he'd never settle on an actual date. Shall we proceed now with the sale in your own name?" He asked the question of Jane but turned for an answer to Dorothy.

"No," Mrs Lanyon said at once, again to their surprise. Then, with a smile, she turned to Jane. "I can understand your father, my dear, not wanting to return to that house, where the memories were more of separation from the bosom of his family than of your time together. Also his age. And yet I was never happy at the thought of entrusting the sale entirely to a Parisian agent." She turned to Vosper. "Imagine a Frenchman who owned some property here ..."

"In Frenchman's Creek?" he suggested, naming a local cove.

She laughed. "Anywhere. But imagine him entrusting it to some local agent. Could we put our hands on our hearts and swear he'd get as good a price as if he were here in person, looking over the fellow's shoulder, and with fire in his breath?"

Vosper nodded. "There's truth in that."

She turned then to Jane. "So, my dear, I thought that perhaps in the spring we might go over to Paris and see for ourselves. Wouldn't you like that?"

Jane closed her eyes and breathed out the one word, "Oh!"

"The place is empty now," Vosper told them. "Esterhazy's lease still has years to run but I'm informed he's already moved out and is seeking a subtenant. There are just four servants left on board wages."

"Perhaps we'll go sooner, then," Dorothy said. "Let's see how you feel, precious."

"Let's talk about it after Christmas," Jane said. The thought of going to Paris again, of seeing once more that most beautiful and beloved of homes, was too wonderful even to acknowledge. "It is mine, isn't it?" she asked Vosper.

"Outright." He nodded. "You signed an agency agreement, allowing your father to keep it or dispose of it as he thought fit. But its ownership remains yours."

Later she escorted him to the door. "I dreamed about you last night," she said.

"I know. You told us."

"Did I? I didn't!"

"You said you had a very disturbed night."

She gave him a playful punch. "I dreamed I saw your face as if it were in a portrait and you know how in dreams things can be two things at once? Well, your face was like a portrait on the wall but it was also on a much bigger canvas in the garden or in a field or on the beach or somewhere."

"I do go about!"

"Just listen!" She hugged his arm and shook him.

He realized that although she was being playful, this dream had quite a hold on her; he listened with more interest.

"It must have been on a beach, though I don't remember any actual water. It was all sort of misty, anyway. Except your portrait, which was, you know, needle sharp, as dreams often are. And while I was gazing at it, telling myself the artist hadn't quite caught this or that feature, a great ship came tearing through it from behind – and then got stuck in the sand."

"Is that it?" he asked after a short pause.

"Yes. What does it mean d'you think?"

"Who was the captain of the other ship?"

"I don't know," she lied. "I saw no one. All I saw was this bowsprit piercing through the middle of your face from behind ..."

He laughed as he took up his hat and cape from the occasional table in the inner porch. "Turning me into a unicorn."

"No, it came out through where your nostrils are."

They were in the gloom of the outer porch. He touched his nose and winced.

"I'll kiss it better," she said and, before he could react, she stood on tiptoe and gave him a swift peck there.

Instinctively he put an arm around her – to support her as much as anything else; but when she went back on her heels he did not remove it. Then she put her arms around him and hugged for dear life. He bent down and kissed the top of her head. How dear she was, how ultimately, utterly dear – and yet how unknowable, too. He would have given his right arm simply to know what was going on in her mind at that moment; just inches from his lips, what thoughts were whirring away?

"This is wrong," he murmured, kissing her again.

"I know." She hugged him even tighter.

"The force that drives me to this," he went on, "cannot be ..."

"I know."

"He would have understood."

"He was the kindest, wisest, most upright man I ever knew," she said simply.

19 THEY SPENT MOST of the following week sorting through Wilfrid Hervey's clothes. Nothing in that vague category we call "personal effects" is more redolent – and reminiscent – of us than our clothes. Throw a jacket carelessly over a chair and we throw a likeness of ourselves; something about it – the curve of the arm or the stretching at the shoulder – will make people say, "Oh yes, that's so-and-so's jacket, all right." And because the object itself is three-dimensional, its evocations can be even more powerful than those of a photograph.

Time and again over those first few days Jane would take up a morning coat, a dressing gown, a smoking jacket, and, with the work of imagination three-quarters done, she would almost feel her father's presence within them, substantial though invisible. Then came the hammer blow of realizing she would never again see him in this suit, that coat, those cloaks – of which there were so many. And then the tears would start anew. And thus she overburdened her grief until it could respond no more, and she was left marooned in a desert of exhausted feelings.

It was not the least of God's mercies at such a time to have a friend like Dorothy Lanyon. A shoulder to weep on, a shield against loneliness and the distortions to which the lonely, grieving mind is prey – even a source of laughter when sorrow made room for it – she was all of these to Jane as they worked their way slowly and methodically through his large wardrobe.

"He had some really beautiful clothes," she commented more than once. And then an explanation struck her. "Of course, Leeds is the capital of the woollen industry."

"He had lots of friends 'in wool,' as he always put it." Jane laughed at a sudden memory. "Mr Caldecote used to travel in ladies' woollens, he said." The laughter was nipped off by tears.

Dorothy squeezed her arm. "That's how he lives on, my dear – when we remember some amusing thing he said or some special little characteristic of his. That's how we all may hope to outlive our earthly span."

The quality was so good that they decided they could not possibly send it for distribution among the local poor. "We'd see Old Hodge turned out finer than our own husbands!" Dorothy commented. Of course, there were a few items, a couple of dozen or so, that were well worn and just about ready for turning out; they'd do. But as to the rest, they considered selling them and giving the money to the local church mendicant fund instead; then Dorothy remembered a home for distressed gentlefolk in Penzance and they decided to let them have at least some of it.

"One feels so sorry for them," Jane said.

Dorothy smiled fondly. "It does your heart great credit, my pet. Yet do not forget – they are some of life's failures. We should help them, of course, but no too strenuously."

"Because of ... evolution and so on," Jane said casually, remembering her conversation with Jesse.

Dorothy frowned, and then laughed. "Ah, I know who you've been talking with! Well, between you and me, dear – though I love the man very dearly – I have to allow that, like a lot of highly intellectual gentlemen of great distinction, he does not always have his feet quite so firmly on the ground as you and I. And a good thing, too, else what would be left for us to do! No, he and Mr Darwin think you can leave it all to blind chance and, after a few thousand years or so, the improvements will automatically come rolling along! No doubt it's true, but you and I know full well that a farmer would go bankrupt while waiting for blind chance to improve his stock like that. Which is why he picks his herd with care, guards it jealously, builds stout fences to keep out the interlopers. You may think my metaphor somewhat indelicately agricultural, but it's no use mincing these matters. As far as the human race is concerned, society is its pedigree stock, and we women are the farmers. We

151

are the ones who build the stout fences. We determine who is an interloper and who is not. We are the jealous guards. The philosophers may have their evolution, but we know what's what." She held up a garment and, looking at it critically, murmured, "How did we get onto this topic?"

"Clothes for the distressed gentlefolk," Jane reminded her.

"Ah yes." She smiled in satisfaction.

"How big a place is it?" Jane asked. "The home, I mean."

Dorothy had no idea; the place existed, that was all she knew.

"Perhaps we could make up a small parcel and take it to them tomorrow afternoon?" Jane suggested.

Dorothy thought it over. "You could do that on your own, dear. I know you're my ward and so on, but that doesn't tie you to my apron strings. You must begin to cultivate a little judicious independence, I feel."

Jane's heart swelled with gratitude. Dorothy Lanyon answerable to her father might have been a rather strict and fussy chaperone; but the same woman answerable to her own judgement was obviously going to be quite different. "I'm grateful for your trust, Mrs Lanyon," she said.

The woman laid down the suit she had been inspecting. "My dear, I think we know each other well enough by now to drop some of the formalities. From now on it shall be Dorothy and Jane between us. And you may call Mr Lanyon, Uncle Jesse. I know you'll do nothing to abuse the intimacy." While Jane stammered her thanks, she went on, "And as for trusting you – well, you're almost twenty now. A marriageable woman. It is important for you to try out your wings on such little errands as this. Far too many young girls nowadays are reared as pinioned doves, only to be carried to the altar of Hymen and thrown to the tempest."

"*Is* it a tempest?" Jane asked.

Dorothy returned to their work. "It is not one long warm zephyr – I hardly give away secrets in saying that." As an afterthought she added, "I might make a start on your father's papers today – unless, of course, you'd rather be there."

A slight jocularity of tone suggested that she was really saying, "Unless, of course, you don't trust me!" Jane responded to it at once. "Not at all. I'd be quite glad if you did, Dorothy. You could set aside anything that might cause me pain in this immediate ..."

"My thoughts exactly, my precious."

Jane, realizing how ambiguous her remark had been, added hastily, "I don't mean anything ... you know – but you might find letters of his – he always made copies of everything he wrote, you know – letters that refer tenderly to me. Things like that."

"I'm sure I shall find a thousand things of that kind."

Jane chuckled. "You'll find a thousand things of *every* kind. He made a note of everything. Every farthing he ever made or spent is recorded somewhere."

"Not your household accounts, surely? Didn't Mrs Tresidder keep them?"

Her eyes raked the ceiling. "She did. Indeed, she still does. And I had to examine and approve them each week. And it was the same in Leeds, even while my mother was alive, because she quite frankly admitted she was hopeless at all that sort of thing. But he kept a set in parallel, as it were. And woe betide us if our reckonings

152

did not tally with his!" It suddenly struck her that she would never again pause outside his study door and offer up a little prayer before taking the accounts in to him. And how often had she prayed that he would soon trust her enough to leave off that weekly inquisition? And now she would submit to it daily – hourly – just to have him back. She felt an impulse to tears but none were left to weep.

"Talking of your mother," Dorothy said, "it is a thing I often remarked, and meant to ask. You keep no portraits of her, I notice."

"My father would not have it. There are several portraits of her at the villa in Paris. Her friends there were always commissioning them. But he wouldn't bring them back with us. He has a smallish one of her, I know. In a silver frame. But he keeps it locked ... I mean, kept it locked." She sighed. "Anyway, he always used to say that the best portrait is the one we hold in our minds. If we rely on paintings or photographs, they eventually replace the real person. It was almost a superstition with him that her portrait should never be shown."

"Well, he was right, of course." Dorothy went on with her work, feeling inside every pocket and lining in case they might give the distressed gentlefolk rather more than was intended. "And yet," she added lightly, "it has had the effect of piquing my curiosity about her. I often find that, don't you? When a thing is hidden, or forbidden, or simply not talked about, then our curiosity is doubled and redoubled."

Jane nodded but said nothing.

"Pandora's box, eh?" Dorothy laughed. After a while she went on in a brisker, more everyday tone: "When you're at the place in Penzance, you might ask them if there is a similar establishment in Falmouth. I fancy there is. South of the town – somewhere out beyond Swanpool."

The name rang a bell. "Isn't that where Angelica and Jemima Pellew live?"

Dorothy nodded. "I believe you're right. You could call on them, too."

"They wrote me such a lovely letter of condolence," Jane said to mask her astonishment. This was liberality run riot; before now Dorothy hadn't a good word to say for the Pellews – or anyone in Mrs Moore's circle. Chancing her arm, she went on, "I'm still worried about Bessie. I know I behaved in a wicked and headstrong fashion that night, but I was beside myself with ..."

"We were all a little overwrought that night, my dear. I know Lanyon regrets some of the things he said ..."

"I mean to write to him today, by the way."

Dorothy smiled encouragingly. "It need not be too abject, you know. Mild but sincere regret will do. I know he'll accept it." The smile hardened. "Take my word."

"Oh, you are so good to me. But what about Bessie? D'you think I might at least call at Lanfear House and inquire after her?"

Dorothy thought the matter over. "I believe you might permit yourself a degree of concern for her – without actually embroiling yourself in the wretched girl's affairs."

Jane noticed that although this reply did not actually permit her to call at Lanfear, it did not forbid her, either. Only a week ago such ambiguity would have left her uneasy; now, she discovered, she rather liked it.

*   *   *

The following morning, the first Wednesday in December, they assembled a small parcel of her father's clothes as a gift to the home in Penzance: a couple of suits and a good warm winter coat. "I think that's just sufficient," Dorothy said judiciously. "If it turns out they're not gentlefolk at all but just a gaggle of failed tradespeople who like to consider themselves genteel, we shan't have wasted too much."

After an early luncheon Jane and Banks set off to deliver them. It was a bright winter day, mild, as so many winter days in Cornwall are, but dry and sunny, too, which is more rare. Gangs of men on relief were out mending the roads, so the ride was the smoothest they had ever enjoyed on that particular highway. As they passed Lanfear House, Jane could almost swear she saw Bessie sitting in one of the window seats, staring out over the bay – or, more probably, over the ruins of a life that had hardly started. But, since several fields and the bare tops of half a dozen small trees intervened between there and the road, she could not be certain.

The thought reverberated in her mind – *She could not be certain.* Actually, she realized, it would serve as a motto for her entire life since coming to Cornwall, where everything seemed transient, nebulous, fitful. It was like living in a house designed to drive you mad, a house full of windows and mirrors, full of odd angles and walls that didn't meet and doors that opened into nothing or couldn't be opened at all.

"Poor Bessie Wender," she murmured, turning to Banks. "If we have time on our way home, we might just drop by and ask after her."

The maid arched her eyebrows. "Are you left do that?"

Jane nodded. "I asked Mrs Lanyon yesterday. She raised no objection."

"Well, that's a turnabout."

"I think, when she was acting for my father she felt she had to be as strict as he was. But now, she knows ..." Jane's voice tailed off and she fell into a reverie.

"What?" Banks prompted.

"She knows that my father's wishes are more binding on me now than ever they were during his lifetime."

"Ah."

The single syllable was so heavy with disbelief that Jane felt obliged to say, "Oh but they are. Just look where my disobedience led."

"To a whole day on bread and water."

"No! You know very well what I mean."

"If you say so, miss." Banks stared out at the passing scene. "I see they opened Pengersick Mine again."

After a silence Jane said, "I wonder what distressed gentlefolk are like. You keep hearing about them and giving to collections, but I've never actually seen one."

"I should think they're people, same as anyone else." Banks smothered a yawn and then apologized, adding, with a slight edge to her voice, that she hadn't had much sleep last night.

Jane smiled. "Why? Was I restless?"

"That's one word for it."

"I had that dream again – oh, of course, I didn't tell you about it. I dreamed I was looking at Mr Scawen's portrait, down on the beach. It was huge. The canvas must have been a ship's sail. Anyway, a ship came charging toward the shore and as it ran

154

aground it poked its bowsprit right through the middle of the portrait. Tore it in two. And you'll never guess who was at the helm."

Banks stared at her quizzically. "This beach – would it be down Trequean, where you and the Pellew girls ..."

"It could have been. It doesn't matter."

"I don't suppose it was a certain young man who came walking ashore that day?"

"Banks! You're amazing – how did you know that?"

"I wonder." The maid chuckled.

"And what can it mean?"

"It means I know why you passed such a restless night." Then she added, "And it means I shan't fret so much next time you lie there, tossing and turning."

Jane's good humour vanished. "I'm sorry. I don't believe it was that dream. It's my conscience, you see. I think I was more than half to blame for my father's death."

She sat there amazed at herself, listening to the dying echo of words she had intended never to utter. More disconcerting still – why speak them to Banks of all people? She looked up anxiously to see how the maid had taken it. Her surprise was redoubled when she saw the woman smiling. "So that's it," Banks said. "Out with it at last."

"What d'you mean?"

"I mean I've been waiting to hear you say those words, Miss Hervey, because I've also been waiting to tell you you couldn't be more wrong. Your father died a *werry 'appy man*. He died with a certain smile on his lips."

"How d'you know? You said yourself you weren't actually there."

The maid chuckled.

"What are you hinting at? You're suggesting something, I know. What did that barber tell you?"

"Nothing, miss. Nothing I haven't already told you. But you can take it from me as if it was Bible – your little disagreement with your father had nothing whatever to do with his death."

"But how can you possibly know that?"

"His time had come. That was all."

She spoke with immense conviction, and yet simple logic assured Jane it was an assertion the woman could not possibly make – unless there was something more, something she had not yet divulged. However, she had experience enough of these situations to know that blunt probing would get nothing from her, much less a direct order to reveal all she knew. "I'd like to believe that," she murmured, setting the matter aside for the moment.

They stared out of opposite windows for a while; then Jane said, "I wonder why distressed gentlefolk have to go and live in a charity home? Unless they're all very old. But Mrs Lanyon said some of them can be quite young."

"I suppose they're not trained up to any trade or occupation."

"The men can all write, surely? I should think if you're starving, a place as a clerk wouldn't be beneath one's dignity. And every woman can use a needle, can't she?"

Banks looked at her pityingly. "Is that what you'd do?"

"Yes – why not?"

155

"How many buttons would you have to sew on at a farthing a shirt to buy even one bonnet, one sack of coal, one loaf of bread, one gill of milk ...?"

"They could paint water colours, then." Jane spoke less certainly. "Or open a little teashop. Or write signs, or tie fishing flies, or bind books ... there must be dozens of things a woman could do that don't require the brute strength of a man."

Banks eyed her shrewdly. "Here! You've been thinking about it, haven't you."

Jane blushed and denied it.

"What got you doing that?" the maid persisted.

"You go too far," Jane snapped.

"I'm sorry, miss, I'm sure." Looking not the least bit sorry she resumed her gazing out through the window.

Jane felt both annoyed and mortified. She simply wasn't patterned to be a mistress of servants; she was too curious about people and all their different little ways. "No, I'm the one who's sorry, Banks. I encourage you to talk, because you always tell me interesting things, and then I snap your head off." She smiled. "Am I forgiven?"

Banks pulled a comical face, rolled her eyes, and nodded.

"You're quite right. I have been thinking about it. If I tell you, will you promise never never to tell another living soul?"

"That's a big promise, miss."

"I won't say a word otherwise. Go on – promise – because I'm dying to tell you. I thought I could keep it to myself, but I can't."

"I suppose I'd better promise, then."

"All right. I'll tell you. Despite your comforting words just now, I simply know I'm the one who's mainly to blame for my father's death. No, no – hear me out! I've decided I couldn't possibly profit from any legacy he's left me. Of course, at the moment, I have no choice. Mr and Mrs Lanyon control it all and dole it out to me as they think fit. And anyway, they mustn't gain the slightest inkling of what I have in mind. But when I turn twenty-five and become a free agent, I'll ask Mr Scawen to go through all the accounts and tell me how much was my mother's originally and how much my father's. Then I'll renounce all interest in my father's legacy and just live off my mother's. The thing is, it may not be very much. There may have been annuities and things that died with her. I don't know, you see, so I've got to be prepared for the worst. We shall have some capital, however, because I'll be able to sell the villa in Paris. So we could ... I don't know – open a small hotel? Start a garment factory – a farthing a shirt sounds as if the labour would be cheap, anyway. Or a domestic employment agency? The thing is, we've got five years to plan it all out. Only you see now why you've got to keep it a secret."

Banks closed her eyes and gave out a weak laugh. Where could one begin to oppose such a torrent of madness? And yet at the core of it there was an undeniable streak of common sense. The really lunatic part of it was all in the beginning – her reasons for going off like this. "What's all this 'we,' then?" she asked.

"I was rather hoping you could help me."

"And what's Mr Scawen going to say to all this?"

Jane shook her head lugubriously. "I shall never marry, Banks. That's part of what I must accept for having behaved the way I did. You know when you found me

156

unconscious last week? Well, what I was actually doing was trying to punish myself all in one night. But I've realized since that it's got to be much less dramatic than that. It's got to be lifelong. So it's just you and me. You may get married, of course. In fact, you'd better, because we'll need at least one man in it, too. And you may tell him the secret."

"Thank you, miss," Banks responded gravely.

"Have you anyone in mind?"

She suppressed a laugh. "I might."

"Well, I shan't pry. But don't think you'll lose your place by marrying." She smiled craftily. "If you're at one with me, that is. If not, you'd better say so now, and I'll start looking for someone else."

The maid laughed good-naturedly.

"D'you think I'm not serious?" Jane asked.

"No – that's the whole thing. I believe you are." And she laughed again.

The home for distressed gentlefolk was out on the road to Sheffield. Jane thought it amusing that one of Yorkshire's mighty cities should share its name with such a tiny hamlet. The house had only five inmates at present: two elderly gentlemen who seemed to quarrel all the time; two even older ladies, who egged them on and then told them they were behaving disgracefully; and Miss Leslie, a woman of around thirty who had been left penniless by the death of her parents and who partly earned her keep by acting as companion-housekeeper to the other four. The warden's wife, a bluff, angular woman with a protruding lower jaw, said that Miss Leslie had gone into a decline and would probably never recover; Jane thought it dreadful to dismiss someone's entire future like that, but held her tongue.

"Look at her now," the woman murmured.

Miss Leslie was going about the room putting everything precisely in its place. She moved a paperweight half an inch, she set a little brass letter tray at right angles to the wall, she moved a picture an eighth of an inch, and then moved it back again.

The two old men were still quarrelling over the clothing when she left, but the image of Miss Leslie, establishing her pathetic claim to that teeny kingdom, was the one that lingered. She resolved to return soon and leave her some clothes to enliven the drab fustian of her present wardrobe.

Banks, who had been turning their previous conversation over in her mind all this while, said, "Can I ask you something, miss? Only don't take it wrong, now, but it's about what you were saying before. About not getting married and that, and taking up an occupation instead."

"Yes. Actually, there's something I didn't say. Of course, if it turned out that my mother had left me very well off, then I wouldn't take any money out of our hotel or agency or whatever it might be. You'd have your share, naturally, but I wouldn't touch mine. I'm not so shameless and indelicate as to take money I don't need. I expect that answers your question, eh?"

Banks shook her head. "It only makes it more necessary, miss. The thing I was going to ask was, do you truly want to get married at all?"

Jane nodded in bewilderment. "Naturally I do. Every girl wants to marry, surely?"

"I hope I'm not being impertinent."

"Of course you are. But do go on." She laughed at her memory of just such a reply from Mrs Moore. "What makes you ask?"

"Oh" – the maid shrugged and stared awkwardly about – "I just wondered. Something in the way you spoke."

The question made Jane pause and think. She was quite certain she did want to marry, otherwise there'd be no sacrifice in her decision not to. On the other hand, she had to allow that there was a certain excitement in planning and daydreaming about an independent life ...

No. That was just the novelty of the thing. It would soon wear off. And her decision not to marry – that was a genuine sacrifice.

But she was still pondering the matter as they went back down Market Jew Street. Suddenly, before she could stop herself, she asked the question she had not dared speak on their way in: "Where is this barber's shop, Banks?"

The maid's eyes filled with alarm. "Oh, I can't 'zackly recall, miss. I was in such a dalver when they sent for me. I think we've passed it – back up the top of the town."

Jane rapped on the panelling above her head. "Veryan will know," she said. "He drove the carriage that day."

They pulled to a halt. Banks, seeing the determined glint in her mistress's eye, gave in. "Well!" she exclaimed. "I'll go to Hellvelyan! That's the very place." And she indicated a narrow archway between two shops. "There's a little courtyard the other side, and the barber ..."

"How extraordinary!" Jane descended and measured the street with her eye, seeking Mrs Brown's bonnet shop. "Yes – that is the very place where my father met Miss Wilkinson that day. You remember?'

"If you say so, miss." The maid joined her in the street. "Myself, I'd have said it was that arch there." She pointed to a very similar feature two doors up. "There's half a dozen of them, look."

Jane shook her head. "It was this one and I'll tell you how I know." She crossed the narrow street and patted a lamppost just across the footpath from the arch. "He leaned a hand against this while he was addressing her. I remember thinking it showed he must be on quite intimate terms with Miss Wilkinson."

Banks, not knowing what else to do, examined the lamp post minutely. Jane grasped her arm. "Don't think me morbid," she said earnestly, "but I would so like to see that barber's shop. And the man himself, of course. And I'd like to thank him."

In desperation, the maid said, "It's not a very salubrious area, miss. If I was you ..."

"It can't be so very *un*salubrious, either, Banks – not if my father went there."

"Oh dear. Let me just ask Veryan if he thinks we can go in safely."

"Well ... very well. Only hurry."

Banks ran back over the road and, speaking so softly that Veryan had to bend down and cup his ear, said, "Here's a how d'ee do. Miss Hervey wishes to go and thank the barber.

"Oh my gidge!" the man exclaimed. "You can't leave she do that."

"How am I to stop her? She has a nose for fish like my old cat. I can't never lie to she. Anyroad, I was thinking it mebbe wouldn't be no bad thing – just so long as ... what's his name – the barber?"

158

"Bassett. George Bassett."

"Just so long as he do play his part fitty-like. You think he will?"

"How?"

"Miss Jane do think 'twas she as killed the old feller. Disobeying him and that. She thinks she broke his heart." She looked at him and almost shouted. "'Tin't funny, man!" – and then almost burst out laughing herself. But she calmed down enough to add that her mistress was ruining her life with guilt and worry. "So I think she might so well hear as he died laughing in Bassett's chair, don't you?"

He shrugged, as trapped in the dilemma as she. "S'pose so."

"But I don't think we shall tell anyone else, like as it might be Mrs Tresidder. There's no call to tell she."

He nodded his agreement.

"I'll be quick as I can," she said over her shoulder as she tripped back to Jane.

The "courtyard" was, in fact, the upper remnant of a street that had once been accessible from the quays below. The building of the gasworks had, however, truncated the street, whose only remaining access was by way of a narrow lane along the back of the works or the arch through which Jane and Banks now walked in some trepidation. A thin, winter mist rose off the harbour, acquired a tang of sulphur and ammonia from the coal stills, and then hung between the houses, adding to their sense of squalor.

"He must be the best barber in Cornwall to entice my father down here," Jane commented, taking Banks's arm and drawing closer to her for comfort.

It was by contrast a pleasure to pass the workshops of the small tradesmen who occupied the row of dwellings to their left – the saddler, smelling of leather and neatsfoot oil; the colourman, reeking of linseed and turpentine; the jobbing joiner, ankle-deep in fragrant shaving of pine and cedar; a dyer, whose windows gave out the aroma of wet, steamy wool; and, at last, the premises of George Bassett, barber and tooth-puller. The perfumes of pomade, cloves, and macassar oil gave him away even before Jane saw his sign.

"It's all men in there," she said, peering nervously through the window.

"It usually is, miss."

"Well, I can't go in." She tapped on the glass.

Everyone looked at her except George Bassett, who was in full flight with rather a good story. She gesticulated toward him and made the others understand what she wanted. He paused, glanced at her wearily, and slip-slopped reluctantly to the door. The moment he saw Banks, however, his demeanour changed. He glanced from her to Jane and surmised at once, from her full mourning, who she was. "Ah," he said.

"Mr Bassett?" Jane took the initiative. "You don't know me, but ..."

"Begging your pardon, miss, but I think I do. Miss Hervey, is it not?" He had the conversational confidence of a lifelong barber. Banks began to relax.

"Yes, I just wanted to thank you for coping so well with what must have been a most distressing incident."

He tilted his head. "I did little enough, I fear, Miss Hervey. If I may, I'd like to express my sorrow at all your trouble. He was a ... a good man."

"Thank you. That is so kind. He was a regular customer of yours?"

159

He pursed his lips and stared at the house opposite, as if the answer might be chalked on one of its walls.

"He belonged to come Penzance every week," Banks informed him. "Was he as regular as that here?"

He smiled gratefully at her. "Pretty much, I'd say. Yes, about once a week." Jane said, "And he died with a certain smile on his lips, so I'm told?"

The man looked at her in startled bewilderment. "You do *know*, then?" he asked.

Behind her Banks shook her head vigorously – so vigorously, indeed, that Jane saw the gesture reflected in the glass of the darkened doorway. What was the maid's other phrase? "Yes," she continued, "was it you who told Banks that he died a 'werry happy man'?"

In the impromptu looking glass she was surprised to see Banks sinking her head into her hands. Bassett smiled sheepishly and said her father had always seemed a cheerful sort of cove.

"Well, I see you have several customers waiting." Jane held out her hand. "I just wanted to thank you for all you did."

He recovered his poise at that. "I wish it had none of it been necessary, miss, but I'm glad to have been of some small service."

They bade each other good night. The two women started to retrace their steps. As soon as she heard Bassett's door clang shut, Jane again grasped Banks's arm, but this time with a predatory fierceness. "And now," she said sternly, "you are going to tell me the truth."

Before the maid could reply, however, she felt her mistress's grip grow even tighter. She looked up to discover the cause but Jane was already hauling her into the side doorway of the carpenter's shop, which, like Bassett's, was unlighted. The man popped his head out into the passageway.

"May we shelter here a minute, please?" Jane asked him. "There's someone coming down the street I wish to avoid."

He chuckled. "There's many like that down here, maid. As long as it's not the law on your tails."

He was gone before Jane could protest.

"Who?" Banks asked with sinking heart.

"I think you know very well," Jane said. "You'll see her in a minute, anyway." A few seconds later she whispered, "There!"

Across the street, walking slowly into the circle of light from the gaslamp that stood almost opposite the barber's shop, was Miss Esther Wilkinson. Jogging along at her side was a short, tubby man with a walrus moustache and a bowler hat a size too small for him.

Banks drew breath to speak but Jane silenced her with a tap on the arm. "Let's see where she goes. It's something to do with her, isn't it. She's at the heart of all this mystery."

When the couple had passed, Jane grew bolder, finally stepping right out into the street again. "There!" she said triumphantly. "Right opposite the barber's! Now I'm certain of it." And before Banks could stop her she called out, "Miss Wilkinson! A moment, if you please?"

20 MISS WILKINSON SPOKE a word or two to the little man, who scurried across the street into the barber's shop as Jane and Banks approached; Banks kept saying, "No," and "Please!" and tugging at her mistress's sleeve, but Jane paid her no attention.

"Good evening, Miss Hervey," the woman said as they drew near.

"Oh," Jane replied, with a mixture of pleasure and surprise. "I didn't for one moment suppose you'd remember me. I don't mean to drive your friend away."

"He'll be back." There was an edge of sarcasm to the prediction. "May I say how sorry I am about your bereavement."

"Thank you. The support of friends and acquaintances, and, indeed, of comparative strangers, has been a great comfort. I've been overwhelmed with the friendliness of people."

"I'm glad to hear you say so. I, too, lost both my parents, so I know what you must be going through." She was, just as Jane remembered her, immaculate – not a wisp of hair out of place; she seemed to have the knack of walking through the streets without picking up a single fleck of mud.

Jane smiled awkwardly. "I don't know whether to call you friend, acquaintance, or comparative stranger, Miss Wilkinson. I believe you knew my father?"

The woman smiled, too – but it was glacial. "That is his business, Miss Hervey – or it was." She saw the anguish in Jane's face and relented somewhat. "Believe me, anything I might be able to tell you about ... anything, would only cause you more pain. For your own sake, ask me nothing further. It is over and done with."

"So there *is* something." She turned to Banks. "You know what it is." Then back to Miss Wilkinson. "And so do you. And even Mr Bassett knows it." She gestured across the narrow street.

The woman, now at bay to her own tenderness of heart, closed her eyes and spoke softly. "It is a trivial, commonplace, nothing, but ..."

"Then it can do me no harm to be told of it – and so have done with the whole mystery. It is *not* knowing that plagues me so. Can you not understand?"

"Most easily."

"Then where's the harm?"

Miss Wilkinson gave a mirthless laugh. "In my view, none at all. But you and I inhabit different worlds, Miss Hervey. In your world they would flog me at a cart tail for saying one word of it, if that were still in fashion."

"So you still won't tell me?"

She half-turned toward the barber's shop. "I detest the hypocrisy of your world more than anything. But I would not visit my loathing on you, who, I believe, are more victim of it than I." She walked to the shop and tapped on the window.

Like a bolt from a crossbow the podgy little man sprang to the door; gales of manly laughter speeded his exit. "Evening, ladies!" he chirped, gripping Miss Wilkinson firmly by the elbow and propelling her back across the street; he did not even look at the other two. "All the better for a little anticimipatience, eh?"

Miss Wilkinson took out a key and unlocked the street door immediately opposite Bassett's. To Jane's horror the revolting little man put his hand to her bustle and shoved her inside.

The moment they were gone Banks ran after them. Jane, still dazed at this rapid turn of events, was slower to follow; by the time she reached the door the maid was coming out again. "What did you do that for?" Jane asked. "What did you tell her?"

"I asked her if she wouldn't spare you just a little more time," Banks lied. She took her mistress's arm and started walking her firmly back to the main street.

"What did she say?"

"She said she has a living to earn like any other."

"With that nauseating little man? Is he part of it?" She shuddered.

When they were back in the carriage and on their way home, Banks, thinking to have the last word on the subject, commented, "It's all for the best, perhaps. You'll never get anything useful out of that sort. They're only ever out for themselves."

"She is an enigma," Jane stated, as if her words agreed exactly with Banks's judgement. "She is as well-spoken as I or anyone I know. To look at her and listen to her you'd swear she was a complete lady. And her sentiments, too, at the beginning, were as refined and as well expressed as the most polished gentlewoman could make them. And yet look at where she lives! And she never has a chaperone. And the people she associates with ..."

One image stayed with her for which she could find no words: that little man with his foxy eyes, grinning like a Cheshire cat, and touching her in that offensive way. It repelled her almost to the point of nausea, and yet her mind could not let it go.

"D'you remember the day we went up Trigonning Hill?" she asked Banks. "I thought at the time – there's the Atlantic on your right, and the Channel on your left, and the end of England in front of you, and you can see it all without even turning your head. It's almost as if you could reach out and hold it in your hand. And yet just think of all the passions that are being expended in that one tiny area – all the love and hate, the greed, the jealousy, the envy ... all the people scheming to get one up ... people desperate for invitations to this and that, and others determined not to give them one ... people plotting murder ... children thinking up pranks." She laughed at her own enthusiasm. "Doesn't that ever strike you?"

Banks nodded. "Now you put it like that."

"It makes me wonder what it's all for. We're all so certain of ourselves." After a pause she added, "The Ancient Greeks used to believe that the gods made men and women for their laughter. There's something in it, don't you think?"

The maid nodded again and stared out of the window. The sky had clouded over before sunset; now the world was quite dark, with just the occasional candle or oil lamp burning in a cottage window. The interior of the carriage suddenly seemed timeless to her, a small, dimly lighted oasis wandering through an endless, eternal void. "I wonder if we come back," she said. "If we get another life, and then another. There's some old religion says we do. A missionary preacher once told us that."

"What would you like to be?" Jane grinned and settled to what she thought would be a pleasant game to while away the journey. "A grand lady of leisure, I suppose."

"A man," Banks said at once.

"Why?" Jane asked in surprise. But even as she put the question she felt a surge of agreement run through her. Suddenly she felt a little afraid of this conversation and the turn it had taken – without being able to say why.

"I'd like to see the world from their point of view," Banks said thoughtfully. "Just to understand them, I suppose. Why do so many of them hate us?" After a pause she added, "'Course, there's a lot of women *I* can't stand, but I don't mean that. I mean why is there so many men who just hate the lot of us?"

"I hope I can't think of any man who hates me," Jane said dubiously.

"The exception proves the rule," Banks replied vaguely. "What would you be if you could choose your next life?"

"Oh, I haven't given it any thought at all." She half rose in her seat and rapped on the carriage ceiling.

Veryan pulled up the horses.

"Just pop your head out of the window and tell him we'll go back by way of Lanfear House, will you?" Jane said to the maid. "I want to see how poor Mrs Moore is."

Banks did as she was bid and then said, "Mrs Moore?"

"I meant Mrs Wender, of course. I can't think why I said Mrs Moore. 'Poor Mrs Moore' is hardly an apt description of her."

Banks eyed her shrewdly. "If I had to come back as a woman," she said, "that's who I'd like to be. Mrs Moore. She's got the best of both worlds."

Jane nodded and went on staring out of the window.

Mrs Moore, despite her surprise, welcomed Jane with every sign of affability. "You've come to see Bessie, of course. I'm afraid she's taken to her bed. Nothing very serious, just a rather nasty cold in the head." She smiled. "I ignore such things, but you know how fussy some *doctors* are."

"May I see her?"

"If you don't mind the risk. Hers is the first door to the right at the top of the stairs. Did you come alone?"

"Margaret Banks, my maid, has gone round to the servants' entrance. How is Bessie ... apart from ...?"

Mrs Moore thought briefly before she replied, "She is more resilient than we once dared hope, my dear. Seeing you will do her a power of good." She watched Jane all the way upstairs.

Jane knocked hesitantly at Bessie's door. There was no reply. Mrs Moore gave her an encouraging nod. She knocked louder and this time Bessie cried out a froggy, "Come in!"

The moment the door upstairs closed, Banks stepped from the doorway to the servants' hall and cleared her throat. Mrs Moore peered at her and said, "Yes?"

The maid came forward into the light. She put a finger to her lips and pointed upstairs. "May I have a word with you, ma'am?" she asked.

Mrs Moore glanced up the stairs and then at Banks, who nodded in confirmation of the unspoken question. She pushed open the morning-room door. "In here, then."

There was a good glowing fire in the hearth and the pleasing smell of well-trimmed lamps filled the air. "Sit down." She pointed to a chair beside the fire.

"Oh, I don't hardly like ..." Banks began.

"What you have to tell me obviously isn't going to be easy, so you might as well be as comfortable as possible."

Banks sat. Mrs Moore seated herself opposite and, reaching her hands toward the fire, said, "You wish to tell me something about Miss Hervey? I don't know how long she'll be up there."

The maid looked at her, pretending to gather her thoughts, though she knew well enough what she wished to say; it was just that she needed a moment or two to adjust to this formidable woman. "I don't hardly know where to begin."

Mrs Moore smiled. "The beginning is usually recommended."

Banks chuckled. "I suppose the beginning was the evening she and her father arrived at Penzance station. She had no maid with her, and her father – I don't know what he was thinking of – but he sent her to wait at the top of the platform while he fussed over their bags. Well, she went out to have a look at the sunset and the harbour and ... all that."

"Yes, I know the scene." Mrs Moore spoke with a certain emphasis.

"Well, as it happened, there was only one lady of the town there at that moment, a Miss Esther Wilkinson, and she ..."

Mrs Moore's head jerked up in surprise. "Who did you say?"

Banks repeated the name.

"Good heavens!" exclaimed Mrs Moore. "A tallish woman in her early twenties? Mid-brown hair? Handsome, with rather striking features? Always very neat?"

Banks confirmed each detail with a nod. "I didn't know you knew her, ma'am."

"I met her a time or two at around the time her parents died. You know who they were, I suppose?"

Banks shook her head.

"He was freeholder of the Crown Hotel in Redruth. You've got cousins down Scorrier, haven't you?"

"My mother has, yes."

"Well one of them – she was called Margaret, too – Margaret Vean – she was housekeeper there. She'd tell you all about Esther Wilkinson. A very headstrong, independent young miss."

A sudden memory struck Banks. "Were they the man and wife who died in their own cellar?"

Mrs Moore nodded. "It was terrible. I wanted to buy him out. That's how I came to know them. There wasn't a penny left when all the debts were paid. But I thought the daughter went as governess to General de Buisson's children, up in Wadebridge." She stared into the fire. "I wonder if it is the same woman. Anyway, I'm sorry to have interrupted. Do go on. This Miss Wilkinson was there, plying her trade. I suppose she took Miss Hervey for a new recruit?"

Banks shrugged. "I don't know what conversation they may have had, ma'am, but knowing Miss Jane it was all to cross purposes. She hasn't the first notion about that sort of thing. She's as innocent as a babe."

"Ignorant," murmured the other.

"So you can imagine the conclusion she leaps to when her father comes out, sees them chatting like two friends, and starts shouting and cursing at Miss W for daring to talk to his daughter. She thinks the woman is somehow mixed up in their family affairs – part of it, you might say."

164

Mrs Moore smiled at the thought. "Well, no great harm done, surely?"

"Not if that was the end of it, ma'am. But then back in the fall – October, I believe it was – we were in Penzance looking at bonnets and things in Mrs Brown's little shop and who should be in there too but Miss Wilkinson. She's standing down the back in the dark so Miss Jane doesn't recognize her straight off. But when she hands her card to Mrs Brown and she reads out 'Miss Jane Hervey' – well, Miss W can't get out of the shop fast enough! Miss Jane goes to the door after her, but she's already across the street – and talking to ..." Her eyes raked the ceiling. "Well, I promise you – I nearly died!"

Mrs Moore frowned. "Not Mr Hervey?"

Banks nodded.

"Good heavens!"

The maid, thinking she detected disapproval, said, "Well – he was lonely and she's a pretty woman. He must have taken à liking to her looks that first evening."

Mrs Moore's eyes narrowed. "Whereupon, of course, Miss Jane's earlier suspicions that the woman is somehow mixed up in her family's affairs harden into a certainty. I see it. And now, with her father gone, she's beginning to show a certain curiosity? Is that it?"

Banks gave a single, ironic laugh. "If only it was, ma'am." She closed her eyes and shook her head. "God forgive me for telling you this, but I must. Poor old Mr Hervey, God rest him, died, as they say, with a certain smile on his lips, if you take my meaning?"

Mrs Moore suddenly gripped the arms of her chair. "With ...?"

"Yes. She lives directly over the way from Bassett's the barber's. Fortunately, I was in Penzance because it was my afternoon off, and I saw Bassett himself running to Tom Veryan. So I knew it was something amiss. Anyway, we had a bit of a conflab and we decided to get him over into the shop, into the chair."

"Yes, that's what I heard. They said he had a heart attack there."

"Don't ever breathe a word of this, ma'am. Because I've made out I didn't get there till it was all over. But the thing is, you see, Miss Jane was a bit headstrong the night before. It was over wanting to see Mrs Wender, in fact. She said she would and her father said no, and locked her in her room on bread and water. But *she* thinks it was her wickedness and self-will that killed her father."

"Oh, dear."

"And now, well, we've just come from Penzance because we went over there to leave some of the master's old clothes for the distressed gentlefolk. And Miss Jane suddenly took it into her head to go and thank old Bassett for all he did. And he behaved so shifty, like, she knew something wasn't up-and-down straight, as you might say. And *then* ..." The maid shook her head as if she could still hardly believe it. "Then, just as we were leaving, who should come down the street but ... give you one guess."

"No need! And I suppose Miss Jane asked her outright. What did she reply?"

"Well, she was very good. She never gave anything away. She never denied she knew Mr Hervey, she just said it was his business and hers and no one else's. And anyway it was all over and done with. Got very hoity-toity at the end, she did."

"She's nimble in her wits, then," Mrs Moore commented. "It must all have seemed a bit of a mystery to her."

"Well, I slipped back and told her. I said Miss Jane blames herself for her father's death. I couldn't say much because she had someone with her."

Mrs Moore frowned. "But why did you do that?"

"Because I know Miss Jane, ma'am. She won't let this be. She'll worry at it and worry at it like a puppy with a rag – till she's torn it to fletters. So I thought I'd give Miss W time to prepare herself. I only hope I did right."

The frown turned to a glance of shrewd approval. "You think quickly, Miss Banks. I'm sure you did the right thing. Is that what you wanted my opinion on?"

Banks shook her head. "I know she's unwed and all that, ma'am. But I don't believe she should stay in ignorance about ... I think she ought to learn what makes the world go round. And it's no good asking Mrs Lanyon – not that I could ever work around to it, anyway. But I was wondering ... do you believe I should do it? Which I'm willing enough to do, though I could lose my place for it. But I'd even sacrifice that."

"I'm sure there's no need for anything so heroic." Mrs Moore stared into the fire, twisting her wedding ring round and round her finger. "You say she wishes to punish herself?" she asked. "In what way?"

Banks glanced at the door, as if she now feared her mistress would suddenly appear. "The first night, the night he died, she stripped herself stark and tried to kneel all night on the bare floorboards. She's got some old book on medieval chivalry where it says knights of old used to purge themselves of sin before they got their sword like that."

The other chuckled. "Well, these moods don't last long in young girls. It'll pass."

"But now she says it's got to be lifelong. She says when she inherits her father's estate in five years ..."

"Oh? Is that the terms of his will?"

"Seemingly. Mr and Mrs Lanyon are her guardians till then. Anyway, she'll renounce it all and take up some line of work. She'll kill me if she ever hears I told you this."

"What line of work?" The chuckled deepened.

"Oh, she says we've got five years to plan it, and no one must know. She talks of a hotel or a domestic employment agency or a garment factory." Her eyes raked the ceiling. "She's not short of ideas. I'll say that."

Again Mrs Moore was dismissive. "With money behind her she might just manage. Otherwise, I'm afraid she's in for a shock. People have no idea. Hardly a day goes by at the brewery without my having to explain to some poor middle-class woman that the world is awash with legal copyists, and proof readers, envelope addressers, needlewomen ... and all the other hopeful things they think of after I tell them I can offer nothing. It is quite desperate for some of them, I know." She smiled wanly. "I expect Miss Wilkinson discovered as much – though I'd have found something for her if she'd approached me." She shook her head as if to dismiss these gloomy thoughts and went on more brightly, "Anyway, I'm sure that in five years' time Miss Hervey will have forgotten all about it."

But now Banks was adamant. "I think not, ma'am. The fact is, I believe it's what she really wants to do anyway, only she wouldn't dare. I believe she's giving herself this excuse."

"But how can you possibly know that?" Mrs Moore asked skeptically.

"Because you should just see her eyes all aglow when she talks about it. She swears she's all penitence and punishing herself and yet, shut your eyes and just listen to her voice, and it's like the way most girls would talk of their wedding day and their dresses for next month's ball and things like that." She glanced shrewdly at Mrs Moore. "And she talks about you as the luckiest of mortal women."

Mrs Moore shook her head at such folly. "So what were you hoping I'd do?" she asked. "Talk her out of it?"

Banks shook her head. "Just talk to her ma'am. Tell me if I'm all of a dalver and worrying for nothing."

The woman looked over her shoulder at the clock. "There'll never be a better chance," she murmured. "My husband is spending the night at the clinic in Redruth, and the young lady herself has called on an altogether different matter. Will she stay to supper, d'you think?"

*　　　*　　　*

Despite her cold, little Bessie actually looked healthier than Jane had ever seen her. "Well," she told her jovially, "you found a shilling and lost sixpence. That's better than the other way about. How d'you feel, really?"

Bessie stretched out beneath the covers and wriggled herself slightly more upright. "It's such bliss to be away from Skyburriowe." She sniffed glutinously.

"It must be." Jane pecked her swiftly near her ear. "But let's not talk about that. Dr and Mrs Moore are nice people?"

"Absolute saints. They say I'm not to worry about anything and I can stay as long as I like ..." Suddenly she froze and stared at Jane in horror. "I forgot," she murmured. "I forgot. Your bereavement! I'm so sorry."

"But you wrote, darling. Such a lovely letter. It's I who am remiss. I should have thanked you at once."

"No, I should have spoken. I should have spoken ..."

"Oh, well," Jane said sarcastically, "if you wish to wallow in an orgy of self-blame when you're not at fault at all ..." She grew uncomfortable with the thought and abandoned it. "Anyway, let's talk about the future. When you're up and about again, which won't be long, I thought I could come and collect you and we could go out on such jolly drives. I don't know the country at all, and you can tell me everything you know about all the villages and farms as we pass."

For a while they spoke about all the places they could go to and how different they were – the wild, treeless moors around Carnmenellis, between Helston and Redruth; the dark, thickly wooded valleys around all the creeks of the Helford River; the prehistoric landscapes of Land's End; the soaring, majestic cliffs of the Atlantic coast; the rich, fertile valleys that ran out like splayed fingers from the estuary of the Fal – all so different and each within an easy carriage drive of Breage.

167

And when these plans came to a happy exhaustion they sat in smiling silence, casting about for some other topic. "Tell me about the ball," Bessie said. "Who else was there? And who did you dance with? I'll bet simply everybody asked you!"

"Haven't your sisters told you?" Jane asked.

"They haven't been to see me." She picked at a knot in the counterpane. "I wish you'd tell my mother I only stuck it as long as I did for my sisters' sakes – and her. I don't know how I can make her understand." A slow tear rolled down her cheek.

"Oh, dear." Jane snatched out her handkerchief and dabbed it. "I didn't wish to distress you, darling. I had no idea they haven't visited you. Tell me. What d'you wish them to understand? Tell me and I'll make sure they get to hear of it, I promise."

Bessie stared at her and simply shook her head.

Jane gritted her teeth. "I didn't sleep that night – the night of the ball – worrying about you. I defied my father and fell out with the Lanyons because I wanted to come here and sit at your bedside. And now I shan't sleep again tonight, either."

The words clearly tore poor Bessie in two. Half of her longed to tell someone; the other half of her remembered that Jane had not yet crossed that great divide in a woman's life and was Not To Be Told.

"All for nothing," Jane added.

These almost meaningless words did more to tilt the balance in Bessie's divided mind than any direct appeal or threat might have achieved. "You promise you won't tell anyone I told you?" she whispered, glancing fearfully at the door.

"Of course I won't. I'll tell you a secret, too, if you like. But you go first." She leaned nearer her would-be confidante.

"Well, Dr Moore says I'm not really married and we'll be able to get it annulled. So I'll go back to being Miss Elizabeth Delamere again."

"Is that your name? Well, of course it must be. I've only ever heard anyone call you Bessie."

The girl pulled a face. "I don't like it."

"What would you rather?"

"I always wanted to be called Liz, but my mother said it was common."

Jane, who didn't think "Bessie" any less common than "Liz," said, "Well, I shall call you Liz from now on if that's what you prefer. Anyway, how can Dr Moore know you weren't really married? Was the vicar unfrocked, or something?"

"No." The murmur fell back to a whisper again. "It's because Wender never properly con ... something ..."

"Consecrated?"

"Something like that. He never properly consecrated me." Her face screwed up. "It's a word like that."

Jane giggled. "Not constipated?" She blushed as soon as she spoke.

"No," the girl replied with surprising vehemence. "He took care of that, all right. It was his way of not giving me a baby, you see." She closed her eyes and shook her head. "I shouldn't be telling you all this."

"It's all right." Jane's heart missed a beat, and then made up for it in double tides; she realized that, all unwittingly, she had strayed into the very centre of that awesome mystery which had obsessed her lately.

"You understand what I'm talking about?" Bessie – or Liz, as she must now think of her – would not look up. She barely spoke her words, delivering them instead in a kind of half-whispered intoning.

"Of course I do."

"You're lucky, Jane. No one told me a thing. Just after the wedding breakfast my mother said I wasn't to be surprised at anything Wender did when we were alone, and I should drink all I wanted that evening because it wouldn't harm me for once. So, of course, I thought *that* was what she was talking about. And I put up with it five or six times a day, all those months. And now it turns out I needn't have because I wasn't really ... consummated! That's the word! He didn't consummate me – and Dr Moore can prove it." She turned her eyes to Jane at last. "Just see if there's someone at the door, will you?"

"I'm sure there isn't." But Jane checked nonetheless.

When she came back, Liz continued, "The thing is, you see, what Wender did with me was a criminal offence. Not even a *husband* can make his wife do that. So it was criminal, you see."

"But you didn't know it," Jane protested. "I'm sure a thing can't be criminal unless you know it to be so." A further thought struck her and she brightened. "But if *he* knew it ..."

"Yes, that's the point. He did know it. And Dr Moore and Mr Scawen have threatened him that if he opposes the annulling or whatever they call it ..."

"Annulment."

"Yes. If he tries to stop it, they'll expose him in court and he'll be ruined. They also made him sign a promise never to marry again, because they think that's how his other wives died, though it could never be proved. So" – she gave a charmingly girlish smile – "some good came out of it after all."

*　　　*　　　*

Banks was back in the servant's hall by the time Jane returned downstairs. Mrs Moore called out, "Come in and warm yourself before you set off, Miss Hervey."

Jane closed the door behind her. "Are we likely to be disturbed," she replied.

"No." Mrs Moore looked at her askance.

"Good." Jane stood with her back to the fire and hitched up her skirts behind. "I love the feeling of this," she murmured. "Don't you?"

"I haven't done that for years." She checked that the curtains were well drawn and then followed suit. "Not since the nursery."

"Oh," Jane said. "That puts me in my place."

Mrs Moore laughed. "You're quite right, though. It is a rather delightful sensation. I'd forgotten. Well, what d'you think of our patient?"

"Better than I've ever seen her. I wondered if, when she's a little better, when she's up and about, I wondered if I might take her for a drive?"

"Well," Mrs Moore said hesitantly, "let's see what Mrs Lanyon says about that."

"Oh, you know about them, do you."

"News travels fast. She may have ideas of her own on the subject."

169

There was a noise out in the passage; Jane dropped her skirts at once. "Is that the doctor?" she asked.

"No. He's spending the night in Redruth. He often does on a Wednesday. My grass-widow day, I call it." After a pause, while Jane hitched up her dress again, she went on, "I don't suppose you'd care to take a bite of supper with me, my dear? We needn't dress for it. Your maid could go home and tell them not to prepare anything and then come back for you at around ... ten, shall we say?"

Jane, who wished for nothing more in all the world, made a few feebly dubious noises for politeness' sake.

Mrs Moore put in the coup de grace. "You remember you asked me a question – and I begged time to consider my answer? I think I may give it you now."

21 JANE RUBBED HER hands gleefully as she entered the dining room. "I think I have never in my life sat down to an evening meal without first dressing," she said. "Since leaving the nursery, I mean."

"That puts *me* in my place!" Mrs Moore smiled. "Does it feel terribly wicked?"

"No." The discovery surprised Jane. "It happened once when some slates blew off the roof and the rain poured in and the whole house was in turmoil. And my father, with the utmost reluctance, said we might dine without dressing."

"Otherwise you always dressed?"

"Always. He was punctilious in such matters."

They seated themselves without ceremony. "D'you think you will miss it?" her hostess asked. "I'm sorry if that seems unfeeling, I meant ..."

"I wonder?" Jane replied. "I'll miss it in connection with *him*, of course. But will I miss it in my own life? In a way, that's the question I asked you in Helston the other night, isn't it. I don't seem to have had 'my own life' until now. First I had my mother's life in Paris, or the bits of it I was punished for trying to glimpse through banister railings and upstairs windows. Then the utterly different life in my father's household in Leeds."

"Tell me about Paris. What d'you remember of it? I can't imagine two places more different than Paris and Leeds."

And so the first half of the meal, which was a beefsteak and kidney pudding, passed in sharing their memories of childhood. Mrs Moore described her early years near Hayle, over on the north coast, and how, when her parents had both died, she was taken in by her aunt and uncle who then owned Lanfear House. It had been a very grudging adoption. Her aunt had made it clear she could expect no dowry and so would not marry particularly well – if at all.

She paused in her narrative, seemingly lost in a reverie.

"And yet ..." Jane prompted, waving a hand vaguely at their surroundings.

Mrs Moore smiled. "What have you heard about me?"

"Oh, nothing ... really." Jane was caught on the hop.

"Nothing?"

She gathered her wits. "Well ... what I have heard suggests that you would not be particularly concerned at what people said about you."

The woman laughed. "Well spoken! You, too, are a nimble thinker, I see."

"Too?"

Mrs Moore kicked herself mentally. "I mean like me. I hope I don't sound boastful, but it's the one quality you need above all others if you wish to run against the herd." The phrase troubled her. "And yet," she went on, "that is something I never set out to do – run against the herd. I always thought of myself as the very soul of conformity and moderation. In a way I still do. D'you find that strange?"

Jane shook her head. "I can't imagine how it was possible to go from being a poor orphan to owning the biggest brewery in Cornwall. How d'you decide to do something like that?"

"I didn't, of course." Mrs Moore looked her guest up and down, as if wondering how much to tell.

"There was never a moment when you said to yourself: That's what I'm going to be in life?"

She shook her head. "I don't think people set about building their lives in that elementary sort of way."

"Argus Nicholl does. He told me he's going to be a bishop. He even offered me a part in his Grand Design."

"Lucky you! The awful thing about wanting something like that so desperately when you're young is that you'll probably get it. And then what d'you do?" She dismissed Mr Nicholl with a waft of her hand. "Actually, there was one moment when I determined I would brew and sell beer, though I meant it in the way of a little cottage industry, you understand – to keep body and soul together. Funnily enough, it was, on the face of it, the worst day of my life." A faraway look came into her eyes. "It was a Sunday in November about ten years ago. I was then a housekeeper at the Golden Ram ..."

"Yes?" Jane prompted again when the silence became almost unbearable.

Mrs Moore laid down her knife and fork. She gripped her right hand in her left and squeezed until all her knuckles showed white. "D'you want the full truth of it, Jane?" she asked.

Jane realized they had suddenly passed beyond the bounds of conventional reminiscence – the minor sort of bridge-building people indulge in when they find they like each other and wish to move toward a deeper friendship. "Yes," she said.

Mrs Moore nodded with satisfaction. "On that particular day, which began like any other, I was denounced from the pulpit as a public scandal. I'm sure kind neighbours have told you the tale, with all the usual embroideries. It is true that I was carrying a baby, although I was not married – little Hannah, in fact. You met her."

Jane nodded.

"Well, I wasn't the first young girl in that unfortunate condition but very few others were denounced like that. You may also have heard – and this is quite untrue – that I was in some sort of partnership with a man called Charley Vose in running a disorderly house in Goldsithney. You understand what I mean by that?"

171

"Yes. More or less." Jane found that half of her wanted to halt this flow of revelation; it was too intense for the shallow intimacy that so far existed between them. The rest of her, however, simply hung on every word.

"The truth is I barely tolerated its existence. I was housekeeper at the Golden Ram, which was then leased by Charley Vose. The *maison tolérée,* as one might call it, was certainly more than tolerated by the gentry of West Cornwall, including almost every magistrate there was. Anyway, this infamous 'house' was at the far end of the garden. It was, in fact, a row of cottages. I pulled them down later, after I bought the freehold of the inn."

"Now *there* was a change in fortune!"

"Yes. My real sin – in the eyes of all those fine, upstanding gentlemen – was that I did *not* tolerate the *maison tolérée.* I would not allow the girls who worked there to come within half a mile of the inn, and I would not allow even the most casual or oblique reference to it beneath my roof. It annoyed them. Half a furlong away there were a dozen girls who'd laugh at their coarse witticisms and 'spread the gentlemen's relish,' as they liked to put it, yet I wouldn't allow the smallest whisper of it at the inn. But I stuck to my guns and they just had to conform." Her lips curled in a sneer. "The more worldly-wise realized that my puritan reputation was their best protection. If rumours ever reached their wives about their true purpose in visiting the Golden Ram, those women would tell themselves that Johanna Rosewarne could not possibly be mixed up in such an affair."

She smiled at the gullibility of women, the petty duplicity of men. "Of course, when it became obvious that *Miss* Rosewarne was about to become a mother, the floodgates of contumely were opened. And that's why I was denounced from the pulpit. I had pricked their hypocrisy and it hurt." She frowned. "What was I saying?"

"Your decision to brew beer."

"Ah yes. It was that same day. I arrived back from church to find my belongings had all been put out in the rain. I never saw such rain, before or since. The skies just teemed down all day. I came into Helston and I tried to see ... a very dear friend, Lady Nina Brookes of Liston Court. But I ... well, I wasn't able to. She was dying, though I didn't know it. And for some strange reason, which I've never been able to explain, I set off in that absolute downpour – walking – and eventually crawling on hands and knees – making for the home of another friend, Hamill Oliver ..."

"I danced with him at the ball," Jane said. "I think."

"You'd not forget it."

"He's very keen on all things Cornish?"

Mrs Moore grinned. "You danced with Hamill Oliver. But why I was making for his cottage in that downpour I cannot say. I fell unconscious somewhere near his gate. Dr Moore, who was out scouring the countryside for me, happened to find me there, carried me to the cottage, and delivered me of little Hannah."

"Goodness!" Jane's eyes glowed with excitement borrowed from the older woman's telling. "Nothing so thrilling will ever happen to me, I'm sure."

Mrs Moore checked herself and laughed. "I didn't mean to go into all that. What I meant to say was that somewhere on that nightmare journey I resolved to myself that I would brew beer, in an old outhouse somewhere, and go around selling it door to door. When I woke up, after it was all over, and I gave little Hannah her first feed, I just lay there telling her all about this wonderful decision I'd reached."

"But the courage it must have taken," Jane said.

"Yes! That's another rule in life: The more stupid you are, the more courage you need. Goodness, I am sounding philosophical."

"Well, it also shows that if one is determined to do something, one can do it."

"At least you'll never face such a choice, my dear." She beamed at Jane. "Yours is the primrose path of virtue, marriage, and affluence."

"Yes." Jane picked up her fork, moved a bit of food, and laid it down again.

"Well, I declare, I never heard a girl so positive!"

"About Dr Moore," Jane began hesitantly.

"Yes?"

"Did he try to dissuade you? Did you even tell him?"

"I had to tell him. I wanted to rent the gardener's cottage here from him. He had bought Lanfear from my uncle by then – I should have explained that. I wanted to rent the cottage and use the old stables as my brew-house."

"And did he encourage you?"

"Not directly. I don't think he relished the idea very much. But like everyone else he thought it a bit of a nine-day-wonder, a joke that would soon pall." She glanced all around and then leaned forward, as if about to yield up a dark secret. "You can get away with quite a lot if people think it's just a bit of a joke, you know."

"I see," Jane said thoughtfully.

The other straightened again and said, in an altogether brisker tone, "Well, does my little bout of autobiography answer your original question?"

"Certainly," Jane assured her.

"More to the point, does it raise any fresh ones?" She put her head on one side and waited.

Jane bit her lip. "I must think."

Mrs Moore gave her a moment or two, saw the courage failing her, and added, "By the way, that man I mentioned, Charley Vose, he was later convicted of owning the house I mentioned, the *maison*-no-longer-*tolérée*. He served six years in the penal colony in Australia. But he's back here now and managing the Golden Ram for me. The ups and downs of fortune, eh?"

Jane took her courage in both hands. "Those girls," she said, "the ones you mentioned, who ..."

"Yes? I knew one or two of them. You'd be surprised. Some of them were of extremely good class, as well spoken as you or I."

"What did they ... I mean what *exactly* did they ..."

"Do?"

"Yes."

"Once the house was closed down, you mean? Most of them went to work in other houses. There are two or three in every town, you know. I see you're surprised. I remember how unbelievable I found it, but it's true – sad to relate. A few of the girls 'went freelance,' as they say. I used to see them trawling for custom outside Penzance Station, by the quays." She smiled. "I'm sure you know that's the place for

173

respectable ladies to avoid – or traverse as swiftly as possible, since one can't literally avoid it. But the men who go there seeking those women won't accost you if you're walking away to some purpose."

Jane swallowed heavily.

Mrs Moore sighed. "I know this is hardly the most delicate subject to be discussing with a refined young lady. But, on the other hand, you must know of these things, even though you must then pretend not to. But I'm sure someone has warned you?"

Jane, still somewhat dazed, shook her head.

"It was probably difficult for your father. But not Mrs Tresidder?"

Another shake of the head.

"Nor your lady's maid – what's her name – Banks? Of course, she wasn't trained up as a true lady's maid."

"She's the best maid I ever had," Jane said stoutly.

"Of course, of course. She's full of other good qualities. But people in general down here are fairly prudish. She might not like to mention such things, even in the way of duty. I'm sure a good French maid would have spotted it at once and warned you off. Once you know what to look for, it's unmistakable." She smiled affably.

"I had a good French maid once," Jane said.

The door opened. "And here's a good Cornish maid!" Mrs Moore said heartily. "Mary Blight of Carleen. What's for pudding, Mary?"

"Spotted dick, please ma'am."

"The doctor's favourite," she commented with relish. "That'll teach him to desert his proper hearth. Wheel it in!"

Over pudding Mrs Moore canvassed her opinion of the Delamere girls. "I'm told that the oldest one ... Rose?"

"Rosa."

"Ah, the wild rose! Then she's well named, or so I hear?"

"In what way?"

"Someone saw her winding an imaginary handle in the back of her dancing partner at the ball. That's not the way to get a husband, is it."

Jane shrugged. "I suppose not."

Mrs Moore eyed her cautiously and said, "Hmmm. And what of the youngest? I try asking Bessie these things but she's too loyal to say much. The youngest is a bit of a shrinking violet, by all accounts."

Jane stared at her pudding. "I must take her that doll," she said.

"I beg your pardon?"

"Sorry." She smiled wanly and explained what had happened. "I'll give it to her at Christmas. I'm sure that once Mrs Lanyon understands, she'll agree."

"And if she doesn't?"

Jane's eyes levelled in hers. "I think I must still give it her." Then, aware that the situation was acquiring an unwelcome edge of drama, she added, "I'd have done it earlier but there's been so much else happening."

The general air of intimacy that had now grown up between them encouraged Jane to one final assault on her own ignorance. "Going back to what we were talking about earlier," she began.

"Yes?"

Looking into those kindly eyes Jane suddenly realized she could ask anything of this woman and she would receive a frank reply; she had never felt that before about any other person in her life. "About ... outside Penzance station and so on."

"Yes?"

"The men who go there *seeking* those women, as you said, what do they actually ... I mean, *why?*"

The woman laid down her spoon and wiped her lips in the napkin. "It is a mystery I have never really fathomed, Jane. You don't mind if I am utterly frank?"

"Please!"

"Some, of course, are widowers who have only the happiest memories of their wives and of the bliss they found in their ... in the union of their bodies. And since, in the dark, anyway, and in that most basic of all human activities, since one woman's body is very like another's, I suppose they can close their eyes and imagine things as they were. But for the rest – the men who are supposedly happily married, with wives they claim to adore waiting for them at home – why they go out and pay anything from five shillings to ten guineas for a mercenary affection and the most fleeting of pleasures ... as I say, I cannot fathom it. The women themselves are the least able to explain it. I suppose it would not be in their interest to do so. Their contempt for the men is great enough as it is."

She smiled at her own intensity and took a final mouthful of pudding. "Some more?" she offered.

"No thanks." Jane was still wrapped up in her thoughts.

"No, you're right. Save it for the lord and master. That should be every wife's motto, before we grow too smug and complacent about our own virtuous state. The men who go lusting after those women – what does it tell us about their wives, eh? Perhaps they are the ones who are really to blame. Remember that when you marry, Jane – keep a welcoming bed and an upright smile for your husband and he won't stray down Penzance quays."

Jane nodded fervently enough but Mrs Moore was still left wondering how much she had truly comprehended. She patted her arm affectionately. "You did ask me to be frank," she reminded her.

They took an apple each, the last of the season's pippins, and went back to sit by the fire. "Eat them like we used when we were children," Mrs Moore said, taking a small bite, skin and all.

Try as she might, Jane could not avoid glancing about her before she did that most unladylike thing. But it did taste scrumptious, she had to allow. "D'you ever get the feeling," she murmured as she gazed into the glowing hearth, "when you look back on your life ... I mean, even when you look back on ... only yesterday ... d'you ever feel how ... *simple* you must have been? And yet it didn't seem like it at the time."

Mrs Moore closed her eyes and breathed a deep sigh of relief. "I remember thinking that," she confessed. Then she laughed. "As if it were only yesterday."

20 IN THE SECOND week of that December a violent storm ran a three-master, the *Good Hope*, ashore at Praa. She had, however, remained intact and there was a prospect of refloating her on the afternoon tide, especially if the wind backed toward the southeast. Banks told Jane it would be "some burr old spectacle," which she ought not to miss, so, since the rain had passed over, she decided to take the carriage down to Rinsey Head and watch the excitement from a respectable distance. If the day remained dry, they might walk the mile or so along the clifftop to Megaliggar, where she and the Pellew sisters had gone swimming that morning.

They arrived at the headland with half an hour to spare before the very peak of the tide. The grandeur of the scene surpassed anything Jane's imagination had led her to expect. The dense pall of storm clouds had given way to chunks of towering cumulus, upon which the low, wintry sun struck almost horizontally, throwing every detail into sharp relief; they seemed like mountains torn from some fairytale kingdom and liberated to wander overhead. As part of the magic, the temperature had risen several degrees since morning, so that for December it was almost balmy. But the wind remained turbulent and unruly, goading anyone who had no direct hand in the business to seek the lee of the nearest rock, bush, carriage, or friend. Jane was almost bowled over the moment she stepped from the shelter of the brougham, and had it not been for the stout stone hedgerow, the vehicle itself might well have been toppled. Even with that protection, the violence of the motion unnerved the horses, so she told Veryan to go and shelter behind a little chapel they had passed a half-mile back.

She herself chose a position behind the tall stone pillar of the gatepost at the very end of the lane, and there she stood and marvelled at the power of the gale; Banks settled in behind her. The hedge was low enough at that point to allow them to see the whole of Praa Sands, whose nearer end was almost a mile to their west. The *Good Hope* lay half way along the beach and a cable's length offshore. On the flood tide she was so nearly upright you would think her at anchor; only the slight but unvarying tilt of her masts gave the game away. She had grounded prow-first on a mighty sou'westerly and would have to be sailed off backward; and even then the wind would be scant on her starboard beam. The sails were already set for the manoeuvre; on top of which, three of the largest fishing boats from Porthleven had lines aboard and were preparing to assist her at the most critical moment.

The strand was packed with onlookers, a goodly few no doubt hoping for the failure of the exercise – to be followed, in hallowed tradition, by a plundering spree.

"I've seen men too drunk to stand," Banks said, "up to the armpits in water, which was their only means of keeping upright. And holding kegs of brandy above them, pouring it down their gullets. And nine-tenths of it going to waste. And the excise men standing by powerless. I'll lay there's a lot of tongues licking a lot of lips this very minute, down there in that crowd of emmets."

"How heartless," Jane exclaimed.

The maid replied it had always been the way of things and at least they no longer stripped the poor seamen naked, which had continued into her grandfather's time.

Nothing seemed to be happening – which, if Jane had thought about it, was just what she should have expected. The sails were set, the lines strained; the rest was a matter of wind and tide; the men themselves could do little more than stand ready to slacken off if the sheets looked like parting – and pray. She passed Banks the binoculars and turned to gaze at the vaster natural drama that was going on all around the bay. She had seen some of it from her bedroom window earlier that morning, but it was nothing compared to this majestic panorama of nature's overwhelming turbulence.

Immediately before them stretched a furlong or so of wild scrub, part of it despoiled by a tin mine whose dirty engine house and belching chimney nestled in a clifftop hollow, a few hundred yards to the east. A half-mile beyond it she could just see the foot of the towering cliffs at Trewarvas Head, where a larger mine spilled an even grubbier trail across the landscape. There she could see the real power of the elements, where huge seas reared to dash themselves at the foot of the cliff; they reared but never fell, for the restless hand of the storm swept them up and carried them in vast sheets of trembling water right over the clifftop, where at last they shattered into a myriad fragments and fell like driving rain.

Farther along the shore, in the sandy coves beyond Porthleven, the surf broke in mighty turmoil and you could almost believe that the sea was boiling there. Loe Bar, a colossal sandbank a mile long, closing off what had, many centuries ago, been a navigable sea-creek all the way up to Helston, was under constant assault. Each successive wave hurled itself at the shingle while its predecessor was still retreating headlong down those towering banks. They and their fellows all around the bay set up a constant roaring that vied with the wind to deafen the rash souls who had ventured forth to witness what would no doubt be one of the memorable sights of 1860 - no matter how things turned out.

"She's afloat!" Banks cried excitedly. "Now who's going to win?" She passed the binoculars back to her mistress, but Jane declined them; they were so high-powered it was impossible to keep the scene steady in this blast.

"Come here, where you can lean against the gatepost," she said, changing places with her.

It was strange, she thought as she turned her gaze back upon the *Good Hope,* how you could tell the difference between a ship listing under the wind and the same vessel leaning over on a sand shoal. She was definitely alive now. You could see her stern coming about to windward as the fishing boats began to haul her off. Unfortunately, the action put the gale even more onto her beam and thus reduced the effectiveness of her own sails, without which she had no hope of getting offshore.

"She's gone back," Banks cried gleefully. "They've gone and hauled her into the wind and she's been driven aground again. They'll never get her off at that angle."

The crew were letting free as fast as they could, for every blast of wind now served only to drive them harder into the sand. She was all sheets to the wind on two of her masts already.

"Now those fishermen'll have to come downwind of her and pull her back broadside-on, like she was before." The maid jumped up and down in her excitement. "Another twenty minutes and they'll lose this tide."

Jane watched her in amazement. "You actually want them to fail," she accused. "I'm astonished at you."

177

Banks glanced at her briefly before she returned her gaze to the impending debacle. "'Tis a bit of excitement, miss. I shouldn't mind so much if they succeed at the last minute. Oh my gidge!"

The two women held their breath and stood on tiptoe, every sinew stretched to its limit. A mighty wave, vast even by the standards of this storm, had washed right over the grounded vessel. For a moment it seemed that she must capsize entirely, but then, as the white foam drained from her decks, she shuddered upright again – and then a great cheer went up, audible even at this distance and despite the crosswind; for that monstrous wall of water had, seemingly, lifted her across the shoal and put her into one of the numerous shifting channels, different with every tide, that abound along that stretch of shore. Moreover, she was once again aligned toward the sou'west, and with the wind scant to starboard.

The master, doubtless realizing how little time was left, took the bold decision to cut her free of the three fishermen – which almost leaped out of the water as the boatswain's axe severed their lines. The loose sails were quickly gathered in and set once more, but for a long while nothing seemed to happen; yet the very fact that the ship was not drifting helplessly downwind was the best evidence that something, indeed, was afoot. Banks, aided by the glasses, was the first to confirm it, for she could see the mastheads slipping past small landmarks in the hedges and fields beyond. "Oh," she said, letting out her pent-up breath, "I'd swear a babby could crawl faster."

Soon even Jane's unaided eye could mark her progress. "She must have a good clean keel," she commented, hoping to impress her companion with a nautical tidbit she'd picked up on the cross-Channel ferry a few years ago.

"She's still not going to clear Hoe Point," the maid said.

The master must have been of the same opinion, for no sooner had he reached the safety of the water beyond the shoals than he dropped anchor and, swinging round to face the gale, settled to ride out whatever remained of it.

The black swarm of emmets on the sands below began to disperse. On any other day they'd have stood around in knots and slandered absent friends for half an hour or so - passing on all the news that somehow slipped between the lines of the local papers; but today the wind defeated them - which was a measure of its strength rather than of the frailty of the Cornishman's liking for gossip.

"Well?" Jane asked. "Would we be mad to walk back along the cliffs?"

Banks grinned. "I'm so buffeted by it now, I don't hardly seem to notice it. Shall I go up and tell Veryan he may go home?"

But the man himself saved them the trouble, for he had left the horses in charge of a boy and, a penny the poorer, had come back to watch the fun for himself. At that moment he was standing in a gateway about twenty paces up the lane.

"Wasn't that exciting!" Jane said as they drew near him.

The man agreed, though he had seen some spectacular wrecks in his day and privately thought that this afternoon's proceedings had been as exciting as watching flowers open.

She told him of their plans, whereupon he said he'd come with them, sending one of the grooms back later to collect the carriage. He returned to Rinsey, to stable the horses properly, and then cut across the fields to catch up with them just before Trewarvas Head.

When the two women had gone some way from the gate, a dog cart came lurching down the lane. "Well, look who that is, then," Banks said.

Jane turned and saw three figures silhouetted against the sky. "Mrs Delamere?" she asked the maid.

"And her daughter Susie – and who might that be in the seat behind them?"

"It looks remarkably like Mr Argus Nicholl of Antron. What can this mean? we ask ourselves." They glanced at each other and laughed.

But the laughter died when Nicholl leaped from the car and came bounding toward them over the springy turf. "Well, I'll go to Hellvelyan," Banks said.

"Good afternoon ..." he began when he was still several bounds away. The gale snatched off his hat for him and it was several moments before he completed his greeting, this time with its brim clutched tight between his fingers. "... ladies! What a storm, eh?"

"How d'you do, Mr Nicholl. I'm afraid you've missed what little excitement there was. She's afloat and at anchor now."

"Ah." He seemed at a sudden loss for words.

Jane said, "Convey my good wishes to Mrs Delamere and Miss Susie. I'm afraid we must press on."

"Yes," he replied uncertainly, making no move to go.

"It was kind of you to come so far out of your way to greet us," she added. "Perhaps you thought we were in difficulties? But, as you see, we are trimmed and braced for all weathers."

Banks, ever the blunt one, turned to resume their interrupted walk.

"You are never out of my thoughts," he said – and then spun on his heels and ran before the wind.

When she felt sure he was was out of earshot, Jane laughed. "What on earth was that all about?"

"We do call it 'simmering two pots on the one hob'," Banks remarked.

Walking crabwise for a pace or two, Jane watched him turn into a silhouette once more as he rejoined the other two. "I hope something comes of that," she said. "They are admirably suited."

"The easiest work in the world – matching others."

They set off once more into the teeth of the gale. By the time they reached Trewarvas Head, they were quite sure that their walk was insane – and they were therefore enjoying it even more than they had the refloating of the ship. More than once they were knocked to the ground by a gust so powerful they could not believe it was the mere movement of air. They lay in the dense, sedgy grass and laughed as much as any two women could with the breath knocked out of them. Fortunately, the ground sloped upward from the cliff edge, in places as steep as forty-five degrees, so they had little distance to fall; and the path, even at its nearest, ran some twenty paces from that same edge, so they were merely flirting with danger rather than actively courting it. Nonetheless, it was more exciting than anything else they had done in many a long day.

When they reached Trewarvas and that part of the headland where the wind lifted the waters right up over the point, they ran screaming through the salty showers to reach the dryer ground at the very edge of the mine workings. Until the gale blew itself out, all work at the surface – *grass* work, as they call it – was suspended; down in the sumps the day's haul of ore was being stockpiled against a quieter morrow, but here on the surface a strangely unpeopled calm prevailed amidst the storm's rages. The tables where the bal maidens usually stood and picked the ore from the useless *gozan* were empty; the little bogeys that carried the ore to the stamps and the gozan to the halvans were motionless; the buddles and vanning frames, whose racket was usually loud enough to carry for miles, were uncannily silent. Only the smoke from the chimneys and the slow, unremitting rise and fall of the beam engines revealed that this was, indeed, a living mine. The nearer engine house was a hundred yards down the cliff at their feet, precariously balanced (as it seemed) on a ledge; they could almost peer directly down its chimney and watch the puffs of smoke swirl and dart up the steep cliffhead like black sprites in a madcap game of tag.

An engineer came out of the building wiping his hands with a bundle of cotton waste. He saw them and tried to shout something but the wind tore off his words and whipped them away. He gave up and, with a friendly wave, went back indoors.

Jane's eyes wandered the path they still had to tread; her heart fell when she realized they had covered barely a third of the distance to Megaliggar - or, even more dispiriting, less than a quarter of the entire way home. She wondered how far it was by road from Rinsey to Trewarvas and whether to send Veryan back to bring the carriage down here; but then the cloud that had darkened them for the past ten minutes passed on and the entire stretch of headland gleamed in its brilliance. Then her spirit rose once more to the challenge.

But she grew sombre again when, with the mines behind them, they arrived at the spot where her father had stood on that day when she first met ... no, she wasn't even going to think about him – the day she went swimming with the Pellews.

Since her conversation with Mrs Moore the previous week her mind had veered away from the entire subject of her father, her feelings of guilt at his death, her innocence of life in all other respects. It was not that she understood everything clearly now; far from it. Indeed, in some ways, her ignorance was more profound than ever - but at least its focus was sharper. She knew *whereof* she remained in doubt, whereas before she had known only that there existed a great, formless Question she could not even articulate.

One phrase of Mrs Moore's repeated itself again and again in Jane's mind, whether she willed it or not: "the joyful union of their bodies." Curiously enough it made no pictures in her mind; the means of that union were beyond her imagining. But the *idea* of it held an astonishing sway over her imagination.

After her mother died she had heard someone reciting a Shakespeare sonnet in which the poet spoke of "friends hid in Death's dateless night," and those six words had so exactly captured all her feelings about the mystery of death during those grim weeks that they had assumed an almost magical power in her mind. Now something similar was happening with Mrs Moore's much more prosaic formula - six more words that took on a potency their literal meaning could not explain.

She thought of her father and mother, and this mysteriously "joyful union" – and it somehow completed the happy picture of them which her mind had always treasured. But then there was a more shadowy image – of her father and Miss Wilkinson – and her mind shied away from that.

She took the binoculars from Banks and scanned the little cove where she had swum with Angelica and Jemima. She was delicately testing those memories when her attention was suddenly caught by something that had not been there that day. "Goodness!" she cried, passing the glasses to Veryan. "I hope that doesn't mean something awful's happened."

"Lobsterman," the coachman replied. "I don't see no one there, not fast by her, anyroad." He passed the binoculars on to Banks.

She found the little craft at once. "That's some burr old mess," she commented, twiddling the focus knob. Then she drew a sudden breath and darted an anxious glance at Jane. "I reckon we'd best go see if she had anyone aboard."

"D'you recognize her?" Jane asked, alerted by something in her manner.

"Can't be sure," she replied, leading the way down the path to Trequean Zawn, the next small headland, from where the land fell to the marshy hollow that gave easy, if messy, access to the beach below.

With the spur of possible tragedy to hasten their feet, they made better progress over this remaining ground. Even so, they almost passed by the one poor soul who had survived the wreck, who was covered in rich black mud from head to foot. Somehow he had struggled up the winding path to the brow of the low cliff. The stream, which had been so sluggish on Jane's last visit, was now a lively torrent; yet he had fought his way through it – twice – where it dashed across the zigzag path. Now he lay collapsed and unconscious, but breathing, at the edge of the marsh, where he was lucky not to have drowned.

There was congealed blood about his head. Veryan stooped and turned him over. It was Daniel Jago.

Jane gave out a cry and fell to her knees at his side, oblivious of the marsh and the thick, black mud that half swallowed her.

23 THEY FASHIONED A ROUGH stretcher from an oar, a broken spar, and Daniel's own greatcoat, which they found abandoned half way down the cliff; between them they somehow got him up the steep slope to Trequean Farm, where they borrowed a trap and hastened on to Montpelier.

Dorothy Lanyon, who had not been there when they left, came running out in consternation when she saw the strange vehicle rolling up the drive. "My dear, what has happened? I was on the point of sending out Tom Collett to ..." Her voice tailed off as she saw that Jane was not sitting but kneeling, tending a wet and filthy bundle of a man who lay cushioned on straw in the body of the trap. "What on earth is that?" she asked.

"I'll explain later," Jane told her. Before they had even drawn up at the portico she was issuing commands – one was to go for Dr Armstrong, another to prepare a warm bath in her father's old bedroom, still others to heat the bed and strain some broth ... It was a Jane whom Dorothy had not seen before.

Two footmen gritted their teeth as they grasped the rude stretcher in their white-gloved hands and bore it aloft; but they demurred at laying it on the fine Turkey rug, until Jane shouted at them, "Never mind that, just set him down gently and go and get the bath and hot water."

Daniel gave out a small groan as they complied – the first sign of his returning consciousness. She took her father's old penknife and began cutting off his buttons. At that Dorothy protested: "My dear child! What can you be thinking of?"

"I'm thinking of a man in danger of dying of exposure," she replied – though actually, having watched him so keenly all the way home, she did not think the danger very great. He had been badly mauled by the waves and rocks, especially about the face for some reason; but she did not suppose he had lain in the marsh longer than ten minutes before they found him. He must have been struggling up the cliff path at the very moment they first spotted the wreck of his boat.

"But nonetheless, my dear, a *man!*" Dorothy insisted. "It is unthinkable you should remain present while he is bathed and reclothed."

Jane half-turned and stared up at her; the depths of resentment in those green-brown eyes, usually so soft and mild, astonished Dorothy. Banks crouched down beside her mistress and nudged her hand for the knife. Jane turned that same chill gaze on her, but the maid was ready for it. She simply nodded and touched Jane's hand again.

That little nod held an obscure, inarticulate promise – enough to persuade Jane to abandon her resistance. She rose and made at once for the door, saying, "I'll see to the broth, then. And some iodine for those cuts."

Dorothy, who had witnessed every detail of the unspoken exchange, stared thoughtfully at Banks after Jane had gone; but the maid appeared not to notice. She calmly finished cutting off Jago's buttons, severing his bootlaces, too, for good measure. "That's a burr sharp knife," she commented laconically.

"Wouldn't you expect it to be?" Dorothy asked. "We'll get those boots off first."

The "we" was more royal than practical, for the hands that actually did the tugging belonged to Banks and Kemp, one of the other maids. A footman had meanwhile spread a thick carpet of newspapers, upon which he now aligned the discarded boots with a fastidious prod of his patent-leather toecap.

"Now his shirt," Dorothy was saying – needlessly, since the two maids already had the sodden garment half off.

Meanwhile the fire was beginning to roar and the bath was filling nicely, as pail after pail was relayed up the stairs.

Daniel's body, wiry and strong, contrasted so strangely with his battered face and head that it seemed the two could hardly belong to the same person. The whorls of black hair, pressed to his broad chest by the damp, seemed more painted than real.

"Can you feel any heartbeat?" Dorothy asked, crouching at his side and placing her fingers between his ribs, an inch or two below his left nipple.

"'Tis more here, surely?" Banks said, touching him gingerly, just to the left of his bare breastbone.

"Here's where I do feel mine the most," Kemp put in, pressing her fingers beside Mrs Lanyon's but an inch or two nearer Daniel's side.

None of them found a heartbeat, which suddenly made them all feel a little embarrassed at what they were doing.

"Yes ... well ..." Dorothy withdrew fussily. "The doctor can see to all that. Let's ... ah ... get on with it."

The two maids shuffled awkwardly on bended knees toward his feet.

"You left his belt," Kemp said.

Banks nodded. "Shame to cut 'n. That's good leather, that is." She drew a deep breath and began to tug the loose end through the buckle. She tried to give the impression that it was all in a day's work to her – yet also that she had never done such a thing in her life before now.

When the belt was loose, she and Kemp sat back on their haunches and stared at him uncertainly. Banks had picked up a splinter, which she had to bite and suck from the fold of her finger. The taste on her hand left her somewhat puzzled.

"Well," Dorothy said at length, "we certainly can't bath him until ... I mean, we can't bath him like that."

The maids grasped a trouser leg each, and pulled.

Daniel proved to be wearing long woollen underpants.

The maids again glanced at Dorothy. "Everything," she barked, turning to the door and telling the footman there to be careful whom he allowed in.

The two maids fixed each other ostentatiously in the eye as, with the help of the other footman, they manhandled the naked Daniel into the hot bath. The shock of it brought him momentarily back to consciousness. His eyes opened but had difficulty in focussing; soon they furled skyward again and his lids fell. When Banks took a sponge to his contusions he winced briefly and then relapsed into complete stupor.

"Best thing for him," Dorothy said.

"That's a bad one there, ma'am." Banks pointed to a deep cut in his scalp, above his right ear. "I think I should leave that for the doctor. That needs stitches, that do."

Dorothy bent to examine it and nodded her agreement. "Still," she said, "if that's the worst the sea did to him this day, he's got off lightly."

"How much shall us wash then, ma'am?" Kemp asked.

"Just his face and hands. His feet look all right. Just the dirty bits." She permitted herself a brief, official inspection of the rest of him; her eye tarried on that dark, languid orchid, looming beneath the stained and soapmottled water. "The muddy bits," she corrected herself.

There were so many stories about the Jagos. They couldn't all be true, of course, and yet there was no smoke without fire. The father, Kinghorn, had been the greatest womanizer of his day, by all accounts – and there were many who said his day wasn't yet done. And now his son Daniel was treading the same primrose path of dalliance.

Funny word, she thought – dalliance. There was something innocent about it, excusable almost. She darted another brief glance at his unconscious body. *What would it be like?* she wondered before she pulled herself angrily together.

183

"That'll do," she snapped. "Spread out those towels, girl, and you, footman, what's-your-name, help those two get him out. And help them rub him dry, too." She didn't need to specify the precise division of their labour.

Daniel's eyelids fluttered constantly as they dried him and got him into one of Mr Hervey's nightshirts. Sometimes they opened to reveal only a thin crescent of white, sometimes he stared about him with those large, dark eyes, seeing nothing.

"He'll come to hisself soon enough," Kemp said.

"With enough headaches for a week of wet Sundays," Banks agreed.

Kemp glanced up at Dorothy. "We'd just so well put he to bed now, ma'am?"

She nodded. The maids held up the sheets while the two footmen managed the transfer between them.

"Very well!" Dorothy clapped her hands like a school dame. "This is a sickroom now. Clear everything out, including yourselves."

Jane returned at that moment; behind her were two maids, one carrying a pan of broth, the other a tray on which was a moustache cup, a plate of thin, unbuttered toast, and a small vase holding a single white fairy rose from the hothouse.

Dorothy's eyebrows shot up. "You have been busy," she commented. "Banks, you'd better take your mistress to her boudoir and change all her clothes. And then the same yourself."

"I'm all right," Jane assured her, staring at Daniel and trying to edge around the maids who were now busily emptying the bath.

Mrs Lanyon merely nodded at Banks.

"Now *she's* going to insist on doing everything," Jane fumed as the maid hurried after her down the passage.

"And welcome to him," Banks replied.

"Well, if that's all you can say, you'd best say nothing at all."

"Pilchards in a box, that's all they Jagos are."

"She shan't nurse him back to health. This is my house, isn't it. I'll say who does what under this roof. No, no – you go and get my clean things. And hurry! I can undress myself for once."

In fact, she managed it in about a quarter of the time the operation usually took.

"My dear soul!" Banks exclaimed. "Aren't you going to wipe off that mud then?"

Jane snatched up her flannel and scrubbed away vigorously. "Lick and a promise," she said. "Come on! Come on! He might rally at any moment."

"He'd think the more of you for keeping your distance," Banks advised.

"Time enough for that later. The poor man won't know what's happened to him, and Mrs Lanyon wasn't there, so she can't tell him ..."

"I believe he'll know very well what happened to him, miss," Banks said carefully.

Jane hesitated; the chemise, which had been resisting her hasty struggles, fell about her of its own accord. "Why d'you speak in that tone?" she asked.

The maid offered her a woollen chemisette, but Jane brushed it aside. "I shall be too warm in there. I want that fire kept going day and night. Why did you speak in that odd way?"

Banks helped her into the first of several underskirts. "When Kemp and I pulled his clothes off of him ..."

"Oh, so Mrs Lanyon didn't ... never mind. Go on."

"... I got a little splinter, just here. Little thorn, it was." She held up her right little finger. "So I went to suck it out" – she gave a token demonstration of how to suck out a thorn – "and then I thought to myself, I thought, that's a bit odd, that is – no salt."

"What d'you mean – no salt?"

"It never tasted of salt, see? Here's a man been knocked around something cruel by the waves, and no salt in his clothes."

"You must have been mistaken."

Banks shook her head.

"Well ... the marsh is all freshwater. It probably got washed out while he lay there – or diluted enough to ..."

Banks went on shaking her head. "None of his clothes had any trace of salt. And the soap lathered, too, which it never does in salt water."

"That's enough," Jane told her. "You may put my dress on now. What does it matter, anyway – salt or no salt? I can't see it signifies anything."

The maid plied the buttonhook deftly. "If it wasn't the sea as dealt him they bruises ..." She left the sentence unfinished.

Jane broke away impatiently. "Come on. You go and get changed yourself now."

"But I've not done."

"You can button the rest of them later. I'll cover it with a shawl." She was already half-out the door.

Banks gave a sigh and hurried off to her own room to change as fast as she could.

When Jane arrived at ... she still thought of it as her father's bedroom – the *sickroom*, she told herself firmly – when she arrived at the sickroom she found Dorothy sitting alone at Daniel's bedside. The pan of broth was wheezing on the trivet; the tray was still as she had left it, on the bedside commode.

Dorothy raised a finger to her lips and darted it toward their patient, matching the gesture with an encouraging smile. "I think I heard Collett returning just now, dear," she whispered as Jane drew near. "Would you be an angel and go and discover what news of the doctor?"

Jane hesitated. Dorothy saw the anguish in her eyes, glanced at the unconscious Daniel, and murmured, "Well, I don't suppose there'll be a safer moment to leave you alone ..." She rose and gestured Jane toward the chair.

Jane, overwhelmed by this amazing show of liberality, sat down without a word.

"Ring for a maid the moment he comes to. Promise?"

"Yes."

"You understand what I mean now? You are never, never to be alone with him, not for one moment – not while he's conscious." She left the door wide open.

Poor Daniel, she thought, and poor, poor wounds. Now that the mud had been cleaned off, they looked worse than ever. She remembered him at the ball, only a few weeks ago, though it seemed like half a lifetime. How handsome he had appeared to her then, this wild, dangerous, strangely alien, yet utterly beautiful young man. And how woebegone he looked now, with his face all swollen and cut and that great gash above his ear. Her heart bled for him; and yet she could not suppress a certain savage delight, too – to think that those same wounds now held him here in her care. Ashamed of herself, she anticipated with relish the long days of his convalescence.

She noticed that the largest wound was oozing blood into his hair – or not so much blood as a pinkish sort of lymph. She took out her handkerchief and dabbed its lower margin as tenderly as she could. He gave a moan, stirred, opened an eye, gazed a second or two at the ceiling, and closed it again.

"Mr Jago?" she whispered.

There was no response.

"Daniel?"

Still nothing.

He was sweating. That couldn't be good, surely?

She rolled the quilt down toward the foot of the bed. Then she counted the blankets – six. He'd never cool off under all that, especially with the fire roaring away. She reached across him and stretched them taut, to draw some cooler air in over his body. When she let it go slack again, the blast that came out was like a furnace. She repeated the operation several times more, until her arms ached. The blankets were just too heavy; she folded them down as far as his knees.

Then, after a pause, the sheet.

His nightgown was drenched in sweat and the skin of his thighs – or as much of it as was visible between the thick, dark curls of hair – was lobster pink. She became suddenly aware how fast her heart was beating. This was what Dorothy had banished her from the room rather than ...

This was the great ...

This was what they always ...

This was The Secret.

If the hem had ridden up just an inch or two more ...

Before she could stop herself she reached out and gave the material a tweak.

Daniel began to stir and groan. Hastily Jane dropped his nightshirt and tugged it down to his ankles. She pulled the sheet back over him, too, and started to fan the cool air about him. Her action was well timed, for, in the very next moment, Dorothy returned. "My dear child!" she cried. "What on earth d'you suppose you're doing?"

"Trying to cool him. The perspiration is just pouring off him. It can't be good."

Dorothy gave her such an odd look that, for one guilty moment, Jane supposed she had been observed satisfying her curiosity; but calmer reflection told her that could hardly be. If the woman had seen her doing *that*, she'd hardly have confined her comments to the trivial matter of fanning their patient with a sheet.

"Well ..." Dorothy seemed mollified. "It's having some effect." And she nodded toward the bed.

Jane followed her gaze and saw that Daniel's eyes were not merely open but were actually looking directly at her. He tried to smile but the pain from his lacerations made him wince. A shiver of fear ran through her; suppose he had recovered consciousness just ten seconds earlier! She would have *died* of shame. What an idiotic thing to have done, to risk his respect and Dorothy's wrath ... and all for what? For the most disappointing damp squib of a revelation she ever experienced.

186

Oddly enough, it made her angry with him, as if he had deliberately cheated her of something more profound.

Dorothy spoke slowly and distinctly, as to a simpleton. "Your boat was driven ashore in the storm, Mr Jago. You were almost drowned. Your face and head were quite badly cut on the rocks."

"Or so it would appear," Jane added. She spoke in the same tone as Dorothy; it gave the words a ring of sarcasm that surprised the other two. Daniel eyed her warily.

"Some good hot broth?" she offered.

He nodded. "I'm obliged, Miss Hervey." He spoke as though his mouth were obstructed with pebbles.

"Dr Armstrong will be here as soon as he can," Dorothy assured him.

"I hardly need trouble him, surely?"

"You haven't seen the wound on your head," Jane told him. "No – don't touch it. It should be stitched."

"Have you a looking glass?" he asked.

"You'd best eat first," Jane said as she crossed to the fireplace and took up the pan of broth. "It's not a sight to encourage the appetite." Again, her sharpness made him and Dorothy exchanged slightly bemused glances while her back was turned.

The handle was hot and she had to wrap it with an antimacassar. She was struck with the thought that her mild jest was truer than she had realized: The man was no longer a sight to encourage any sort of appetite. The swollen and distorted visage on the pillow was still recognizably that of Daniel Jago; and yet it no longer possessed that strange, haunting power over her emotions. Until now she would have said that power resided in his eyes, yet they were as dark and piercing as ever. So was there a change in him, or in her?

It was odd to be sitting beside him, feeding him broth by the spoonful, as one might a baby, and finding herself able to look at him quite dispassionately at last. But what about when he recovered, she wondered? When that superb nose, those wonderfully chiselled lips, and that strong, manly chin were restored to their undamaged beauty, would he once again be able to set her heart all a-flutter just by looking at her? But if so, what price those feelings, anyway?

"What possessed you to put to sea in such a storm?" Dorothy asked. "And in such a frail craft?"

"I was not at sea at all," he assured them. "I went down to Megaliggar to see if she'd slipped her moorings. Not that I could have done much about it if she had."

"Instead it was you who slipped," Dorothy commented.

He smiled grimly. "You may say as much, Mrs Lanyon."

She became aware that she was missing some point in this whole business, something to which Jane was privy – or so her sarcasm suggested. He saw the annoyance in her eyes and was surprised by it. In his groggy state he had assumed she was the one who had tumbled to what really happened. He turned to Jane. "Did you see it all, then?"

She shook her head. "You were alone when we arrived."

He nodded. "Nonetheless, I believe I owe you my life. They would not have scrupled to kill me."

"Whom do you speak of?" Dorothy stared from one to the other. "And if you didn't see them, my dear, how d'you know of them at all?"

Banks came in at that moment and hitched Jane's shawl up a little higher, covering her unhooked buttons, which were in danger of revelation.

"Ah," Daniel said, "here is the one who twigged it. They were your kinsmen, Miss Banks, I believe?"

"An incautious claim, sir," she replied warily. "Especially for one so far from his own country."

He chuckled. "But poaching's a pleasure all its own, no matter how far the country." His eyes turned casually to Jane. "Nor how unattainable."

She feigned incomprehension. "Countries are not *attained,* Mr Jago."

He bowed slightly, seeming to accept her correction. "You are right. It is altogether too weasel a word – *attained.* They are won in battle, by invasion and conquest. Ouch!"

"I'm so sorry!" In removing the spoon Jane had tweaked his lip just at the point where it was split.

Dorothy turned to Banks. "Are you implying he did not acquire those wounds while being washed ashore?"

The maid turned to Daniel. "The man himself is best judge of that, ma'am."

"It was a monstrous great sea," he said ruefully. "But it has taught me to respect its power. I shall not treat it so lightly in future."

"A lesson well learned, then," Banks told him.

He nodded. "I believe so, miss. And I'd be humbly obliged if others might be brought to believe it of me, too."

The exchange added a new layer to Jane's annoyance; but this time it was a kind of frustration with herself, to realize that a completely unknown, exciting, challenging – dangerous – sort of life was going on somewhere out there, and she had no part in it. Daniel Jago lived at its very heart; Banks on its fringes; but she herself was nowhere.

Into all these cross-currents strode the benign and reassuring figure of Dr Armstrong. He took a needle and thread from behind his lapel and sutured the one bad cut above Daniel's right ear; he put iodine on the rest, and then dismissed the ladies while he conducted a more thorough search for less visible damage. This revealed a lightly fractured rib, whose pain Daniel had taken for no more than a bad bruise. He recommended a day or two in bed and promised to call by on the morrow.

This advice led to a bitter argument between Jane and her guardian, who said it was out of the question for Jane to stay in the house overnight in such circumstances. Jane thought it far more important for her to be on hand in case their patient took a turn for the worse. The dispute came to a predictable conclusion: Jane took a resentful farewell of Daniel Jago and smouldered in silence at Dorothy's side all the way back to Parc-an-Ython.

24 JESSE LANYON, STARTLED AT the intrusion, looked up from his papers; he could not remember the last occasion on which Dorothy had disturbed him at his studies. "My dear!" He rose and went to her. "Are you feeling quite well?"

She sighed and allowed herself to be assisted toward a chair by the fire. "I hardly know what I feel. Thank heavens you are here, Jesse, my love."

He gave an awkward laugh. "And where else should I be on a Thursday evening?"

"No, I mean ... *here*. Thank God you're here at all."

He drew up a chair, sat himself down at her side, and took her hand in his.

"One knows the principles well enough," she mused, "but putting them into practice is quite another thing."

"Is it some trouble with Miss Hervey?" he risked asking.

"A minor contretemps. It will pass. I brought her home with me, by the way. You may have heard her stamping through the hall just now. She's dressing for dinner." She gave his hand a confidential squeeze. "I want you to keep a particular eye on her while I'm out this evening."

He frowned and then remembered. "Your committee meeting. Must you go?"

She nodded and went on to explain what had happened that afternoon.

"It has clearly disturbed you," he commented.

She looked into his eyes a while before she replied. "I am far more disturbed by her father, actually."

He frowned.

She went on: "The man was so thorough ... so dangerously thorough. Jane thought him meticulous, I know – and even I, at times, would almost have gone so far."

When she volunteered nothing more, he asked, "Are you sure you have the word, my dear? 'Meticulous' implies an absurd and ludicrous degree of care."

She sighed. "Perhaps I don't, then. What is the word for an absurdly *dangerous* degree of care?"

He noted it was the second time she had used that word. "You're talking in riddles," he said gently.

She stared into the flames. "Perhaps I shouldn't be talking at all. Yet if not to you, then to whom?" There was a further pause before she said, "I begin to wonder if anyone – any of the decent, respectable, upright people we know – if any of them leads a normal sort of life at all."

His eyebrows parodied a vast surprise. He chuckled, to encourage her out of this sombre mood.

Her gaze returned to the fire. "Remember what you always say about the truth?"

He rose and put the blaze at his back. "What do I always say about the truth?"

"That it can do no harm to pursue it. That half the world's troubles ..."

"Yes, yes. What of it?"

She stared up at him, her eyes intense and troubled. "Is it really so? Can the truth honestly never harm us?"

"Perhaps if you told me in what particular ..."

"No!" she cried. "Then I'd never know whether you tailored your answer to the situation or not."

"Do you not trust me?"

She could hear the anger in his voice, though his face remained a dark silhouette against the lights in the mirror behind him. She did not reply.

"The truth can never harm," he said quietly at last. "It can hurt. It can reveal that we are not as courageous, as generous, as large of soul, as we may fondly have supposed ..."

"Or as mature?" she added.

"It can reveal all of these things and more. And, as I say, it can hurt. But it is the hurt of the child chastised. It is a hurt by which we may profit in the end."

She nodded, and stared once more into the fire. When he saw her relax again he said, "Now perhaps you will favour me with the particulars?"

She gave a faint smile and nodded, though still she did not look at him. "It concerns our dear, late friend," she said.

"Hervey?"

"Yes. He was, as I say, so dangerous-meticulous." She stood up suddenly and began to pace around the room – not swiftly, not nervously, but with a slow, measured tread, as if that were the only way she could force herself to remain calm. "He kept a note of everything, literally everything. Letters to the Postmaster General asking why a parcel was damaged ... to the Chairman of the Great Western Railway complaining that the train to Long Rock was three minutes late ... to the ..."

"Just a mo'. Why did he take a train to Long Rock – one stop from Penzance?"

She smiled grimly. "Just wait till I come to it. You'll understand without my telling you. What I mean is, he kept a record of everything he ever did or said or thought. Even his dreams."

She was close enough at that moment for him to reach out a hand and touch her arm. "Have you been reading his diaries?" he asked warily.

"I'm coming to that, too." She flashed him the ghost of a smile. "I trust you know me well enough to be sure I would not do such a thing out of mere wanton curiosity."

He nodded.

She resumed her peregrinations, and her tale. "There is a ... person," she said. After a pause she added, "In Penzance. A ... young person."

"Yes?" he prompted when nothing more seemed forthcoming.

"A female young person. She was a ... I don't know what to call her. *He* called her *ma petite fille de joie.*"

"*Gay* is the more usual term, I believe," he said. He spoke calmly enough but a swift glance revealed to her how tense he was suddenly.

She explained how the Wilkinson creature had first swum into the Hervey family's ken - all of which had been recorded in those exhaustive diaries. "But obviously he found her attractive enough to cause him to return to Penzance a few weeks later," she went on. "And after that ... well ..."

"Quite," he said.

"He paid her several pounds a week," she added.

"Several *pounds?*" he was startled into asking. "I mean, I know little enough about such things but whenever cases come up before me, it's usually a matter of pence or shillings, not pounds."

"Well he paid her pounds," she asserted.

190

"Perhaps he was keeping her then? Exclusively, I mean. Having to compensate her for loss of ... anyway – good heavens! What does it matter any longer? The poor old fellow's dead. He'll be pleading his cause in the only court that's now entitled to ..."

"Please!" she interrupted him. "That's not what I mean. I'm not judging dear old Hervey. I'm not judging anyone. Indeed, I no longer feel I *understand* anyone enough to judge them." Again she fell silent.

"He was a widower," her husband said. "He was lonely. The girl was ..."

"It's nothing like that, my dear." She waved him to silence. "I mean, I can accept all that – to a degree. But that's not my difficulty."

"What then?"

She had come back to her chair by the fire; now she sat down on its arm. "He wasn't keeping her, this ... Esther, her name was. Esther Wilkinson. He wasn't paying her all that money to persuade her to reserve herself ... I mean, not to ... go with other men. Quite the opposite. He was paying her to do precisely that – to go with other men."

"My dear Mrs Lanyon!" He laughed.

She knew that laugh so well, and never had it grated so much as now. It was the laugh he made – the laugh so many man made – when they were sure she had somehow got hold of the wrong end of the stick. *Dear, sweet, muddleheaded little thing!* it implied. *Now let me set you right.*

It was all she needed to stiffen her backbone and bring her to the nub of the matter. "Yes!" she insisted. "He paid her to keep a diary. To record every one of those ... *encounters!*" She shivered at the word. "He used to sit in the barber's opposite – the place where he died." She sniffed. "Or where he is alleged to have died. He used to sit there and watch her go in and out, in and out, with all those men. And then, after half a dozen or so, he'd spring up there himself, and she'd describe everything they'd done, those other men ..."

"My dear! Do we really need to ..."

"Yes we do, Jesse! Or you'll never understand what I ... why I ..." The words eluded her. "The point is, he *relished* it, Jesse. He revelled in it. Nothing was too foul or odious. The worse it was, the better he liked it. And it's all recorded there. He came home and wrote it all down. And in a way, the most gruesome thing of all is that his hand remains as fine and as neat as when he's writing a letter to *The Times* correcting them on some small point of detail concerning the wholesale tea trade. And yet this is our dear friend, Wilfrid Hervey! A man who, I would have said, occupied the very pinnacle of respectability. Why he even insisted that Jane should retire to her boudoir to change her gloves! He told me once it would horrify him to see her disrobing even that much – just changing her gloves – in public. The day I first met them he apologized to me for walking hatless across twenty paces of lawn, while his valet fetched his hat. He was ... he was ..."

"Meticulous?" Jesse suggested with a grim smile.

"You are obviously not as shocked as I," she said.

He turned and stared at the flames. "Do not forget I am a magistrate, my dear. I hear things in court, and am told things by the police, that I would never dream of repeating to you – quite apart from any question of confidentiality."

191

She nodded slowly, with a kind of wistful understanding in here eyes – as if it were exactly what she had expected him to say.

So, there was another world – a whole secret world – going on out there, all the time. A world of which she knew nothing. A world about which people had lied to her from birth.

No, not people – men.

A new question suddenly struck her: Which was the conspiracy? Was it their silence? Or could it be their conventions of respectability? Was that other world, perhaps, the real one? The honest one? Had she lived all her life in the comfortable sham of its outer shell?

Until that moment she had wondered – all through her conversation with Jesse – why she could not bring herself to tell him the *real* secret she had unearthed that day. It was a secret beside which her revelations concerning poor old Hervey and this Esther Wilkinson would pale into merest tittle-tattle. Indeed, she had only meant them as the curtain-raiser to that far more dramatic and disturbing truth. Now the Inquisition itself would not drag it from her. In fact, if any kind of inquisition were now the order of the day, *she* was going to conduct it – in her own good time and in her own sweet way.

"Well?" he asked, adopting his kindliest tone, "is it quite as bad as you thought, my dear? Come – be honest now, with yourself and me. Don't you feel better already for having spoken of it?"

She forced herself to smile. "You are right, my darling – as always." A loving twinkle crept into her eyes, augmented by the firelight's glow. "I end as I began – thank God you are *there!*"

He nodded sagely. "The truth, you see," he said. "It may hurt. It does hurt. Yet it can never harm!"

Dorothy could only hope he was right, for the truths she had discovered that day threatened to tear the whole fabric of her world apart. It was disturbing enough to have uncovered Jane's origins at last – but to have that discovery so swiftly confirmed by the girl's own behaviour seemed like an omen from on high. She had been shocked enough at the way Jane had gone into Daniel Jago's bedroom, with her clothing all unbuttoned, and feasted her eyes on his naked body. But if she had not learned the truth from Wilfrid Hervey's papers, she would have taken it as a simple act of casual wickedness. Now, however, she could see it was evidence of something far worse – an inherited depravity that could eventually destroy the girl, no matter what precautions she, Dorothy, might take.

Jane herself did not realize it yet, poor dear. Her parents, notwithstanding their own vices, had done their best to preserve her innocence. But perhaps all was not lost. If the girl could be made to see what great danger she was in, she might yet be saved from the very worst of it. But first she must understand what a dire inheritance of vice was hers. It was now Dorothy's plain duty, as she saw it, to give scope to that most wretched discovery.

*   *   *

After a rather frosty dinner, when Dorothy had gone, Jesse said he felt too jaded for his studies and asked Jane if she might care to join him for a round or two of bezique or else two-handed whist. She, having dreaded an evening alone with her distemper, readily accepted. They played for a button a trick, which they agreed would be worth one thousand pounds each.

Jane proved the better gambler in that she could devise her strategy as she first sorted out her cards; she was then able to play her hand almost automatically – freeing her tongue for anything that crossed her mind. Her opponent was less nimble and needed to correct his earlier decisions after every three or four tricks. She thus had the advantage not only of the game but also of their conversation; so it was extremely foolhardy of him to try, though ever so delicately, to verify his wife's earlier revelations.

"What do you think of us Corns now, eh?" he asked jovially.

She had heard him speak of the Cornish as "Corns" before, so the word itself raised no more than a tolerant smile. "One certainly has the feeling of not quite being in England," she replied.

"Ah!" He nodded. "You're not the only one to notice that. But tell me, when did it strike you? In fact" – he gave a diffident little laugh – "what was your very first impression of us, the very first thing that struck you as being different?"

He led low in a suit where she would have expected him to lead high; she had to adjust her plan quickly. He, misinterpreting the pause, prompted: "You came down by train, of course. Did you get off at Redruth or ... Penzance?"

His careful offhandedness alerted her to his more-than-casual interest in her reply. In a flash too swift to be called "thought," she realized that Dorothy must have told him about that encounter with Miss Wilkinson. She tried to remember what she might have revealed to her guardian but could not be sure; it had obviously been enough for Dorothy to make further inquiries – of Banks, most likely – and then to tell her husband. Jane, despite her newly acquired feelings of maturity, was still naïve enough to think she might now squeeze some amusement from the situation.

"Oddly enough, Uncle Jesse," she replied, "my very first impression was of how *similar* Cornwall is to the rest of the world. My father, God rest him, sent me to wait for him by the station entrance ..."

"Good heavens!," he remarked.

She refused the bait. "... and I thought the reek off the harbour was like Dover and Calais and every other port I've ever been in. And the sight and smell of the gasworks wasn't exactly unique, either."

Now – would he make something of that, or would he try to steer her back to what seemed to be on his mind?

He lost the trick but, instead of making a joking parade of his annoyance, which was his way, he placed the discard on her pile without comment, saying instead, "Who was the first Cornishman you met – or woman, to be sure?" He took the next trick and then played what he must have thought was a strong lead.

She trumped it. "The porter at the station, I suppose." She laid down her four remaining cards. "And the rest are mine, I believe."

He stared at her ruefully. "What do I owe you?"

"Twenty-five thousand pounds," she replied without even counting. "I'll take a six-month bill, if you prefer."

"Oh no!" He rubbed his hands. "I'll win it all back this time, you'll see."

"Double or quit?" she offered.

He chuckled. "You *are* a gambler. Very well. You're on."

She dealt a new hand. While they were sorting out he said, again in the most offhand way, "Your father cannot have known Penzance at all well at that time – I mean, to send you to wait in *that* particular place."

She concentrated on her cards and said "Mmmm," as if she had only vaguely heard him. "Actually, the first Cornish person I met was there, 'in *that* particular place.' A most respectably dressed young lady, a little older than me. She, too, was waiting for someone." She laughed. "It was only a few weeks later, and quite by chance, that I learned she was actually waiting for my father." She stared at the card he had led and added, "Are you sure you mean that?"

He looked at it and said, "No!" in a rather vexed tone. "Still – what's done is done. Play on."

She took the trick. His failure to follow up her astounding revelation amused her – and also confirmed that he knew precisely what she was talking about. She went on: "She introduced herself as Miss Wilkinson – though, oddly enough, my father didn't know her by that name at all. It later became clear she had once played some part in our family's affairs."

She lost the next three tricks, one of which she could have taken. Happier with himself he asked, "How do you know that? Did she tell you so?"

"No, but he was furious when he saw I'd even learned of her existence. He said if I'd still had Manette, my old French maid, she would have recognized Miss Wilkinson at once and would not have permitted us to speak. I wonder what the connection was?" She sighed. "Now, I suppose I shall never know."

He nodded sagely at his cards. "Sleeping dogs, eh?"

They played another trick or two and then, when it seemed the subject was fading into oblivion, she added, "He was so furious he absolutely forbade me to even think about it."

"He must have had his reasons. This Esther Wilkinson can't have been a very salubrious person to know." He spoke as if he truly had lost all interest in the topic.

She chuckled as she gave him another winnable trick. "It's a funny thing about prohibitions like that, don't you find? They make one want to break them. I wonder if there'd be any smuggling if it were all made perfectly legal?"

He nodded sagely as he accommodated himself to this new twist of her thoughts. To fill the silence she said, "In which case, poor Daniel Jago wouldn't be lying in such pain in my father's bed at this moment." She laughed. "And I shouldn't be here, keeping you from your studies and talking such scribble."

He scooped up the last trick, winning the hand by a single point.

"I should never have offered double or quit," she complained. "Now I must start all over again."

"And I!" – he glowered jocularly at her – "must be on my guard. You are far more nimble of wit than I suspected."

194

"Indeed!" She adopted his tone. "Let battle commence! Your deal, I believe, sir." She cut the cards to him.

There was silence while he dealt and then she said, "Suppose *nothing* was forbidden. Suppose anyone could do anything they liked?"

"It would be chaos," he replied. "Anarchy. Anyway, what are *you* forbidden to do? Precious little, it would seem to me."

"To sleep under my own roof tonight, for instance."

He smiled. "But that is not really a prohibition, Jane. It is a decision which – forgive me for saying so – a decision which, if you were just a *little* more grown-up, you would make for yourself. Tell me, are you specifically forbidden to stand at the edge of a crumbling cliff?"

She shook her head.

"There's no need, is there," he pointed out. "You're mature enough to forbid yourself. You see, philosophically speaking, you are quite right. The Anarchists have an unassailable moral position. In an ideal world nothing would be forbidden – because we should all be mature enough to realize that society's prohibitions are for our own good. And we should then abstain from those acts for that very reason rather than for fear of the law or society's disapprobation."

He lost three tricks while explaining this.

"It all goes back to Adam and Eve," she murmured, thinking of a recent sermon she had heard.

"Eh?" he asked uneasily.

"Well, God wanted them to be like the other animals and not to acquire knowledge. He forbade them to seek after knowledge, didn't He. And that was fatal. Perhaps if He'd explained *why* knowledge was bad for them, we'd all still be living in the Garden of Eden."

He cleared his throat and concentrated on trying to win.

"But forbidding it only made them more curious. It was as good as saying 'Eat of the Fruit!' in my opinion."

She took the trick without appearing to notice it. He scooped up the cards and placed them on her pile.

"The thing I can't understand is why it's no longer wrong."

"Isn't it?" he asked cautiously.

"Surely not? I mean, don't *you* now spend night after night doing the very thing for which Adam and Eve were expelled from Eden?"

"Jane!" He almost choked; the quicks of his nails drained suddenly of blood that all rushed to the tips of his ears.

"Monday, Geology," she said, gabbling to cover his embarrassment, which had taken her completely by surprise. "Tuesday, Engineering. Wednesday, Natural Philosophy ... isn't it all the Fruit of the Tree of Knowledge?"

"Ah," he said, licking his lips and losing yet another trick. "In a way, I suppose you're right." He smiled at her and exhaled hugely in relief. "Yes - charmingly, charmingly right."

*　　　*　　　*

Much later it occurred to Jane that she had never mentioned Miss Wilkinson's Christian name to him; yet he had said "Esther" without even noticing it. Therefore he must have been discussing it with ... it could only be with Dorothy.

Unless men confided such things to each other far more readily than one supposed they did.

This qualification made her realize that, for the first time in her life, she was beginning to think of men as ranged in a kind of conspiracy against her. Well, not specifically against her, but against all "sweetly innocent" young girls. She tried to imagine her father digging Uncle Jesse in the ribs and chuckling over his – what could one call them? – his exploits with Miss W. Two weeks ago it would have mortified her to discover herself capable of so foul a suspicion; now it seemed so firm a probability that the name "suspicion" dignified it with an aura of uncertainty.

Was there a conspiracy, then? Perhaps she was being unfair to single men out in that way. Dorothy was part of it, too – but was she a dupe or a willing conspirator? Was it all-men-and-married-women *versus* the rest? Especially *versus* young spinsters? That was the point to be decided next.

She turned over and settled herself to sleep. Often, she had been told – though she had never personally had such luck – you could drop off into the profoundest slumber with a question ringing in your mind – and when you woke up, it was miraculously answered.

If there were any truth in that other old wives' tale – about your ears burning when people talk about you – she ought to have set the pillow on fire. For at that very moment she was the prime topic of conversation in at least three different places not five miles apart.

25 JESSE STARED REFLECTIVELY at his wife, who had been oddly silent since her return from her meeting. "Was it not a success, my dear?" he ventured to ask.

"It was certainly very brief. I spent more time on the road than on ... than seated. Mrs Troy is still unwell and sent her apologies. But we can't go on holding meetings in her absence for ever. How was Jane?"

"Bright as a button – or bright as you'd wish in the circumstances. She beat me. I owe her forty thousand pounds."

"*What!*"

"Or all the buttons you're likely to use in the next two years."

"Oh." She shivered. "I don't think it's amusing, my dear, even in jest."

"Then I must try to *ingest* some of your solemnity."

She winced, and then, out of the blue, said, "D'you think, perhaps, we've taken on rather more than we bargained for?"

"Your committees?"

"No, with Jane, I mean. We don't really know an awful lot about her, do we."

He was astonished. "I would have thought her ... her goodness and innocence ... and ... and purity of heart spoke for themselves. What more do we need to know about her? She is, as it were, an almost empty slate on which the world has yet to write its Song of Experience."

After a pause Dorothy said, "I was thinking more of her mother. What breeding had she?"

He frowned. "What is there to know about the mother? I mean, how can one think about someone one never met and ... and ..."

"... and of whom one has been told next to nothing? Precisely. What has Jane ever told you about her mother? I'll wager you could set it all down on a postcard."

He looked at her askance, as if he doubted not so much what she was saying as her reasons for saying it. "She speaks of her quite often, my dear, and quite openly. There's no hint from *her* of anything to hide."

She ignored the accusation behind his stressing of that word. "But it's always the same few memories, isn't it: Stuck in the nursery. Forbidden beyond the green baize door. Glimpses of a life far more dazzling than anything you and I might have associated with wholesale tea – if, perhaps, we were not the trusting people we are?" She let the words rise on a questioning tone.

He laughed dismissively. "My dear! We're hardly justified in leaping from Jane's rather sketchy memories of her childhood to dark suspicions of immorality and ..."

"Immorality, Jesse?" Her amusement had a victorious edge. "But I said nothing as to immorality. And yet how interesting that you should have made the connection."

"You implied it."

His face froze. "I believe I borrowed any such implication from you, my dearest – with your talk of our over-trusting natures, and 'what do we really know about her?' and so on."

"All I'm saying is there's a seed of a doubt there."

"And it appears to have found fertile soil upon your tongue."

She bridled at the injustice of this jibe. "You do not seem to understand," she responded with some heat. "We have accepted responsibility for the girl. *We* are now the ones who must see her safely and wisely matched."

He waved his hand dismissively. "I'm perfectly aware of everything you say ..."

"Well, one would never imagine it, to hear you speak. And now that she's a double orphan, her period of mourning will be no reason for her not to marry."

"She can hardly attend any more balls this season."

"Of course not." Dorothy's tone turned weary. "It will all be arranged much more discreetly – but it will be arranged nonetheless. So, tell me – what when Mrs Lemon, or Mrs Vyvyan, or Mrs Fox, or Mrs Bolitho ... what when they ask me – as would be perfectly natural, and, indeed, right and proper – what is known of her mother? What do I say?"

His eyes recruited patience from somewhere up beside the chandelier. "You say that what is known of the mother is that she was a considerable heiress in her own right, and that she lived in Paris at a level of opulence commensurate with her purse. What of it, eh? She certainly was no spendthrift, if we may judge by what she has been able to leave Jane."

"And why was she estranged from her husband?"

"On the two occasions Hervey spoke to me on the matter, he said that was not so. He visited her as often as he could."

Her only response was a knowing grin.

"Did he ever say different to you?" Jesse asked.

She shook her head. "I was remembering that Jane once told me her first clear memory of his visits is at the age of twelve. Even at the time – when she told me, I mean – I remember thinking it just a little bit odd."

He soaped his hands. "And how did you explain it to yourself – at the time?"

"You must remember that I then considered Wilfred Hervey to be the very soul of propriety. I knew nothing of ..."

"Yes, yes!"

"I considered that such a *beacon* of rectitude might have excellent private reasons for not wishing to unsettle a young girl with infrequent and unpredictable reunions and partings."

"There you are! A perfectly reasonable explanation."

"I know, Jesse. I know. The trouble is, there are rather a lot of disturbing features connected with that somewhat bizarre marriage. And though it is true each one of them can be explained away in the same perfectly reasonable fashion, yet, taken all together ... well, it becomes rather a large pill to swallow."

He still was not swayed. "With her inheritance, not to mention her beauty and figure, the pill will be swallowed 'though it were huge as high Olympus.' Take my word on it."

"Yes," she sneered, "the men might indeed be so obliging. But I doubt their mothers will show the same complaisant gullibility towards her. And you may take my word on *that!*"

*   *   *

At around that same hour, when Jane's ears ought to have been burning, Dr and Mrs Moore were taking their leave of the Pellews, with whom they had dined. Mr and Mrs Menadue completed the party. It was the protracted sort of leave-taking that begins while all are comfortably seated and the glasses of mulled wine are still three-fourths full – when one or other guest says, "Good heavens! Is that the time?" and then the conversation flows back around the interruption. Such phrases are polite signals that anyone who has anything of significance to say or ask had better say or ask it soon.

The speaker on this occasion was Johanna Moore herself; and the one with the unasked question was Mrs Menadue, who, apropos nothing, murmured, "Did anyone see the Hervey gel at the ball in Liston Court?" She squinted at Johanna. "Come to think of it, I didn't see you there, my dear. Your own place, too."

"My own place, too!" Johanna echoed in amusement. "I had business that night, or all the king's horses wouldn't have kept me away. Even *this* man promised me a polka." She indicated her husband, who nodded solemnly all around to confirm it.

198

Their host, Squire Pellew, wagged a finger at her. "You are a dreadful woman, Mrs Moore. And quite the worst example in the entire district. Business first, trade last, and pleasure nowhere."

Mightily offended, Johanna turned to her husband. "Hand him your card," she commanded. "Pistols for two, brandy for one."

But he shook his head and said mildly, "Not at all. I agree with the fellow. You're an appalling influence."

"About the Hervey gel ..." Mrs Menadue repeated.

Johanna laughed. "Oh, come on, you're dying to tell us."

"Not if no one's interested," she responded huffily, but then immediately went on: "I was just wondering if anyone saw her dancing with Daniel Jago?"

She turned to Mrs Pellew, who nodded warily.

"Did anything strike you about them?" Mrs Menadue asked.

"Well, of course, they made a handsome couple," she allowed – desperately trying to recall the scene, or anything particular about it. "I suppose he's as hopeful as any other. Not that he stands a chance, mind. My money's still on Richard Vyvyan."

"But you noticed nothing else?" Mrs Menadue pressed.

Johanna's eyes narrowed shrewdly. "Why d'you ask?"

"Oh," the other said airily, "no particular reason. Probably pure fancy. Don't say you're at last taking an interest in the romantic toing and froing of the district?"

Johanna smiled knowingly. "Not at all. She may marry her own bootblack for all I care. But speaking of Daniel Jago, do you know where that particular young man is at this very moment?"

Mrs Menadue chuckled. "He's hardly out smuggling in this weather."

The knowing smile grew broader. They all sat up a little and leaned toward her. "We may be quite certain he'll do no more smuggling this side the Lizard – *ever*. The public story is he was wrecked in this morning's storm and took a terrible battering on the rocks at Megaliggar. But the little birds are saying that the rocks had several dozen knuckles – and all were of the Penaluna clan."

"And where *is* he now?" Mrs Pellew asked, remembering Johanna's question.

"Nursing his wounds in the late Mr Hervey's bed at Montpelier."

Sensation.

Further questions soon satisfied the company that this was no mere servants' tattle. "Of course, his hostess is passing the night at Parc-an-Ython," Johanna added, as if it went without saying. The disappointment was considerable but the story then became all too mundane and believable.

"I'll wager she didn't like being dragged off to La Lanyon's Lair," Mrs Menadue said. "I saw the look in her eyes at the ball. Infatuation wasn't the word." She turned to Anthony Moore. "Was he badly hurt? Will he be there long?"

"I'm not their doctor," he told her.

"Long enough, perhaps, to cure an infatuation," Johanna replied for him.

"Or to permit it to ripen into friendship?" her husband suggested quietly.

She grinned. "Now wouldn't that set the cat among the pigeons!"

*   *   *

The third place where Jane was being discussed that night was back at Lanfear House, where Rosa had called to keep her sister company while the Moores were out. Having ascertained that there could hardly be a more miserable family on earth than theirs, they naturally turned their attention to the one person they considered the luckiest in all the world – Jane Hervey.

"One ought to hate her, I know," Rosa said. "And yet she's so ..."

"Hate her?" Bessie echoed in surprise. "But why?"

"Oh ... because she's so ... I don't know. Because everything's been made so easy for her. And she doesn't seem to appreciate the fact. I mean, if I didn't know her, and I heard there was this rich young heiress who'd spent all summer and autumn meeting absolutely everyone, all the eligible bachelors this side of the Tamar, and still hadn't made up her mind ... well, I'd say what a typically spoiled young miss, and want to scratch her eyes out."

"Perhaps she doesn't wish to marry at all?" Bessie suggested.

Rosa's eyes gleamed at the notion. "Has she been talking to you about it? Did she tell you that?"

"Of course not. Why?"

Rosa's smile vanished. "No, she wouldn't stand out against convention like that. I don't suppose she has the courage."

"Courage? Sometimes you choose the oddest words, Rosie." She burst into a smile. "She calls me Liz now, you know."

"Does she, indeed!" Her sister grinned. "It'll be interesting to see what Mama says when she hears of it."

"Which of them would you pick if you were her? Argus Nicholl?" Bessie's eyes bubbled with amusement.

Rosa pulled a face. "Don't! It'll be bad enough having him for a brother-in-law."

Bessie's amusement faded. "Oh, did she tell you, too? She made me promise not to breathe a word to you. She said you'd only go and spoil it."

Rosa shook her head. "She didn't need to. Susie couldn't keep a thing like that secret to save her life." She shuddered. "I'll tell you the worst of it, though – we're going to have to *kiss* him, you realize."

"I've known worse," Bessie said woodenly.

Rosa's hand went out and petted her sister's arm. "I know, dear. I know. I shouldn't joke." She brightened again. "And yet why not? It's that or go mad."

"You didn't tell me who you would pick." Bessie grinned conspiratorially. "But I bet I can guess. Daniel Jago."

Rosa's eyes gleamed once more – and yet she shook her head. "I wouldn't marry him. I'd run away with him, but I'd never marry him."

Bessie stared at her wide-eyed. "How can you say such a thing?" The very idea horrified her.

Rosa closed her eyes and daydreamed. "I'm sure we'd have a marvellous year or two together. You have to allow – he's one of the most ..." She sighed and a frown creased her brow. "But pity the poor woman who puts her whole life and heart into that man's hands."

"What about babies?" Bessie asked.

"Oh, you know about them now, do you?"

"You're mingy." Bessie pouted.

"What of them?" Rosa shrugged. "Look at the Jago household. It used to be alive with children of all sorts of unions. They all got brought up somehow. They survived. I'll bet they're a jolly sight happier than we are, anyway."

"Mama would have a fit if she could only hear you. And you *still* haven't said who you'd marry."

"If I had Jane Hervey's money?"

Bessie nodded.

"I jolly well shouldn't marry at all in that case. If I had money, I'd just spend it and spend it and ..."

Bessie gave a superior smile. "You're like Mrs Moore's cousin Selina. Lawyer Visick's sister. Not about money but about marrying. She swore she'd never marry, but within three days of meeting the right man – or the right one for her – she was off to America with him and they got married on the ship."

A faraway look stole into Rosa's eyes. "That's who I'd really wish to be like – Mrs Moore." She frowned. "How d'you know all this, anyway?"

"She told me. She makes no secret of it."

The smile returned. "Yes. That's how I'd be if I had Jane's money. I'd behave just as I liked – and I wouldn't care a fig who knew about it."

After a pause Bessie reminded her, "Mrs Moore had no money at all."

Rosa was silent quite a while after that. Then, brightening again, she said, "Wouldn't it be amusing to try and get Jane to see it like that."

26 THE FOLLOWING MORNING Jane was up with the lark and ready to return to Montpelier before Dorothy had even appeared for breakfast. "Such a busy bee!" Jesse Lanyon commented abstractedly while the other nine-tenths of him dithered between the devilled kidneys and the kedgeree.

"We saw Mrs Delamere at Rinsey yesterday," she told him. "Susie was with her – and guess who else?"

He smiled. As always, her childlike effervescence charmed him – the way she made little games out of quite ordinary events that, to his much duller soul, would simply pass by in the muddy stream of life. What a threadbare world it would be without the women, he thought. "A gentleman?" he asked.

"Mr Argus Nicholl of Antron! I do hope something comes of that. If it does – I've been thinking about it – d'you suppose it would be possible for me to make them a little wedding present? Something to start them off in life?"

He chose the devilled kidneys and returned to the table. "An admirable thought, Jane, my dear – and so characteristic, if I may say so, of your generous heart. A silver canteen, perhaps? Or a tantalus of three decanters and some crystal?"

"I was thinking more of something like four or five hundred pounds."

He choked on a kidney.

"I was thinking it might have been the sort of dowry her father might have given her, had he been spared," she explained.

He laughed as he recovered. "Ah, Jane, Jane – now you see why your wise old father entrusted the management of your inheritance to me. Your dear, sweet, kind heart would empty the treasury in weeks. It is a lovely, lovely thought, my dear, and I'm sure it will be pressed in that book of mementoes of your soul which the Recording Angel is writing at this very minute ..."

Jane allowed the matter to rest.

Shortly after breakfast Vosper Scawen called with some papers that required her signature. She tried to read them but gave up. "Technicalities connected with probate," he assured her as she signed away.

"I'll just see Mr Scawen to his carriage," she told Dorothy, who was at that moment descending the stairs.

Leaving her bonnet strings dangling, Jane took Vosper's arm the moment they were out of doors – mainly to slow him down. "Tell me," she said, as if it were a matter of the most casual interest, "do I actually own the villa in Paris?"

He assured her – yet again – that she did.

"Absolutely? Lock, stock, and barrel? And it's not administered or whatever you call it by my guardians?"

He chuckled. "Are you chafing already, Jane?"

"I don't know what you mean."

"Ah, forgive me. I felt in my bones that you were already finding your guardians' control over your inheritance somewhat irksome. It crossed my mind that you were looking for a source of money beyond their control. For a fleeting moment, I even imagined you might be considering a mortgage on the villa." He stared up at the clouds, all innocence. "Without having seen the place, of course, it's hard to say what you might raise. But, considering the usual term of such loans, and your expectations at the date of maturity ... well, it would be several thousand." His smile went a shade acid as he turned to her at last. "Of course, you have other things on your mind at the moment. Your thoughts are miles away. Three and seven-tenths miles away."

"Vosper!" Her tone was neatly divided between delight and annoyance.

"What?" He was as unreadable as ever.

"Why do you always go all about the houses like that?"

They had reached his gig, the hood of which was up. She diverted him around the farther side and, in the brief moment they were in its shade, she plucked his sleeve and said, "Kiss me."

He stared at her in disbelief.

"Come on," she urged. "Don't you want to?"

He needed no second bidding but folded her in his arms and pressed her to him.

She had kissed other young men before, of course – playful little pecks or hasty brushes during well-chaperoned games and dances; but this was her first in earnest. To begin with she was overwhelmed by the sheer physical novelty of it – the warmth of his lips, the soft, silkiness of his neat little beard, the strange sighing of his disordered breathing in his nostrils, so close to her ears. Then, just when she was in danger of becoming a spectator to these novelties, some much deeper response rose from within and engulfed her. It was like feeling faint – and yet she never felt stronger. It was like wanting to cry – and yet she never felt closer to laughter. It was like – no, it was like nothing she had ever felt before.

So it must be love, she thought. What else? She had experienced all those lesser emotions like friendship, amity, companionship ... it was like none of them. *I love you.* She practised the words in her mind but something prevented her tongue from forming them. Because she was unsure? No, she thought, the silence was part of her very nature – cautious, wily, female. "You'd better go now," was all she said.

He lifted a hand to her face, tucked a stray lock beneath her bonnet, and let his knuckles caress her cheek as he withdrew. The gesture gave her the strangest feeling of being hollow, of a great falling inside her. "I'll make some preliminary inquiries about the villa," he murmured – at least, those were his words, but their tone said what she herself had withheld.

She watched him to the bend in the road, knowing very well he would not turn and wave. What an odd man he was. Would her love for him last? Would they end up sharing their lives for ever? Could one love two men at the same time?

She sighed as she turned back toward the house; every new milestone seemed to double the distance to that vague haven of love and marriage.

Would she have kissed him at all if he had not dropped those hints about Daniel? And why should his jealousy evoke so unusual a response in her?

Oddly enough, her ignorance about herself – her inability to supply her own motives – worried her not at all. Quite the contrary. It was, if anything, rather comforting to know that, although her conscious mind might be hopelessly bogged down in reasons-for and reasons-against, not to mention the great sea of unreason that separated them, nonetheless *something* within her was capable of rising to the occasion and doing the right thing.

It had been the right thing; of that she was certain.

*   *   *

Daniel Jago was in fighting form again and beginning to regret his meek surrender of yesterday. "You tell your people I'll meet any one of them in a fair fight," he informed Banks as she changed the poultice on the worst of his wounds, the one Dr Armstrong had sutured.

"I would," she sneered, "if I could think of one of them who'd lower hisself so."

"Oh? You wouldn't call eight-to-one low enough, I suppose."

She sniffed. "'Twas five-to-one yesterday. By the time you get back home you'll be saying 'twas the whole of the Duke of Cornwall's."

He laughed. "Give us a kiss, Meg. You're a woman after my own heart."

"It's not your *heart* I'm after, Mr Jago." She loaded the words with apparent significance – to which he was swift to respond.

"Oh?" His eyes acquired a speculative gleam.

"More like your head on a plate," she told him.

203

He smiled and caressed her arm with one fingernail. "Come on – show there's no hard feelings."

Despite her opinion of the man, Banks found herself responding to some brute magnetism within him. She shivered slightly as she withdrew, taking up the old poultice and the roll of lint. "No feelings of any kind," she assured him.

He smoothed down his blankets. "Well, that's an improvement on yesterday at least. By next week we'll be in clover."

"By next week you'll be back in Falmouth. You'll go today, if they'll heed me."

"You're a hard woman, Meg. It's what makes you so irresistible." He chuckled. "Fortunately, your sweet mistress won't heed you."

Banks set down her tray on a little occasional table near the door; she strode purposefully back to the bed. "You just leave she be," she warned.

To her surprise no ribald comment rose to his lips; he simply looked at her and shook his head.

"I mean it," she assured him.

His silence began to undermine her self-confidence.

"Poor thing," he murmured.

His gaze was so distant she could not tell whether he referred to her, to Miss Hervey, or some some imaginary version of her, treasured in his mind alone. "Anyway," she said as she took up the tray and pressed the door handle with her knee, "the doctor'll say you're fit – and then there's no call for you to stop here a minute longer."

Out in the passage she met her mistress and Mrs Lanyon, coming from the stairhead. "Fit as a frog," she replied to their one chorussed question. "All steamed up like a yard bull. He's no call to stay another hour."

"Has he made any trouble?" Dorothy asked sharply.

The maid's eyes raked the ceiling. "Wants me to carry a challenge to any of Penaluna's gang to meet him in fair fight." She sniffed. "Men!"

"He mustn't think of fighting until his wounds are healed," Jane exclaimed.

They stared at her in surprise. Dorothy patted her arm gently. "He mustn't think of fighting at all, dear. This is eighteen-sixty, not *eight*-sixty."

There was a sudden brawling in the hall below, with one of the footmen crying, "No sir! You may not enter … come back, I say!" and a great bellowing of: "Where is he? Where have you put him?" and sounds of a heavy tread upon the stair.

"Kinghorn Jago!" Banks whispered, more to herself than anyone. She set down her tray in the nearest doorway and ran to the head of the stairs. "Go back!" she cried. "Go back out of here!"

The racket stopped. For a moment perfect silence reigned. Then came a great laugh and the footsteps continued. A moment later a head appeared in the space between the maid's skirt and the top newel-post of the banister - a great, wild head fringed by a luxuriance of dark, curly hair and a flowing black beard. "Banks?" he roared. "Margaret Banks? You've a cool nerve to stand there and order me out."

"You've no right in this house," she told him

"And you've no right in this kingdom – not after what your kinsmen did to my son. Where is he?"

204

Dorothy and Jane started for the stairhead. Jane spoke first: "Mr Jago - if that is indeed who you are - your son is upstairs and under the care of the doctor. There is no need for this violent intrusion. If you will return to the front door and knock in the usual fashion, you will be admitted in the usual way."

Banks gasped and looked around for some handy weapon. Dorothy turned pale. Little as she knew of the Jagos, it was enough to tell her that no one ever addressed the patriarch himself like that.

There was a silence you could have carved.

The man shielded his eyes from the overhead light, filtering down from the lantern, and peered into the gloom where the three women stood in outline. Then he threw back his head and laughed. "If that's the way of it, mistress," he cried, "why, 'tis your house and so be it."

And, meek as a lamb, yet still with an air of amused truculence about him, he turned and descended to the hall.

"Well, I'll go to ..." Banks's voice tailed off in disbelief.

"Hell ..." Jane suggested with a smile – which broadened when Dorothy's shocked eyes turned upon her and she added, "... velyan?"

"I never thought I'd live to see the like of that," Banks murmured.

A thoughtful look replaced the shock in Dorothy's eye. "Better safe than sorry," she commented enigmatically, and then, adding, "I shall only be a moment," went into Wilfred Hervey's old dressing room, whose door was only yards away.

Kinghorn Jago was walking calmly back upstairs by the time she returned. "Miss Hervey?" he said to Dorothy from the half-way landing. "I'm delighted to meet you at last."

Jane, realizing he could not make them out, standing as they were in the gloom of the corridor, while he was still in the light of the stairwell, stepped forward into the edge of it.

The moment he clapped eyes on her the most extraordinary transformation came over him. He faltered in mid-stride and reached out for the banister rail. His eyes blinked rapidly and seemed to experience some momentary difficulty in focussing upon her. "Miss ..." He swallowed audibly. "Hervey?" Of his former truculence there was no remnant; he was like a man confronted with a ghost.

She had intended not to shake his hand – to make it clear to him that his was not a social call and that he was not to presume that any kind of acquaintance existed between them hereafter. But suddenly he looked so lost, so pathetic (a word no one had associated with him in all his half-century of existence), she found herself descending the half-dozen stairs he had yet to climb and taking him by the arm.

For a fraction of a second he flinched at her touch; then, peering at her more closely, he was obviously reassured by something he alone saw in her. The smile returned to his lips, along with some of the colour that had deserted his cheek. "You gave me a start," he murmured, taking her hand between his and patting it reassuringly – though half the reassurance was for himself, she guessed.

"I realize that." She turned at his side and, holding his arm, started to remount the last few steps.

"A trick of the light," he added.

With something of a shock Jane noticed that Dorothy was carrying a poker. She made no attempt to hide it, but nor did she refer to it when she nodded warily at their visitor and said, "Mr Jago."

He smiled affably. "Mrs Lanyon. I see you now. I didn't recognize you at first."

"Well," she replied frostily. "I won't pretend you're the most welcome guest this house ever saw, but as your son is here, you'd best come in and talk with him."

Although Jane – or, rather, Miss Hervey, the well-brought-up young lady – agreed with these sentiments, a goodly part of her rebelled at their application; however, she did no more than give the man's arm a surreptitious squeeze to imply that a different welcome lay beneath this glacial surface. To her surprise, he stiffened rather than relaxed.

A most peculiar man in every way, she thought.

But then she herself was feeling most unpredictable this morning, too. Though she wanted nothing more than to witness the meeting between father and son, something in her shied at the prospect and she heard herself saying, "I'll leave you, if I may, Mr Jago. Please stay with your son for as long as you wish. I must attend to my flowers."

She expected Dorothy to follow her; after all, Banks could see to whatever needs might arise. But, for some reason, Dorothy now took it upon herself to play the hostess and conduct the man personally to his son's sickbed; since she still clutched the poker in her hand, it was an odd combination of signals.

Jane actually had very few flowers to attend to. The conservatory at Montpelier was not large and she was trying to husband their meagre stock of blooms for Christmas, which would be upon them the week after next. However, an invalid in the house was, she thought, sufficient cause to cut enough to fill a small vase.

With annoyance she remembered she had intended inviting Vosper to dine at Montpelier on Christmas Eve; if he declined, she wouldn't bother asking any of the other intended guests, the Delameres and Mr Nicholl – and Richard Vyvyan, who would be home on shore leave. Now she'd have to send Tom Collett into Helston with a note. The whole venture was absurd, anyway. Much too last-minute. Like everything else in her life. She planned great projects, undertook the most sweeping revolutions of her soul, set herself the most sensible goals ... and the next puff of wind would blow it all away!

No, that wasn't fair. The "next puff of wind" was actually a new bit of experience or a shattering discovery or a mighty overturning of all her previous understanding – something, anyway, that she simply couldn't ignore, something that made all her previous ideas and resolves out of date.

Talking of new experiences ... she glanced all about her and then raised her fingers to her lips, pretending their touch was Vosper's. It didn't work for more than half a second. If it did, of course, you could kiss the men goodbye. She wondered in what circumstances she would next embrace him like that. Probably not until Christmas Eve – if even then. Suddenly it seemed a lifetime away.

While she arranged the flowers for Daniel she enjoyed a little daydream in which heavy snows fell all afternoon on the 24th, and only Vosper managed to fight his way through to her dinner. And the darling flakes went on falling and falling until it was quite unthinkable for him to return home that night ...

Kinghorn Jago stayed for only half an hour. He found Jane in the library when he came to take his leave. He was rather subdued, she thought, and it made her wonder if Daniel were less well than Banks had so scornfully maintained.

"You're not taking him away with you, then?" she remarked.

"I would do," he replied, "but Mrs Lanyon is of the opinion Dr Armstrong should see him first." He eyed her cannily. "One thing I should warn you about him, Miss ... Miss Hervey," he went on. "Don't be alarmed now if he starts lolling out his tongue and rolling his eyes and making little yelps like a dog."

"Goodness, Mr Jago!" she exclaimed.

"He probably won't do no such thing – now I've gone and let the cat out the bag." He laughed reassuringly. "But he's not had a fit for some months now, so" – he shrugged – "you never know. I'd hate for it to spring on you unawares, like."

"Well ... thank you for telling me."

"Don't breathe a word to him, mind," he begged.

"Of course not."

"And another thing – if he seems to lose his temper for no reason, 'tis best to give his humour scope. You're a maid of some spirit, as I've cause to know." He laughed and patted her on the arm. On the surface he made it seem like a ritual renewal of his submission; and yet, or so Jane felt, there was an odd sort of pride in the gesture, too. He became serious again as he concluded: "But it wouldn't do to goad young Daniel like that. He's lifted his hand to many a woman in his time, and blacked their eyes and broken their teeth. I don't know where his mother and I went wrong."

Jane suddenly realized that the man was doing his level best to warn her off his son. Of course, nothing was more calculated to raise her hackles than that. However, she showed no sign of annoyance as she replied, in her sweetest tone: "Perhaps he has not yet met the right woman, Mr Jago?"

Quick as silver he came back with: "Not for want of trying, miss, I do assure you. His mother and I are fostering three results of his search this very minute. We dread a knock at the door sometimes, for I'm sure those three are but the merest sample. Still" – he lifted his head and rallied with a smile – "he'll be gone from this house directly and that's the end of that."

Dr Armstrong came shortly after Jago senior had departed. On his way out he told Jane that the young man had made an extraordinary recovery, even allowing for his youth and vigour; there was no reason for him to remain in bed (nor in this house, his tone implied). Dorothy, at his side, nodded vigorous agreement. Jane, who had looked forward to spoiling him for a day or two, hid her disappointment. She wouldn't send Tom Collett into Helston; she'd go there herself, with Banks to chaperone her, and see young Daniel onto the Falmouth coach. That was the least she could do.

She told Banks of this arrangement when the maid passed her, carrying Jago's washed and pressed clothing up to their ex-patient.

She expected Dorothy to demur, but all her guardian said was, "Don't take those things into the dressing room. Put them behind the screen and let him dress in the bedroom. I won't say don't let him out of your sight, but at least don't let him out of your company."

"Yes ma'am."

To Jane she explained: "We don't want him poking and prying all over the place." Banks wondered what was the difference between now and last night, when the young man had had the run of the house, if he had wished it. She said nothing of that, however, and followed the instructions to the letter. Daniel made some ribald suggestions as to other purposes for which so elegant a screen might be intended. She ignored him and wandered as far away as possible, back near the door. She paused in front of the little table where she had earlier set down her tray, during their altercation. It was exactly as she had seen it then – but not at all as it had been when Kinghorn Jago was there.

She was still running her fingers idly over its polished surface when Daniel emerged from behind the screen. "What's the matter?" he asked – meaning why was she so far away?

"The picture that was here?" she risked asking.

"The one of Miss Hervey?"

The maid suppressed a smile. "The one in the solid silver frame."

He thought he understood her question. "Better search me," he advised solemnly. She went on staring at the table.

"I'd steal a kiss," he admitted, "because it's easily hidden, see?"

"Easier than a bruise," she agreed.

He laughed. "If you really want to know – Mrs Lanyon removed it."

She smiled, as if that was precisely what she had expected to hear. "That's all right then," she said.

But it wasn't. That picture had never been on display in this house. It lived in the second drawer down – the *locked* second drawer down – in the master's writing desk in his dressing room. Yet when Kinghorn Jago had gone into the room, or sometime between the moment he entered and the moment he left, that picture had somehow materialized and had stood there prominently, where he could not fail to see it on his way out.

And the only person who could have devised all that was Mrs Lanyon. Whatever her purpose, the sight of it had certainly shocked the father – especially when she had murmured, "Miss Hervey's mother." Banks would never forget it. And she'd bet a year's wages the picture was already safely back under lock and key.

What sort of game was afoot here?

27 AS SOON AS DANIEL was dressed he went back to Megaliggar to see what wreckage might be salvaged from his boat. Jane, who had been waiting-without-seeming-to-wait in the morning room, went at once to Dorothy, pointing out how dangerous it was to go from the warmth of a sickroom to the icy blast of …

She need not have bothered. Her guardian agreed heartily. Daniel Jago was to be found and brought back as swiftly as possible. "Banks will accompany you," she said.

Banks, pausing only for a brief word with Mrs Tresidder, stuck to Jane like a leech.

The wind had got up again to a half-gale blowing out of the east, and it bit into the flesh as cold as most winds from that quarter. Jane was glad of her stout cape of linsey-woolsey, though she wished she had remembered her ear muffs. She covered her head with part of the blanket she had brought for Daniel. Banks looked like a scarecrow – but a warm one – in a heavy coachman's overcoat she had borrowed in haste from Tom Collett. Despite these defences, they were both ready to turn back less than half-way to the cliffs.

"Pity the labourers who have to be out on such a day," Jane commented.

"And the fishermen."

Jane remembered how cold the sea had felt in summer; what must it be like now? She shuddered even to think of it.

They reached the coastal road, from whose seaward hedge they ought to have been able to see Daniel, unless he were actually down on the rocks.

"You don't suppose he's met with your relations again," Jane asked.

"They're no relations of mine, miss. More like kinsfolk, really. But I shouldn't hardly think so." Her face hardened and she pointed down across the field. "Why there he is now."

At the marshy hollow where they had found him unconscious, the edge of the cliff formed a sort of U-shape – into the base of which Daniel's head and shoulders were now emerging. He spotted them almost at once and waved.

"Now we must stand here and attend him, I s'pose," Banks grumbled.

As if he heard her, he broke into a loping trot, zigzagging steeply up the slope. Cheated of one grumble, Banks started another: "Should ought to have slapped a drop of iodine on him and lent him the coachfare home," she muttered.

"Are you behaving like this because you think I might be – how shall I put it? – turning a little tender toward him?" Jane asked.

"Shall us go back in that-there field?" was all she replied. "He's a bit more sheltered in there."

Jane walked crabwise as she followed the maid, so as not to lose sight of Daniel. "Look at him!" she commented. "No overcoat and shirt open at the neck. I don't know." When they were in the lee of the other hedge she drew the blanket loosely over them both and added, "You didn't answer me. *Is* that what you fear?"

"I don't know what I fear, miss, and that's a fact. And yet I'm full of misgivings."

"Well, I'm sure I can't think why."

"Nor yet can I, but 'tis so."

Their eyes dwelled in each other's for a moment. Jane looked impatiently away.

"Was your mother ever in Cornwall, miss?" Banks asked suddenly.

Jane shook her head. "I don't believe so. Why?"

"I just wondered."

Jane frowned. "What a strange thing to 'just wonder'. You must have a reason."

"Didn't you once tell me she kept a little map of the county always?"

Jane shrugged. "I don't know about *always*. I remember finding such a map once. In her pocket book."

"And she never said why?"

"Good heavens!" Jane laughed. "I never dared ask her. She'd have skinned me alive if she learned I'd been going through her things like that."

"She never liked folk peeking and prying, then?"

"I'm sure most people don't."

"Not even you, her own daughter."

"Well" – Jane gave a little defensive laugh – "I'm sure most people ... I mean, did *your* mother let you rifle through her things?"

"That she did, miss," Banks assured her. "She made a sort of game of it, like."

"Horses for courses," Jane said vaguely. "My mother was a very *private* person."

"Like your father."

"That's enough of that now," she said severely. "I'm surprised at you."

"I wasn't referring to that, miss." But Banks had no time to explain, for Daniel had reached the road.

"It was worth it," he cried as he leaped atop the hedge and then dropped into the field. "See!" He held up a pair of brass rowlocks as if for their approval.

"Those stitches will open if you're not more careful," Jane warned.

There was a roguish light in his eye as he thought of something to say to that; but whatever it was, he kept it to himself.

"Where's your greatcoat?" she went on.

He shrugged. "Still wet."

"Put this up about you," Banks snapped, tugging the blanket from her mistress before she could offer the service. "And come us on! Else we'll surely be late for the Falmouth coach."

He stole a swift squeeze as she slung the material around him. "I shouldn't go short of a ride to Falmouth," he promised.

She punched him playfully hard in the stomach but he rode it and laughed again.

"What *do* you look like?" Jane asked crossly as she turned to lead the way back to the house. Actually, she thought, with that arrogant grin, and his body all aglow from the exertion of running up from the shore, he looked like a faun. And not just any faun, but a particular one in a painting her mother had commissioned from a young painter called Jalabert when she had first come to Paris: *Nymphs and Fauns,* painted in the style of Fragonard. There had been many such canvasses around the house at that time; she could only just remember them – woodland scenes, *fêtes champêtres,* embarkations for Cythera – all filled with frolicsome young men and women in diaphanous clothing. Later, as tastes grew more sober, they had been taken down and replaced with classical scenes – still with plenty of flesh, but white as marble and quite bloodless. *Nymphs and Fauns,* however, had remained.

The horses were spanned to the carriage by the time they returned. "We'll proceed at once," Jane decided. "I don't need to change, I think."

Banks was furious, for she could hardly say the same. As she trudged to the yard door Jane called after her: "And bring my father's second-best overcoat for Mr Jago. Also find a cravat of some kind."

"Fifth-best'll do," he added with a laugh. When the maid had gone he turned, opened the carriage door, and, offering his arm for assistance, said, "You, at least, should go inside, Miss Hervey."

She accepted his support but the moment she was in she grasped his wrist and pulled him in after her – a feat which, it should be said, called for hardly any effort on her part. The interior was tall enough to allow her to stand but he had to stoop slightly. For a moment they faced each other, letting their eyes adjust to the gloom. "Well?" she said. And, "Well!" he replied.

She moved the barest inch toward him and then his arms were about her and his lips closed on hers. This time that strange new emotion was ready to claim her; so, although it was more immediate, she found it less overwhelming. That same melting hollowness invaded her. The same pounding seized her heart. She experienced the same curious and contradictory impulse to surrender and to resist ... but, in some indefinable way, the emotions seemed intrinsic to *her* rather than to anything in him. She doubted now she could call it love.

She stirred slightly, not really intending to break off their embrace. He drew a little apart and then let go of her, as if the mere touch of her would undermine his resolve. "We must be mad," he said tightly.

She took her seat; he stepped a pace back and stood with one foot on the running board, holding the door slightly ajar against him. "And I imagined I'd have to fight you for that,"

"I kissed another man this morning," she told him, "I just wanted to see if it was the same."

"Ah." He was so crestfallen that half a dozen comforting white lies rose to her lips – where they died unspoken.

"And was it?" he pressed.

"No. It was different," she allowed.

"Then I don't know what to say."

"It's because I don't really know you. Tell me about yourself. This smuggling business is just a kind of game, isn't it? What d'you really do? Or, better still, what d'you intend to do – in life, I mean?"

Banks returned at that moment. His foot on the running board was apparently enough to satisfy her, since she passed no comment on the fact that the rest of him was inside.

"I didn't think to ask Mrs Lanyon," Jane said with a show of retrospective guilt.

"She raised no objection," Banks told her, with just an edge of sarcasm in her tone.

Jane let it pass. While they arranged themselves, she thought back over the emphatically pleasant experience of kissing Daniel Jago. If it had not been love, then what might she call it?

It was, she decided, simply the unaccustomed sensation of being kissed by an ardent young man – in both cases – for whom she felt ... what? Attraction? Yes, certainly that. Something deeper .. something closer to an obsession? Yes, that was so, too, though she was less willing to concede it. And friendship? Ah! Now there was a difference. For Vosper Scawen she certainly had the most cordial feelings, older than whatever it was she had mistaken for love. But toward Daniel Jago she could discover no such stirrings. But then, that was only natural, wasn't it? After all, she hardly knew him.

"You were about to tell me ...?" she prompted him.

He smiled at her, a kind of smile she had not seen before. His smiles usually carried the promise of some kind of jocular combat – as though he saw her, or perhaps all women, as amiable opponents in an obscure battle of wits. But not this smile. "Now there, Miss Hervey," he said, "I believe we are poles apart."

"In what way?" she inquired.

The carriage set off smoothly and he relaxed. "I have no plan as to what I intend to do in life."

"And you suppose I have?"

"On the contrary. I suppose that even if you had, it would all be set at naught. Your life is pretty well planned for you. Or am I wrong?"

"You got no call to talk on such matters," Banks snapped at him.

"If I'm asked a civil question ..." he responded.

A silence fell.

"Miss Hervey can do as she pleases," Banks added. "No one can tell her what to do or ..."

He chuckled at her failure to complete the antithesis – which he now mockingly supplied: "... or what not to do?"

"Be quiet, Banks," Jane said, more in weariness than in anger. "Mr Jago is right. My life *is* planned for me, from first to last."

"And for good reason," the maid murmured.

"Just because I'm not a man, you mean?"

They both stared at her in surprise.

Her surprise was equally great. "Isn't it obvious?" she asked. "It is to me." She turned upon Daniel. "If you were nineteen years old and you'd just inherited a considerable fortune, what would happen to you?"

He laughed. "We Jagos do not inherit, Miss Hervey. We merely spend."

She continued to stare at him, a level, unblinking stare.

"Very well." He shrugged. "If pigs flew and snowdrops flowered in June – and I was a rich young heir to a fortune ..." He closed his eyes and frowned. The situation was so unthinkable he had no ready-made answer. "I suppose my benefactor would have arranged for it to be put in trust until I reached twenty-five. Or thirty-five. Or forty-five. Or whatever is a trustworthy age for a Jago."

"See!" Banks cried in triumph.

"Do be quiet!" Jane snapped. "Let him finish."

"And then I'd be free to spend it, I suppose," he concluded lamely.

"And marriage?" Jane asked.

"Ah!" He caught her drift suddenly – and turned to Banks with a smile and a nod, as if to say, "I told you so!"

She tried to remember such an occasion but could not – unless it was that strange, half-whispered, "Poor thing!" when she had warned him to keep his distance from her mistress.

This exchange of glances was not lost on Jane. Though she passed no comment, it doubled her determination to discover from one or other of them what conversation had passed between them to cause it. "Exactly so," she said grimly. "His life would not be *ridden* by kindly ... friends – more eager to see him wedded than suited."

"That's a truth, indeed." Daniel grinned. "My father would sooner get his own hands on my inheritance than see it all pass into the control of some scheming harpie. He'd play prosecutor against them all."

Jane took her heart in her hands and said, "He'd make a bad job of it, though. That I may swear."

He turned to her in surprise at her vehemence.

"Tell me, Mr Jago," she went on. "Are you by any chance subject to fits?"

"Of drinking ... spending ... melancholia ...?"

"Be serious. Does your tongue loll out and do your eyes turn white? Have you struck defenceless women and broken their jaws?"

His face darkened as her catalogue unfurled. "Why do you ask me these things?" he growled.

His anger was strangely thrilling. She had intended to stop at that but now she went on: "And are your parents now rearing three love children of yours?"

"Miss!" Banks almost screamed.

He was so taken aback by the frankness of her question that words deserted him for a moment.

And Jane, too, was astonished into silence – not that she had asked such a question but that she should have used the words *love children*. She had never consciously made the connection. Yet something within her had done so. Something had drawn a line between that ancient scrap of family arcana – Uncle James's love children – and her more recently acquired understanding.

Something similar happened for Daniel, too. The shattering silence allowed him to see a connecting line between these brazen questions of hers and the assertion which preceded them: that his father would make a poor prosecutor of any girl who seemed likely to take his fancy. "Did my father tell you all that?" he asked slowly.

She began to regret her frankness, since she did not know him well enough to guess what he might now do. She glanced at Banks – and was surprised to see that the woman hung upon her answer even more anxiously than Daniel. She quizzed the maid with her eyebrows, only to see the familiar servant's mask descend. "He must have taken a dislike to me," she explained. "He came bursting into the house and I'm afraid I ordered him back out."

"You *what?*" Daniel asked in a voice laden with disbelief.

Banks leaped in. "That's true as I'm sitting here, Mr Jago."

Mister Jago? Jane thought. The mystery deepened.

"Go out and come in again properly. We were all set for him to pull the house down about our ears."

"And?" Daniel was still incredulous.

"He obeyed her. Meek as a lamb, he went and did as she bid."

Daniel turned and stared at Jane as if there were twenty important things he had so far failed to notice in her. "Really?" he asked.

She nodded. "So that's probably why he spoke as he did. After all, what man wants his son to take up with a shrewish, self-opinionated woman – heiress or no?"

Daniel laughed. "The old curmudgeon!"

Jane tuned to Banks. "Don't you think that must be it?"

213

The maid shrugged awkwardly. "If you say so, miss. I mean – you were there, after all, and I wasn't."

"So he didn't pass any remark to you about it?"

Banks shook her head.

"I believe no harm was done," Daniel put in. "In fact, I believe he was quite taken with you."

"I believe we should talk of other matters," Banks said swiftly.

Jane ignored her. "Why d'you say that?" she asked Daniel.

"Well, he was certainly pretty taken with that portrait of you on the table in your father's room."

Jane felt Banks stiffen at her side. Oh dear, she thought, there was so much going on here that she did not understand. But if she just kept picking away at it, something would surely emerge. "Portrait of me?" She frowned.

"In the silver frame, on the little table by the door."

"Ah." Jane spoke in as neutral a tone as she could manage. "I didn't know that photograph had been placed there. It's certainly the wrong place for it."

He stared at one and then the other of them with some amusement; plainly a house in which each knick-knack had its precisely allotted place was far outside his ken. "You needn't worry," he assured them tendentiously. "Mrs Lanyon has tidied it away again."

Jane pounced. "Again?"

"Well, she took it away, at any rate."

The reply seemed to satisfy Jane. Banks, however, did not relax, she noticed.

"Actually," he added, "I didn't think it was a photograph. It looked more like a sketch in pastel."

"In a plain silver frame?" Jane asked casually.

He nodded.

"Then you're right," she told him. "That's not the photograph of me. But now I think I know the picture you mean."

PART THREE

Ménage seul

28 THE GALES OF EARLY December ushered in a spell of settled cold weather that persisted right through Christmas. Jane stood at her window at Parc-an-Ython on Christmas morning, staring out at the great brooding blanket of snow that had fallen silently in the windless night and which now covered lawn and shrubbery, rooftop and field, with impartial perfection. It seemed curious that it could render those features so indistinct from each other, despite their crisp delineation in the pale, wintry sun.

Perhaps there was snow all over England? She remembered such vistas in Leeds, where a winter without its blanket of white was almost unheard of. Suddenly, in her mind's eye, there was an image of her mother's grave as she had seen it last January, with just *In Loving Memory of Angwin Hervey* visible above the snow. There was no headstone on her father's grave as yet. Today, when she went to church, it would be ... hid in Death's dateless *white!*

The thought that the dead were merely hidden somewhere – available if you could only find them – was still comforting to her. Her eyes scanned the white world and the cold blue sky, and she shivered. Banks, who entered the room at that moment, saw it and said,"I told them we should set a fire here today. Shall I put one of the maids to it now?"

Jane shook her head without turning round. "It wasn't that. I was thinking how easy it would be to imagine Death stalking this landscape. You know – a skeleton in a black shroud with a scythe and hourglass? If he went walking across the lawn there now, you wouldn't be a bit surprised."

The maid gave an involuntary shudder, too. "You shouldn't ought to dwell on such fancies, miss," she chided gently. "'Tis Christmas – and a new year soon enough."

Jane turned to her and smiled, to show her this was no shallow or passing fit of melancholy but part of something far deeper – too deep for a fleeting smile to disturb. "Both your parents are still alive, aren't they?" she asked.

"By the grace of God."

"It's like a shield against Death, you know. Even if there's only one of them. While they still live, you don't get that thought – *I'm next!* That sounds callous but it's the truth. I feel as if a shield has been taken away from me."

Banks came to her with a heavy woollen stole. "Here, put this up. At least you'll feel warmer."

Instead of letting the maid slip it round her, Jane turned and took it in her hands. "Black," she said with distaste. "Black, black, black!" She waved vaguely about the room. "I've worn the colour too long, Banks. It's beginning to darken my soul. I feel its oppression like ..." No apt comparison came to her, but she did not search very hard. "Do you suppose I should cause an almighty scandal if I dropped it all on New Year's Day?"

217

"You know you would." Banks spoke without enthusiasm. In spirit she was all for the idea.

"But the county of Cornwall would survive the shock, I think?" Her tone was strangely at odds with the sentiment – abstracted, remote, as if her mind had already passed on to other, weightier matters. As if it were all settled. She looked at Banks's bewildered face and smiled. "Don't mind me," she advised. "But it's an interesting speculation, don't you think? What are the limits on my freedom now? What may I decide for myself and carry off successfully? What would merely raise an eyebrow? What would cause a gasp? What would bring a cry of *No!* In short, where will Mrs Lanyon draw the line – when she's pushed to it?"

"Are you asking me?" Banks responded.

Jane, who had meant the questions rhetorically, decided to say, "Yes."

"'Tis hardly my place to speak of it," she began cautiously – but then rushed on before Jane could have second thoughts and agree: "But I do catch the feeling she's lost her way with you."

"Her *sway* with me, d'you mean?"

"No, not exactly, miss. If you cast your mind back to how she was when she first took you under her wing ... I mean, everything was do this, do that, wear that dress, this is right, that's wrong – 'twas all cut and dried, as we do say. But she isn't like that no more, hardly."

Jane pulled the stole about her and was glad of the sudden warmth, no matter what its colour. "You've noticed it, too," she commented.

Banks bit her lip. "Jump down my throat if you like, miss, but I think she's gone and found something in your father's papers that she doesn't know how to ... well, she doesn't know *what* to do." She eyed her mistress warily.

"Go on," Jane encouraged her.

"You must have seen it yourself, now. While your father lived she was like a steam tug with a line fast to you – pushing you and pulling you so you never hardly had time to draw breath. But now ..." She faltered.

"... it's like she's lost her rudder," Jane said after a pause. "You're quite right. At first I thought it was just that she wanted to be gentle with me because ... well, for obvious reasons. But now I don't believe that's so at all. What have I done to make her ... doubtful like that?"

Again Banks made several gestures of placatory caution before she replied. "I don't believe 'tis anything you've done, miss. Or not done, neither. She's just the same with mister, if you noticed. She's like a bulgrannick with all her horns pulled in. Mild as a plucked goose. I believe she's learned something, somehow. And it's taken all the starch out of her."

The thought struck such a disturbing resonance in Jane she was suddenly filled with the greatest reluctance to pursue it. She turned and stared out of the window again and said, with a sigh, "I suppose this appalling weather will put paid to my little supper party tomorrow."

"Never fret," Banks assured her. "If there's no fresh fall tonight, the roads'll be clear tomorrow."

Jane did not follow. "D'you mean it'll all melt?"

218

"No, they'll put gangs on it all day today."

"On Christmas Day?"

The maid smiled grimly. "It doesn't mean much in the labouring houses hereabouts, miss. Just a day of unpaid idleness. They'd be glad of the wage. Women and children, too."

* * *

There was no thaw, but Banks was right about the roads being cleared. The Highway Commissioner had opened his coffers and gangs of ill-clad wraiths, some of them scarcely more substantial than the steamy breath they exhaled upon the motionless air, swarmed up and down the turnpike to shovel it clean. It was, by general acclaim, the best Christmas for years; the baker worked double tides to halve the bonus with the publican.

Jane decided to wear a magnificent black-silk ball gown her mother had worn on the death of Honoré de Balzac, some ten years ago. Banks almost burst a blood vessel in her exertions to lace her mistress into it, but she managed it at last. And then it was, "My, don't you look a picture!" and "You'll take their breath away!"

"Then it'll be honours even," Jane gasped as she tried to draw breath against the impossible confinement of those cruel laces. "Oh, why do we torture ourselves so?"

But, looking at herself in the mirror, she could see her answer. The dress, as Banks had pointed out when they selected it in daylight, was not actually black. If you took a good glass to it, you could detect fine threads of dark crimson and ultramarine shooting in among the general warp and weft of undoubted black. Though invisible to the unaided eye at its more customary distance of some three or four feet, something of its vibration yet remained and gave the cloth its mysterious fascination.

Its *couture* had that same curious duality. The bodice was cut very low across her breast; but there was a kind of sleeved halter of dense black tulle that erupted in a froth of dark gray lace at her wrists and was constrained in a broad band of velour around her throat, making her neck seem even longer and more elegant. This same tulle spilled outward and down to cover her breast and back, so that her exposed *décolleté*, though hardly on show, contributed to the overall effect that same vibrant excitement as the visible-invisible colours in the silk.

Two diamond earrings and a small diamond clasp in her hair completed the magic. Banks held her breath and stared at her in undisguised awe. There were no words to describe the transformation, yet neither could doubt that a new Jane Hervey had somehow been conjured up by the triple sorcery of silk, candlelight, and diamonds. No – quadruple sorcery, for there was a fourth ingredient, something less tangible, in that bewitchment.

I am a woman, she thought, looking at herself in surprise. She had, to be sure, made such private boasts before, but never with such cause as now. She moved slightly, a little quarter turn, swaying to one side with a sinuosity that felt new. And it looked new, too. No mirror-image Jane had ever moved quite like that before.

And then she recognized it for what it was. Often at balls and garden parties, at the theatre or simply out walking in the *Bois,* she had noticed that certain ladies possessed a strange power to compel all eyes to follow them. Many were beautiful, but not all. Many wore striking costumes, but not all. Many behaved in the most animated fashion, but not all. And the most irresistible among them were those who were neither beautiful nor gaudy nor flamboyant – and yet somehow they demanded the homage of that fascination, from men and women alike.

It was something of that same compulsive quality which Jane now recognized in her looking glass, a little bewildered, more than a little frightened.

"Well, if you don't gather three proposals tonight, Miss Jane," Banks murmured at last, "then Cornwall's dead. That's all I can say."

Jane realized she meant it as the ultimate sort of compliment, but the literal meaning of the words jarred oddly with her own expectations – which was another surprise. What *did* she expect from this evening, then, she asked herself? She could not tell – except that it was something less obvious than a simple proposal.

As she moved toward the door, gliding across the floor like a stately black clipper, she was seized with a sudden, almost overwhelming feeling that her mother had experienced some of these odd new sensations, too, on the day she had first put on this very dress. Later her rational mind explained it away as an effect of sudden movement ... forgetting to breathe ... tight lacing ... excitement – all the running dogs of female intuition; but at the time she was almost overcome by an overwhelming conviction that her mother was there, physically there, in that room.

Curiously enough, only moments later, that same conviction filled her with a profound sense of calm. It suddenly seemed the most natural thing in the world, and not the least bit disturbing or frightening, that the ghostly mother should somehow be evoked by her daughter's putting on of this particular gown. As Jane recovered from the immediate shock she became aware that she had never before thought of her mother as a woman – or not as this sort of woman, the sort she now felt herself to be. She had always been ... just Mother, Mama, *Maman, ta mère,* your dear mater ... a remote figure of authority and reward whose caprice was more like that of fate itself than of anything identifiably feminine.

And now, as she strove to capture her mother's feelings – wondering what loves and hates, what desires and fears were running through her life in the hours when she had donned this dress for the first time – she felt her comforting shade recede, as though the effort of rising from her eternal sleep could not sustain any inquiry, especially into emotions so long extinct.

At last she knew she was alone once more. The shield had gone. Yet this time the realization was not so bleak as before. To be alone was also natural.

As she left she told Banks she could now put out the dresses and things for the Delamere girls.

When Dorothy saw her, she, too, recognized at once some new and compelling quality in her ward. She stopped and put her hand to her breast. "Oh, my dear! You ..." She fell to silence.

"What?" Jane prompted.

"... look simply beautiful."

Jane took her arm and laughed as they walked toward the stairhead. "What were you really going to say?"

"That," Dorothy assured her.

"It was to do with my father, wasn't it."

Dorothy came to a sudden halt. "How did you know?"

Jane shrugged and edged her forward again. "I just did. I think it's my night for just knowing things."

Dorothy laughed, not at all easily. "You're right as it happens. I was thinking of your father, of something he told me. Are you sure you ...?"

"Go on."

"He once told me how it always gave him a shock to see you in any of your dear mother's dresses – how alike you are. And, seeing you there just now, I suddenly knew exactly what he meant." Then, realizing that her words suggested an acquaintance she had not shared, she added, "I do wish I'd known your mother."

The sentiment – conventional enough – was delivered with a curious flatness that was almost wistful, as if her desire had some particular reference.

"I wish she'd seen me in this gown," Jane said. "It's the one she wore when the whole of Paris was in mourning for Balzac, you know."

Dorothy suddenly gripped her tight – and then apologized. "I thought I was going to turn my heel on a stair rod," she explained – none too convincingly to a Jane who was growing daily more attuned to the nuances of her guardian's behaviour.

"I wonder where she wore it?" Jane mused. "Who danced with her? And where? What did they talk about? What little Parisian scandals could this dress reveal if it could only speak? Did she ever dance with my father in it?"

There was a little twitch at that; so now Jane knew this dress had some significance in her parents' lives; and it was important enough to have caused him to tell Dorothy about it. Or perhaps she had discovered it in his diaries? Yes, that was more probable. She remembered Banks's suspicion that those diaries had caused Dorothy to change, to lose her sense of purpose.

"Who's going to arrive first?" Dorothy asked. "And will it be a good omen or not? Did you sleep on the champagne cork last night? I forgot to ask."

Jane chuckled. "Yes, I dreamed of Kinghorn Jago. So there's another old wives' tale hit on the head."

But Dorothy appeared to take it all quite seriously. "It's what you dream that counts, my precious. There'll be a clue in it, mark my words. Did he tell you Daniel had run away to sea or something like that?"

Jane sighed wearily, wishing this nonsense had never begun. "I was sitting by an upstairs window in a house I've never been in before – in an ordinary suburban street – and Kinghorn Jago walked by outside, looked up, spotted me, and asked where was the nearest public footbath. And that was it." She laughed at its absurdity.

"He needs to launder his conscience, you see," Dorothy assured her.

"Not in my champagne." Jane was determined to go on making light of it all.

"What d'you know about bathing in champagne?" Dorothy asked tartly.

Jane pulled an exaggeratedly contrite face and said, in a stagey, sepulchral tone, "Only what I read in the servants' newspapers."

Dorothy dropped her arm in vexation. "I hope you're not going to be frivolous all evening, my lamb. Remember, you are still in mourning."

221

Jane, her face quite serious now, stared her out – thinking it a most extraordinary thing to be doing. If Dorothy had been as cutting and as peremptory as that on any previous occasion, she'd have been mortified.

A knock at the door saved them. Jane put on her most welcoming smile and nodded to the valet du jour that she was ready to receive.

"I'm sorry," Dorothy said at her elbow. "I expect we're both a little on edge this evening. How I hate Christmas!"

Jane took her arm but continued to smile toward the door. "Tight lacing," she said. "There must be some little grain of truth in all those articles by all those clever doctors." She felt Dorothy grow tense again; her guardian, she realized, simply did not know how to respond when she said such things.

The caller was Richard Vyvyan, who flung his cocked hat and cape across the footman's arm and came forward stamping the snow off his boots. "Hah! It's more like Canada than Cornwall," he declared. "Happy Christmas, one and all!"

He shook Dorothy's hand first, which piqued Jane – until he took hers and did not let it go.

"Oh, you'll steal all the girls' hearts in that uniform, young man," Dorothy said. The promise, jocular though it was, slightly embarrassed him.

"Oh no he won't," Jane said quietly, staring him full in the eye. "For this heart he'll pay full measure."

He laughed then, finding her humour more to his liking. "Steal, pay, or win," he said truculently. "So long as I get 'em, what?"

Dorothy laughed louder than Jane.

He let her hand go at last, but their mutual inspection of each other continued a moment longer. On her part, Jane realized, it was cool – not in the sense of being unfriendly (far from it), but it was calmly made, without fear or awkwardness. And its conclusions were fairly warm. Successful suitor or not, she decided, Richard Vyvyan would make a jolly good friend. "Thank you for your letter," she said.

He gave a genial little smile and nodded. "I wasn't going to say anything."

"Well, it was very kind and thoughtful. Now I'm going to desert my post and get you some mulled wine." She took him by the arm and led him toward the dining room, where a small buffet was laid out. "I hope you're feeling as queasy about food as we are," she warned. "There's very little, as you see."

He laughed heartily – a little too heartily, allowing his relief to show. "You're a tonic, Miss Hervey," he told her.

So he had expected a sticky passage this evening. Jane thought it an insight into the sort of person she had been all those *years* ago last summer. He held his glass while she emptied the ladle into it. "It is a splendid uniform," she told him. "It must take at least two valets to keep it looking so immaculate."

"You wouldn't have thought so an hour ago," he replied. "I swear I all but murdered the scoundrel."

Idly she touched the buttons and braid across his chest. "He made up for it since."

"Jane, dear!" Dorothy's rather imperious call came from the door, where she stood, a darkish silhouette against the brilliance beyond. "Another carriage is approaching. Duty calls."

222

"Coming," she cried with determined gaiety; under her breath she added to him, "I don't wish it to be half so formal. Help me every chance you get."

"Gladly," he murmured as she went to obey the summons. There was a hint of bewilderment in his tone.

Was she really so different from the Jane he remembered? she wondered. The odd thing was, she could feel no great difference in herself; to her it was much less profound, more like the difference between wearing one kind of bonnet or another. The thought of bonnets reminded her of Mrs Brown in Penzance, and then, by inevitable progression, of an interview she must soon seek with Miss Wilkinson there. Not in Miss Brown's shop, of course ... though, come to think of it, why not? Now she knew all about the girl, they could hardly meet anywhere else.

The carriage was the Lanyons' own, bringing Jesse and the Delameres, – including, Jane was overjoyed to discover, young Bessie, looking brighter than she had ever seen the girl. "Come on upstairs," she cried when the more formal exchanges were done with. She spread her arms like a goose girl and swept them all before her. "And deal with the ravages of your long and tedious journey."

"Jane, dear!" Dorothy gave a brittle laugh.

"Sorry, Uncle Jesse." She paused briefly in her ascent of the stair. "I'd forgotten its was such *ages* since we met. There's a wassail bowl in the dining room – and Mr Vyvyan to keep you company."

"That isn't quite what I meant," Dorothy said even more brittly. "We are expecting further guests."

"Only Lawyer Scawen and Mr Nicholl. I want to surprise them."

"Well, you're going the right way about it, I must say."

Jane smiled at her as if she took the words for agreement. At the half way landing Mrs Delamere murmured, "I think Mrs Lanyon is right, my dear – if you don't mind my saying so. You ought to be there to greet ..."

"No, no." Jane patted her reassuringly on the arm. "This is much more important. You'll see."

"How *did* you get into that dress?" Rosa asked in a stage whisper. "It's not fair. It looks simply magnificent."

"After yesterday's excesses? With great difficulty, I can assure you." They had reached the door of her bedroom. She turned for a moment and guarded it with her back. "Now let me go in first, and don't follow. I just want to make sure everything's in place. Come in when I call you."

They exchanged glances of bewilderment, but the promise in Jane's smile and voice was so marked they could not help smiling, too.

A moment later came the cry, "Ready!" and they pressed forward eagerly, almost crushing one another between the doorjambs.

A moment later still, the cries were all theirs. "Oh, Jane! ... How utterly, utterly ... you shouldn't have ..." and so on.

But the sight that most gladdened Jane's heart, the memory that remained long after the shallower excitements had dwindled and died, was of young Fanny, standing alone, still and silent in that sea of raucous delight, clutching the fashion doll with the porcelain head to her bosom, eyes clenched, tears of joy streaming down her face.

223

It was too much for Jane, who turned and ran – or tripped as fast as her lacing would allow – back downstairs. There, Dorothy looked daggers at her, though she had obviously decided to say nothing until the festivities were over. Jane saw no other remedy than to take the bull by the horns – or, rather, her guardian by the arm. "Oh, come on, Dorothy," she pleaded. "I don't want that sort of stuffy ... gathering. You could hardly call it a party. I want a jolly evening where a jolly group of friends have a jolly time together."

A fortuitous shower of golden laughter fell on them from above. "You see?" she said, looking Dorothy full in the face, now in one eye, now in the other ...

And Dorothy, staring back into those bright eyes, those all-too-adorable features ... feeling the radiance of her joy – and the monstrous, egotistical will that gave it such power – Dorothy knew she had lost the battle to keep alive the pure and sweet young creature she had once fancied she saw in Jane. In that moment it was as if some obscure wand of office passed from her to her ward.

From somewhere she plucked up a smile. "You are right," she said. "It is not an evening for standing on ceremony."

"Oh, bless you, dear, dear Dorothy!" Jane threw her arms about her and gave her a passionate hug.

To Dorothy, swallowing her tears, it was like the swansong of the dear young girl who had so briefly lighted up her life.

29 THEY BEGAN WITH dumb crambo as soon as Vosper Scawen and Argus Nicholl arrived. Jesse Lanyon gave out the words, he being considered too dignified to make a fool of himself in front of the Delamere girls. To Jane he gave *Montpelier*, which she thought easy enough. *Mon* would be the way the Scots pronounced *man*, so she'd do a man in a kilt for that. *Pel* would be like *pelt* – not the skin but hurling things at people. And *lier* ... well, anyone could *leer*. And if they couldn't get Montpelier from *mon-pelt-leer*, they really were dumb crambos!

Richard Vyvyan had the easiest, with *grog; G* was a horse, which he mimed very comically; *R* was Ah!; *O* was Oh!; the whole was a drunken reel, again very comic – and he was bathed in a shower of congratulations in less than thirty seconds. Rosa had to do *automaton*, as a punishment for her unseemly gesture at the ball in November. Through a chorus of "wonder ... admiration ... praise ... seasickness ..." they narrowed the first syllable down to *awe;* then it was "kitten ... puss-puss ... circus strong man ..." down to *tom*. And there was no need to mime the rest.

But when it came to *Montpelier* Jane paid dearly for her guesses of "seasickness" and "circus strong man." Somehow, without saying a word, Rosa managed to induce the rest to feign near-idiocy. As a result, her *mon* brought the company no nearer the syllable than "Balkan goatherd" – the only kilted figure they could think of, it seemed. By a similar misdirection, the whole became "Balkan goatherd – throwing snowballs – simpering." She had to admit defeat and forfeit the point, greatly to Rosa's satisfaction.

"Now *that's* what *I* call simpering!" Jane pointed an accusing finger at her. Everybody laughed. In the end the formalities were so shattered that Jesse Lanyon himself, Justice of the Peace or not, insisted on taking part. Jane gave him *evolution,* hoping that *Eve* would fox him; but he did *evil,* instead, followed easily by *you* and (atten)*shun* – and he did it so well, they had to concede him the laurels,

After that, it hardly mattered what they did; everyone was in such a good humour. So much so that when J. Lanyon Esq. Justice of the Peace, met Miss Hervey, Noted Heiress, in the taproom at the Queen's Arms and he said to her, "Put more coal on the fire, girl," and she replied, "Please allow me to adjust your cravat, sir," and the consequence was that they had to hide in the broom cupboard for the rest of the evening – well, even Mrs Lanyon could not help laughing.

Before they broke for a bite to eat, J. Lanyon Esq. suddenly remembered his grandfather's favourite game and insisted they should play it at once. It was clearly not a tradition in his own household, for Dorothy was as mystified as any.

"What we do, you see," he said eagerly, "is we all go down on our hands and knees around this square in the middle of the carpet."

They complied with a will. The square was only four foot by three, so there was much jostling and giggling.

"Now we all place our hands outstretched, exactly on the perimeter. Fingers just touching it. No fingers inside the square."

He then spent a good minute, correcting them minutely, making them line up their fingers precisely. By now, of course, everyone was wondering what significance it could possibly have.

Then he said to Fanny, who was at his left, "D'you know this game?"

"No, sir," she replied, more than slightly bewildered.

Then to his wife: "Do you know this game, my dear?"

"You know I do not," she told him sharply, finding it most undignified to be down on all fours like that.

And so it went on, right around the circle. Each player was asked if he knew the game, and each had to reply that he did not – even Vosper Scawen, whose grin showed that he did. That grin, and the increasing speed with which Jesse conducted the ritual inquest, soon piqued everyone's curiosity to screaming point.

Which was precisely the moment when Jesse, having completed the circle, said, "Nor do I. Let's play something else."

Such an idiotic conclusion, coming as it did from a person of such dignity, left them helpless with laughter.

Even the refreshments became part of a game. Jane had pinned up slips of paper all about the room containing anagrams of the names of the food; no one was permitted to eat an item until they could tell her where its anagram was located. *Geg* was easy, and the egg sandwiches went quickly; but *no cap, clod* ensured that the cold capon remained uncarved until almost the last.

Then Dorothy finally had her way, with everyone doing their party pieces. But by now the ice was so thoroughly broken that no one felt nervous, no one dried up, no one shrivelled in a blaze of blushes. She herself pushed the boat out with a lovely contralto rendering of *Angus Macdonald* ... "Oh sad was my heart when from

225

mountain and glen ..." Fanny and Rosa played a duet by Handel in which they crossed hands very effectively. Richard Vyvyan folded his arms and glowered all the way through *Drake's Drum*. And Jane, who had prepared *The Heart Bow'd Down* from *The Bohemian Girl*, changed her mind at the last minute and sang instead, *I Dream't I Dwelt in Marble Halls* from the same operetta. She sang one verse to Richard, the other to Vosper; there being no third verse, she sang nothing at all to Argus Nicholl – which was as kindly a way as any of telling him how he stood. When his turn came, he and Vosper surprised everyone by pulling on caps borrowed from a pair of stable lads and singing, *Goin' up Camborne Hill Coming Down* with great comic effect.

Everyone contributed something, but once again Jesse Lanyon stole the crown by telling one of the most chilling ghost stories they had ever heard – because, until the very last line, no one knew it was a ghost story at all. He dressed it up as a reminiscence of his youth when he had been caught out on Bodmin Moor during a torrential downpour. He had taken refuge at an inn, where one of the locals had entertained him with a most graphic account of the saving of the bridge on the Launceston turnpike, a good half-century earlier and on just such a wild night as that. The structure was then only half completed and was in imminent danger of being swept away. Twenty wretched souls had perished in securing it against the flood – twenty, carried off by the engorged waters and drowned. The old fellow described every piteous moment – each one of which was now retailed by Jesse Lanyon to a hushed and wide-eyed company at Montpelier.

"And then I noticed something exceedingly odd," he concluded. "We had been sitting by that roaring fire above half an hour. I who had been as wet as a herring was now bone dry. Not so my interlocutor, however. He was as soaked and sodden as when I entered. Why, you would have supposed that someone had dashed a pail of water over him not ten seconds since. And the vast, dark pool beneath his chair would merely have heightened that same impression. 'My dear sir,' I exclaimed to him, 'you must have been caught in an even worse downpour than I. For I am now dry – yet look at you.' He smiled at me, a twinkling, genial smile, and asked if I had understood nothing of his tale. I would have grown angry and told him I grasped every word, but a sudden and terrible chill clamped itself about my heart and I found I could not utter a word. I stared at him, with some overpowering but nameless horror clawing at my innards, and he just sat there and stared back at me, smiling that ancient, enigmatic smile. And at last he spoke again. 'You do understand, then,' he said simply. 'The likes o' we do *never* dry.' "

Young Fanny gave an involuntary little cry of terror and had to be comforted in her mother's arms. It was Dorothy who unwittingly broke the spell when she said, quite seriously, that he must be making it up, because he had never said a word before tonight about having been on Bodmin Moor. Most of them supposed she was simply prolonging the joke – giving it a different twist – and they laughed. Then, of course, she had to pretend that she had meant it in just such a spirit, but Jane could see that she was annoyed at having been taken in.

After that it was dancing – country dances, mostly, quadrilles and eightsome reels with all holding hands in a ring. At the end there were more modern dances for couples only. Jane enjoyed one each with the three young bachelors. Argus Nicholl, cool as a moss house, asked her if she had given his proposal any further consideration. She replied that her answer was precisely what she had predicted it would be. He accepted her rebuff philosophically and asked at once whether she thought Susie Delamere had the makings of an ecclesiastical wife. Jane, behaving as if the notion would never have crossed her mind in a million years, told him how much she envied his grasp of character and quality; of course, now that he had made the connection, she realized that Susie was perfectly moulded to the life – but it had needed someone with his acuity to see it.

He deferred to her and said that *she* was the one who possessed truly sharp insight into character. "All I did was pose one simple question, Miss Hervey. Yet from it you have deduced one of the most profound and fundamental truths about my character and faculties. Few indeed are the people who realize how subtle and discerning a mind is mine."

He proposed to Susie the very next dance. She swallowed her answer before it leapt off her tongue and promised it before the next day's sun had set.

Richard Vyvyan, who danced as if he had learned the art on a heaving deck – "all rubato and no bars," as Rosa described it – told her he'd had a bit of luck recently: "A kinsman of mine, a Commodore Jago, has been appointed naval attaché at our embassy in Paris and he's asked for me on secondment as his ADC. Not bad, what!"

"But that's even better news than you think," she told him delightedly. "At least for me – and I hope for you, too. It seems that I still own my mother's old villa in Paris, in the Faubourg-St.-Honoré ..."

He pursed his lips and whistled soundlessly. "Was it her family home?" he asked.

"No, she was from Cardiff, but she inherited ... oh, it's too complicated to go into all that now."

"And none of my business, anyway!"

"Oh, I didn't mean it like that, Mr Vyvyan. But believe me, it is all highly involved. And rather dull. But the thing I was going to say is that Mrs Lanyon is of the opinion that we should not sell it without first seeing it – to be sure we get a good price and aren't cheated."

He cleared his throat delicately. "I'm afraid the life of an ADC to a naval attaché in so important a capital as Paris will hardly leave me time to ..."

She laughed and shook his arm. "Dear man! I'm not going to ask you to *sell* the place for us! Merely to reserve an evening or two while we are there!"

He joined her laughter, rather sheepishly, scratched his head, lost what little grasp of the rhythm he had enjoyed until then, and brought them to a halt. "Of course," he said. "When?"

"When does your secondment begin?"

"In April, I believe."

"Then I think you have just had commission of your first unofficial duty."

He recovered some of his poise and told her he now looked forward to the posting ten times more than before.

She remembered then that she wanted to ask him about that name Jago, but the piece ended and there was no time.

227

"By rights you should have the next three dances," she told Vosper as he swept her away for the waltz. Five steps later she added, "And if you dance them all as nimbly as this, you shall!"

He really was superb – better, even, than Daniel Jago.

"Why so?" he asked.

"Because I still owe you two from the Liston House ball."

"Ah yes." His eyes swept around the room, seeking Bessie Wender. "I think she is looking exceptionally well this evening. Good people, the Moores."

"Don't let Dorothy hear you say so."

"I don't live in her pocket."

She shook his arm aggressively. "I wasn't even suggesting it."

"Good."

"What's come over you?" she asked, staring into his eyes with an odd mixture of annoyance and concern.

"I'm sorry." He smiled and made a visible effort to brighten up.

But she was not about to let him go so easily. "You have to tell me now," she said.

He pulled a rueful face. "I haven't been able to forget that kiss."

"Nor I," she assured him warmly. "D'you think we'll get a chance to slip away and do it again?"

"I don't imagine so," he answered glumly.

"I know what," she said, hoping to cheer him up. "You know Dorothy's talking about her and me going to Paris in the spring? Well, why don't you make up some important lawyer's reason for accompanying us? Throw in a few French legal terms and frighten her to death."

Suddenly he was grinning like a sandboy. On an equally sudden intuition she said to him, "You were listening, weren't you!"

"What?" His features gathered to protest.

"You were," she persisted. "You overheard me talking about it with Mr Vyvyan."

His ears went pink but he made no direct answer.

"Oh, Vosper!" She hugged him briefly. "Don't go all … like that!"

"Like what?"

"You know jolly well. Oh, by the way – here's another thing you might know – he mentioned a kinsman of his, a Commodore Jago. Would he be related to the Jagos of Greeenbank?"

"Jago just means James in Cornish, you know."

"That's not exactly an answer, Vosper. I wonder what Vosper means, anyway."

He chuckled. "A rich pasture beside a stout rampart."

"I'm sorry I asked," she informed him. "Cornish is obviously a very concise language. I suppose the whole of the Lord's Prayer is over in three words! Anyway, about Commodore Jago?"

"I don't know." He shook his head apologetically. "I suppose they must all be related if you go back far enough. Just as all the various branches of the Vyvyans are." He frowned as if some puzzle had just occurred to him, but did not volunteer what it might be.

"Well?" she pressed.

He shook his head in vexation – at himself, not her. "There's something at the back of my mind about Vyvyans and Jagos. He said this Commodore Jago is a kinsman of his?"

She nodded.

"It doesn't ring a bell – and yet I'm sure there's a link somewhere." He smiled. "It'll come to me. Probably at four o'clock tomorrow morning and then I shan't get back to sleep."

The vigour of the waltz disordered her hair and she went upstairs to repair it. She found Rosa sitting before the mirror. "There's a face!" Jane commented.

"Precisely what I was thinking," the girl replied.

"No, I meant glum. No one's allowed to be glum at my party."

"I was just wondering – what *use* am I to anyone?"

"Oh, poor ickle Wosa'a all despaiwing! You're not expecting sympathy from me, I hope? Not after your disgraceful behaviour during my dumb crambo."

Rosa chuckled at the memory. "Go on," she urged. "You're cheering me up already." She stood and yielded the chair. "Allow me," she added, taking the comb from Jane's hand.

"Well," Jane risked saying after a moment or two, "you'd make a first-class ladies maid, anyway."

"Don't!" she replied with theatrical alarm. "It's too close to the bone."

"You will go about, doing these funny things. You'll have to let the memory of that simmer down now. Such a waste of time."

Rosa pulled a disgusted face. "You sound like every country walk I've taken for the last three years." She stopped combing and started to massage Jane's neck, pressing her thumbs hard on each side of the bone.

"Oh, that's wonderful," Jane told her. Then, casually, "D'you actually *want* to marry, Rosie?"

The girl pulled a face. "When I hear doors shutting against me all over the county, just because of a bit of high spirits – yes, then I want to marry. I want to show *someone* it wouldn't exactly be a prison sentence. If you were a man, would you think it such a terrible thing to be my husband?"

"I think life would never have a dull moment," Jane replied cautiously.

"There you are, then. Surely there must be some man out there who'd quite like a bit of zest in his life?" She ceased her massage and picked up the brush, with which she arranged and disarranged Jane's curls to no great effect. "But then, when I actually think of being married to just one man for the rest of my life – I mean, picking him now, or, even worse, being picked by him now, and then that's it! Over and done with! Just him and me for the next fifty years."

"And your children."

She pulled an even glummer face. "That, too!"

"What *do* you want, then?" Jane asked.

Rosa glanced at her warily in the mirror. "Don't take this amiss, darling, but d'you remember telling me once about the life your mother led in Paris? Well, that's what I'd like."

On an impulse too sudden to check, Jane blurted out, "Would you like to see it?"

"What?" Rosa stared at her in bewilderment. "See what?"

"The villa. In Paris. Dorothy and I are going there in the spring. Would you like to come, too?" She laughed. "You might as well. Everybody else is."

But Rosa hardly seemed to hear this last. She had gone white as snow and now clutched at Jane for support. "Do you truly mean it?" she whispered. "Because, if you're just joking, it would be ..."

"I truly mean it," Jane assured her.

"Oh!" She flung the brush into the air, not caring where it fell, and began to pirouette around the room. "In Paris in spring, in spring, in spring ..." she sang to the tune of the Viennese Waltz. She stopped as suddenly as she started and, taking Jane by the hand, said, "Tell me again tomorrow. I shan't believe it until I hear you say it by the cold light of day."

Jane smiled. "We'd better go back down. They'll be leaving, soon."

"They? Shan't you be going with them?"

The smile grew a shade conspiratorial. "I shall have a sudden ague or something. There is a letter I wish to write. A rather difficult letter. And I don't wish Dorothy to know of it."

Rosa broke into a slow grin. "You're a dark 'un, aren't you! Actually, watching you and her tonight ... something's happened, hasn't it. Something's changed."

"In her."

"And in you. I can see it now, too. Something in your eyes." She simpered, deliberately, as she had done earlier that evening. "Of course, if you'd rather not tell me, I'll *quite* understand."

Jane chuckled. "I don't know what there is to tell." More hesitantly she added, "I do know what the difference in *me* is, though."

"And?" Rosa prompted after a short silence.

"You're going to think I've been very childish up until now."

Rosa shook her head encouragingly.

"I mean, for all I know everybody else stopped thinking ... what I thought, when they left the nursery ..."

"Namely?" Rosa was having to grit her teeth against her impatience.

"It's not an easy thing to explain."

Rosa hung her head and pretended to fall asleep. "Perhaps it's another thing for the cold light of day?"

"I'll tell you," Jane said quickly. "Until very recently, you see, I've always believed ... oh dear!"

The other's bright eyes encouraged her; and the nodding head and the knowing smile said that she knew exactly what was going to come next ... and it wasn't so difficult, honestly ...

"I always believed that being a grown-up ... that the difference between grown-ups and children ... no, it's no good."

"Let me help," Rosa suggested in the tones of a gracious dowager. "It's to do with men and women, isn't it."

Jane nodded. "About the real business of living."

"Yes – about our bodies."

For a moment Jane stared at her in total incomprehension; then, as understanding dawned, she laughed. "No, no," she said. "I know about *that*. No, it's a much more jealously guarded secret than that."

"Oh," Rosa said weakly.

"Yes. Good heavens, did you think I meant ...! No, what I'm talking about is the business of having to *fight* for everything – for every last little thing. I wasn't brought up to think that."

3O ALL THAT DAY JANE'S feeling of dread at what she had done grew stronger. It was now the second Thursday in January, 1861. More than two weeks had passed since she had written to Miss Wilkinson, and, though she had asked the woman not to acknowledge the letter (except by complying with its suggestion that they should meet at Mrs Brown's on this particular day), the silence unnerved her and left her uncertain how to proceed. She knew what she wished to achieve by it – indeed, that ambition had grown stronger than ever – but whether by appeal or threat, browbeating or bargain, she had not the faintest idea.

She had also written to Mrs Brown, asking if she had a small workroom or store at the back of the premises where she, Jane, might meet Miss Wilkinson in privacy – and again had asked her not to acknowledge the letter. It had all seemed so straightforward at the time, as enthusiasms and hobby horses often do; but mature reflection, for which she had had ample scope, told her what a thoughtless and perilous act it had been.

She now put herself in Mrs Brown's shoes – pictured herself as an insignificant shopkeeper, struggling to make a living and utterly dependent on the goodwill of a few dozen married ladies, without whose custom the rest of her trade would dwindle. And here was a bizarre request from a young, unmarried girl who had no circle, ruled no clique, set no fashion; her standing, as far as Mrs Brown was concerned, was very much that of the unmarried daughters of her clientèle. And what should Mrs B – or any sensible tradesman – do if one such daughter wrote asking for a clandestine meeting with a "lady of the town" and using her shop as a cloak for the affair? Jane knew that if she were that shopkeeper, she would inform the girl's mother by return of post.

So Jane had studied Dorothy Lanyon most closely these past two weeks, seeking the faintest sign that Mrs Brown had alerted her to what was intended. Outwardly, at least, her guardian seemed as affable as ever, but that did nothing to still Jane's fears. Ever since Dorothy's extraordinary behaviour during Daniel Jago's enforced visit, Jane had lost all belief that her superficial actions in any way mirrored her true thoughts and intentions.

When the day arrived, and she and Banks mounted into the carriage, she thought of telling Tom Collett to go about by way of Goldsithney; but a moment's reflection showed her how useless that would be. If Dorothy knew of the meeting, as to both

231

time and place, no amount of misdirection would deflect her; indeed, it would give her the chance to slip into Penzance ahead of Jane and conceal herself somewhere where she might overhear. The odd thing was that, although Jane felt sure Dorothy would approve of everything she was about to say and do – or try to do – she would be horrified at the cause of it all and at Jane's understanding of the whole business. In Dorothy's view, she felt sure, the phrase "lady of the town" ought to mean the mayor's wife or something like that (which is what Jane had assumed it *did* mean on the one previous occasion she had accidentally heard the words being used).

Nonetheless, as she and Banks walked up Market Jew Street, she found her tread growing heavier and slower, and her interest increasing in the most out-of-the-way items in other shop windows. "Look at that," she observed as they passed the undertaker's a few doors down from the bonnet shop. "Isn't that amazing?"

"What?" Banks saw nothing of interest.

"It's a patent clip that allows the driver to remove the white plumes from a harness and insert black hearse feathers instead. So he can change from a wedding carriage to a funeral carriage in a matter of moments."

Banks stared at her, shook her head sadly, and said, "Let's go home again."

"No, but it is clever," Jane insisted as she resumed her reluctant walk up the hill.

The worst moment of all came when her fingers closed around the handle to Mrs Brown's shop. *You can still go back,* she told herself. *Not a word has been said as yet. You've committed yourself to nothing. Just turn and go. Send a note from the nearest café - Sorry, changed my mind! Forget it.*

She grasped the handle and turned it forcefully.

Mrs Brown nodded gravely; her face was unreadable. Jane realized that in all her fearful anticipation of this afternoon she had not given a moment's thought to meeting Mrs Brown; all her fears and anxieties had centered around Miss Wilkinson. So it was all the more gratifying to hear herself saying, in a voice that sounded almost unruffled, "Mrs Brown! This really is very good of you. I'm afraid I acted most impetuously, without a moment's thought for the difficulties I might be putting your way. So please tell me at once – if you would rather I did not pursue my intentions, please say so now and I shall not take it the slightest bit amiss."

There was a strange weariness, almost a world-weariness, in the woman's eye as she assured Jane she had no qualms whatever about permitting such a meeting.

"When you know your own motives are of the best," Jane continued, "you're apt to forget that others might put an entirely different construction on ..."

Mrs Brown's smile broadened as she ushered Jane on down the narrow passage between her stock and her displays. "Live and let live," she said. "That's always been my watchword. You'll find your party waiting there, my lover." She gave a significant nod at the door to the workroom, or whatever it was that lay beyond. All Jane's terror returned over those last few paces, but she stepped out more lively and gave herself no time to dither.

Miss Wilkinson must have been standing the other side, waiting, for the moment Jane's hand touched the knob, it turned and the door was pulled inward quite vigorously. "Welcome, Miss Hervey," she called out in a truculent tone, which suggested that she, too, was uneasy at this encounter.

By arrangement, but only after much bitter argument, Banks had remained near the entrance, ready to alert her mistress if anything untoward happened. Jane, staring into Miss Wilkinson's cool blue eyes, almost wished she had not been so insistent on conducting this interview alone.

"Miss Wilkinson," she said pleasantly. "I must apologize for deranging your day."

"Not at all." She closed the door in a more gentle fashion. "As it happens, I'm off work this week, anyway."

"You're not unwell, I trust?" Jane stared about her and was surprised to find that the room was neither store nor workroom but a kind of parlour, with an elegant little table and two chairs, a fire, with a kettle singing on the hob, and a rather luxurious chaise longue. The tall looking-glass, adjustable and free-standing, seemed out of place until Jane realized that it gave Mrs Brown the ability to say to a very fastidious customer that she could come in here and inspect herself in privacy and at full length – and in much better light than was available in the shop.

"On the contrary," Miss Wilkinson replied with a laugh. "This is always the most welcome day of the month – if you take my meaning?"

"Ah." Jane stared awkwardly at the window; every pane was of frosted glass.

"A cup of tea?" the other asked, moving toward the fire. "Or ...?" She opened a small cabinet that was filled to overflowing with liquor bottles.

Jane was agog; she would never have thought someone of Mrs Brown's apparent temper and habits would have so much in the way of ardent spirits. "Tea would be most welcome," she replied.

Miss Wilkinson wet the pot and tipped it into a slop bucket beside the chaise longue. Jane noticed there was a jug and ewer on a washstand in the corner – which struck her as rather odd for a parlour.

"What was all that about 'not pursuing your intentions,' or something of that sort? With Ma B just now?"

Jane gave a self-deprecating smile. "I'm afraid I was rather impetuous in making this arrangement. I did not think of her good name, you see."

The other burst out laughing.

It stung Jane into exclaiming, "I know it must be a small matter to you by now, but Mrs Brown is surely dependent on her good name?"

"Surely, indeed!"

"Why say it in that tone?"

Miss Wilkinson brought the teapot to the table. "Do sit down," she said. "If, indeed, that's what you're waiting for."

Jane, who was standing near the chaise longue, sat down there.

"If you prefer it so." Miss Wilkinson lifted the delicate little table and carried it to Jane, who thought of pointing out that she was perfectly capable of holding a cup and plate; but, not wishing to continue on so shrewish a note, she held her peace. "Why did you speak of Mrs Brown like that?" she persisted.

The woman gazed at her – an odd mixture of sadness and affection in her eye – and said, "I believe that the more we confine ourselves to matters in hand, and the less we bother with inconsequential questions like that, the better it will be for us both. Don't you agree?"

233

Jane could hardly help realizing she had just been snubbed, even though it had been in the gentlest fashion. She was so crestfallen that Miss Wilkinson felt compelled to add, "I may as well confess – I have gone in dread of this meeting ever since I received your letter."

"*You've* gone in dread!" Jane blurted out. "How do you suppose I have felt?"

"Smug? That at least was my guess."

Jane stared at her in astonishment. "Tell me," she murmured at last, "why do you imagine I asked to see you?"

Miss Wilkinson shook her head sadly. "I cannot imagine. I cannot think of one topic, one single point of interest we might share in common, Miss Hervey. I assumed you wished to ask me questions about your father and his ... connection" – she smiled faintly at the word and passed Jane her cup – "with me." She gave the creamer and sugar bowl a token push. "Help yourself. I refuse to play hostess. Or guest, come to that."

"Why would you dread talking about my father?" Jane asked. "Do you think I don't know what took place between you?"

Her eyebrows shot up, more with interest than in surprise; but she said, "No, I imagine you've learned enough to work that out for yourself by now. Or that excellent maid of yours has contrived to put the knowledge in your path. But that only makes it worse."

"Well, it certainly wasn't easy to accept ..."

"No, I don't mean that. I mean ... who said, 'A little learning is a dangerous thing'? There is no field of human ... how may I put it? ... *activity* in which that is more true than mine. My *chosen* field."

Jane closed her eyes and intoned, "I want to know everything you care to tell me. Mine is no idle curiosity, I assure you. Nor is it that kind which pretends to be shocked and is secretly delighted ... what's the word for that?'"

Miss Wilkinson smiled. "Prurient?"

"Yes. You are ..." She hesitated to complete the thought.

"Well educated?" The smile became thinner. "About prurience? I could write the textbook." She shook her head and the smile vanished altogether. "I accept what you say, Miss Hervey. You have discovered that your father, who was a good man, a decent man, a gentleman – and no one will beat me into second place in asserting as much – you have discovered that he behaved in a way that this hypocritical world ..." She checked herself, closed her eyes, shook her curls. "No," she told herself crossly, "let us leave such adjectives out of it." She opened her eyes again and smiled at Jane. "You have discovered that he behaved in a way that runs utterly at odds with everything he ever taught you ... everything you ever learned about the proper way for a gentleman to behave. And yet you, too, know he was a good and decent man – so you wish to understand. Isn't that it?"

Jane shook her head in amazement. "How do you know so much?" she asked.

Miss Wilkinson lowered her eyes. Her lips trembled a little. "Please don't say kindly or admiring things," she murmured. "It's something I've forgotten how to cope with." She drew a sharp breath and became brisk again. "Let me come to the point I was going to make, which is that, even if I told you every last little ... everything I

234

possibly could about your father – even then, I should leave you in a worse state of ignorance than you are now."

"I can't see that," Jane asserted.

"No," she agreed wanly. "It took me weeks to grasp the point – and I was in the very thick of it, day and night. It isn't your father you have to understand. It's the whole ... the matter of being human, of being men and women." She stared into the fire and said, as if she were asking the flames, "More tea?"

"If I don't start somewhere ..." Jane said hopefully. "If I don't even try ..."

Still staring into the flames, Miss Wilkinson said dreamily, "D'you suppose Ma Brown makes her living out of bonnets?" She waved a hand vaguely about them. "Did bonnets at a shilling or two each buy all this, for example?"

Jane stared at her in alarm, not daring to crystallize the guesses that were already stirring her imagination.

"Why *two* doors?" Miss Wilkinson continued the catechism. "One from the leather shop next door, one from the bonnet shop here. A man's shop and a woman's shop – each with access to a room with a washstand – two sets of towels, notice – a cabinet full of stimulating beverages, and ..."

Jane sprang up, almost dashing her teacup to the floor. "And a chaise longue! Good heavens!" She stared wildly about the room, seeing everything in it with new eyes. "Do you mean people actually ..." She stared at the woman, thinking even now that this might be some test of her gullibility.

"Take it from One Who Knows," she replied tersely. But then, as she saw Jane absorbing the notion, tucking it neatly away in the compartment where her new-found knowledge of *that* kind of woman was stored, she added, "I hardly ever use it. Girls like us don't like dividing the fee with women like Ma Brown, you see."

Jane interrupted her. "Did you ... did my father ...?"

"Once." Miss Wilkinson stared at her with expressionless eyes. "Would you rather not stay here now? Shall we go for a drive in your carriage instead?"

Making a defiant gesture of it, Jane seated herself again upon the chaise longue and said, "No."

The other nodded admiringly. "Let's try, then," she murmured. "Most of the women who use this room are married ladies who are wearied with their husbands – with their carelessness, their inattention, their refusal to believe that a wife can possibly be a flesh-and-blood creature with all the normal desires of flesh and blood. Most of the men who use this room are married gentlemen who are fatigued beyond bearing by their wives – by their endless prattle about their brilliant children, their wicked servants, the extortionate tradesmen of the district, the fading curtains, and those dreadful, dreadful neighbours ... Without such a place of assignation as this, they would die of spiritual prostration."

Jane shook her head. "I can hardly believe it," she said.

Miss Wilkinson nodded. "Eight months ago I was the same. I remember being appalled at what I discovered."

"And are you not so still?"

"No," was the simple reply.

"Oh," Jane said.

After a silence the woman, who had not taken her eyes off Jane, added, "I am not ashamed of what I do, you know. I was when you first met me – that evening by the station, if you remember?"

"Of course I remember."

She smiled. "Ashamed and therefore truculent. I shouldn't have addressed you at all. I would never do so now – but that's because I now have" – she paused and weighed Jane up before concluding – "confidence in it."

"For a moment," Jane told her, "I thought you were going to say pride."

"I was, but I didn't think you'd understand."

Jane looked away. "I don't."

"Didn't I warn you?" she reminded her.

After a silence Jane added, "Nor my father. I don't understand him. And I don't understand you."

Miss Wilkinson said nothing.

Jane went on, "The first time he came and sought you out – he must have sought you out – he knew nothing about you, except that you had angered him by engaging me in ..."

The woman laughed. "But that was when he decided! He came back and 'sought me out,' as you put it, the very next week. But I already knew he was coming."

"Did he write to say so? I don't follow ..."

Miss Wilkinson tapped her cheek just below her eyes. "I saw it in him here. There's a certain look men get in their eyes. I know it very well by now."

"But even so – he didn't know you and you didn't know him. The thought of going somewhere private, with a stranger ..." She shuddered.

"I was sick the first time," the woman responded, and then shook her head as if she hadn't meant to start going down that line at all. She went on hastily, "I suppose you expect me to trot out all the usual excuses? The poverty and wretchedness that forced me to it. The dozens of honest positions I sought and failed to get until I found myself staring at my last stale crust of bread ..."

"Yes," Jane chipped in eagerly, "surely there were honest positions open to you."

"I believe what I do now is honest," she replied quietly.

"Yes, but you know what I mean." Jane smiled encouragingly. "Did you really and truly try?"

Now Miss Wilkinson's smile was almost scornful. "Oh, Miss Hervey, do you really and truly wish to know?"

"Yes." Jane bridled.

"Very well. I first took a position as governess in a most *respectable* household in North Cornwall. The master was a ... well, a very senior military man. For two months I fought to keep his hands off my person and *all* of him out of my bed."

"But why did you not go to his wife? Surely she would have put a stop to such deplorable goings on?"

The woman smiled at her sadly. "Women are strange enough creatures," she said. "Wives are the strangest of all. She *knew* all about it. She knew exactly what was taking place. I wasn't the first by any means. She couldn't wait for him to succeed with me, whereupon she'd turn and cut me to fletters."

"That was the time you were made sick?" Jane asked hesitantly.

"No, he never 'had his way with me.' I'd written to Miss Rye, who is a prominent member of the Society for Promoting the Employment of Women. D'you know of her? No, I didn't expect you would. She herself is the owner and manager of a law-stationery firm in Portugal Street, Lincoln's Inn. She employs a large number of educated women to copy legal documents and sermons, writing circulars, addressing envelopes – four thousand envelopes for one pound, if you're interested. Her reply was sympathetic but unhelpful. She told me that every single day she receives at least twenty applications like mine – from the daughters of professional men up and down the kingdom. She has scarcely twenty new vacancies a year, so the chance of finding employment with her is several hundred to one against."

Jane sat in a silence that bordered on shock; it was not so much Miss Wilkinson's flat recital that appalled her but the thought that such a level of frustration existed, 'up and down the kingdom,' and she had not the first inkling of it.

"There were others, of course," the woman continued. "I must have written to well over two dozen possible employers, all of whom replied in the same damning terms. Though, strangely enough, Miss Rye did correspond with me later. She is trying to set up a scheme that will advance money to educated ladies who are willing to go out to the colonies as teachers and governesses. There is a great deficiency of them, it seems." She chuckled. "I could certainly teach a thing or two now!"

Politely Jane joined her amusement. "All the same ..." she ventured.

Miss Wilkinson knew what she meant. "Yes," she said, "all the same – how did I progress from my twentieth letter of no-hope to selling my one commodity down on Penzance quays." She stared ruminatively at her. "There is, of course, a moment when you do actually make that choice. Yet even I, who considered it for weeks beforehand, who thought of it endlessly once the Rubicon was crossed, and who was never more alert to myself and my innermost thoughts and feeling than at that particular moment ... even I would not care to say what those thoughts and feeling were. I imagine, when they tell a prisoner he is to be hanged – I imagine that nine parts of him are filled with dread and terror, but there is a tenth part that leaps up in the strangest sort of joy at the news."

The ruminative stare intensified. "I wonder if you, Miss Hervey, will ever be faced with such a choice as that. Don't cry, *Impossible!* for that is what I would have cried only a year ago."

"I did not come here to speculate about my own responses to ..." Her lips curled in disgust but the words in which to express it would not form.

"Oh yes you did," Miss Wilkinson said quietly, almost mockingly.

"I came here to try to understand my father and you. Also to ..."

"And you suppose you can do that without understanding yourself, too?"

"Yes."

"If your only yardstick is the comforting lies ..." She paused as if a brand new thought had just struck her. "We call them *comforting* lies. In fact, the only person they comfort is the teller – as you are beginning to realize." She laughed, not unkindly. "If your only yardstick is those comforting lies, what can you ever hope to understand, eh? So of course you came here to learn something about yourself!"

237

Jane closed her eyes and shook her head. Nothing had gone as she had planned it. All her certainties had started to sink in the shifting sands of this woman's morality.

Miss Wilkinson took pity on her perplexity. "I'm sorry. I interrupted you a moment ago. You were about to say you had some other purpose in wishing to see me?"

Jane eagerly seized the bait. "It occurred to me just at that moment. When you spoke of the great deficiency of educated females in the colonies, well, I did just wonder ... suppose I were to advance you the fare to Australia, say, or the Cape – or wherever you might care to go – together with enough for your subsistence for three months upon your arrival – so that you did not need to snap up the first thing you were offered ... would you consider it?"

It was almost as if the woman had not heard her. She stared into the fire, her face a blank, for several long moments before she said, barely audibly, "How odd! How very ... very ... odd."

"It was on the spur of the moment," Jane explained.

Still in that same faraway voice she went on, "I would never, never, never so much as breathe your father's name to another living soul, you know."

"Oh, but I wasn't thinking of that!" Jane protested.

Miss Wilkinson chuckled. "Little liar! Of course you were – and quite right, too. More power to you! However, I hope I've set your mind at rest on that score. No – I was thinking *how odd* because I asked myself the identical question only yesterday. You see, I have accumulated, in the past eight months, I have accumulated enough to pay the first-class boat fare to Australia and to live frugally without stipend for the best part of a year. I could pass myself off, too. You'd get me several impeccable references, wouldn't you?"

"Yes!" Jane promised ingenuously.

Miss Wilkinson closed her eyes and laughed. "There's absolutely no defence against simple goodness, is there! Well, bless you, dear Miss Hervey, but I must regretfully decline your kind offers to damn yourself with bribery and forgery. I shall remain ... what I am."

"But how can you?" Jane cried in disappointment. "That awful little man I saw you with ..." She shivered theatrically. "How can you?"

The other went on smiling at her, not the least bit put out. "At the risk of stating the obvious," she said, "that's my business. However" – she rubbed her hands briskly and made those petty movements people make when preparing to end a conversation and leave – "your wishes will be granted in any case, as it turns out, for I am, indeed, leaving Penzance shortly. In fact, I am never willingly going to ply my trade on the streets again. It was the most foolish thing ever."

"Oh, but I am so glad to hear it," Jane started to say.

The woman held up a hand to halt her flow. "I don't think you will be, when you hear why. It is a desire not for reform but for betterment that has shaped my choice." She relaxed again, exaggerating the movement to show that her earlier gestures of departure had been premature. "I have lately met a young officer in the French navy who has done me the honour of asking me to become his mistress."

"In France?"

"Of course."

238

"Oh! You are lucky at last then."

She shrugged. "We shall see."

Jane frowned. "D'you mean, you do not love him?"

Miss Wilkinson's eyebrows shot up at once. "Do *you* mean that, if I did love him, then becoming his mistress would be all right in your eyes?"

Jane had not thought the matter out at all, but, seeing that her instinctive response had committed her, she said, "Yes."

The eyebrows shot even higher. "Well now, you have at last said something to surprise me. I suspect I have underestimated you. Anyway, I'm sorry if I lose your esteem for it (though I possessed it for a mere second or two, I quite enjoyed it), but I have to say I do not love him. I like him immensely, of course. And I believe I shall enjoy being his mistress all the more for that very reason." She smiled sweetly. "So, this Saturday I take up new lodgings in Falmouth – and wait for his pinnace to put ashore sometime in the middle of next month. What a happy settlement of your worries and mine!"

31 JANE SANK BACK into the soft embrace of the carriage upholstery and stared moodily out of the window; the now familiar streetscape of eastern Penzance and the Green trundled by.

"The days are definitely getting longer," Banks said.

"Mmmmm."

They were level with the gate to the railway goods yard before the maid spoke again. "Food for thought, was it?"

"It did not go at all as I expected," Jane told her.

"If it'd've been me, I don't know what I might have expected." She studied her mistress carefully out of the corner of her eye.

"She was certainly very candid."

After a pause, Banks prompted, "Brazen, you might say?"

Jane shook her head. "Just ... matter of fact."

At last Banks came out with it: "What was it you were hoping for, miss – if I may make so bold?"

Jane scratched the lobe of her ear. "It's hard to remember now. I hoped to understand it better, I suppose – in fact, to understand it at all. And, on the practical side, I intended to offer her the fare to Australia or Canada or somewhere, and enough subsistence to enable her to look around for the right position. I just wanted to get her away from ... the whole district."

"And she wouldn't take it?" The maid's tone held a curious mixture of surprise and I-could-have-told-you-so contempt.

Jane shook her head. "She was really very pleasant about it, and ... forthright ... and everything." Her voice was remote, as if she still had not comprehended all she had been told. "But I can't believe that there was no other way, can you?"

239

Banks shrugged.

"I mean ... to be a servant is an honourable thing, surely? Do you feel demeaned because you are my lady's maid? Do you go around thinking yourself inferior? I most certainly hope not."

"It's second nature to me, miss," Banks replied guardedly. "But then, I was never reared to think of myself as anything else. Lady's maid is a step up for me."

"And it would surely be a step up for her – from her present degrading occupation? A *step* up? It would be an impossible leap now, for who would employ her even as a scullery maid?"

Banks noted that "even," but said nothing.

"Misfortune may happen to anyone," Jane went on. "I remember my father pointing out to me a clerk in our solicitor's office in Leeds and saying he was once the richest man in Yorkshire, with a house and a deerpark and three carriages and I don't know what. And he lost it all in the railway bubble. And there he was, a humble clerk, but uncomplaining. He still had his dignity and self-respect, you see."

"It's very important," Banks agreed.

Jane shook her head. "And there's Miss Wilkinson, behaving for all the world as if she still has hers."

"The hussy!"

"No! That would be understandable. I mean, one could understand it if she tried to brazen it out. But *hussy* is the very last word. She's so neat and tidy ... almost meticulous." She shook her head at the seeming impossibility of conveying the superiority that woman had radiated – amused but not contemptuous, firm in her opinions without flaunting them.

"Her mother and father, they belonged to own the Crown Hotel over to Redruth," Banks told her.

Jane nodded. "She told me she lost them both."

"Same day, it was. About a year back. Just before Christmas, I recall." Jane winced.

"They went down the cellar to check the stock and, seemingly, it was bad air down there. Something off the barrels. And it smothered the pair of them. And she was the one who found them – Miss Esther. Almost died herself. My mother's cousin, Margaret Vean, over Scorrier, she was housekeeper there, so we heard all about it."

Jane clenched her eyes and held her breath a moment; she had never imagined it could have been something as awful as that. When a person says she's "lost a parent," you think of natural or sudden causes, like fevers or runaway horses. But to walk into a room in your own house, where your parents were doing something they've probably done a hundred times before, and in perfect safety – and to find them dead ... it was beyond all imagination frightful. "In the aftermath of such a tragedy," she murmured, "one can understand anybody making a foolish decision." But then it struck her that Miss Wilkinson had done the *right* thing at that time; it was four or five months later, when she ought to have been over the worst of it, that she had gone wrong.

"I did hear," Banks said casually, "as she found a position with General de Buisson's family up Wadebridge way somewhere."

240

Jane, who had been on the point of telling her Miss Wilkinson's early experiences, simply said, "Oh."

"I wonder what happened to that?" the maid added.

"It seems he was not quite the gentleman one would have expected."

"Ah," Banks said bitterly, "when it comes to those capers, I don't s'pose a governess'd be all that different from any other servant."

Jane frowned at her. "I don't understand?"

The maid's laugh hsad little humour. "If you were to stand near the girls at next hiring fair, miss, you'd hear them 'tipping the wink,' as we do say: 'Don't 'ee go near that old boy! He've got more hands than the clocks at Seven Dials.' Things like that."

"Good heavens! I had no idea."

"You can't blame the men really, I s'pose."

"Indeed? And why not, I'd like to know?"

"Well, miss, they got the power. It's only natural they'd use it."

"What power?" Jane asked. "Good gracious, has conscience no power? Or their own sense of honour?"

"There's always more applicants than places, miss. *Even* for scullery maid, as you might say. If a girl won't cooperate, she'll get given no Character, and then what'll she do? You ask Miss Wilkinson, next time you meet ..."

"I hope I may never meet her again!" Jane blurted out.

"Yes, well, if it should happen you ask her what sort of character the general gave her!"

"But what about the wives of all these wretched men? And the sisters? Have they no influence? And have the men no shame?"

Banks shrugged eloquently. "An ounce of prevention is their best motto. Like Mrs Wilmot over Gwinear. She do meet the girls off the train and Willy Bowden, the porter there, he says to her, 'Shall I bother to fetch 'er bag out the van, missis?' And old Ma Wilmot, she do look the girl up and down and if she's ugly as Satan or disfigured or pocked, she says, 'You may carry it to the trap, Bowden.' Else she puts the fare home into the girl's hand and sends her straight back." She laughed.

"It's hardly funny," Jane commented. "I think it's appalling – though I can still hardly believe it."

"'Course, I wouldn't say it happens everywhere. Nor yet in most places. I never met it, not myself, and I worked in nigh on a dozen houses since I was twelve ..."

"And you're hardly 'ugly as Satan or disfigured' or anything."

"God be praised. Mind you, I've had the young masters chance their luck. They push you in a dark corner and try stealing kisses and that."

"Well, I don't suppose there's too much harm in that," Jane commented, remembering how pleasant her own clandestine kisses had been.

"But then they try and go further, see. That's when you got to be firm. A lot of girls, they're too frightened to say no. And then the damage is done."

Jane stared out of the window, at the field gangs still working in the gathering dusk. "Everybody's fighting," she murmured.

"And for what?" Banks rested her eyes on the same dour scene. "Just to hold on. Not to go sliding back down."

As they drew into Marazion, Jane said, "All the same, I don't think it exonerates someone of Miss Wilkinson's education and breeding. She 'slid back down' a good many miles to get where she is now."

Banks nodded but said nothing.

"And d'you know what's almost the worst thing of all? She isn't really ashamed. She was in the beginning But now she says she's proud of it."

"And you say she's not brazen!" Banks commented drily.

"She doesn't say it in a brazen way. In fact, I put the word *pride* into her mouth. She just says she feels confident in herself. But how can she!"

"Feel confident?" The maid seemed surprised that Jane should question it.

"No. How can she *do* it. In all this cacophony of explanations and excuses, that's the question we lose sight of: How *can* she bring herself to do it? Surely you remember that awful, awful little man we saw her with? I mean, if I'd realized then what was happening, I think I'd have been sick just to look at him. Like a little ferret. A fat little weasel. Eurgh!"

Banks nodded and shuddered in sympathy.

"How can *any* woman allow her person to be polluted like that – let alone one with some claim to education and sensibility?"

Banks nodded again and drew in her breath between her teeth.

"And d'you know what she says about it all now? She says 'it was a great mistake'! Not a great sin, mark you – no moral judgement at all. Just a mistake. She's going off now to be ..." She shivered. "I can hardly bring myself to tell you. A sudden thought occurred to her: "Another military man! A naval officer. The only military men I've known were all French, of course – and the very soul of honour." Her rambling ended in confusion when she remembered that Miss W's new paramoor was also French. "She says she's going to be his *mistress,*" she went on. "Though it seems a singularly tasteless use of the word to me."

Banks turned away to hide her smile.

"An officer in the French navy!" Jane added, as if that were the least credible part of all Miss Wilkinson's tale.

After a moment's thought Banks asked which she considered worse – going with every Tom, Dick, and Harry on Penzance quays or keeping herself exclusively to one, seeing as both ways it was for money?

"That's like asking if it's worse stealing one pearl or many," Jane replied. "Surely any woman who allows her person to be defiled in that way has put herself beyond such judgements as 'better' or 'worse'? She is absolutely base and irredeemable."

"Even just with one man?" Banks asked in surprise.

"Even so. D'you think that's harsh? I don't believe there can be shades of good and bad. There is an absolute line, and once you cross it, you're on the other side. And no going back."

"I suppose you're right, miss." Banks kept a straight face as she added, "You're the one who understands these things."

"I have always held these beliefs," Jane told her fervently.

They were silent again, all the way through Marazion, until the business of paying the toll released Jane's tongue again. "The worst thing of all," she said, "the one thing I shall never forgive her for – the Wilkinson creature – was right at the end, after we'd bidden each other goodbye. She just happened to open her handbag and I saw an old red cummerbund in it. A red-flannel cummerbund like the one I gave my father used to wear. I'm sure it *was* his, too. You helped lay him out, didn't you – did you find it?"

"I'm sure I can't recollect a thing like that, miss."

"I suppose not. Anyway, I'm sure it was his and she'd brought it along to flaunt in my face in case I tried taking a high moral line with her. So you see the level of depravity to which her mind has sunk! A tarnished mind in a polluted body – that's her true wages. And never mind if it's enough for the first-class fare to the antipodes *and* a year in idleness when she got there ..."

Banks whistled soundlessly. "Is that what she put by, then?"

"Tainted gold," Jane sneered. "Just like its owner."

At Rosudgeon, ten silent minutes farther on, she said, "It must amount to over a hundred pounds!"

"In eight months," Banks said at once, showing that she, too, had been ruminating on the subject.

"And she's bought fine clothes and lived well meanwhile. I wonder how many ..." She hesitated; she had been going to say "fat little weasels," but then remembered that her father had been among them. Even as the thought surfaced she felt her mind thrusting it away. She turned her head aside sharply and stared out at the last of the twilight; she cringed, as if the thought were physically present and might assault her at any moment.

Banks, who knew well enough what question she had intended, held her peace.

At Higher Kenneggy, Jane said, "And to think I was so calm! I just *sat* there, and not a squeak of protest!"

It made her even angrier to know that, if she had to go through it all again, Miss Wilkinson's presence would once more dominate. Jane had never known anyone who could impose herself with so little outward insistence. Actually, she realized, she had known one – her mother. But then most people would probably say that was true of their mothers. Miss Wilkinson, on the other hand, was only the same sort of age as Jane. She began to seethe with fresh resentment.

"If ever I do meet her again," she said, "I'll give her such a piece of my mind."

32 THERE WAS NO HOME for distressed gentlefolk in Falmouth but Jane made her long-promised visit to Angelica and Jemima Pellew nonetheless. The name of their home, Pennance Hall, looked rather forbidding on their note of invitation, but when she heard Banks pronounce it the Cornish way, P'naance, it became a different sort of place altogether. From what the two sisters had said, she knew it was somewhat smaller than Montpelier, situated in fields that sloped down to a low cliff and a rocky foreshore, over a mile south of the entrance to Falmouth harbour.

The quickest way from Breage would have been via Gweek and Mawnan Smith, going no nearer to Falmouth than its outer fringe at Swanpool; but, since Jane had not yet seen the port, she told Veryan to take them by the main road and to go right through the town.

"Up over Penwerris Beacon," Banks suggested. "You can see the whole of Falmouth Roads from there, and all across to Roseland ..."

"Roseland!" Jane exclaimed. "What a pretty name!"

"Pretty place, too, miss," the maid told her. "It isn't hardly like Cornwall. And you can see across the river to Flushing." Apropos nothing she added, "There's a ferry there, between Flushing and Greenbank."

Jane frowned, as if the name were familiar, but for some reason she could not quite place it. "Greenbank," she murmured. "Now would that be farther away still? Beyond Flushing, I mean?"

"No, miss. Greenbank is right at the foot of Penwerris Beacon. You can stand up there and look down in the chimney pots of Greenbank."

"I see," Jane said thoughtfully.

When they crossed the bridge at the head of the Penryn river, a mile or so from the outskirts of Falmouth, she looked out of the window and exclaimed, "Gracious! Is that your Penwerris Beacon?" – pointing to a moderate hill on the skyline. "But it's a veritable mountain! The poor horses! Is there no way round for us?"

"Only through Greenbank, miss." Banks spoke as if she thought her mistress's common sense would rule that out.

Jane thought it over. "I suppose we should still see quite a bit of the harbour and Roseland and all that ... if we went on the lower road?"

Banks shook her head. "No more than you'd fit on a postage stamp. Once you get past Greenbank there's tall houses both sides of the street, see. You'd just get a little slant now and then between."

After a little further thought Jane said, "All the same, the horses have had a long and exhausting drive - well, an exhausting one, anyway - and we don't know what hills lie ahead. I think, to be fair, we should forego the pleasure of the panorama and take the gentler route through ... what was it called?"

"Greenbank, miss."

"Yes, of course. Pop your head out and tell Veryan, would you?"

Greenbank proved to be a straggling village, all on the uphill side of the road; the lower side, which was to their left, sloped sharply down, a hundred yards or so, to the estuary shore, and was occupied by vegetable plots, a few shanties, and a couple of small boathouses. One sweep of the eye was enough to take it all in; after that Jane turned her attention to the dwellings on the upper side.

"That's Flushing, see." Banks pointed across the river.

"Mmm." Jane hardly glanced at it. "Pretty little spot."

"Sunniest place in Cornwall, they do say."

"Really. How nice for them. Who lives in all these houses, I wonder? What do they do for a living?"

"That's lovely country there in behind Flushing, from there to Perranarworthal. That's mostly the Carclew estate."

"The Lemons of Carclew," Jane said abstractedly, still not taking her eyes off the houses on their right. Half the village had gone past by now. "I remember a Horace Lemon." She smiled. "Rather sweet."

"You can see the prison hulks from here, too," Banks told her. "You want to change places? I got the best view this side."

They were now approaching the end of the village. Craning her neck Jane could see the road rise over the long, sloping shoulder of the Beacon, from which crest, presumably, it led down into Falmouth proper. "I don't suppose you know where the Jagos live," she asked at last.

Banks suppressed a smile. "I believe it's the last house before the chapel, miss."

A moment later Jane could have kicked herself. She needn't have asked at all. For there, in the garden of 'the last house before the chapel' was Daniel himself. He stood with his back to her, studying the roof of their house through a pair of binoculars. Kinghorn stood beside him, making jottings in a notebook. Glancing briefly at the roof Jane understood their business at once, for it was a patchwork of broken or missing slates and areas of tarred sailcloth.

"They must have had a little windfall if they're thinking of mending that at last," Banks commented.

"Or even a big windfall," Jane added. "What a decrepit old pile!"

It had once been a fine place, though – and it didn't need the faded legend *Greenbank House* on the gate to confirm it. Three storeys high and with a small porticoed entrance, it towered over all its neighbours. But decades of neglect had taken their toll, so that nowadays people would look at it and say, "If it were mine, I'd raze it and build afresh." The garden was shoulder-high with the brown stalks of last season's weeds; bleached whorls of old man's beard festooned what had long since ceased to be a carriage. Beside it stood an upturned rowing boat, half painted. Two seagulls rooted for scraps in beady-eyed ill temper.

Just as they drew level with the place a woman came to the front door and stood there with her arms folded, staring at the two men; insofar as Jane could read her expression over the fifty-odd paces that separated them, it was a mixture of incredulity and contempt.

"That's missis," Banks informed her. "She could tell a tale or two. She was some burr old woman in her day."

"She doesn't look so tottery now," Jane said. The woman was in her late forties, perhaps, angular and strong, with long, dark hair gathered into an unruly bunch at the nape of her neck.

Having seen enough of the two men to challenge her distrust of their earnestness, she turned her attention to the fine carriage passing by. Her eyes found Jane's and held them, filling the younger woman with a curious disquiet. Kinghorn Jago followed his wife's gaze, but when he saw Jane he scowled – so menacingly, indeed, that she instinctively drew back into the dark of the interior. She hadn't expected him to dance a jig or call out a greeting, but at least he might have nodded.

A moment later he astonished them both by leaping on the running board and opening the door a crack. "I'll thank you to stay away from my house, Miss Hervey," he said curtly.

245

She stared frostily over his head, saying nothing.

"You hear me?" he asked.

Without being bid Veryan cut at him with the whip; but he was ready for it. He simply grasped the tail of it in his hand and held it tight, like an angler's line snagged in an old drowned boot.

"I had no idea you lived here, Mr Jago," Jane began ...

Suddenly he was hauled off the running board by someone outside – by Daniel, Jane presumed. A moment later it was confirmed, when, glancing back, she saw the pair of them, father and son, arguing fiercely in the middle of the highway. The carriage turned into a slight left-hand bend, cutting off her view from that side window. She hastened to the other, where Banks made room by drawing up her skirts and kneeling on the seat. Now, she saw, they had actually come to blows – not a serious fight but more of a shouting match punctuated by open-handed pushes to the shoulder and chest. At last Daniel flapped a dismissive hand at the older man and turned to run after the coach, which had reached the crest and was about to pass out of view entirely.

Jane's heart began to race. However, he had not gone half a dozen paces when his father shouted something that made him stop. He simply turned and stared at the man, who spoke a few more words, perhaps a repetition of what he had just said, and nodded vigorously. The hillcrest then cut them off from mutual view.

"What was that?" Jane asked. "What did he tell him?"

"I couldn't hear a word, miss," Banks assured her. And it was the truth; no words, even shouted at the top of the voice, could have carried into the carriage over the rumble of the iron tyres on the cobbled street.

She waited with her cheek pressed to the window, to see if he might yet come after them; eventually Banks's hesitant tap on her shoulder made her realize what a spectacle she offered, and she withdrew and sat like a lady once more. "Well! And what are we to make of all that?" she asked breathlessly.

"One look at the house and you know what to make of *them*," the maid sneered.

"I thought *she* had rather a fine face." Jane said defensively. "What's her family? Tell me what you know about her."

"Nothing, really," Banks replied in an equally guarded manner – but then, Jane reflected, she often said things like that, and immediately went on to disprove it.

This occasion was no exception. "Drusilla's her name. Drusilla Collet, she was before she wed. If Tom Collet was driving us now, he'd be the one to ask. His father is brother to Drusilla Jago's grandfather, who used to live up Playing Place, near Truro. But there's no more than thirty years between them so he'd be more like an uncle to her than a great-uncle. She's from Truro way herself – from a place called Come-to-Good."

"What a droll name!"

"'Tis Cornish, really. *Cum* ... something. I don't know what it do mean. Anyroad, that's where she's from. She was some wild thing, too – like him. She was a seventh daughter and her mother was a seventh daughter before her. She was a Moyle, from Kea. Her father had the King Harry Ferry there. But they say she do have the Sixth Sense – Mrs Jago, now, I mean."

"And what's that?" Jane asked.

Banks shrugged her shoulders and laughed. "I don't know, I'm sure. But whatever it is, she's got it. And they say she can scull a boat in the dark, or in a mist, and she could pass within a dozen yards of 'ee and you'd never be the wiser."

Jane remembered the woman's lithe, sturdy frame and believed it.

"And she knows every inch of the Fal," Banks went on. "She given more excise men the slip than any other smuggler, man or woman. She's never been caught."

"Is that how they make their living then?"

Banks pulled a face. "Who can tell how that family shifts? Talk about nine lives! He's some great singing man, Kinghorn. He's often up Plymouth, singing in operas and such like. That's one way he'll *admit* to earning his daily bread. But I should think there's many a day in that house with not a penny in the box and not a crust in the pantry."

Jane shivered at the thought of a life lived so close to the edge.

"Yet they're content enough, I s'pose," the maid added with some reluctance.

"We're missing the town," Jane said, peering eagerly out of the windows again. "I must say, it's rather poky."

The contrast with Helston, with its broad streets and fine stone buildings, could hardly have been greater. Here the way was narrow and the shops tull and cramped. Now and then a vaulted archway gave glimpses into a dingy court or narrow passage, with even dingier premises beyond – pie shops, laundries, and ship's chandlers. The road widened a little and the gloom lifted as they neared the bottom of the hill, or "Falmouth Moor," as Banks now named it to Jane, who remarked that it must be the only moor in the kingdom to be cobbled over and bordered by houses.

"We can go directly out to Swanpool now, if you're minded," Banks told her. "Or?"

"Or continue on through the town to the harbour and castle and then out to Swanpool. That's like two sides of a triangle to one."

"I think we'll go directly to Pennance House," Jane decided. "We've taxed the poor horses quite enough for one day."

Banks smiled as if she had been quite certain that would be her mistress's decision.

Twenty minutes later they were in sight of their goal. The lie of the land and the arrangement of the house in relation to the cliff and sea was more or less as Jane had imagined it; what she had not expected, however, was the much gentler aspect of the coastal vegetation on this more sheltered side of the Lizard peninsula. The clifftop, for instance, was adorned with a fine stand of oak, ash, and whitebeam – not one of which could have survived on the wilder headlands of Mount's Bay.

The road wound down to the edge of Swanpool, which, like the Loe at Helston, must once have been a tidal creek. Now it, too, was a landlocked pool, but a mere quarter of a mile long and only a furlong or so in width. At its seaward end, to the south, its gullet was choked by a broad beach of fine white sand across which the road meandered to climb steeply onto the headland of Pennance Point.

The main approach to the house was from the west, or landward, side, so they had to follow the road round for another mile, sometimes losing sight of the house altogether, before they arrived at the gate lodge. The keeper welcomed them cheerily and followed them up with a rake, removing all trace of their tyres in the gravel; he raked the near side going up and the off-side going back; the carriage sweep immediately before the house, however, appeared to be the responsibility of the gardeners.

Whatever this fastidiousness might have promised in the way of general order and propriety, it was swiftly shattered by the irruption of Angelica and Jemima, even before the carriage had drawn to a halt. "Jane! Oh Jane!" they cried, hatless and gloveless, as they scrabbled at the door handle and trapped their fingers in the folding steps. "Welcome to Pennance!"

And it was a welcome, too. Agnes Pellew, a jovial, pneumatic woman of near fifty, stood beaming at the door, smiling tolerantly at her two indulged but unspoiled darlings, waiting to honour their guest in a more sober fashion.   However, the moment Jane faced her and folded back the hood of her cape, the woman turned pale. Angelica noticed it at once. "What is it, Mama?" she asked. "Do come in out of the cold."

But Agnes Pellew was smiling again. "Just a little turn. Miss Hervey reminded me of someone I knew years ago." She linked arms with Jane and brought her up the last couple of steps. Jane had rarely felt such warmth, especially of such an immediate and spontaneous kind, before.

"What an idyllic setting!" she exclaimed as they went indoors. "I have often wished Montpelier were just half a mile nearer the cliffs – and now that I see Pennance I know why."

"If the weather is kindly," Mrs Pellew promised, "we shall take many walks in the district. Oh, Jane – may I call you Jane? – it is all I have heard for days: Jane, Jane, Jane! – there is so much to show you."

"We saw a little of Falmouth on our way in."

Angelica sniggered. "Such as it might be Greenbank, for example?"

The two sisters collapsed in laughter.

"They're just silly and excited," their mother told Jane. "Take them upstairs and calm them down. Your maid will attend to your things."

She smiled at Banks, who said, "Banks, ma'am."

"You're welcome, too, Banks. Yours is the little room at the back off the same landing as your mistress. My daughters will show you."

But her daughters were already half way up the stairs, bustling Jane with them. "You're in our room," Jemima said.

Jane was about to protest that she didn't wish to drive them out of their own bedroom when Angelica added, "Because it's much too large even for us." She flung open the door as she spoke and Jane saw that it was, indeed, a huge chamber, with a grand french window leading to a balcony with views eastward over the whole of Falmouth Bay.

"It is, in fact, the principal bedroom," Angelica explained, "but our parents don't like it. My father says he hates sleeping in a room with a French *widow.*" She pulled a naughty-girl face and waited for Jane's response – which was one of mystification until Jemima pointed toward the balcony and said, "He's fond of puns and acrostics and things. You must be sure to laugh at them."

"I'm sure I shall like him immensely," Jane replied. "I think your mother seems ever so jolly."

"She's not bad as mothers go," Angelica admitted.

"But she doesn't go often enough!" Jemima laughed.

Jane looked around and saw only two beds, a double and a single, side by side along the long wall.

"Which d'you want?" they asked. "Normally we take turns. A week in the big one and a week in the small. But we can go in the big one, if you like, and you can have the small. Or ..."

"Or what?"

"Or not," Angelica said.

"As the case may be," Jemima laughed.

Jane, who had never shared a bedroom except when ill, did not relish the idea of sharing a bed – even one as large as that. But it seemed churlish to say so.

"We could take it turn and turn about," Angelica suggested, seeing her hesitation. "You go in the small one tonight. Not that we shall sleep much, anyway. Oh, Jane, there is so *much* to tell you!"

"And so much to hear as well," Jemima added "Who are you going to marry? Is it decided yet?"

"Give her chance to breathe!" her sister chided. "All in good time."

"Well, she could at least give us a hint."

They stared expectantly at her. Jane slowly drew off a glove, with a smile that promised to reveal the most magnificent diamond ring they had ever seen. With bated breath they watched her tug at each finger in turn. And then, with a dramatic flourish, she almost struck them with a hand whose every finger was unadorned. "Broad enough?" she asked pugnaciously.

Laughing they tripped downstairs to the waiting tea and the madeira cake. Banks found her own room without any assistance.

*   *   *

Jane lay in her single bed and watched the firelight flickering upon the ceiling. A large spider walked slowly across that vast expanse of plaster, following an almost perfect diagonal; it reminded her of standing on the top of Trigonning Hill, watching a farmer crossing a pasture far below. The dim light combined with her happy exhaustion to turn the spider into that man and the ceiling into his field; Jane lost all sense of orientation and felt herself floating, neither up nor down, but just floating somewhere near her physical body, which was still in the bed.

That sensation of floating, in turn, reminded her of the night she tried to punish herself for her father's death. It was the first time she had cared to think of it since then. What a child she had been!

And what had Miss Wilkinson done that night? she wondered. Had she felt any responsibility at all? Probably not. When a woman sank to that level of depravity, she lost all her finer feelings.

"Amen," Angelica murmured loudly at her side; she was the nearer of the two sisters. She added in the same stage whisper, "Jemima always takes ages, but then she has so much more to confess and expiate. Ouch!"

"Amen," Jemima said. "Don't you love sleeping with a fire, Jane? It almost makes winter bearable."

Jane told them she never had a fire unless she were ill.

They couldn't understand it; she was mistress of her own house and could order a fire to be kept burning night and day if she wished.

"I like *your* fire," Jane told them. "It's different when one comes away on a visit."

"Aha!" Jemima said, as if Jane had just made a significant concession.

"You're like our Scotch cousins," Angelica told her. "They seem to live entirely without fires, and even the ones they do have seem to put more smoke than heat into their rooms."

"Didn't you like Scotland?" Jane asked.

"We adored it."

"Or we'd hardly have got engaged there," Jemima added.

"Which means having to live there after we're married."

Jane wondered what they'd do when marriage separated them and they were no longer able to finish each other's sentences. "You didn't tell me how it all happened," she said. "Was it terribly romantic? I imagine it all taking place among snow-capped turrets and ghosts flitting along the battlements and the aged retainers telling you it was a good sign when the Lady of the Black Tower walks on Martinmas ... and all that sort of thing."

Jemima chuckled at her fancy. "In my case, you couldn't be further from the truth. Angus proposed to me in the cellar!"

"Gracious!" Jane exclaimed. "I hope it was well ventilated."

"Eh?" Jemima said.

"I mean, unventilated cellars can be dangerous. It's well known."

They both roared with laughter and told her she was priceless.

"But it's true!" She could hear the increasing desperation in her voice. "Banks was telling me only last week of a tragic case in Redruth ... anyway – never mind. Do go on." She gritted her teeth and told herself she must get that wretched Miss Wilkinson out of her mind. Why did she keep cropping up like this, anyway?

"We'll take your word for it," Jemima promised. "Anyway, they sent Angus down to the cellar to get some special whisky – three thousand years old, or something ..."

"We can't make jokes about it after we're married," Angelica told her, as if it were an item on some unseen agenda.

"Why didn't they send the butler?" Jane asked.

"Because, for one thing, Scotchmen are more than a bit funny when it comes to special, rare whiskies."

"And also they wanted to give him a chance to propose to Jemima."

"You mean you were already down there?" Jane asked in astonishment.

"No, no. It gave him a chance to say, 'You've never seen our cellars, have you, Gem?' He always calls me Gem – the jewel in his diadem, he says." She sighed and lapsed into silence.

"Anyway," Angelica went on, "when they got down there ..."

"No, I'm going to tell it," Jemima insisted.

"Well, get on with it. You just lie there sighing about him."

"It's just the same as you and Dougall."

"No, it isn't."

"'Tis!"

Jane's thoughts drifted off once more. If she happened to bump into Daniel Jago on Falmouth Moor, would he say to her, "Oh, by the way, Jane ..."

Jane! What a dull name!

Plain Jane! No jewel there.

"... by the way, you haven't seen our cellars in Greenbank House, have you!"

"What d'you think about when you think of Angus?" Jane asked. "Or Dougall."

She heard Jemima stretching luxuriously as she replied. "Oh ... I think of a man who imagines he's the hardiest, toughest, bonniest, brawniest fellow north of the border and yet underneath he's as soft and sensitive as the most consumptive poet you ever saw. I think of his great shaggy eyebrows and those freckles, which almost *scream* – you know? – and his eyes, which are ... mmmm! You can't explain it, and if you're not in love, you can't possibly imagine it. When he takes me in his arms I feel like a bit of thistledown, and yet when I think of him, he's like a little toy to me. How can you explain that? Did you ever have a little dolly when you were young and you used to pet it and preen it and ... and *do* everything for it? Well, that's what it's like. I want to devote my whole life just to *doing* everything for Angus. And he feels the same about me, of course. We're going to have the happiest house ever."

"Almost," Angelica interrupted. "But I think until Jane has seen Dougall, she won't really understand what true love is. Angus is very dashing. I grant that. Everything he does has a certain style – which you couldn't say about Dougall."

"Certainly not!" Jemima chuckled.

"Now then! I said nothing untoward about Angus – and believe me, I could."

"For instance?" Jemima challenged coldly.

"Well, darling, you have to admit he is rather *fond* of that whisky and it does rather take the edge off his brilliance after half a dozen glasses."

Jane drifted off once more. "I don't love him," Miss Wilkinson had said. "And therefore I think we'll be very happy together." Something like that, anyway. But why "therefore"? How could happiness depend on *not* being in love. She had said it with such confidence, too – like everything else she did. It was hard to shake off the feeling that her somewhat raw and brutal contact with life had taught her secrets not available to girls who had led a more sheltered existence.

Jane tried reminding herself of the awful men with whom that woman had consorted, but all she could think of now was that her own father had been among them. He must have seen something in her. More than just *that*. Or else he'd hardly have kept going back to her, time and again.

The sisters had finished politely shredding each other's fiancés and were once again answering Jane's original question. "I like thinking about our house," Angelica confessed. "Dougall's promised to build me one and I'm permitted to tell the architect anything I want. And I simply can't stop thinking about it ..."

"Don't we know it!" her sister cut in.

"Well, you're just as bad with all the alterations you want made to that gloomy old castle of yours."

"I know. I'm only teasing."

"*Are* you going to live in a castle, Jemima?" Jane asked.

"Just a mo," Angelica interrupted. "I was telling you about the house Dougall's promised to build me."

And that took care of the next half hour. When she'd finished, Jane heaved a great sigh and said, "Oh, I do envy you so!" – which, in a way, was true of what she had heard during the first fifteen minutes, before her attention began once more to wander. She didn't envy the girl her beautiful villa so much as the utter certainty with which she contemplated her joyful life within it.

"Your happiness will come, too, Jane," Angelica assured her kindly.

In the silence the glowing embers of the fire settled with a kind of muted sigh.

"There must be the perfect man for you," Angelica went on. "There's one for all of us ... somewhere out there." She gave a great yawn and resettled herself in a new valley in the feather mattress.

To Jane it seemed a strange term – the *perfect* man. She knew she was a far from perfect woman, so it had never occurred to her to hope for, or even think of, the perfect man. Of the three men who might be called serious contenders for her hand – at least in the sense that she would consider them, whatever their intentions in the matter might be – none could be called anything like perfect.

Richard Vyvyan, socially the most obvious choice, was more of a good friend than a worship-you-until-death partner. He'd be attentive, loving, considerate, good company ... and then he'd vanish for three years. Not her idea of married bliss. But then what were her ideas worth, anyway? What had she ever seen of marriage? And there must be plenty of women to whom it was quite acceptable – since most sailors, officers and men alike, were married.

Daniel Jago, the least socially acceptable, was the opposite in every other way, too. There'd never be peace or mere friendship in a life with him; it would range to the extremes of joy and fury. She had no doubt she'd find a kind of ecstasy with him that no one else could ever provide; but she'd also taste the very pit of despair. Perhaps that was what she had seen in Drusilla Jago's eyes in that brief moment of meeting today? She had gone through the same ordeal with Kinghorn. But why had it disquieted Jane so much, that cool, sharp gaze? Perhaps the human soul was born knowing its destiny. Perhaps her soul knew that in her case it lay with Daniel. Had she therefore recognized in Drusilla's eyes a kind of judgement?

She gave an involuntary shiver and turned to thoughts of Vosper Scawen – on the surface the most in-between choice of all; yet underneath the most complex. She had a fleeting intuition that he was the most frightening of the three – because he made no demands on her as to how he expected her to behave. The other two, different as they might be, were quite positive in that respect. Richard would expect her to be the snug little wife ashore, waiting for the sailor's return. Daniel would always demand more than she could possibly give. Passion, love, dedication, *rapport* ... no matter what she yielded of these qualities to him, he would seek more. Yet even that impossibility was somehow less frightening than Vosper's unvarying desire that she should simply be herself. The others gave her a goal, a pattern of a person – easy or impossible as the case may be, but, either way, something *out there* to aim at. Vosper simply handed her a mirror and told her to peer through it and see all that was presently invisible.

And what if it turned out to be nothing! So many of her experiences recently were tending to nudge that dreadful possibility to the fore.

She shook her head angrily and the thought fled, for a while.

"Now what about your castle, Jemima?" she asked dutifully.

The only reply was the steady breathing of the two happy young sisters, deep once more in their domestic dreams.

33 THERE WAS A LIGHT snowfall that night. Jane knew it even before Banks came in and drew the curtains; there was that unmistakable pallor upon the ceiling and a muted crispness in the air.

"At least there's no ice on the jug," Angelica said – a reference, Jane presumed, to the rigours of Scottish baronial life.

With girlish shrieks they exaggerated the icy shock of their clothing and then raced down to warm themselves on porridge and kedgeree by the breakfast-room fire.

"A man was seen hanging around the grounds during the night," Mrs Pellew announced as she sailed in.

"A poacher?" her husband asked, rising to help her into her seat. "I wish you'd invite him in to poach our eggs. They're quite ruined again."

She laughed dutifully and said this particular scoundrel must be a very apprentice at the trade, for he'd left his footprints in the snow all over the lawns and flowerbeds.

"Perhaps he's a burglar!" Jemima suggested. "We must lay soot in all the doorways tonight." Since no one felt like asking her how that might help, she added, "That's what it said in the *Police Gazette.*"

"I do wish you wouldn't read those awful servants' rags," her mother said abstractedly as she opened her morning post. "Oh! Betty's littered six! And we can have one if we want."

The entire meal was conducted in that same bland fog of inconsequential and contradictory declarations. Jane, who had been reared on Golden Silence or Instructive Intercourse, at first supposed that her presence had unsettled them, but it soon became clear that this was, indeed, their everyday fare. And, somehow, useful information was shared and significant decisions were reached – for instance, that, though they could undertake no long walks in this pretty but inclement weather, they might go for a brisk half-hour to Swanpool Beach. And after luncheon they might take the carriage and drive into Falmouth to look at the shops.

"Is the tide in or out?" Jemima asked. "It's very important." She picked up the newspaper and hunted for the tidal tables.

253

Mr Pellew took Jane gently by the elbow and guided her to the window. "See?" He pointed at the long stretch of southerly coastline, all the way to Rosemullion Head. "The tide is, indeed, out. Acres of wet barnacles and seaweed proclaim it to the very heavens! The question is, dear Jane, how do we persuade lost souls like that" – he nodded at Jemima, who had rolled her eyeballs upward into her skull and was counting off her fingers against her thumb – "how do we persuade them that the *Police Gazette* and the *Western Morning News* are not the repositories of all wisdom?"

Jemima pulled an excruciating face as she rolled the huge boulder of her calculation to the very summit of its difficulty. "No," she announced in a blend of relief and disappointment – relief that the mathematical ordeal was over, disappointment at its conclusion – "it'll be high water in quarter of an hour."

Her father took her by the hand and led her to the window. "One great advantage of the tide tables," he said, "as you have most ably demonstrated, is that they allow one to predict conditions a week in advance."

The girl laughed in delight and, throwing her arms around her father's neck, kissed him effusively.

"All she cares about is gathering limpet shells," Angelica commented scornfully.

Guiltily Jane caught herself wishing her own father had been a little more like Mr Pellew; but then perhaps it was something you couldn't just start at the age of twelve. Both her parents had been very affectionate toward her ... well, *quite* affectionate – but not in that demonstrative sort of way.

The three girls dressed warmly against the rigours of thirty-one degrees Fahrenheit and set off for the beach, a walk of about half a mile over the fields. "Is it always like that?" Jane asked. "Life at Pennance Hall?"

"Like what?" Angelica countered.

"So ... busy and confusing."

The sisters frowned quizzically at each other. "Is it?" Jemima asked.

"If you've grown up alone like me."

"I suppose so, then. I've never really thought about it."

"You should have come a-visiting when we were all still living at home!" Angelica told her. "Now that *was* anarchy. Even father had to put his foot down."

"I do like him," Jane commented. "Didn't I say I would. He's so amusing."

"Yes and no," Angelica said.

"You mean there's another side to him?"

"Not at home. He's always like that with us. But I remember the first time I sat in court and listened to him passing sentence. I couldn't believe he was the same man. You heard him joke about poachers at breakfast? I'm sure there are a couple of dozen of that profession hereabout who'd drop dead with surprise to hear him talk like that – considering what he said to *them* when he put them away."

"So he's like two people?" Jane asked, wondering if it were true of all fathers, indeed, of grown-ups in general.

"Not in the way of being two-faced."

Jemima chuckled. "Remember when he caned Tommy that time? And he said, 'Now, my boy, this is going to hurt you much more than its hurts me.' And they both laughed – but he swished him good and hard nonetheless."

254

"But compared with most parents," Angelica added hastily, "he's very light on the rod. I was never smacked." She stuck her nose in the air and lolled her head loosely. "I was only smacked once," her sister pointed out. "And that was your fault as much as mine."

Angelica put the tip of her nose against Jemima's cheek. "Oh, and it still rankles, doesn't it!" She turned laughing to Jane while her sister recoiled in mock annoyance from that cold touch. "I gave her my best doll and all my humbugs for that week, but still she's never forgiven me."

"I think that *did* hurt him more than it hurt me." Jemima was serious now. "He always hated punishing us girls. It was the same with Sally and she really was naughty at times."

"Your older sister?" Jane asked.

They nodded. "She's dead now."

"She died with her first baby."

Then, after a pause, "The baby died, too."

Jane drew breath to express her commiserations but Angelica smiled at her and said, "It was five years ago now. She was only seventeen when she married. That's why they've waited a bit with us."

"He lets women off in court," Jemima said "They pray to come up before him."

"He thinks we're angels!" Angelica pulled a face as if to ask, *Don't you find such naïvete charming?*

"Anyway," her sister said vehemently, "I don't see why *that* should be a crime – nor why it should always be the women who are brought up for it."

They turned to Jane as if they expected her to determine the next phase of this particular conversation. Jane said, "Why have you brought that bag?"

"Oh, well may you ask!" Angelica got in before her sister. They had reached the beach by now and she waved Jemima away, saying, "Go on! Get your portion for today. I'll give Jane a hundred guesses." She turned to Jane herself. "And you still won't be within a million miles."

Jemima walked briskly down to the tide line and began a search of the sand, working toward the rocks that fringed the beach on the Falmouth side; every now and then she stooped and picked up something, which she either threw away again or popped into her bag.

"We're having *moules marinières* for supper," Jane suggested.

"Guess again."

"She is picking up shells?"

"Yes, but they're dead ones. Empty."

"Ah, then she's going to build a grotto, like Mrs Harris at Rosemerryn."

Angelica raised an admiring eyebrow. "How did you know about her?"

"Oh ... one hears things, you know." Jane was proudly offhand. "Am I right?"

"Well, you're certainly within a million miles. I'll tell you. She's determined to have a *bathroom* in this villa-to-end-all-villas! You know, with the water running in pipes and everything. And the *pièce de résistance* is to be a grand basin in the form of a giant cockleshell, all in mother of pearl. And it is to be set on a plinth studded with limpet shells!"

"Which is what she's collecting down there?"

Angelica nodded. "She has enough to stud the entire room, but they're to be picked and graded until you'd think one machine made them all." She shook her head despondently. "In one way it's funny but in another I think it's dreadfully sad. They haven't even chosen where to build this house of their dreams, and yet look at her! She's quite unhinged on the subject of her marriage, you know. And between you and me and that seagull, he isn't a terribly nice man."

"I gathered that was your opinion last night. Fond of the bottle, is he?"

Angelica pulled a face. "If only that were all! He makes my flesh crawl. There's an air of debauchery about him. D'you know what I mean? Surely you've come across men like that?"

"Yes." Jane nodded as she struggled to think of a particular specimen. Briefly she remembered the fat little weasel.

"I'm afraid she's going to end up very bitter and disappointed. I know it worries my father, but my mother just says he'll turn over a new leaf once he's married. She says all bachelors are a bit like that. Of course, one can't say a word about it to Jemima herself. She just says I'm jealous." She gave a dry chuckle. "And, on the face of it, I suppose I'd have every reason."

"Why d'you say that?"

"Well ... between the two men, I'd be the first to admit, there's no comparison. Angus is an Adonis ... debonair, charming ... whereas Dougall is ... well, *not!* To be blunt, he's actually quite ugly."

"But if you love him ..." Jane offered.

Angelica sighed. "That's it, you see. I don't think I do. Not if that nonsense going on down there" – she pointed at her sister with one toe – "has anything to do with love. I like him more than anyone else I've ever known. He's so warm and witty and ... oh, when you get to know him, you'll see for yourself. He's a wonderful man. Yet I can also be quite detached about him. And he's the same about me. We go at each other hammer and tongs at times. You'd imagine there were no worse enemies in all the world. And yet I think about him all the time. And I absolutely know that my life and his life belong together. But I don't swoon about it." She nodded at her sister again. "D'you know what I mean?"

"You make it very clear," Jane told her.

"And what about you? Have you really made no progress at all? Oh dear, she's coming back. Let's talk about it another time."

But Jane did not want to allow a situation to develop in which she was Angelica's especial confidante to the exclusion of Jemima. "Oh, I don't mind discussing it," she replied. "In fact, I'd rather talk about it with both of you."

"What?" Jemima asked, arriving at that moment. "Talk about what?"

"The trials and tribulations of an heiress with more suitors than she wants," Angelica said severely.

"Oh, I knew you'd talk about that the moment my back was turned!"

"Fear not," Jane declared. "We've waited for you. Your sister has merely been passing the time with a *catalogue raisonnée* of the virtues of a certain Dougall ... d'you know, I'm not aware of his surname. Isn't that dreadful?"

"McDougall," Jemima said sweetly. "Dougall McDougall. He not only sounds like a steam engine – *mcdougall-mcdougall-mcdougall-mcdougall ...!*" She laughed and nimbly sidestepped her sister's boot. "He looks like one, too!"

Angelica assumed a basilisk mask and turned to their guest. "Jane," she said.

They started to walk home again, up the steep bit of road to the field gate, where they picked up their tracks in the snow. And as they went, Jane told them the events of the previous day and the thoughts that had briefly kept her from sleep. She made the account slightly jocular, to hint that such conundrums of the heart were not uppermost in her mind these days; but to her surprise, the sisters had put off their teasing banter and were treating the business quite seriously.

"You see the gate back there?" Jemima asked suddenly.

Mystified somewhat, Jane said that she did.

"Now follow with your eye from there all down the hedge to the clifftop. Then all along there to the point. Then right up the skyline to the house and down again across the fields, back to the gate. Have you got that?"

Jane smiled and nodded. "But why?"

"That's thirty-seven acres," Jemima went on. "Now just imagine a woman standing here. And a woman standing here. And a woman standing here. And a woman standing here ... and so on, right throughout that area. One woman in each square yard. D'you know how many women that'd be?"

"I haven't the first notion!" Jane laughed. "It'd be approximately five thousand times thirty-seven. Say forty. Two hundred thousand? So it's about a hundred and eighty thousand?"

The sisters stared at each other. "That's something we keep forgetting about the rich," Angelica said. "They *can* do sums."

"But what has this to do with my uncertainties?" Jane pressed.

"Everything!" Jemima was picking up the shards of her broken surprise. "The precise answer is just over one hundred and seventy-nine thousand. And that's the number of surplus women of marriageable age in the British Isles at this very moment. Isn't it awful?"

"How on earth do you know that?" Jane asked scornfully.

"Because before we went away to Scotland our father told us. We were actually walking on this path – which is what reminded me. And he showed us what I've just shown you. Look at it, Jane! You haven't really looked at it yet. Just imagine it – one female to every yard as far as the eye can see. And not one of them is going to get a husband! Not ever. I think of it every time I gaze out of our windows." She dramatized her response with a shiver.

"So that's where all our discussions of marriage should begin," Angelica added.

Jane could hear their father's jovial solemnity behind the words. "It doesn't actually help me choose, though," she pointed out.

"All right, then." They set off on a brisk march to the hillcrest.

"I certainly think Richard Vyvyan's ruled out," Jemima said. "Don't you?" She stared past Jane at her sister, who smiled and replied, "Yes! A husband can be a very comforting thing on a cold winter night."

"And a warm summer one," Jemima chuckled.

"Not to mention spring and autumn!" They both laughed and turned to Jane, not quite looking her in the eye. But Jemima broke their sly concord by adding, "Pay no attention to her. It's all hearsay." Under her breath she added, "In her case." Moving until Jane's bonnet hid her from her sister, Angelica winked at Jane. "Anyway," she said. "Richard Vyvyan's definitely out – which is a pity, because he's a sweet boy."

"I thought Horace *Lemon* was rather *sweet,*" Jane told them with an impish smile. They gazed at her wearily. "Do make sure you repeat that to our father," Angelica advised. "You'll be his favourite for weeks. Anyway, that leaves the lawyer and the scoundrel." She shook her head in vexation. "I must say, my dear, you're a great disappointment if that's the best you can do."

Jemima, thinking the remark slightly heedless of Jane's bereavement, added swiftly, "Do you actually want either of them? Or any husband at all?"

"Of course I want a husband." Jane was scandalized at any notion to the contrary.

"Sorry, I'm sure!" Jemima laughed.

"I didn't mean ..." Jane stammered.

"But do you want either of *them?*" Angelica cut in.

"I think if I married Vosper, then every time I saw Daniel Jago, I'd feel such a wrench inside me. But if I married Daniel, I'd be in such misery half the time, I'd never stop thinking of Vosper."

"I'd pick Daniel," Jemima said decisively.

Angelica nudged Jane on the other side. "Why?" she asked.

"Because men who can stir one like that are rare." She turned to Jane with a kind of panic in her eyes. "Just imagine it if he married someone else!"

Jane closed her eyes and bowed her head. "Don't!"

The sisters' eyes met; Angelica made a helpless face. "Did you steal a moment alone with him when he was at Montpelier?" she asked.

Jane nodded but did not directly take up the point. "I believe he was the mysterious poacher who left his footprints all over the flower beds last night," she said quietly. "He was hanging around Montpelier in the same way when his enemies set upon him."

"How d'you know?"

"He as good as told me so. You see – he behaves as if ... well ... absurdly. As if he can't live without me. As if he'll wilt out of my company. But when we meet, he's so ... contemptuous and ... I don't know. Angry."

"He's angry with himself, not you," Jemima said.

Jane looked at her sharply.

"He's never been truly smitten by a woman before, and now he doesn't like it. I know Daniel Jago!"

"You've met him?" Jane asked excitedly.

"No, but I know him to look at. And everybody knows his reputation. He's a typical Jago, just like his father. Everyone knows them."

"Yes, but what do they know? He's damned by reputation, it seems."

Again the sisters' eyes met; this time Jane saw it. "Don't be afraid to tell me," she pleaded. "I want to know, whatever it is."

"To put it as delicately as possible," Angelica began hesitantly ...
"He's made more feet for baby's boots than any other man in Falmouth. There!"
Jane turned to Jemima. "But how can you possibly know that?"

"Because I heard my father telling my mother one day when they didn't know I was there. Six different women have served paternity summonses on him, so that's how I know."

Jane stared at her, first one eye, then the other, hoping to see her burst into laughter and say she was teasing. "Why that smile?" she asked at length.

The smile grew broader but she made no other reply.

*　　　*　　　*

They left the carriage in a little square just above the Church of St Charles the Martyr, which lay in that part of Falmouth she had not seen yesterday. They had brought Banks along because there were sure to be parcels to carry – and also because Jane privately wanted her opinion of these two strange young ladies.

They wandered first down Arwennack Street; not that the shops there were especially exciting, but they thought that Jane ought not to come to Falmouth without seeing "the King's Tobacco Pipe" – a gaunt stone chimney at the end of the Custom House where they burned the contraband and tormented the populace with the honeyed reek of its waste. Today, however, the monster was cold. They strolled back up the other side of the street. They had almost reached the bend by the church when Jane stopped dead and murmured, "I don't believe it!"

"What? Don't believe what?" They stared at her and then at the little *parfumeur* across the street, which seemed to be the focus of her incredulity.

"Lapin," she told them. It was the name over the door.

"Well?" Angelica asked. "She's been here years. I say – d'you wear perfume?"

"Very seldom. My mother frowned on it – though she wore some every day. But the extraordinary thing is that her *parfumeur* was also called Lapin! They must be related. Is she French?"

"Very!" The sisters laughed. "Let's go and see."

Jane had only once accompanied her mother to Lapin's in Paris, but the aroma of musk and ambergris inside its Cornish namesake unlocked more of her memory than any other key might have done. Indeed, it was so overpowering that for a moment she hesitated, half resolved to make some apology and leave at once. But the look on the woman's face prevented her. Her curiously French mixture of suspicion and affability struck such a chord of nostalgia in Jane that she felt compelled to stay. *"Bonjour madame,"* she called out.

The affability increased; the suspicion remained until Jane had delivered herself of several paragraphs of her native French. And even then it did not so much vanish as change character. It soon became clear that Mme Lapin had recognized her, or something about her, but couldn't quite place it.

Jane, now more certain of her ground, asked if Madame were in any way connected with a wonderful Parisian *parfumeur* of the same name, adding that her mother had never bought her perfume anywhere else.

"I knew it!" Mme Lapin cried happily. "That shop was my father's. Indeed, it still is. Just near l'Étoile. But I knew I had seen Mademoiselle before. You used to accompany your mother, perhaps?"

Jane admitted she had once done so.

"Don't tell me her name," Madame said. "It's on the tip of my tongue. I remember you had a fine villa in the Faubourg-St.-Honoré. Oh, my father will be so pleased when I write to tell him I have seen the daughter of the celebrated ... ach! La ... La ... what was it? I only worked in the establishment one summer, before I got married. But I remember her so clearly."

Jane, growing weary of the guessing game, gave her a hint. "It has two syllables," she said, "and the second one is -vey." She pronounced it in the usual English manner – which, to a French ear, sounds like vie.

"La Vivie!" Madame cried. "Voilá! I knew it. My father's most favourite customer of all. La Vivie, oh yes." Her smile grew a shade conspiratorial. "But she was from Cornwall, too, no? Aha! And so you are back among your people – to rub it in, eh?" And she laughed as if the notion were highly piquant.

Jane, though mystified at this last remark, felt that her companions must be growing bored by all these reminiscences in which they could have no share – and all in an unfamiliar tongue; so, with a vague smile, which Madame could take as signifying agreement if she wished, she asked if by any chance the woman remembered her mother's own personal receipt for perfume.

Madame Lapin, being a shopkeeper to her very fingertips, said it was engraved on her heart. Jane ordered an ounce of it. She was shocked at the price, and not really mollified at being told that her mother had ordered it by the demilitre. "Oh, but I remember her so well. She'd never send her maid – though she had dozens! She always came herself. Always most particular ..." And thus the garrulous, self-absorbed, and utterly Gallic monologue continued, edging swiftly away from Jane's mother (whom, Jane suspected, Madame did not, in fact, remember at all well) and toward her own good self. She explained how she had married a sea captain (God rest him), who had retired here to Falmouth and left her to practise the only trade she knew and for which, God be praised, there was great need in Cornwall ...

Jane thought of mentioning that she was intending to return to Paris in the spring but decided against it since she had by now successfully edged herself within a foot of the door. She could tell her when she came back to collect the perfume – which, like her mother, she intended to do in person.

"Wasn't that extraordinary!" she said when they were back in the street.

They agreed that it was. "Though it would be more likely in Falmouth than anywhere else in Cornwall," Jemima pointed out.

Jane looked about her and realized that the girl had put her finger on something that had been at the back of her mind ever since she had set eyes on this end of the town. "You're right," she said. "It does feel more cosmopolitan than anywhere else down here."

"What does retourner le poignard dans la plaie mean?" Angelica asked.

"Rub it in," Jane replied. "In the sense of rubbing salt in the wound. I have no idea what she was talking about. Didn't she ramble! I thought we'd never get away."

They wandered into a haberdashery, where they made a few small purchases of ribbons and silk thread. Banks acquired the first of her parcels. She slipped back to the carriage rather than be burdened with them for the rest of the afternoon.

"Come to think of it," Jane said as they contemplated the choice of hat shops, "shouldn't you both be buying furiously for your *trousseaux* and things? I expected to find your house in a frenzy of guest lists and caterers in attendance."

The sisters laughed and explained that they had three years to think about it; Angus had a tour of duty with his regiment in India and would not have leave to marry until he returned; and Dougall had to spend at least two years on his family's estates in Canada, in circumstances which no gentleman would dream of asking a lady to share. So that was that. "The main thing is – we've gottem!" Angelica parodied a harpy and twiddled her engagement ring.

In all three hat shops, Angelica, the only one seriously considering a purchase, dithered so much that they bustled her out of the last and would not hear of going back, even though she swore she knew the one she wanted. Later, when they were having tea together (Banks having been sent to a cheaper café a few doors down), Angelica's regret surfaced again and nothing would satisfy her but she must go back and buy that hat.

"Well, we're not traipsing back all that way just for you," Jemima told her. "You can jolly well wait and buy it on our way back."

But no, it might have gone by then – and any way she could borrow Banks to chaperone her so they needn't stir their bones on her account. She had reached the door before Jane called after her. She turned and waited. "You *may* borrow Banks," Jane said. She pulled a contrite face and left.

"It's not like her to be so insistent," Jemima remarked. "However, I'm glad of it for it gives me a chance to unburden myself to you."

"Oh dear."

Jemima laughed. "Not about me. About her. I'm rather worried about her, in fact. Did she talk to you much about Dougall this morning?"

Jane made a reluctant, so-so gesture. "I presume you have no great secrets from each other?"

"None whatever."

"Well then, she did talk about him, quite a bit ..."

"Oh, I know! She never stops."

"I don't think she's – what's the English phrase? Speaking French again has un ... un ... *unworded* me! She's not blinded by stars. Is that English?"

Jemima smiled. "It'll do very nicely. But don't be taken in by her. She *is* blinded by stars. She pretends to be terribly matter-of-fact and cool in her estimate of him, but really she's absolutely besotted and obsessed by the man. And – honestly, Jane, I don't know how I can convey it to you – but he is the dullest, dullest clod you can possibly imagine. And what I'm afraid of, you see, is that she won't wake up to the fact until it's too late. I fear she's going to die of screaming boredom. Did you ever meet a man who's so dull he gives you the shivers, just to be addressed by him? Well, that's Dougall."

"It's sad, if that's the case," Jane responded. "But it is her choice."

Jemima shook her head. "It isn't, you know. Not really. It's Father's choice. Not that he selected those two men in particular, but when he told us that story – imagining all those women standing on Pennance cliffs. If only he hadn't put them standing on the cliffs! I keep thinking of them hurling themselves off in despair." She closed her eyes and clenched her fists. "There is an awful lot of quiet despair going on, you know."

"I know," Jane agreed. "I have three friends in particular ... well, one is safely engaged now." She caught her own words and laughed without humour. "Hark at me! *Safely* engaged! Susie is at least happily engaged."

"Are you talking about the Delameres?"

Jane nodded. "You heard about poor Bessie, I suppose?"

Jemima licked her lips, glanced briefly around, leaned a little closer, and asked, "Is it true – what he used to do to her?"

"The marriage is to be annulled, anyway."

She slumped. "But who will have her now? There's one for the clifftop!"

"Don't!" Jane reached forward and clutched at her arm.

"Sorry." She smiled sheepishly. "I didn't mean it – well, not literally, you know." Her eyes brightened. "And is it true about the other sister? Rose, is it?"

"Rosa."

"Is it true about her dancing round the ballroom floor at Liston House, pretending she had to keep winding up her partner's mainspring?" She giggled. "Isn't it what we've all longed to do at times? When I heard it I nearly died! I know I shan't be able even to look at Dougall in future without thinking of that." The humour faded as swiftly as it had flared up. "But she's cooked her own goose for all that."

Now it was Jane's turn to smile. "Not Rosa. She's the one I worry least of all about. I don't know what it is – a certain *je ne sais quoi* – but she's ..." She sought for the word a moment or two and at last chose: "Robust. She's a cork in a millrace."

The strange thing was that, as she thought of the word *robust,* it was not Rosa in her mind's eye but Miss Wilkinson. Give her her due, she was robust, too.

Jemima suddenly asked, "How often do you think of Daniel Jago?"

Jane rocked back in her chair and lifted her eyebrows. "Honestly and truly?"

Jemima nodded and held her breath.

Jane grinned. "I suppose about every fifteen minutes."

The other whistled. "And you still don't know whether or not you love him?"

"I don't know whether such love is worth anything or not."

"If he wanted to ... you know. Would you let him?" Jemima asked the question and then flushed scarlet.

Jane felt more embarrassed for her than for herself now; she shrugged.

"You must have thought about it," Jemima went on – since there was now no way of turning back. "Every girl does."

"Would you?" Jane asked.

She nodded slowly, not taking her gaze off Jane. "I did." Now that it was out she smiled weakly, fanned her face, and heaved a small sigh of relief. "Fortunately without any drastic consequence."

"What was it like?"

She grimaced. "Confusing. Too brief to ..." She gave a single laugh and shrugged. "What about you?"

Jane shook her head.

"But would you?"

"I don't think so."

Jemima gave a brief, rather superior smile. "Well, I didn't think so, either. But I'll tell you another thing: If it came to the point again, I'll say no next time. It's simply not worth the anxiety."

After a silence she went on, "Some people say that if you let a man do it, he loses all respect for you and that's the last you'll see of him. But it's not true, is it?"

Jane made a sympathetic face and said she didn't know.

"It's not been true of Angus, anyway."

"And that's all that matters," Jane said.

Jemima nodded morosely. "Don't tell Angelica any of this, will you."

Jane laughed at the very idea. "What, your opinion of Dougall?"

"No. I know you won't tell her about that. I mean my Confession of Shame."

"But you as good as confessed it yourself, this morning, when you said it was all imagination in *her* case."

"Oh, but I've told her all about it. Only she's convinced I'm making it up. That's often the best way with Angelica. Tell her the truth and she'll reply that she's not as green as her cabbages. But coming from you it might be different."

So Jane promised not to do what she would not, in any case, have done for a king's ransom: discuss either girl's confidences with her sister.

*   *   *

At supper that night there occurred one of those incidents that, though trivial in itself, changes all future relationships between those involved. In this case, although they were all seated round the table, the only two who were involved were Jane and Mrs Pellew. They were eating a sort of hotpot containing, among things that Jane could only guess at, pork and butter beans. The pork was rather gristly, but apparently Mr Pellew liked it that way so nobody else complained. In any case, the cook had chopped it up fine, so it was edible if not precisely palatable.

Mrs Pellew, however, found a piece in her mouth that was much too large to be swallowed; and Jane just happened to be looking at her when she made the discovery. She raised her hand to her mouth and glanced slyly round the table. Immediately before their eyes met, Jane turned to Angelica at her left and asked for the pepper. When she looked back she saw to her absolute horror that her hostess was dropping the lump of chewed gristle *back in the tureen.*

She just sat there transfixed. A moment later she found herself staring into the equally horrified eyes of Mrs Pellew – who now knew beyond peradventure that she had been observed. As victims of drowning are said to see all their past in a flash, Jane, drowning in this social nightmare, now saw all her *future* with this woman, in an equally vivid flash. Neither of them would ever be able to mention it, of course; and yet they would never meet without the awareness of it hanging there between them, like a silent scream; they would never again exchange another ordinary, casual, unguarded word.

What could she do? Mimic Oliver Twist and ask for more? She was far too young. It would be impossibly patronizing. Refuse a second helping – which she would have done in any case? But now it would look so different. And yet there was no third possibility. It ruined the rest of the meal for her, and she knew it was going to darken her entire stay with the family.

Yet there was absolutely nothing she could do about it.

After supper the master of the house went down to the conservatory to smoke his pipe; his two daughters scampered into the drawing room to get out the stereoscopes of Paris, which they had promised to show Jane that evening; Jane herself, going at a more sedate pace, felt a pluck at her sleeve from behind. Uncertain as to whether she could face the woman as yet, Jane reached behind her, without looking round, and gave her hand a squeeze.

Moments later she was saved by the sight of Banks, hovering at the kitchen door. "D'you want me?" she asked.

"Just a minute, if you please, miss? It's to do with two of your dresses."

Jane made her excuses gratefully and led the way upstairs. But the moment the bedroom door closed behind them Banks said, "Never mind the dresses, miss. I only said that. But I thought you ought to know something as happened this afternoon, when you sent me back with Miss Angelica to get that hat. Well, as we left the shop, she gave me the hatbox and told me to take it back to the carriage. Of course, I didn't like to leave her alone in the street, so I was quite willing to carry it to the café and back again to the carriage. But she wouldn't have it. 'You take it now,' she says, 'while we're down this end. I don't mind waiting. I shan't come to no harm here.' That's what she said."

"Well, that was surely considerate of her?"

34 THAT NIGHT JANE shared the large bed with Angelica, who proved very cold-blooded and said Jane didn't know how lucky she was not to suffer each winter. Jane turned her back to her and let her warm the soles of her feet against her calf muscles. Then, as a special act of kindness, she changed places with her. Angelica made the sort of noises normally heard from people as they sink into a good hot bath. "Oh!" she exclaimed. "If I were a queen, I'd pick half a dozen handmaidens like you, Jane, and send them to my bed a half an hour before me. D'you suppose that's what handmaidens were? I've often wondered."

Jane, sniffing the pillow Angelica had just vacated, said, "Are you wearing perfume?"

Angelica giggled.

Jemima, braving the cold, got half out of bed and snuffled at her sister's head. "You are!" she said in a scandalized tone.

Angelica giggled again. "I couldn't resist it. After I'd bought the hat, Madame Lapin's was just too to temptingly close. Banks caught me out, actually. Didn't she tell you?"

"So that's what it was," Jane replied. "I suspected as much."

"Did you know all perfumes have names?"

"Balm of Gilead, attar of roses, eau de Cologne ..." Jemima began.

"No, I mean particular names. This one is called La Pompadour after the famous ... whatever she was. Empress or something. Just think – this is the same perfume, the *exact* same, as she used to buy. And it was only five shillings an ounce!"

There was a choking noise from Jemima's bed. *"How* much?"

"Well, one expects to pay for quality," Angelica retorted. "Just think – the same perfume as Madame de Pompadour!"

"She was the king's mistress, actually," Jemima said. "I don't know if that adds much to its lustre."

The words struck a chord of memory in Jane; perhaps it was a general usage, then, not just one of Miss Wilkinson's little jokes.

"Didn't you know?" Jemima asked maliciously when her sister remained silent.

"Of course I did," Angelica said hastily. "What of it? I dare say she also wore silk. Does that mean no one else can ever wear silk again, just because she did?"

"I didn't say you shouldn't wear her perfume just because she wore it."

"You implied it, didn't she, Jane?"

"Excuse me, but I did no such thing – and I'm sure Jane will bear me out. Did I imply there was anything wrong in wearing a perfume called Madame de Pompadour, just because I said she was the king's mistress?"

"Was it Louis xv?" Jane asked. "Her real name was Poisson, you know. Fancy being called *Fish!"*

"What about being called Lapin? *Rabbit* is just as bad, surely?"

"In fact," Jemima persisted, "I don't see anything wrong at all in being a *king's* mistress, do you? Charles II made four of his into duchesses and they're some of the most respectable families in the land today."

"Why should kings be any different?" Angelica asked. "If it's sinful, it's sinful. Don't you agree, Jane?"

"Because kings can't marry for ..."

"Oh, do be quiet, Jemima, and let poor Jane get a word in edgeways."

"I was only going to say that a king can't marry for love and so it's only fair he should be allowed to have a mistress. That's all."

Angelica could not resist the argument. "A lot of men can't marry for love," she pointed out. "Not just kings."

"And a lot of men keep mistresses. So there you are."

"Oh, and I suppose you consider that's all right, too! I don't know what Jane must think of us, hearing you say such things."

Jane heaved a sigh. She was obviously to be allowed no peace until she had voiced her opinion. "I blame the women in all these cases," she said. "It takes two to make that sort of bargain. And if the women held firm and simply said no, that would be an end to it. After all, a lot of queens can't marry for love, either, but no one says it's all right for them to keep ... *masters,* or whatever you'd call them. At least, I've never heard of it."

They absorbed this opinion in silence.

Jane, feeling none too certain of her ground, added, "Women have always led the way in matters like that. In all civilized refinements. If it had been left to the men, I'm sure we'd all still be sitting round the communal cooking pot, dipping our hands ..." Her voice tailed off as she remembered what Mrs Pellew had done that evening.

"I think that's a counsel of perfection," Jemima said. "It's like saying nobody should tell lies – whereas we all know the world would come to an end if we went around telling the truth all the time."

"There's certainly something in what you say," Jane agreed wearily.

Jemima laughed. "It's easy to tell you're an only child, my lover," she said. "The whole point of an argument is not about being right or wrong. It's all about sticking to your guns and beating the other girl into surrender. It's even better when you know you're wrong – as, indeed, *you* are in this particular instance."

"Indeed, I am not," Jane said stoutly.

A surreptitious pinch from Angelica told her she had fallen into Jemima's trap; but there was no turning back now.

"You are!" Jemima wriggled with delight at the prospect of a good old ding-dong with someone other than her sister. "What queens can and cannot do is completely beside the point. If kings and aristocrats go about the countryside spreading their wild oats, they do no real harm at all. In fact, they raise the general pedigree of the human stock, if anything. How could a queen possibly do that? The two cases are quite different, you see."

"Not in simple morality," Jane objected. "And what about the poor girls who have to carry the harvest of all these wild oats?"

"They usually get paid jolly well for it."

"I didn't mean *those* girls," Jane blurted out, remembering how much Miss Wilkinson had been able to put by.

After a silence Jemima said, "Nor did I, actually. But there! Now you've mentioned them, don't they prove my point even more strongly? It's not just kings and lords, it's everybody."

"I think it's beastly beyond ... beyond all imagining," Jane said. "I don't even like to think about it – much less talk about it."

"You're just afraid of showing your ignorance," Jemima taunted.

And though Jane knew ·it was spoken in a good-natured provocation, it nonetheless stung her into saying, "Well, that's where you're wrong. It just so happens that I know one of them quite well." The moment the words were out she could have bitten her tongue off. How could she possibly explain such an acquaintance? For a heartbeat or two she toyed with wild inventions. She had met the creature while engaged in charitable work with Mrs Lanyon. The woman was no longer one of *them.* She had been, years ago, but now lived blamelessly in ... where? The home for distressed gentlefolk!

Jane was rescued by a memory of Manette, her French maid in Leeds, who had once said, "When a lady is forced into telling a little fib, it is generally best for her to steer as near the truth as possible." So she described, with perfect accuracy, her first meeting with Miss Wilkinson at Penzance station last summer – including the fact that she then had no idea of what the girl did for a living. Then she described their later meeting in Mrs Brown's hat shop – the one in which Miss W had, in fact, hastened out of doors on seeing Jane again (as Jane now described it). By means of further embroidery, this odd behaviour had led to a conversation in which Mrs Brown had reluctantly mentioned the girl's occupation. "I thought her guilty response revealed a soul that was still within reach of salvation," Jane added modestly. "So I ... sought her out."

After a thoughtful silence Angelica echoed, "Sought her out?"

"Yes. You know ... sought her out."

"Gracious!" Jemima exclaimed, completely bowled over at these revelations. "You mean, you actually went and *spoke* to her? Knowing what she was?"

"Yes," Jane replied simply.

"You mean you actually went to ... well, whatever is the equivalent of Vernon Place in Penzance?"

"What's Vernon Place?"

"It's where all those special houses are – you know – with women like that – here in Falmouth."

Jane remembered her conversation with Mrs Moore and said, "Oh, no. She doesn't work in one of them. She's a free lance, as they express it. Or was, rather."

"You mean, you talked her out of it?"

"I like to think that my few words, poor and inadequate though they were, helped tip the balance. People have to want to be helped before you can achieve anything, you know."

"Gracious!" Jemima squirmed with excitement once again. "You're going to be one of those crusading women, aren't you. Carrying hope and enlightenment into the darkest dens of iniquity and being absolutely fearless because you know that Right is on your side."

"What d'you mean, 'going to be'?" Angelica asked scornfully. "If she's done what she claims, then she already is. Oh, I'm sure I'd *die* before I could bring myself to talk to one! What are they like? What was her name, by the way?"

"I don't believe I should tell you that. Call her Miss W."

"*Miss* W! One doesn't think of them as Miss – or Mrs, either. What did she say? I expect she was terribly, terribly contrite and so on?"

"Distressingly ordinary," Jane replied. "As I said, the first time we met, I took her for a lady like myself. They don't reek of sulphur and have horns sticking out of their foreheads, you know."

"All the same!" Angelica was determined not to be done out of her admiration. "To actually seek her out, and talk to her! What did you talk about? Did she tell you ... you know, what it's like?"

"She admitted it had been a dreadful mistake. She didn't wish to discuss it at all. And nor, of course, did I."

"What?" Jemima asked. "You mean you weren't just a teeny bit curious?"

"What about?"

267

"Well – the men, for instance."

"Oh, but I had seen some of them already. Believe me, there was nothing about them to prick the slightest curiosity."

"What is Miss W going to do now that you've saved her?" Angelica asked. "Go and tend lepers in the colonies or something like that?"

Jane chuckled. "She is waiting for a boat to France, where she has ... relations, waiting for her."

"And I'll bet you gave her the fare. Oh, Jane, you are so good – and so quiet about it."

"Please!" Jane protested, happy merely to have recovered from her potentially disastrous revelation and not in the least wishing to reap this extra reward.

"No, I mean it," Angelica enthused. "I can't think of anyone else I know who, after having been trapped into such a mistake, would deliberately beard the lion, or the lioness in her den like that. And to bring about such a happy outcome, too!"

"Did you give her the fare?" Jemima asked. "They never save anything, do they, that sort of woman. It all goes on their backs. They're like squirrels." She chuckled.

"Eh? What's that?" the other two chorussed.

"Mary Beauchamp told me that. Can't you guess?" She giggled even louder. "They cover their backs with their tails, of course!"

The others laughed, Jane more dutifully than in earnest. Then, feeling she now had some sort of reputation to keep up, said, "We laugh, of course, yet it isn't really funny. Our bodies are not ours to do as we like with. We are no more than their stewards and one day we must account for our stewardship. I come back to what I said before: Women are the leaders in the long march from barbarity to civilization. We have an innate understanding of what is fitting and decent and what is loathsome and disgusting. Even such a creature as Miss W has it."

*   *   *

The following day was bright and sunny, but still cold enough to prevent a thaw; so their planned walks to Maenporth and Pendennis Castle were ruled out.

"Why not drive into Falmouth and take one of the ferries to St Mawes?" Mr Pellew suggested. "You can visit the other castle there. It'll be no more than half an hour in this wind, so you can't get very seasick. And you'll surely find a fisherman's cottage over there where you may get a cup of tea and some heavy-cake."

And so it was decided. "Isn't it funny?" Angelica commented. "We've lived in sight of St Mawes Castle all our lives and yet this'll be only our third-ever visit there. We only ever go there when we have visitors."

Also, as there would be no shopping of any kind to be done in St Mawes, it was decided to leave Banks at home, where there was plenty of darning and ironing for her to catch up on.

A half an hour after the girls had left, Mrs Pellew came into their room to sort through some of their things. She appeared to have forgotten that Banks would be there for she gave a little start on seeing the maid, sitting in the good light near the window and making a tiny darn in one of Jane's silk stockings.

"If you'd rather I left and worked elsewhere, Mrs ..."

"Not at all. Stay where you are, by all means." She was at Banks's side by now. "I say, that's beautiful work. Who taught you to sew like that?"

Banks held the darning at arm's length and tried to appear modest. "I don't know, I'm sure. I always have liked sewing. Funny thing is, though, I can't abide knitting."

"You're just the person I need to help me sort out my own needlework. There's one particular thing I've never been able to do."

Banks smiled but the woman seemed serious. "What, now?" the maid asked.

"Strike while the iron is hot, they always say – unless, to be sure, you truly cannot spare the time?"

"I could at least have a look, I s'pose." Highly flattered, she rose and followed Mrs Pellew to her bedroom.

"You'll laugh, I know," the woman went on. "But it's the business of buttonholing. Of course, there's a little woman in the village who does most of my sewing, but I don't like to be beaten by something so elementary. And yet ... well, look at it!" She snatched up one of her blouses and showed Banks the cuff, where the buttonhole – only half completed – was, indeed, nothing to write home about.

Banks took it over the the window. The locking part of the stitch, which should lie neatly along the outer edge of the slit, was all over the place. "Show me how you do it, if you mind to, ma'am," she said.

No sooner had the woman done two stitches than Banks saw where the problem was: She was pulling the needle clear of the material before passing it through the loop to make the lock. And sometimes she drew it tight against the front edge of the loop, sometimes against the back, so no wonder it was all over the place.

"Well, now, this is the way I belong to do it," Banks said, taking the work from her. And she showed her how to pass the loop over the needle while it was still in the material. "That way, see, he's got to pull tight against the same part each time. So he's difficult not to get her even, see?" Five stitches later, even a child could have seen it.

Mrs Pellew tutted and shook her head in vexation. "As simple as that, eh?"

Banks nodded sympathetically.

"Well, you inspire me, Banks," the woman continued. "I think I'll unpick all those buttonholes this very minute and do them properly – with you to help if disaster looms again. May I come and sit by you?"

Banks thought it such an extraordinary question for a mistress to be asking in her own home that should could only nod and hope it didn't seem like permission.

There is one thing that all Cornish people, from the humblest to the most exalted, will do on finding themselves in company together: sort out their respective genealogies. Within ten minutes Mrs Pellew had the entire Banks clan anatomized, from a third cousin in Mousehole to her mother's relatives in Scorrier. Then she started on her own.

She was a Vyvyan. Not one of the rich Vyvyans from Wendron; one of the poor ones from Mawnan Smith.

Banks reflected that in the class of gentry to which Mrs P belonged, "poor" and "rich" were highly relative terms.

269

"I believe a nephew of mine, Richard Vyvyan, is on Mrs Lanyon's short list of eligibles?" she added. "He's one of the poor ones, too."

Banks admitted that she had seen the young man from time to time.

Mrs Pellew stared briefly at her, but she continued sewing as if unaware of it. "Yes, very diplomatic," the woman went on. "My father is Redvers Vyvyan. He lives with my brother and his wife in Somerset."

"I've heard tell of him," Banks admitted carefully.

The other chuckled. "Yes, he was quite a firebrand in his youth ..." Bit by bit she pushed out the bounds of her family to first, then second, then third cousins – at which point they discovered they had several distant relatives in common.

Then, having unpacked the treasure chest, they began to gloat over one or two of its prize contents. Banks had an aunt who was strictly teetotal but who kept "sugar bees" working away in a bottle on the top of the dresser, "because they're never wrong about the weather." Banks laughed. "Her washing got so wet as anyone's else, though she swore by they bees. And when they died, she'd drink off the liquor because it was good for her rheumatiz – and sing like a linnet from dawn to dusk. Drunk as a lord. But she'd swear she never touched a drop, not of the demon drink."

Mrs Pellew had a second cousin the same. A fiddle maker in Constantine who would drink nothing but glasses of whey all the week and then lie in bed all Sunday, drunk on port and brandy, both smuggled by the Jagos. He used to call all his customers by the names of composers. "One would come in and pick up the instrument he'd ordered and he'd play a bit of Bach, say. Well, ever after that he was 'Mr Bach,' and no use protesting that his real name was Witherspoon or Murgatroyd or whatever it might be, he was Mr Bach."

When they had finished chuckling at the strange ways of folk, she added, "There are those who claim we're related to the Jagos – us Vyvyans, I mean – but it's not so, you know. Have you ever heard it said?"

She seemed to place enormous importance on the maid's reply, though Banks could not for the life of her see why. She told the woman she'd never heard it said anywhere. But Mrs Pellew went on staring at her as if unable to decide on the truth of her assertion, to Banks's discomfort. Then, as if it were a continuation of the same topic, she went on, "I suppose you know very little about your mistress before she and her father came to live down here?"

"Very little, missis," Banks agreed. "I do know they lived in Leeds a while. And before that, Miss Jane, well, she lived all her early life in Paris."

"Paris?" Mrs Pellew echoed dubiously.

"Oh yes, she can speak French just so well as what you and I can English. You should have heard her yesterday."

But the other was only half listening. "Of course," she mused, "French is fairly widely spoken on the Continent. Are you sure she's never mentioned anything about living in Vienna?"

Banks shook her head. "I never heard tell of that."

The older woman nodded. "I'm sorry – you were about to tell me something about yesterday? Why was she speaking French yesterday?"

Banks described the scene in Mme Lapin's.

"So, Madame Lapin would have known Jane's mother!" Mrs Pellew said, with rather more interest than the prospect would seem to warrant. "What an incredibly small world it is at times, isn't it!"

* * *

"Why is our mother a little offhand with you, Jane, all of a sudden?" Jemima asked. They had decided that the best way to avoid seasickness was to sit somewhere amidships, just forward of the mast, where they'd be out of the way of the boom – "In case they luff or do those other mysterious, nautical things," Angelica had said.

"I don't know," Jane replied. "I hope I've done nothing to upset her."

"I shouldn't worry," Angelica assured her. "She blows hot and cold all the time. They're like that, all her side of the family."

"Ah! Those Vyvyans!" Jemima said portentously – as, in Florence, one might say, "Those Medici!"

Angelica laughed and stared at the sea. The other two stared at her. "Out with it," her sister said at last. "Don't keep it to yourself."

"Oh ... nothing really."

"Is your mother a Vyvyan, too?" Jane asked eagerly.

Angelica almost pinnical on her "Why d'you say 'too' like that?"

"I mean is she related to Richard Vyvyan of Mawnan Smith?" She smiled coyly. "People have tried to link our names, you know."

Angelica looked disappointed, but her sister grew even more enthusiastic. "Why don't you marry him, Jane? Then you'd be our *somethingth* cousin." She laughed. "And then dear Mama would have to be nice to you again."

"Talking of Vyvyan," Angelica said. "That's what I thought Madame Lapin said yesterday. At first, you know. It just shows how we hear what we expect to hear, or what we're most familiar with. But why was your mother called La Vivie, anyway? D'you know?"

Jane shook her head. "Certainly nothing to do with Vyvyan. I mean, I only knew it as a man's Christian name, Vivian, you see, before we came to live down here. I just assumed she took the last syllable of our surname, Har-Vie, and doubled it up. Except ..." Whatever she had been going to say, she thought better of it.

"Except what?" Angelica asked off-handedly.

"Oh dear! It's all very complicated and excessively boring." And she went on to explain all about her parents' clandestine marriage, and how his family were not to hear of it – which was why, when they lived in Paris, they had taken his mother's maiden name.

"So you weren't even known as Miss Hervey there?" Angelica said.

Jane laughed and, putting on a Parisian flourish, said, *"Ah, mais non. Si vous permettez, je vous présente Mademoiselle Révair! A votre service!"* She curtseyed low – to their amused applause.

On hearing the name, Angelica lost all interest in the topic. Indeed, as they drew near St Mawes, the girl became absorbed in a smaller sailing boat off their port beam. She had the general look of a fisherman, though there was something too stylish about her for that. And whoever was sailing her certainly knew his ropes, for she was coming up fast and, if her destination was St Mawes rather than somewhere up the coast in the open seas beyond, she'd get there before the ferry.

However, these feats of helmsmanship were of only passing interest to Angelica, who was far more interested in the helmsman himself. She had recognized him – quite literally by the cut of his jib – long before his features became discernible to her. "There's a fellow knows how to sail," she called out admiringly to the other two, who were now at the starboard rail, looking back at Pendennis Castle, high on the peninsula whose sheltering arm makes Falmouth the finest deepwater port in the West of England.

"Much she knows about it!" Jemima muttered scornfully to Jane.

"And do you?" Jane asked.

"No, but at least I make no pretence of it."

"He'll overhaul us long before we reach St Mawes," Angelica added.

"Could it possibly be that he's smaller and lighter?" Jemima shouted.

"At least Jane should come and look – if she wants to see a fine bit of seamanship at close quarters."

Jane shrugged at Jemima and heaved herself off the rail with a sigh. But Angelica was going on: "He must have left Greenbank a good ten minutes after us ..." And then she laughed, for Jane was suddenly at her side, asking, "Where?"

"One has almost to hit you with a hammer before you'll say ow," Angelica commented wearily.

"The one with the yellow stripe around her gunwale?" Jane asked. But then she saw the man at the helm and her question was answered. "D'you think he is going to St Mawes, too?" she asked.

Angelica chuckled. "I'm sure he decided on that the very moment he saw us board this ferry."

Jane looked about at their fellow passengers for the first time – all pretty ordinary people by their appearance. No one who mattered. She drew a deep breath and shouted, "Daniel!" as she waved large.

The wind was in her favour and he waved back.

"St Mawes?" she yelled next.

Whether or not he made the words out, he waved again – which had to serve as confirmation until their converging course brought him nearer.

"I heard somewhere recently," Angelica said, "perhaps it was in one of Canon Watkins's boring old sermons or one of my father's journals, but I distinctly remember hearing that woman have led the march from barbarism to civilization. For refined behaviour there's none can beat us."

Jane dug her hard with her elbow and went on staring at Daniel's boat.

"Ouch! Yes, that sort of thing," Angelica added.

Daniel tied up in St Mawes harbour five minutes before they rounded the breakwater. He was sauntering up and down the quay, pretending he was there for no particular purpose – and that he was surprised beyond measure to see them there. But behind the bonhomie Jane could sense a great uneasiness in him. He was too charming, too effusive, to be Daniel.

"Come to see the castle, have you? Then I'm your man. I know every stone."
"When was it built?" Jane asked as he led them off up the narrow lane that connected the fishing port to its now-crumbling defences, which had started to fall into disuse with the final defeat of Napoleon.

"Good Lord, I don't know *that* sort of history," he replied in disgust. "I mean real history. I can show you the very cleft down in the rocks from which I directed the landing of forty hogsheads of the best Amontillado sherry while an excise man was standing not twenty feet above me on the castle battlements and telling his superior all was well and they'd scared us off for the night. Now that's history!"

He was as charming and attentive to the two sisters as he was to Jane, which so won them over that, by the time they had scanned the horizons half a dozen times from those same battlements, it seemed only kindly for them to slip away a few minutes in advance of him and Jane.

"What's the matter?" she asked the moment they were alone.

"Why should anything be the matter?" he responded truculently.

"Aren't you even going to kiss me?"

He closed his eyes and bowed his head.

"That's why they've so tactfully vanished," she added.

Still he did not move. She edged closer to him until their forearms were touching. How brown and strong and bony his hands looked. She wanted to feel them on her body, pulling her to him, caressing her. "Daniel?" she murmured.

"I hope we may always remain friends," he said tonelessly.

"What?" The words seemed to mean nothing.

"I mean ... I'm ... well, I'm to be wed, if you must know."

There was another string of words. They seemed to have even less meaning than the last. She stood there, still touching him, still wanting him, more desperately than ever now – while the meaningless words lined themselves up invisibly on the stones of the parapet, and danced invisibly before her eyes, and tormented her invisibly in every rebellious corner of her being. "No," she said at last.

"Yes," he replied.

"But why? Surely you know ..."

His hand closed over hers. "Don't say it. Not another word more. Listen. I'm no good. Not for you. Not for any woman. And never have been ..."

"Why d'you have to marry?"

"Why d'you think?" he snapped. "If I don't, her father'll kill me. I thought he was joking, but he came round and shot my dog last night. So" – he heaved himself off the wall and turned for the stairhead, which led back indoors – "that's all about it."

For a moment she just stood there and watched him go. It was the one nightmare for which she had never prepared. She had no response ready for this moment. Back in the good old days, ten minutes earlier, there had been a certain luxury in thinking of Daniel as one of three possible men in her life. A certain delicious self-indulgence in *not* choosing any of them. But now, seeing him walk away from her, and with that mocking message still ringing in her ears, the time for such games was over. Her mind being vacant, her body took over. It chose Daniel for her, on the spot and without a second thought.

273

"Darling?" she called after him, in a voice that sounded astonishingly cheerful, even to her.

It surprised him into turning around and staring at her, when every particle of him wanted to be out of her way – out of temptation – as soon as possible.

"Is it really the truth?" she asked, taking advantage of his immobility to close the distance between them. "That's the only reason you're marrying ... this woman?"

He nodded, no longer trusting himself to speak.

"Do you love her?"

He shook his head.

She smiled. "Then there's no need for this meeting to be our last."

"What are you saying, woman?"

"You know very well what I'm saying. We can continue to meet."

"And?" He stared at her almost as if he were beginning to doubt her identity.

She stood on tiptoe and kissed him briefly, her lips barely brushing his. "I love you, Daniel. When I saw you go just now, I realized I can't live without you. So ..."

She was going to say more, much more, but, with a look of anguish, he raised his hand to her face and clamped it over her lips with a cry of "Stop!" Then he turned from her and dashed his forehead against the stone wall at his side.

She saw the blood spurt from the cut and cried out his name. But his howl of agony drowned hers. "You do not know!" he moaned. At her. At the stones. At the indifferent blue of the sky. At the demons that tormented him. "You do not know!"

And he turned and ran from her, leaving her, bereft and marooned, among those stones and that indifferent blue sky.

35 IF ANGELICA HAD NOT been polishing her engagement ring and gazing at it so admiringly when Jane returned, she would have behaved rather differently. But the thought of confessing that she, Jane Hervey, the noted heiress, had been jilted (which was how she now thought of it) by Daniel Jago, helped summon up all her reserves of self-control, to put a smile on her lips, and to force her to say in the most jovial tones, "Well, shall we go and look for our tea and heavy-cake?"

"Where is Mr Jago?" Jemima asked.

"He slipped and cut his head on the parapet. Nothing serious. I think he went to bathe it in salt water."

"Shouldn't you be with him?" Angelica asked.

"He appeared to think not," she replied coolly. "He's one of those people who don't like to reveal their weaknesses."

Angelica raised an eyebrow but neither sister said another word on the subject of Daniel Jago for the rest of the outing.

They were back at Pennance in time for a proper high tea, with pikelets toasted at the fire and gentlemen's relish to spread upon them. Looking at the white porcelain jar standing in the hearth, Jane remembered Mrs Moore's use of that phrase, "spreading the Gentleman's Relish," in quite a different context; she realized she would never again be able to look at a pot of the stuff and simply see it for what it was; it was now shaded with another meaning. And it suddenly struck her that the same applied to everything else in her life. The most commonplace objects and actions were steadily acquiring new outer layers of meaning. And it was affecting her memories, too. This morning at breakfast, St Mawes Castle had been no more than a romantic little pile of historic masonry, perched on a headland across the bay – a goal for a day's outing; but now ... She shied away from the reminiscence. Later. Later. When it was dark and the world was asleep.

Mrs Pellew's voice cut across her reverie. "A little bird tells me, Jane, dear, that you have quite won over our charming French *parfumeuse*, here in Falmouth?" She turned to her daughters. "Neither of you mentioned it."

"We didn't buy anything there," Angelica said swiftly.

"I should hope not."

"We visited so many shops," Jane added in support. "I only went into Mme Lapin's because the name was the same as my mother's favourite perfumer in Paris."

"Ah yes. Paris. Tell me – were you born there by any chance?"

"I think so," Jane replied. "At least, that is what I was told."

"Doesn't it say on your birth certificate?" Angelica asked.

Jane shrugged. "I don't know. Am I spreading this too thick? It's very piquant, isn't it. Should I scrape some off?"

"You mean you haven't ever seen your birth certificate?" Angelica pressed her. "What about when you were confirmed?"

"I suppose I did," Jane agreed.

"And?"

"And what?"

Angelica pretended to tear her hair. "What did it say about your place of birth?"

Jane laughed at her intensity. "I told you – I've no idea. What does it matter, anyway? Paris is the only place I remember before Leeds."

"Was your mother a Parisienne, then?" Mrs Pellew asked. "Do say if you think we're being too inquisitive – but you probably know by now our dreadful Cornish habit of family-tree climbing. Did you realize, for instance, that I am related by three different lines to your lady's maid?"

"Gracious!" Jane exclaimed.

"It's not uncommon to find that sort of thing down here. I say, do eat one of those pikelets yourself. You're giving them all away."

When Jane's mouth was sufficiently empty to permit her to speak again, she said, "I don't think you'll find any such links between us, Mrs Pellew – not unless you have a branch of the family in Wales. My mother was a Thomas from Glamorgan, where, if you go by names alone, she must have fifty-thousand relations."

"I knew a Myfanwy Thomas once," the woman replied. "She married the present Lord St Aubyn's maternal uncle. A long time ago." She sighed, as people do when they encounter nostalgic memories too remote and complex to be shared. "Myfanwy," she added, "that's a very Welsh name."

"So was my mother's," Jane put in. "She was Angwin Thomas."

Mrs Pellew closed her eyes. Her face remained expressionless. "Did she spell it with an *i* or a *y?*" she asked at length.

"With an i," Jane replied, thinking such detail a little pedantic. "I didn't know it could be spelled with a *y.*"

The woman nodded. "Indeed, yes," she murmured, almost absently. "Well, tell me about your day in St Mawes. Did you see the ghost?"

"Oh – I know a ghost story," Jane said. "Shall we turn down the lamps and sit round the fire and I'll tell it?"

The two girls agreed with great enthusiasm; with rather less of it, their mother went along. She sat in her chair, a little distant from them, and when Jane began, she gazed at her as if she did not wish to miss one syllable. Mr Pellew came in before the story was too far advanced; he sat on the arm of his wife's chair and motioned to Jane to continue.

It was, of course, the story Jesse Lanyon had told at the Christmas party. She realized she had spoiled its surprise by saying in advance that it was a ghost story, so she threw them off the scent by adding little details about a curious scratching and groaning that came from behind the wainscot while the "wet local" was telling his fantastic tale. In that way she restored the surprise and made both Angelica and Jemima give out little squeals of horror when the ghost revealed himself.

When they put up the lamps again, Angelica noticed that her mother's cheeks were wet with tears. Her husband saw it, too, and asked if anything were the matter; but she just shook her head and said, "Nothing ... nothing."

"D'you know any others?" Jemima asked eagerly.

Jane laughed. "I'll tell you one tonight, in bed in the dark." She threw her voice down as low as it would go and added, "I wants to make your flesh creep!"

All this while she had been watching herself in amazement. Her heart was breaking. She could feel it inside her, literally and physically aching in her chest. She knew that if she were on her own for a minute, she would break down in uncontrollable weeping. And yet, while there were others about her – before whom she was too proud to reveal her loss and humiliation – then she was cheerfulness incarnate. From where had she suddenly culled these reserves of ... what could one call it? Not character. The only honest word, she decided, was stubbornness.

Why was it so important that no one should guess how heartbroken she was? How would their sympathy demean her? She had no answer to these questions, but she knew she would rather die than reveal the depth of her sorrow. And yet she had never concealed one iota of her grief at the death of her mother, nor of her father. But even as that thought came to her, she knew this grief was different. It was the death of something within her, something she had conceived and grown and nurtured – and she alone. That was why it had to remain so private: No one else could help inter it properly.

The rest of the evening passed in a normal fashion. That night Jane recounted a ghost story her mother had told her once, on one of her precious visits to the nursery. It was of a man, a wanderer in a forest who had lost his way and came upon an old crone gathering firewood. And when he asked her the best path out of the forest, she told him, pleasantly and directly enough. In return, he helped her carry her burden back to the door of her cottage. But then, on remounting his horse, he glanced over his shoulder to thank her again ...

"And she laughed. And she passed her hand upwards over her face, and though the skin above her hand was all craggy and wrinkled, below it, all was featureless. And when she reached the crown of her head, he saw she possessed neither mouth nor chin, neither nose nor eyes. And her visage was as smooth and as pale as the side of an egg. Seized with terror he spurred his horse back into the forest, away from that odious place."

Jane described the terror of his journey, the wanderer who no longer cared what path he went as long as it took him away from that old crone, whose transformation had left him filled with an overpowering sense of having encountered Evil Incarnate. At last, disorientated beyond all rescue, deep in the deep, dark heart of the forest, he came upon a clearing with a charming little cottage – where he saw a beautiful young damsel drawing water from a well. He told her his tale and she replied that he was the luckiest of mortals to have escaped one of that ilk.

Of what ilk, pray? the man quite naturally asked.

But the damsel replied that they were so evil that no denizen of the forest had ever dared say their name aloud, and so it had been forgotten. However, she promised him a goodly supper and a safe and comfortable lodging for the night. And when he was in bed, she brought him a nightlight and a soothing draught, to help him sleep, and to forget that day's terrible events.

"And as his eyelids were beginning to droop," Jane concluded, "with the world spinning around him and the most delightful lethargy invading his limbs, the damsel leaned forward to kiss him tenderly. But just before their lips met, she smiled and said, 'By the way, the old crone you met this morning – when she passed her hand over her face, was it something like this?' And she passed her hand over her own face – which immediately became as smooth and as pale as the side of an egg."

Standing outside their bedroom door, listening to her daughters squealing with delighted terror, their mother laid her forehead to its polished woodwork, closed her eyes, and wept once again.

*   *   *

After breakfast Mrs Pellew said, "Now, you two girls, you have an act of sheer pleasure to perform before you may embark on the solemn duty of entertaining our charming young visitor.

"Oh no!" Angelica moaned, knowing very well what her mother meant.

"Oh yes, young lady! Good heavens, when you first became engaged you were going to write every single day. If you slip below once a week, it will cause some comment within the family."

"It's worse than being back at school," Jemima added. "I hope you won't want to read them before we seal them?"

"Not if they contain secrets you'd rather not share," was the sweet reply.

"That's bullying and coercion," Angelica complained. "Anyway, what's Jane going to do?"

"I think I shall show her my scrapbook. Would you like that, Jane?"
Jane said she'd like nothing better.

But when they were alone, Mrs Pellew seemed in no hurry to carry out her threat. Indeed, she stood at her writing desk so long, staring out over the slush and sodden snow, that Jane wondered if she had had a silent seizure; she cleared her throat with polite delicacy.

"I know," Mrs Pellew said, not turning to look at Jane. "But I just cannot decide."

"Oh." Jane said. And then, "Ah."

"Sit down, my dear," she said at last. "I don't know whether what I have to say to you will come as a surprise or whether it's as ..."

"If it's about the other night ..." Jane began.

The other woman frowned at her, genuinely puzzled. Then the penny dropped. "Oh ... that!" She laughed. "You may not believe this, but nothing has been further from my thoughts. However, since you mention it, let's get it over with."

"Oh, please ... " Jane faltered. "If you'd rather not. I mean, I ..."

"I don't know why I did it," she said. "I can only ask you to believe I have never done such a thing before in all my life. I was flustered. I didn't want anyone to see me laying down ... well, you know. In fact, I didn't want *you* to see me. But then" – she gave an enigmatic smile – "you always did have that effect on me, didn't you!"

"I beg your pardon?" Jane asked in astonishment.

Mrs Pellew's gaze was level and even. "You honestly have no idea what I mean – or what I might be hinting at?"

Jane shook her head.

"Then I'm going to show you a photograph. One of the earliest photographs ever taken in Cornwall. It's no longer very clear, I'm afraid. But when I showed it to Mme Lapin yesterday, she had no difficulty in recognizing its subject. I don't expect you will, either."

Without further ado she handed Jane a cardboard folder, tied in faded pink silk ribbon. "Open it." She nodded.

Mystified, and not a little apprehensive, Jane tugged at the bow and laid the folder open. What she saw among the blotches that marred the brown and fading image knocked the breath out of her; it was almost like a physical blow in the midriff. "How did you come by this?" she asked.

"Tell me first who you believe it is."

"You know who it is, else you would not be showing me."

"Say it, or I can tell you nothing further."

"It is my mother," Jane murmured.

Mrs Pellew let out a great sigh of relief, as if a long ordeal had ended.

"But she's so young here," Jane went on, peering more intently at the photo and now beginning to smile. "She can be no older than I am now."

"She was nineteen."

"But I never saw a photograph as early as this – not of her, I mean."

"No," the woman said quietly. "She left it behind." Almost in a whisper she added, "Here in Cornwall."

Again Jane could only stare at her in bewilderment.

278

"You still have no idea what any of this may mean?" the other asked. "Then I will tell you – trusting to God and whatever angels He has set over our family that I am doing the right thing."

She drew up a chair and took Jane's hands in hers. Jane offered no resistance but sat there, looking almost hypnotized, ready to hear anything.

"Your mother, darling Jane, was my sister. My younger sister. My darling little Angwin. That's why I was so inquisitive yesterday at teatime – though truly I had no doubt of it from the moment I set eyes on you." She went on talking in this way – not burdening the girl with new facts – to give her time to absorb this most shattering news of all. "I cannot believe it is mere chance has brought you here. If I did, I would probably say nothing – and let you go on your way again, none the wiser. But if it is not chance ... then why? Surely it is to enable you, at last, to know the truth about yourself." In a quieter voice she added, "and for me to ..."

She paused. Jane asked her to continue.

"I have been mainly worried that you would find it too much of a shock, that your constitution would not withstand these revelations. But, seeing how well you have coped with ... what happened yesterday at St Mawes Castle ..."

"How do you know that?" Jane asked her sharply.

"I don't know, of course. But I can easily guess."

Jane gave a mirthless laugh. "Are you sure that's not what you're doing with the whole fantastic ...?" Her eye fell on the old photograph and she was silent again.

"My guess is that Daniel Jago told you he could not marry you, or have anything further to do with you? Something of that sort?"

Reluctantly Jane confirmed it. "He said he was going to marry another ... that the girl's father was forcing him to it."

"He was trying to let you down gently, then. I'm sure there's no such female."

Jane looked up sharply, fresh hope kindling in her heart.

But the woman shook her head sadly. "The truth is, my dear, that Daniel Jago is your brother."

"No!" Jane cried out in horror.

"Your half-brother," she corrected herself. "And Kinghorn Jago is your father."

Jane rose and went to the window.

"Jane?" There was an anxious noise behind her.

"I'm all right," she said, though, of course, she had no way of knowing if that were true. She could feel nothing at all. She stared at the thawing world and all that came into her head were the names of things, spoken with an echoey sort of resonance into the emptiness behind her eyes: oak, cow, cliff, gravel, water ... The names tumbled on into the numbness.

"Jane?" There was that question again.

She said, "I want to hear everything you can remember."

Nothing happened. Or, rather, everything seemed to be happening back to front. Only after she spoke these words did she realize what memory had unlocked them. It was of Kinghorn Jago running after Daniel, outside their house at Greenbank, and shouting something to him – something that had stopped him dead. The only difference was that she could now supply the actual words.

She returned to her seat, took Mrs Pellew's hands between hers this time, and said, "I want to hear everything you can remember." Then she added, "Didn't I already say that?"

"No dear." Mrs Pellew smiled encouragingly. "Would you like a little brandy? Your face is" – she smiled even more broadly – "as smooth and as pale as the side of an egg. Oh, I can remember the very day, the very hour, when Angwin told us that tale. Just as you told it."

"Am I very like her?"

Tears welled into the other's eyes and she could only nod.

"I'll have some brandy if you will," she added. "Do I call you Aunt Agnes?"

Her aunt went gratefully to the tantalus and poured out two generous measures of spirits. "Better not," she said. "Or not just yet. We'll have to think of all the implications of this before we do anything so public. I'm not even sure that we'll tell the girls. Mr Pellew knows, of course." She sighed. "We were up half the night discussing the pros and cons of it. By the way, I think your maid has a pretty good suspicion of it, too. D'you suppose she's been rifling through your father's papers?"

The hair bristled down the nape of Jane's neck. "No," she said. "But I know who has!" She lifted her hand to take the proffered glass, amazed at her steadiness. "Thank you. Now I must know it all."

"I only know what happened at this end." She sipped at her brandy and smiled. "The bare facts I've already told you. But what I can never convey is what a wonderful young girl your mother was. She was like the *weather* of the whole house, you know? When she was happy, which was most of the time, it was like ... sunshine in all the rooms. And when she was sad, you could feel the very air hanging around you like lead. She was always the centre of every crowd. Society was not so stiff in its joints then and she ... how can one put it? She tweaked its nose and made it laugh. She did the most outrageous things, but with such infectious gaiety that nobody tut-tutted or tried to slap her down. I expect she was like that in Paris, too?"

"Very much." Jane agreed.

"Well, the time came for her to be married off – and that's the way it was in those days, more so than now. And my father, Redvers Vyvyan, decided ..."

Jane sat bolt upright. "Pardon me, but who did you say?"

"Redvers Vyvyan, why? Did he ever write? He swore he'd never so much as ..." Her voice tailed off as she saw the girl shaking her head.

"During our early days in Paris, before my parents could openly acknowledge their marriage, the name she took was Redvers! I was known as Mlle Jane Redvers – or Révair, as the French say it – until I was twelve."

"And what happened then?"

"Oh, just that it was at last possible for my father to take us back to England."

"I see." She nodded, took another sip, and continued. "My father ... She was the apple of his eye, you know. He took it as a deep and bitter personal betrayal." She shook her head and was lost in some private reverie for a while. "Anyway," she went on at last, "it all began when he arranged for her to marry a young man called Victor Bolitho. Angwin seemed perfectly happy ... by the way, that was another small confirmation: Angwin with an *i*. The Welsh always spell it with a *y*. No matter.

Angwin seemed perfectly content with the arrangement. Victor was a charming fellow. No longer a callow youth, of course, but desperately in love with her. Not that he was alone in that!"

She reached over and touched the photograph, which now lay at Jane's side upon the little sofa. "It was the very same day as that was taken. Exposures in those days lasted five minutes! Can you believe it? So you didn't just 'drop in' and have your picture taken, as one does nowadays. Our mother, God rest her, made an appointment in Stanton's for one Thursday morning ..."

"Is that the studio on the corner by the gasworks?" Jane asked excitedly. "Half way along the main street?"

Her aunt nodded. "The very same – and still with the same chairs, the same clouds, the same scene from the Tyrol ... the same moon! They'd only just been open a few months then, of course. And who was the photographer's assistant but a very young and excessively handsome Kinghorn Jago!"

"Did he look like Daniel?"

Sadly the older woman shook her head. "Wouldn't that be nice! But no – Kinghorn was fair in those days, a golden youth with the sort of face you want to *touch*. D'you know? Almost as if you don't believe such perfection can be real. Of course, the inevitable happened. Five minutes is a long time to sit stock still ... staring into the eyes of such a beautiful young Adonis. That same evening they were 'up the line,' as we say – except that there was no line then. They eloped in a little chaise, changed horses every four miles, and got to Plymouth in time for the Royal Mail to Bristol – where they must have thought they were safe."

"Did they get married there?" Jane asked eagerly.

The other shook her head. "Five more minutes and no man could have put them asunder. But my father and Victor Bolitho followed their trail and were just in time to prevent it. However" – she cleared her throat delicately – "they had already, er, behaved like man and wife ..."

"Was there a fight?" Jane interrupted. "I mean, how did they stop the ceremony? There was no just cause or impediment, surely?"

"Your mother was only nineteen," Mrs Pellew reminded her. "But it was simpler than that. A prominent Cornish magistrate and the son of the Lord Lieutenant of Somerset against a renegade photographer's assistant! Poor Kinghorn hadn't a chance against them."

She lowered her gaze, and her voice, as she went on, "I shall never forget the look in your mother's face when they brought her home. It was heartrending. She was locked up in her room and kept on bread and water until they could arrange ... Have you ever seen a sweetwater pearl that has lost its lustre? That was your mother in those dreadful days. Her skin, even her skin, changed. We were forbidden to go near her. She was treated like an absolute pariah until they could arrange for her to travel to Vienna."

"Vienna?" Jane echoed in surprise.

"Yes, my dear. You were born in Vienna. That's why I asked yesterday evening. I knew she later went to Paris, but I thought you might have some faint memory of the earlier home."

Jane shook her head. Try as she might, she could remember no other home but the villa on the Faubourg-St.-Honoré, which her mother had bought out of ... "But just a moment," she said. "Something here doesn't quite square. If my mother isn't from Wales, and never had that wealthy grandmother in Glamorgan, then ... how did she afford our villa?"

Her aunt smiled. "Naturally, there were all sorts of scurrilous explanations! But Angwin would never have stooped to that. I believe your mother's little white lie about a legacy from a wealthy grandmother may not have been too wide of the mark. Only she was a great aunt – one of the rich Vyvyans." She gave a humorous frown. "You know there are rich Vyvyans and poor Vyvyans?"

"I've heard Richard mention ..." Her heart missed a beat. "Good heavens! He's not a brother, too, is he?"

Mrs Pellew chuckled. "No, my dear. You're well outside the forbidden degrees of consanguinity there. He'd be ... let me see ... his father is a cousin to me. So you are, in fact, second cousins. Quite safe and proper – if that's what's now on your mind?" She let her voice rise in a questioning tone.

But Jane was shaking her head, lost in amazement at it all. "It's the most extraordinary thing," she said, "but of all the men I have met since coming down here, he is the one who felt more like a brother than anything. D'you think there's a sense of these things in us? Kinship, I mean?" But then she immediately answered herself. "No! Else how could I *not* have felt it in Daniel, who truly is my brother? And why does Kinghorn Jago not feel even remotely like my father, even now I know it?" She smiled. "I'm sorry. I shouldn't ramble so. You were telling me about my mother's rich great aunt?"

"Great Aunt Cicely, yes. One of the rich Vyvyans, as I said. A cantankerous old ... B, if you'll pardon me. She left all her money to another cousin of mine – and, naturally, of Angwin's, too. Luxon Vyvyan was his name, and he was, at that time, Second Secretary at our embassy in Paris."

Jane drew breath to interrupt but the other waved her to silence. "I know what you're going to say, my dear. Richard's just off to Paris, too – and will there be no end to these coincidences? But actually, that's no coincidence at all. Luxon has been pulling every string in sight ever since Richard got his commission. The boy was never destined for anywhere else. However, be that as it may, at the time you were born, Luxon inherited something well over a hundred thou' from Great Aunt Cicely. The most extraordinary thing is, he has never behaved like a rich man at all. You'd think he'd inherited no more than a shilling or two, to judge by the change in his way of life. In short, there's been no change at all. Now it's my belief that, having seen how money had ruined several of his friends and cronies, he decided to let Angwin have the lion's share – or lioness's." She laughed. "In fact, I wouldn't even put it past the old girl to have left him the money on that condition. She'd have made him give his word on it – which, naturally, he would have kept. She absolutely doted on your mother and never spoke to my father again after he sent her away. It would be just like her to leave Angwin the money in that roundabout fashion, just so that the rest of the family would tear out its hair, trying to guess what was what." She downed the last of her brandy and chuckled at the old woman's duplicity.

"Well, my dear," she went on after a brief pause, "that's all I know of your mother's tale. It has cast a long shadow over my life – losing her like that. But the moment I set eyes on you ... I began to hope ..." She could not quite articulate the thought. "Did I do right?" she asked simply.

Jane reached across and squeezed her hand, remembering that it was precisely what she had done after that awful incident with the lump of gristle. By some instinct she knew it was what her mother would have done. Not to her, Jane. Indeed, her mother had always avoided passing or petty intimacies of that nature. But it was what Angwin would have done to her sister.

That same sister now patted her niece's hand contentedly – except (that same instinct now told her) it was more like Angwin's hand to her.

"I don't think we'll tell anyone else just yet, Mrs Pellew," Jane said. "There is so much else still to be resolved."

"You are so like her," the woman replied, "in so many ways. It's quite uncanny."

36 IF ONLY MISS WILKINSON had not dropped that little aside about going to Falmouth and waiting for her paramour to come and collect her. It hung like a threat over Jane's every visit to the town. She found herself peering into shops and looking up and down each street and side alley, always half-expecting to find the woman there.

It was not that she wanted to see her. Far from it. But the prospect of an accidental meeting was a damper on each expedition.

One appointment Jane could not resist, however, no matter how great the risk of an encounter: a visit to Stanton's to have her likeness taken. The photographer, Mr Stanton himself, told her he had a cancellation and could take her in at once, but she said that was not convenient and she would prefer to return some time that afternoon; in point of fact, she wanted an excuse for being in Falmouth without the constant attendance of Angelica and Jemima. The appointment was set for four.

Jane left directly after lunch, managing to convey to the other two girls that she hoped to see Daniel once more, and that Banks would provide all she required in the way of chaperonage. Banks, having that devious sort of mind, had leaped to the same conclusion unaided. "Greenbank?" she asked with a smile as they set off.

"No!" Jane replied, enjoying her surprise. "This time let's go up on the Beacon and enjoy those views you were so keen for me to see."

As they drove in, Banks told her mistress what had happened at Pennance on the day she went to St Mawes; so vividly did she describe it, Jane almost felt she had been there. "She's fishing for something, miss," she concluded. "That I'll swear to."

Jane drew a deep breath and said, "Not any longer, Banks."

But the maid was still impelled by her own surmises. "I wonder," she mused, "has she been speaking with Mrs Lanyon?"

"Why d'you ask that?"

"Or perhaps Mrs Lanyon wrote to her? The reason I say it, miss – now, strike me dead, if you mind – but I'm sure as I'm sitting here that Mrs Lanyon found out something in your father's papers ..."

"She wasn't nosing around," Jane said quickly. "I did ask her to go through them for me."

"I know it, miss. But she's found something out – that I know, too. And she can't fathom what to make of it."

"What sort of thing?" Jane asked.

The girl shrugged. "That's what's got me meezy-mazy. 'Tis something to do with Cornwall, else how did Kinghorn Jago recognize your mother's photo at Montpelier straight off? Your mother must have been in Cornwall sometime. Or can you calculate it out some other way?"

In that moment Jane decided to tell Banks everything. In fact, "decided" is not quite the word. An instinct whose force she could not withstand urged her to do so; later she was able to justify it with reasons – that, in any case, the maid had speculated her way close enough to the truth ... that she, Jane, needed someone she could trust with whom she could discuss the whole bizarre history, especially its implications for her. But she knew that even if every reason had been against it, she would still have done as she did. She was learning more and more to trust her instincts and let reason make its own adjustments as and when it could.

Banks heard her out in near-silence, throwing in the occasional, "Oh ah," and, "Did you ever!" to ease the tale along.

"The one thing that has puzzled me most deeply since learning all this last night," Jane concluded, "is why on earth my father – knowing what we now know – why did he bring us down here of all places? We could have stayed in Leeds. We could have moved to London. We could have gone anywhere in the kingdom – anywhere in Europe. But no, he chose Cornwall. Now why?"

Banks nodded, but ventured no answer.

"He even ... I remember this quite clearly. On our very first night in Montpelier, he said to me, 'I hope you'll be safe here, my dear.' But why would he have said that after bringing us to the one place where there was any real danger of discovery? It's so unlike him, or the man he was."

"What did you think he meant?" Banks asked.

"I had no idea. Parents are always saying vaguely threatening things to their daughters ... you know – hinting at all sorts of unmentionable dangers that we're supposed to know about without actually being told in so many words. I just thought it was part of that vague cloud of *dread* they surround you with." Her frown intensified. "Surely he did know, Banks?"

"Ah-ha!" the woman responded.

"You mean, you think he didn't?"

"That's what it begins to look like, miss."

Jane nodded in reluctant agreement, and said no more for some time. But there was no baulking the inevitable conclusion: "So her little white lie about having come from Wales ... I mean, she even told it to him. Otherwise this is the last place on earth he'd have chosen to retire to." Her memory put up a sudden new hare to chase:

"Of course! That's why she always carried that little map of Cornwall around in her pocket book!" She closed her eyes and shook her head. "I know I'm going to start remembering one incident after another like that. Things that make it perfectly obvious how blind I've been." The sudden bitterness in her tone surprised her. "Even La Vivic," she added. "Of course that was from Vyvyan. She must have told someone there her true name. Or perhaps it was her friendship with her cousin Luxon. I'll bet all the tongues in Paris wagged themselves delirious over *that!* Aren't people disgusting at times!"

Banks cleared her throat. "Turn me out in the street if you mind to, miss, but may I ask how *you* feel about it? I mean not being Mr Hervey's daughter after all?"

Jane drew a deep breath, and then let it out again – as if she had hoped that its mere passage through her larynx would somehow have prompted an answer. But there were no words for it. How *did* she feel? Delicately she probed inside herself for a response of some kind and found ... nothing.

"I got no call to ask," Banks mumbled.

"I suppose," Jane said slowly, "that I'm reluctant to face the fact that, deep down inside me, I never truly felt he was my father. It often seemed we were like stage actors who'd been given those parts to play. But I was always ashamed of those feelings, too. I explained them as the result of his absence throughout my childhood. I don't remember seeing him at all until I was eleven or twelve. And yet they behaved as if he'd often been there before. Like when we went to the *ménagerie* at the *Jardin des Plantes* and my father – Mr Hervey, I mean – reminded me of the time he had brought me there as a little girl. And I couldn't remember it. And he was so insistent that I burst into tears ..." Her voice tailed off as other memories assailed her. After a pause she went on, "And I remember my mother telling me, ever so gently, that I'd had a recurring illness as a child, the effect of which was to erase some of my memory, which was why I was prone to forget things that she and my father could remember so vividly." She stared at the maid in horror. "They *lied* to me, Banks. Isn't that dreadful? I never had such an illness. My memory is true and faithful. They deliberately lied to me."

"I'm sure they thought it all for the best, miss," she replied, beginning to feel slightly alarmed at her mistress's agitation.

"Indeed!" Jane sneered. "Best for whom? Not for me. I don't believe my mother even knew my ... Mr Hervey until I was twelve. That's the truth. Before that she was ..." She swallowed heavily and went white. "Oh, Banks! She wasn't married at all!"

"But she brought you up as strict and proper as she knew how," the maid was swift to point out.

Jane closed her eyes and pressed her palms to her forehead. "I don't wish to think about it any more. It's too horrible."

They had arrived at the Beacon by now. The last of the snow had gone and the ground was mired and wet. A little way off, slightly in the lee of the summit where the carriage had drawn up, a gang of unemployed men were playing a game that involved throwing halfpennies into the air and betting on their fall. They stared incuriously for a moment at their unusual visitors – the Beacon was not considered a salubrious place in which to stop – and then resumed their raucous amusement.

Jane accepted the mud on her hem rather than show an inch or two of ankle, which, she felt sure, would only provoke ribaldry from behind, and walked to that part of the crest from which Greenbank was visible. The maid had been right; one could, indeed, look down into the chimneypots. The main difference between the imaginary picture and the real one was in their scale. She had imagined the Beacon to be much higher than it was; the chimneypots were less than a furlong away, whereas she had pictured them as little specks in the distance. Indeed, now that she raised her eyes to the whole panorama of the harbour and the mouth of the Fal, everything seemed remarkably close today. Trefusis Point, a mile away on the opposite bank, and Roseland, more than twice as distant on the far side of the great deepwater anchorage known as Carrick Roads, seemed almost near enough to touch.

She drew Banks's attention to it. "That's a sure sign of rain," the maid replied. And then she drew her mistress's attention to the village below – whose inspection Jane had been deliberately avoiding, even though that had been her intention in coming up here in the first place.

She spotted Daniel at once. It was not difficult, for he was standing on the roof, hacking at some tarred-canvas patching with a kind of short-handled adze.

"They'll need some loose canvas over that before nightfall," Banks commented.

My brother! she thought.

The trouble was that no amount of mere knowledge would ever make him feel like her brother. In a way there were now two Daniels – the one with whom, only two days ago, she would have forsaken all propriety, shed all her standards and scruples, and run away, just as her mother had with his father; and the other, who, as a matter of plain history, was of that same man's loins, and thus denied to her forever. But that first Daniel was not dead – not safely hid in some dateless night. To her unreasoning body he was still the only Daniel there was; she could feel the longing for him coiling itself within her now, just at the sight of him.

It would not do. She realized she had to meet the second Daniel and get to know him, too, otherwise the first would haunt her forever. "I'm going down there," she said. "Fetch me the photograph from the carriage. I want to show him. You may go into the town, if you wish. Meet me at the photographer's at half-past-three."

Banks shook her head, sure of her duty. "I can't do that, miss, and you know it."

"But of course you can!" Jane laughed. "Who ever heard of a woman needing a chaperone to meet her own brother!"

There was still some token resistance but Jane prevailed, mainly because the maid had no liking for the Jagos and would rather not meet them if it were at all avoidable. Banks brought her the photograph and departed.

"Ahoy! Daniel!" she shouted as she set off down the winding network of footpaths, seeking the ones that led toward his house.

"Go away!" he called back the moment he saw her.

She smiled but made no reply. When she was only yards from the back wall, she saw that there was, in fact, a gate, all festooned in trails of old man's beard.

"Go away," he said again. They were now within ordinary talking distance.

"No," she replied.

He picked up a small piece of slate and hefted it in his hand.

286

"You wouldn't dare," she told him.

He flipped it down at her, as a card player might flip a winning trump onto the table. It came straight for her. At the last moment she turned and took its impact just above her shoulder blade. It hurt only briefly; the pain was already fading when she turned back and laughed. "You've been longing to do that ever since last June, haven't you! Honours even, all right?"

He stared down at her, not knowing what to say.

"Daniel," she went on, quite serious now, "I know."

"What?" He seemed incredulous.

"I know the entire story. I know why you told me ... what you did. But there's no need for such lies between us now. Can't we talk?"

Reluctantly he stared at the sky. "It's going to rain."

"Pull some canvas over it then. Which is more important?"

Still irresolute he stood there, looking alternately at her and the sky.

"Anyway, how long have those repairs been needed? Will one more hour make any difference?"

"My mother would kill you for saying that." He pulled a face. "She'd kill you anyway. Or scratch your eyes out."

"But she doesn't even know me.'

"She'd guess. They've bickered over little else since your carriage went by."

"Is she within?" Jane asked in alarm.

He smiled, for the first time. "She's gone up Truro for the day. I suppose we may go indoors a while." He disappeared over the ridge. Jane wondered what reason Mrs Jago had to be angry with her. Then it struck her – the single most obvious fact about the whole relationship: Daniel was her senior by several years! And he had at least two sisters who were older still. No just cause or impediment, indeed! Kinghorn would have been a bigamist. It was a little odd that Aunt Agnes had not mentioned it. Out of kindness, perhaps? Not wanting Jane to realize that no matter what had happened she would have remained a ... she had not said the word yet, not even in the most secret recesses of her mind. But she said it now: *bastard.*

It was oddly ... liberating, she found, this new truth about herself.

Daniel returned, unfurling a roll of sailcloth behind him, the ends of which he reefed to the plank on which he had been standing. When he let it go it slid down the remaining yard of roof, struck the cast-iron gutter, and sent it crashing down into the yard below, where it broke into a dozen pieces. He pulled a disgusted face. "That launder needed renewing anyway, but my father will say I did it deliberately."

Remembering the force with which he had let the plank go, she wondered if that had not, indeed, been the case. There was, she realized, a large and unclaimed territory in all of us, between deliberate and purposeful action and decisive inaction. "Is he indoors?" she asked.

In a highly risky manoeuvre that brought her heart into her mouth Daniel stood upon the ladder and "jumped" it over to a stretch of undamaged launder. Its rungs were ricketty enough, anyway, without this provocation; her heart did not return to its place until he was back on firm ground. "Is he?" she repeated as he broke open the gate for her.

287

"No," was all he said.

"And your sisters?"

He shook his head.

Their eyes dwelled in each other's. "Well," she offered at last, "we are brother and sister, I suppose."

He nodded gravely, took a token pace back, and ushered her through the gate. "Or so they tell us," she added as she passed. The reek off him was a heady mixture of tar and fresh sweat. On impulse she took his arm, his lean, wiry arm, and walked him at her side. The touch of him was electric.

"You'll excuse this mess," he said laconically, pointing at a collection of rusty baths, broken sinks, decrepit mangles, and a bewildering array of nautical *things*.

Surveying it rapidly, she realized it was quite different from the mess one sees outside the homes of the poor; in simplest terms, there was nothing here to nurture a rat or any other vermin. It was a collection of items that had once cost money – and a goodly few of which could be salvaged for the same commodity, too. "Don't you ever have a clear-out?" she asked.

"When we're desperate. What d'you think there is for us to talk about?"

"I want to show you something." She lifted the cardboard folder by way of promise as he leaned in front of her and pushed open the door – whose only means of closure was the friction between it and the stone of the threshold. "Anyway, I never had a brother before," she added.

"And I already had three more sisters than I ever wanted."

She chuckled. "And where *is* your father?" she asked.

"Let's say he's ... keeping up his reputation elsewhere in the town. What's this I'm to look at?"

It was dark in the kitchen. The windows were grimy from years of frying and neglect. Jane grasped the handle of the knife polisher as she passed, not so much for support as to avoid its catching in her sleeve. It proved to be stuck fast. "Can't we go to some other room?" she asked.

"This is the best. Your eyes will get used to the gloom." He placed a chair for her. She took a cloth off the dresser and wiped its seat before she sat. "Ah!" He took the cloth from her. "I was searching high and low for that."

"Perhaps *it* got used to the gloom, too," she commented acidly. "You know that knife polisher is stuck?"

"I keep meaning to take that abroad and see what's wrong," he replied.

She passed him the folder. He put a surprisingly deft finger and thumb to the loose end of the bow and gave it a tweak. Two tweaks. Three ... In a sudden vision, too swift to prevent, she saw those same fingers tweaking other bows. She swallowed hard and closed her mind to the thought.

He unfolded the card with the same deliberation. The photograph, which was loose, slipped out and lay upon the table. He stared at it a long moment. As she watched him she felt all her old longing return – together with something new and much sharper. A poignancy for what could never be?

That thought was more of a hope than a suggestion. She knew very well what the new feeling was. And its vocabulary did not include words like "never."

He rose and carried the picture into the light by the back door. "Unbelievable!" he murmured at last.

"Your father took it."

He looked up at her sharply and returned to his seat, which was diagonally across the end of the plain kitchen table from her. "My father?"

"Didn't you know? He used to be Stanton's assistant."

"I don't believe it."

She repeated the tale as her aunt had told it her. "And I can't see that Mrs Pellew has any cause to lie," she concluded. "What was your father's tale?"

He shook his head.

"You've got to tell me," she insisted.

"Why?"

"Because we've got to make sense of it. We've got to know the truth – and we're not going to get it from any of them. But perhaps between them ...?"

Avoiding her gaze, then, he told her: "According to my father he was hired to sing at a concert given for Redvers Vyvyan's fiftieth birthday in the Pendarves Arms. He said it wasn't your mother, Angwin Vyvyan, that he took up with, not at first, but one of her sisters. He said she ..."

"Which one?"

"He lowered his head still further and said, "Your aunt."

"They'd all be my aunts."

"But you know the one I mean. That's why she'd have cause to lie to you. Anyway, he ran off in the end with your mother, Angwin." He looked briefly at her then. "And the rest you know."

"But it would have been bigamy."

He shook his head. "He and my mother weren't married in those days. He was a free-thinker in his youth – no marriage, no property, that sort of thing."

"But he would have married my mother?"

Daniel shook his head. "It wasn't a real vicar. Just someone he knew in Bristol, dressed up."

Jane sank her head into her hands. "Dear God! The deeper we go ..."

His hand stole round her wrist and gave it an encouraging squeeze.

Melting at his touch, she looked up into his eyes, which were almost incandescent in that gloom, and said, "Have we deserved this, Daniel? All my life, as I now discover, I've been living a lie. And now I learn that it started even before I was born. Lies, lies – I feel the weight of them now. I want to pick them up ... roll them up ... and just ..." She subsided into incoherence.

"We'll never know," he agreed morosely.

"To Hell with them!"

He raised his eyebrows and then smiled at her vehemence.

It stung her. "D'you remember what you said to me that night of the ball?"

He looked down again and drew his hand away. But hers snaked after it and caught it again. "Do you?" she insisted.

He nodded.

"And d'you still feel like that?"

He nodded, even more miserably.

"So do I," she told him. And, in the teeth of his mounting astonishment, she continued: "If I hadn't been such a spoiled little ... *moppet,* so smugly playing the game of come-and-get-me ... if I'd only had the sense to listen to my own heart, I'd have gone away with you, there and then." She pulled his hand to her. "We still could, Daniel. Let's do it now. We could take the next ship that calls for orders. The Cape. America. Australia. What does it matter? The main thing is, we'd have left it all behind. All the lies and deceit. It would be just you and me. No one would ever know."

He was shivering violently now. Gritting his teeth and grimacing as if he hated himself for doing it, he said, "But *we* would know."

She gave a single, harsh laugh. "Would we? I ask you – what would we know? Daniel, they have lied to us and lied to us and *lied* to us. And for all we know, this may be their last, desperate ... Anyway, can't you see a kind of Providence in all this? My mother and that man tried to build my whole life on a lie. But one of those lies gets turned back upon them – when she told him she came from Wales. So where does he pick as the safest haven from discovery? Leeds? London? Constantinople? No! He picks Cornwall! Now surely that is Providence having a little joke. And why choose Montpelier? Why did you come ashore there on that particular day? Why have I been unable to get you out of my mind from that moment to this?"

He squeezed her hand. "Please, Jane, stop this now," he begged.

But nothing could stop her, not now, not ever. "How can you fail to see the hand of Providence in it? But why? That's the real question. Was it all just so that we could say hail and farewell? I can't believe that, my darling."

"Jane!"

"Yes! My darling still! I am calf sick and moon sick for the love of you. If I really thought I was to live the rest of my life without you, I'd go straight from here and drown myself."

"Jane!" His tone was suddenly sharper, angrier, as he raised a hand to strike her – not in anger but as one might strike a hysteric, to restore some calm.

But she caught his hand and pressed it to her lips, covering it with her hot, wet, passionate kisses.

"Jane?"

She heard the note of panic in his tone and knew that she had won. Heedless now of all consequences, she rose and went to him, meaning to seat herself upon his lap. But he half sprang up to prevent it, so that her action bore him down at an angle that swept the chair backward and deposited them both on the floor.

And there, amid the splinters of his chair, she lay upon him, with her skirts all in disarray up about her knees, and together they tasted ... laughter! The saving grace of laughter.

And that was the moment Drusilla Jago returned. "Bitch!" she cried, the moment she saw Jane. Dropping her bags in the doorway, she ran across the kitchen to where they lay, now desperately struggling to rise. She seized up a broken leg of the chair and lashed out at them indiscriminately, all the while crying, "Whore! Child of Satan!" and other such abuse.

Jane took several painful whacks before she gained her feet, whereupon she caught the weapon in full flight and twisted it from the woman's hand. She drew it back to give as good as she had got.

"No!" Daniel roared, placing himself between them. "No, Jane!" He held out his hand for her to yield him the stick.

Seeing that his attention was all on the girl, something primitive in his mother snapped. With a screech that was barely human she hurled herself upon him and sank her teeth into his neck, just behind his ear. He, for his part, gave out a bellow of pain. Unthinkingly Jane lashed out with the chairleg and caught her a resounding blow on the skull.

The woman fell at once and Jane was quite sure she'd killed her; but Mrs Jago didn't even lose consciousness. And then, as she climbed groggily to her feet once more, her eyes caught sight of the photograph, still lying on the table. She could not possibly have made it out in that light, but Jane gave it away by crying out, "You dare! You just dare!"

Alas, it was all the encouragement the woman needed, and, before Jane could deliver another blow, she had torn it, once, twice ... She was tearing it for the third time when Jane hit her across the neck with the chairleg – and this time she was well and truly knocked out.

"She's wrecked it!" she cried, too angry and too shocked for tears. "My mother's picture – and she's wrecked it." She fell to her knees to pick up what had fallen to the floor.

Daniel was meanwhile gathering up his mother's body and preparing to carry her to her bed. "She's all right," he said. "I mean, at least she's breathing."

Jane was about to say she wished she'd killed her when the meaning of the words struck home. She stood there, staring at the chair leg, still in her grasp, and then at the fragments of the photograph. Then, with a sudden, spasmodic jerk, she cast the leg from her. "Daniel," she murmured.

He was already on the stair. "I'll come straight back," he called.

"How did it happen?" she asked the emptiness he had left. Then, slowly, as if in a trance, she began trying to reassemble the scraps of paper.

He returned to find her standing at the sink, working the pump. "You'll need some water to bathe her head," she explained.

Without a word he placed the enamel pail beneath the spout.

She looked down and saw that she had been pumping directly to waste. Then at last she wept. And then at last, too, he put his arms around her, turned her to him, and hugged her for dear life. "I didn't mean it," she said through her tears.

"I know."

"I've never felt such anger before. Where did it come from?"

"Never mind. It's over now."

"But ... your mother! I didn't mean ... she's the last person on earth ..."

"Shh now! No one can blame you ..."

Finally she was calm again. The touch of him and the nearness of him was a feast for a body so long starved of affection. She just stood there, allowing herself to melt into him, feeling the dear pressure of him everywhere they touched. It was a new sensation for her. She tried to think what it was like – certainly it was *un*like any other embrace she had ever experienced with a man.

Then suddenly an image popped into her head. It was of Jemima and her father ... the way she had turned laughingly to him and kissed him after that mistake with the tide tables. So easy. So natural. That was what this embrace was like. And so at last she discovered that other Daniel. But even more, a part of the loneliness that had seemed to be her burden in life was dissolved away. She had *family* once again.

Safe and warm in his arms now, she clung to him even more tightly and let out a great sigh of relief.

He sensed the change in her, misunderstood it, and pulled slightly apart. And she, with so little practice in expressing her tender feelings, said nothing of them then.

37 DANIEL HELPED HER look respectable once again by brushing off her back. He had to use his hands because, as she swiftly told him, the brush he had discovered after a lengthy search was, in the first place, a scrubbing brush, and, in the second, fit only for yard work. He was not ashamed of the brush but he was of the feelings she still aroused in him. As his fingers worked over the black wool of her dress, picking at splinters of wood, brushing away the dust and gravel, he could not help picturing the lissome young body beneath. So near ...

And because he still longed for her in that elemental way, it transformed her most innocent movement into provocation. His mother's cries of *harlot* still rang in his ears. Though every particle of him protested their unfairness, when Jane innocently stuck out her bustle for him to seek among its folds for more bits of the kitchen floor, the protest was blunted. *You see only what you wish to see,* he told himself, but the truth of it merely deepened his disgust.

"You're going to make a wonderful lady's maid, brother dear," she told him as she gave him another kiss. "Except that you'll have to shave more frequently."

"I didn't know you were calling," he said gruffly, rubbing the stubble on his chin.

"Then be warned, I shall call every day from now on. And people will say that at least one of your sisters is a good influence on you."

"Dan!" his mother called from above. "Is that harlot still here?"

"Perhaps we'll meet on neutral ground instead," Jane said drily.

"Miss Hervey is about to leave," he called back up the stairs.

"I mean it," Jane told him. "Where can we meet? Tomorrow. Somewhere in town. I know – Stanton's at eleven, when I call to approve the prints."

He nodded warily.

"Promise?" she insisted.

"Promise."

He saw her to the front door; as they passed the foot of the stairs, Drusilla Jago shouted down at her: "Your mother was nothing but a common prostitute and you've turned out the same. Don't you ever dare show your face here again!"

Jane clutched the folder with the torn-up photograph more tightly but made no reply. "She'll understand in time," she murmured to Daniel as she gave him one final peck at the door.

"You might need this," he said, handing her an umbrella from the hallstand. She hesitated.

"Give it me back tomorrow."

He watched her all the way to the crest of the road, where Greenbank becomes Falmouth, knowing it would be the last time he would ever see her.

But she, blithely happy in the discoveries she had made and the true wealth that now was hers, walked with the lightest tread. To test herself she tried to think of Daniel as he had been to her only an hour or so earlier, before their laughter had rescued them. To her surprise, he was still there. But immediately on the heels of that realization came another: He was still there *in her mind.* In the real world outside he had no place at all. He had become what he perhaps always was: a figment of her desires. He already had little enough in common with the kindly and slightly bewildered brother who had helped her tidy herself up just now; he was more like the buccaneer of her dreams – the swashbuckling figure who had driven his ship straight through the image of Vosper Scawen ...

What about Vosper now?

She pushed the question away. There was too much to explore in the strange no-man's-land between buccaneer-lover and dear brother. She had an intimation that every imaginary lover whom she might henceforth base on a real live man would, on ripening acquaintance, lose in excitement as he gained in humanity. For that, she realized, was what had happened with Daniel, quite apart from all question of their kinship. The more she saw of him, the more it was forced upon her that he had his own life, independent of hers, his own foibles and opinions, his own will. And it would be the same with all the others, too.

All the others? Was she expecting to run a gamut of them now?

Well, even if there were only one more, it would happen with him, too. The only lover she could totally control was the one who remained forever a figment. In that case, she asked herself, what was she controlling?

Her own desires.

Was it normal for a woman to feel such desires? And to have to control them by such elaborate means? Nobody ever spoke about it. Every word she'd ever read on the pleasures of womanhood was devoted to the home in general and the nursery in particular. Dorothy Lanyon never mentioned it, nor even hinted at it. Mrs Moore had spoken of "joyful union," and "greatest pleasure"; but then no one put her forward as a model woman. And in between there was Jemima, who had said it was quite good fun but not worth the anxiety. All of which brought her back to the nub of it: What is normal?

As a solo woman of outward respectability but walking alone, Jane had attracted – and ignored – a transient interest among the passing manscape. Her set face and purposeful walk had nipped it in the bud – except for one slightly drunken sailor, a foreigner by his dress, who would not leave her alone. He offered no great threat but, like a tipsy puppy, he scampered along in the gutter beside her, giggling and saying,

"Jigajig ... jigajig!" over and over again. Several men looked as if they might intervene on her behalf, but the brawn of the sailor and the glint in his eye gave them second thoughts. One fellow asked if the "dago" was bothering her, but he himself had such a leer that she didn't want to become beholden to him instead. She thanked him and declined.

Brave thought! In fact, she had not the first notion what she might do. As the approached the bottom of the hill, he became even more importunate. He knew by now that he hadn't a chance, of course; he was simply making her suffer for spurning his wonderful offer. She looked around for someone to help her – anyone, even the leering rescuer. But they all avoided her eye. The sailor's foul-mouthed insults were transforming her into a street drab, one of that tribe of women well able to look out for themselves. Lord, she would even welcome the sight of Miss Wilkinson now!

At last, goaded beyond endurance, she turned and prodded at the creature with her umbrella. She intended to poke him somewhere vaguely in the midriff, but the handle was more slippery than she realized and the point of impact was an excruciating few inches lower. The man gave a bellow of pain and fell writhing into the gutter. She stood and looked at him in dismay; a crowd was gathering. A butcher came out of his shop, immediately beside her, and touched her arm. "That's all right, my lover," he said quietly. "You go on now."

Jane turned. Someone, a woman, linked arms with her and said gaily, "We have come a long way since last June, haven't we!" It was, of course, Miss Wilkinson.

"Where did you spring from?" Jane asked, wishing the woman's intimacy were not quite so comforting.

"I was behind you all the way from the top of the hill."

"And you did nothing to help?"

"Why should I?"

Jane struggled crossly and freed her arm from the other's clutch.

Miss Wilkinson laughed and took hold of her again. "Of course I'd have helped you! If you had shown signs of needing it. Don't you feel proud of having coped on your own?"

Jane gave a little shrug, not wishing to admit it.

"But what a feeble lot of men, eh?" the woman added. "You were quite right to refuse the one who did offer his help."

"If only that were all he offered," Jane commented.

"Quite!" Miss W faltered for a pace, caught up again, and added, "I say!"

"I knew our paths would cross," Jane said in the sort of vexed tones in which a woman might "know" it would rain the moment she hung out her washing. "As soon as you said you were coming 'to Falmouth for orders'."

"Did I say that?" the other asked in surprise.

"No. That's the traditional owner's orders to his *vessel*. Didn't you know?" She laughed. "Is there actually something in the world that I know and you don't!"

"Lots, I expect," Miss Wilkinson said, so equably that Jane now felt a little childish.

"Well, it's true, isn't it," she said grumpily. "This French officer you're waiting for, you're just his vessel. He'll give you your orders."

294

"Will he!" Her eyes sparkled with superior merriment, which only increased Jane's annoyance.

"The man who pays the piper and all that," Jane added.

"I see." Her tone was so light it suggested that the argument wasn't even worth the bother of refuting.

"No answer, eh," Jane countered.

"Obviously not," she replied, as if they were talking about a third party now. In the same breath she added gaily, "I've been having my portrait painted. Did you know there's a very good painter who lives out along Greenbank? Roger Moynihan. Just a few doors down from that derelict house I saw you coming out of. He noticed me in the street and asked me if I'd sit for him. I thought, 'Oh yes!' At least it was a novel approach. But I couldn't have been further from the truth. If I meet just one more man like him, I shall have to revise my opinion of the entire species."

"Well, I'm very happy for you, I'm sure," Jane interrupted. "As it happens, I am about to have my portrait taken, too." She pointed her umbrella at Stanton's, which was now within sight, a hundred yards or so ahead.

"I haven't finished yet," Miss Wilkinson said evenly. "Mr Moynihan talks quite a lot as he works. He believes that the mind must be distracted from what the demon artist is doing or it tries to dabble in the work itself. Anyway, he told me today that when one of the popes was having his portrait painted by the great master Titian, the painter dropped a brush. And the pope leaped out of his chair, picked it up, and handed it back to him! There, what d'you think of that!"

Jane looked to see if she were joking.

"Who calls the tune when the piper is a Titian?" the woman asked.

"I see!" Jane said wearily. "Well to me it only confirms my view that all artists have much too high an opinion of themselves."

Miss Wilkinson laughed and said "Oh!" several times and squeezed her arm encouragingly – and generally behaved as grown-ups do when a child unintentionally says something clever or funny.

They had reached Stanton's by now, where Jane held out her hand to bid Miss W farewell and pointedly sever all future intercourse between them. Instead she heard herself asking the woman if she would kindly wait and then join her for a cup of tea. Even worse, Miss W herself did not appear to relish the prospect, either. "Unfinished business?" she asked.

Jane nodded, not having any clear idea what it might be.

"Oh, very well," she said. "Half an hour. I'll go and do some marketing."

Jane stood awhile and watched her walking away up the street. There was no swagger about her, no showy truculence, yet she owned every inch she touched. People, even other women, stepped aside to let her pass.

"Miss?" Banks said at her side.

"It's not only me, you see," Jane told her as she went within.

That brief vision of Miss Wilkinson lingered with Jane all through her portrait session with Mr Stanton and his assistant. It was an argument more powerful than a dozen tracts, precisely because it was so unconscious. Miss Wilkinson dictated the terms on which the world was to accept her; and she managed it without bravado, vanity, or any taint of self-importance. Jane could not help comparing it with her own situation – all those petty rules. Though they were second-nature to her now, so that she hardly ever thought of them consciously, they nonetheless kept her life crimped and confined.

"You may stop and pass the time of day with these and these people. To those and those you may bow your head and pass on. And if the others are so vulgar as to greet you, you will cut them ..."

"Refreshments are never served to callers until after four o'clock ..."

"Cards are repaid with cards, calls with calls ..."

"You will talk of the weather, the season, the delightfulness of the occasion (even if it be odious), and – in very general terms, of course – your partner's chief occupation or profession ..."

"You will not talk of politics, gossip, scandal, or anything that might smack of an intellectual interest or *cleverness* ..."

"Dull Men Eat Very Brown Bread."

These and countless other maxims had been dinned into her for as long as she could remember. And though, in a way, she could see that they were right and that the world would be a happier place if everyone did what was expected of them and accepted their lot ... all those arguments fell to the devastating and unanswerable sermon of Miss Wilkinson's walk. And that must account for what happened next.

Jane found herself sitting in the idential "rustic seat" that her mother had occupied almost twenty-one years previously, in the May of 1840. She wondered if this Mr Stanton was the same photographer as then, too.

"How old is that camera?" she asked by way of opening.

"It is the very latest, Miss Hervey, from Mapperly of Plymouth."

"Ah. I expect you've seen a good many changes in cameras, since you first opened?" It was hard to talk conversationally with his assistant fretting around her, hiding the little struts that would help her keep her head still for the ten seconds or so that the exposure would require. Mrs Pellew had said that if you kept moving just a teeny bit it would stop your wrinkles from showing on the plate. "Not that *you* have any such problem yet, my dear," she added. Still, it was useful to know these things.

The man agreed that, indeed, he had seen many changes.

"Do I have to hold my pose for long?" she went on. "My mother once told me she had to sit stock still for five minutes."

The man chuckled. "That must have been many years ago, miss."

"True," she agreed. "In fact, I'm not sure it wasn't in this very studio. Would you have been here in 1840?"

The man peered at her through half-closed eyes. "Well, well, well," he said abstractedly. "Fancy that! John, I think we'll move the big reflector a little to the ... yes, that's better."

"It was when Kinghorn Jago was an assistant here," Jane added. "I remember her telling me that."

The man froze. "That *is* going back," he said carefully. "May I ask your mother's name, Miss Hervey?"

"She was a Vyvyan from Mawnan Smith. Angwin Vyvyan was her name."

He stared at her and then murmured, "Of course."

When he said no more she asked him what he meant by "of course"?

He laughed weakly and shook his head. "I mean, of course I should have recognized you, Miss Hervey. And now that I look at you as something other than a photographic subject, I do. Yes, indeed I do."

"You see that folder there? Banks, give it to him please."

"If you're quite sure, miss," the maid replied with a slow and heavy emphasis.

"I am," she said. "Quite sure." She couldn't turn her head to see his reaction but she heard his tut of dismay at the damage.

"People are so unforgiving," she went on, "I suppose it's too much to hope that you still have the negative?"

He smiled over her head and said, "There you are, my lad!" To her he added, "Young Master John here wanted to throw them out, only last month. But no, I told him, you never know. It was a flimsy paper negative but I can expose it up onto a wet plate and then make as many prints as you require."

"I'd like one for every Vyvyan in the county," she told him. "But I'll content myself with one and a spare, if that's agreeable?"

After that there was a subtle change in his attitude toward her. Earlier, it had been a mixture of command and servility. Would she ever so kindly mind tilting her head ... so − or raising her eyes ... yes, like that! But these were clearly his orders. Now, although he was still the one who placed her and moved the lights and reflectors, he added the all-important explanations: This would make her seem vapid, that too juvenile, or sentimental. He asked her how she wished to appear. He made her a party to his decisions rather than the pampered and flattered object of them. In that day of startling revelations, it was by no means the least.

Before they left, he dug out the original negative of her mother's portrait and showed it to her. There in the ticket in the corner were the pencilled initials, KJ. She was glad Aunt Agnes had been shown to tell the truth − even if not the whole truth. She took out her purse to pay the deposit, on which Stanton had been most insistent; but now he waived it, saying that, in the circumstances, it was hardly necessary. "A family with such an old and valued custom here," he added with a twinkle.

"What was all that about, miss?" Banks asked as soon as they were outside again.

"I have lit a fuze," Jane said.

"I should just about think you have! What did you go and do it for?"

Jane was about to reply that she just wanted to stir things up a bit when she was seized with the most spine-chilling thought she had ever had in all her life. The maid saw her hesitation and said, "What?"

Jane shook her head. "I promised to meet ... someone else for tea. A woman. You needn't worry. Well, in fact, it was Miss Wilkinson." Seeing the look in the maid's eye, she added, "I could hardly do otherwise. There was a man pestering me in the street and she ... got rid of him. She's eager to talk to me. What could I do? I won't be long. Where's the carriage?"

"At St Gluvias ..." Banks turned to point out the direction and saw Miss W herself, approaching them. "There she is now." Her tone indicated a slight surprise that her mistress had been telling the truth after all.

297

Jane had already seen her. "We'll be thirty minutes or so, I expect. I'll also call on Mme Lapin."

She chose a small café with a view over the harbour from Fish Strand Quay. Respectable enough, it looked nonetheless as if few really respectable people would choose to meet there. "Well?" Miss Wilkinson asked impatiently as soon as the waiter had gone with their order.

"Once upon a time," Jane said with a smile, "there was a respectable young Cornish lady who, while having her photograph taken, fell desperately in love with the photographer's assistant."

The woman smiled, too. "Has this just happened ..." Her question tailed off when she saw Jane's upraised finger.

"They eloped that very afternoon," she went on, "and soon put many miles between them and their pursuers. Unfortunately, they had not gone far enough – in terms of distance, you understand, though in all other ways they had already gone much too far."

Miss Wilkinson's eyes went wide in alarm. "Miss Hervey! I beg you will remember I am an unmarried lady!"

"Much too far," Jane insisted. "They separated the young lovers, threw him in jail, and sent her to Vienna."

"Ah!" Miss W relaxed. "Until now I have been wondering if you were attempting a sentimentalized account of my own ..."

"To Vienna," Jane interrupted, "where, she was soon delivered of a daughter. Shortly thereafter they moved to Paris, helped by a legacy from a great-aunt who had been scandalized at the family's treatment of our heroine."

Miss Wilkinson rubbed her hands with glee. "I love fairy tales – and the more improbable, the better."

"The daughter was brought up in the strictest manner. No hint of her ... her bastardy was ever let fall."

Miss Wilkinson, who had been about to pass another sarcastic remark, suddenly turned pale· and silent. After that there were no more such interruptions.

"When the daughter was twelve, her mother must have realized that the truth could not be forever concealed. Quite fortuitously she – the mother – was befriended by a kindly old gentleman from England, who offered to take her back there, give her an honoured name and a place in society once more. Between them they devised a tale to satisfy 'his' daughter as to why her 'father' had been so long absent. She believed them, of course. They returned to England when she was around fourteen. By the time she was eighteen ..."

"I think I know the rest," Miss Wilkinson said quietly. "Her mother died. Yes? And her father brought her" – she tapped the tablecloth – "here? To Cornwall?"

"What disturbs me about this story," Jane said slowly, "is its very improbability. Ever since I was told it, I could not believe that they came to Cornwall by sheer chance. And yet, knowing the character of the man in the tale, I could not believe he chose it deliberately – not if he knew the mother's background." She drew a deep breath, closed her eyes, and said, "But *suppose he didn't!*"

"Exactly," Miss Wilkinson whispered, having got there already.

"Ah! You think it likely?" Jane hung upon her answer.

It was a reluctant nod.

"Go on," Jane urged. "Myself, I hardly dare."

The other sighed. "I imagine it was ... when? Not in Vienna. While she was there she would, of course, be seething with resentment, dreaming impossible dreams of revenge upon her family ..."

"No!" Jane exclaimed. "Upon the whole of society."

"Ah!" Miss Wilkinson smiled a sudden understanding smile. "That is why you ask me? Me in particular?"

"Yes."

"Oh, Jane Hervey! Have you considered all the implications of that reply?"

"Yes, Miss Wilkinson, I have."

The woman reached across the table and gave her arm a brief, friendly squeeze. "Then I think it must have been when she came into that legacy. I'm sorry I said that was a fairy-tale. In fact, it is the most immediately credible element of all. I believe that money inside families is far more often used for spite than for any other purpose. But you can imagine her, can't you – enough money to live like ... well, in France, they'd say the *haute bourgeoisie*. And yet in England, in Cornwall, she will be an outcast forever. But wait! She has a daughter. A Trojan horse, perhaps ..." She frowned. "But that wouldn't work. How can she get her husband and her daughter to go while she herself stays behind?"

"In a little country graveyard," Jane said.

Her evenness of tone made Miss Wilkinson shiver. "She knew she was dying?"

Jane nodded. "I didn't, of course – not until it was ... distressingly obvious. But I think now that she was told some time before."

"And then she said to your father ... or perhaps he asked her first – yes! He asked her would she like to go back to her own people ..."

"In Wales!" Jane put in.

"Wales?"

"Yes. That's what she always told us. She had an entire family in Glamorgan – all invented. But you're right, I think. He asked her if she'd like to go back and die on her native soil. And she said no, somewhere else, similar, perhaps ... Celtic, too. Cornwall! The very place. There was something safe and remote about it on the map. Of course, when it came to it, she was too ill to make the journey."

"And after her death," Miss Wilkinson concluded, "the wish would assume the proportions of a sacred trust. He would uproot himself from all his friends and bring you down here."

"Where, with my inheritance, I would be sure to marry into one of the great county families ... a little fuze to an enormous bomb ... fizzing away. Angwin Vyvyan's long-delayed revenge!"

Miss Wilkinson swallowed audibly. "My dear, d'you suppose there's a word of truth in it all?"

Jane closed her eyes and shook her head. "I think I long ago abandoned all hope of learning the truth. There is no such thing as truth, except what is in people's minds. And they guard it so carefully. And let it out in such careful ways." She

299

smiled. "I'm not being especially personal, now. I'm just the same, I know. So I have no hope of learning *the* truth. All I want, in my modest fashion, is enough of it to make sense."

"What can I tell you?" Miss Wilkinson asked hopelessly – and then brightened. "I can tell you that I'm sure your father – Wilfrid Hervey, I mean – I'm sure he had no part in the deception."

"In *that* deception," Jane said. "He was the heart and soul of all the others."

"You poor girl. You mustn't let it make you bitter, you know – take it from one who has sojourned in that land."

The waiter brought them their tea and toasted buns.

"What do you feel about men in general?" Jane asked when he had gone.

"Contempt," Miss Wilkinson replied simply, and then laughed. "See what I mean?" As she spread the butter upon her bun and watched it melt and soak in, she went on, "You mean what tender feelings do I have? If any? Pity, I suppose. I pity them in a way."

"Why?"

"Because they are so easily duped. Because they are so obsessed, so enslaved by their need for us. Did you ever see a dozen dogs going up the street with a bitch on heat in their midst? That stupid grin on their faces? Panting and drooling and egging each other on? I never see a procession of aldermen without thinking of that. Or bishops in solemn conclave. Or judges and barristers in wig and gown. Or Penzance football team coming down Market Jew Street all singing and covered in mud. They're all just different packs of dogs to me."

Her eyes levelled in Jane's, who smiled and said, "That's contempt, all right. But you also mentioned pity?"

Miss Wilkinson laughed. "There's no difference, is there."

Jane saw there was no hope of a balanced answer from her and gave up. Suddenly she became businesslike again. "Listen! You know you said you're off to France?"

"Y-e-s?" It was a most guarded agreement.

"Paris?"

Miss Wilkinson smiled wickedly. "I don't know, do I! I've come 'to Falmouth for orders' – as the saying goes!"

Jane made a contrite face. "But is there a chance?"

"I suppose so. Especially if I get bored with him rather quickly."

"Because I'm going there, you see. As soon as I can now. And if you're there at the same time, well, it'd be fun to meet, don't you think? Anyway, meet or not, let's keep in touch? You could write to me *poste restante* at the embassy, care of Lieutenant Richard Vyvyan ..."

Miss Wilkinson suppressed a smile and Jane knew they were no strangers. One in every port, indeed! "What are you going to do there?" the woman asked.

Jane grinned and said, with delicate precision, as if it were the most refined and ladylike of sentiments: "Whatever I damn well please!"

38 EVEN WHEN SHE SAW the envelope, propped up and waiting for her, Jane did not guess what it might contain. She supposed it was from Daniel, suggesting a different rendezvous, since he was not there in person. She slipped it into her pocket book, to read at the first suitable opportunity.

The prints of her mother delighted her. They were far superior to the fading original; indeed, their crystalline sharpness made it hard to believe she was looking back at a scene captured more than two decades gone – older than herself. That sense of awe was only increased when Mr Stanton, saying no word but with a gesture that spoke volumes, laid her own portrait beside them; it was the identical young woman who sat there, so composed and calm, staring at the lens. Jane, who knew only her mirror image, was quite taken aback. "I've never seen closer," he said. "Not in all my years."

She paid him and returned to the carriage in something of a daze. "I understand why my aunt was so certain, now," she said to Banks. "But why can I not see it in the looking glass?"

"For the same reason you can't read anything in the glass, I suppose," was the practical reply.

"My letter!" Jane cried. "How could I forget?"

Hastily she tore it open and turned it to the light from the window. It was dated the previous night, Sunday, and read:

My darling Jane,

By the time you read this I shall be on the high seas and gone. You, with your want of family found it easy to accept me as your brother despite any earlier desires you may have had, and claimed you had. Was it to test me in that regard you suggested we run off together? You did not say as man and wife but that was in your eyes. Well, a man may test himself in that way, too, in his mind, which I have done and found myself grievously wanting. I cannot think of you as sister, already having three too many of that sour and cheerless clan. All the while I was brushing your clothes yester afternoon, I could not stop myself recalling why that soil was on them, for what reason we fell – and so nearly Fell, and would indeed have Fallen but for my mother's return.

I cannot think it common lust tho it has all its marks. I touch your dress and tremble. I think of your sweet body and ache to hold it. And this is all as any Lover might, not to hold you for an hour and then begone, but for ever and always – and still count that too short a time together.

I will forget you. I mean to forget you. But never while you are there, near me, moving near me, filling the air with the enticement of you, smiling at me and thinking yourself no more to me than my dear, smiling sister, when in truth you are all I desire. Farewell! I sign myself what I know in my heart I can never be:

Yr affec. brother,
Daniel

Silent tears were coursing down her face by the time she finished. The letter fell from her nerveless fingers. Banks darted a hand forward and caught it before it reached the floor. She folded it, and offered it back to her. "Miss?" she prompted when Jane made no response.

"Read it," Jane said. Her voice was salty, strangled.

"I don't hardly ..."

"Go on."

She, too, was close to tears by the time she finished. "The poor edjack," she muttered, taking out a handkerchief and blowing her nose. "Couldn't he have striven himself down? He only needed a bit of time, surely?"

Jane stared out of the window. How drab and weary everything looked. "Where can we find out what vessels have sailed since last night?" she asked.

Banks thought for a moment. "There must be some office down by the harbour," she suggested. "The pilots and that, they must know."

"Then lean your head out and tell the driver that's where we want to go."

But the man, being Cornish, wished to know why. When Banks told him, he tightened the brake, leaped to the ground, and vanished into a nearby public house. Five minutes later, reeking of malt, he was able to tell them only one vessel had sailed last night – the *Jupiter,* bound for Genoa. Jane, though grateful enough for this information, was immediately assailed by fresh uncertainties. How would they know if she arrived or if any mishap befell her on the way? And after that, how could they keep track of her? And was there a faster boat leaving in the next few days, also headed for Genoa? How could she get a message delivered ...?

He told her.

From that day forth, she resolved, *Lloyd's Register* would be her daily reading. She diverted the carriage back up the main street in order to buy her first copy at once. The newsagent came out to her carriage to tell her   the issue for that day would not arrive until four in the afternoon. He agreed to keep her a copy; Jane received the impression she was not the first distraught young lady who had ever presented herself at his door with a sudden lively interest in the movements of the world's merchant fleets.

They rode back to Pennance in a desultory silence as Jane pondered the loss of Daniel for the second time within the week, first as lover, now as brother. To her surprise, she discovered that the second was the worse of the two, for brother-sisterhood is permanent, immutable, in a way that love is not. Why could he not see that? The more she thought of it, the less of a surprise it became.

She remembered Banks's phrase, that he could have "striven himself down." How perfectly that expressed it. And it would have been easy, too, since the love that unites siblings is far nobler than that other kind. She could see it so clearly now. It was even more frustrating not to be able to tell him. "At least it doesn't blow hot and cold," she said aloud.

"I beg your pardon, miss?"

"Losing Daniel like this, it's not the same as losing him ... the other way. I mean, it doesn't change any of the facts, does it?"

"I'm not quite sure I follow, miss."

"Well, this time it's just annoying. More than annoying. Infuriating. We've got to find him, write him a letter telling him how foolish he's being. Make him understand that running away doesn't change anything. Oh!" She grasped his umbrella in her rage and shook it. "If only he were here, I could make him see it. Why couldn't he just tell me? He didn't give us any chance at all."

"That's true," Banks said, glad to find one of her mistress's utterances that made immediate sense.

There was another silence before Jane burst out with: "Love!"

The maid stared in surprise at the scorn in the word.

"What has it ever done?" Jane went on. "Just think of the people we know, and what it's done for them. It ruined my mother's life, and my grandparents' too, and whoever she was intended to marry. It drove her into exile. It's left me branded with her shame for life. The pursuit of it killed my father. Its demands put Esther Wilkinson on the streets and have left her with nothing but contempt for all men. Look what it did to Bessie Wender. And now look what it's done to Daniel and me! I tell you, Banks – and I'll swear it on anything you like – I am *finished* with love. It is nothing but a delusion."

"Yes, miss."

"Don't you agree?"

The maid smiled. "I wouldn't say as I'm not content, the way things are going along with me."

"You never say anything."

"Ah well, there's very little to say. I'm just well suited, I suppose. Not having too much time to get into agonies, like."

Jane considered her reply carefully. "You're right," she said at last. "I need an occupation. Ever since I left the schoolroom my thoughts have been directed at one thing only – love and marriage. It can't be healthy. What's the best marriage we know of? I exclude Mr and Mrs Lanyon because it wouldn't be proper for us to discuss them. But in any case, they'd hardly qualify as ... no, I mustn't say that. But who has the best marriage? Come on!"

The maid eased the band of her collar and said, diffidently, "I should think Mr and Mrs Moore do clink pretty well."

"Exactly. She's the one to go and see."

There was another fairly lengthy pause before she burst out with: "How *can* I make the Lanyons do what I want?"

Banks sniffed. "I should think the fuze you lit back there at Stanton's will go a good long way."

Jane smiled. "You've been thinking about these matters, too!"

"I think about it all the time."

Jane smiled gratefully at her. "I simply don't know what to do. I'm in such confusion now. If only Daniel hadn't run away like that. There's another reason why it's so infuriating."

"You can't just cut loose from it all," the maid warned.

"I know. That's the great temptation, of course. But I have too many ties, and I don't just mean the money."

303

"Money's important."

"But so are the other ties, too, old and new. Take my Aunt Agnes. I can't do anything to hurt her now, can I – not after her kindness to me. You see, the thing is I'm really on my mother's side. You know what I told you last night – what I told Miss Wilkinson on Saturday?"

"About your mother tricking you and the master into coming down here?"

"Well, you may put it like that. But I agree with what my mother did, even though I'm its victim. Or pawn, perhaps. When I think of the way she was treated, it makes my blood boil. I want to *do* something. Like Mrs Moore. She had the whole world against her. And hasn't she just ... rubbed ... salt ..." She closed her eyes. "My goodness! That's what Mme Lapin meant. Even she thought of it!" She shook her head and gathered her wits again. "Anyway, Mrs Moore has certainly made the world eat humble pie. That's what I want to do, too. If my mother had only taken me into her confidence, I'd have been her delighted accomplice instead of her pawn." Her eyes gleamed at the thought, but the light went out of them as she added, "Yet I'm saddled with the Lanyons until I'm ... until I've got one foot in the grave, practically. What can I do?"

She stared hopefully at Banks, who replied guardedly, "That'll take some scheming out, miss."

Jane sighed and gazed out of the window. "I know. The thing is, they've got to go on believing they're making all the decisions. But the decisions they actually make must be ours."

"Ours?" Banks echoed.

"You know what I mean."

Privately Banks was only too afraid that she did.

*   *   *

The visit to Pennance lasted a further ten days, which were as devoid of incident as the first five had been packed – for which Jane was grateful. She needed that time to absorb all that had happened. The bright chatter of her two young friends was a grand tonic, too, as they took their postponed walks to Maenporth and Pendennis Castle. Their obsession with their forthcoming marriages grew a little wearing toward the end, mainly because it was so inconsistent. They would daydream endlessly about their future homes, papering each room a dozen times between noon and supper. They spoke of their children (a variable quantity but never fewer than a half-dozen each), of the demure and dutiful girls and the tough, awkward, chivalrous, adorable boys, of the pets, the servants, the carriages ... in short, they lived in a world of phantoms and illusions that, to Jane, seemed all too depressingly attainable. And yet, when it came to writing to their beloveds, you would have thought it Greek grammar for all their enthusiasm. Could no one read such omens?

She imagined them at forty, plump and garrulous, living their unlived dreams through their children and scarce able to exchange a civil word with the darlings they now claimed to worship. Who would then remember the two sweet nymphs who had taught her the Ophelia Game? *I will*, she thought.

But what was the alternative? For each to live on at "home" into that same grim decade, a pathetic burden, ostentatiously tolerated, earning her unchaperoned freedom only by her undesirability.

Yet they seemed as happy now as the day was long. At the very end of her stay, in the middle of February, they rode over to Helford, a winding and deeply divided saltwater estuary to an insignificant freshwater stream, where they borrowed a rowing boat from one of their father's friends. The Clerk of the Weather, having given Jane a taste of winter on her arrival, now decided that late spring was more in order for her departure. So, between the high, wooded banks of the river, they sweltered in their winter clothing, and caught crabs, and soaked themselves, and lost both oars (though fortunately not at the same time), and laughed until they begged one another for mercy. But to Jane it was doomed laughter, such as pretty butterflies might make in their one summer day if they were but given the voice.

The following morning she left for Parc-an-Ython amid more laughter, with long and repeated expressions of gratitude, all genuine – and yet there was an ineffable sadness in her soul.

39 BECAUSE JANE COULD NO longer meet Daniel as a brother, and so become day by day more familiar with him in that character, she found herself slipping back into thinking of him in his previous role. Perhaps "thinking" is not quite the word. She spoke his phrase over and over again in her mind: *I think of your sweet body and ache to hold it.* She remembered the moment in which she had been ready to set aside all scruple and become his lover. At first her mind would approach it with a sort of dread, as her conscience cast about for some distraction, some alternative enticement even. But, of course, there was none. Then came a sense of resignation, as an exhausted swimmer might feel in being swept toward the midstream of some mighty cataract. But at last there was an inexpressible sweetness as she passed beyond the bounds of memory and into the realm of fancy, as she yielded her sweet body to him and made him hers. It was no use then to recall that he was her brother; those elemental stirrings within her lay much too deep for such a meticulous challenge. And though she could not, or would not, acknowledge the name of this still-unrequited passion, she now realized it had always been there, even when she had been innocent of its purpose. But whereas it had once been formless and vague, it was now both sharp and poignant.

This regression began even before she departed from Pennance, where her busy days and chatterbox nights left scant time for any pining. On the journey home, it almost overwhelmed her. By the time they drew near to Helston, she knew it would be quite impossible for her to return to her semi-reclusive state of mourning. She told Veryan to stop at Lawyer Scawen's office; she wanted to know whether he had yet learned the likely price of the old villa in Paris. It was, as she saw it, her only hope of independence from the controlling hand of the Lanyons.

Jane hardly ever bothered to take out her fob watch; indeed, it often stopped for lack of winding. Her life ran on an internal clock whose hands pointed to hunger or tiredness but otherwise told no time at all. She was therefore surprised to find Vosper on his way out for luncheon; she herself felt not the slightest hunger. He had intended going for a chop to The Blue Anchor, where he knew he would find a particular client of his, a farmer, whom he urgently wished to see. However, though he had no news at all for Jane, he changed his plans on the spot and invited her and Mrs Lanyon, whom he presumed must also be somewhere in town, to eat with him at The Angel instead.

She, knowing he would never agree to eat alone with her, and that Banks could hardly join them at The Angel, and that she herself could hardly eat at any inferior place, tried hinting that Dorothy was undergoing a difficult fitting and wasn't very hungry but would probably join them later. But he shook his head sadly before she was half-way through this persiflage and asked her if she really thought him so naïve. He sent one of the lads down with orders for a meal to be brought up to his office. She told him Banks could go for it, but he wouldn't even have that.

"What has made you so suddenly careless of your reputation?" he asked as they went into his office.

"I don't suppose I shall be enjoying it for very much longer, anyway," she replied. "Not that *enjoy* is the word I'd choose in any case."

"I'm not sure I like the sound of this."

"You may not like the substance too much, either."

She stood a long moment at his window, watching the horses as they laboured up Wendron Street. How exhausted they must be at the end of the day's work. All they'd want is a bellyful of oats and then they'd sink into the straw and oblivion. It was the same with humans, too. The women in the field gangs, lifting turnips all day in the wind and rain – or the two little girls in the milliner's across the way, sometimes they'd be working until gone half past ten at night, according to Rosa; you'd see them there, exhausted, all haggard and drawn. But at least they'd have no time to torment themselves with vague fancies of things that could never happen, dreams that could never be.

She turned round to find that Vosper had calmly gone back to the papers on his desk. "You are a most infuriating man at times," she said.

He smiled. "If you wish to tell me something, you will. If not, I have no right to press you on the matter."

"No right to press me!" she echoed scornfully. "I walk in out of the blue, I'm probably interfering with some important affairs, and all you can say is you 'have no right to press me'."

His smile did not waver. "Oh, well, if we're going to split hairs, then let me rephrase it: I do not *claim* such a right. Satisfied?"

Jane rounded on Banks. "And you can just wipe that stupid grin off your lips." The maid pulled a theatrically contrite face.

"I'm sorry, Miss Banks," Vosper said, suppressing a laugh. "How remiss of me. Do please be seated."

"D'you know anything about French law?" Jane asked suddenly.

"Only as much as you yourself could find in any good encyclopedia under *Code Napoléon*. Probably less. Why?"

"If I went to Paris and sold the villa, could Mr and Mrs Lanyon ..." She hesitated and then tried a different tack: "I mean, they are appointed my guardians under English law, aren't they."

He stared at his fingers for a while and then showed her a scratch on one of them. "Cats, eh!" he said.

"Aren't they?" she insisted.

"Perhaps, if you were to tell me what you hope to achieve, Jane? Why these sudden preparations for war?"

"Because I think that's what it's going to be. No! I don't know what it's going to be." Her eyes narrowed. "How well do you really know Mrs Lanyon? Can you say how she's likely to behave in extreme circumstances?"

"Earthquake? Fire? Flood ..."

"You know what I mean."

He shook his head and waited. Jane stared at Banks, who, unable to read her mistress's expression against the light from the window, piped up, "If you're asking my opinion, miss ..."

"Well, I'm not," Jane snapped. Then, after a lengthy silence, she said, "Oh, very well. What is it?"

As if there had been no interruption at all Banks replied, "I think 'tis a bit of a miracle play, if you ask me – for you to go and tell the likes of that Wilkinson creature and not Mr Vosper."

Jane turned angrily away, back to her perusal of the passing traffic. Her anger was not so much at Banks as at the fact that the maid was right. If she should tell her shameful secret to only one person in all the world, that person ought to be Vosper Scawen, the one most likely to help. She could not really understand her reluctance – except that she did not wish to pollute herself in his estimation. Without turning round, she asked, "Do people still talk of an Angwin Vyvyan in these parts?"

"Ah!" he replied.

His tone made her turn and stare at him. "You know" she accused.

He shook his head. "I have made certain guesses – but I've been a lawyer long enough to know how dangerous that can be."

"What d'you *know* of her, then? Never mind the guesses."

"I know only what whispers and gossip ..."

"Oh, Vosper, don't start splitting hairs now. Either the story is widely known, or it isn't. Anyway, the original truth doesn't matter now. It's what people believe that's important. What have you heard people saying about her?"

He sighed. "Certain facts are matters of public record. She eloped to Bristol with Kinghorn Jago and was apprehended before their marriage could be solemnized. After that, all is conjecture. It's fairly certain that she was discovered to be with child and that she was sent out of Cornwall, probably out of England, until after it was born. Rumour says to Vienna. She appears not to have returned."

"And that's all you know?"

"That's as far as the generally agreed gossip goes."

"So why did you say *ah!* in that knowing tone?"

"Why don't you come and sit down?" he suggested.

At that moment their luncheon arrived – pasties wrapped in spotless white linen and still piping hot. Jane tackled hers with a knife and fork; Vosper, out of deference to her, followed suit; but Banks said she'd "eat 'n fitty-like," the proper Cornish way, and held it in her hands.

Vosper opened a bottle of hock, which he took from a cupboard behind him, and poured a glass each, diluted with seltzer.

"I didn't feel at all hungry until this arrived," Jane said as she carved away with gusto. "Oh, that wonderful aroma!"

"The reason I said *ah!* like that," Vosper went on, "is that Mrs Lanyon happened to say in passing that if ever I came across a portrait of Angwin Vyvyan, she would be very interested to hear of it."

"There!" Jane said to Banks.

"I think I'm breaking no confidences," he added. "She did not ask me as her lawyer. Just as an acquaintance, you understand."

"I understand only too well," Jane replied. "And I suppose you've put two and two together? Well, I shan't ask you to guess. I'll tell you."

And, over the next five minutes or so, that is what she did, leaving nothing out – not even Daniel's extreme response to the news.

His first question surprised her. "May I ask why you have this sudden eagerness to go to Paris?"

"Surely you can understand that?" she responded.

He shook his head. "I would have said that if ever there was a sleeping dog that ought to be let lie, that was it. I understand your desire to leave Cornwall. If word of this came out, you could hardly continue to move in society down here."

She smiled. "Not the sort of society in which the Lanyons move, no."

"Is there any other?"

"Mrs Moore's."

"Oh yes." He gave a roguish smile. "How easy it is to forget her."

"Perhaps for some," Jane replied crossly.

He finished his pasty, wiped his lips in the napkin, and took a sip of wine. "I think," he said slowly, "you may be underestimating Mrs Lanyon."

"I don't underestimate the power she holds over me."

"No, I'm sure you don't – and I agree it's considerable. But I believe you underestimate ... how can I put it? Her moral sense."

"Hah – very likely!"

"Just hear me out. There are some people who think of themselves as highly moral, but who, on finding that the world is not as it should be, or not as they were taught to believe, will close their eyes and ears to such evidence and blindly insist on their teaching. In fact, they are moral cowards. I believe Dorothy Lanyon is as far removed from them as it is possible to be." He smiled. "Mind you, I don't believe *she* knows it yet. In fact, I think she is in the very throes of making the discovery. So – if you were to go to her now in a more open frame of mind, I think you might be agreeably surprised at her response."

308

"In what frame of mind? I mean, what d'you think I should say?"

He dipped his head uncertainly. "That's entirely your affair. All I can say is that if you go in with your fists flailing, I don't think you'll do half so well." He took her plate and stacked it on his. "I could be quite wrong, mind," he added helpfully.

*   *   *

"Oh!" Jane exclaimed when they were back in their carriage and on their way to Parc-an-Ython. "Did you ever know such an infuriating man? One day I shall either kill him ... or ..." She abandoned the thought. After a moment she said to Banks, "There you go again! These secret smiles you keep making – I wish you knew how stupid you looked."

The maid tried to appear solemn.

"I bitterly regret having asked him to come with us to Paris now," Jane went on. "I can just imagine what would happen if we discovered something dreadful there, and I'd say I might as well go and throw myself in the Seine, and he'd say, 'That's entirely your decision, Jane.' I can just hear him."

"You like a man who'll tell you straight out what to do, eh, miss? Then you can just knuckle under and obey?"

Jane nodded, but it was a struggle to keep a straight face. "Or," she said at last, "disobey. But at least I'd know what I was disobeying. It's not fair the way he keeps leaving all my decisions to me. He's not like that with Mrs Lanyon. I've heard him give quite straightforward advice. He's my solicitor, too. Don't you think I've an equal right to get advice?"

"And don't you think he gave it?"

She shrugged and stared angrily out of the window. "There's such a thing as being too clever by half," she muttered vaguely.

Dorothy, who had parted with her on somewhat strained terms, was now over the moon to see her back. "Your letters were so gay and fulsome," she said, "I almost felt I was there, too. Which, of course, I was, in spirit. But do come and sit by the fire now, and tell me all over again. Banks will see to all your unpacking, won't you?"

"Indeed, ma'am," the maid responded with surprise. Mrs Lanyon had never before pitched her commands in the tones of a request.

"I had my portrait taken," Jane told her guardian when they were alone by the drawing-room fire.

"I know. So you said."

Jane passed over the new print of her mother and held her breath.

"Oh, but that's charming!" Dorothy started to say ... then her voice tailed off. "Jane?" she said in a small, questioning voice, staring straight at her young ward.

Jane nodded. "Angwin Vyvyan."

Dorothy rose and carried the print to the window, but Jane doubted she could actually see it even then. The woman's hand trembled so violently she had to hook a little finger round the curtain to steady herself. Jane drew breath to speak but Dorothy heard her and shook her head. Then, looking far out across the fields, she said, "I have imagined this moment a thousand times and in a thousand different ways. I have made myself ill with the worry of it."

"I wish ..." Jane began.

"No. Let me finish." She gave a little laugh. "I never imagined it would be so ... such an anticlimax." She drew a deep breath and stared at the picture, which she could now hold almost steady. "It is astonishing."

"Even Mr Stanton remarked on it – once I mentioned the connection."

"You told him?" Dorothy was scandalized.

"How else could I have acquired that copy?" She described how she had come by the original and what had happened to it, adding, for the sake of a little light relief, "Between you and me, I believe Aunt Agnes herself had a teeny *affaire* with Kinghorn Jago some time before his eyes happened on my mother."

Dorothy's expression hardened at this news. "I hold no great respect for her, in that case, for she was already married by then. A faithless woman is surely the worst of all abominations."

"Oh, I don't suppose it was much more than the odd glance, the occasional sigh, you know," Jane added hastily. "All I meant to say was that I don't think it all happened between him and my mother during the five minutes it required to expose the plate. Can you imagine! Staying still for five minutes!"

Dorothy became pensive once more. "How much of your mother's history do you now believe you know?" she asked.

"Everything," Jane replied – and then added, "Except the single most important thing of all."

Dorothy did not ask her what that might be. In fact, her troubled eyes dwelled in Jane's as if she did not dare to ask. Jane knew then that the same worry had crossed Dorothy's mind as well. "We have to go to Paris," she said quietly.

Dorothy nodded slowly. "I know."

"And we have to try not to ... not to think the worst meanwhile."

"I know."

PART FOUR

ᴏ FALMOUTH FROM THE BEACON ᴏ

Ménage complèt

40 THEY CROSSED THE CHANNEL from Dover to Calais in the teeth of a March gale, a west-sou'-westerly that battered their little steamship broadside-on, pushing it from side to side "like a rook's nest on a withy," as Banks expressed it. Jane, who had experienced such conditions before, though in the opposite direction, could not understand why the constitution that, at fourteen years of age, had laughed at the discomforts of her fellow passengers could not, at twenty, repeat the performance. Dorothy lay in laudanumed stupefaction in the Ladies Cabin. Jane tried it for a while – the stupefaction without the laudanum – but found the stuffiness unbearable and went back on deck. There, Rosa paced up and down, anxiously saying, "I *think* I'm going to be all right." Banks sat on a tethered life raft in the lee of the after deck housing, waiting for the galley to open and muttering that she couldn't see what all the fuss was about. A fat, smug little boy, endlessly circumnavigating the deck, stopped each time he passed and informed her, "I've seen twenty-seven people sicking ... twenty-nine ... thirty-one ..."

About half-way over, just when no one imagined it could get worse, the seas began running diagonally at the little vessel, coming up from behind her on the starboard beam. As a result, instead of just rolling along between neatly parallel waves, with more-or-less level decks fore-and-aft, she broached, or went corkscrewing across them, and never hit a moment with an even keel. Rosa stopped saying that she thought she'd be all right and joined Jane at the rail, where she, too, parted with her meagre breakfast.

"Banks has gone below to *eat,*" she said in disgust.

"Thank heavens Vosper didn't come," Jane told her.

"That's a change of tune! Oh, why did nobody warn us at breakfast!"

"How can you even mention breakfast? I'd have hated him to see me like this."

"Oh, I'd welcome him," Rosa said dully. "*Any* man, almost. Just someone to hug me half to death and promise me this'll all be over soon."

They stared into the swollen, greeny-white banks of water that rolled beneath them and hurtled onward, rank after rank; every now and then a sudden congruence of wind, wave, and iron sides would send up a great sheet of spray, which would be plucked aloft by the wind and sent hurtling across the watery hills and valleys. Then the face of the deep would seem to shudder at the onslaught, as if bracing itself against an unbearable cold; and the sharp, tangy effervescence that danced briefly in the air would send shivers down the spines of the two miserable young ladies.

"We surely cannot go on to Paris tonight?" Rosa asked. "I shall just want to collapse into the nearest bed. Can travellers have their own rooms in France or is it like the coaching inns in England?"

"I'm sure we can have our own room. But I don't think I could go indoors. I just want to stand on a hilltop, on firm, firm ground, and let the wind fill my lungs. Don't you feel you can't breathe enough air here?" She stretched her chin skyward and drew in the deepest draught she could manage; then she let it out in a rush, saying, "I still can't get enough."

As they drew nearer to Calais the wind, at least, abated. Without its incessant roaring in their ears, they found that the swell had somehow become more tolerable. "Or perhaps we're getting our sea limbs," Jane commented hopefully.

"To be honest, I'm not sure I have any limbs of any kind," Rosa complained. "I'm *frozen.* Aren't you?"

Banks came above at that moment. "The best blow-out I've had in years," she said cheerily as she handed back the change from the florin she had been allowed.

"I can well believe that!" Jane ostentatiously weighed the single threepenny bit in the palm of her hand.

Banks giggled. "I had wine, too. The steward says they all do it over there. Funny taste, though – like sour aglans. Whoops!" She lurched with the bucking deck and fell against the rail.

Jane returned the coin to her, with orders to go below for a coffee.

"I must say – you're very tolerant," Rosa remarked when the maid had gone. "She was as tipsy as a cuckoo."

"She's the salt of the earth," Jane replied. "There's more good sense in that brain of hers, tipsy or sober, than in a whole bench of judges."

"I say!" Rosa looked at her askance.

"What?"

"It's not what I'd have thought of you. Your reputation is ..."

"Heavens!" Jane laughed. "Do you say I have a reputation?"

"Well, moving in La Lanyon's circle, you know." She frowned. "Actually, *she's* changed a bit, too, just lately. I don't know what it is."

A sudden blast of wind caught the vessel on the crest of a wave and made it shudder; they clung to the rail until it had passed.

"Can you answer me one thing?" Rosa went on. "Why, in fact, are we going to Paris at all? Not that I'm not eternally grateful and so on, but ..."

"Why do you ask?"

"I just wondered. You and La Lanyon seem to ... I mean, I just get the feeling it's about something more than just seeing the old family home."

Jane stared at the sea for a while. "Just when you get used to the swell coming from one direction, it changes," she commented. Then she sighed. "I suppose it's not fair, leaving you in the dark. And anyway, the whole of Cornwall will probably know soon enough ..." And she went on to tell Rosa something of her story, with one or two embellishments. She made the legacy from Great-Aunt Cicely seem a matter of historical fact, rather than of Aunt Agnes's conjecture; she said nothing of her inability to remember her father's visits before she was twelve; nor did she say that the villa had been an apparent gift from Baron de Puisne. Such topics were unlikely to arise now, anything up to twenty years after the event, so there was no need to complicate the tale with them.

To Jane's surprise, Rosa seemed overwhelmed with gratitude to be made party to such a confidence. "That's why you're out of mourning already," she said. "I was afraid to ask."

Afraid to ask! It made Jane realize what a barrier to true friendship her wealth still was; how it coloured everything that happened between them. Yet she saw no way of overcoming it.

Rosa's nimble wits, however, were soon at work on the tale. "She was an extremely fortunate woman, your mother," she said. "Given the first bit of bad luck, I mean."

Jane smiled. Conversation was certainly a good distraction from *mal-de-mer.* "You think it was bad luck to have been prevented from marrying someone like Kinghorn Jago?" she asked. "I shudder every time I remember he's my father. I still cannot feel it in here." She tapped her breast.

Rosa chuckled. "No – I meant *you* were the bad luck, if you'll pardon my saying so. But many a lady in those circumstances has to leave her baby with some Italian or French peasant family and return to a diet of very 'umble pie."

"Many?" Jane questioned in surprise.

Rosa seemed equally surprised that it was news to Jane. "Even I could name three. And nobody breathes a whisper of such things to a virtuous young lady. I'll wager La Lanyon could name a dozen."

"I'll ask her," Jane said as a matter of passing interest.

"For heaven's sake, no!"

"Why not? She's become quite frank with me since ... you know."

"No doubt. But it used to be quite common for a wife to prove she was ... well, that the baby-making bits of her were all shipshape – if you see what I mean."

"Ah!"

"Quite. I don't know, but it may be a bit of a sore point between her and Mr L."

Jane closed her eyes and shivered at the thought of the gaffe she might have made. The white cliffs of the Pas de Calais were now well up on the skyline. The shallower seas were starting to make the swell shorter and steeper, but, since it was now attacking them from full astern, the decks were at least even across her beams. One of the hands told them that the smoothest ride was now to be found amidships, so they removed themselves there, upwind of the smoke from the funnel.

"Anyway," Rosa went on, as if no interruption had occurred, "those little gambles in ... what can one call it? Husbandry? Human husbandry?" She laughed. "They must sometimes have led to tragedies. Often, perhaps. Don't you think?"

"I suppose so, though you make it sound all rather matter-of-fact. I think, in my mother's case, anyway, it was sheer impulse."

"Well, of course," Rosa said guardedly, "you knew her."

"Not really. But I can remember how I felt about Daniel – in the days before I knew he was my brother, of course. I think I felt like that the moment I saw him." She described the occasion, omitting to mention that she had been clad in nothing but seaweed at the time. "And that's why I threw that stone at him – it was like throwing those feelings away ... damaging the thing that was causing them." She drew a deep breath and added, "And even now, you know – even when I know he's my brother – there's part of me that ..." She allowed a shrug to complete the sentence for her.

Rosa leaned forward and looked into her face to see if she were serious. "Honestly?" she asked.

315

Jane nodded. "It would be different if he were here, mind. I'm sure it would. Even in that single afternoon, when I was ... just hopelessly trapped between thinking of him as my brother and ... the other thing, I managed it. To make the leap, I mean. There was a wonderful moment when I realized that the world had a thousand possible lovers but only one brother. Only one, *ever!* It's a different kind of love, but, oh, it's so strong! That's what I hate about his being away now – I can't enjoy the uniqueness of it. Of course, it's not unique for him. He's already got three other sisters and he can't stand the sight of them. I know exactly what sort of turmoil it threw him into. He couldn't make that same leap. He couldn't relinquish his feelings about me as, you know, a lover and all that."

"How can you be sure?" Rosa asked in what she intended as a kindness. "A lot of men are just waiting for some excuse to vanish over the horizon. I don't mean from you, but from home."

Jane shook her head. "I just know. Because, as I say, there's some part of me that cannot help longing for him as I used to. Don't you ever feel that? A sort of longing that is against everything else you believe in – all your finer judgement, your scruples, even your sense of ... you know?"

"No." Rosa was fascinated at her intensity.

"You've never been in love? Never felt that ..." She shook her head at the impossibility of portraying it more clearly.

"No. Not if what you describe is love."

"What do you feel, then? Don't you like the company of men?"

"Company?" Rosa echoed with a laugh. "Say *regiment,* rather! I adore them. But not deeply like you. I'd hate to be tied to just one of them like that. I'd pine away thinking of all the others whose society I'd be missing." After a moment she added, "And their jealousy, too. I'd hate it if one of them got all jealous."

Watching her, looking into her eyes and seeing them come alive as she spoke, Jane had a sudden intimation that her mother, the young Angwin, must have been very much like young Rosa as she made this same cross-Channel journey, twenty-one years ago now. She found herself wondering which of them was going to evoke more memories when they arrived in Paris and began meeting old friends: the one who merely looked like Angwin, or the one who truly was like her?

*   *   *

They missed the Paris train in any case and had to send a telegraph down the line to Richard Vyvyan, who would be expecting them at the Embarcadère du Nord. First a number of trunks had burst open in the baggage hold – none of theirs, fortunately, but people had to go below and identify them. Then, when everything was duly arranged in the customs hall, a clerk came to tell them that the officer had gone off duty and would not return until seven that evening.

A tall, angry Englishman in an Inverness cape waved a fist in the man's face and shouted, "Vous avez swindled us, m'soo. C'est un conspiracy pour les hôteliers de Calais." His face was red from drink and the salty gale.

316

The clerk remained impassive. The gentleman stared around at his compatriots and explained, for the benefit of those who had not followed his fluent French, that this business of the customs officer vanishing until it was too late to get to Paris was always happening. "I shall sit here all night in protest," he exclaimed. "And I urge you to do the same."

Sheepish and shamefaced, they sidled out in search of hotels, hot baths, and deep feather beds.

"If this is what it's like to be swindled," Rosa commented as they came stamping their muddy feet into the reassuringly named Hôtel des Anglais and stretched their hands toward the blazing fire, "I'm just going to surrender and enjoy it."

Dorothy, still numbed by the laudanum, allowed herself to be led up to her room and put to bed. The porter brought down a truckle bed for Banks, who was now quite clear-headed again and looking forward to her next voyage.

Jane and Rosa had the adjacent room, accessible by a connecting door. There they swilled their faces and gargled away the last disagreeable memories of the crossing. Then Jane said, "Can you keep a secret?" to which Rosa replied, as always, "No. What is it?"

"Well, you'd better keep this one, because you're to be part of it, too." And she led her over to one of the smaller suitcases, which she unlocked and opened. "Pandora's box," she chuckled.

"I'm part of what?" Rosa asked.

"This. And this. And this ..." She put a series of mysterious parcels on the counterpane. "Carry them over to the dressing table." She took out several more, saying, "When I was in Falmouth last month I just happened to see a little French perfumer's and the name over it was Lapin, which was the same as the *parfumeur* my mother always patronized in Paris. And it turned out to be his daughter, who had married a Cornish sea captain and been widowed. Anyway, I ordered some of my mother's old perfume and when I went to collect it – thank heavens I'd sent Banks back to the carriage – the old devil had done up a whole parcel of things she swore my mother used to employ."

Rosa had unwrapped some of them by now – a powder called *Poudre de la Comtesse,* a little box of rouge, something called *Mascarade,* henna ... she stared at them aghast. Jane added more: a red sort of grease for the lips, a bottle of *eau de toilette,* and a small phial of her mother's own perfume.

"Jane!" Rosa exclaimed.

"It's different in France, honestly," Jane assured her.

Rosa's speed of adjustment took her breath away. One moment she was fingering them as if they might explode, the next she was opening them, seating herself before the looking glass, and gabbling excitedly about all the things they could do with them – all except the *Mascarade,* whose purpose she could not even guess. "It's a kind of blacking for the eyelashes," Jane explained off-handedly.

Side by side, stroke by stroke, they transformed themselves into as raddled a pair of harridans as ever skulked in a side-alley doorway on a moonless night. At first it was hilarious to possess bright red lips, twice as generous as life; but as one desperate attempt at rescue succeeded another their panic mounted – along with a giggling hysteria – until, at last, they could only sit and stare at themselves, saying, "What on earth do we think we look like!"

"Let's go down to supper like this and see what happens?" Rosa suggested. Jane pulled a face, which was no mean feat under that disguise. "I wouldn't dare stick my nose outside the door! We've done it all wrong. I vote we just wipe it all off and start again."

But Rosa was reluctant to part with her new persona so swiftly. "I wish I could have a photograph of me just like this. It shows what you can do, doesn't it. If someone knew what they were about, they could make themselves unrecognizable."

Jane laughed. "From the evidence before us, I'd say very little skill would be needed for *that!*"

"No, but you know what I mean. Don't tell me your mother used to look like this." She kept touching her face and turning it this way and that, as if she still couldn't believe it.

"No!" Jane exclaimed. "You'd never suspect she was wearing a bit of it until she bent down to kiss you goodnight or something like that. That's the secret of it, I'm sure. We've just overdone it."

They wiped it all off and started again. This time they watched each other like cats and as soon as one could see the powder or colour or whatever it was, she would call out, "Too much, too much!" and the other was obliged to remove some of it.

This time the transformation was even more fascinating – because it was so subtle. "It's like the way you only *think* you are," Rosa murmured, afraid to touch her face anywhere now for fear of undoing the effect. "You know – that moment when you draw a deep breath before you go into a crowded ballroom and tell yourself you look quite dazzling? This is what you mean." She pointed at the pair of them.

"It's like a portrait in a salon," Jane agreed. "You know how you look at them and you say to yourself, 'Hah! I'll wager *she* wished she could really look like that!' And here it is. I don't feel sinful about it, do you?"

"Only a little."

"Oh but you shouldn't feel any. It won't be right if you feel the slightest bit. I told you – we're in France now."

"All right," Rosa agreed with naughty reluctance. "It feels ... just right. D'you think we may go down to supper like this?"

"Of course. That's the idea." Jane drew herself up and composed all her features. "I believe, if we are decorous – and aloof – enough ... I'm ravenous, aren't you?"

Rosa frowned and wagged a reprimanding finger.

Solemnly Jane accepted the rebuke and amended her statement: "I believe a little refreshment would be highly acceptable."

But Rosa's face was still pained. "Not 'highly,' Jane, dear. These wild excesses of thought and language simply do not become a young lady."

Their demure solemnity lasted as far as the door, where Jane impetuously took Rosa by the arm and said, "Oh, I do wish I had had a sister all these years."

"Me, too!" Rosa said heartily. "Where are you going to hide all that ... disguise?"

"In a little travelling writing case I also bought in Falmouth. It has a secret drawer that Dorothy will never suspect."

In public they found it easier to sustain a patrician aloofness. In the beginning they watched anxiously, though not obviously, for any sign that their appearance was giving rise to scandal, either among the servants or with their enforced fellow guests. But there was none.

The moment he heard Jane speaking French, the patron's attitude underwent a marked change. He showed them to a prominent table in the centre of the room; and, rather than simply tell them the *table d'hôte* as he had with all the others, he brought out the chef from the kitchen, complete with chopping board, bits of pork and kidney, and cultivated mushrooms. A commis chef stood by to show them how beautifully the vegetables had been julienned. Jane, knowing what was expected of her, asked intelligent questions about the precise method of cooking and *garniture*, and, all being to her satisfaction, gave in the order.

Their fellow travellers, at first a little resentful of so much favouritism, now understood they had a foreign princess, at least, travelling incognito with her maid and two ladies of the bedchamber; the only sign of this understanding was that neither Jane nor Rosa ever caught the eye of any of them – though the moment she glanced away, she could feel all eyes upon her.

The ritual was intensified when the meal itself was served. The chef and his commis stood in agony at the half-opened kitchen door; the patron hovered nearby, cracking his finger joints one by one and looking as if he was standing on tiptoe. His wife planted herself in the doorway, one hand to her mouth. The royal delusion now appeared to have spread among the staff.

Jane took a soupçon onto her fork and raised it to her mouth, sniffing its aroma without giving the slightest appearance of doing so; that alone told her how good it was going to be. The rest was easy since it involved no sham at all. She chewed it once, twice, slowly rolling it around her mouth and breathing in discreetly; she swallowed and smacked her lips with amazing finesse; she put her head on one side and frowned – but only a little. The wife's stays creaked audibly in the doorway; you could have scrubbed wet washing on the patron's furrowed brow. Jane nodded, once, twice, and looked up with a judicious smile at the man.

You would have thought that Jane was a banker, saying the patron's bill could run for another three at the same rate. The man burst into an ecstatic smile, blew a kiss at his wife, and waved small congratulatory circles of approval toward the kitchen. Normality returned.

"Rum lot, these frogs," said a voice from an alcove.

They peered into the gloom and could just about discern the protesting Englishman from the customs hall.

"All the same," Rosa said, "I have to agree with him. What was that all about?"

"It's a local religious ceremony," Jane told her. "Like all such things, you can't really ask what it's *about.*" She grinned. "Lucky I knew the ritual, what?"

As the meal (which thoroughly deserved to be the object of any veneration going) wound through its many small and delicate courses, their thoughts turned to the days ahead. "Don't think I'm prying, but ... what are you actually expecting to find when we get to Paris?" Rosa asked.

"The dust covers removed. Extra servants taken on ..."

"No! You know what I mean. I suppose there'll be plenty of people around who'll remember your mother still?"

Jane pulled a face. "I honestly don't know. One suspects that memories in her sort of circle are notoriously short. If one misses one opera and two meetings at Longchamps, people no longer ask, 'Where's soandso?' They say, 'Didn't we once know someone called whatsizname?' Six or seven years could be several lifetimes ago to them. It almost is to *me.*"

"Yes, but it must be ... what? Twenty years since she first came to Paris?"

"I don't know. That's one of the things I hope to find out. She acquired the villa in 1843 – and, for some reason that none of us can explain, she conveyed it to me within the month."

"So you've been the proud owner of a grand Parisian villa for the past" – she rolled her eyes upward – "eighteen years!"

Jane nodded modestly. "And I didn't know it until a few months ago."

After a pause Rosa asked carefully, "Does it change your view of your mother at all, when you find out things like that?"

Jane considered her answer and then nodded. "I hadn't really thought about it, but it does. In a funny way, it's almost as if I've got two mothers now. There's the one I always thought I had, the one I remember – and now she's dead, it's as if nothing can ever change her. But alongside all that there's another sort of mother beginning to emerge. She's the one I hardly knew, whose life was a closed book to me. I only know her by what I'm slowly discovering. People tell me things, or I find them out from ... old deeds, old photographs. And it's a completely different picture. I don't mean worse. Or better. Just different. I know this other woman was my mother but I can't feel it."

Rosa looked at her shrewdly. "And feelings are always more important to you – than knowledge, I mean – aren't they."

Jane nodded.

"Just as well, perhaps ... in the circumstances."

"Indeed." Jane gave rather a grim little smile.

41 THE VILLA STOOD AT the leafy end of the Faubourg-St.-Honoré, just north of the Étoile. In fact, from its attic windows on the garden side, which had also been Jane's nursery windows, you could see the Arc de Triomphe towering over the neighbourhood, so close you felt you could reach out and touch it. On the other side, just visible between a pair of elegant houses across the road, was the Parc de Monceau, where Jane had first learned to walk. Every view from every window brought back some memory, renewed some old association.

For the first half hour she forgot all her duties as a hostess and went from room to room, exclaiming with delight as this or that forgotten detail came back to her. The thing that astonished her most was that so little had changed. Not a single drop of new paint had sullied the weatherstained bargeboards and shutters on any of the the neighbouring houses – or the villa itself, come to that. Iron railings that had shown signs of rust in 1856, showed more of the same in 1861. Broken paving had been repaired, both in the road and along the footpaths; but that, Jane guessed, was a matter of public order; bits of stone make handy weapons for unruly mobs.

"It all looks just a teeny bit run down," Rosa commented over Jane's shoulder. "Like Greenbank House."

"Where's that? Oh! Is that where *he* lives?"

Jane nodded. "Lived, actually. Look at this painting over our bed, *Nymphs and Fauns* by a friend of my mother's, a man called Jalabert. Doesn't that faun remind you of anyone?"

Rosa stared at it briefly and said, "No."

"Not even faintly?"

Rosa shook her head.

Janeane sighed. "How long is it going to take for *Lloyds Register* to get here each day, I wonder?"

Rosa gave a small sigh of compassionate exasperation. "It's no good, Jane."

"I know." Jane sighed, too. "Something perverse in me won't ... or can't ..."

"What did you think of Richard Vyvyan?" Rosa tried a hearty change of tack.

"The same as always. I've got on famously with him from the word go. He's one of the jolliest and decentest men I know."

"But that's all?"

Jane laughed. "Before you say it, I'll point out that he's only a very *distant* cousin to me – obviously nothing like close enough to be of the slightest romantic interest!"

"Jane!" Rosa was not amused.

"I'm only joking, darling. You're very prudish all of a sudden."

"It's nothing to do with prudery. It's just common sense. If you start talking about yourself like that, even in jest, you'll start estimating yourself like that, too. What I meant about Mr Vyvyan was, didn't you think his behaviour just a little odd?"

Dorothy came in at that moment. "Are you going to risk leaving all your unpacking to Banks and that French maid?" she asked. "And which of us is to give instructions to the housekeeper?"

"No one, I hope," Jane said swiftly. "We must call them all monsieur and madame and mademoiselle. And we certainly don't *instruct* Mme Tisserand. We discuss her arrangements and approve them. D'you think I'd better do it?" She made the suggestion as tactfully as she could, expecting a clash of wills. But, to her surprise, Dorothy yielded the office almost gratefully, giving as her excuse that Jane's French was so much better than hers.

"Did I hear you discussing Richard Vyvyan?" she asked. "I, too, thought there was something a little odd about him at the station today – as if he were bursting to tell us something and yet knew he couldn't."

"Yes, that's what I meant." Rosa looked at Jane, who said she had noticed nothing. "But then I was too intent on seeing Paris again."

"Ah yes." Dorothy went and sat in the window seat. "A beautiful city, but somewhat faded, don't you think?"

"It's just one of those differences," Jane said. "The English peasant puts fresh lime on his cottage every year because he thinks it ought to stand out. It's his castle. But the French peasant prefers to let the weather and the seasons do their work, until his home is in harmony with everything around." She went to the window and stood at Dorothy's side. "Look – when *every* shutter is flaking and peeling, and *every* bit of stucco is streaked and ... well, like that out there – don't you think it has a charm and elegance all its own?"

"No, I do not!" Dorothy replied with an emphatic laugh. "It's all part and parcel of the deplorable French character, I'm afraid. Laxity, laxity on every front. But I'm shocked to discover that they don't even bother to keep up *appearances*. We have to be on our guard here, my dears. It will be all too easy to say, 'Oh, things are different here in France,' and then slip into their lax ways. The moment we start thinking like that we're done for." She turned to Jane. "You may laugh all you like, my dear, but you know I'm right."

"No, I was just thinking," Jane told her. "There was a couple in Leeds, neighbours of ours, who painted the house from top to bottom every year – on the street frontage, anyway. But every time we visited them my mother would secretly point out to me one or other little filth packet she had discovered."

"What's a filth packet?" the others asked in chorus.

"Little piles of fluff and dust that the servants push into out-of-the-way corners. What do you call them?"

"Grounds for dismissal," Dorothy said firmly.

Jane sighed, knowing she would never make her point. She just stared out of the window at the beautiful mellowness of everything. "It's as if they had got a painter, a real artist, I mean, to paint it all," she said.

"Precisely," Dorothy rejoined. "I couldn't have put it better myself."

Richard Vyvyan joined them that evening for a light, four-course dinner, which they ate without formality. Then he took them out for a quick drive through the city. It was a fine night so they used an open carriage and wrapped up well against the frost. It was a tour of famous names rather than of the sights to which those names referred, since even the brightest gaslamps revealed little more than the presence of this or that grand palace or church or public monument. Most of the windows in these magnificent edifices were dark. Here and there a candle guttering in a servant's attic or a single ground-floor window would hint at some kind of life; but in general, the grander parts of Paris at eight of an evening were reminiscent of an English provincial town at three in the morning.

They drove down the Champs Élysées, home of the better class of horse dealer, past the Palais de l'Industrie – a hive of inactivity at that hour – and round to the north side of the Louvre by the Rue de Rivoli. Here at last there were signs of life in abundance as they drew near to the city's markets, which, Richard assured them, were a sight not to be missed. He appeared quite bowled over by Paris. All the tales that had circulated in England for years – the appalling paving, the complete lack of footpaths, the medieval sewerage, the violence of the mobs, the ramshackle markets – all had proved false. And Les Halles Centrales, it seemed, were where his eyes had been opened. Jane, too, was eager to see them since Louis Philippe had only just

322

begun to build them when she was last here; she remembered well the wretched sprawl of huts and sheds that had once been on that same site.

"It's going to be nearly five acres when they've finished," Richard said as he leaped out and held the door open for the three ladies.

"We are surely not going to descend?" Dorothy was aghast.

"It is perfectly safe, I assure you. And we must see the vaults. There's a huge tank for live fish, and they're starting to build tramways to all the principal railway stations. It'll change your views about the French, Mrs Lanyon. Honestly."

The endless ranks of pavilions, one for butter and eggs, another for meat, another for fish, and so on, all ranged beneath massive arched roofs of iron and glass, was, indeed, prodigious – though Dorothy believed that the new Crystal Palace in London would far outshine it in grace and beauty. But the vaults, she had to agree, were without parallel. The fish tank was especially impressive, though it seemed to her a vast and possibly immoral expenditure when its only purpose was to ensure a slightly improved flavour at the table. French food had thrown her principles into a whirl. She could not deny it was superb, and yet she could not help feeling there must be something wrong when so much care was devoted to what was, after all, a fleeting sensual pleasure.

They went next to the Palais Royal, where they sat in a café, on a kind of glazed terrace, and watched the *monde*, both *haute-* and *demi-*, go by while they sipped their coffee and a small liqueur. Dorothy chose one that tasted of peppermint, which the waiter assured her was sovereign for the digestion. And then they drove back by way of the Madeleine and the Boulevart des Malesherbes so that Jane could at least get a glimpse of her beloved Parc de Monceau.

"Do they still have those beautiful flower markets here every Tuesday and Friday?" she asked Richard as they crossed the Place de la Madeleine. Then, to Rosa, "We must get up early and see that. It'll take your breath away."

Dorothy reminded her that they had come to Paris for a rather more serious purpose than mere sightseeing, not to mention stuffing themselves on truffles and liqueurs. In the dark, Richard handed Jane a small packet – the promised letter from Miss Wilkinson, she guessed; she squeezed his arm in silent acknowledgement and, halfway between the next pair of lamps, hid the letter in her pocketbook.

When they arrived at the villa he declined their invitation to join them for some chocolate, apologized that embassy affairs would occupy him until Friday evening, but promised that on Saturday and Sunday he was theirs to command. Jane saved the letter until she and Rosa were tucked up in bed and settling to sleep. As hostess she had naturally occupied her mother's old bedroom, putting Dorothy a few rooms away in the principal guest room – the most luxurious thing of its kind that her guardian had ever seen. Again it threw her into a quandary. She both relished the luxury and felt guilty at it. Yet what else could she do? She could hardly insist on sleeping in one of the attic rooms – just as, at table, she could hardly send the food back and ask for stewed cabbage and boiled bacon instead. If fine things were the *only* things available ... well, it was hardly her fault, was it?

"Are you getting letters from admirers already?" Rosa asked gleefully when Jane produced the packet with a conspiratorial flourish.

"You didn't see Richard pass it to me?" she asked anxiously as she drew up her knees beneath the sheets to make a rest for the letter.

Rosa shook her head. "But surely he's not ..." Her voice tailed off when she saw the look of bewilderment on Jane's face.

"It's from England," she said. "Mrs Moynihan? I don't know a Mrs Moynihan?" And yet the name did ring a faintish sort of a bell. The stamp was, as usual, cancelled in an illegible hand.

It read:

Dear Miss Hervey,

You will rightly scold me for giving no hint of this at our last meeting. I am as you see married by special licence (and never was licence more special to me!) to my darling Roger Moynihan who says that his asking to paint my portrait was a mere ruse (didn't I tell you!) and that he determined we should be married from the moment he set eyes on me. And yes indeed he knows all about me. No skeletons are left to rattle in my cupboards at least, and he I think is too utterly dedicated to his art to have any of his own.

So that is to explain why I shall not be visiting you in Paris, at least not this once. Roger is eager to go there on his own account so I make no doubt we shall be there soon, one way or another. But my gallant naval officer Gerard de Guy must look for favours elsewhere – which I am sure he would have done anyway even if ... But no I will not contemplate that if any more.

Well then there it is! I am a respectable woman once again. A girl I met when I first began that way of life assured me that most of "us" ended up in a respectable marriage, quite contrary to the popular picture of a starving, drunken wretch expiring in the poor house. If like me you can forget my unhappy past, then do please be sure to call by on your next visit to Falmouth.

I nearly forgot! Your half-brother Daniel has turned up again. There was a rumour in the town that he had signed on aboard some merchantman and gone to foreign parts. In fact he took charge of a little coaster that was tied up at Greenbank jetty when her master took a bad bout of colic. He sailed her to Plymouth then Poole then back and is once more risking his neck – I can see him now as I write – on the roof of that dreadful house of theirs. Roger would reproach me for writing so. He admires the Jagos more than any other family in Falmouth. He says they have the right attitude to life and he wishes to cultivate their acquaintance. The world has come to a pretty pass when a woman like me proves more censorious than a man like Roger eh!

So, adieu – or is it just au revoir?
I hope the latter but would understand the former.

Esther Moynihan (nee Wilkinson)

PS I was on the point of sealing this when I realized I owe you something of an explanation. Just before we parted I delivered myself of a most shallow opinion on the subject of men. I did not lie. What I said I truly felt and deeply too. But now it

324

has all evaporated. It frightens me to realize how much my opinions are dependent on the whim of the moment. Forgive my arrogance.

But even now, in confessing the foregoing, I feel myself skirting to avoid an even more uncomfortable memory. The reason I was so firm and dismissive was to make you be quiet. I felt you edging ever closer to asking me about your father and it was a subject I did not wish to face. Do not at this point dash my letter from you. I assure you the reason for my reluctance was all to his credit and little to mine. So, at the risk of letting the tale of this PS wag the dog of the letter, let me explain:

The first man I went with for money was only after my most careful choice. A young fellow, very debonair, very handsome, charming, courteous, good company ... as far as I could see, the perfect man. And indeed he was everything he promised – gentle, considerate, patient and et cetera. I only just managed not to be ill while he was still with me. After that I simply thought that's the way of it for us women. I swallowed my disgust and counted my earnings. Then one day four months later I was picked up by a man who was the very opposite of my first in every way. He was old. He had missing teeth. Withered shanks. Bald ... et cetera. He talked about his late wife. A lot of them do that, of course, but his loss somehow touched me. It was like my own. He was kindly and gentle with me. And proficient. It is an accomplishment, too, you know. He was an accomplished lover. And he made me [the words were scored through] He brought out within me [that, too, was scored through] All I will say is that I had never been so shaken by any experience in all my life. I wept when he died and for some time after in my private moments. You, for your part, must be proud that he was that same very good man who chose to call himself your father.

"Sad news?" Rosa asked as Jane folded the letter away.

"Not really." She dabbed at her eyes with her sleeve. "Just a very kind little note from someone who remembered my father. Mr Hervey, that is." She forced herself to brighten. "And she says that Daniel wasn't on that merchantman, after all. He took charge of a little coaster just while the master was ill. He's back in Falmouth again." She galnced at the painting above the bed. "I wonder."

"What? Blow out the candle so we can lie in the dark and talk."

Jane did as she was bid and they lay there for a while listening to the muted roar of ten thousand iron-tyred wheels on the stone paving. "It makes such a change," Rosa said, "from listening to the screech owls and every little breeze that comes moaning through our ill-fitting casements at home. No! I don't even want to think of home."

"I use to lie ... up there" – Jane pointed diagonally at the ceiling – "and listen to this every night. I simply couldn't imagine why so many people were on the move about the city while I was in bed. Why don't you want to think of home?"

"Would *you?*" she asked drily. "The whole future's just ... blank."

"Cheer up. Someone will come along, you'll see."

"I think, when we get back, I'll put about a tale that I won half a million francs while I was here."

Jane chuckled. "You wouldn't want the sort of man who'd come sniffing after that. Take it from one who knows."

"You started to say, when we were talking about Daniel, you said, 'I wonder ...' What was that?"

"Oh yes." Jane stretched out fully in the bed and tweaked the sheets in around her neck. "I wonder if it takes men longer to accept a change like that? Did he actually have to run away before he could do it? And what's he thinking now? I almost want to take the next train to Brittany and the next boat to Falmouth."

"You wouldn't?" Rosa asked in a shocked voice.

"Of course not. It's just that it's always so hard to know what men are thinking. I mean, really thinking. Even Richard tonight. He behaves as if he's an absolutely open book. But I agree with you – there's something he's keeping back. He wants to tell us but he won't. And if you asked him straight out, he'd ... I don't know."

"He'd go all bluff and hearty and you'd never be told."

"That was the thing about Daniel, you see," Jane went on. "He wasn't like that. He made no secret of his feelings. I think that's the right attitude to life. When he looked at me it was pure ... why is *desire* such an ugly word?"

"Is it?"

"It is when some people say it."

"People who never felt it themselves – if you know who I mean. And I'm not going to name her, so don't worry."

"Poor Dorothy! Oh, isn't it all just so *confusing!*"

They contemplated Confusion in silence for a while; then Jane said, "Talking of Dorothy, I think ... underneath it all, you know ... I think she is actually more passionate than anyone. But she's frightened of it. You remember when I said I threw that stone at Daniel? That was the same thing, Fear, you see. And this letter from one of my father's old friends. She reminded me ..."

"Oh, it was a she-friend?"

"Yes, Rosa, it was a she-friend. And she reminded me of an occasion when we met recently and she was rather short with me. She apologizes for it now and says it was because she thought I was getting too close to some rather tender memories."

Rosa cleared her throat. "Really?"

"Listen, my dear. He was a widower and a lonely old man. I'm not going to condemn him. But can't you see what I'm driving at? These feeling that almost overwhelm us at times, they also make us frightened. That's when we throw stones, make cutting remarks, and start laying down the law as if there could be no other possible point of view."

"Mmmm." After a pause Rosa giggled. "Dorothy Lanyon, eh? I wonder if you're right about her. What did she mean, you've got more serious business on hand than sightseeing in Paris, or whatever she said? It sounds as if you're going to sell the villa after all."

"Can you keep a secret?" Jane asked.

"I keep telling you no."

"And you keep on not breaking them anyway. The fact is that we came here to discover ... about my mother." And she went on to reveal those things she had omitted from her earlier explanation.

Rosa lay there and listened to her in mounting horror, which Jane was aware of but which she misinterpreted completely. "I didn't realize it would shock you so much," she said at last.

326

Rosa swallowed heavily. "I'm not shocked at all at what you say about ..."

"Oh yes you are. I can feel it coming at me in waves."

"Will you let me finish? Not about your mother. That's not what shocks me. It's the thought of letting Dorothy Lanyon find out, too."

"She is my guardian."

"Precisely! What d'you think your life will be worth if your worst misgivings turn out to be true? You know she's almost insane on the subject of pedigree. Breeding is the be-all and end-all of her life. She'll watch you like a cat with a mouse."

"I don't know," Jane objected. "She's been quite liberal with me up until now – especially after my father died. I was quite surprised."

Rosa snorted in scorn. "You've obviously never watched a cat with a mouse."

Jane had, of course, and the assertion made her suddenly very thoughtful.

"Plus the fact," Rosa went on, "that she probably wanted you out of the way while she went right through your father's papers. All with your best interests at heart, of course." Her voice went faraway and pensive. "No – we've got to be ready for her if the worst comes to the worst."

"We?" Jane echoed.

"Of course. Why else do you suppose your guardian angel insisted on your bringing me?"

42 BEFORE THEY HAD even left Cornwall, Dorothy wrote letters to a number of people whose directions she had culled from Wilfrid Hervey's papers; she, in turn, had directed any eventual replies to the *Poste Restante* at the General Post Office in the Rue Jean-Jacques Rousseau – just across the road, in fact, from Les Halles. She had noted it the previous night on their visit to the markets, an ugly building, astonishingly ugly for Paris, and she had longed to pop in and see if her efforts had met with any reward. The following morning, despite her stern remarks of the previous evening, she told Jane that she ought to take Rosa to see the splendours of Versailles, a suggestion to which neither girl objected. The moment they had gone, chaperoned not only by Banks but by a splendid *valet de pied* and his wife (both, naturally, recommended by the embassy), Dorothy took the carriage and went to examine her trawl.

If she had known how dirty, mean, and crowded the *Poste Restante* office was, she would have made some other arrangement; but at last she was called up to the poky little *guichet*, where, on production of her passport and after a further interminable wait, four letters were produced. She could hardly contain herself for excitement and almost ran back to her carriage, where she began opening them at once.

One was from her correspondent's widow, and written in terms that made her glad her French was no better than it was; it was still good enough to reveal that the lady held no very high opinion of "La Vivie."

The second was from Count Esterhazy. She and Vosper Scawen had already engaged in a more open correspondence with the Count on the matter of the lease; having had scant success in finding a subtenant at short notice for so grand a property, he had gladly relinquished it to Jane as his ground landlord. In this present letter, from his family home in Meulon, some thirty miles away down the Seine, he simply noted that he intended coming to the city the following Monday, the 18th, and putting up for a few days at the Club des Pommes de Terre on the Quai Voltaire. He would gladly attend upon her then but did not suppose he could do much to further her inquiries.

"We shall see about that!" Dorothy said grimly as she tucked his letter away.

The third was from a house in Ville d'Avray. It struck her as curious to think that Jane and Rosa might well be driving past it at that very moment on their way to Versailles. The letter was not, however, written by her correspondent, the Baron de Puisne, but by someone claiming to be his nurse – an English lady by her hand and command of the language, though she signed herself Mme Elinor Duret. She explained that the Baron was now elderly and somewhat erratic in his health. On some days he was as lucid as one might wish; on others he couldn't even tell you his name. In either condition, Mme Lanyon would readily understand, it was out of the question that he should undertake the tedious journey into Paris. All that Mme Duret could suggest was that Mme Lanyon should herself call at Ville d'Avray, at eleven o'clock on any morning, prepared to hear that the Baron was not well enough to receive her that day.

These replies left Dorothy feeling somewhat deflated. Eighteen letters she had written and got only four in return: one from the relict of her correspondent; one from a member of something called the Potato Club, who disclaimed all helpful knowledge in advance; and one from the nurse of a man in his dotage! She hardly dared open the fourth now. Good gracious, she thought, it was no more than half a dozen years since Angwin Vyvyan – or Hervey as she was by then – had departed from one of the most glittering social circles in this most glittering of cities. Where had it all gone?

Perhaps it was no more than make-believe? Yet there was the villa – solid enough evidence to the contrary. If only its *Toile de Jouy* and gilded plasterwork could talk! Fleetingly it crossed her mind to wonder why she was going to so much trouble. Then, startled by this vacillation so early in the game, she angrily thrust the self-doubt aside. It was *infinitely* worth while to discover the truth about Jane's parents and origins. The girl herself understood it well enough. They needed to know what dire inheritance they were pitted against.

Yet Dorothy was uneasily aware of a further set of reasons for being here – if one could call anything so vague by the name of reason. Until last November she would have said that Wilfrid Hervey was the man who, after her husband, was the very soul of probity and decency. What she had discovered in his papers had shaken her to the very core; and her husband's calm acceptance of it had done nothing to reassure her, either. It was not that she doubted her principles now, but she was aware that their application was not the simple matter she had once assumed. This time in Paris was a time for finding out. In that spirit she turned to the fourth and final letter.

It was from a Chevalier de la Villette, who entreated her to call upon him any Thursday or Friday morning while she was in Paris, but not, please, before ten o'clock. His house was in the Rue Castiglione, next to the hotel of that name, between the Tuileries and the Place Vendïme. She tutted with vexation for she had been within walking distance of the place when she left the post office, ten minutes ago. Now she was almost back at the villa. She was on the point of telling the driver to put about when fresh doubts assailed her and she held her tongue.

What sort of man was this Chevalier? His invitation was certainly cavalier! Suggesting that a lady might visit him any Thursday or Friday morning. An English gentleman would automatically have written "you and a companion" – but perhaps that was the automatic assumption here in Paris? Then again, he was a friend of the celebrated Vivie. What would he make of her, Dorothy – a *petite bourgeoise* from some remote corner of Perfidious Albion. No, a visit to such a man required a little preparation, both mental ... and (she tested the thought delicately) physical.

As soon as she was indoors she summoned Mademoiselle Nancy, her maid for the duration of this visit. This female, who was in her early twenties, had hopes of a recommendation in England and was therefore most eager to please. Dorothy led her to Jane's bedroom, where she took out the new wooden writing case that Jane had bought in Falmouth. She moved two of the "knots," as they were fashioned to seem, and out sprang the secret drawer. "Are you familiar with these ... substances, mademoiselle?" she asked.

The maid turned over the jars and bottles of perfume, powder, rouge, and mascarade, assessing each with a professional eye and nose. *"Mais oui, madame,"* she replied simply. "It's good."

"You mean these are ... substances of good quality?"

"Yes. It's French."

"And what sort of ladies might employ such ... assistance here in Paris?"

"All sorts. But a lady will be very ... *discrète."* She smiled knowingly. "Especially a lady like madame who have such little needs of it."

"And do you know how to apply it?" She asked the question hesitantly, as if the woman might take justifiable offence.

"But of course. Madame wishes that I shall show her?"

Dorothy sat at Jane's looking glass and watched with amazement as Nancy wrought the most subtle transformation of her face with those simple materials. It was not that she looked any different when the work was complete; and yet she looked entirely renewed. "You are a sorceress, mademoiselle," she murmured. "Tell me, do you know of a shop here in Paris where such items may be purchased?"

"But it's where these came from, madame. Lapin - it's round the corner from here, in the Rue de Tilsit."

So the little minx had sent for them in secret, from Paris! Unless these were remnants from the stock of La Vivie? The stock-*in-trade?* But then many respectable women employed such artifices, too, according to Nancy. In that welter of confusion Dorothy looked for one certainty – and found it in the knowledge that a gentleman like Wilfrid Hervey would never have permitted Jane to ... and then she remembered the other certainty about Wilfrid Hervey.

Like Jane before her, Dorothy was staggered at the price – a hundred francs, or almost four pounds sterling. But, like Jane before her, and ten million Janes and Dorothys before and since, she paid it nonetheless. And then, feeling as secure as a knight in armour, except that this armour was discreetly invisible, she went back to her carriage and gave directions to the Rue Castiglione.

No more than twenty seconds after she had handed in her card, the Chevalier himself was standing on his doorstep, smiling broadly and looking as if he, personally, were about to escort her within. From the points of his tightly waxed moustache to the tips of his burnished shoes, he was a Parisian swell. Yet he was not languid in the weary affectation of his English counterpart; his smile was roguish and his eye bright and alert. She glanced up and down the busy street in alarm but nobody seemed to be taking the least bit of notice. He observed her gesture and came forward, across the footpath, to stand at her carriage door. She now noticed that he was carrying his hat and cane. "Mrs Lanyon," he drawled in an English accent that was almost too perfect, "I am delighted to make your acquaintance."

She swallowed heavily and managed to say, "Chevalier," as she stuck out a hand toward him.

He kissed the air an eighth of an inch above her glove. "Madame, I should be honoured if you would consent to visit me at home but I have another suggestion. A friend of M. Corot, the painter, you know? He is in Paris and he has two small landscapes for sale which I would dearly love to buy. I was just on my way there now. Will you accompany me, perhaps? It will be amusing for you, I hope?"

"By all means, Chevalier." Her relief at not having to go alone with him into his house was overwhelming. "Shall we take my carriage? Tell the driver where you wish to go."

"Palais Royal," he called out as he slipped into the seat at her side. "What a lovely brisk day! You were so right to choose an open carriage. Oh, you English ladies! You are the cream of the cream, the salt of the earth. The way you just accepted my suggestion and put your carriage at my disposal – *formidable!* You are so wonderfully independent."

"You are too kind," she replied, feeling it a most inadequate response. Should she raise the topic of her inquiries first, or would it be better coming from him?

They soon covered the few streets between his house and the Palais Royal. It was, in fact, the same way as Richard Vyvyan had taken them, along the Rue de Rivoli, but the grandeur of the buildings, now revealed in the bright March sunlight, took her breath away. "We came here last night," she told him as they entered the forecourt of the Palais. "My two wards and I and a friend from the British Embassy."

"It was a good choice for a first night in Paris," he replied. "You are probably burdened down with invitations, madame, but if you have a spare evening or two, please call on me to escort you anywhere you desire. Would you like to visit the catacombs? You know they're closed to visitors now, but I could take you and your two wards there, if you wish. But don't decide yet. The offer is made, that's all."

Dorothy began to warm to him, and, more importantly, to lose some of her fear. She blessed Providence or whatever instinct it was that made her put on a little circumspect colouring; the confidence it imparted was truly amazing. Despite his urbane exterior and suave manners there was something quite boyish in the Chevalier's character – the way he made these impetuous offers and suggestions, and then immediately told her to pay no attention if they weren't to her liking. At first sight she had taken him to be at least forty; now he might be as young as thirty. It was really impossible to tell. "You are fond of art?" she asked.

"There's our fellow," he said, nodding toward a crowded café. "Oh yes, madame. It is the one redeeming feature in a life that is otherwise not particularly admirable, I fear. Perhaps you would prefer to see the weekly parade at the École Militaire rather than the catacombs? I can secure you excellent seats for that. The uniforms are always so inspiring to the female heart. But ask your wards before you decide."

The café was two doors away from the rather grander establishment they had patronized last night. She pointed it out to him and again he said it was a good choice "for one's first night in Paris." But this time his tone held the suggestion that she was now an *habituée* who could exercise greater discrimination.

He introduced her rather casually to M. Bertot, the great painter's friend. For the next ten minutes or so she sat and watched in fascination as the commercial man, out to get a good deal, vied with the *connoisseur*, the liberal patron of the arts – the Chevalier himself playing both roles. The paintings, two small landscapes, as he had said, were, indeed, charming, though he appeared to think they were something greater than that. Neither man was the least bit squeamish about conducting a business conversation in the presence of a lady

However, the Chevalier must have felt some small twinge of unease on that point, for the moment M. Bertot had left – to take the paintings to be reframed after the Chevalier's wishes – he turned to her and said, "Is it not extraordinary? If I were, let us say, a large importer of coffee, like the proprietor of this little restaurant, I should not discuss the purchase of a single bean in the presence of a lady. But art ... ah, art! It sanctifies all, eh?"

"Indeed," Dorothy agreed uncertainly.

His steady gaze was like an audit, but his eyes twinkled once again. "You don't truly think so, I can tell." His tongue was a brief flash of rosebud pink on his lower lip. "I wonder?"

Dorothy wondered, too. Had he just noticed the minute quantity of colouring on her countenance? There was a subtle change in his attitude toward her.

"You probably have a busy day arranged, madame?" he asked. "Already I have stolen too much of your valuable time."

"In fact, no." She tried to sound as if it surprised her. She explained that she had written to many other old friends of "La Vivie" and had set aside today to meet them, but ... *alors* ... She made a gesture more Gallic than English. Now surely, she told herself, he must take up the subject.

But all he did was smile. "I would be greatly honoured, Madame Lanyon, if you would permit me to be your guide for a visit to the Louvre. Not the entire Louvre, I hasten to say, just the chambers of the modern French paintings."

Dorothy demurred politely, saying that she hardly felt she could trespass on his generosity in that way, but when he appeared to be on the point of accepting it as a polite refusal, she quickly said, "On the other hand ... if you're quite sure ..."

331

At his suggestion she sent her carriage home with instructions to return to the Rue Castiglione at three that afternoon; it would give them time to discuss all her questions over luncheon, he explained. She felt alone and vulnerable once the coachman had gone, yet she knew it was absurd. After all, she had not been within sight of the man for the past half hour. Yet, on the other hand, he had been *there*. And now he was not.

The northern entrance to the great museum was immediately opposite the Palais Royal; as they crossed the Rue de Rivoli, Dorothy fumbled for her passport but he laughed and said it would not be necessary. "Is it a day for all classes?" she asked with distaste.

"No, but you are with me," he said.

The *guardien* saluted them and waved them through. Immediately behind her Dorothy recognized a lady who had been a passenger on the ferry, the day before yesterday – a rather grand lady, by her own estimate, at least. To Dorothy's delight, *she* had to show her passport before the man would allow her in, which she did with ill grace.

Unthinkingly, Dorothy took the Chevalier's arm while she explained to him in a near-whisper what had just happened. He laughed and said that the whole secret of life was to have the right keys – or to know how to open doors without them.

The French school of the Revolutionary and Imperial periods was up on the first floor, in the magnificent *Salle des Sept Cheminées*, another of Louis Philippe's inspirations. To Dorothy it was a revelation. If someone had told her that she would find herself able to stand for full twenty minutes before a painting, however dramatic, showing the crew of a shipwreck clinging to a raft that prolonged their miserable lives by a few hours or days, she would simply have laughed. If that same informant had told her she would come away from it understanding that such a painting could be one of the greatest revolutionary declarations in history *and* an artistic revolution in its own right, being one of the great sources of the fire and thunder that reverberated through French art to this very day ... she would have dismissed him as a madman.

Yet that was only one of several great paintings by means of which the Chevalier opened her eyes and gripped her imagination. And he was a different man, too; in the clothing of a swell he spoke to her with a passion and an idealism that was as incongruous as his earlier boyishness had seemed. But somehow they were united, these seemingly jarring and disparate elements. For a while she wondered what it was that could hold such a strangely mixed character together; just before they left the gallery she decided it was his absolute enthusiasm. Whichever one of his conflicting personalities was dominant at any given moment, he somehow had the knack of playing it with absolute conviction. No, she corrected herself, he did not *play* it – nothing so calculated as that – he threw himself into that part so wholeheartedly he truly became ... whatever it was.

How was she ever going to describe such an encounter – such a man – as this to Jesse? Darling Jesse, whose world had no room for such fleeting changes, to whom water was wet, fire hot, iron hard ... who thought this person good, that one bad ... who knew this crime was worth seven days, that one five shillings. Even as she posed the question, she knew she would not even try. It was one of those cases where revelation would be a greater deception than simple silence.

For lunch he took her to Philippe's in the Rue Montorgeuil, the favourite restaurant, he said, of the true *gourmets* of Paris. The portions were small, he warned, but exquisite. Dorothy hesitated at the door but was reassured to discover that she would by no means be the only lady there, as would almost certainly have been the case in England. The Chevalier was apparently well known there, too, for he was shown to the sort of table restaurants like to keep in case royalty calls. And, indeed, he treated the gesture very much as an emperor might treat the offer of the keys to the city, as a symbolic act, which, while it would be shocking if omitted, was not to be taken too literally. He touched a chair in a ritual of acceptance and asked if madame might not prefer somewhere a little less conspicuous.

"No," Dorothy said at once, which caused him to smile.

"You are magnificently decisive," he told her when they were seated at that most conspicuous table.

She was aware that their arrival had caused a small ripple of interest among their fellow diners. "But to have moved into some dark corner," she replied, "would have suggested that I feel uneasy at being seen in public with you."

"Then you honour me, madame, in almost every possible way."

The word "almost" jarred slightly with the rest of the sentiment but she did not openly remark upon it. She glanced briefly at the menu and resigned the selection to him. For a while they talked of the paintings he had shown her and she tried to convey to him what a revelation it had been. "It almost makes me afraid to go back to a gallery now," she confessed.

"Yes!" he agreed, his eyes sparkling with admiration – as if he had not expected her to progress to that depth of understanding for some time yet. "Madame, you are *formidable!* You see things so quickly."

"No, dear Chevalier," she replied. "It is you who guide me so well."

He smiled a rather feminine smile – the sort that a woman might give when she knows her partner has been too extravagant with his compliments, and *why*. "You are surely Cornish?" he asked slyly.

"Indeed." She laughed in surprise.

"That must be it," he went on. "I have only ever known one other Cornish lady."

"Ah!" she said, and her smile invited the rest.

"What can I say of her? That she was unique? But each woman is unique. I am not a religious man – forgive me if I offend you? It is a very tenable position in France. But if I were a believer and I wished to persuade someone like me of the existence of a benevolent God, I should advance only one argument: the existence of woman. I wish our bishops would do the same. Half the miseries of humanity would vanish overnight. Three-quarters, even." He smiled. "I don't know whether the same argument in reverse would be so convincing to a woman. The existence of man?"

"The existence of some men," she said archly.

He beamed. "You are not offended?"

"I ought to be, yet you express it so elegantly. Perhaps these things are different here in France."

333

"Certainly they are. La Vivie said it so often. Now she was the one I would have chosen for my example, for the goodness and mercy of God." He looked to see if his use of "would have" had registered and then continued: "Even in Paris she was ... extraordinary. In this city, you know, there are many ... oh, how to put it? May I be utterly frank, madame?"

"Please! I desire nothing more."

He chuckled. "Never say that." The waiter placed the first course, a small serving of *consommé carmélite*, before them. "As with these dishes," the Chevalier added, "one should always wish for a *little* more. You take one sip, you see." His nod encouraged her to do so; when she obeyed, he followed suit. "And you think, 'Oh, this is perhaps not so good. I'm not sure ...' Then you take another." Again they did so. "And you think, 'Mmm. It's possible. Possible' And so you savour it a little more." He allowed her time to do so. "And then you take the third *soupçon*. And now you know you are close to greatness. 'Oh, this chef!' you say. 'Surely he is from Parnassus!' You take a further sip – and with dismay you note it is your last but one. You savour it as before, but this time there is no improvement in your estimate. How could there be, for you had already tasted perfection, no? And your last spoonful confirms it. *Voilà!* The wise gourmet then bids the soup *adieu* and does not look for more. A second bowl would be a disaster, even from the same pot."

Dorothy's heart was now beating doubles, for, half way through this lesson in *cuisine* she suddenly realized what he was really talking about – even worse, she knew he had seen that realization in her face. Now he looked at the pulse in her neck; he watched it refusing to abate.

"La Vivie understood it so well," he murmured. "For, of course, it applies to all our appetites."

Find some way of putting this idea right out of his mind! she told herself. *Before things go too far.*

"Do you eat like this at home?" she asked. Immediately she could have died of shame. What a gauche, stupid question! Now he would see what a little simpleton she was.

"Like this? No," he said decisively. "There is no substance, no great nourishment in this food from Parnassus. We eat it simply to know something of what it is like to be a god. Or goddess. But for simple nourishment we must eat *à la provençale* at home – which I do with my wife once or twice a week."

"Ah. Your wife. Yes. Does she ... never dine in Parnassus?"

"She has her own favourites. Restaurants, I mean." He smiled reproachfully at her, as if she had trapped him into forgetting his metaphor.

"And La Vivie?" she went on. "You say she understood this need for small helpings? She must have said a lot of *adieux* in her ... how long was she here? A dozen years?"

"Yes and no," he conceded. "Look at it this way – I shall say no to a second helping of this *consommé carmélite* if I am offered it now. But if at some time in the future I am invited back *chez Philippe*, I shall certainly taste it again."

Dorothy tried to remember the sort of questions she ought to be asking about Angwin Hervey but they somehow kept slipping just beyond her grasp. She gave up at last, contenting herself with the realization that, even if they did occur to her, she could not possibly frame them in the terms of his elaborate and frivolous metaphor.

The meal progressed from one superb dish to another, each pathetically small by what one might call the "roast beef of old England" standard, but all of them perfect by those of the Chevalier's Parnassus.

With the next dish, a mouthwatering *rougets beurre fondue*, he changed the subject entirely and you would have thought him nothing more than a very attentive uncle entertaining his niece to luncheon – except that, since she now felt sure he was closer to thirty than forty, they were more like cousins, really. At all events, there was no more sly innuendo, no flirting even.

She felt its withdrawal keenly and wondered if she had unwittingly broken some rule of the game? In which case, how could she tell him that – as long as that was all it was, a witty little game – she quite enjoyed the play. But he talked of every other subject under the sun, asked her questions about England, her home, her childhood – and seemed to hang on her replies. In short, he behaved as if she were one of the most fascinating women he had ever had the good fortune to meet.

So that when, at around twenty past two, he suggested they stroll back to the Rue Castiglione to await her carriage ... perhaps to enjoy a demitasse of coffee and a little liqueur ... and to admire his Corots, which would have been delivered by now, her acceptance seemed the most natural thing in all the world,

"The most natural thing in all the world," seemed to be the only words her mind could utter as they returned to his home. Their way led through a maze of little streets that opened at last into the Place des Victoires and so onward to the Petits Champs on the northern side of the Palais Royal. Everything was so different here. People lived in buildings with walls, stairs, windows, and roofs, just as they did at home, and yet you could see at once that it was ... different. She was grateful for the walk, anyway. It gave her time to settle everything in her mind. She was quite calm again by the time he tapped his cane at the door and the *valet du jour* instantly admitted them. Where were her qualms of but a few hours since!

The room into which he showed her was opulent in a style that was quintesentially French. When other nations tried to copy it, they caught only its grosser features. The finesse, it seemed, would not travel. And finesse was certainly the word for his behaviour. He dismissed the footman at once and served her the liqueur and coffee himself. He showed her the Corots, which did, indeed, look magnificent in their new frames. He showed her several more paintings beside. He spoke of other interests, from the opera, through horse-racing, to rowing. And all the while she was thinking, *My coach is coming in twenty minutes ... fifteen ... ten ...*

He mentioned that there was a grand production of the new opera by Wagner, *Tristan et Isolde*, at the Opéra Français this coming Saturday. And all of a sudden it struck her: Today was *not* the day. And nor was it to be some giddy occasion after which she might have the excuse that he swept her off her feet, she didn't know what she was doing ... all that good food and wine ... No such luck! Today was the day for making the offer and showing her the locations, no more than that. Now the choice was hers. It seemed extraordinary, even at the time, that she never entertained the slightest doubt which way that decision – and she herself – would fall.

43 THE STRANGE BEHAVIOUR of the man caught Jane's and Rosa's attention some time before he approached them. They had seen their fill of all the state apartments and were standing outside on the Parterre d'Eau, gazing over the Tapis Vert and the Grand Canal, awestruck at the vastness of that entirely man-made landscape, when Rosa saw him approach a family party down by the Bains d'Apollon. He raised his hat, asked a question of the paterfamilias, which was answered by a grave shake of the head, and then withdrew – only to repeat the procedure with another family party walking near by.

And so it went with several more – the polite question, the polite denial, the polite withdrawal – until at last he had exhausted all the possibilities on that level of the gardens.

"Have you been watching that man?" Jane asked.

"Yes," Rosa replied. "You notice he doesn't approach single persons."

"Nor couples, nor families with young children, nor with only boys."

"I do think it's unfair of him to exclude us. I'm simply burning to know what he can possibly be asking such a varied assortment of ..."

"He's seen us," Jane said. "And he's coming towards us. Look away."

"Pretend you don't know any French if he ask us. Otherwise it's not fair. You and he will just gabble away. I say, he is *very* handsome."

"You're not supposed to be looking."

"I'm not. He's a bit old. He must be thirty. And there's a sort of military cut about him. And a little bit of a swell, too, though it's held in check today."

"Rosa!" Jane said with amused annoyance.

"What? Am I the only person in the world who can see everything she wants out of the corner of her eye? What d'you think, Banks?"

The maid admitted she had seen worse.

The man began to mount the grand flight of steps, making straight for them.

"Oh," Rosa said, "if he asks me, I know I shall just stand here with my mouth open, blowing bubbles. You answer him."

"In French?" Jane asked sweetly.

"In Greek if you wish."

But the man – although he could not take his eyes off them – went to their footman and his wife and asked, in French, if either of them knew a Mlle Hervey. Jane turned about in surprise and faced him. "Sir?" she said. Rosa had not exaggerated; he was, indeed, a most handsome young man. She would have put him on the younger side of thirty – the difference, she supposed between the perception of an eighteen-year-old girl and a mature young woman of twenty.

"Miss Hervey?" he asked with a light bow.

She nodded. He handed his card to the footman, who glanced at it and then, quite impassive, passed it on to Jane; it told her that this was none other than Gérard de Guy, with directions to the Naval Club on the Quai d'Orsay. She passed it on to Rosa, who was crowding her elbow. "M. de Guy," she said. "You are an acquaintance of Miss Wilkinson, I believe?"

He gave an icy smile. "I was."

"And what is it you wish of me?"

336

"Information, Miss Hervey, if you will be so kind. But I don't wish to delay you in your tour of the gardens. There is so much to see. May I perhaps accompany you briefly, in whatever direction you intended?"

"We were looking for somewhere that serves hot chocolate," Rosa ventured. He turned to her with an amused smile, and a lightly raised eyebrow.

"Well!" Jane said in annoyance. "May I present Lieutenant Gérard de Guy of the Imperial Navy. Miss Rosa Delamere."

"De la mer?" he murmured, raising her hand to his lips. "Then we already have something in common, mademoiselle." To Jane he said, "The only café I know of within the park is the Café de la Comédie, down near the Bassin du Dragon." He pointed northward. "It is in the general direction of the Trianons, if you were intending to visit them, too?"

Jane saw that it was adroit of him to make the choice seem hers, but she was annoyed at his familiarity with Rosa. "Why have you sought me out like this, sir?" she asked.

For reply he handed her a piece of notepaper – a letter, in fact, from Miss Wilkinson, or, rather, Mrs Moynihan. In two sentences it informed him coolly of her marriage and added that, if he desired any further information, he was to apply to Miss Jane Hervey, c/o the British Embassy in Paris.

"And they supplied you with my directions?" she asked in surprise as she handed back the note. He merely smiled, so she guessed he had done it all by bribery. Meanwhile she was wondering what possible motive Miss Wilkinson might have had for playing this trick. Was it a misplaced joke, an act of petty spite, or what?

He stared at her. "Forgive me for saying this, Miss Hervey, but you bear the most uncanny likeness to an English lady I knew in Paris some years ago. And since you now live in the same villa as that lady, it is not ..."

"You mean, you knew my mother?" Jane's entire attitude changed.

He inclined his head gravely.

"Why didn't you say so at once, monsieur?" She turned to her chaperones and explained that the gentleman was a friend of her late mother's and had known her, Jane, when she was a child. Satisfied, they withdrew to beyond eavesdropping distance; Banks went with them but Jane called her back to her side as they all set off for the café.

"Vous parlez très bien ..." de Guy began.

"D'you mind if we continue in English?" Jane interrupted. "Tell me, did you ever mention my mother to Miss Wilkinson?"

"Well ..." He gave an awkward little laugh.

"It's only fair to add, monsieur, that she told me all about you."

"Ah," he said.

"And to be fair to her, too, I don't suppose she ever imagined we'd meet."

He grunted. "You are more charitable than I, Miss Hervey. I confess I am now covered with embarrassment. I thought ... well, I didn't know what to think."

She told him what little she knew of Roger Moynihan and the circumstances of Miss Wilkinson's marriage. "But," she added, "I don't suppose she sent you on this errand simply to hear that."

337

"Nor do I," he added heavily.

"Forgive my curiosity," Rosa cut in, "but had you yourself hoped to marry the young lady, M. de Guy? If so, it was dreadfully callous of her and I do feel for you." Jane stared at her in astonishment and then turned to the young man with a laugh. "May I tell her?" she asked.

That simple question, she saw, went part way toward resolving a doubt he must have felt – about what sort of young ladies he was dealing with. That she was surrounded with chaperones should have made it quite clear; so what had put any other possibility into his mind? Most probably it was her association with Miss W. But could it also be that she was the daughter, and fair copy, of La Vivie? He would never tell her as long as he suspected the best. It was going to be a delicate interview.

He leaned forward a little and looked her up and down, in a manner he would not have attempted earlier. "I myself would be most interested to hear your explanation, Miss Hervey," he replied.

Jane turned to Rosa. "When Mrs Moynihan was just plain Miss Wilkinson," she explained, "she found herself an orphan and quite destitute. Having little in the way of education – and nothing in the way of training – to equip her to earn a living, she did what many another has been forced to do in those circumstances, and ..."

"I believe very little force was required," de Guy interrupted.

"In that case, I believe she could have found a great career upon the stage," Jane said coldly.

He raised his hands in an almost priestly gesture, deferring to her.

"Mr Moynihan, who, I ought to say, knows all about that unfortunate episode in her life, has rescued her from it. M. de Guy here had also proposed a form of rescue to her – not quite all the way into wedlock, shall we say, but, nonetheless, a great step up from a life on the streets. Am I putting it fairly, monsieur?"

"I doubt the ... *ange-archiviste?*"

"Recording angel."

"I doubt he could be more scrupulous. But it is not, you will understand, a subject a gentleman would choose to discuss with young ladies."

In short, Jane thought, *nail your colours to the mast, miss!*

"Sometimes a lady has no choice, monsieur," she replied. Then, turning in frustration to Rosa she said, "Forgive me, I have to say this in French. English is much too blunt." And she went on to explain that young people, in the slow unfolding of their understanding, came under the influence of certain historical eventualities, an influence that was subtle and all too often unnoticed but which nonetheless permeated ...

In short, by means of a long and polished sequence of French sonorities, all glittering with abstraction, she managed to convey to him that she was interested in her mother's past. And she managed it all without descending to anything so particular as herself, her mother, or life as it was once lived at the villa.

But the walls of Jericho did not fall at the first blast of the trumpets. He, for his part, spoke of the essential uniqueness of each individual soul, of the memory of the dead, the fallibility of memory, the inviolability of memory, and of the need in each generation to shed the past lest it choke the present. Which brought them, somewhat

338

breathless from all that chasing after allusion and illusion, to the Café de la Comédie. Jane asked de Guy to join them – which, naturally, he was only too pleased to do.

Expecting little custom at that season, despite the glorious sunshine, the proprietor had set up no more than one brazier among the tables. The footman and his wife went to stand in the lee of the café wall, where they were allowed a glass of mulled wine and a cognac to chase it. De Guy watched Jane with amusement as she consented to these uncommonly liberal arrangements; when she turned to him and said, "And you, monsieur?" he laughed openly – much as to say she would not loosen his tongue *that* way. He settled for coffee, which he paid for at once, without offering to pay for theirs; it was a way of underscoring the fact that he regarded them as the sort of young ladies with whom he would never dream of discussing the likes of Miss Wilkinson, no matter how many steps above the street; in other words, he would not embarrass their guardians by putting them in his debt – not even by the price of a cup of chocolate.

He gazed out at the neatly tamed landscapes of the Sun King and said it was hard to imagine it as it must have been in the days when it was an entirely private garden – when "the likes of us" would probably have been flogged for trespass.

"I don't see why you can't talk sensibly to us on a topic of some interest," Rosa said bluntly, determined to try the English approach. "We'll probably never meet again in our lives, so why not?"

He glanced at her and smiled, but then saw the seriousness in her eyes and became serious himself, turning back to Jane. "I cannot talk of your mother like ... like" – he waved an arm vaguely toward the palace – "Marie Antoinette or some character from history. I was in love with her, insofar as it's possible for a youth of twenty-one to be in love with a lady a century older in wisdom and ... *conpassion?* I do not mean to sound ungallant."

At last Jane saw a chink in his armour. "Of course," she said as if she agreed absolutely with him. "If there were things in her life of which she was deeply ashamed, then you, as a gentleman ..."

"No!" he cried. "There was nothing in her life of which she could be ashamed. She was rightly proud of ..." He turned to Rosa as if she represented a means of escape from this intolerable situation. "What do you wish to know, mademoiselle? On the understanding that we shall never meet again, I will tell you – whatever it is."

Her eyes gleamed. She licked her lips and drew breath to speak ...

But Jane was remorseless. "Then you hurt me deeply, monsieur, by your suggestion that *I* would be ashamed of things that made my mother 'rightly proud' – your very own words."

He closed his eyes and shook his head.

"When you ..." Rosa began, but Jane nudged her arm and she fell silent.

"What is it you wish to know?" he asked woodenly.

"Not what, monsieur. Whom. I wish to know my mother."

The man opened his eyes and gazed, not at her, but at Rosa. Then Jane knew that her intuition had been right – that Rosa was more essentially like Angwin Vyvyan than she, her own daughter, despite all misleading resemblances.

"And if you knew?" he asked, turning to her at last.

Jane shrugged. "Then I would know."

"But what would you *do?*"

She sighed. "Continue to lead my own life, I suppose. But without this ..." She mimed a large, heavy *something* on her back.

"If only I could be sure of that." He turned to Banks. "Tell me what you think, mademoiselle. You must know her better than she knows herself."

Banks stared steadily at her mistress, smiled, and said, "There is no one and nothing on the face of this earth could make that woman there deviate one hair's breadth from her own chosen path. I've seen a few as tried it and came to grief. But I know of only one ..."

He held up a finger. "It's enough. I will tell you." He stared out into the trees and said, "La Vivie was the sun and moon to all who knew her. Superficially, Mlle Hervey, you are the living image of her, but I believe it is no more than that – superficial. If what your maid says is true, you could not be more different, in fact. She was consumed by a rage for life – because she could never find more than half of it. She was hard. She could be cruel. She was always capricious. And yet at the heart of her, just every now and then, I thought I could glimpse someone quite different – frightened, vulnerable, curious ... and sad. No. *Triste.* To me it's different from 'sad.' I always had the feeling of a *tristesse* – as if other people had discovered some secret which they could never share and she could never learn from them."

"They were her lovers, these other people?"

He nodded.

"And she had many?"

He tilted his head awkwardly. "That was part of her search. I don't mean she didn't love them, too. She had more love in her than ..."

"How did she support herself? Did her lovers support her?"

He shook his head slowly, not so much in denial as at the impossibility of expressing it in such elementary terms.

"Did *you* ever give her money?" Jane asked brutally.

"No," he replied at once.

"Thank you, monsieur."

But he shook his head sadly. "And now, mademoiselle, I believe you know even less about her than before."

"I know she had lovers and that some of them supported her. And that is something I ..."

"Oh yes! So now you believe she was ... *courtisane! Une grande horizontale!* If so, you are truly even farther from understanding her. Some of those who gave her money were never her lovers in that way. Some who loved her in that way, including me, would never have insulted her so. She was a woman of infinite subtlety. To have proposed to her the sort of arrangement I might propose ... that, in fact, I *did* propose to Miss Wilkinson, for example, would have been ..." He waved his hands around in a hopeless search for something stronger than "impossible." Then he smiled reassuringly at her. "Abandon your search, mademoiselle. The Vivie I knew can never replace the mother you knew."

She smiled, to show she recognized his kindness. "But I didn't know her, you see. Else I should not be here now. One thing more: Why do you suppose she married my father and returned to England?"

"For you, of course," he said at once.

"Then there was some degree of shame there, after all."

"Not in the slightest!" He tapped his heart. "Not in here. But she knew the way of the world. She had taken her chance and enjoyed it. True, she had not found what she was looking for but ... *alors, c'est la vie*. Now it was time to think of you. *C'est la vie, aussi*."

"And why do you suppose my father married her? Mr Hervey, I mean."

"I did not know Mr Hervey, mademoiselle." He pulled out his watch and looked at it. "But, if you can spare me a week, I could furnish you with sufficient reasons why any man might move heaven and earth to marry your mother."

Jane smiled and stared into the brazier.

"Or," he said, rising to his feet, "I could be very French and say who knows why any woman chooses to do anything. As a matter of fact, the man who could probably tell you – the man who was her lover more times, now hot, now cold, over the years – lives not half a dozen miles from here at Ville d'Avray. You will pass his house on your way back."

Jane was all attention again. "D'you know him, monsieur? What is his name?"

He made a self-deprecating face. "As well as any younger man may know one of his grandfather's generation, but yes, I know him. The Baron de Puisne."

"Ha!" Jane cried out in delight.

"Why so?" he asked.

"Nothing. Could you ... may I trespass yet further? Could you possibly see your way to effecting an introduction? D'you suppose he would receive me?"

"Oh, I make not the slightest doubt. But" – he patted his pockets – "I have no paper about me. We could go into Versailles and ..."

"No, I mean now. On our way back to Paris. Will you ride with us ... how did you get here?"

"By train."

"Ride back with us, then, and see if the Baron will receive me? Please?"

He laughed. "Perhaps, mademoiselle, your similarity to your mother is not so superficial after all. How can I refuse?"

*　　　*　　　*

Before they could see the Baron, however, they had to get past a sour young Cerberus called Mme Duret, an Englishwoman, despite her name. The house was built on a short, steep hill at the narrowest part of the road, so they were compelled to leave the carriage lower down and walk back up. Thinking that four might be a forbidding number, they left Banks behind – which contented her well enough once she spied an interesting row of shops a little farther down the hill.

Mme Duret was on the point of slamming the door in their faces when de Guy let drop the fact that Jane's mother had also been known as La Vivie.

341

"But I thought I told you ..." she said with a frown – and then changed her mind and smiled. "No. Of course I didn't. How could I!" She sighed. "I suppose the Baron would never forgive me if he heard that his darling Vivie's daughter had called and I had turned her away. But I must insist on being present. His heart is not strong." She turned to the other two. "And there can be no question of your seeing him today. Old friend or no."

"May we walk in your garden?" Rosa said at once.

"You may do as you please," she replied over her shoulder as she led Jane off down the passage.

The house was built in an L-shape, in rather a colonial style, with a broad verandah on the inner sides of the L, looking into the garden, which straggled down the hill for a couple of hundred yards. As they walked out into the little gravelled space that squared off the L, they saw Jane being ushered into the Baron's presence.

"And now your question, Mlle Rosa?" he said lightly.

She swallowed hard. "Me?"

"Isn't that why you suggested this little stroll? You were on the point of asking me a question back there at Versailles when Miss Hervey interrupted."

"Oh! Gracious! It'll sound very ... I mean, I was only going to ask ... you know ... Miss Wilkinson and so on. When you make a proposal like that to a woman, I mean, d'you just ... out with it? How do you put it? I just can't imagine it."

"Can't you? I'm sure you can."

"Honestly."

"I'm sure you *have*. But, since you ask, and since we have a few minutes at our disposal, let me try to tell you. In the first place, it is not at all like hiring a servant – despite the obvious similarities, the exchange of payment for services, and so on. With a servant there are well-understood, quite formal ways of making the contract. But when the woman is one with whom you hope to share the most joyful and intimate moments of your life, then it must be different each time. It is a very personal contract, after all. So, tell me, which young lady is doing me the honour of considering my proposition? I need to know that before I can begin."

"Goodness!" Rosa laughed nervously. "Let's say Miss Wilkinson. What did you tell her?"

"D'you know the lady?"

"No."

"Then it would have no meaning. It must be someone you know."

She held her breath.

He took her arm then. "Yourself, for instance," he said quietly. "Then you would truly understand it." After a pause he added, "You would like that?"

"Go on," she told him.

"It's true I hardly know you, yet, between men and women there are ways of knowing that do not depend on time. Between some men and some women. And from the moment I met you, Miss Rosa, just a few hours ago, I have ..." He gave a little laugh. "You recall what I said to Miss Hervey, about the difference between her and her mother? What I hesitated to tell her, and what I will now confess to you, is this: You are far more like La Vivie than Miss Hervey ever will be, though she

342

looks the very copy of her mother. But you have that spirit. Tell me, do you look forward to the prospect of marriage?"

"No!" Rosa replied emphatically.

"And yet you enjoy the society of men. It's not a question, so don't answer. *Alors*, I said for each woman the arrangement proposed must be slightly different. In your case it must be very different. To Miss Wilkinson I proposed a beautiful *apartement* on the Rive Gauche, where I would visit her four afternoons each week and one night, Saturday or Sunday. And for that she will receive four thousand francs a year." He felt her arm grow tense and added, "For one like that it must be a very commercial arrangement. 'Commercial' – it's the right word?"

"I couldn't think of a better," Rosa agreed.

"But for you it would be quite wrong," he added hastily.

"Oh, well, I wouldn't say ..."

He ignored her protest. "For you it must be the same as for La Vivie." She fell silent then.

"First you must understand that here in France *les plus grandes horizontales* can never be for one man alone. But nor can they be for all mankind, like any *poule*. Impossible, you say with your English logic. But let me tell you now."

They had reached the foot of the garden and started a slow turn across the grass that would bring them back along its farther fringe. "The Baron, to whom we owe this charming recreation ... this little *jeu d'esprit* ... game of make-believe? He was the first lover of ... a certain lady."

"You mean La Vivie?"

"A certain lady," he insisted. "He gives her a villa. He gives her jewels ... clothes ... he pays her servants ... but never a penny does he give her. They never talk of money even. She knows not to want too much, and he knows not to give too little. And he also knows he cannot possibly reserve so superb a creature to himself alone. So he invites his friends to little parties *chez* La Vivie – people in his same political circle, financiers, officers of middle rank with their ears to the wall, *entrepreneurs* who know of safe speculations. And it is understood that, if the lady wishes it – and only if she wishes it – she is free to conduct little *affaires* with them, too. Of course, because she is so grateful to the Baron, she will wish it more often than not. Much more often than not. And these men, unlike the Baron, are free to leave little *cadeaux* of money. Somewhere in the room, you understand. Never to her personally. So you see how important such a woman becomes to such a man? That she is also his mistress is the very least of her value to him. She can also make or mar his career. She is more important than his wife, who is no more than his brood mare."

"Do you have a wife?" Rosa asked.

"No more than a brood mare," he repeated ambiguously. "But why have I been talking about this anonymous lady? After all, I am making this proposal ..."

"Why won't you admit who it is? We both know you're talking about La Vivie."

He lifted his hand gently to her face and chucked her under the chin. "Because, *mon ange* – and you must understand this very well – the reputation of such a lady remains inviolate. Everyone knows about her but her name is never ... how do you say? Assaulted in civilities?"

"Bandied about?"

"Perhaps. Her name is never bandied about. Therefore she is accepted in all societies, even at court. You should think of that with comfort, no? As I said, I am making this proposal to you. For the next three years I shall be *aide-de-camp* to Admiral Lequesne here in Paris. I have found favour with someone and this is my first step to higher things. A mistress like Miss Wilkinson would have been a great error. I can admit it now. She would not have served me well, except in the most obvious way. But you, mademoiselle, will be perfect, I think. You have that rare quality. For you I will do what the Baron did — except I am not so rich that I can buy a villa. But I will rent La V... Miss Hervey's for you and furnish the servants and everything else that's necessary for your immediate needs."

"And your friends?" Rosa asked hesitantly.

"They will furnish what is necessary for your old age."

They strolled on in silence quite a while before Rosa said, "It is a big engagement to undertake on so slender an acquaintance." She turned to him suddenly and pulled his face down to hers. He kissed her. She responded as passionately as she knew how. When she drew away he was plainly shaken. For once he was at a loss for words. She whispered, "If only we could ... you know ... just to see."

He regained some of his aplomb. "It would be very easy to arrange!"

"For you, perhaps," she said glumly.

"And for you, too."

She shook her head. "We have to be sensible. We have to ... face the possibility that the very worst might happen. Suppose, for instance, we, you and I, simply didn't ... you know?"

His smile showed how unlikely he thought that would be.

"But it could happen," she insisted. "And suppose La Lanyon found out."

"She's your ...?"

"Guardian, unofficially. She's Jane's official guardian, in fact. Suppose she found out what we'd done. I'd have to go back to Cornwall with her ... and my life would be as good as finished. Pffft! The End!"

"I see," he said thoughtfully.

"She's so strict. Such a puritan — d'you understand the word?"

He nodded. "We say *puritain de puritain.*" He stared uncertainly at the trees.

Judging her moment she added, "And yet, like a lot of puritanical women, I suspect she's really extremely passionate underneath it all."

He turned that same uncertain gaze on her.

She smiled, not at all uncertainly. And then so did he.

▼

44 JANE AND ROSA LAY on their backs and marvelled at the patterns where the street lights shone up through the lace curtains. Jane laughed suddenly. Rosa asked why. "She numbers the stars while he counts the blades of grass — something Banks said to me once. And I hadn't the faintest idea what she meant."

"Really? How on earth did you get onto the subject, then?"

"Something cryptic she said about not accepting ginger fairings from a man at Harvest Fair or something. As I say, I couldn't make head nor tail ..."

"D'you think she's been slyly educating you all this time?"

"I suppose she has. Isn't that what a good lady's maid is for?"

"I wouldn't know," Rosa said archly.

"How did you find out about It, then?"

"I always knew."

"No, you can't *always* have known. There must have been a ..."

"Ever since I was a child, anyway. There was a farmer called Lory who used to take the workhouse girls out of the field gangs and put them down Tolmenor Woods. When we lived near Tintagel."

"And you used to watch?" Jane asked in horror.

"It was by accident the first time. But after that I used to go and watch. And Susie, too, though she denies it flatly now."

"So you've actually *seen* it!"

"Scores of times, me 'ansum," she replied in her best North Cornish. "It's not very edifying, actually, but when one's a child, you know how one is. I used to go and watch the butcher slaughtering cattle and the blacksmith burning the horses' hooves, and never turned a hair."

"Goodness gracious! I hope it's like none of those things." Jane exclaimed.

"It is quite violent and noisy. Listen – what we were talking about earlier – I'll make a pact with you: If you tell me what the Baron told you, I'll tell you what M de Guy said to me."

"Don't change the subject," Jane said petulantly. "I'd really like to know what ..."

"I don't think I am changing the subject, am I?"

Jane lay silent awhile. When she spoke it was flat and weary. "In a way, he told me nothing. He's a bit what the French call *gah-gah* now. The moment he clapped eyes on me he mistook me for my mother, of course. Laughing and crying all in one. I tried to explain but that Mme Duret caught my eye and then I had to play the part."

"Is it true he gave her this villa?"

Jane stiffened. "Did de Guy tell you that?"

"Not in so many words. They're all so civilized and gentlemanly. All these codes of honour and pretending to be so chivalrous and *suave*. But in the end it's just Farmer Lory dragging a workhouse girl into the woods. There's no difference."

"You sound like Miss Wilkinson. 'All men are just packs of hunting dogs'."

"Perhaps that's the attitude you need to be successful at it. I don't know."

"Successful at what, Rosa? If you don't tell me, it's only going to fester inside you."

"You haven't finished telling me about you and the Baron yet."

Jane sighed. "There's nothing actually to tell. I had to sit on his knee and kiss him – just *pour souvenir*, you know. But it hurt his legs, so that was soon over."

"How grisly!"

"No, he's quite sweet, really. I can see what my mother liked in him. He's very humorous, very forthright. The sort of man who's got no doubt about what he wants – nor that he'll get it. Mme Duret says he's a devil."

"Yes, but what did he *tell* you?"

"Nothing! Because, of course, he assumed I already knew it all. But just reading between the lines, from the sort of things he said, I mean, it's quite obvious that my mother was his ... mistress." She gave a dry laugh. "Which, I must admit, is not the earth-shaking news it might once have been. D'you know what I think today's greatest revelation has been?"

"What?"

"Banks. What she told de Guy. That I am impervious to the truth."

Rosa laughed. "But that's an absolute travesty of what she said. What she actually told him was that no truth, however painful, would break your spirit. What interested me was the bit he interrupted. She said she'd seen two people try to break your spirit and fail. But there was one who ... and that's where he cut her off. What d'you suppose she was about to say?"

"I have no idea. She must be blind."

"A fashion set by her mistress."

"D'you think Dorothy's right when she says blood will always out in the end, no matter how people try to fight it?"

Rosa reached a hand out into the cold and patted Jane's curls in playful contempt. "Yes, dear, you're utterly doomed. Perhaps you should have taken that stroll with M de Guy instead of me."

"Why?" Jane turned excitedly on her side.

"Because he proposed to me what ..."

"He *proposed* to you!" Jane began the usual spinster rituals of delight.

"Listen!" Rosa continued flatly. "He made the same sort of proposal to me as I imagine the Baron once made to your mother."

"Oh."

"Yes, oh. It was, of course, terribly civilized and *suave* – I've got that word on my brain. But it was."

"But you can be terribly polished, too, when you want," Jane said encouragingly. "I'll bet you let him down lightly and it was all smoothed over."

There was no reply.

"Rosa?"

There was an audible swallowing noise.

"Rosa!" Jane was shocked. "You didn't!"

At last she spoke. "The thing is, you see, I intended it as a sort of trick. I knew what was on his mind. I mean, I could just feel it there. As soon as we started talking about Miss Wilkinson and his frustrated arrangement with her ... oh, but he's clever! He told me all about what he'd proposed to her. An absolutely ravishing little apartment on the Left Bank, with everything she could possibly want for her comfort – her own maid and everything – and four thousand francs a year. And she'd only have to entertain him four afternoons a week and one night ..."

"And he told you all this? Just like that!"

"Every word. Just like a contract at a hiring fair. And he got me thinking, you see – that doesn't sound such a bad sort of life ..."

"Rosa! But you didn't ..."

346

"Just wait. The best is yet to come. As soon as he feels me thinking that – I don't know how, except that he's one of those men who know exactly how women feel – he says, 'Of course, I wouldn't propose anything so dull and ordinary as that for a girl like *you*, Rosa!' Apparently, I'm much too rare!" And she went on to tell Jane precisely what de Guy had proposed.

After she had finished Jane was silent awhile; then she said, "Of course, he was only telling you all that so you'd tell me. He didn't mean it, so I wouldn't worry if I were you. It was his way of telling me – through you – how the Baron once spoke to my mother. You know what their code of honour is like ..."

"No, Jane, he meant every word," Rosa said quietly.

"But that's awful! We must give instructions that he's never to be admitted here, and we must cut him dead if he has the impudence to ..."

"You don't understand, Jane. I told him I would consider it very seriously."

"To get rid of him?"

"No." There was a silence before Rosa went on. "You see, it started as a sort of trick – and it still is." And she went on to explain how matters stood with de Guy. "*That's* all I intended to happen, when I began. I could feel he wanted to make some proposal of that nature, and so I thought I might be able to use him to knock La Lanyon off her high horse. But that was all. I never imagined the effect it might have on me if such a handsome and dashing young man, with the entrée to the entire *haute monde* of Paris ... if he whispered such seductions in my ear."

"But it's disgraceful," Jane said.

Rosa, who had had more than enough of morality by now – and from someone who could so easily afford to take a high tone – stretched herself luxuriously and said, "And yet it is a beautiful villa!"

She referred, of course, to de Guy's offer, but Jane, equally naturally, took it as a hint that she, living in this conspicuously ornate glass house, was the last one to start throwing stones. Suddenly, all the tensions, anxieties, and uncertainties of these past weeks overwhelmed her. She tried not to let Rosa become aware of it, but soon the whole bed was rocked by her sobbing.

Rosa was mortified. "But, darling! I didn't mean that! Not that! Oh, please ..." Hesitantly she reached across and stroked Jane's arm.

Jane, desperate for comfort, struggled over the fleecy billows of swansdown and collapsed into Rosa's embrace, cradling her cheek against the girl's neck. "I meant *me*," Rosa murmured, petting and stroking her head. "I was talking about me. I was being sarcastic – about how shallow my emotions are, you see – that I could be swayed by the offer of these bricks and mortar ..." Suddenly she realized what she was saying, or *also* saying and she cast about for some way of honeying her words.

Jane started to giggle, even though she was still weeping.

"I'm hopeless," Rosa said lugubriously.

"No, you're not. You're honest." Jane sniffed back a great salt stream and became serious again. "I'm the one who ought to stay and ... go back to that way of life."

"What d'you mean, go *back* to it?"

"You know – take over where my mother left off. I feel such a hypocrite."

Rosa shook her arm quite fiercely. "Jane, dear, you're just talking nonsense ..."

347

"No! All that horror I was expressing just now, while you were telling me what de Guy said ... all that, 'Rosa, you didn't!' and, 'We must cut him dead.' Hah! D'you know what I really felt? Envy. I thought, 'Why did he ask her? Why not me? Aren't I good enough?' So you can just see what I'm like really." She tried to summon up the courage to confess her ultimate shame – that when she had fallen into Rosa's arms a few moments earlier and felt her warm body against her cheek, she had tried to imagine it was Daniel's.

But honesty drew its own line. A passing whim, once confessed like that, becomes enshrined in infamy, and something within her had sense enough to realize it and step back from the brink. And yet she could not so easily unconfess it to herself.

She eased a little apart and reached out for Rosa's hand, to show there was no rejection in it.

"Let's both stay, then," Rosa said with the sort of experimental chuckle she could quickly disown if Jane took the proposal seriously.

"Easy enough for you," Jane pointed out glumly. "You're not anybody's ward – at least, you've no inheritance worth fighting over."

Still as if they were pursuing some airy fancy, Rosa replied, "We'd have to ask de Guy to find you a very powerful protector, high in the French government."

"He'd be bound to be old and fat."

"Yes, but powerful. You can always close your eyes and think of that! With one stroke of his pen he can send men to Devil's Island for life. Whole regiments quake at his name. But you'll hold him in the palm of your hand. Just say no and he'll be on his knees, begging you. And no one will dare cut you or insult you because they'd have to answer to him for it ..."

Jane felt her shivering with excitement at the prospect. "I hadn't thought of that," she said.

"Nor had I – until de Guy spoke to me this afternoon."

*   *   *

To Gérard de Guy the seduction of an unwilling woman was like a military engagement. Even a mediocre general would set out to discover the terrain where the battle was to be fought; a wise one would know far more. So, when Dorothy set out the following morning, "to see a dear old nurse who is now looking after a former owner of this villa," she had not the faintest notion that the occupant of the carriage which drew out of the Rue de la Reine Hortense a moment later was in any way interested in this act of charity. Had that been the case, she would certainly not have driven directly to the Rue Castiglione – nor given the driver most of the day off in order to visit his nephew at Vincennes, nor greeted the Chevalier with quite such warmth, nor allowed him to escort her at once to the Luxembourg, nor hung on his every word with such conspicuous delight, nor have taken so sybaritic a luncheon with him at the Vachette on the Boulevart Montmartre, where she would surely not have taken quite so much wine. And of all these quite positive negatives, the most unequivocal of all is surely this: that she would never, never have returned to the Chevalier's home a full two hours before her carriage was due.

Poor de Guy, who had followed and watched all this in mounting dismay, went to seek solace at a place on the Rive Gauche where that commodity was *une spécialité de la maison.*

*   *   *

The eye of the tiger sparkled in the glow of the fire – profoundly knowing, deeply approving, in all its feline sensuality. Catlike herself, Dorothy rubbed her cheek against its ear. At her other side a heavy-lidded Chevalier stroked her hair and murmured, *"Tigresse! Que vous êtes tigresse, madame!"*

She turned lazily to him, nuzzling his cheek with her lips. "I had no choice," she whispered. "I was caught between *two* tigers."

Their lips met, brushed each other, parted ... returned hungrily to the encounter. His fingers toyed with the hem of her chemise, began drawing it back down over her naked breasts.

"No," she moaned.

"No?"

"More. Just once more."

"Oh!" he begged. *"Je vous en prie – non!"* But it was a forlorn cry. Her suddenly all-knowing fingers were already at their maddening, gentle work. Moments later, empty, aching, groaning, he was once again raising her to pinnacles of a pleasure whose existence she had never suspected.

That was the true miracle of it all. These thrilling new sensations were actually there inside her, in the very core of her being; they must have been there all these years, just waiting for this order of release. She had never even suspected it. And yet the Chevalier had realized it at once – the moment he saw her. He had told her as much, promised her ecstasies such as she had never known.

What a man! What a truly remarkable man! She could not stop thinking about him, all the way home. What was going to happen to her now? She could not possibly go back to Jesse, dear, kindly ... clumsy, fumbling, unfeeling Jesse. It would be like walking out of the light of day forever ... deliberately locking herself away in a dungeon. No, she would stay here and be the mistress of the Chevalier. Why not? It was almost respectable here. Indeed, it *was* respectable. He had as good as said that La Vivie ... well, he hadn't mentioned her by name, of course, but that just went to prove it, didn't it! Although she had been the Baron's mistress, she was also a respectable lady whose good name he could not possibly blacken. Oh, yes – things were certainly different here in Paris.

And tomorrow – the opera! It would be the most passionate music, he promised, that the world has ever known. The legend of a legendary love. And they would sit in his private box and see and hear the drama unfold – and at its magnificent climax he would ... no, even to think of it, to remember the words of his glorious boast, would spoil it.

*   *   *

"And how was Mme D..." Jane bit her tongue off. "I mean, Mme Dauphine?"
"Who on earth is she?" Dorothy asked.
"Oh," Jane laughed, "it's a nickname for any old nurse. You were going to see ..."
"Oh, yes." Dorothy became grave all of a sudden. "Jane, my dear, I believe you should compose yourself to hear what is really some rather ..." She paused and then her face cracked in a smile. "... splendid news."
"Really?" Jane did her best to conform to Dorothy's obvious expectations.
"Yes. It seems that your Aunt Agnes's surmise was correct all along. The poor Baron was unable to see me. He's not at all well – in fact, he's been in a coma for some days past and I fear the end is nigh ..."
"Oh, poor man," Jane said. "And I should so love to have seen him."
Dorothy shrugged sympathetically. "I fear it may never be. But I had such a long and interesting talk with his old nurse – Mme Dauphine, as you say. No! Duret, of course! Mme Duret. A wonderful old lady, too. English by birth, funnily enough, but she's been part of the Baron's household since he was a little boy. Fancy that!"
"Yes ... just fancy. Anyway, what did she say?"
"Oh, it would take from now till Christmas next to tell you everything, but the long and short of it is this: It seems your mother's great-uncle ... what was his name?"
"Uncle Lyon?" Jane asked.
"Lion?" The name seemed to distract her for a moment. "Yes, that was it."
"L-y-o-n," Jane spelled it out. "It's Cornish, I think."
"Yes, to be sure. Anyway, she distinctly remembers a legacy from him ..."
"But it was actually from Great-Aunt Cicely, according to my aunt."
For a moment Dorothy was nonplussed. Then she brightened. "Yes, but Mme Duret wasn't to know that, was she! Anyway, it wasn't far short of a hundred thousand pounds. And, as she left you, out of *her* estate, only little over half that ... well, there's a measure of the scale on which she lived while she was here! And so, though we may deprecate such extravagance, it nonetheless assures us that nobody *else* was supporting her in that style." She beamed. "So you may sleep easy, my child. Your mother was – as, indeed, one would guess from her daughter – an upright woman." She smiled naughtily and added, "Not a *horizontale* one."
Jane heaved a great sigh of relief, threw her arms around her guardian, and hugged her passionately, unable to utter a word.
Dorothy, feeling the girl shiver, was astonished at the strength of her response. "Poor child," she murmured tenderly, stroking her back and smoothing her hair. "I had no idea ... I mean I thought you were resigned to ... oh, my dear! I'm so glad to be the bearer of these tidings! So glad!"
The door opened at that moment, rescuing Jane from total collapse. "Jane!" Rosa called out excitedly, just poking her head into the room. "You'll never guess who has just come a-knocking at our door! He says he was a childhood friend of yours and used to come and play here with you in the nursery."
"Hardly that!" de Guy objected loudly.
Jane, recognized his voice and saw that Rosa had got just a little carried away. She went swiftly to the door, greeted de Guy as if they had not met in a dozen years, and brought him in to meet Dorothy.

"Enchanté, madame," he murmured, raising her hand to his lips. When he looked into her eyes he was almost overwhelmed with what he detected burning there. And in that fraction of a second he revised the tale he had decided to tell Rosa to excuse his failure; indeed, he wiped the very idea of failure entirely from his mind.

"When this young man was an even younger man," Jane was explaining meanwhile, "I used to torment the life out of him for piggyback rides." She grasped his arm and led him a pace or two to the window. "It's marvellous to see you again, M de Guy, and so kind of you to call."

"Please!" He smirked. "Can it not still be Gérard and Jane?"

"If you wish." She spoke warmly and stared daggers. "Look, there is the lawn where I so tormented you."

They invented and exchanged several more "childhood memories," and then he said it was time to go but he hoped they might have the chance to meet again while they were in Paris ...

To everyone's surprise, it was Dorothy who pressed him to stay and dine with them that evening. He demurred, of course ... had several appointments which, though tedious in the extreme, were *de rigueur.* However, it might be possible to call by for a small, *late* supper?

*　　　*　　　*

Banks did not strike the match until she had closed the door behind her. She put the candle down and saw the flame well established before she lifted the holder again.

"Well?" Jane asked impatiently.

The maid nodded grimly. "He climbed up that creeper stuff, up to her balcony."

"When?"

"Only now."

Jane shielded her eyes from the direct light of the flame and peered at her. "Do I detect a note of disapproval?" she asked.

"You do, miss. I say it's a scandal. Mrs Lanyon! Who'd ever of thought it?"

"I wonder what she was doing this afternoon? She most certainly wasn't at Ville d'Avray talking to sweet old grey-haired Mme Duret!"

Rosa laughed. "Is that what she told you?"

"That and more. She's a dark horse, our Dorothy. A dark mare."

"A nightmare," Banks commented.

Rosa giggled again. "Certainly not a brood mare!" Suddenly she turned pale. "What if he comes along here afterwards? To claim ... I mean ... he is ..."

"Yes?" Jane prompted. "He is what?"

"Well, he's making it very obvious that he's keeping his part of the bargain."

"Bargain?"

Rosa looked at her with renewed hope. "You're right. It wasn't *really* a bargain, was it. No."

Jane shrugged diffidently, suggesting that the last thing she wanted was to disagree, but ... on the other hand ...

"He won't," Rosa said confidently.

351

"I'll go and sleep with Banks," Jane said comfortingly. Rosa clutched at her arm. "You wouldn't! Please, don't leave me. If he comes ..." Banks gave an exasperated sigh. They both turned to her. She shook her head and said, "I dunno."

"What?" Rosa asked.

"What good do you think he'd be after a time or two along there." She jerked her head in the direction of Dorothy's room.

In the silence, nine-tenths drowned by the roar of traffic which they must have hoped would complete the work, came the unmistakable sounds of two in ecstasy.

Banks stared at them, darker than ever in her dissent. "The sooner we get back home to Cornwall the better," she commented.

45 THE STEAM LAUNCH made heavy going against the swollen waters of the Seine, for, despite the fine weather in Paris, there had been heavy rains in the east and the river was now taking the brunt of it.

"It's a good thing, really," Jane said. "The one civilized amenity Paris still lacks is proper sanitation."

"I had noticed," Richard Vyvyan replied. "It reminded me of my father's descriptions of the Stinking Thames of his youth. I say, why doesn't Mrs Lanyon come and join us on this side?"

"I don't know. I hope she doesn't imagine she's being tactful."

"Ah." Richard cleared his throat uncertainly.

Jane, who had meant she thought Dorothy was giving her time to tell Richard about their kinship, realized that he thought she was harking back to an earlier period of their acquaintance. In which case her words must have seemed like a heavy hint to get on with his proposal. She wondered how she might gently disabuse him of the notion. They both spoke simultaneously: "Is this ..." and "Talking of ..." They laughed. "You go on." "No, you." Jane broke the impasse. "I was only going to ask if this boat belongs to the embassy?"

"Good heavens, no. Why?"

To ask how else an impecunious young naval attaché would get the use of it would seem churlish. She cast around for something that might justify the link – a sign in English, for instance. But there was nothing.

"Actually," he said, "it belongs to some count at the Italian Embassy. He came a cropper at the races. Or baccarat, or something. Anyway, he needed a bit of a bunk up so I ... sort of hired it from him for the day. Just for us."

"Hired it?" she echoed in surprise.

He laughed awkwardly. "I know. As a matter of fact, Jane, that's really what I wanted to talk to you about. You see – now you probably weren't aware of it – but one of the reasons we were rather thrown together last summer was ... well ..."

"Yes, I know," she told him.

"You do?"

"I did sort of ... twig it."

"Well!" He gave a small, slightly baffled laugh. "You see, one never can tell. I would never have guessed."

"We're all taught to hide our true feelings, aren't we."

He started to pull his fingers, making his knuckles crack. "Please don't!" Jane gritted her teeth and touched his hand gently.

"I'd have given anything to reveal mine at the time, Jane, but ..." He sighed. "I don't know. The poor suitor and the rich heiress, don't you know. It smacked of mercenary ... motives."

"Richard!" she chided.

"I know, but I couldn't help it. However, that's all water under the bridge. Things are different now, you see."

"Are they?" She began to feel a touch uneasy.

"Yes. I'm not supposed to say anything yet, but I can't hold back any longer, Jane. I must tell you."

"Richard, please, I think you ought to know ..."

"No. Let me say my say. I've been thinking of nothing else ever since you came to Paris and if I don't get it off my chest now, I'll burst. The thing is, you see, in a few months' time I shall come into quite a bit of pelf."

"Richard! But that's marvellous!" Her misgivings grew with his every word.

"I don't know exactly how much because they're still working it out, but ... well, one doesn't wish to sound vulgar, but it'll be at least a hundred thou', they say."

She drew breath to squeal her delighted congratulations, but he put up both hands and begged her to be quiet. "I want to tell you first, you see. I mean, in the days when I had nothing and you were the wealthy one ... well, it made it very hard to talk. Really talk, didn't it."

"I don't know about that, Richard. I always thought you were far and away the easiest conversationalist among ..."

"Yes. All right. I grant that. But it's nothing like now, is it. I mean, now we need have no ... there'll be no suspicions of an ulterior motive."

"Y-e-e-s. All the same, I think I ought to say ..."

"In a mo, my lover. Please, just let me have my day in court. You see, if this had happened to me ... dash it, here's Notre Dame. We'll have to join them on that side if you want to see it."

"No, for heaven's sake, Richard, do go on now you've started."

"You don't mind?"

"I'll scream if you don't"

"Goodness, Jane, you are a right-down regular brick, you know! I was going to say, if this had happened to me last summer – this legacy business – I'd have dropped to my knees and fired the question."

She clutched a hand to her breast. "And you'd have scored a bullseye in here," she replied. "Last summer."

He did not catch the note of qualification. But, to her surprise, his face fell. "That's the thing, you see. It started to happen a little bit at Christmas. At your party.

353

But, of course, I couldn't do anything about it then, either. I mean, if there's anything more cringing than a poor swain making sheep's eyes at a wealthy heiress it's the same idiot swooning over a girl without a farthing to her name."

"I'm sorry, Richard. I am now utterly at a loss."

"Oh." He bit his lip uncertainly. "I was hoping you'd be able to tell me."

"Tell you what?"

"D'you think she'll have me?" His eyes strayed surreptitiously toward the opposite rail, where the other two were staring up at the cathedral towers. "No, I don't mean to put it that way. I mean, boot's on the other foot, you see. No longer poor little ensign sighing hopelessly after rich young heiress – but lucre-laden lout browbeating poor but beautiful ..."

"Richard!" Jane both laughed and struggled not to, which resulted in a near-explosion. "Are you struggling to say you'd like to ask Rosa to marry you?"

"Yes!" He stared in amazement. "Haven't you heard a word I've spoken?"

"And you'd like me to ask her for you?"

"Yes. No! I don't know. Just tell me what she'll say." He gnawed his lip in a frenzy of indecision. "There isn't anyone else, is there?"

"Hardly!"

He drew himself back and stared crossly at her. "Why d'you say it in that tone?"

"Well, my dear, far be it from me to pour cold water on your enthusiasm, but I, too, am inordinately fond of Rosa. Part of my intention in asking her to join me here – quite aside from the pleasure of her company – was in the hope that Dorothy Lanyon would take such a liking to her she'd agree to my providing her a dowry out of ... well, never mind. I had a silly notion then that I didn't deserve any of my father's legacy ..."

"Good heavens!"

"It's too *mazy,* as Banks says, to go into it all now. And anyway, it was so long ago and so much has happened since. What was I saying? Oh yes! You do realize what a handful you'll be taking on?"

"I think so," he replied warily.

But she pressed him harder. "Little as I know of the world, Richard, I do think I understand what qualities go to make a good diplomatic wife. And, with the best of wills, I don't believe dear Rosa could muster a single one of them."

He nodded. For a moment their eyes dwelled in each other's and she became aware that she was seeing a new Richard, or new to her – cautious, even secretive. "I'm resigning, in fact." He turned away and stared out at the Left Bank – as if she might read too much if she could still see his eyes.

"And going back to your family's estates in Cornwall?"

"Estates!" He chuckled at the word.

"Well what, then?"

He waved a hand at the city. "I'll pay off the old family mortgages, of course – back home – but this is the place for me, Jane. There's a fortune to be made here by those in the know. The thing is, I can't imagine life without Rosa at my side. I don't suppose you'd sell me your villa? D'you think that would make me more acceptable in her eyes?"

"Richard!" She threw up her hands in despair. "Where does one begin?"

But he would not be teased out of his gloom. "The thing is, I feel quite at ease with you – or anyone else. But when I think of Rosa, asking her the question, and the way I know she'll just look at me ... I feel almost sick. Perhaps I should stick to the original plan and marry you, instead?"

The boat lurched round the end of the Île de la Cité.

"We still shan't see Notre Dame," he added lugubriously. "Let's change sides."

But the other two had had the same idea a moment earlier. "All change!" Rosa shouted in their ears.

"What a good idea!" Jane grasped Dorothy firmly by the arm and propelled her back to where she had just come from. She began to protest but a squeeze from Jane's hand silenced her.

"Jane!" came Richard's agonized cry.

"My answer's yes," she called back.

"Oh, but look, I say ..." he began.

"Sell or rent," she added. "I don't mind."

And at last he laughed.

"Well," Jane said to Dorothy, "it's a beginning. I think ... I hope ... I *pray* he's going to propose to her."

"Really?" Dorothy could not have been more delighted if she had truly had Rosa's interests at heart. "But he hasn't a bean."

"He's had a legacy. It's rather dirty, isn't it – Notre Dame."

"That's why we wanted to change. Still, for this news I'd put up with any old view. Oh! To have that girl off our hands at last – not that she isn't the dearest ... once you get to know her." She turned and peered over her shoulder. "Are you sure? I always thought Richard such a sensible young fellow. Indeed, I had rather sort of hoped he and you ... you know?"

"Well, Dorothy!" Jane laughed. "And I'd never have guessed it." The laughter redoubled. "I thought he was proposing to me just now, in fact, but it turned out he was only asking me what I thought Rosa would say if he put the question to her. He doesn't know whether he's on his head or his heels."

The view was now filled with government buildings, all rather cleaner and more imposing than the old cathedral in their midst. "Are you sure he said *legacy?*" Dorothy asked after a while.

"Yes, Mrs Lanyon," Jane replied evenly.

"Why d'you say it like that, dear?"

"Because I think we both know the source of it. It was Luxon Vyvyan, by the way. I misremembered the name."

Dorothy let this glib explanation pass, in the circumstances. "So there was no point in my trying to shelter you," she commented flatly.

"Not much. But I have so many more reasons to ask your forgiveness, Dorothy."

When she volunteered no more, Dorothy said, "I'd like to hear them."

But Jane shook her head. "It doesn't matter now. It was all part of this absurd wild-goose chase – coming to Paris. We hoped to unravel a conspiracy of half-truths and found ourselves getting tangled up in them, instead."

355

"You're not suggesting we leave?" Dorothy asked in alarm. "I have ... er, written to people. I have made engagements with them. Even if our search is ended, I still cannot ... just break it so abruptly."

"By no means!" Jane was emphatic.

"Why, even tonight, I have an engagement to visit the opera to meet a friend of your mother's. An elderly ..."

Jane made her tone even more soothing: "We'll stay as long as we dare – until Mr Lanyon sends us a vial of his tears."

Dorothy laughed at that. "He'd never do anything so romantic." Then she became serious again. "But if you think this is all a mistake ..."

"No!" Jane interrupted. "Not being in Paris. That's not the mistake. Our mistake was to suppose that we might still be able to discover a woman who left here a century ago – in the butterfly minds of all who knew her. Not to mention these ... *thickets* of gentlemen who are all such outward models of rectitude they won't even breathe her name ..."

"How do you know that?" Dorothy asked sharply. "To whom have you been ..."

"It doesn't matter, Dorothy. That's what I said. The search is finished. It was never anything but futile."

"But then we have no reason to stay in Paris," she said bleakly.

"We have the best reason in the world – to enjoy ourselves. If you want something a little worthier than that: We are chaperoning Rosa until her courtship is well enough established to profit by a little separation from her one true love."

Dorothy smiled. "Do I detect a note of jealousy, my dear?"

Jane blushed and stared down into the water. "There's bound to be a little, isn't there? It would be only natural."

"Don't worry, my lamb. Someone will come along."

Jane gave a single dry chuckle. "I can't deny it. I said those very words to dear Rosa, not a week since, and just look what's happened!" She sighed, almost angrily. "But, really, that's what's wrong with it all."

"Wrong with what?"

"*Who* will I marry? *When* will I meet him? How *long* before he asks me? Waiting, waiting, waiting ... Well, we've got three weeks, a month, whatever we like ... in Paris – and no point in watching or waiting for anyone. Three weeks of pure, simple fun!"

She waited for an explosion but none came. "Don't you agree?" she prompted.

Dorothy cleared her throat. "I agree the search has become a little futile, dear. It's funny. I had such a clear picture of how it would go but the minute we got here it all started to dissolve. Even Richard, whom I always considered the most dependable boy. I suppose I can confess it to you now. I asked him to look out a copy of your birth certificate in the Embassy records ..."

"But I was born in Vienna."

"Yes, but there's two months' grace to register. You were registered here – it's all in your father's papers, including the ledger number. Anyway, Richard said there'd be nothing easier. But then he came back and blithely said all those records had been sent to London. Not true, of course, but there he is – he's now been drawn into this web of courteous lies."

"A plague on them then," Jane said stoutly. "I vote we turn our backs on it all and simply content ourselves for the next month or two, eh?"

But Dorothy was not so sure. "I don't think it would be wise," she said judiciously, "for me to spend every hour of every day with you."

"Oh!" Jane sounded disappointed.

"No, dear. At home it would be different, of course. You would not want to get a *reputation*. But there is little fear of that here."

You hope, Jane said to herself.

46 THE SERVANTS AT THE VILLA were as delighted as any at the news of Rosa's engagement to Richard Vyvyan, especially when it became known that he was to buy the property. Being true *citoyens et citoyennes* they were incapable of acting in concert, so Jane became a sort of domestic chamberlain, receiving individual petitions to the new mistress, asking if their present temporary positions might now be confirmed as permanent.

"Keep them dangling," Rosa replied.

The change that came over her was the most startling thing of all. The young girl who had come skipping into the villa and declared herself charmed with simply everything, now developed an eagle's eye for the slightest blemish. Venerable wall silks from the First Empire were suddenly anathema and endless visits were made to Aux Villes de France in the Rue Richelieu in search of something better – something a great deal better.

And that was only one among dozens of little shops and *grands magasins* on which Rosa had seemingly become an overnight authority. A new long-case clock was needed in the entrance hall? Of course, the only possible place was Leroi et Fils at the Palais Royal; however, for the smaller timepiece that was lacking on the mantelshelf in what would be her salon, one would never dream of going anywhere but Wurtel's in the Passage Vivienne. Her new boots were from Meier in the Rue Tronchet, her dresses from Mme Servot in the Boulevart Montmartre, her silks from Au Grand Condé in the Rue de Seine. And her hats? "Aha!" she would say with a knowing smile. "No true Parisienne will tell you that!" When Dorothy was rash enough to give as her opinion that perfumes from Lapin were among the best in the world, Rosa commented that *she* had always heard people speak very highly of the Société Hygénique in the Boulevart des Italiens.

Richard watched it all with an equanimity that could only be called saintly. "It's amazing," he said to Jane one day, after going through her latest batch of bills. "I chose her because I love her and could not help myself. You remember how you tried to warn me she was not the most practical or domestic of females? And I must admit that was a secret qualm of mine, too. Yet look at her now! We could not have been more wrong, could we! She understands, absolutely by instinct, that the sort of business I and my associates will shortly be conducting needs a house like the one she is presently creating here. Such luck! Such luck!"

Yet even he was observed to turn a trifle pale when, after he had remarked that twelve thousand francs seemed a *little* excessive for a marble nymph, even one by Canova, she replied that he was, as always right. "Shopkeepers in this city are utter bloodsuckers," she said. "We must resist their extortions in every way. I think I shall start making tiny, tiny excursions, two or three days at a time, you know, to Lyons, Metz, Rouen, Strasbourg ..."

Jane, who had encouraged this new-found domestic passion in its early days, soon after it became clear Rosa had *carte blanche* with Richard's legacy, at last gave up. Dorothy declared she would never have believed it. Jane, remembering how Angelica and Jemima had changed after their betrothals, said she would not have believed the scale of the change. "I'm sure I shall never go mad like that," she added. "If a clock keeps good time, why bother to change it – just because you don't like the expression on the face of the full moon! No, to me a chair is a chair and a table's a table, and that's that."

All the same, she enjoyed her shopping expeditions with Rosa ... the vicarious pleasure of spending someone else's money ... the pampering civilities of the tradespeople ... the feeling of importance it induced. She became familiar with a new Paris during those weeks, one that had never impinged on her childhood here. But the novelty palled in the end; her only lasting impression was of the revolting rubbish that was offered for sale, through which poor Rosa had to wade in search of something tasteful.

Then, with Banks to chaperone her, she renewed her acquaintance with the more permanent city. She sought out old friends of her mother's, some of whom were pleased to see her – and, to be sure, uncomfortably amazed at her resemblance; others, for whatever reason, were less welcoming. But one had to be charitable; it was anything up to twenty years ago for them; over such a span it is surely harder to remember one's pleasure than to recall the heirlooms that were sold to pay for it.

Only one of her school friends was still in Paris. In fact, it had not been a school – just a few daughters of friends who shared her governess. This particular classmate, a girl called Jeanne, was the only one apart from Jane who remained unmarried. She was now an almoner at a religious hospital in Billancourt, on the banks of the Seine. They met a couple of times and tried to reestablish the old bonhomie but with only moderate success; the last of Jane's cards to her received no reply, and that was the end of that.

"Actually," she told Banks, "I find I enjoy being alone most of all. I am not indifferent to company but I find I don't need it. Perhaps I shall remain a spinster by choice. What d'you think?"

Banks said it was "a good enough arrangement to be going on with – so long as it's strictly adhered to."

Together they wandered around Père Lachaise, the Louvre, the Jardin des Plantes, the Bois de Boulogne, the poky little streets of Montmartre, the city's own little village ... and in general did everything that adds up to "seeing Paris." Sometimes Dorothy accompanied them but more often not. In the early days, she was careful to provide explanations for her absence ... she was still meeting the odd friend of La Vivie with whom she had made appointments it would be discourteous to break ... then those friends recommended her to others ... and so on. But in time she abandoned these pretences and merely said she was "going shopping," or "meeting a lady I ran across at Galignani's Reading Rooms." In reality she continued to see the Chevalier and M de Guy several times a week. De Guy, a frequent visitor to the villa, was never anything but formal and correct with Rosa, who thus understood that their conversation at Ville d'Avray had never occurred.

At first Dorothy's puritan soul was horrified at what she had let happen – as if one lover were not bad enough. She tossed coins and drew straws and raced raindrops called "de Guy" and "Chevalier" down the window panes, to see which she would give up. But finally she persuaded herself that infidelity was infidelity and did not grow better or worse by the tally. Indeed, the very fact of having two lovers simultaneously only emphasized that she was taking neither of them very seriously. Her dewy-eyed adoration of the Chevalier had not survived the visit to the opera, when, despite his living up to his every promise, he had, in so doing, revealed himself for what he was: a grand master of what he frankly called *l'artifice d'amour.*

The two men soon knew of each other's involvement with her; not that they spoke of it – and Dorothy certainly did not tell them! – but they had shared mistresses before and swiftly recognized each other's style in *bonnes bouches.* De Guy always gave little ornaments in amber from Schiedel's in the Boulevart de Sébastopol; the Chevalier favoured silver trinkets from J. Welse In the Rue de l'Arbre-Sec. They, too, were content to know she was not falling singlemindedly in love with either.

The Chevalier often pressed Dorothy for an introduction to Jane, at which Dorothy equally often demurred. In wounded tones, he pointed out that a Frenchman's sense of honour was identical to that of an English gentleman, and that an unmarried lady of good class and breeding would be inviolate with both species "even for a year on the island of Robinson Crusoe." Dorothy had no doubt of it, but that was not her principal worry. Eventually he won by sheer persistence – and also because de Guy's little spell of leave would soon be up and they desired to make the most of what remained.

The Chevalier was therefore invited to tea at the villa, where he made arrangements to take Jane to the Louvre the following morning. It was a revelation to her. If someone had told her that she would find herself able to stand for full twenty minutes before a painting, however dramatic, showing the crew of a shipwreck clinging to a raft that prolonged their miserable lives by a few hours or days, she would simply have laughed. If that same informant had told her she would come away from it understanding that such a painting could be one of the greatest revolutionary declarations in history *and* an artistic revolution in its own right, being one of the great sources of the fire and thunder etcetera etcetera ... she would have dismissed him as a madman.

"It just shows, doesn't it," she said. "We never know which minute will be our last. D'you suppose those sailors, as they climbed into their hammocks before the wreck happened, thought to themselves, 'I wonder if this is the last time I'll ever be doing this?' I often think that, don't you?"

"It's rather a morbid notion for such a charming young lady," he chided with a smile, and led her to the next great revolutionary work.

He was like that all morning. Anything she said that did not exactly accord with his rather strict notion of a well brought up young lady met with a sharp, though smiling, remonstrance. At first she was annoyed. But then it struck her that perhaps he was trying to conform to some promise that Dorothy had extracted from him – that his behaviour with her would be impeccable down to the smallest detail. Therefore when she, for her part, failed to conform to his notion of gentility, even in the smallest detail, he had to set her right.

He took her to luncheon at the Rocher de Cancale, opposite Philippe's in the Rue Montorgeuil, where he continued to play the part of the perfect gentleman to the last spoonful of sorbet. After that it was a concert at the Conservatoire, tea at the Palais Royal, and then home. At various moments during that excessively tedious day, Jane had considered the possibility of a little gentle teasing; in the end, she found it more interesting to wonder what could possibly drive such a man to behave as he did. The situation was bizarre, to say the least.

He had been her mother's lover. She, Jane, resembled her to an astonishing degree. So what were the thoughts that passed through his mind as he sat opposite her at table, strolled with her down a boulevart, watched her response to one of his favourite paintings? Did he derive some strange satisfaction from contrasting the lover's abandon with the daughter's purity? Did licentious memories acquire some new and exquisite gloss in the serene light of her innocence?

Only once did the mask slip – and then by the merest fraction. She made some remark to the effect that if she lived in Paris, she wouldn't keep a chef at all but simply dine out at the Rocher de Cancale all the time. He smiled his superior smile and told her that the secret of the true gourmet was to keep moving on before the *table d'hôte* grew wearingly familiar. A moment or two later, apropos nothing it seemed, he asked how much longer Mrs Lanyon intended to stay in Paris. The question was barely uttered when she saw a tiny panic in his eyes as he realized that the *apropos* was all too plain to her. After that he was even more careful than before.

That night, in the minutes before sleep, she imagined the many conversations she might have had with him – all beginning with, "Now see here, Chevalier, we both know my mother was your mistress, so let's stop all this pretence, eh? What I want to know is ..."

Unfortunately, almost everything she wanted to know turned out to be unutterably trivial when answered – for she imagined his answers, too, in many variations. When he told her that La Vivie had only one, only three, at least half a dozen, lovers a day, a week, a month ... what did it matter? What did any of those answers mean, here, now, to her daughter – even though that daughter lay in the very bed where those encounters presumably took place? And who cared that it was always – or never – La Vivie who initiated the process? Jane began to realize that even if the Recording Angel took her through every second of that unimaginable life, the insight to explain it to her own satisfaction would still be lacking.

That in itself was a discovery – perhaps a grand discovery – perhaps worth coming all this way to achieve.

Imperceptibly, then, her mind slipped away from the dry catalogue of questions she might have asked the Chevalier to a much more pleasant fantasy about the situation to which those questions, in turn, might have led. In this new mental playlet, the Chevalier brought her back to his house (to show her some more paintings, of course) and there his memories of passionate hours with La Vivie overwhelmed him and he forgot himself at last. Their eyes dwelled in each other's for one long, incandescent moment ... their hands touched ... their knees trembled ... and then, when the physical pictures gave out, she was whirled off into a lilac storm of delicate sensations where his voice and his touch became like threads of shimmering sweetness, stretching all through her in a golden skein.

To her surprise, it was as pleasant as when she pictured Daniel in that role. Perhaps it was worth coming all this way to learn that, too?

*　　*　　*

One evening toward the end of May, Dorothy's friend the Cardinal failed to pay his customary visit. She had spent each month of her married life watching anxiously for just such a failure, so she was alert to it within a day rather than a week. She went straight to the Chevalier with the news. He embraced her warmly, for the best part of an hour, knowing it was their last time, and told her that this was the other reason why a young *un*married lady was always safe with a gentleman. Dorothy responded that it might be possible for her to stay on in Paris; he replied that in that case it *might* be possible for them to meet, as old friends ought to meet – from time to time. The following morning a small packet was delivered to the villa; it contained a silver napkin ring; in the cartouche was engraved a single letter *L;* the space for the initial of the Christian name was a blank.

That evening, when her friend de Guy *did* pay his customary visit, she told him, too. He embraced her warmly, for the best part of the night, knowing it was their last time, and told her that until this news he would have said it was a thousand pities she was already married. "But now?" she asked. "Only nine hundred and ninety-nine," he replied. The following day he was sent on a diplomatic mission to the court of the Kaiser. He had argued most strenuously against it, he assured her in the note that accompanied his final gift of amber, but "we *all* have our duty."

*　　*　　*

"Duty calls, I fear," Dorothy told Jane one morning toward the end of May. "I have neglected my poor dear Jesse far too long."

Jane, who was surprised the call had not come four weeks earlier, set Banks to packing at once. There was a maudlin moment or two on their final evening, especially when Jane realized she was saying farewell for ever to this childhood home; but it soon passed. The childhood she remembered no longer found its shrine there, nor even in the city of Paris at large. Now and forever it was hid in that dateless summer's day of her memory, where neither alarm nor discovery could mar its serenity; and that was the best place of all.

There were tearful farewells at the Embarcadère du Nord, promises to write often, visit often, remember one another always. The French habit of penning the crowds

361

back until about five seconds before the train departs gave them a chance to repeat these promises many times. But there were, in fact, no crowds for that particular boat train, so the Chevalier's carriage was able to draw well within the concourse. He did not alight, and nor did Dorothy go to him, but at the last, as they filed through the opened barricade, she turned and saw a flash of grey behind the carriage window, as he took off his hat and lowered it with ceremonial gravity. She bowed lightly in his direction – and that, for all she knew, was the last of their intercourse.

The Channel was as smooth as glass, with not even the faintest swell to disturb the most delicate stomach. But "delicate" hardly seemed to be the word for Dorothy's stomach these days. She started the voyage with one of the heartiest luncheons Jane had ever seen her eat – including pickled walnuts and a large helping of sourkrout with spicy German sausage. When Jane remarked on it, Dorothy said that Paris had given her a taste for something new.

Afterward they spread their parasols and promenaded round the deck.

"We came with nine trunks and we're going with twenty-three," Jane commented.

"I have bought lots of things for Jesse, remember," Dorothy replied.

Jane did not point out that those "lots" had filled only two of the smaller trunks.

"And also things for our home," Dorothy added. "We shall have one of the most *è la mode* homes, and I one of the most stylish husbands, in the whole of Cornwall."

"And when is the wedding to be?"

Dorothy looked at her askance. "What may you mean by that, my dear?"

Jane laughed. "You were talking like Angelica and Jemima – and Rosa before she got the bit between her teeth."

Dorothy sighed. "I wonder how long that marriage will last! It's not a question one asks very often, is it – but *that* one ...!"

"They've made their bed, as Banks says. Now they must lie in it. Richard only has himself to blame. He could have chosen me."

"You're really regretting that now, aren't you."

"Of course not! I'm only joking. I'd never have married Richard – and I said as much, if you recall, before there was any question of his choosing Rosa. No, if they're happy, I shan't cavil, just because she's mad and he's a fool."

"Who are you considering at present, then – dare I ask?"

"If you do, I shall throw you overboard. I don't even want to think about it. If you press for an answer, I'll just say I'm not going to marry anybody – ever!"

She expected a small explosion from Dorothy over this outburst, but there was none. Instead, Dorothy's pace faltered to a stop and she turned to lean upon the rail. Jane took a step or two back and joined her. For a while they stared at the mirrored sea in contented silence; then Jane became aware of a certain tension in the air. She drew breath to make some trivial remark but Dorothy got in first: "Funny you should put it like that," she said pensively, "asking me when the wedding will be. In a curious way, I feel it's going to be like a new beginning."

"We have been away a good long time," Jane agreed.

"It's more than that."

There was a slight tremor in her voice. Looking out of the corner of her eye, Jane saw that the woman was shivering, although the day was warm. She realized then that if she did not allow her to say what was on her mind, this sort of heavy-sighing-and-hinting conversation would last from here to Penzance. "Starting with a new honeymoon?" she suggested.

"What may you mean by that?" Dorothy asked sharply.

"I think it had *better* start that way, don't you?" Jane replied evenly.

"I can't imagine what you're talking about."

Jane closed her eyes and shook her head gently. "Please?" she said. "I am no longer a child."

"Worse and worse!" Dorothy murmured. "I hope you're not implying you've been ..." She could not finish the sentence.

Jane chuckled. "I believe my response to your earlier question ought to set your mind at rest on *that* score."

Dorothy was silent a long while. "I've been such a fool," she said at last.

"I don't agree," Jane replied at once.

"What do you know about it?"

"Not as much as I hope you're going to tell me."

"I shall confess it all. It is the only way."

Jane waited for her to fulfill the promise.

"I'll simply throw myself on his mercy."

Suddenly all Jane's faculties came alive. "*His* mercy? I hope you mean God's and not Uncle Jesse's?"

"It is my duty. It would be the duty of any wife."

"Dorothy, you must be mad!"

"Hoity toity, miss! Kindly remember who ..."

"You'll ruin his life. Can't you see it? You'll destroy his peace of mind for ever." Dorothy clutched at the straw. "D'you think so?"

"I was never more sure of anything in ..."

"But what about me? What about my peace of mind? How can I face him, day after day, with that sin unconfessed between us? And unforgiven, too?"

It would never have occurred to Jane to confess such an infidelity; therefore she had no ready answer. She replied on the spur of the moment: "Because there are some sins you confess and some you forgive, but this isn't either of those."

"How nice! I'd like to know what else one may do with a sin."

"What's the word?" Jane clenched her fists and hit the rail. "You know, when you work to make it better ... *expiate!* That's the word. If this is a sin – and only God could tell you that – then it's the kind you expiate in silent service. I mean, in *love.*"

Her self-assurance left Dorothy speechless for a moment. Then the seed of an almost unthinkable transformation began to germinate within her. "Of course it's a sin," she murmured at length. "How can you suggest it might not be?"

"Why did you do it?" Jane asked equally quietly.

"I don't know" The anguish sounded highly conventional. "I wish I never had."

"Why did you do it?" Jane repeated in the same monotone.

"Because!"

"Why did you do it?"

"Don't keep saying that!"

"Why did you do it? I shall go on asking until you give me a proper answer." She laughed despite herself. "It's like putting the same plate of uneaten greens back in front of a recalcitrant child!"

It allowed Dorothy to laugh, too. "Do you really think I'm behaving like a child?" She thought for a while and then went on, "I know why I allowed it to happen the first time – with the Chevalier. It was because ... No! It's no good. I really cannot discuss this – with you of all people."

"Why not me of all people?"

"I seem to hear your father's voice in my ear – telling me that the purity and innocence of a young girl are ..."

"Dorothy! I really will throw you overboard – and I'm not joking."

Dorothy stared at her in something close to real fear. Her tone when she next spoke was almost pleading. "But I should be telling you things that I've never told another living soul, not even my nearest and dearest married friend."

Jane shrugged. "Whoever she may be, she's not here. And I am."

Dorothy drew a deep breath and closed her eyes, as if that would somehow reduce her difficulties. Even then she made several false starts. "When I first married Jesse ... when he explained what we ... You know what a wonderful sense of humour he has? I thought it was another of his jests. I mean ... what I really mean is that my parents told me nothing. Anyway, it was awful. When we returned from our honeymoon there was a little circle of ladies over in Hayle at that time, all of us newly married, and they'd formed a whist club and they asked me to join. Actually, all they wanted to do, really, was talk about the pleasure of ... you know" – she swallowed heavily – "being in bed with their husbands."

"There!" Jane said, as if Dorothy had at last drawn a splinter from her finger.

"I couldn't understand it." Dorothy began to gabble now she had breasted the summit and reached the downhill run. "I thought they were making it up – because, of course, when their attention turned to me, that's precisely what I used to do."

"But now?"

Dorothy smiled at the sea. "Now I know it was ... they were so overwhelmed by it ... I mean, you know how women love to talk? It's our way of coping with things." She turned to Jane and smiled a dreamy, faraway smile. "Oh, my dear, I hope you have the fortune to marry a husband like ... some of theirs."

Jane knew she had other originals in mind but all she did was smile.

Hesitantly Dorothy touched her arm. "How have you become so wise and knowing? You haven't ..."

Jane shook her head. Then, judging her moment, she asked, "Meanwhile, how do we explain a few hundredweights of amber and silver?"

Dorothy nodded ruefully but offered no answer.

"I think – a little letter to Rosa ... reminding her how grateful she was to you ... how she rather overdid it, perhaps?"

Dorothy pulled a face. "It means letting one more person in on my shameful secret." She saw Jane's smile and added, "You mean ... she, too?"

"I'm afraid so."

"And Banks?" Dorothy was suddenly wide-awake in alarm.

"Safest of all with her."

"Even so – just the thought that she knows. How shall I ever be able to look her in the face again?"

Jane allowed a short silence before she went on, "What I'd really like to talk about, Dorothy, is the sort of life I wish to lead when we're home again."

"Indeed?" Dorothy asked nervously. "I'm afraid we shan't enjoy anything like the freedom we've just ..."

"I wish to sell Montpelier ..." Jane interrupted.

"Sell Mont...!"

"And buy a much smaller property somewhere. You see, I've decided I don't really wish to marry anyone. Not for the moment."

"But Jane, dear ..."

"Please just hear me out."

Dorothy fell silent, but it was not Jane's words that achieved this near-miracle – after such an astonishing declaration – it was the serene, almost seraphic, look on her face as she marshalled her thoughts. "I suppose it began," Jane said at last, "on the evening we arrived in Cornwall, as we drove along that straight road by Praa, and Mrs Moore overtook us in her smart little fly and put that absurd trumpet to her lips – you know how she does."

Dorothy's eyes did a quick, skyward lift.

"She looked like burnished copper in the setting sun. I'll never forget that image of her." Her eyes suddenly pleaded with Dorothy to understand, for she knew she would never be able to convey the power of it all. "Isn't it amazing what a hold a sudden image like that can exercise! Whenever somebody paints a picture for me of the meek and modest little Angel-in-the-Home sort of woman, I also see Mrs Moore as she was on that evening."

"She has much to answer for," Dorothy could not help saying.

"I'm afraid you're right. That image of her certainly misled me for a long time – because her way seemed to offer the only possible alternative for me. I must have driven poor Banks to distraction with my ridiculous schemes for little ventures I could start, è la Moore!"

"You did what?"

"Private hotels, legal-copying services, small schools ..." Jane listed half a dozen in a voice that would out-scorn any echo Dorothy might attempt. "You see, that's all I could think of – something commercial."

Dorothy shuddered at the very word. "So what is it to be instead?"

"I don't know. At least, I'm not sure. But I know what I'd like to try for a year or so." She stared uncertainly at her guardian, who responded with: "I'd better hear the worst, I suppose."

"It came to me about two weeks ago when I was walking through the Jardin des Plantes with Richard, listening to him trying not to complain about Rosa's bills and telling me what a marvel she was. Well, I had actually heard it all before. So I started looking at the botanical beds all around me ... there you are, you see. Botanical beds! You can't even call them flower beds. Anyway, it suddenly struck me that that ... military style was utterly, utterly wrong for a garden. So what I want to do is take about forty acres of Cornwall, somewhere, I don't know where, and turn them into *my* idea of a garden. Even if it takes me all my life."

Dorothy, prepared by Jane's preamble to hear something dreadful, was rather taken aback at this ... this ... what could one call it? Her worst objection, on the spur of the moment, was, "Don't you think it's perhaps a little ... *eccentric?*"

Jane jabbed her in the arm, harder than she intended, though it helped make her point. "And if I marry at all, Dorothy, it'll be to a man who would neither say that nor even think it. Because I don't believe it's in the least *bit* eccentric."

"What is your idea of a garden?" Now that the first shock of it was dwindling, Dorothy found herself irresistibly drawn on by the girl's enthusiasm.

"I don't know. I want water and rocks and ... profusion! And ... swirly things! And light and shadow. And sudden bends and surprises. And vistas. And secret corners. I don't know! But I will know it the moment I see it. I want to do for gardens what Géricault did for French painting – there!"

Dorothy's jaw dropped.

Jane stared back in surprise. "Is it so shocking?" she asked.

"No, not that. But what you said about Géricault. Did ... he ...?"

"The Chevalier?" Jane nodded. *"The Raft of the Medusa* – the great revolutionary statement of ..."

Dorothy's nostrils flared. "The unspeakable swine!" she cried. A moment later she was seized by a further horrible thought. "And afterwards, did he take you ... he didn't take you to a restaurant in the ... tskoh! what was it called?"

"In the Rue Montorgeuil."

"Yes!" Dorothy spat out the word. "Oh, the traitor!" Then, sick with apprehension, she put the final question. "And after that ... did he ... did you ...?"

"We went to a concert at the Conservatoire and tea in the Palais Royal and home. The dullest day since we left Cornwall."

"Never mind dull!" Dorothy relaxed a little.

"He just seemed to want to carry me round like some little marble angel under a glass dome all day."

And at last, after a relieved and thoughtful silence, Dorothy pronounced a sentiment upon which they could both heartily agree: "One thing I shall never understand," she said. "And that is *men.*"

47 THE TWO WOMEN arrived in London on the evening of the 30th of May, which was a Thursday. The following morning there was nothing to prevent them from going straight to Paddington to catch the Penzance train. But Jane took a sudden, sentimental notion to time her return to Cornwall exactly one year to the day after she and her father had first arrived. Knowing that Dorothy, in her present state of anxiety, would hardly consent to a delay on such frivolous grounds, she invented a peculiar form of travel sickness – "more of a lassitude, really" – induced by the endless counting of trunks and boxes, the banging of carriage doors, the

queasiness of a supernaturally calm sea, the mewing of gulls ... and anything else she could think of.

It began to pass of its own accord about an hour after the departure of the Penzance train, which did, however, carry eighteen items of their luggage as well as letters to Uncle Jesse and Mrs Tresidder, giving notice of their intended return on the morrow. Jane then declared that she thought some fresh air might clear her distemper – and why not kill two birds with one stone by paying a visit to Kew Gardens? Which is how they passed the remainder of that wasted Friday.

Over luncheon in the Orangery, Jane told Dorothy she would not go back into mourning. Instead of expostulating, Dorothy asked if she remembered the black ballgown she had worn at Christmas.

"The one my mother had made on the death of Balzac?"

Dorothy nodded. "The seventeenth of August, eighteen-fifty."

Jane chuckled. "How on earth d'you know that?"

"She wore it on the nineteenth, and on that same evening she met your ... she met Wilfrid Hervey for the first time. He records it in his diary. You shall read it when we return. It is one of the most beautiful things I ever saw. Of course, he had no idea than that she would one day accept his proposal, so it is full of despair. A man of fifty-nine, overwhelmed with love for the very first time in his life ... your mother was the most ethereally beautiful creature he had ever seen. He just poured his heart out onto the page."

Jane swallowed heavily. "One would never have believed so much ardour was there within him."

"And yet," Dorothy concluded, "on the very next page he records in the most matter-of-fact way that Balzac wore eight rings, one on each finger, which were given to him by his mistresses. And he wonders if that is not the secret of happiness – to have a wife who's an angel and eight happy mistresses." She sighed. "Shall we ever fathom them?"

Saturday the 1st of June was so *un*special that Jane's conscience began to prick her: How unfeeling she had been ... what a dreadful ordeal Dorothy was about to face ... to have made it worse, even by a single day, was unforgivable. Indeed, she was now so especially kind and thoughtful toward her guardian that Dorothy had to reprove her for it. "You will give it all away at once if you are not your usual surly, wayward self, my dear."

"I am never surly," Jane protested.

"Try!" Dorothy urged drily. "Indeed, try anything but this winsome tenderness."

The nearer they drew to Cornwall, the greater the excitement Jane felt building up within her. Her dream of taking a large slice of the Cornish landscape and reshaping it after some barely glimpsed vision in her mind had really seized her now. Until she had spoken it aloud to Dorothy it had been one of those myriad pleasing little daydreams that flit through the mind but never outgrow it. Thus she had often promised herself that "one day" she would see the Pyramids ... the Taj Mahal ... icebergs taller than a ship ... the inside of a Cornish tin mine ... wolves in the snow ... a myriad sights and experiences lay out there, just waiting their moment. In the same spirit she had often resolved that "soon" she would truly master the piano, learn

367

German, collect a complete herbarium of all the plants to be found on a single Cornish headland ...

The pleasure of these promises and resolutions was that the mere making of them seemed, in some curious way, to leave them already half-completed – as if the difficult preparatory work were now over and all that remained was to get on and complete the project. Her landscape-garden might have lodged forever in that category had she not nailed the colour of it so emphatically to her mast when Dorothy had pressed her for an alternative to the serious business of husband-catching. But now, as always happens when a new enthusiasm takes one over, everything she heard and saw became grist to the mill of her scheme.

She kept her eyes glued to the windows for most of the journey. Small, haphazard details of the landscape suggested a score of new ideas to her – a lacy canopy of branches hanging over an outcrop of boulders ... a tumbling, tossing, restless little gorge, almost certainly man-made – an ancient quarry, perhaps ... a rush-girt stream meandering over a marshy meadow ...

At Kew yesterday Dorothy had ridiculed her for not knowing the names of all the plants; and it was true that the visit had brought home her ignorance of botanical Latin in a most depressing way. But now these little glimpses of England helped her realize that in *her* kind of gardening the most important thing was to know what effect you wanted. Then you could easily go out and find the plants to produce it. In time, to be sure, it would work both ways. While swotting up about one plant she'd discover half a dozen others; and then she'd say to herself, "I know where that would fit perfectly." And so, bit by bit, and with many a disappointment, no doubt, it would all come together – given her health and strength over the next forty years.

"I suppose I ought to learn about blasting powder and rock boring and things like that," she said aloud at the conclusion of one especially ambitious daydream.

Dorothy merely looked at her and shook her head. As they crossed the Tamar into Cornwall – almost as if it were some kind of symbolic welcome – they passed through a stray summer shower, one of those small, forlornly weeping clouds that wanders disconsolate over the countryside looking for a properly organized rain cluster to join. "That's Cornwall!" Dorothy said.

Jane nodded and rubbed her hands with pleasure. "Home."

"Really?"

"It's beginning to feel like it. We've proved that Paris *isn't*. And it's months since I've even thought of Leeds."

*   *   *

Uncle Jesse was waiting for them on the platform at Penzance, with a smile that almost split his face in two. "My dears! My very dear dears!" he cried, hugging them by turns and beside himself with joy. It was too much for Dorothy, who burst into tears, though that only pleased him the more.

"Well, well, well!" He took out a large kerchief and blew his nose like a trombone. "You must be exhausted. Such a journey. Now why don't the pair of you stroll up the platform and leave me to count off your boxes?"

368

Dorothy grasped his arm and said nothing would part them now.

Jane laughed and said, "I'll be back in half a shake. There's a small ritual that must be observed."

When her meaning had sunk in, Dorothy called after her: "Jane! No!"

"Don't *worry!*" Jane called over her shoulder as she pressed on toward the arch that led out onto the quays.

With every step of the way she had to keep reminding herself that it was only a year ... only a year ... only a year. And still it seemed hardly believable. As she went under the archway, where the hot breeze of that summer evening assailed her with the reek of tar, coal gas, and rotting fish, it was so powerfully reminiscent that for a moment she could not go on. Half fearfully – prepared, even, to see the shades of herself and Miss Wilkinson chatting innocently in the sunshine – she took the last few steps and, nervously, spied around the brickwork.

The sight that met her eyes was, in a way, just as incredible as her wildest fancy: Standing almost where she had stood, leaning lightly against the pillar of the arch, talking to one of the porters, was Vosper Scawen. Her movement attracted his attention. He turned, smiled, and said in the calmest voice, as if she had only been gone a week or so, "Hello, Jane. Welcome back."

"Vosper!" She skipped the pace or two that separated them and would have thrown her arms about him if he had not put out both his hands and grasped hers, shaking them warmly. And now he was laughing at the success of his little surprise.

"But how did you know?" she asked him several times.

All he would say was, "Aha!" He pointed toward Veryan, who was waiting with her carriage on the far side of the forecourt.

"But I must tell the Lanyons." She turned toward the arch.

He, however, kept a hold on her right arm. "Lanyon knows. It's all right. And here's the party complete. Miss Banks, you're very welcome home." He gave a light bow, not at all mocking.

She responded with a cheerful little curtsey. "You're a welcome sight, too, Mr Scawen, if I may say so, sir."

Jane thought he was carrying gallantry a little far, however, when, after handing her into the carriage, he performed the same service for the maid. But Banks had no sooner got her face inside than she withdrew it again and fanned it with her hand. "'Tis like a bakeoven in there. I'll just so well travel outside with Veryan if you mind, Miss Hervey?"

Jane neither assented to the arrangement nor forbade it.

Vosper climbed in, sat opposite her, and smiled. "Well!" he said.

"Well!" she replied.

There was a moment of unexpected shyness. "And you look it," he went on. "It's nice to see such colour in your cheeks again. Paris must have suited you."

"You could have come over," she answered reproachfully. "Even for a week."

He nodded but said nothing, watching her carefully as if waiting for more.

"Anyway, I came back," she added. "For good now. Good or ill. Paris is over and done with."

He smiled with satisfaction.

369

"How did you know?" she asked.

He pursed his lips diffidently. "I'm afraid I had to go through all your father's papers – the task that defeated poor Dorothy Lanyon."

"And it's all there? My accidental meeting with ... my ghastly ..."

"Everything," he told her.

"How did he describe *her?*"

"Do you really want to know?"

She stared out of the window a moment. They were taking the bend down onto Penzance Green already. Her father's words at that precise spot, precisely a year ago, came back to her: "The sooner you're safely married, the better!" She smiled at Vosper. "I suppose not," she said. "Funny – you said the same about Paris. Did I really want to know? And in a way you were right about that, too, my dear."

"Only in a way?" he asked with playful belligerence.

But she continued in her serious vein. "It's true I learned all the facts, or enough to go on with. But I'm no nearer to really understanding her. The most important thing I discovered, I suppose, is the pointlessness of it all."

His expression was a blend of surprise and pleasure. "And Mrs Lanyon? Has it changed her at all?"

Jane chuckled. "You'll hardly recognize her as the same woman, Vosper."

He nodded thoughtfully. "I believe it."

"Why d'you say it like that?"

"I'm sorry." He smiled rapidly. "I meant nothing in particular by it."

But she felt she was onto something. "You did," she accused.

He heaved a weary sigh. "I spoke hastily, that's all. Listen, one day next week I'm going over to ..."

"No, don't change the subject. It doesn't matter a fig whether you spoke hastily or after a lifetime's reflection – you meant something by it. Something to do with me."

He pushed himself back into his seat – the gesture of a trapped animal. "What did you think I meant?" he asked.

"I don't know. You were implying that Dorothy would only need to spend s few weeks with me and of course she'd come back completely changed."

His shrug implied that he could not deny it. After a silence he said, "I suppose I'd better say it all."

"Yes."

"Despite the risk."

Jane merely stared at him and waited.

"I watched your father trying to break your spirit, poor man. He went through agonies, you know – not so much at the thought of the suffering he was causing you, though he was affected by that, too. But far worse was a nagging conviction that you were actually in the right."

"This is all in his diaries?" Jane asked.

"There's page after page of argument, proving in a dozen ways that he was right and you were wrong. But at the end of it all he cannot shake that suspicion that it was the other way around. Dorothy Lanyon was subtler, I suppose. I mean, she tried to work on you in subtler ways. Feminine ways. But she has come off worse, too. No?"

370

She shook her head. "I honestly can't think what you mean, Vosper. If Dorothy ..."

"Let me put it this way, then: When you and she left for Paris, she was a woman of extremely firm views on ... all sorts of matters. Don't you agree?"

Jane nodded warily.

"And so were you. And those firm views did not always precisely coincide?"

Another nod, even more wary.

"And have *you* changed at all? Have you changed as much as you say Dorothy Lanyon has, for instance?"

Now it was Jane who wriggled back in her seat. "Yes," she said defiantly.

"Careful now," he warned. "Are you saying you're a different person? Or are you essentially the same person but with a much clearer idea of what you want to do?"

There was no more upholstery left to squirm into. "I can't see where all this is leading, anyway," she answered tetchily. "Let's talk of something else."

"Yes," he agreed eagerly. "If you remember, I didn't want to talk about it at all. So" – he rubbed his hands as if the evening were chill – "what *are* you going to do?"

"Nothing," she snapped.

"What, just ... carry on as before?"

"Yes!"

"Living at Montpelier?"

"Yes!"

"Shopping excursions with Banks? At Homes? Visits to Swanpool?"

"Yes! Yes! Why d'you keep on so?"

"Good," he said enthusiastically.

After a silence she added, "I'm glad you think so. I don't see what's particularly good about it."

"At least it's something you've had lots of practice at."

She turned and stared out of the window. "Sometimes," she told him coldly, "you can be most aggravating."

He kept his eyes on her; she, knowing that, refused to look at him. At last he directed his gaze toward the window; then she turned to him. "Oh dear, Vosper, I didn't want this to happen at all."

"Nor I," he replied mildly.

After a pause she went on, "I might slightly alter the gardens at Montpelier."

He nodded. "Some of those beds have been there a long time."

"In fact, I might alter them quite a bit."

"Even the most trivial-seeming change can transform a place," he told her. "About ten years ago, when Lady Nina Brookes was still alive, Hamill Oliver talked her into setting up an old Cornish menhir on her front lawn. And you'd never believe ..."

"Or I might not," Jane cut in. "I mean, it might be better to start on some completely virgin bit of land."

"She blew it up a year or so later, though. Did a colossal amount of damage."

"Blew it up?" Jane echoed, suddenly interested.

"Yes. For no reason at all. It took years to settle all the claims."

"What ... with her own hands? I mean, she just went out and bought some blasting powder and ..."

"No, no. She hired three drunken louts from Praze, unemployed miners."

"Oh." Jane was momentarily disappointed. Then she brightened again. "Still, I suppose if she'd wanted to learn how to do it properly, they'd have taught her?"

"Not that gang! Look at the mess they made of it themselves. No, she'd have done best to take a proper course in blasting at the School of Mines."

"The School of Mines," Jane echoed thoughtfully. "Yes, of course." She smiled at him then and all her anger was forgotten. "What were you going to say, just when we were leaving Penzance? Something about next week?"

"Oh yes. I'm going over to Falmouth and I thought you might like to come with me. It's legal business on my part, but I don't imagine you'll be bored."

His smile promised so much more. "Come on, then," she urged. "I can see you're dying to tell me."

"Officially I'm to take a deposition from a witness – the only witness in a case of slander. It's one of those stupid affairs in which, if only people would get down off their high horses, it could all be settled with a handshake and a round or two of drinks. So, although I'm going, as I say, to take this witness's deposition, I'm actually hoping to persuade him that his memory is nothing like as clear as he now supposes."

"Who's insulted whom?" Jane asked. "You seem to be implying I'd know them, or one of them. Is it Mrs Moore?"

He laughed at the thought. "No. It's the witness who'll interest you. His name ... well, he lives in Greenbank."

Jane turned suddenly pale. The smile remained on Vosper's lips but it deserted his eyes entirely. "Roger Moynihan," he said.

"Oh, him!" Jane swallowed and breathed again. "I don't actually ... I mean, I've never met him."

"But you know Mrs Moynihan, I think?"

Jane frowned. "Did she tell you so?"

"I've never set eyes on her – on either of them. But I put two and two together, you know. Specifically, your father's diaries and a recent wedding announcement in the *Falmouth Packet*. So ... will you come along? Especially now that you know it's *only* Mr Moynihan?"

She heard the sadness in his voice and flinched from it, forcing herself to be bright again. "Of course I shall. I've a crow of my own to pluck with Mrs M." She tied a mental knot in a mental handkerchief to remind her to spend a pleasant hour or two planning that woman's discomfiture for the trick she had played on de Guy. "Anyway," she said, returning to an earlier theme, "you haven't told me what you think of my idea."

"Which idea was that?" he asked uncertainly.

"The one I was telling you about. To take forty or fifty acres of Cornish landscape and turn it into a garden of wonders"

"Oh *that* idea!" he said, as if it had merely slipped his mind. Then he laughed.

"Is that all you can say?" she asked in a wounded tone.

"It may surprise you to hear it, Jane, but you didn't actually tell me."

"I most certainly did."

"You mentioned moving the odd flower bed at Montpelier."

"Well ... all right. But I as good as told you. So what do you think of it?"

"On the spur of the moment?"

She nodded and held her breath.

"It all depends," he replied. "I mean, what particular bit of Cornwall do you have in mind?"

Her face relaxed into a cherubic grin. And, for once, Vosper Scawen, who prided himself that he understood Jane Hervey better than any other living soul, man or woman – and certainly better than she understood herself – for once – had no idea what lay behind that happy smile.

48 Mrs Moynihan led Jane from room to room in her new little empire. "Of course, Roger won't let me *touch* his studio," she explained after opening the door to give Jane a brief glimpse of what looked like the aftermath of a storm. What she meant was, *but just look at everything else!* And well she might, for nothing was out of place; not a speck of dust could Jane discover. Every fringe on every rug was combed in parallel regiments; each pleat in the lace curtains was balanced by its mirror twin. "It's beautiful," Jane said. "And you keep it looking so immaculate."

"Well enough," Mrs Moynihan said. "If I had known you were coming, I'd have made a little extra effort."

Jane laughed and challenged her to find one more chore – anything at all – that still needed doing. The woman shrugged and said, "It's small, but it's cosy. It suits us. It's a home."

"I can see that."

"People are quite wrong, you know. They think artists thrive in disorder, but they don't. Roger is coming round to my point of view on that. He's working ever so much harder now than he used to. He's off into his studio every daylight hour."

Jane could believe it. "What a warm day," she commented.

"Yes." Mrs Moynihan frowned. "I hate opening the windows because of the pollen, you see."

"Shall we take a little constitutional, perhaps?" With annoyance Jane heard herself slipping into this middle-aged lingo. "Totter down to the old jetty," she added in a heartier vein.

The woman frowned. "I know what you wish to discuss," she said. "You needn't have gone to all this elaborate trouble ..." She waved a hand vaguely toward Vosper and her husband.

"Esther!" Jane said reproachfully.

"What?"

"You haven't relaxed or smiled from the moment I crossed the threshold." Esther's lip trembled as Jane added, "I've never seen you like this."

At last she looked away. "I just feel so ashamed. So ashamed."

"But why?"

"You're right. Let's go for a walk." She went to get a mantilla, despite the heat, which almost felled them as they stepped from the shade of the house; quickly they raised their parasols and Esther let the mantilla hang down her back. With a smile, Jane eased it gently from her and, opening the door, folded it lightly on one of the hall chairs. On the way out she stole a surreptitious glance at the Jagos' house; Daniel was nowhere in sight but his paints and ladder were there. "They did quite a good job on that roof," she said to explain her interest.

"They? The father did nothing but stand in the street and mock."

"Well ... Daniel did a good job, then."

"Mmmm. Listen, I suppose I'd better say it at once. I'm sorry. There!"

"Are we talking about de Guy now?"

"What else?" A six-horse cart went by laden with heavy timbers for the Ponsharden shipyard. "It was a scurvy trick."

They sauntered across the road and started down the steep, unpaved path to Greenbank jetty. But Esther cried, "It's no good. I'll be back in ten seconds." She dashed back across the road and into the house. A moment later, Jane saw her briefly at a window. When she returned she smiled feebly. "I just couldn't leave that mantilla lying there so untidily."

"I'm so *awfully* sorry," Jane said sarcastically; but it was lost on Esther, who merely observed, "You were only trying to be kind and not delay us, I know."

"Anyway," Jane went on as they started once more down the path, "as I was about to say, you needn't even dream of apologizing about Gérard de Guy. He proved to be a most charming man and an amiable companion. Even my guardian thought so – and I must have told you how censorious she can be."

After a silence Esther said, "I don't deserve it ... Jane. I don't deserve anything that's happened to me."

They had arrived at the level part of the jetty, beside the hotel. The ferryman looked up at them expectantly. "Over to Flushing, ladies? Only a ha'penny." Shrewdly he added, "There's a touch more breeze that side, too."

Jane looked at Esther, who said, "We didn't tell the men."

"He'll let them know." She turned to the boatman and handed him his penny. He nodded and said he knew Mr Moynihan very well.

They sat in restful silence over the creek. Jane trailed her hands in the water, luxuriating in its coolness. As they disembarked she told Esther of her two distant cousins who lived at Pennance and how they had played the Ophelia Game.

"I often wonder what it would be like to drown," Esther said. "One of the girls I knew in Penzance threw herself in the harbour one night, stone cold sober. She looked quite peaceful when they fished her out."

They circumnavigated the stone quays and wandered up a little cut between a pub and a net store to reach the main street – which was, indeed, almost the only street of the village. "Right or left?" Jane asked.

"Right is level. Left goes uphill."

They turned right and sauntered on between the sunbaked houses. Nothing stirred. They were the only things that moved in the entire village. Jane thought of commenting on the boatman's promise of more breeze, but was prevented by the fear that Esther would merely use it as an excuse for one more lugubrious comment.

"What has happened to you, my dear?" she asked gently.

"What have you noticed?" the other asked sharply.

"What *haven't* I noticed! When I last saw you at the beginning of February, you were a proud, self-contained, dignified woman. When I last heard from you – in March, was it? – you sounded over the moon with happiness at your forthcoming marriage. But now ..."

"One year," Esther commented glumly. "That's all it was. Not even that. Eleven months. And it's going to hang around my neck until the day I die."

"What nonsense!" Jane exclaimed.

Esther seemed not to hear her. "I can't keep the meanest sort of scullery maid. They all get to hear of it. Everybody knows by now. They all snigger at me."

"But I thought you said your husband knows all about it?" Jane was beginning to feel alarmed.

"I started having a kid but I had to get rid of it."

"Oh no!" Jane clutched at her but who was supporting whom was a moot point.

"I could just imagine the look on its face when it came back from school one day. It wouldn't say anything but I'd know someone had whispered my shame to it. I couldn't face that."

"Oh, Esther – that was so wrong, such a wrong thing to do!"

"It's easy to talk. It was all so long ago and far away for you. Or are you going to go round Cornwall ringing a bell and shouting out your old lady was a whore?"

"Of course not."

"No! I didn't suppose you would." After a short pause she said in a slightly less belligerent tone, "What would you say?"

It struck Jane as extraordinary that the question had never even crossed her mind. She gave the first reply that came into her head. "If anyone was impertinent enough to raise the matter, I'd say I was proud of her. I'd say she was proud, as well. Too proud to starve, and too fond of life. And too popular to be allowed to do so."

Esther pulled her arm away. "That's just so much glib talk," she sneered. "It's not *you* the maids snigger at. How dare they, anyway. Most of them have turned a gay trick or two when their luck was down." Again her wrath abated a little as she said, "I'd like to know what you'd say if it was you that had been the whore."

"I've never even thought about it," Jane confessed. "But what's done can't be undone. You've got to find some way of making the best of it."

"The best of it!" she scoffed. "Thank you so much! Here endeth the lesson!"

"All right. I'd carry the fight into their camp. You catch them sniggering behind your back, you say?"

"Not actually sniggering," she admitted uncomfortably. "They're too smart for that. But I can see it in their eyes."

"Have it out with them, then – the moment you detect the first sign of it."

"Oh yes! Just walk up and say to them, 'Listen, my girl, it's plain to me you've learned I was once a whore ...' Very clever!"

"Dear God!" Jane raised her hands in loose supplication. "Attack! Never defend. Just come straight out with it. Say to them, 'Listen, my girl, do you feel unhappy having to work for me ... and take orders from me? Because I couldn't have a girl like that in the house, d'you understand?' Crack the whip."

Esther was silent and sullen – but at least she *was* silent. Jane let it work for a while and then told her of a little scene she had witnessed in Paris. "I was strolling with Banks through the Bois de Boulogne, and they graze a small flock of sheep there, in one part, to keep down the grass. And of course it was lambing time and lots of people like to go out and watch them gambolling in the grass. And quite a few of them gambol in the grass themselves, but that's another story."

Esther, much against her will, laughed slightly.

"Anyway, there was this one couple with a ferocious dog, and it slipped its leash and went for one of the lambs. My heart was in my mouth, I needn't tell you. But the ewe, the mother – it's something I never thought I'd see – she leaped straight up in the air, about five feet up. Imagine! A fat woolly sheep leaping that high! And down she came with all four feet straight on that dog's back. How she didn't break his spine, I'll never know. But that dog, who could have turned round and torn the whole flock to shreds, he just gave out one almighty yelp, put his tail between his legs, and fled. You should have heard the people cheer."

"Hurrah!" Esther said tonelessly.

Jane ignored her. "But the thing that struck me was why can't that sheep remember that triumph even after her lambs have grown up and gone? She could scare the liver and lights out of that dog any day of the year."

They had reached the end of the village by now. Jane asked whether the lane led anywhere in particular. Esther replied that it went to Trefusis Point, anyway. They decided to go that far and turn back.

"Talk's easy," Esther commented morosely as they set out with a brisker pace.

"I'm glad you agree that *something's* easy."

"I wish you lived nearer."

"Perhaps I will. I'm going to leave ... *bree-ahje!*" She laughed. "Remember?"

Esther nodded. "Happy days!" she said sarcastically. "Here, don't tell Roger what I said, about getting rid of the kid. He still thinks I'm carrying. Won't come near me in bed. It's driving me mad, needing him."

"Can't you say you had an ordinary miscarriage?"

Esther looked at her in surprise. "Hark at you!"

Jane froze suddenly. The lane at this point was long and straight; she had glanced the length of it not five seconds ago and found it empty; yet now, not twenty paces in front of her, facing her in equal shock, stood Daniel Jago.

For a moment neither of them moved. Then he turned and glanced at the bushes to his left, on the seaward side; he must have come up that way.

"Daniel!" she cried at last.

He leaped back among the bushes; moments later they heard him crashing through a thin stand of saplings beyond.

Jane ran to the point where he had disappeared. "What's down there?" she asked.

Esther shrugged. "Just rocks and water. He must have rowed over here."

"But why? D'you think he saw us on the ferry and then rowed ahead of us to waylay us? But then why just turn round and run?"

"It does seem unlikely," Esther said – though she had seen hundreds of men falter and pass on in the last moments of their approach. "Perhaps he *didn't* see us and brought a maid over with him. It's a handy place for a gambol." She turned to Jane with a smile, thinking this echo would amuse her. The anguish she saw in the girl's eyes was a shock. "He is your brother, isn't he?" she asked.

Jane nodded. "I just wish he could accept it, too. Until he does, until we can ... well, anyway, I'm stuck with all my old feelings about him."

"But that's ..." She gulped.

"Yes!" Jane agreed angrily. "And that's another thing I'm not going around with a bell, shouting out. Come on, let's go back to the ferry."

"But why?"

"If he's gone home, I can have it out with him once and for all."

"And if he hasn't?"

"I'll camp on his front lawn."

As they set off, Esther took her arm. "I didn't mean to be so cross with you, Jane," she said. "You've been very good to me. You're the one person – well, you and Roger – you're the two people who never looked down at me."

"And you want it to go on being exclusive?" Jane asked.

It caught Esther on the hop. "I don't quite ..."

"You don't seem to want to give anyone else the chance, do you."

For a while there was no reply. Then Esther heaved a great sigh and said, "When you talk like that you make it sound so easy, and you make me think it's easy, too. You make me ashamed of all my fears. But the moment you go, I know they're all going to come crowding back upon me and this time tomorrow I'll be as bad as ever."

"Well, at least that's twenty-four hours. Next time it might be thirty-six."

*   *   *

The men were waiting for them at the jetty on the Greenbank side. They parodied their relief at finding the ladies safe and well, and spoke as if Jane and Esther had been walking through bandit-infested country. Esther was so jolly that Jane began to feel a little hope for her at last. There was no sign of Daniel, either on the water or up by his home.

When they reached the road Jane drew a deep breath and said, "I'm just going up to ... Greenbank House for a second. Start tea without me if I'm delayed."

Vospe took a few paces with her. "Shall I accompany you?" he asked out of hearing of the others.

With their arms linked she could feel the tension in him. She was so torn between a soothing reply, which would hint that he had good grounds for worrying, and a joke, which might so easily backfire, that she said nothing.

He let go her arm and stood there, holding the image of her in his eyes, seeing it diminish. And she, knowing his anguish, and not wanting to lend it colour by some solemn reassurance, merely turned and repeated her earlier injunction: "Don't wait." In the circumstances it had an unfortunate resonance.

She knew his eyes were upon her but she did not turn again. Drusilla Jago was standing at her front door. "What d'you want?" she challenged.

"I wish to speak to my brother."

"More criminal conversation!"

"Mrs Jago, I do understand your resentment of me. I know the pain is still there for you. But I think you might try to understand how painful it is for me, too." The woman's eyes looked at everything but Jane. "Who's that fine gentleman you were talking to?" she asked, nodding toward the Moynihans' house.

"That's no business of yours."

"He's still standing there."

"He's the gentleman I intend to marry."

Without a further word Mrs Jago turned and went inside, slamming the door behind her. Jane looked up and saw Daniel standing at an upstairs window, gazing down at her. She smiled at him. He, too, vanished without a word. A moment later another window on that same floor was opened and his mother stood there, holding a pail of slops with obvious intent. Jane turned and went back to Vosper.

Half an hour later, when they took their farewells of a much happier pair of newlyweds, Vosper told his driver to go on through the town. Jane, realizing that this would take them directly past the Jagos, asked why.

"We're going back a different way," he replied. "There's something I wish to show you. We might also call on the Pellews."

As they passed Greenbank House, Drusilla Jago came running out. Knowing she was capable of any devilment, Jane raised her parasol to strike her down; but Vosper grasped it and took it from her. The woman leaped onto the running board and, clutching at the door for support, looked Vosper contemptuously up and down. "Lawyer Scawen!" she sneered, not even looking at Jane. "And that's the thing you're going to marry – that object of pity! A little country quill-sharpener who'll never be of service to man nor beast – nor yet woman, neither." She turned to Jane at last and gave a maniacal laugh. "Well, Miss Vyvyan-Jago, full of airs and graces, let me just tell you one thing: You could have had your Daniel if you'd wanted, for there's no Jago taint in him at all. The great Kinghorn wasn't the only one with a light pair of heels!" She turned again to Vosper. "And you consider it careful, Lawyer Scawen. Here's a rod for your back. When you and she bed down each night, what'll she be thinking, eh?" She leaped backward and stood in the dust of their wake. "She'll be thinking she could have had my Daniel after all!" She repeated the taunt several times, her voice rising to a shriek of pure malevolence.

Until they reached the brow of the hill, where she passed out of view, Jane was transfixed by that sharp-etched bundle of angular spite. When she turned back to face Vosper again, he glanced at his watch and said, "I don't think there'll be time to go and see the Pellews now. We'll press straight on to Mawnan Smith."

"What a shame," she said flatly.

She knew he must be dying to ask her about what that mad woman had said – especially her opening remarks – but she also knew he was trying to force her to speak first. After that it became a clash of wills between them, a point of honour not to yield. So all the way out to Mawnan Smith they talked of everything under the sun except what was uppermost in both their minds. Just after they had passed through the village, at a sharp bend in the road, he told the driver to stop. Then he leaped over the door, opened it, and held out his hand for her to alight.

"What's this?" she asked, intrigued.

"A rather splendid view of the Helford River. Now you've decided to settle down here, you ought to start getting to know the county a bit."

He led her down over small fields and patches of wild, untouched land to a cliff that overlooked the very mouth of the river. There beneath a cloudless sky a faint breeze stirred, drowsy with the mingled aromas of woodland, river bank, and open sea. To her left stretched the sparkling waters of Falmouth Bay, shimmering in blue and emerald, purple and ultramarine, until they were lost in the haze, somewhere beyond St Mawes. Falmouth itself was no more than a quivering blur from there, but she could just make out, a mile or two nearer, the pale, square smudge of Pennance House. How long ago *that* now seemed! To her right, the contrast could hardly have been more marked, with the lush, verdant greens of the steeply wooded hills that formed the estuary and its many tiny creeks, and the hot browns of slow decay that marked their meeting with the waters.

Viewed from that place, the whole earth seemed at peace, glad of the sun, the laziness, the life-bringing warmth. She felt it invading every part of her being, soothing away all her cares.

"Possibilities?" he murmured when he saw her begin her survey for the third time.

The hair rose on the nape of her neck as she realized what he was talking about.

"It belongs to a local family whose son, or so I understand, does not intend to keep it up. It's mortgaged to the hilt. He was going to pay it off – the son – but I believe he's had other calls on his money lately ..."

"Vosper!" She turned and put her arms about him. The feel of his body, its warmth and solidity, were suddenly overwhelmingly dear to her. She raised her face for him to kiss her.

But he held off as yet. "About Mrs Jago ..." he said.

Their eyes met and dwelled in each other's. "All that hate!" she told him. "To live at that ... screaming pitch of passion all the time! I could never withstand it."

He lowered his lips to hers then and at last she felt the strength and fire of his love. It was not the dark-bright ardour that Daniel professed but a fervour more cosmic and profound – an inexhaustible love that a lifetime could not consume.

"And, talking of Mrs Jago – or what she said ..." Jane whispered when they broke.

"Yes?"

"Will you?"

"Spur of the moment?"

She butted him playfully and said, "I don't think!"

He smiled and kissed her again, lightheartedly now. "If you're sure you can put up with me. I doubt if many women could."

"I don't know any other man who could put up with me."

He hugged her and laughed. "Now there I think you may be right."

"I mean ... without wanting to change me."

"Yes," he said. "That's what I meant, too."

THE END